The Diamond Brooch

The Celtic Brooch Series, Book 7

Katherine Lowry Logan

Copyright © 2017 by Katherine Lowry Logan
Print Edition

This is a work of fiction. Names, characters, places, and incidents are the product of the author's imagination, or are used fictitiously, and any resemblance to actual persons living or dead, business establishments, events, or locales is entirely coincidental.

All rights reserved. No part of this book may be used or reproduced in any manner whatsoever without written permission of the author, except in the case of brief quotations embedded in critical articles or reviews.

Story consultant and editor: Faith Freewoman
Cover art by Damonza
Interior design by BB eBooks

Website: www.katherinellogan.com

"It's great to be young and a Giant."
−*Laughing Larry Doyle*

CAST OF CHARACTERS

Alphabetical Order

1. Allen, Mr. and Mrs.: Kevin's parents

2. Allen, Kevin: fiancé of JL O'Grady, VP of Finance for MacKlenna Corporation, biological son of Elliott Fraser and brother of James Cullen Fraser (appears in all books except *The Ruby Brooch*)

3. Arées, Carolina Rose: (mentioned only) love interest of Jack Mallory (appears in *The Three Brooches)*

4. Arées, Gracie Morrison: (mentioned only) wife of Dr. Arées and mother of Carolina Rose and Catherine Lily, Kit MacKlenna Montgomery's aunt

5. Bennett, James Gordon: publisher of the *New York Herald*

6. Brady, Diamond Jim: (mentioned only) businessman, philanthropist, and Lillian Russell's longtime companion

7. Carter, Mr.: Providence Loan Society employee

8. Cate: Meredith's assistant and Montgomery Winery's office manager (appears in *The Last MacKlenna, The Broken Brooch* and mentioned in *The Three Brooches)*

9. Chester, steward on the *SS New York*

10. Collins, Mrs.: Elliott Fraser's longtime cook and housekeeper at MacKlenna Farm (first appeared in *The Last MacKlenna*)

11. Cooper, Laurette: (mentioned only) Amy Spalding's thrice-removed first cousin, Catherine Lily Taylor Sterling's granddaughter

12. Digby, Mr.: (mentioned only) mysterious Edinburgh, Scotland solicitor (discussed in *The Sapphire Brooch, The Emerald Brooch, The Broken Brooch)*

13. Duffy, Emily: Kit MacKlenna Montgomery's ward from the

nineteenth-century (appears in *The Three Brooches*)

14. Fraser, Elliott: Chairman of the Board of the MacKlenna Corporation, husband of Meredith Montgomery, father of James Cullen Fraser and Kevin Allen, equine vet (appears in all Brooch books)

15. Fraser, James Cullen: son of Meredith Montgomery and Elliott Fraser (appears in all Brooch books except *The Ruby Brooch*)

16. Gilbert, Joe: (mentioned only) Amy Spalding's boyfriend (mentioned in *The Three Brooches*)

17. Kelly, Olivia: Connor O'Grady's new girlfriend in Colorado

18. Lilla: Maria Ricci's sister, owner of the restaurant in Little Italy

19. Mallory, Charlotte: surgeon, wife of Braham McCabe and mother of Lincoln, Kitherina, and Amelia Rose, sister of Jack Mallory (appears in all Brooch books except *The Ruby Brooch, The Last MacKlenna*)

20. Mallory, Jack: *New York Times* best-selling author (appears in *The Sapphire Brooch, The Emerald Brooch, The Broken Brooch, The Three Brooches*)

21. Mathewson, Christy: (mentioned only) New York Giants pitcher

22. Mathewson, Jane: wife of New York Giants pitcher Christy Mathewson

23. McBain, Alice: (mentioned only) David's mother (appears in *The Last MacKlenna, The Emerald Brooch, The Broken Brooch, The Three Brooches*)

24. McBain, David: veteran, author, President of MacKlenna Corporation, husband of Kenzie McBain and father of Henry, Robbie, and Laurie Wallis (appears in all Brooch books except *The Ruby Brooch*)

25. McBain, Kenzie: veteran, West Point graduate, MacKlenna Corporation attorney, wife of David McBain and mother of Henry, Robbie, and Laura Wallis (appears in *The Emerald Brooch, The Broken Brooch, The Three Brooches*)

26. McBain, Henry and Robbie: Twin sons of David and Kenzie (appear in *The Broken Brooch, The Three Brooches* and mentioned in

The Emerald Brooch

27. McCabe, Braham: former Union cavalry officer, lawyer, senator, husband of Charlotte Mallory and father of Lincoln, Kitherina, and Amelia Rose, Jack Mallory's brother-in-law, Kit MacKlenna Montgomery's first cousin (appears in all Brooch books except *The Last MacKlenna*)

28. McCabe, Lincoln: son of Braham McCabe and Charlotte Mallory (appears in *The Sapphire Brooch, The Emerald Brooch, The Broken Brooch, The Three Brooches*)

29. McGraw, Blanche: wife of New York Giants manager John McGraw

30. McGraw, John: New York Giants manager

31. Montgomery, Cullen: lawyer, author, founder of Montgomery Winery, husband of Kit MacKlenna Montgomery (appears in *The Ruby Brooch, The Sapphire Brooch, The Three Brooches* and mentioned in all but *The Emerald Brooch*)

32. Montgomery, Kit MacKlenna: founder of Montgomery Winery, wife of Cullen Montgomery, goddaughter of Elliott Fraser, guardian of Emily Duffy (appears in *The Ruby Brooch, The Sapphire Brooch, The Three Brooches* and mentioned in all other books)

33. Montgomery, Meredith: owner of Montgomery Winery, wife of Elliott Fraser and mother of James Cullen Montgomery, breast cancer survivor (appears in all *Brooch* books except *The Ruby Brooch*)

34. Moretti, Gabriele: dealmaker, shipper/importer, friend of Amy Spalding and the Ricci family

35. Mustache Cop, New York City policeman

36. Members of the New York Giants 1909 team: (mentioned only)

37. Nightstick Cop, New York City policeman

38. O'Grady, Austin: University of Kentucky incoming basketball player, son of JL O'Grady and Chris Dalton—power forward for the Golden State Warriors (appears in *The Broken Brooch, The Three Brooches*)

39. O'Grady, Connor: former NYPD detective, Director of Global

Security for MacKlenna Corporation, brother of JL, Shane, Patrick, and Jeff O'Grady, son of Retired Deputy Chief Lawrence "Pops" O'Grady (appears in *The Broken Brooch, The Three Brooches*)

40. O'Grady, Jeff: (mentioned only) former NYPD detective, Director of Global Security for MacKlenna Corporation, brother of JL, Shane, Patrick, and Connor O'Grady, son of Retired Deputy Chief Lawrence "Pops" O'Grady (appears in *The Broken Brooch, The Three Brooches*)

41. O'Grady, Jenny "JL" Lynn: former NYPD detective, Vice President of Global Security for MacKlenna Corporation, fiancée of Kevin Allen, mother of Austin, sister of Connor, Shane, Patrick, and Jeff O'Grady, daughter of Retired Deputy Chief Lawrence "Pops" O'Grady (appears in *The Broken Brooch, The Three Brooches*)

42. O'Grady, Julie: wife of Jeff O'Grady (mentioned in *The Broken Brooch, The Three Brooches*)

43. O'Grady, Retired Deputy Chief Lawrence "Pops": (mentioned only) father of JL, Shane, Patrick, Jeff, and Connor (appears in *The Broken Brooch, The Three Brooches*)

44. O'Grady, Shane: (mentioned only) Director of Global Security for MacKlenna Corporation, brother of JJ., Connor, and Jeff O'Grady, son of Retired Deputy Chief Lawrence "Pops" O'Grady (appears in *The Broken Brooch, The Three Brooches*)

45. O'Grady, Susan: (mentioned only) daughter of Jeff and Julie O'Grady

46. Parrino, Pete: former NYPD detective, Director of Global Security for MacKlenna Corporation, JL O'Grady's former partner (appears in *The Broken Brooch, The Three Brooches*)

47. Potter, Mr.: Providence Loan Society employee

48. Ricci, Isabella: granddaughter of Maria

49. Ricci, Maria: widow of Micky, grandmother of Isabella

50. Ricci, Micky: (mentioned only) deceased friend of Gabriele Moretti, husband of Maria Ricci, grandfather of Isabella Ricci

51. Russell, Lillian: actress, companion of Diamond Jim Brady (mentioned in *The Broken Brooch,* appears in *The Three Brooches*)

52. Spalding, Amy Rebecca: former Olympian, ESPN baseball analyst (mentioned in *The Broken Brooch, The Three Brooches*)

53. Spalding, A. G.: (mentioned only) Co-founder of A. G. Spalding sporting goods company

54. Sterling, Edward: husband of Catherine Lily Taylor Sterling, Amy's three-times great-grandfather

55. Sterling, Catherine Lily Taylor: Amy's three-times great-grandmother

56. Taylor, Alison Morrison: (mentioned only) Catherine Lily Taylor Sterling's mother, sister of Gracie Morrison mother of Carolina Rose Arées

57. Ted: Elliott's trainer (appears in The Last MacKlenna and mentioned in other books except The Ruby Brooch)

58. Thomson, Stephen 'the widower': President of Providence Loan Society

59. Wallace, Madame: salesclerk at the Iron Palace

60. Wilson, Patrick: street urchin

"I see great things in baseball. It's our game—the American game."
—Walt Whitman

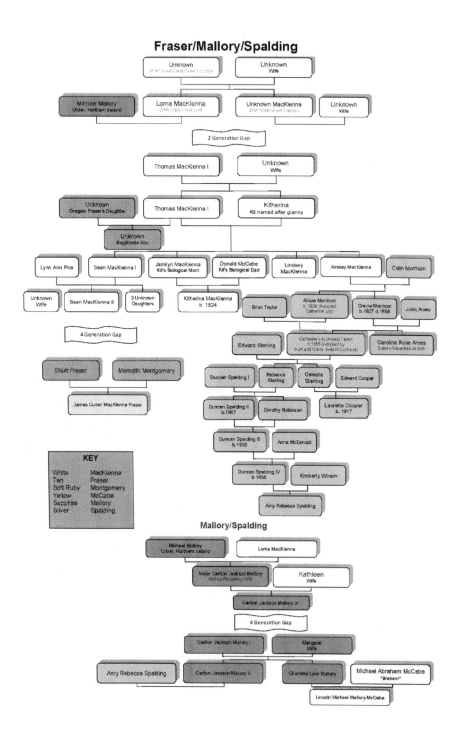

1

Present day (October) New York City—Amy

THE OVERCAST DAY had turned gunmetal gray by the time the yellow cab turned off Broadway onto 107th Street in New York City.

"You can drop me at the corner," Amy Spalding told the driver. She opened the Arro app on her smartphone to be sure the tip amount defaulted to twenty percent. At the end of the trip, a receipt for the total charges would go directly to her email, where it would have gathered dust until tax time.

But, as of two hours ago, her tax return would be too difficult to calculate and file on her own. She needed to hire a CPA, a tax lawyer, a bookkeeper, and a stockbroker to manage—get this—her multi-million-dollar estate.

A text message from her collector friend, Chris, popped up while she was deciding how much to tip the driver. She read the message quickly, before the cab reached the corner of Riverside Drive. *Found a Marquard with a Sweet Caporal back. Interested?*

Interested? Was he kidding? Of course she was. A Rube Marquard would be a fantastic addition to her PSA-graded T206 set. She started collecting 1909-1911 tobacco baseball cards almost twenty years ago, and she now had all the New York Giants pitchers except Marquard, Christy Mathewson, and Honus Wagner.

She replied: *How much?*

He responded: *$250.*

She replied: *Send the link.*

The taxi pulled to a stop at the corner. She gathered her purse and a file folder, looked around to be sure she wasn't leaving anything behind, and climbed out. Directly in front of her was an imposing four-story, white marble, French Renaissance-style mansion overlooking the Hudson River.

She whistled. "That's some house." She opened the folder to double-check the address. Yeah. She was in the right place.

Chris sent another text along with the link: *If you don't want it, I'll contact the next collector on my list.*

Two-fifty fit her budget. Her old budget. The budget she had before she became an heiress.

She clicked the link in the text message, studied the photograph, and read the description and details. The card had a Mint 9 rating. *That's good.* It exhibited only one minor flaw—a very slight wax stain on the reverse side—which was okay with her. There was no need for an internal debate about the most appropriate use of her reserve funds. This was a must-have. She clicked the buy button and mentally checked Marquard, or, as he was tagged—the $11,000 lemon—off her list.

She responded: *Bought it. Will send you a finder's fee. Still looking for a 1909 Mathewson.*

A Mathewson with a Mint 9 rating could cost $65,000. To buy it, she would have to sell a portion of her collection. The card would be worth the sacrifice, though, and would feed a lifetime passion bordering on obsession. The hobby was an intoxicating combination. It blended interesting artwork and the thrill of the hunt with the sport of her heart—baseball.

Chris replied: *If I find a Mathewson, you won't hear about it until AF-TER I buy it!*

Yeah, right. They were both all talk. Neither of them would spend that kind of money on a baseball card, even though she now had the funds. She shook her head, still unable to wrap her brain around how her life had changed in the past week.

Her first cousin thrice removed, Laurette Cooper, whom Amy never met, died without a will. To Amy's surprise, she was Laurette's only living heir. The entire estate—a mansion and twenty million dollars—had fallen into Amy's lap. She studied the thirty-five-room residence looming in front of her, neglected and forlorn.

What in the world was she going to do with a hundred-year-old New York City mansion? As a baseball analyst for ESPN, she was on the road from April through October, and could barely keep up with her hoped-to-be fiancé, Joe Gilbert—the founder and executive producer of GBC Sports—much less a mansion in need of a makeover.

This monstrosity could easily become an albatross—a four-story Victorian albatross.

She shoved the folder into an oversized leather bag and walked the width of the fenced-in property, looking at the house and yard from different angles. In 1974, the mansion received a National Historic Landmark designation. It was the only privately owned single-family residence in Manhattan. Amy's attorney had warned her that Cousin Laurette spent the last two decades of her life as a reclusive invalid, and during those years the house had fallen into disrepair. If the outside was any indication of the mansion's deterioration, the inside probably had more problems than peeling paint and pops and bangs from an old furnace.

Amy's limited knowledge of fixing up old houses came from watching a flip show on HGTV. Based on the cost of renovating those homes, the expense of restoring the mansion to its early twentieth-century grandeur could exceed her cash inheritance. If she spent all the money to renovate the place, she wouldn't be able to pay the real estate taxes.

She had to be realistic. Her lifestyle wouldn't support a mansion on the Upper West Side. Her boyfriend lived in a gilded penthouse on 5th Avenue. The apartment suited him, and he didn't want to live anywhere else in the city. Her taste leaned toward historic Southern homes with verandas surrounded by the scent of magnolias. So far, she hadn't seen a veranda or smelled any magnolias, which left the imposing white marble mansion with at least three strikes against it.

Was she ungrateful? She hoped not, but the truth was, her life's goal was to one day return to the South. As a child, she lived in Charleston, South Carolina, until her dad took a coaching position at a college in California. Then she stayed on the West Coast to attend UCLA on a softball scholarship. The South was a siren call, but playing in the National Pro Fastpitch League and on the USA Softball Women's National Team had delayed plans to return there. When she was offered her dream job two years ago at ESPN, she traded one dream for another.

Even an outside chance of living in the South again was as slim as owning a 1909 Mathewson or Wagner. It just wasn't going to happen. She was a New York City girl now.

If she was going to turn the mansion over to a realtor to sell, which made the most sense, she needed to go through her cousin's possessions to see if there was anything she wanted to keep. She knew nothing about Laurette Cooper, other than she and Amy shared a three-times great-grandmother—Catherine Lily Sterling.

The one important fact, though, was that her cousin had just a single heir—Amy Rebecca Spalding. It was sad to think a woman could reach the age of ninety-seven and be left with only one distant relative. And how sad the distant relative was alone in the world, too. If Amy had known about Laurette, she would have visited. But Laurette hadn't known about Amy, either. Her will stipulated if an heir couldn't be found, then the entire estate was to be liquidated and the proceeds paid into the Riverside Park Conservancy.

Amy passed through the mansion's wrought iron gate. The ends of the gate were capped with lion busts posed on pedestals. Each received a cursory glance and pat on the paw. Who would put the Lion King near the entrance to their house? If she renovated the mansion, the busts would be the first to go. The pedestals needed pineapples, a Southern welcome tradition, not lions.

She jogged up the steps to the front porch and unlocked the door. When she stepped inside the marble foyer, she was hit with a swirl of musty, old age smells—mothballs and dust, Ben-Gay and rubbing alcohol.

Based on information in the short bio prepared by her attorney, Amy knew Cousin Laurette recently died in the house following a lengthy illness. Not only had she died in the mansion, but she was born there as well, a foreign concept to Amy. She had lost count of the number of houses and apartments she'd lived in since leaving home for college.

Based on the foyer, it didn't take much of an imagination to see the beauty beneath the outdated fixtures and furnishings, cracks in the plaster, peeling wallpaper, and dust thick enough to show footprints. A cleaning service would make an enormous difference. Maybe renovating…

"Stop it," she said with a shake of her head. "I don't need a twelve-thousand-square-foot mansion."

Her mind shifted from imagining possibilities to exploring what was there, taking her time to inspect the house as she made her way through the downstairs. When she reached an Egyptian marble hall inlaid with Turkish glass, she sat in what looked like Cleopatra's throne perched atop a short, square mount with hieroglyphics carved into the wood. This would be an interesting piece to keep. She ran her fingers down the side of the chair, wondering what kind of exotic wood was used in its construction.

Remembering the information packet from her attorney, she dug into her bag to retrieve the folder. Inside was an inventory of her cousin's property. She thumbed through the pages until she reached a tab titled "Egyptian Hall." She perused the list of paintings and statues until she came to a chair identified as a "Throne Made of Cypress." She ran her finger along the dotted line across the page to the right-hand column listing values.

"Sixty-five-thousand dollars? Seriously?"

She hopped out of the chair before a three-hundred-pound gorilla dressed in a guard's uniform came charging out of her imagination and caught her sitting on a museum piece and tossed her out. Then she felt stupid. No one was going to throw her out. Everything in the house belonged to her, and she could dispose of the property however she chose. She could even set the chair on the curb for the garbage men. Or, she thought, tapping her chin with her fingertip, she could sell it and buy a Mathewson, if one became available. She patted the seat of the throne with renewed appreciation.

Moving on, she found the Louis XVI drawing room, a mahogany dining room, smoking room, bathroom, kitchen, and a library. The library was decorated with teak panels, marble, mosaics, and at the ceiling, an oval dome. A portrait of one of the most beautiful women Amy had ever seen—regal and angelic, with a sweep of red hair—was hung above a floor-to-ceiling fireplace. But it was the woman's violet-colored eyes that held Amy's rapt attention. Beneath the portrait an engraved gold plate identified the woman as Catherine Lily Sterling, 1855-1935.

"She's beautiful." Amy had none of her three-times great-grandmother's features. Not her violet-colored eyes or long red hair or tip-tilted nose. Amy was nothing like the beauty in the painting. Sure, she was pretty enough, or else she would never have gotten a TV gig, but she wasn't the glamorous type.

She wandered out of the library, skipping the other rooms on the first floor, and made her way up the grand staircase. The house was eerily quiet and stuffy, as if holding fast to the tail end of summer.

An alcove at the top of the stairs exposed a partial view of the river. Next to a comfy-looking chaise lounge was a small table with a pair of reading glasses and a book she'd seen on display in airport bookstores. The alcove must have been the caregiver's hangout.

Amy picked it up and glanced at the back of the book jacket. A hot guy leaned against the knotted trunk of a large oak tree, a linen jacket neatly folded over his knee, and one foot propped on a wrought-iron bench.

She ran the tip of her finger across his face. The perfect smile was meant to impress, but it didn't impress her. She'd seen smiles like his on early round draftees—cocky and arrogant. If she had time to read fiction, she'd read this book just to see if the author's writing style reflected his cocky expression, but her reading time was limited to studying stats and player profiles.

She returned the book to its place on the table, picture side up.

Before moving on, she checked out the view from the window. The trees were awash in majestic golds and reds, making it a prime leaf-peeping view. On impulse, she raised the window, and the sound of children's voices from the playground on the other side of Riverside Drive filtered in. She took a deep cleansing breath, then closed the window, and continued her exploration.

Paintings and sculptures lined the second-floor corridor. Four doors were partially open and each led to a bedroom with peeling wallpaper and dust. The last room she entered had the strongest old-people smell, but there was no peeling wallpaper or dust. This must have been Laurette's room.

A sofa and two big, comfy chairs in a bright, flowery print were positioned in front of the floor-to-ceiling marble fireplace, and the coffee table held copies of current ladies' magazines, pill bottles, and a TV remote.

Two long windows flanked by heavy brocade drapes blocked out most of the sunlight. She gathered up the panels and tied them back with tassel pom-pom cords, then raised the windows to air out the room.

What a view. Much better than the one from the alcove. She lingered there, breathing deeply of the fresh air and taking in the sights—runners, dog walkers, nannies pushing strollers, kids on bikes, a UPS truck, and a helicopter flying low above the river. Someday she was going to take a helicopter tour and soar above the congested streets to see all the major sites in thirty minutes. She made a swishing move with her hand as if shooting a basketball, and the tour idea sailed into her bucket list. Swish. She'd been living in the city for three months and hadn't even been able to manage a visit to the National September 11 Memorial and Museum.

Time. She never had enough.

She turned to tackle the room. The lawyer had recommended that, before she did anything else, she should go through her cousin's jewelry and put the valuable pieces in a lockbox. Amy wasn't a jewelry person. In her teens, she left her mother's pearl earrings in her gym bag, and they were stolen. Watches, rings, and necklaces got in the way at practices or games, and she didn't want to tempt another thief, so she went without.

Between the windows was a dressing table with an attached mirror in a molded frame with carved supports. The seat to its matching chair was covered with blue velvet. Vintage perfume puffer bottles in a variety of shapes and colors filled an oval glass tray and sat on the right side of the table. A pristine jewelry chest, about fourteen inches square, with carved decorations on all sides and a large "S" monogram on the front sat to the left. An ebony hairbrush and comb lay side by side in the center.

Amy settled on the corner of the chair to inspect the perfume bottles. She sprayed the contents of a green-glass, fan-shaped bottle into the air and immediately coughed and fanned away the scent. "Yuck."

She opened the lid to the ornate box and peered inside. Her breath hitched. "My God."

The box wasn't just a jewelry box. It was a treasure chest filled with extravagant necklaces and bracelets made with emeralds, rubies, sapphires, and diamonds. The jewels glinted against the blue felt lining, and truly represented the grandeur of a bygone era, when New York society was at its most regal.

With her hand shaking, she removed the top tray and set it aside. The next tray held pearl earrings, necklaces, and rings. She removed that tray and set it aside, too.

On the bottom of the chest was a single piece of jewelry—a diamond brooch. It was by far the most exquisite piece in the collection. It wasn't the brilliant diamond that made it so spectacular. It was the age of the piece, the workmanship, the design, the materials used, and an unexplainable energy, as if the brooch knew it was the most magnificent piece in the keepsakes chest.

She carried it over to the window and turned on the reading lamp, then sat in an upholstered chair and studied the brooch in better light. Holding it in her palm, she rotated her hand to view the jewelry from different angles. The fiery diamond threw off rainbows in the lamplight and heated in her hand.

She was trained to notice the slightest shifts in body language, changes in the sky, or small objects as they twisted and turned. Almost instantly, she noticed something significant about the diamond. It had a crack around the circumference that would certainly affect its value.

"What a shame." What could have caused it? It had to have been man-made. It was too perfect to be anything other than intentional. She followed the crack around the stone until she found a teeny, tiny hinge. But how did it open? The brooch was becoming almost too hot to hold.

Using her fingernail, she pried open the stone. Inside were letters written in a foreign language. She could read French and Spanish, but whatever this was…possibly Gaelic…she couldn't translate it, but she could sound out the words.

"Chan ann le tìm no àite a bhios sinn a' tomhais an' gaol ach 's ann le neart anama."

An earthy-scented fog rose from the floor in thick tendrils, enveloping her. She jumped to her feet and tried to run, but when she moved, the cloud moved, too. It jerked her left, then right, then back again, tossing her about like a ship in a tempest.

Until finally she was swept away, screaming, "Help!"

2

Present day (June) Mallory Plantation, Richmond, Virginia—Jack

SUMMER HAD ARRIVED in the Commonwealth of Virginia, and the wildflowers growing on the shore of the James River were in majestic bloom. Enjoying the view, *New York Times* and international best-selling author Jack Mallory picked up his pace. He ran alongside the river on a running path he and his sister had carved through the grounds of his home, Virginia's first plantation, founded in 1613 by their ancestors.

Jack noted the time and distance on his Garmin watch, pleased to find both had improved over the past month. He wasn't yet at peak performance, but he wasn't in training mode, either. He'd been selected in the lottery to run the New York City Marathon in November, but training wouldn't begin until July. Until then he would continue his non-training schedule, which included running twenty-five miles a week and lifting an hour a day at the gym. Previous training schedules had cut into his social life, but right now he didn't have one.

One of the most eligible bachelors this side of the Mississippi was off the market.

The death of Carolina Rose Arées eight months earlier had left him stranded in a deep pit, wondering if he would ever be able to climb out. Never, not even in high school, had he lost a woman he loved until Carolina Rose died in his arms. She left her fingerprints all over his soul, and those fingerprints refused to fade, as if in death she held on to him, while in life he held on to her.

When he reached the oak tree in his backyard, he slowed to a cool-down walk through the garden to enjoy the heavily scented flowers. Those post-run minutes were his favorite part of a morning run. Later, after three or four hours of focused writing, he'd return to prune them, much like the monks at the monastery—where he spent at least a month every year for the past twenty years—pruned him.

He had a host of hobbies, chief among them, after meditating and caring for his garden, was sports, both playing and attending events. He was a trivia master in Thoroughbred racing, basketball, and baseball—which reminded him, the Yankees and Red Sox were playing at seven o'clock. He had a box at the stadium, but didn't get to New York City as often as he liked. Time to call his brother-in-law, Braham McCabe, and invite him over to watch the game. Jack used to watch televised sports at a downtown Richmond bar, but since Carolina Rose's death, he avoided places where women gathered to meet men, and men gathered to watch games and, during commercials, meet women.

His lack of interest worried those closest to him, like his sister and brother-in-law, and his friend David McBain. But when he asked them why, they'd only shrug and say, "We want the old Jack back."

That was a lie. None of them wanted the old Jack back. They wanted a new, revised one. Their problem was, they couldn't pinpoint or explain exactly what it meant. Did they want him to lose his insatiable curiosity and boyish charm? Did they want him to harness his impulsiveness and acquire some wisdom?

Wisdom? Really?

Wisdom had little to do with intelligence. It wasn't a byproduct of schooling, but of the experiences of a lifetime. How could anyone expect him to acquire a lifetime's worth of wisdom overnight? They couldn't. As for curbing his impulsiveness—he let out a heavy sigh—it was part and parcel of his curiosity and his success as an author.

What they really wanted was for him to stop being so selfish. He'd be the first to admit he had a selfish streak. But not in the usual sense. To a fault, he was loving and generous. The problem was when his curiosity—the untamable beast—teamed up with his selfish side. Then, wham. He became a rail-thin dog walker dragged down the road by a lunging Saint Bernard.

That's what his sister and Braham and the entire clan wanted him to fix. They wanted the Saint Bernard to go to obedience school. They still wanted to see Jack's smile and ogle the eye candy on his arm, but if he ever put anyone in danger again, the clan would disown him.

His cell phone rang, and he crossed the lawn to the bench beneath the oak tree behind his house and snatched up the phone before it went to voicemail. It was Connor O'Grady, Director of Global Security for MacKlenna Corporation.

"Hey, Connor."

"I'm in New York and found something you need to see. The jet will be at the Richmond airport in an hour. Pack an overnight bag. I've booked a suite at the Plaza. A car service will pick you up. See you this afternoon."

"Can't. I'm on deadline."

"The deadline can wait. The Yankees are playing the Sox tonight. Let's use those tickets of yours."

"You're killing me, Con," Jack said. "I've got work to do. Maybe next week."

"Not a chance. You need to come up here. How can you say no? It's gonna be a great game. Get your ass to the airport."

Connor was right. Jack couldn't say no to the game, and two hours later he boarded the MacKlenna Farm jet for the ninety-minute flight to LaGuardia. A limo was waiting on the tarmac when he deplaned.

He called Connor. "Where are you?"

"I'm on Riverside Drive. Your driver has the address. I'll see you when you get here."

Jack pocketed his phone. Riverside Drive? Didn't Amy Spalding disappear from a house on Riverside? The hair on the back of his neck stood on end, sending a stark warning. Something big was about to happen. He considered racing back to the plane and getting the hell out of town.

He'd exceeded his limit for life-altering events. All he wanted to do now was work on his next book, spend time with his family, and enjoy a long vacation in the mountains.

If he turned around and went home, Connor would only call him again. Since Jack was in town and the Yankees were playing, he might as well stick around and find out what was on Connor's mind.

After a stop and go drive through the congested city, the limo driver pulled to the curb in front of a sprawling mansion on Riverside Drive. Jack scrolled through his messages from Connor to confirm the address. Yep. He was at the right place. The thought of a mystery spiked Jack's curiosity, but he quickly restrained it. He wasn't going to get sidetracked. Not now. If he wanted an adventure, he'd go back in time to find Amy Spalding.

He sent Connor a text asking where he was. Instead of responding, Connor opened the front door of the mansion. "What took you so long?"

Jack mounted the steps. "I stopped for lunch." He stepped into a vestibule built with veined Greek marble and a faience tile ceiling and was instantly hit by a stale, musty odor. "Did somebody die in here?"

"What gave it away? Your nose or your ESP?" Connor asked.

"Both," Jack said.

"Breathe through your mouth. It's a rose garden compared to some places I've been." Connor waved his arm in a follow-me motion. "This way. I want you to see something."

"Not a dead body, I hope."

"I haven't been all over the house, but my brother Jeff has. The New York cops haven't found one so far."

Jack followed Connor through a large foyer. "Who owns this

place?"

"A woman named Laurette Cooper. She died a few months ago."

"Okay. So what are we doing here?"

Connor led the way into a library decorated with East Indian teak panels, Tinos marble, bronze, mosaics, and at the ceiling, an oval dome of lacquered gold in iridescent colors.

"What are we doing here?"

"There's something I want you to see." Connor stopped in front of the floor-to-ceiling marble fireplace and pointed at a portrait hanging above the mantel.

Jack stared at the painting, drawing a series of deep breaths. He blinked. Stared again. Blinked. Shook his head. Refocused his eyes and stared again. Impossible. Was it Carolina Rose? No, it couldn't be. But…the resemblance was uncanny, and seeing it stoked raw memories, painful raw memories.

Words caught in his throat. "She…looks…like—"

"—Carolina Rose," Connor finished the sentence. "Last night Jeff was looking at my phone, going through pictures I took of the Colorado ranch. He saw the picture of you and Carolina Rose at the Hopkins' party in San Francisco in 1881."

Jack was struck dumb by the comment. After a few seconds, he forced himself to ask, "What picture?"

"The one Cullen found on the internet. He was researching the *San Francisco Chronicle's* archives for articles written around the time of his disappearance. He found a picture of Lillian Russell with you and Carolina Rose. You haven't seen it?"

Jack held out his hand, his face hot with anger. "Let me see it," he said tersely.

Connor scrolled through his pictures, found the one he wanted, and handed over his phone. "I thought Braham would have shown it to you."

"My brother-in-law won't even mention her name." Jack stretched the picture on the cell phone, enlarging it. His stomach cramped. She was even more beautiful than he remembered. He forwarded the picture to his device, then slapped the phone back into Connor's hand. "You should have sent this to me."

Connor pocketed his phone. "It wasn't mine to send. Take it up with Braham."

"I will." Jack understood why Braham hadn't told him, but it didn't mean he wasn't going to give Braham hell about it. "Finish your story about Jeff," Jack said.

"When Jeff saw the picture of Carolina Rose, he said she resembled the woman in the portrait hanging in the Riverside Drive house where Amy Spalding disappeared. I asked him if I could see it, and he agreed. As soon as I saw it, I knew you would want to see it, too. I thought you'd be interested in the mystery."

"I'm out of the mystery-solving business."

"Yeah, sure. Which is why you're already compiling a list of questions in your over-active brain. You've got the twitch thing going on at the corners of your eyes, like a camera snapping pictures to puzzle through later."

Jack walked over to the fireplace to read the brass plate attached to the portrait's frame: Catherine Lily Sterling, June 1, 1855 – June 1, 1935. "Who is she?"

"She's Laurette Cooper's grandmother. Look, I didn't want to bring you up here until I knew all the players. Laurette Cooper is Amy Spalding's cousin, and Catherine Lily Sterling is Amy's three-times great-grandmother."

Connor's statement sucked the oxygen right out of the room. "Amy's ancestor looks like Carolina Rose. Is that what you're telling me?"

"Yep."

Jack's head felt like a whacked-up piñata. This couldn't be happening. For the second time since entering the room, he was dumbstruck. Then, although he wasn't sure he wanted to hear the answer, he asked, "Did you find a connection between Catherine Lily and Carolina Rose?"

"Sorry, pal. Dead end. Catherine Lily was adopted as an infant and grew up in Scotland, not France. There's no record of her birth mother."

Jack sat in the nearest chair, breathing heavily now, and put his head in his hands. He had spent the last several months trying to move past his grief. Now, just as she had done when he met her in San Francisco, Carolina Rose blindsided him again.

He couldn't connect the dots just yet, but his heart told him Carolina Rose and Catherine Lily looked enough alike they could be sisters or cousins. Although there was one problem. Carolina Rose told him her uncle was her only relative. Which could have been a lie. After all, she had lied to him about other things.

"Catherine Lily and her husband moved into this house when it was completed in 1909. If you go back for Amy, you could arrange to meet Catherine Lily and ask her if she knows Carolina Rose," Connor said.

After four adventures back in time, enough was enough. Jack had been shot at, held prisoner, almost died in the belly of a crashing B-17, and the woman he loved died in his arms. No, he was done with time travel. "I'll find another way. Have you searched the house for letters or journals?"

"Amy Spalding's disappearance isn't my case. I don't have any authority to search the house."

"Who needs authority? We're here now."

"You sound like McBain," Connor said. "I'm a retired NYPD detective. I won't cross the line. Besides, I told my brother I only wanted to visit the library."

"Okay. You stay here. I'll do a quick search."

"What do you think you can find?"

"There could be correspondence, or reports from an investigation into Carolina Rose's disappearance in San Francisco. There could be a journal, or even a family tree written in the front of a Bible connecting the women. There could be letters from Catherine Lily's mother mentioning her adoption. The possibilities are endless."

"Our time here, however, is not," Connor said. "A beat cop will be here in five minutes to lock the door. Even if I wanted to search the house, we don't have time."

"You don't have time," Jack said. "But I do. You said you didn't tell anyone I would be here. You leave, and I'll stay and search. I might find evidence to help us locate Amy."

"She's been gone since October, Jack. If there was any evidence to shed light on her disappearance, it would have been found by now."

"Maybe. Maybe not. I need a few hours to search the house. And no one knows where Amy got a brooch. Was it sent to her or did she find it here?" A few hours would give him a good start. If he needed more time, he'd call in reinforcements.

"If Jeff finds out I let you in here, I'll get reamed out. If he finds out I left you here, he'll lock me up."

Jack wasn't ready to leave, but he didn't want Connor to catch hell, either. "Ask Jeff if you can come back tomorrow."

"He'd really be suspicious then." Connor's phone beeped with a text message. "The cop is here to lock the door."

"Is this still a crime scene?"

"No, but the police still have the key. The estate lawyers don't know what to do with the house, the furnishings, and the jewelry collection since Amy doesn't have any relatives. You've got to leave."

The front door opened and a voice yelled, "Detective O'Grady. Are you ready?"

"Crap," Connor said. "I've got to go. Find a way out and lock the door behind you."

Jack stepped into the shadows so he wouldn't be seen by the cop. "I'll send a text when I leave."

"Be right there," Connor yelled. Then he hissed at Jack. "Don't screw this up and get me into trouble."

Jack removed an envelope from his jacket pocket and handed Connor two tickets to the game. "Jeff's going, too. Right?"

Connor took the tickets. "Yeah, so don't be late. He thinks you're in town to meet with your agent."

"My agent is in DC."

"He doesn't know that. Just...." Connor swatted at the air as he turned and hurried away. "Never mind."

Jack returned the envelope to his pocket. "I'll be in my seat by the time they play the national anthem."

Connor looked directly into Jack's face, flashing his toughest badass cop look. In any other situation, Jack would have been intimidated. "If you're not there…" Connor left the threat unspoken.

"I will be," Jack promised.

As soon as the front door closed, Jack loped up the steps, barely winded by the time he reached the fourth floor. He jogged down the hall, opening each door until he found the one leading to the attic. Before climbing the narrow steps, he set the timer on his watch. He only had two hours to search as much of the house as he could, so he'd focus on the attic, the master bedroom, the library, and the basement.

If he left for the ballpark any later than two hours, he'd miss the pregame warm-up. Not only did he not want to miss it, but it was important to keep his word to Connor. Jack had screwed up royally when the family went back in time to San Francisco. So far his apologies, although sincere, hadn't repaired the damage to several relationships. No one trusted him now, and he needed to prove he deserved their faith in him. He might never get it back, but he had to try.

He allotted fifteen minutes to search the attic. His big feet barely fit on the treads of the narrowly curving steps, and he had to climb sideways to reach the top. He was relieved to find the attic clean and well organized. If the boxes were accurately labeled, he'd be in and out in five minutes.

Tables and chairs were stacked on one side, boxes on the other. Each box was labeled and dated. None were marked photographs or personal. He rushed out of the attic and buzzed through the fourth floor, picking through closets and dressers. He rifled through book boxes, finding mostly bestsellers from the 1980s and 1990s. None of his. He was always disappointed whenever he dug through boxes of books and none had his name on the cover. But he knew his writing didn't appeal to everyone, and as long as he stayed on the best-seller lists, he didn't take it personally.

He looked at the time, feeling pressure to hurry. Fifteen minutes had elapsed. The third floor took longer. It had fewer rooms, but they were larger, and had room-sized closets. He made it back around to the stairs in fifteen minutes, and checked off the third floor.

The minute he stepped onto the second floor, his senses went on full alert. Although his intuition occasionally got him into trouble, it was rarely wrong. He glanced at his watch. He would allow an hour to explore this floor. Which left fifteen minutes to search the library, and before he left the mansion he wanted to see the portrait again. On a good day, he could go several hours without thinking of Carolina Rose, but since seeing the portrait of Catherine Lily, he hadn't been able to get her out of his head.

Catherine and Carolina with flowers as middle names? Too much of a coincidence for him.

He moved quickly through the first four bedrooms on the second floor, finding nothing more remarkable than evidence a Giants fan once lived in the house. In the second bedroom, he found a box of baseball memorabilia: a 1951 team-signed baseball, Willie Mays and Casey Stengel-signed baseball cards, a 1942 Baseball Magazine with a picture of Hall of Famer Mel Ott—one of the game's most feared sluggers—on the front. If the contents of the house were auctioned off at some point, Jack intended to bid on a few items. He closed the box and left the room.

The last bedroom on the floor was the master suite. It didn't have a sign above the door, but it was the largest room, with a seating area facing a fireplace, and a TV mounted over the mantel. Bookshelves artfully arranged with knickknacks and photographs bordered the fireplace. A dozen novels, stacked three high, formed bases for several Limoges boxes. One was a black London taxicab. He picked it up, chuckling at the clever design. Then he set it down in the exact same spot, marked by a dusty outline.

The canary yellow upholstery on the sofa and chairs went out of style in the 1970s, but while they weren't threadbare they did show wear, and the oriental rug had a desirable patina from walking across it with outdoor shoes.

Then he noticed an ornate dressing table, with a large jewelry chest with carved designs on all sides and a large "S" monogram on the front sitting squarely in the middle. He made a beeline there and opened it. Empty.

Below the mirror were three small drawers. One contained an ebony comb and brush. Another held several pairs of white gloves. The third drawer was caught on something and wouldn't open fully. He pulled on the handle. When it still wouldn't budge, he wedged his hand inside and felt around for whatever was causing the obstruction. A piece of paper. He tugged gently until it came unstuck, and he eased it out between his fingers.

He straightened the crumpled paper, and, while he wasn't surprised by what he found—a mailing label from Mr. Digby, an Edinburgh solicitor—he was surprised by the date the package was sent. It had been mailed on June 1, 1935, the day Catherine Lily died. Digby sent the brooch to Catherine Lily's heir, Laurette Cooper.

The brooch wasn't sent to Amy Spalding. She found it accidentally. The MacKlenna Clan's theories about the brooches were a work in progress, and what this meant for Amy was cause for concern. If she wasn't the intended recipient, what did it mean for her? Was she in danger?

No, he didn't think so. While she might not have been the intended recipient, she was heir to both Catherine Lily and Laurette, which meant the brooch did belong to her.

Finding family letters or journals was even more important now. And because of their importance, they would almost inevitably be harder to find. The old house could have any number of hidden compartments, maybe even hidden rooms.

Jack took pictures of the mailing label, the jewelry box, and the room. He needed help with this, and he couldn't count on Connor, JL, or Pete. As former NYPD detectives, they wouldn't risk crossing the ethical line in their home city. Jack wasn't sure they would take the risk anywhere, but he knew someone who would.

He sent a text to David McBain, MacKlenna Corporation's president: *Amy Spalding disappeared from a house originally owned by her three-times great-grandmother Catherine Lily Sterling. Catherine Lily was adopted as an infant. She could be Carolina Rose's sister or cousin. Found a mailing label from Solicitor Digby dated June 1, 1935. Need help ASAP. Where are you?*

David responded: *MacKlenna Farm. Can leave within the hour.*

Jack replied: *OK to tell Kenz and Frasers.*

David responded: *Will get Meredith started on genealogy.*

Jack then sent photos of the portrait and the mailing label, along with the Riverside Drive address. The jet had been scheduled to return to Kentucky after it dropped him off at LaGuardia, so it should be back in Lexington by now. If David left right away, he could be in the city in two hours. What was Jack going to tell Connor? If he cancelled out on the game, Connor would be pissed. Jack didn't have a choice. He had to go.

Instead of sending another text message, Jack sent David an encrypted email with instructions. If there were letters or journals hidden in the house, David would find them. Jack shot videos of all four floors, and sent those, too. Before he broke into the house, McBain would have the layout memorized, and would probably have a few ideas where important papers could be hidden.

Satisfied he'd done all he could for now, Jack left through the rear door and walked up 107th Street to Broadway, where he caught a taxi. He sent David a text to let him know he had a park view suite at the Plaza and would meet him there after the game.

Forty-five minutes later, Jack was sitting in his box at Yankee Stadium drinking beer with Connor and Jeff.

3

Present day New York City—David

David McBain used a bump key to unlock the back door of the Riverside Drive mansion and let himself in. During the flight, he studied the videos Jack sent, and had the layout in his mind. He also had a few ideas about possible hiding places. If Catherine Lily hid sensitive information, he was almost certain the location would be somewhere she could control, probably her bedroom. The fireplace pilasters, dressing table, floorboards, and bookshelves were all possibilities.

He made his way through the darkened house. His first stop was the library. He wanted to see the portrait for himself. When he saw the picture Jack sent of Catherine Lily, David had to agree that the resemblance to the photograph of Carolina Rose was undeniable. He'd run images of Catherine Lily and Carolina Rose through facial recognition software and surface texture analysis. The results were a ninety-nine percent match. Since Carolina Rose was dead, she couldn't be Catherine Lily. While it would have been helpful to have Carolina Rose's date of birth, it wasn't necessary. Based on the results of the tests, the women were likely identical twins. Which meant Amy Spalding's three-times great-aunt was Carolina Rose Arées. Talk about small worlds.

How did the twins get separated? Did they know about each other? And what was their relationship to the MacKlennas? David hoped his snooping would turn up some answers.

Since the trip to San Francisco, Jack flatly refused to consider going back in time to rescue Amy. Would he change his mind now? And if he did, could David dissuade him? Jack had no business getting involved with Amy Spalding, considering a possible relationship to Carolina Rose. He needed to move forward not stumble backwards.

After stopping at the library and viewing the portrait, David made his way up the stairs to the master bedroom. He pulled the heavy drapes closed, then flipped on the light switch. He would start with the fireplace, then the walls, then the floors. If he didn't find anything in those places, he'd reevaluate.

He shrugged out of his backpack and unloaded his supplies, including a radar scanner to map the areas he wanted to search. If using radar scanning helped archaeologists find a hidden room in the three-thousand-year-old burial chamber of King Tutankhamun, surely, he could find a hidey hole in a hundred-year-old mansion in New York City.

Working quickly, he set up his laptop and scanner. He watched the multicolored bars on the computer screen as the specially modified Koden-brand portable scanner moved up and down along the full width of the fireplace. Watching the data line closely, he determined there wasn't a chamber or cavity in the wood fireplace surround.

So much for the fireplace.

He moved furniture and reset the scanner along the fireplace wall first. Nothing. He moved to the two interior walls and, finding nothing there, stopped to recalibrate the equipment. With two floor-to-ceiling windows taking up almost half of the wall space, scanning the exterior wall went faster than the others. When he finished, he sat back and reviewed the data to be sure he wasn't missing something. He wasn't.

To scan the floorboards, he would have to keep moving heavy furniture out of the way. It would take much longer, but hidden storage between the floor joists had always been a popular hiding place. The data would be harder to read because of the empty spaces between each joist, so the challenge would be finding unidentified objects in those spaces.

He took a break to send his wife a text while he ate an energy bar and drank a bottle of water. He'd been at it for a few hours, and would probably be working through the night, so he needed to stay hydrated.

Kenzie sent back a hugging meme. He kissed his finger and tapped the phone. God, he loved the woman more than life itself, and his body ached when he was away from her. After a moment, she sent another text: *If you're having problems, reevaluate your assumptions.*

How did she know he was having problems? Simple. He hadn't sent a progress report. Reevaluate, huh? Was it possible his assumptions were wrong? He had assumed Catherine Lily instigated an investigation into Carolina Rose's identity. But what if it had been Catherine Lily's husband? If he ordered an investigation, David was looking in the wrong room.

And, of course, it was also possible the Sterlings never heard of Carolina Rose Arées, and he was on a wild goose chase.

But he didn't think that was the case.

If Carolina Rose worked at the Metropolitan Museum, the odds of someone noticing the resemblance between the two women and mentioning it to Catherine Lily and/or her husband were high. If Mr. Sterling hired an investigator, and the investigator discovered Carolina Rose disappeared and was believed to be dead, then Mr. Sterling would have...what? Thrown the report away? No, he would have kept it in case his wife ever mentioned a woman named Carolina Rose.

Jack sent a text: *Any luck?*

David responded: *No hiding places in the master bedroom. Moving to the library.*

He repacked his equipment, then moved the furniture back into place. As he scooted a small chest, one of the legs wobbled. He reached underneath to tighten the screw, and felt something he wasn't expecting. He dropped to the floor and peered underneath.

Wedged between the back of a drawer and the rear leg was a small, brown leather journal. He carefully lifted it from its hiding place, his heart thumping. Turning to the first page of the journal, which was bound by a leather cord, he read the inscription:

I will succeed by striking out on my own path instead of following the ones well worn.

Catherine Lily Taylor – April 4, 1878

Did she immigrate in 1878? Meredith's genealogy team would be able to find out. David pocketed the journal and grabbed his bag. He made the executive decision not to tell Jack about the journal until he had a chance to read it. Catherine Lily's musings might answer their questions, but the information might also hurt Jack. If that was the case, David wanted to be prepared.

He did, though, send Kenzie a text: *Found Catherine Lily's journal. Will send pictures of each page once I get to the hotel. Love, D.*

Kenzie replied: *Woohoo. Can't wait to read it. Love, K*

4

1909 New York City—Amy

AMY CRAWLED OUT of the fog with her head swimming and a godawful taste in her mouth that made her stomach roil. She gagged but held down the contents. Barely. She didn't have a weak stomach, but she had a contrary one which occasionally reacted to anxiety. And, she was sore, as if she'd slid into second, third, and home plate all at the same time.

If she'd been on a three-day drunk, she couldn't have felt worse. What in the world happened to her? She slowly opened her eyes, and was so taken aback by what she saw, she snapped them shut again.

I must be dreaming.

Like Alice, she had fallen into an alternate universe. The landscape looked identical to the early twentieth-century painting of New York City hanging in the lobby of her apartment building in SoHo. She risked a second look and opened her eyes.

A few hours ago, Riverside Park had been thickly forested. What happened to all the trees?

And Riverside Drive was filled with horse-drawn carriages and funny-looking cars and funnier-looking bicycles ridden by women in long dresses and fancy hats. Was someone filming a movie? A movie could explain the cars and bicycles, but not the landscape. No matter how much money a producer wanted to spend, the Conservancy would never allow the deforestation of Riverside Park.

She turned in circles. "Holy crap."

She was standing in front of Grant's Tomb, sitting high atop a rocky slope where the air held the sweet, balmy scent of springtime. In her universe—not the alternate one she'd fallen into—the tomb was surrounded by acres of undeveloped land.

Just like the painting in her apartment building. This wasn't a movie set. This wasn't a dream. She closed her eyes and squeezed both tightly, and then very slowly opened them again.

But nothing changed.

This would be the time to panic. But panicking wasn't in her nature. She had a reputation for being unnaturally calm and cool under pressure. Fear, however, was a different matter. Fear took courage to conquer. And right now, her stores of readily available courage were closed for inventory, or on the verge of being purged.

She considered her situation.

If she wasn't on a movie set, and she wasn't dreaming, and she hadn't fallen into an alternate universe, then there was only one option left.

She must have inhaled a hallucinogen while inside the mansion. That had to be it. She was on a drug-induced trip back in time. She had never taken drugs, and other than beer after games, rarely drank alcohol, so a psychedelic drug was bound to have a strong effect on her.

She had to think about this for a minute, and while she thought, she swung an imaginary bat like some golfers swung imaginary clubs. What exactly had she been doing before she ended up at Grant's Tomb? She mentally placed herself back inside Laurette's room.

The brooch. She had opened a diamond brooch, read an inscription engraved on the diamond, and poof.

She stopped swinging and looked around for the jewelry. There it was, on the step, glinting in the sun. She snatched it up, clutched it close to her chest like it was the most precious thing she owned. In her time-warped world, it was.

In direct sunlight, its age was even more apparent, but she had no way of knowing how old—three or four centuries, maybe older.

It was delicate and finely made of silver with tiny, twisted threads soldered together to form a Celtic design. Her brain hadn't retained much of the three credit hours of art history she took during her sophomore year in college, probably because she spent her time in class studying player stats instead of the course textbook.

Wasn't four hundred years ago the time of witches and magic potions? Maybe the brooch came from Scotland or Ireland, or someplace else with a history of witchcraft. She didn't know for sure if the inscription was Gaelic. For all she knew, it could be Icelandic or Old English.

All in all, it was easier to buy into the idea of a mind-altering drug than witches, warlocks, and magical stones. One thing was clear, though. If she wasn't in the middle of a drug-induced hallucination or unconscious, then she was on a paranormal jaunt through the cosmos.

To test her hypothesis, she could wait for the drug to wear off, or, she could take immediate action and read the inscription again. If the stone was responsible, could it reverse its power and take her home? Or would it carry her to another place on the time continuum? If she had accidentally unleashed the brooch's power, was she doomed to hopscotch through time for the rest of her life, like the guy on that TV show? What was the name? Oh, *Quantum Leap*.

Amy's attorney mentioned Laurette spent most of her life traveling the world. Where had she gone? To other lands...or to other times?

Amy heard the theme song to the show Dragnet. "Da-da-dada-da. Ladies and gentlemen, the story you are about to see is true..."

Well, Laurette was dead, and Amy would never know. But! If her cousin had traveled through time, she also traveled back home again, because she died in her bed. Relief settled in Amy's bones. She was going to operate on a possibly false assumption; unless she was hallucinating, Laurette had traveled through time, and for Amy, the assumption meant she had her return ticket home, right in her hand.

She decided to give it a go and see what happened.

Her hand shook as she held the brooch in her palm. However, it didn't heat up. She read the inscription, and once again the Gaelic words tangled on her tongue. Nothing happened. There was no fog, no earthy smell, and...

No going home.

Despair stirred the fear simmering in the pit of her stomach, churning it up and swirling it around until her entire body quaked. How could this happen? There had to be a way to reverse this mistake. She could try again, but wasn't that a sign of insanity? Doing the same thing over and over and expecting a different result? She could try one more thing, though. Read the words backwards. Stupid idea maybe, but...

She did. The reverse approach didn't work either. Now what was she going to do?

It wasn't easy, accepting she was stuck. The universe just didn't carry people off and drop them into alternate worlds. There had to be more to this. If the brooch didn't work here and now, then where, and when? She didn't think hanging around Grant's Tomb was the answer to her problem. The cliché "return to the scene of the crime" seemed more apropos. The idea was fraught with potential disappointment, but it was her only option. If the brooch didn't work at the mansion, it wouldn't work anywhere.

At least not right now.

Anxious to be on her way, she jogged to the sidewalk, then stopped abruptly. A quick glance around the park at the men and women strolling there made her realize her outfit—black pants and blazer, white silk blouse, and black flats—would stand out like a neon sign. Could she be arrested for indecent exposure?

What were her options? She always considered options, but today they were limited to one. She pulled her shoulder-length hair back into a ponytail and looped it into a knot at her nape. If she thought she could pass herself off as a man, she might as well start laughing now. With her boobs and butt, she didn't even look like a softball player. Her teammates often joked she belonged on the cover of the *Sports Illustrated* swimsuit edition, not in a Nike ad.

She unbuttoned her blazer and untucked part of her blouse to give it the half-tuck, boxy look, to hide her silhouette. The eye would be drawn to the dangling edge of the blouse and not to her boobs. She had a closet full of ball caps and would gladly trade a week's salary for even her grungiest one. But since she didn't have a cap, she put her head down and plowed ahead. A car drove by and splashed mud on her trouser legs. She turned to flip off the driver, but instead gawked at the motorized horse buggy.

What year *was* this? She didn't know enough about cars to identify the make or model. But based on her research of baseball cards, she put the clothing styles anywhere between 1905 and 1912. If it was before 1909, the mansion wouldn't have been built yet, which could complicate matters. Whatever year it was, it was a warm, sunny spring afternoon.

Before disappearing in an earthy-smelling fog, it had been October and the start of the World Series was only two weeks away. She'd be in the broadcasting booth for the first game, but only on the radio, and she couldn't miss it.

She had to find a way home, and fast.

Instead of walking along Riverside Drive, she turned up 118th Street, crossed at West End, and turned right onto Broadway. The road was a mix of markets, saloons doing a brisk business with inebriated customers lolling around the doorways, plus apartment buildings, and the occasional farm. Dozens of horse-drawn carriages, automobiles, a few bicycles, and trucks loaded with merchandise lumbered down the street, all sharing the road with electric trolleys.

Before she reached 115th Street, the broad dome of the Low Library at Columbia University came into view. The campus wasn't yet enclosed, and the view of the buildings which survived well into the twenty-first century and beyond was extraordinary. She'd give a week's salary for a ballcap, but she'd give a year's salary for a camera.

At the corner of 114th and Broadway, a flyer swept across the sidewalk and butted up against her leg. She kicked the paper away. As it fluttered to the curb, she realized the flyer was a baseball advertisement. She snatched it up before it drifted into the muddy street. The handbill advertised the Giants' season opener against the

Brooklyn Superbas (now known as the Dodgers) on April 15, 1909. The 1909 opening game was one for the ages. But had they already played?

A woman pushing a wicker baby buggy walked by. "Excuse me," Amy said. "What's today's date?"

The woman looked Amy over, backed up a few feet, and gave her a dark stare. "April 15."

Really? She landed in an alternate universe on April 15? The game hadn't taken place. The Giants were playing that afternoon. "Oh. My. God!" The excitement nearly bowled her over. Losing herself in the moment, she gave the woman an air five. "It's opening day. I'm here. And it's opening day."

She did an infield dance, then instantly sobered, remembering she was stranded in the early twentieth-century, and the wide-eyed woman pushing the carriage was on the verge of yelling for help from men in white coats carrying straitjackets.

"I can't help it. I love baseball," Amy tried to explain.

The terrified woman was in such a hurry to escape Amy, she almost crashed the baby carriage into the side of a food stand.

Amy cupped her hands next to her mouth and yelled, "Beautiful baby, by the way."

At the corner of 112th Street, she passed a vendor stacking newspapers. The headline read—*New York Giants play season opener at the Polo Grounds.*

She looked at the flyer again. The game started at three o'clock, but what time was it now? She faced south. The sun was on her left, but heading toward high noon. After playing in the sun for almost three decades, she was on a first-name basis with the hot, yellow ball of glowing gases, and could read its position in the sky with an eighty percent accuracy rate.

The game started in about three hours. Leon Kessling "Red" Ames would pitch the opening game and achieve the remarkable feat of losing a no-hitter. Ames didn't give up a hit until the 10th inning, or a run until the 13th, but he still received credit for nine no-hit innings, until they changed the rules in 1991, and eliminated his no-hitter from the record books. But that rule change didn't affect the outcome of today's game. If she bet on the game, she could win enough money to buy dinner.

She searched the pockets in her pants and blazer. She was dead broke, without even a lint-covered penny in her pocket.

As she walked down Broadway with her arms bundled around her, she kept her head down, avoiding the glaring looks from both men and women. She had grown accustomed to the rhythm, mood, and temperament of New York, but this wasn't her city. Thankfully, she wasn't afraid for her safety. She hadn't landed in the middle of the Revolutionary War.

The business establishments lining the road weren't much different from those of the twenty-first century, except there were no signs advertising ATM machines or lottery tickets. For the first time in her life, she had more money than she could spend, and no access to the funds.

That sucked.

The streets weren't quieter than they were in the twenty-first century, but the noise was different. She didn't miss the obnoxious people who thought everyone in God's creation wanted to hear their cell phone conversations. There were no sirens or cabbies honking horns. But there were plenty of jingling harnesses and heavy wagons lumbering down the macadam street. The rinky-dink sound of a piano spilled syncopated ragtime music out of the door of a saloon, and the Salvation Army even had a five-piece band, accompanied by a pert but prim young woman, standing on the corner and singing "Throw Out the Lifeline."

There were no stop lights or stop signs. Wagons, cars, and pedestrians fought for the right of way. A skidding car took the corner at high speed, and she barely had time to jump out of the way. With her heart pumping and her fist waving, she yelled at the driver, "You're gonna kill somebody driving like a maniac. And it just might be me," she added under her breath, remembering again she was in another time. Behavior acceptable in the twenty-first century wasn't necessarily acceptable in the early twentieth.

At 108th, she followed West End as it branched off Broadway, then turned right on 107th for the downhill amble to Riverside Drive.

She stopped short of the corner and crossed the street to avoid the men unloading two horse-drawn trucks with O'Donnell Moving and Storage written on the side panels. Dang. This would make getting into the house more difficult.

Or would it?

She sneaked around the brownstone on the corner, where she could spy on the movers without being seen. There were four men unloading the wagons and carrying boxes into the house. She watched them come and go several times, usually in pairs. From her vantage point, she couldn't tell how much more there was to unload. If she was going to get inside, her best chance would be to pretend she was one of the movers.

She didn't know if she could pull it off, but she had to try.

Her opportunity came when all four men were needed to hoist poles on their shoulders to transport Cleopatra's throne. As soon as they were out of sight, she scurried across the street to grab a box to carry into the house. On the tailgate was a folded tweed jacket and a cap. She peeked around the truck. She had possibly three minutes, five at the max, to sneak inside and get upstairs. The jacket would hide her curves, and the cap would cover her blond waves, but could she avoid detection with the disguise? Probably not, but it was all she could do.

The jacket was two sizes too big, which worked to her advantage. It fit easily over her blazer and fell past her small waist. The beak of the dark newsboy cap sat low enough to shadow her face. To make a lousy disguise even worse, she rubbed her hand over the wagon wheel and dusted dirt on her face. Before shouldering a box, she steeled her nerve. What was the worst thing that could happen if she was detected? Would they call the police?

If they do, I'll wing it. Just don't get caught.

She grabbed a box, heavy but manageable, hauled it up onto her shoulder, and crossed the sidewalk. The breeze caught a corner of the box's lid and snagged it on the lion's paw. "Let go, ugly beast,"

Amy hissed, wiggling back and forth until the lion released its hold. "As soon as I get home, I'm having you declawed."

For the second time that day, she entered the house. This time, though, it smelled of fresh paint and new construction, not mothballs and rubbing alcohol. A heavyset woman wearing a white apron over a black dress inspected the contents of her box.

"Take this to the bedroom on the second floor that overlooks the front of the house," the woman said.

When the housekeeper turned to point the way, the keys, scissors, and thimbles attached to the chatelaine clasped at her waist clinked. The pleats of her long skirt muffled some of the sound, but it was still annoyingly loud. As a child, Amy was given a Victorian doll with a chatelaine. The clinking had annoyed her so much she cut off all the attachments, to her late mother's dismay.

Amy studied the house as she made her way to the staircase. The pristine condition of the white marble floor, gold and bronze moldings, and stained-glass windows confirmed what she already knew. The cost to renovate the Renaissance mansion she had inherited would be astronomical.

She reached the second floor and a man sauntered toward her, his shirt sleeves rolled to his elbows, and in a thick Irish brogue asked, "Boy-o, where ya heading?"

Amy lowered her voice, "Bedroom. End of the hall."

"Hurry up. We'll be going back to midtown for another load."

She dodged him, keeping her head down, but felt his eyes like a hot iron branding her backside with the letter T for thief. Was she wearing his jacket? His hat? She didn't think so. The short, barrel-chested man was too broad for the jacket.

"O'Donnell," another Irishman yelled.

She shifted the weight of the box to her other shoulder and caught a glimpse of the second man. He was too skinny for the jacket. If she hung out in the hall any longer, the perfect-fit Irishman would show up and recognize his clothes.

"Trucks are empty. Ya ready?" he asked.

Before the barrel-chested man could answer, she pushed open

the door to the bedroom and kicked it shut behind her.

Don't let them come after me. Please don't let them follow.

She leaned against the wood-paneled door, breathing deeply to slow her heart rate. It didn't work. She placed her ear to the door and was heartened when she didn't hear voices. The men must have returned to the wagons. Or they were on the other side waiting to barge in on her.

Bring it on. I'll box your ears.

It wasn't just a thief hyperventilating, either. She had the moxie to back it up. She set down the box and did a fast one-two combination, punching at the air. She hadn't boxed since college, and wasn't too much of a threat to anyone, but she had enough power in her arm to make an attacker work hard for the win.

A win? Seriously?

This wasn't about winning. It was about staying out of jail in a foreign world. At least the bedroom didn't seem foreign. The antique furniture was arranged differently, but the bed, dressing table, chest of drawers, and armoire were the same pieces. The wallpaper had shades of brown and beige flowers instead of pale green stripes, and the breeze coming through the open windows rippled the fringe of the pulled-back drapes. She peeked out the window and said a silent thank-you as she watched the wagons drive off.

A sudden sense of doom closed in on her. Coming back in here had been a mistake. It wasn't going to change her circumstances. There was no psychedelic drug that would wear off and restore her twenty-first century reality. The movers were gone, which limited her mobility. She was now stuck inside the house until they returned.

Hey, kiddo. Have you forgotten why you came here? The brooch. Try the brooch.

At least her internal voice was functioning on all cylinders. She opened the stone and spoke the magic words. If the words were Gaelic, her ability to speak them wasn't getting any better. When nothing happened, she tried again, and infused her voice with hope instead of despair.

That didn't work, either.

She was about to try again when the housekeeper's clinking chatelaine, coming down the hall, interrupted her. A quick glance around the room for a hiding place identified only one possibility. She had a split second to dash across the room, go down in a foot-first bent-leg slide, and disappear under the dust-ruffled bed. If it had been her bed, she wouldn't have been able to squeeze in among the boxes of old equipment, jerseys, lost socks, and cleats she refused to throw away, even after they were too worn to wear.

The housekeeper's black polished boots clacked against the wood floor as she entered and moved about the room. Amy lifted the dust ruffle slightly to watch the woman as she opened the box Amy carried to the bedroom and unpacked the contents. Amy slapped her hand over her mouth when she spotted the bill of her cap peeking out from under the dressing table's upholstered chair. In her hurry to slide under the bed, the cap must have flown off and landed there. If the housekeeper glanced down, she would see it.

After the housekeeper unpacked the box, she placed it next to the door, then turned to the lighter weight furniture, pushing one piece here and pulling another piece there. Amy grew impatient with the woman's dawdling. Why didn't she leave?

The housekeeper circled the room, slowly, looking here and there. Amy's guilt assumed the woman suspected something was amiss, and believed she could figure it out if she stayed long enough. If Amy had a way of distracting her, she would, but her last clever idea had been to slide under the bed, and now she was stuck.

The housekeeper snapped her hands to her hips, marched over to the chair, and groaning, picked up the hat.

Amy gnawed on her lower lip. Dang. That was a good hat.

What was the housekeeper going to do with it? Throw it out the window? Toss it in the trash? Leave it on the table for Amy? Good luck with that one.

The housekeeper inspected the inside for identifying marks and not finding any, rolled it up and slipped it into her pocket, scowling.

Amy scooted farther back under the bed, barely breathing.

The housekeeper crossed over to the bed, chatelaine clinking, and lifted the ruffle with her foot. For Amy, it was like standing in the batter's box, bottom of the ninth, down by three, bases loaded, two outs, a three-two count, with the pitcher winding up for the pitch. She held her breath. This could go either way.

The housekeeper dropped the dust ruffle and walked away. A moment later the door opened and closed. Amy didn't dare move. She counted to a hundred. Then counted again. When the housekeeper didn't return, Amy elbow-crawled out from under the bed and pulled to her feet. She put her ear to the door, but couldn't hear a dang thing.

She had to get out of there.

Maybe the brooch would work this time. She repeated the words. She waited. She hoped. She prayed. Nothing happened. Why bring her here? Bad things happened to good people. She knew that. It was part of life, but being launched into an alternate universe wasn't just a bad thing. It was a vast and incomprehensible mistake, and it had to be rectified. But how?

She had no answers.

If she was going to be stuck in the twentieth-century, she needed to get her life in order. Her top priority had to be money to buy food and pay rent. And the only thing of value she had was the brooch. She couldn't sell it, but maybe she could pawn it. If she did, she'd have to reclaim it as soon as possible.

What kind of work could she do? All she knew was baseball. Betting on baseball in the early 1900s was as much a part of the game as hot tempers and fistfights. She could probably earn enough in a couple of weeks, maybe a month, to reclaim the brooch.

She couldn't pawn the brooch looking like a street urchin, though. The pawn shop owner would call the police, convinced she stole it. She checked the mirror, wiping the dirt off her face, and dusted off her pants. Forget it. No matter how clean she was, her clothes would attract unwanted attention. Was there anything in Catherine Lily's drawers she could wear?

The chest held only petticoats, corsets, and hosiery. If Catherine

Lily's undergarments were in here, maybe her dresses were too. Amy yanked open the closet door and nearly jumped with joy. She'd found a gold mine full of dresses, skirts, blouses, hats, coats, and shoes.

She flipped through hangers, searching for an outfit a woman with an expensive diamond brooch would wear, and found just the thing—a medium blue tailored suit made of raw silk, with a long-line jacket and full skirt. It was perfect.

She raced back to the chest to select an appropriate petticoat, then stripped off the stolen jacket, the blazer underneath, and her pants and blouse, folding them neatly before pulling the petticoat over her head and then stepping into the skirt. The suit's jacket was snug, but not uncomfortable. If she wore a corset, she would have a better fit, but visions of Scarlett O'Hara being squeezed into the contraption in *Gone with the Wind* silenced the notion. She would never volunteer to be locked into a steel-boned cage.

A dozen pairs of shoes and boots were lined up on the floor beneath the dresses. She kicked off her shoe and measured her foot against one of the boots. Eyeballing shoes was not the way to determine size, but she could count on it putting her within the half-size-too-big range and, in emergencies, a too-big shoe worked better than going barefoot.

She untied the laces and, using a silver shoehorn suspended on a hook above the row of shoes, shoved her feet into the stiff boots. They weren't the most comfortable shoes she'd ever worn, and if she had to walk a mile or two, she'd have blisters. But the boots were century-appropriate, and, even more important, free. One less item she'd have to buy.

A tooled-leather shoulder bag hung from a hook near the door, big enough to hold her clothes and shoes, but not big enough to stuff in another Catherine Lily dress. But if she folded her clothes into a small bundle, they would fit in the bag along with her shoes and the stolen jacket. At the bottom of the bag was a yellowed and crinkled first-class ticket on the *SS Seneca*, which had departed Kildonan, Scotland, June 28, 1877.

Based on Catherine Lily's birth year engraved on the portrait, Amy figured her ancestor would have been twenty-two. Had she been scared traveling alone? Sailing to America was probably as scary as traveling into the past. The trips led them to a strange new world. For the first time since discovering Catherine Lily's portrait, Amy felt an emotional kinship with her. Maybe their paths would cross while Amy was stuck here.

She put thoughts of Catherine Lily aside for now and packed her few belongings. She wasn't really stealing. In a hundred years, it would all be hers—the house, the furnishings, the fixtures, the clothes, and the brooch. Right?

Who would believe her, though, if she had to explain who she was and where she came from? Not a soul.

A cute tricorn-shaped hat with a ribbon and ostrich plume caught her eye, and she lifted it off the shelf. A ball cap was the only kind of hat she ever wore, but, based on what she just saw in shop windows and adorning women's heads, hats were the height of fashion, and she would look odd without one.

She carried it over to the dressing table and, watching in the mirror, placed it on her head. She adjusted it, front to back and side to side, finally settling on the perfect angle. Pleased with her appearance, she did an uncharacteristic spin in front of the mirror, watching the skirt twirl around her legs, and enjoying the erotic slide of the silk as it rippled against her skin. The gorgeous fabric, so smooth and silky, seemed to melt in her hands. When had she worn anything so elegant? Never. Not until today.

Slowly, she opened the door and peeked out. The hallway was empty, and the doors to the other rooms were shut. The movers hadn't returned with another load, and she didn't want to be here when they did, since there was the trivial matter of a stolen jacket and cap.

She slid the shoulder bag's leather strap over her head, reminding herself that she wasn't really stealing. Although if the housekeeper caught her, she would call the police and Amy would go to jail.

Then she better not get *caught*.

Maybe she could ask the housekeeper for a job. A position of some sort would allow her to work inside the house, where she could keep checking in with the brooch. Surely one day, probably later than sooner, the time travel door would open again and she could escape. But she couldn't interview for a job wearing Catherine Lily's dress, and she couldn't interview for a job without it.

Amy tiptoed out into the hall, eyes peeled, ears sharp, and instincts set to survival mode. No one was there. Feeling like a criminal, she moved as stealthily as possible toward the stairs. The housekeeper could materialize any moment, and if she did, what was Amy's plan? To lie her way out of a confrontation? But what was her story?

Whatever it was, she had to make an unbelievable story both believable and simple. Stick to the truth as much as possible. She was Catherine Lily's descendant, but she couldn't be her granddaughter. Maybe a distant niece from… Where? South Carolina? Sure, why not? She'd follow the adage and fake it till she made it.

Twice a loud bang brought her to a dead stop, but when no one confronted her, she kept going, always listening for the housekeeper's clinking chatelaine. When Amy reached the stairs, she crept down one step at a time, hugging the wall. A door slammed in another part of the house, and she froze while she debated whether to go back upstairs and hide or sprint to the front door and escape. When she didn't hear footfalls or clinking, she stepped off the bottom step and gauged the distance to the door.

She could sprint from first base to second in two-point-seven seconds, or she could when she was playing fast pitch. She couldn't now, but she could get close enough. The distance from the staircase to the front door was about a hundred twenty feet. It would take her six seconds to get there. She glanced down at her boots. Forget that idea. If she ran across the marble floor in these funky boots, she'd sound like a herd of elephants.

She peered around the wall, but didn't see or hear anyone coming her way. The mansion was as silent and still as it had been when she first walked through the front door and became the butt end of a freak cosmic mistake. Mistakes happened. In baseball, there were dozens of ways to make errors. She won a steak dinner recently when a reporter asked her if she could name the player who had the most errors in one season. When she told him Billy Shindle and Herman Long tied at one hundred twenty-two, he didn't believe her. It ended up being one of the most delicious steak dinners she'd eaten in a long time.

Tiptoeing, she inched across the marble floor toward the foyer—which by itself was large enough to host a party—her heart in her throat. Latched onto the doorknob and turned it. Escape was only inches away. She opened the door slightly. The wind whipped across the porch, caught it, and flung the door wide, rattling the stained-glass inserts. She ran smack into a man whose jacket was warm as summer sun and smelled of tomato sauce, which made her stomach rumble with hunger. Caught off-balance, he shuffled backwards, holding tight to her arms.

"I'm so sorry," she said. "Excuse me." She righted herself quickly, an asset honed by years on the ball field.

He tugged off his hat. "*Signora,*" he said with an Italian accent. "Are you Mrs. Sterling?"

Amy wasn't going to stand on the porch and have a conversation with anyone, even a charming Italian. She was wearing a stolen dress, hat, and shoes, and she had to get as far away from the Sterling house as possible.

"No, I'm not. I don't believe she's home today." Amy hurried down the steps and past the lions, patting a paw on her way out the gate.

He rushed after her. "*Mi scusi.*"

"*Non parlo Italiano.*" She knew a handful of Italian phrases, and would use them all up if the conversation extended beyond the sidewalk.

"Do you know when Mr. Sterling will be home?"

She stopped and studied the man she guessed to be in his early thirties. A black bowler hat covered dark, wavy hair, and a broad smile and a gleam in his brown eyes told her she had nothing to fear and no reason to be rude. She pointed toward the front door. "The housekeeper is inside. She should be able to answer your questions. And," she paused a moment. "It's *signorina*. Not *signora*. *Ciao*."

"*Grazie*."

She turned at the corner of 107th and Riverside and shot a glance toward the mansion's front porch. Mr. Italy was standing there knocking on the door. She picked up her pace and very quickly arrived at West End Avenue. Which way? Turn left, or continue to Broadway? West End was all residential, and she needed a pawn shop. If she remembered correctly, she spotted a pawn shop on her way to the mansion, snugged in between two saloons, a block from Columbia University.

She walked by a small grocery store and stopped to peek in the window. Shelves were lined with cans and packages, but she didn't see any vegetables, dairy products, or meat. Did they have separate stores for those? She walked by a meat market earlier, but hadn't thought anything about it. If she was going to survive here, she had to be alert to everything around her, especially the way women behaved. Drawing undue attention could be her downfall.

On the other side of the street, a sign advertising room and board for twenty dollars a week was posted near the door of a brownstone. She needed both.

A quick jaunt across the street put her on the stoop of the last unit in a row of homes. All the buildings were well-maintained, at least from the outside, and the neighborhood seemed safe. Safety was important to her, so was the fact the brownstone was a block from the Sterlings' residence. While she didn't think she had to be inside the mansion for the brooch to do its thing—when and if it decided to open the time portal again—the dang stone could change its frigging mind.

Before she could rent a room, though, she had to know how much money she could get for the brooch. She also wanted to know what kind of salary she could expect to make. Using brooch funds to pay for room and board would put her further in debt, and she might never be able to save enough money to reclaim her property. As soon as she had sufficient funds in her pocket, she would come back and schedule an appointment to meet the owner and see the room.

What if someone beat her to it and leased the unit before she had a chance to see it? Shouldn't she at least make an appointment and express her interest?

The sharp crack of a bat as it connected with a ball interrupted her train of thought. She could tell the batter had hit near the sweet spot from the sound alone, and from experience she knew a ball was sailing over a fence nearby.

Cheering voices came from behind the brownstone. She followed the shouting down the adjoining alley, reaching an empty lot where a dozen young boys were playing baseball. She watched from the shade of the three-story townhome while the batter rounded the bases, and another boy climbed over the fence. The runner tagged home mere seconds before the outfielder threw the ball back onto the improvised field.

"That run ties the game. Next one wins," the pitcher yelled.

"Shut up and throw it," the batter said, wiggling the bat. The pitcher threw a strike, and the batter wiggled the bat again while he waited for the next pitch.

"Strike two," the catcher said.

Amy came out of the shadows, saying, "Time out. I want to talk to the batter."

The catcher gawked at her. "Sorry lady. We don't have time-outs."

"I have a tip to help the batter improve his game," she said.

"Don't need it," the batter said.

The pitcher squared off to the plate, his hand and wrist held deep inside the glove, hiding the grip and ball from the batter. "Step aside before you get hurt."

She moved out of the way, but the itch to intrude grew stronger. If she didn't scratch it, she might break down and cry. While she was stuck in this weird time warp, baseball was the one thing she knew for sure, and by asserting herself, she gained a modicum of control over her life.

"Is there a reason you're wiggling your bat?" she asked.

Without taking his eyes off the pitcher, he said, "I've seen Doyle do it. I want to hit like him."

She had never seen film or photos of Larry Doyle batting, but knew he would lead the National League in hits this year. "It could be a timing device for Doyle, but if you watch him closely, you'll see he always gets his bat back into position before the ball is pitched. Your bat isn't in position, which is why you're striking out."

"I ain't striking out."

"One more and you will. You'll get a hit off your pitcher if you listen to what I'm telling you. If you're going to wiggle the bat, make sure it's for a reason, and not because you're mimicking Doyle. Get your bat into position before the pitcher releases the ball."

He dug in his feet and wiggled his bat, but this time, he popped it back into position before the pitcher released the pitch. He connected with the ball and sprinted to first base. The shortstop turned a badly handled roller into a double, and the batter went to third on a fielder's choice. The next batter singled, and her protégé stayed on third. The player following him popped one to left field. The outfielder caught it on a bounce but sent the orb wide and high of the catcher, and the runner on third scored the winning run.

"Can't you aim any better than that?" the catcher yelled at the player who had thrown the ball from left field.

"Wasn't my aim. It was your catching," the outfielder shouted back.

Her protégé dodged the catcher and outfielder, who were by now shoving each other, and he ran toward her. "Hey, lady. You got any more tips?"

"Good job," she said, holding up her hand to high-five him, but he gave her a puzzled look and she dropped her arm. "I said you'd get a hit if you listened to me."

"Yeah, well…you were right. How'd you know?"

"What's your name?" she asked.

"Eddie Farrell."

Eddie Farrell. Signed by McGraw in 1925. Played for a summer team managed by Larry Doyle. What a small world.

"Okay, Eddie. Wiggling the bat without a reason is a common mistake. But you won't do it again, will you?"

"No, ma'am. What else am I doing wrong? Why can't I hit it over the fence?"

"I'd have to watch you bat several more times, and I don't have time today."

The player who followed Eddie to the plate asked, "What about me? Any tips?"

"A good swing will have a bit of undercut in it, but yours is exaggerated. When you swing, start downward, be level through the zone, and follow through with a slight upper cut." She set her bag on the ground. "Like this." She swung a phantom bat. "See? Keep your front shoulder down on the baseball. You'll have more power if you do."

"What about me?" the pitcher asked.

"When you throw the ball to first base, don't stop and think about it. Just do it." She feigned throwing a baseball. "Imagine the ball you're holding is an egg. Don't crush it. Throw it."

"Got one for me?" the last kid she saw at bat asked.

"Work on your stance. Pry your bat down from the grandstand before you strain an oblique muscle." She poked her side between her hip and rib cage to show him where the muscle was located. "You're holding it too high."

She was now surrounded by a dozen eager-faced young boys. She never thought of herself as a coach, and normally she shied away from giving anyone advice on how to improve their game. But they compelled her as no other player ever had. She wanted…no, make that needed…to share her knowledge and love of the game with them.

"How'd you learn so much?" another player asked.

They'd have no idea what she was talking about if she said she was a national and Olympic fastpitch softball champion. "My dad was a coach. I grew up around the game. They wouldn't let me play, so—"

"Who'd he coach for?" Eddie interrupted.

"A team in California." She changed the subject before they could ask more personal questions. "Here's my parting advice. Hit, run, catch, throw every day, either by yourself or with your friends. That's how you'll get better. Now, I've got to go."

"Wait. What's your name?" Eddie asked.

"Do you live around here?" the pitcher asked.

"Amy Spalding. And, no, I don't live around here." She might end up living in the building whose yard they were playing in, but she didn't want to advertise the possibility.

Eddie had a bewildered look in his eyes. "You're a Spalding? No wonder you know so much about baseball."

"Is Mr. A. G. Spalding your pa?" the pitcher asked.

A. G. Spalding? Oh, my. Growing up, how many times had she claimed a ball was hers because it carried her name? Dozens. "No," she said slowly, thinking how to answer the question so it wouldn't generate hundreds more. "All Spaldings originally came from Scotland, so we're distantly related, but I've never met him."

"Too bad," Eddie said. "He's rich."

She tousled his hair affectionately, and he blushed. "You're right. He is." In her own time, she was, too. Thanks to a woman who hadn't even been born yet. "Now I really do have to go."

"Will you come back?"

The slight desperation in his voice hit her in the pit of her stomach, and she didn't understand why. "I will if I can." If she rented the room, she'd see a lot more of the team. She liked Eddie, and could help him improve his game, and the others, too. His sweet grin and slightly crooked teeth were more than endearing, and she wanted to coach him. If not for the fact she had no money, no home, no food, and no job, she would have stayed and played ball with them for the rest of the day.

He picked her bag up off the ground and handed it to her. "Come back if you can. We're here most afternoons."

"No school? No chores?" she asked.

"We do them first. School, I mean, then chores," the pitcher said.

"My ma hides my glove until chores are done," one of the other boys said.

Amy laughed. "I heard McGraw only wants college boys on his team. He said they're smart enough to figure out their faults."

"I guess if a man is smart enough to figure out his faults, he can change and be a better player," Eddie said.

"That's right," Amy said. "Those who aren't smart try to hide their faults instead."

"They're the ones who never get very far. Right, Miss Spalding?" the pitcher said.

She slung the strap over her shoulder. "You're right. And it applies to much more than baseball. If you're not getting good grades, it's not the teacher's fault. Look in the mirror to see what you can change."

She waved goodbye, thinking of all the opportunities to help disadvantaged kids she had missed in the last few years. Down deep, where resentment and denial grew like weeds in a garden, sat a boatload of bad memories. She resented all the players her dad had coached when he could have been helping her more. If she ever had kids, they would come first—always.

5

1909 New York City—Amy

"Just get me out there and watch my smoke."
—John McGraw

AFTER LEAVING THE BOYS playing baseball, Amy picked up the pace and hurried down 107th Street to Broadway. At the corner, she debated what to do next. She'd noticed a pawn shop near 112th, and a hotel near 113th. If she was successful at the pawn shop, her next stop would be the hotel, and then the brownstone. If she had two choices, she could compare them and make an informed decision. Then she'd go to the Giants' game.

With a destination in mind, she turned the corner.

"*Signorina*, may I offer you a ride?"

She jerked her head toward the familiar, accented voice, smiling as Mr. Italy pulled the cutest little car to the curb.

"You're probably not going where I'm going," she said. "But thanks for the offer."

He turned off the engine and jumped to the ground, landing a mere foot from her. "If not, I'll take you wherever you want to go."

"To the Polo Grounds. Ames is pitching the season opener."

His thumbs found the straps of his suspenders, and he rocked back on his heels. "What luck. I'm going there, too."

She studied his eyes, and they told her he was making it up as he went along. Was he harmless? She didn't know, and if she'd been in the twenty-first century, she would never have considered going anywhere with him. But nervous flares weren't going off, and her spidey senses weren't acting up. Her intuition told her that she was safe with him. If her body washed ashore in the Hudson River, they could inscribe her headstone with the phrase: She should have known better.

She glanced past him and evaluated the car. The cab wasn't any larger than a Smart Car, but the chassis and wheels raised it high off the ground, and it resembled a giant phone booth.

She pointed, asking, "What's that called?"

"It's a Baker Electric Coupe. A favorite style for the ladies. I don't like gas-powered automobiles. They're noisy, smelly, and greasy. You can drive the Baker around town, to a job or to lunch, without fear of soiling your gloves, mussing your hair, or setting your dress on fire." He sounded so much like a salesman in a commercial, she almost laughed. "It's at your disposal"—his eyes twinkled—"if you'll tell me your name."

What a flirt. "Amy Spalding. And yours?"

He doffed his hat. "Gabriele Moretti."

He had great hair and eyes, too. Since meeting Joe, she had become immune to good looks and sexy smiles with perfect teeth. Men like Gabriele were the norm in a game where diamond studs in tight pants held a bat or glove in one hand and grabbed their crotches with the other.

The Polo Grounds stadium was at least two miles away, and, while she wasn't opposed to walking, safety was an issue. And there was the matter of her brooch and finding a pawn shop.

"I appreciate the offer, but there is a stop I need to make before we go to the Polo Grounds."

He opened the car door and offered his hand. "I will stop at every corner from here to the ballpark if it is the *signorina's* wish." He climbed into the vehicle after her, pulled a metal bar down over his lap, and turned the key.

She glanced around the upholstered interior. There was no steering wheel or dashboard or handles to roll the windows up and down. She pointed to the bar across his lap. "What's that?"

"The steering tiller. And this," he pointed to a lever positioned between the door and the bench seat, "is the acceleration lever."

"And the pedals. What do they do?"

"There's one for each rear brake. Do you know how to drive?"

She had been driving stick and automatic vehicles since she turned sixteen, and would love to drive the electric car, but not today. Right now, she had to focus, and driving in a city without signs and signals sounded suicidal. "I do. How fast does this automobile go?"

He merged into Broadway traffic. "About twenty-two miles per hour."

The only electric vehicles she'd ridden in were golf carts. Gabriele's car had more personality, but it didn't go any faster than the carts on the golf course. He easily maneuvered the car around the pot-holed boulevard, dodging other cars, horse-drawn wagons and carriages, and jaywalkers.

"Did you see the Giants play in the playoff game last fall?" she asked.

"I've only been to a few games. I don't know much about baseball. If you ask me a question, I won't know the answer."

"That's okay. I know enough for both of us." Like a kid, she fiddled with the leather strap that held down and closed the window like those used in old railroad cars. She kept looking from one side of the street to the other, noticing business establishments she had missed earlier. An Italian restaurant looked interesting, and there was a hotel right next door. Both were possibilities for tonight. As soon as she pawned the brooch, she'd be able to settle back and enjoy the ride to the ballpark.

"Did you find Mr. Sterling?" she asked.

"The housekeeper said they were returning from out of town tomorrow. I'll go back later this week."

If Catherine Lily wasn't in town, maybe Amy could break into the mansion and steal another dress or two? *Don't be stupid.* She barely got out undetected the first time. Even for another beautiful dress, she couldn't risk being arrested.

"Didn't the housekeeper tell you?" he asked.

"You got more information out of her than I did. It must have been your award-winning smile."

He laughed. "If a butler had been guarding the door, you would have gotten the information, not me."

"Maybe." She had never been very good playing the helpless female card, but she wasn't opposed to trying.

"Do you know Mr. and Mrs. Sterling?" he asked.

How should she play this? Tell as few lies as possible. If she stuck closely to the truth, she wouldn't be as likely to forget her fabrications. "No. I was there…about a position."

"I heard Mrs. Sterling's social secretary married and moved away. Was that the job you were calling about?"

A job as a social secretary hadn't been on her short list of job possibilities, but she would consider it, as well as a hundred other jobs. When a girl had to eat, she couldn't get too picky.

Gabriele hit the brakes to avoid smashing into a car turning left in front of him. Amy would have screamed at the driver, but he just nodded and drove on. "What are you doing now?" he asked, picking up speed once again.

Amy relaxed her grip on the seat. "I just arrived from…" *Stick to the truth if possible.* "Charleston, South Carolina." She had moved home to store her belongings while waiting on ESPN to offer her a job, and, while it had only been for a few weeks, it literally was where she had come from. "I'm looking for employment and an apartment."

"I can help with the apartment. My building has a few vacancies. We could get you settled in there tonight."

She gave him a quick once-over and made a value judgment based on his neat appearance, the quality of his clothing, and, of course, the cute car. "I couldn't afford an apartment in a building you live in."

"It's a modest building on 84th and Riverside." He gave her the same quick once-over, and gently fingered the fabric of her skirt that brushed his leg. "You could rent a lower level unit for less than what you paid for this silk suit. Where's your luggage?"

She sighed, partly for impact, and partly because she was lying. And even though it was necessary to create a cover story, she hated the dishonesty. "My suitcase was stolen from the train." She patted the leather satchel at her side. "All I have are a few personal items, and a piece of jewelry I need to pawn."

"Did the police find any leads?"

"I didn't report it. Finding the thief would be impossible. Other than cash, I didn't lose anything I can't easily replace. I'll never get the money back, so it wasn't worth the trouble of filing a complaint."

She was jabbering and she knew it, but she couldn't stop herself. "The police have so many serious crimes to solve, investigating my case would never be a priority. I know I should have, but..."

"It's not too late. You can file a complaint today."

She shook her head. "All I need now is a pawn shop. I saw one between 112th and 113th."

"Those loan sharks will charge you an outrageous interest rate."

"Beggars can't be choosers."

"Maybe not, but you can choose who you pay interest to. I have an office in the Providence Loan Society's headquarters on Park Avenue and 25th Street. They'll give you a short-term loan using your jewelry as collateral, and at a much lower rate. If you can't repay the loan in six months, they'll auction your property."

"Why would they give me a lower interest rate?"

"It's what they do. It's a not-for-profit company owned by Cornelius Vanderbilt, J. P. Morgan, and others. You'll get a fair deal there."

The property—her brooch—didn't work anyway, but the large diamond had to be worth thousands. Would she really get a fair deal? With a loan, she could rent an apartment and buy clothes and groceries. The rest she could invest. If she got a job and lived frugally, she might be able to save enough through her salary and investments to reclaim the brooch before the end of the term.

"I need a place to stay and food to eat. I can't wait until morning."

"There's a widow in my building. If I ask her, she'll let you stay there. You'll have a clean bed to sleep in tonight, and tomorrow you can get a loan and rent one of the units in the building. After you get settled, you can do something nice for her."

Amy considered his kindness, and wondered why he was helping her. Was he expecting something in return? If he was, she'd get out of the car right now. "I'm a stranger. Why are you helping me?"

He swerved to avoid hitting another car, and her shoulder banged the door. No wonder this traffic was a snarled mess. There was absolutely no rhyme or reason to the way it flowed…no stop lights or stop signs, no speed limits, no traffic cops.

"I was like you once," he said, driving the automobile deftly between two wagons. "I came to the city with nothing. A priest, Father John, caught me stealing an apple from a vendor. Instead of handing me over to the cops, he took me in, gave me a place to stay and food to eat. A few days after he rescued me, he sent me to a parishioner who worked as a foreman on the docks. The man took one look at me, scrappy but clean, and put me to work unloading cargo."

"From the docks to owning a car. That's impressive."

"It took fifteen years. I worked hard and learned everything I could. I own a freight brokerage business now."

"You're the perfect example of the Horatio Alger story—rags to riches." Gabriele hit the brakes to avoid hitting a pedestrian darting across the street, and Amy cringed.

"Father John gave me Alger's books to read to help me learn English."

"You learned it well." If she had landed in a foreign country and couldn't understand the language, she might have jumped off the nearest bridge. "How'd you do it? New country, new language, no family?"

"I wanted to be here. It was hard leaving my family, but I knew if I worked hard, I might see them again."

"I admire your fortitude." She hadn't come here of her own choosing, and she might never see Joe and her friends again. Unlike Gabriele, she just wanted to go home.

Playing sports had taught her how to win, how to lose gracefully, and how to pick yourself up after disappointment or loss. Those lessons would come in handy now, especially the one about picking yourself up after disappointment. In her heart, she hoped she'd wake up and be home again, but in her mind, where reality hung out, she doubted it would happen so easily.

It might be months before her number was called to jump aboard the great roller coaster ride through time. And it might be never. She had two choices: make lemonade out of the lemons she'd been given, or become a sour, defeated person. To Amy Spalding, Olympic champion, it was no choice at all.

It was a beautiful spring day. The Giants were playing their season opener, she had a plan for the next twenty-four hours, and "Red" Ames was pitching, and would lose a no-hitter. If she played it right, she could win enough money to not only buy dinner for them, but pay the widow for a clean bed for the night and a hot bath. If the brooch didn't take her home in the morning, she would proceed with her day-two plan, and pray she wasn't making the second biggest mistake of her life.

6

Present day New York City—Jack

JACK ENJOYED A late-night dinner and a few beers with the O'Grady boys before taking a taxi to the Plaza. During the Yankees game, he had barely contained his frustration with David for not answering his text messages. Had he found notes or letters? If there was anything to find, David would find it. His friend was James Bond and Superman wrapped up in one frustratingly competent Scotsman-superhero.

Jack not only trusted David with his life, he already owed David his life…his sanity, too. Every day for the past eight months, David had emailed, called, or sent text messages. Jack doubted anyone else was aware of the effort David made to stay in touch and provide a shoulder to lean on in the dark days following Carolina Rose's death. Braham's shoulder was always available, too, but Braham lived five hundred yards from Jack's door. David, on the other hand, juggled a family and three residences: Kentucky, the Highlands, and Napa, and yet he never failed to reach out and say, "How ye doing today?"

Regardless of how good David had been to him, Jack was still pissed he hadn't responded to his text messages.

He slid his key card into the slot and opened the door to the hotel suite. The lights were on, and soft jazz was playing on the B&O stereo system. He dropped his jacket and keys on the table in the grand foyer and entered the living area.

David was on the couch, facing the large window with a panoramic view of Central Park and 6th Avenue. Jack stayed at the hotel for the five-star accommodations, but he returned again and again for the incredible view of the city.

"Why didn't you answer my texts?" he demanded by way of greeting.

David set down a half-full highball glass and continued typing on his laptop. "I thought the purpose of my coming was so ye could enjoy the game with JL's brothers. If I'd sent ye updates, ye wouldn't have been able to concentrate on the game."

"At least I wouldn't have worried about you."

David laughed. "Worried? Ye've never worried about me."

"That's not true. I worried you broke your hand when you slugged me in England after the plane crash."

"I should have shot ye and saved myself the pain."

Jack poured a drink from the crystal decanter on the nearby table and sipped. "Well, did you find anything?"

David held up a small leather book and waved it in the air. "Catherine Lily's journal."

Jack grabbed for it, but David held fast to the book, with his finger marking his place. "I'm scanning the pages. Ye can read it as soon as I finish. I don't want ye to get pissed off and rip out pages."

"I wouldn't do that," Jack said.

"I don't trust ye. Ye'll have to wait."

Jack sat in an easy chair next to the sofa, kicked off his shoes, and put his feet up on the coffee table. He tried to appear calm instead of ready to jump out of his skin. "Have you read it? Does it mention Carolina Rose?"

"I haven't read the whole book, but so far there's no mention of her."

Jack turned the crystal round and round, pressing the tips of his fingers into the straight, sharp angles cut into the glass. "If I'd had more time with Carolina Rose, maybe…" He took another sip.

Tonight was the first time he had alcohol in eight months. He picked the anniversary of her death to fall off the wagon. Two beers at the ball game, a few more at dinner, and now whisky. He wasn't an alcoholic or even a problem drinker, and he wanted to keep it that way. Which was why he quit drinking when he did. But since the pain wasn't as raw now, he didn't have the urge to use alcohol to mask the anguish cannibalizing his insides.

"When was the last entry?" There was an odd sensation nipping at him—a feeling of déjà vu. Was this meeting with David at the Plaza reminiscent of the time they spent in 1944 London while searching for Kenzie? Possibly.

David flipped to the last page of the journal and held up a small envelope. "This was stuck in the middle of the book. It contains a lock of hair. There's no note indicating its owner. But ye can have the DNA tested. I'd also test Amy's."

Jack took a deep breath. "I have a gut feeling they were sisters, but what I don't know is why they were separated."

"Catherine Lily's adoptive mother, Alison Morrison Taylor, may be the only person who knew, and she died July 10, 1909."

"How do you know?"

"I asked Alice to look in the parish records to see if she could find anything."

"If you asked your mother to find the Pope's cell phone number, she could. But I thought all the records were in the archives in Edinburgh."

"They are, but the kirk at Inverness keeps its own parishioners' log of births, marriages, and deaths."

David closed the journal and handed it to Jack. "I'm going to take a shower. If ye want to go back to the mansion, I'll go with ye. Otherwise, I'm going to the farm to be with my bride."

"And take advantage of your networks of spies and computer gurus to solve this mystery. I'll go with you. Is Elliott at the farm or the winery?"

"The spring meet starts at Keeneland on Friday. They'll fly to the farm in the morning."

David headed toward the second bedroom, pulling his shirt over his head, flexing thick arm and shoulder muscles. As often as Jack lifted in the gym, he would never have a carved, ripped physique like David's. The man was simply one of a kind, and while Jack envied him, he also loved him like a brother. He rubbed his jaw, which had never been the same since David slugged him almost five years ago.

Jack had deserved it at the time.

David tossed his shirt on the floor next to a duffel bag and unbuckled his belt, flinging it on top of the bed. "I do my top-tier work now in front of the computer."

"I don't believe it," Jack yelled after him. "How long were you in the house before you found the journal?"

"Longer than I should have been." The bathroom door slammed and water pelted the floor of the shower.

Jack picked up the journal and sprawled on the sofa. If he went back in time to rescue Amy, he could take a detour, go to Scotland, and interview Catherine Lily's adoptive mother. He opened the journal to the first page and began reading. In the margins were sketches of roses and lilies. He thumbed through a few pages. If he ever wanted closure, he had to pursue the connection between Amy's family and his Rose, which meant another trip to the past. And while he'd rather not go again, he knew it was the only way to discover the truth.

When David returned to the living room wearing only a pair of boxer briefs and grabbed his mobile off the coffee table, Jack said, "Get dressed. We're leaving."

David checked messages while returning to his room. "The plane is fueled and waiting on the tarmac."

"You already called the pilot?"

"About an hour ago."

Jack jumped to his feet. "How'd you know I'd be ready to leave?"

David grabbed a pair of khakis from his duffel and stepped into them. "We've been through a lot together. I know ye well. Better than ye know yerself. Ye haven't been able to get closure, and without closure ye'll never let Carolina Rose go. This is a chance to find the missing pieces of the puzzle. Once ye put the puzzle together, and it makes sense to ye, ye'll move on, but not before."

Jack picked up the house phone to notify the desk he was checking out. "I hope you're right, because I sure as hell can't go on living like this."

David tucked in his shirttail, zipped his duffel bag, and grabbed the backpack loaded with equipment. "I hope so, too, because this might be yer only opportunity."

7

1909 New York City—Amy

THE TRAFFIC THINNED out as they traveled farther up Broadway. Amy made mental notes along the way, keeping track of banks, apartment rentals, markets, and clothing stores. From what she knew of the city's history, there were plenty of shops in midtown, but unless she had to leave the Upper West Side to go to work, she intended to stay close to the Sterlings' mansion.

She settled back to enjoy the ride and her companion. Gabriele was not only entertaining, but handsome. His deep, probing brown eyes would have unsettled most women, but not her. She had grown immune to sexy men, even if their intellect and sense of humor seemed to sync with hers. They were all so full of themselves.

Joe wasn't much different, and sometimes she wondered why she put up with his selfishness. But she knew why. They had so much in common, including their passion for baseball. Most men enjoyed the game, but few, other than players, lived and breathed it, even rating games ahead of birthdays and anniversaries in importance.

What would Joe do when she didn't show up for their dinner date? He'd call her office first to see if she was working late, then he'd call the lawyer she had visited, and finally the police. The police would find her purse and cell phone at the mansion. When they didn't find any sign of foul play—no blood or overturned furniture—they would rule out murder. Then, when they found the jewels she left behind, they would rule out robbery.

Would she be stuck here for the rest of her life? She could barely swallow past the knot in her throat. She might never see Joe again, and he would never know what happened to her.

The drive through the nose-to-tail traffic of upper Manhattan took them past fewer shops but not fewer vehicles or pedestrians. It seemed the entire city was turning out for the game, riding in automobiles, hansoms, hacks, and sleek, brass-trimmed broughams all jamming the approach to the stadium.

Gabriele turned his electric car onto 155th Street and bounced over the potholed road. He followed closely behind a horse-drawn omnibus, too close for Amy's comfort.

"Would you mind putting space between you and the trolley? You're making me nervous."

Instead of slowing, he sped past a trolley packed with men crammed into the bench seats and hanging out the sides. She put her hand over her eyes, not wanting to see the crash she knew would happen at any moment.

"Why are you hiding your eyes?"

"Because you're going to crash."

When Gabriele laughed, she dropped her hands and glared. She didn't think it was funny at all. His driving scared her, and he was only going twenty miles an hour. If the street had stop signs, she'd bail out at the next one.

"I heard two men talking about the Giants' manager, John McGraw," Gabriele said, turning the tiller to pass a one-horse cart. "They said he eats gunpowder for breakfast and washes it down with blood."

If she hadn't been focusing on the congested intersection ahead, she would have laughed at the description of McGraw. "That's what I've heard, too. But it's rumored that when he's away from baseball, he has a soft side."

Within a block from the Polo Grounds, traffic stalled. Cars, pedestrians, carts, trolleys, and carriages bottlenecked at the intersection of 155th Street and 8th Avenue. "Is this the main entrance?"

"I think so. I've been here a few times, but always took the train to the 155th Street Station and entered the park from that platform." He pointed to the long steps to the station platform just as a train puffed in, its black smoke rising against the sky full of giant, cauliflower-shaped clouds.

"Then park anywhere you can find a spot," she said.

He pulled into an area behind the bleachers where dozens of other cars and carriages were parked and turned off the car. "Are you ready?"

"Tickets to sit in the bleachers cost twenty-five cents, but we can scamper up Coogan's Bluff. It overlooks the ballpark and we can watch the game for free." When it came to games played at the Polo Grounds, there wasn't much she didn't know.

"I've heard you can't see the entire field."

"I've never been up there, but I heard the same thing." She had seen pictures of fans standing on the bluff watching the game. It didn't look like much fun, but she didn't have the price of admission, so she couldn't complain.

"I want a decent seat," he said. "There aren't any on Coogan's Bluff."

"A box seat will cost a dollar. Be sure not to sit behind one of the pillars. It will obstruct your view, and you'll be craning back and forth to watch the pitcher on one side and the batter on the other."

"I'll be sure to get seats away from the pillars."

"Seats? No. Don't get me one. You've done more than enough. You're not buying me a ticket. I can watch from Coogan's Bluff. I'm just thrilled to be here."

"If we separate now, how will I find you in this crowd when the game's over? I insist we sit together. *Capisci.*"

She pressed her lips together in a slight grimace. "Okay, but as soon as I get money, I'm paying you back."

With a sweeping Italian gesture of frustration, he said, "*Signorina, sei testardo.*"

She made a face. "I beg your pardon. Are you calling me stubborn?"

He opened his door. "I'm buying the tickets, and you're going to tell me why you like baseball so much."

"What's not to like?"

He came around the vehicle and made a reasonable facsimile of a courtly bow as he opened the door for her. "Welcome to the Polo Grounds."

She climbed out and joined him on the sidewalk. "It's the only sport that allows time for conversation. It's a shared experience. It's…it's…all-American."

They got in line and followed other fans to the main entrance. "Think about it. The game is played with a ball measuring only"— she formed a ball with her hands—"nine inches in circumference and weighing"—she balanced her hands up and down—"only about five ounces."

"And it travels fast, or so I've heard."

"Your car goes about twenty miles an hour. A pitcher throws a ball at nearly a hundred miles an hour."

Gabriele whistled.

"In those few seconds," she continued, "the pitcher can make the ball twist or spin, rise or fall away. The batter has only a few thousandths of a second to decide whether to hit it or not."

He reached into his pockets for coins to pay for their admission. "Everybody plays it, too. I've seen boys batting at balls in the street."

"Girls have grabbed their bats, balls, and mitts and played the game hard for more than a decade. They refuse to remain in the grandstand. Bloomer Girls want to take part in the American pastime, too."

Gabriele gave the attendant money, and they pushed through the turnstile. "You sound like a suffragette."

"I guess I am, but I remember going to games with my dad. It was electrifying to walk out onto the field together, to hear the crack of a bat when it hits a fastball, and to smell hot dogs and popcorn. I fell in love with the game. The sound of the ball smacking a leather glove haunts my dreams."

"You should be a writer. You would make your readers fall in love with the game, too."

"Who would believe a lady sports writer?"

"You could make them believe," he said.

She did a little bit of notetaking in preparation for broadcasting a game, but not much. During games, sentences came out of her mouth fully formed, as if written in advance. Fans told her she had a gift, a talent for sounding perfectly natural. She wasn't sure the talent could be transferred to the written page.

"I'm not a writer," she said, "but I can share stats and interesting anecdotes about players."

Once inside the stadium, Amy leaned over a railing for a better view. Thousands milled about the grandstand gate, ringed the outfield, spilled along the foul lines, and mingled behind home plate. She soaked in the ambiance, along with the other thirty thousand fans. The thrill of being here reminded her of her first visit to Rome, walking the cobblestone streets and touring the crumbling *palazzi*, fountains, and the magnificent Colosseum.

She had always imagined the early twentieth-century trucked on in monochrome. But after pilfering items from Catherine Lily's multicolored closet, traveling up Broadway where vibrant ads were painted on the sides of buildings, and now, walking into the stadium, she realized life in the early nineteen-hundreds was lived in techni-color.

On a recent trip to Chelsea, a friend had pointed out the oldest and still-visible ad in the city, painted in white on a red brick building in 1900. She now had more appreciation for the old, faded sign advertising the boarding of horses. It made her wonder how many other priceless artifacts she had missed. When she returned home… If she returned home…

She cut the thought short, sliced it off at the knees.

The double-decker grandstand curved around home plate and extended twenty feet beyond first and third bases. Bleachers arched around the rear of centerfield. The stadium had inspired the song "Take Me Out to the Ball Game" and the creation of hot dogs. It was associated with greatness and Merkle's Boner, a spectacular screwup, and, in 1909 alone, more than three quarters of a million people would watch a game, many standing ten deep in the roped-off overflow area in the outfield.

For Amy, this was a five-star moment. Heck no. This was more than that. To see the Giants play would supplant the memory of standing on the podium at the Olympics receiving gold medals.

"Pinch me. I must be dreaming."

He looked at her closely. "No, you're not. Your eyes are wide open." He took her arm and turned her in the direction of the clubhouse. "Let's see if any box seats are left. Then we'll join in the hoopla, eat sausage sandwiches, and drink beer."

Her stomach growled. "A hot dog and beer at the Polo Grounds sounds better than steak and champagne at Delmonico's."

"A game played in the sunshine makes the ideal place to sell suds to the cranks in the hot bleachers. Wish I'd been around to make the first deal between the breweries and club owners." Gabriele made a grand, open-armed gesture, and shouted, *"Mangiamo."*

She got tickled and laughed. "I agree. Let's eat." Feeling light-hearted for the first time since coming out of the fog, she followed him to the grandstand, where he bought tickets for two box seats on the second deck. *Ka-ching.* Her debts were mounting up. She quickly reminded him, "I *am* paying you back."

He mumbled an Italian phrase she didn't understand. He definitely had her at a disadvantage, and she would have to stay sharp to maintain at least a little control over her out-of-control situation.

She led the way through the crowded upper deck, past the vendors in black coats and white aprons charging double nickels for hot dogs, pieces of pie, and beer. After rejecting a few seats because they were too close to pillars, she found two with a good line of sight and to the right of home plate.

Within minutes of settling in, a sea of hats welcomed their team to the field with a reverberating roar. The fielding practice was narrowly observed by the horde of New Yorkers and Brooklynites pushing against the restraining ropes in the outfield and jamming the aisles of the lower field boxes.

Coming off their fall loss, the fans had lofty expectations.

The players were dressed in wool above-the-knee socks, collarless V-neck jersey shirts with a logo patch on the sleeve, a longsleeved undershirt, belt tunnels on the sides of their knickers, and white foot coverings below the ankle, which gave the illusion of stirrups. There were no names or numbers on the jerseys, but she knew them: Schlei behind home plate. Tenney on first. Fletcher on second instead of Doyle. Bridwell at shortstop, and Devlin on third. Murray, McCormich, and O'Hara took up positions in the outfield. She knew their faces. She knew their stats. She even knew how they parted their hair. But she didn't know the sound of their voices.

Warming up, Fletcher fielded a grounder and threw to Tenney, who caught it, stepped on the bag, and tossed the ball high in the air. It caught the sun, dropped toward a thousand reaching hands and disappeared. A moment later, the ball was thrown back onto the field. If the spectator with the ball hadn't thrown it back, the crowd would have chased him down until he did.

"Who's pitching today?" Gabriele asked.

"Red Ames," she said.

"Mr. Kalamity," a man sitting behind them said. "The K doesn't stand for Kessling, Red's given name. It stands for Kalamity."

"He's the unluckiest man in baseball," another man said.

Amy turned around in her seat. "He won't be unlucky today. He'll pitch a no-hitter."

"Doubt that. He has control problems in warm weather."

"The weather won't bother him today," she said.

"How much you want to bet?"

She thought a minute. "I've got a better bet." She whispered into Gabriele's ear. "How much can you afford to bet on a sure thing?"

"How sure?"

"Sure enough. How much money do you have with you?"

"Fifteen dollars."

She turned back to face the man sitting behind her. "I bet Ames pitches a no-hitter and…" *How far should I go?* After the day she'd had, if Gabriele was going to cover her debts, why not go all the way? "The Giants will lose."

"I'll take that bet. Here's two bits," the man behind her said.

She shook her head. "I'm only taking dollar bets, and only the first fifteen bettors. Who's first?"

"Are you sure about this?" Gabriele whispered.

Doubts crept in and skidded across her last nerve. Was it possible her presence could alter history? Had she done anything that could change it? Would her advice to the kids playing ball impact history? She didn't think so, but man, she needed to be careful. "Pretty sure," she said.

Word spread rapidly through the rows directly behind her, and within a minute she was holding fifteen dollars.

"How am I supposed to enjoy the game with so much money on the line? And what makes you so sure?"

"Yeah," the man behind her said. "What makes you so sure?"

"I woke up this morning with a premonition. Never had one before. Hope it brings me luck."

Gabriele leaned over and whispered. "I guess someone up above knew you needed help today."

"Possibly, but it's not my money. It's yours."

"Today it's my money. Tomorrow it's yours."

A band and drum corps helped keep the excitement at a fever pitch until it stopped for the flag ceremony and the Pledge of Allegiance. Then a deep-voiced man with a megaphone announced the lineup and introduced Richard Croker who would throw out the ball in the absence of Mayor McClellan. When Croker threw the ball from an upper box in the grandstand, a great war cry rose from the crowd, and young boys clanged cowbells and blew out three-note huzzahs on cornets. The white ball Croker tossed out onto the field would soon be blackened by tobacco juice.

A day at the ballpark was often fraught with peril, with a mix of alcohol, fistfights, and gambling, but baseball had a softer side belying its rough exterior. Games were generally played between three and four o'clock in the afternoon, and were typically completed in less than two hours. Two hours would seem like an eternity for Amy, while she waited to find out if she had messed with history and changed the game's outcome.

"Why isn't Doyle playing today?" the man behind her asked.

"Contract dispute," Amy said. "He wants to be paid what he's worth. Who can blame him?"

"If we lose, I will," the man said.

She managed to eat a hot dog and carry on a conversation until the seventh inning, when she sat on her hands to keep from beating on Gabriele. He didn't deserve it, but the tension was almost more than she could bear.

A great throw to the plate by Brooklyn in the eighth prevented New York from winning the round, holding the Giants to three singles.

At the top of the ninth, she released her hands and circulation was restored. Ames threw nine innings of no-hit ball before giving up a hit in the tenth. The crowd leapt to their feet and howled, then remained standing. Whitey Alperman, of the Brooklyn Superbas tagged Ames for a one-out double to left center in the tenth inning, but Ames stranded Alperman at third to keep the game scoreless. Brooklyn came back and scored three runs in the top of the thirteenth for the victory. Not until the last man was out did the crowd make any move to leave the grounds.

"At the top of the tenth, I thought I'd win the bet," the man behind her said.

She laughed. "At the top of the tenth, I knew you'd lose."

Gabriele scratched his head. "Ames gave up seven hits, so how'd you win?"

She gave him her winnings, and explained, "A no-hitter is officially defined as a completed game in which a team that batted in at least nine innings recorded no hits, and a pitcher who prevents the opposing team from hitting is said to have thrown a no-hitter. Nine innings is the pivotal part of the definition."

Gabriele gave Amy back the winnings. "This is your money. You won it.

"No, it's yours," she said.

"If you had lost, you would have paid me back. Since you won, you deserve the profit."

"Okay, but I'm paying you back what I owe." She peeled off one dollar and gave it to him. "This is for the use of your money." She peeled off another. "This is for the hot dog. And these"—she gave him two more dollars—are for the tickets and transportation." She closed his fist around the bills. "I'm doing what's fair. But if you want to buy me dinner, I'll let you pay."

The man behind Amy interrupted, asking, "I hope you'll give me a chance to win back my money."

If I'm still here. The Giants would play again the next day, and they would win the second game of the two-game series three-zero, but she didn't remember anything specific about the game. "We'll win tomorrow," she said.

"Another premonition?"

"No, just a guess," she said.

He tipped his brown bowler hat. "Then I'll see you here tomorrow. We'll bet on pitches." He walked away and then turned back. "I'm curious. Who do you think is the foremost player?"

"If you ask John McGraw, I think he'd go to his grave saying Honus Wagner is the best."

"That homely, beer-bellied German? Never. But who do you say?"

"I say…who am I to disagree with McGraw?"

The man with the bowler hat said, "McGraw's a pugnacious man with an extraordinarily combative disposition, and he constantly plays dirty tricks."

"He's a genius at getting maximum performance out of his players," she said, careful not to sound confrontational. "He believes men who lose gracefully, lose easily." Amy didn't know why she was defending McGraw, but she couldn't stop herself. "Namby-pamby methods don't get results. I know his tactics infuriate the fans, and I don't like his brand of sportsmanship, either, but I like my team to win. McGraw will be one of history's greatest team-builders, and one of history's greatest managers."

The man gave her a doubtful stare. "You must know him well."

She shook her head. "I only know of him. Some say he's real and authentic and the most remarkable man in America. I wouldn't go that far, but I'll tell you this… If you're looking for a player and a saint, look no further than Christy Mathewson. He's a power pitcher. On the mound, he'll brush back batters and occasionally argue with umpires, but he'll never trash talk to the hitters he faces. His pitches burst into the catcher's mitt like a gunshot. He's as smart as a Harvard graduate, and as handsome as a Hollywood actor."

"Damn good gambler, too," the man said. "Spends Saturday nights playing poker in a room at the Victoria Hotel. He takes the other players down to their garters."

She laughed. "Are you talking from experience?"

"Let me put it this way," the man said. "If Matty knows you've got a dollar in your pocket, he won't be satisfied until he wins it." The man reached into his vest pocket and pulled out a card. "If I miss you tomorrow, come by my office at your convenience. I'd like to discuss a collaboration."

Amy read his card, read it again, then fanned herself.

"Could I ask your name?" he said.

"Amy Spalding, and I'm not related to A. G."

"You should be. Well, have a good evening, Miss Spalding." He nodded to Gabriele, then walked away.

When he was out of earshot, Gabriele asked, "Who is he?"

She handed over the card, trying to catch her breath. "James Gordon Bennett, publisher and editor of the *New York Herald*."

Gabriele whistled, as she'd already learned he was prone to do when impressed. "And he wants to talk to you about a job."

"He didn't say job. He said 'collaboration.'"

Gabriele framed a pretend headline with his hands "Amy Spalding, newspaper reporter."

She knew writers didn't get bylines in the early days. She didn't care about having her name in print, but she did care about the doors press credentials would open. A reporter's job would be as close to her current job as she could get.

"If I'm going on a job interview, I have to get a new dress."

"After we conclude business at Providence, I'll take you to the Ladies' Mile, and you can shop for new clothes."

The Ladies' Mile Historic District was less than a mile from her apartment in SoHo. "Sounds like a plan." She glanced around at the emptying grandstand. "Let's go down closer to the field so I can get a good look."

They leaned on the fence behind home plate while the wind blew patterns in the rippling grass of the outfield, and the pale light of the afternoon sun played over the rutted, dusty diamond.

She pinched her arm again. Nope. She still wasn't dreaming. She glanced up at Gabriele. What a sweetheart to have rescued her today. Because of him she had a plan, the possibility of a job, and a few dollars in her pocket. She didn't know why the brooch brought her here, but she would try to be a good sport about it.

A single voice issued from the windows of the club house—angry and yelling profanity. Amy moved until she could see who it was, and Gabriele followed. A man not any taller than five-six, pasty face, short arms, and dressed in a blue serge suit, his dark hair fashionably swirled on the sides in a fishhook effect, was shouting through cupped hands.

"McGraw's not happy about something," she said. "I guess he'll rant for a while, then he'll go find a poker game. I've seen enough. Let's go talk to the widow, then have a nice Italian dinner. Tomorrow will be a busy day."

Amy walked slowly back to the car. In the unlikely event the brooch took her home tonight, she wanted to remember everything about the Polo Grounds and her beloved Giants. It had truly been a magical afternoon, and Gabriele made it all possible.

"Thank you for today," she said. "You're my knight in shining armor."

He took her hand and tucked her arm around his. "It was the

most fun I've had since I arrived in New York City."

The late afternoon was cooling and the sky hung low over the bluff by the time they exited the ballpark. Amy caught a glimpse of Mathewson driving away in a Ford Model T. At six-two, with broad shoulders, wavy brown hair, and movie star good looks, he was impossible to miss. If she had to buy every pack of cigarettes in the city, she would find a Mathewson card and get his autograph. The same for Honus Wagner. She might never get back to the future, but she would have something she had spent years searching for. If only the cards were worth as much now as they would be in the future, she wouldn't have to pawn her jewelry.

Tomorrow she would get a loan and hope to God she could reclaim her brooch before the time portal opened again and she missed her ride home.

8

Present day MacKlenna Farm—Jack

JACK AND DAVID arrived at MacKlenna Farm in the middle of the night. Since it was breeding season, the farm never slept, and the doors to the guesthouse were always open. Jack had been coming to MacKlenna Farm for over twelve years and knew all the grooms, security personnel, and staff. He even had his own code for the security gate and password to the server.

After a few hours of sleep, he woke up ready to go for a run, but decided to stop by the mansion for breakfast first and run later. Mrs. Collins, Elliott's long-time housekeeper and cook, could whip up a Southern breakfast to rival any restaurant in Richmond. With a full stomach and a take-away bag of biscuits, Jack walked over to the newly constructed security center.

JL, who was vice president of global security for the corporation, had a large corner office. As president, David had a small office here and a corner office in the corporate center next door. He had been trying for months to divest himself of all security functions, but Elliott, and to some extent JL, kept dragging him back in.

Jack sat down at the computer terminal, logged onto the server reserved for clan members only, and searched for the file titled 1881. He knew it existed because he had emailed JL a report to include with the others. He found it and clicked on the icon, but it had an additional layer of security and asked for another password. He used the same one he'd been given, but it didn't work. He was locked out. What the hell?

He crossed his arms and sat back. To him, mysteries were challenges. Had JL and probably David, too, locked everyone out, or just him? He slammed his fists on the table and pushed back his chair. They cut him out. He knew it.

He marched to the door, shoved it open, and almost knocked JL over.

"Whoa," he said. "Are you okay?"

She rubbed her forehead. "I think. I shouldn't have been leading with my head. I heard you were here."

"Word travels fast."

"I got a text when you came through the gate. Got another one when you logged onto the server."

He held the door for her, and they entered the building. JL stopped at the coffee pot and filled a green MacKlenna Farm mug with black coffee. She was stalling. Jack could see it in her eyes, eyes that avoided looking at him. He followed her down the hall toward her office.

"Do you want to tell me why I'm locked out of the final report of the 1881 trip?" he asked.

She pushed opened the door. "David thought it was a good idea. I agreed."

"Are you going to tell me why?"

She glanced at her watch. "I will in thirty-five seconds." She sipped her coffee and tapped her foot. The main door opened, and she said, "He's right on time."

"Where are ye, JL?" David called out.

"In here with Jack."

"Let me get a cup of coffee."

The clink of glass followed, and while Jack waited he stared out the window at the white-fenced pasture where the grass glittered, varnished with raindrops. He used the landscape as a calming focus to slow the burn rising in his gut. Flowers that had been waiting for hints of full-on summer, were now blossoming in a rainbow of colors. But there was no red more intense than his anger.

David entered the office and sat on the corner of JL's desk. "Ye're getting an early start."

Jack whipped around on his heel. "Why'd you lock me out of the 1881 file?"

David glanced at JL and extended his hand in a gesture that said, "You first."

She accepted the challenge. "Sit down, Jack."

"I'd rather stand."

"Suit yourself." She sat in a leather desk chair with a high back and leaned forward in the seat. "You left town after Carolina Rose's funeral, and before Kenzie figured out where the Confederate treasury was located, at least the general area. You didn't want any part of it. What you don't know is how we discovered the exact location."

Jack looked from JL to David, then back to JL. "I assumed David worked his magic and found the X marking the spot."

"Not exactly," she said. "We did an exhaustive search. We scanned in all of Carolina Rose's sketches, but couldn't narrow it down. Something was missing. There was only one sketch we didn't originally include in the computer search. The one she drew of your tattoo."

Jack would never forget the moment Carolina Rose saw his ink. She had touched his skin and traced the pattern with her finger, a touch so light, yet so intensely erotic. His body still reacted to the memory.

"I'll take it from here," David said. "A hidden picture was drawn into the sketch of your tattoo. When I lined it up—"

"Stop!" Jack demanded. "I was in the room when Kenzie found the first hidden picture. But there's no way in hell one could have been drawn into the sketch of my tattoo."

JL stepped over to him and put her hand, warmed by the coffee cup, on his forearm and squeezed gently. "I know this isn't easy to accept."

Easy to accept? She was right. It wasn't, because it didn't make sense.

"When I lined the tattoo sketch up against the topography maps," David continued, "it led to the entrance of the cave holding the treasure."

"It was the final clue," JL said.

Jack pushed her hand away. "Carolina Rose drew the sketch while she was with you, JL, at the hotel. How could she know...?"

The answer might as well be spelled out in bright lights. Carolina Rose was part of the conspiracy. The truth was a sucker-punch to his solar plexus. How could he have been so damn stupid? Jack dropped to the nearest chair and put his head in his hands. "She was part of it from the beginning. That's what you're implying, isn't it?"

"She had to have known where the treasure was hidden in order to draw the final map into the sketch of your tattoo," David said.

Faced with such utter betrayal, the hole mending in his heart was split wide open again. "Everything she told me was a damnable lie."

"We didn't want to believe it, but it's where the evidence took us," David said.

"You should have told me." Jack hardly recognized the hoarse sound of his voice, a commingling of months of pain and anguish, and now betrayal.

"Ye were so torn up over her death—"

"You didn't think I could handle the truth."

"No, Jack," JL said. "We didn't think you'd want to know the truth."

This revelation was like a bucket of ice water dumped over his head. Without saying another word, he stormed out of the building, letting the door slam behind him. He didn't know where he was going, but he had to get away. He ran through the farm and out onto Old Frankfort Pike, ignoring the endless, rolling hills and beauty surrounding him. He could only see Carolina Rose's betrayal.

And no one, not even David, had bothered to tell him. Elliott could have told him at Christmas. David could have told him during one of their dozens of phone calls. Charlotte could have told him during one of their long walks around the plantation.

But no one did.

After three miles of hills, he turned back toward the farm. He didn't know if he was more devastated over what Carolina Rose did, or what the family did. What surprised him most about Carolina Rose's lies was not that she had lied to him, but the ease with which she told them. Had there been anything good and honorable about her?

Yes, there was one thing. In the saloon, she had turned on her uncle and risked her life to save Jack and the others.

What was he going to do now? He had volunteered to go back for Amy Spalding before he knew she was related to Carolina Rose. Was it going to stop him or propel him forward? He had a half mile before he reached the security center. When he reached the door, he would decide.

For the next four minutes, he weighed his options.

He reached the Security Center's parking lot and stretched while he cooled down. Then he entered the building and paused in the doorway of JL's office. Neither JL nor David had moved from their seats, not even to refill their coffee cups, which sat empty in front of them. They knew he would return to settle this.

Jack wiped sweat from his forehead with his sleeve. "You should have told me. I deserved to know the truth, regardless of how painful it would have been. One of you should have had the guts to tell me."

"You're right," JL said. "We should have. We can fight bad guys all day long, but when it comes to hurting people we love, we're cowards. Every one of us."

"No one wanted to add to yer heartache," David said. "We decided to keep quiet, knowing one day we'd have to fess up. We're not proud of what we did, but it was a decision we made as a group."

Jack flicked his hand in dismissal. "I don't want protection. I want honesty. If no one can give me that, I don't want any of you on my team. I'm leaving in twenty-four hours to rescue Amy Spalding, so make up your minds."

"I'll give you my honesty," JL said. "But with it comes my protection. I'm a cop. That's what I do. And you need me."

"Guard my back then, but everything else is strictly off-limits."

9

1909 New York City—Amy

THE SUN HAD set over the Hudson River by the time Gabriele pulled the car to the curb at the corner of West 84th Street and Riverside Drive. "We're here," he announced, turning off the electric motor.

Amy climbed out, stretching and yawning. Traveling back over a hundred years had worn her out, or maybe it was all the jumping up and down she'd done at the ballpark.

The gas streetlights illuminated the front of a new twelve-story apartment building constructed of limestone and brick. This building still existed in the future with a few alterations to the roofline and the addition of fire escapes. Amy didn't know every building in the city, but she was familiar with this one. She had almost rented one of the renovated units. It would have been a done deal if another client hadn't called the realtor and negotiated a lease shortly before Amy finished touring the apartment. It worked out for the best. She loved her loft in a historic, cast-iron building on one of Soho's prime cobblestone streets.

Light from the streetlamps and the windows above illuminated the park across the street. The river shimmered in the muted light of the stars and the long, curving slice of moon. It was a beautiful evening, cool yet comfortable. If only… She shook away thoughts of Joe and turned toward Gabriele as he joined her in front of the door to the building at 120 Riverside Drive.

"How long have you lived here?" she asked. "It's a nice building."

"It was completed last year, and I was one of the first tenants," he said.

"And how long have you known the widow I'm about to meet?" Amy was uncomfortable with the idea, but her options for the night were severely limited. She could sleep on the street or impose on the widow.

"Maria was married to Micky, the man who gave me my first job on the docks. He died shortly after they moved here from lower Manhattan."

"What about children? Does she have any?"

"One son. He was a cop and was killed on duty. His wife died during labor. Maria and Micky have raised their granddaughter."

"That's so sad. I'm sure she gets lonely. She's lucky to have you in the building."

A strange look came over his face, and he half-shrugged. "I owe Micky more than I could ever repay him."

"Sorry," Amy said. "I didn't mean to remind you of those you've lost."

"You don't have to remind me." He thumped his chest. "They're always here."

Gabriele was a kindhearted person, and he continually surprised her. Meeting him must have been part of the brooch's plan after sending her here with a one-way ticket.

"How old is her granddaughter?"

"Seventeen. She's attending Barnard College."

Gabriele whistled a nameless tune, at least nameless to Amy, as he pulled open the door, and she walked in. On her prior visit, there had been a friendly doorman who flagged a taxi for her, but there wasn't a doorman now. Nor was there a desk where he monitored the comings and goings of the tenants and accepted UPS and FedEx packages in their absence.

"Which floor?"

He pointed toward the stairs. "Top floor."

Amy looked down the long hall, remembering she used the elevator on her prior visit. "Isn't there an elevator?"

"The maintenance men were making repairs this morning. A sign said it would be out of service today."

"All night, too?"

"The sign is still up. I can see it from here."

"Maybe it says, 'Elevator fixed.'"

"The building super would have taken the sign down. Not put another one up."

His blunt logic tickled her, and she couldn't help but smile. "Just checking." By the time they reached the top floor, Amy knew all about the Ricci family, the apartment building, and the efficient building superintendent.

Gabriele knocked on the door to unit 1204 and a beautiful young woman with big brown eyes peeked out. She smiled at Gabriele then looked past him at Amy and instantly dropped it, replacing the smile with a frown.

"Isabella, who's at the door?" a woman asked in a heavily accented voice.

"Gabriele, and he has a *donna* with him." Isabella said the Italian word for woman like it was a four-letter word.

"Don't keep them standing in the hall. Invite them in."

Isabella opened the door wider, stepped aside, and flashed a catlike smile, driving home the point that Amy wasn't welcome. Amy ignored her. She had met her share of divas growing up and, while their energy was attractive, their attitude was not. She gave Isabella a wide berth and entered the apartment. The mouthwatering aroma she'd been smelling since they reached the tenth floor was intoxicating—rich, slightly earthy, and almost narcotic.

"What is that delicious, evocative smell?" Amy asked, sniffing.

Gabriele breathed in deeply, closed his eyes and sighed. "Truffles."

Beneath the scent of truffles was a thick combination of garlic, onions, Parmesan, and homemade bread. As hard as it was, she put the unthinkable into words. "They're getting ready to eat. Let's come back later."

A petite woman with beautiful skin, a striking figure, slightly graying hair, and bright brown eyes walked out of the kitchen. Gabriele crossed the room and kissed her cheek. "Maria, this is my friend, Miss Spalding." He turned to Amy. "This is Maria Ricci and her granddaughter, Isabella."

Amy extended her hand, trying to remember how to say nice to meet you in Italian. Then slowly she said, "*Ciao, è un piacere conoscerti.*"

"*Parla italiano?*" Maria asked.

Amy shook her head to let Maria know she wasn't fluent. "*Je ne parle pas italien.* I only know a few words and phrases."

Maria smiled warmly. "Then we'll speak English, and you're just in time to eat."

The invitation sounded wonderful to Amy. She had eaten a late lunch the day before, went without dinner, and skipped breakfast. The hot dog at the ballpark kept her going, but she was now running on fumes.

"*Grazie,* but we don't want to impose," Gabriele said. "We're going to the Italian restaurant on Broadway for dinner."

Amy's jaw dropped, but she snapped it shut, and tried not to look like what she had become—a starving, homeless person.

"Nonsense," Maria said. "Sit. Dinner is ready. My cooking is better than anything you'll find on the Upper West Side."

Amy watched Gabriele wondering what he would do now? When he removed his jacket, and rolled up his shirt sleeves, Amy raised her eyes and said a silent hallelujah.

"Isabella, set two more places and pour Gabriele and the *giovane donna* a glass of *vino.*"

Isabella sashayed her way to the china cabinet and removed two glasses, clinking them together lightly.

"Don't break them," Maria said.

Isabella poured wine into the goblets. Her expression didn't reflect any enthusiasm for the task until she handed Gabriele a glass, smiling at him. The smile quickly dimmed when she handed one to

Amy. It wasn't much of a stretch to believe Maria's granddaughter had a crush on Gabriele and felt threatened by Amy's appearance.

He carried his wine over to the sofa, where he sat and thumbed through a newspaper.

"Anything exciting happen in the world today?" Amy asked.

"President Taft established a National Monetary Commission to propose a banking reform plan. The panic of 1907 is on everyone's mind. Washington has to bring stability to financial markets."

Isabella sighed dramatically. "Banking is so boring." Then she smiled at Gabriele again, saying, "I bought a new hat at Macy's. Do you want to see it?"

"Maybe later," he said, eyes still on the newspaper.

"All I know about banking is the Federal Reserve was created to regulate banks," Amy said.

Gabriele glanced up. "I haven't heard of the Federal Reserve. What is that?"

"Oh. You haven't?" she asked.

Maybe because it hasn't been created yet.

"It was an idea floated by J. P. Morgan and his business associates. I don't keep up with news like I should." Needing to change the subject, she said, "This is a beautiful room." She couldn't identify the furniture styles, which meant there weren't any early American pieces. The chairs, sofa, and tables had simple, clean lines, without extravagant ornamentation. She ran her hand across the nubby fabric on the sofa. It was a small-scale pattern with multi-tonal colors in charcoal, brown, plum, and green. The room had a modern feel to it, yet was very warm and inviting. Maria had excellent taste in styles and colors. If her taste was any indication of her talents, her cooking would be worthy of any five-star restaurant in the city.

"I'm going to see if Maria needs any help." Amy escaped to the kitchen. The small room was cramped with pots and pans, and packaged food covering the countertop and bulging from the cabinets. The room needed a major overhaul. During her apartment search, Amy toured at least twenty units throughout the city, and saw what creative designers could do with small spaces. She had a few ideas for how Maria could organize her kitchen with just a few tweaks and someone handy with a saw and hammer.

Maria, holding a large wooden spoon over her cupped hand, tasted the tomato sauce before smacking her lips. "It needs more garlic."

"May I help?" Amy asked. "I'm not much of a cook, but I can follow directions, and I'm an accomplished dishwasher."

"No, *grazie*. You are a guest. Enjoy the *vino*." Maria waved Amy away and went back to her sauce, humming.

Amy returned to the living room to find Isabella fluffing pillows behind Gabriele's back.

Oh, good grief.

She sipped her wine while she looked at the framed family pictures displayed on the piano. She pointed to a photograph of a man and woman sitting in a park. "Is this Micky?"

"The picture was taken at their anniversary party. It was their last one." Gabriele crossed the room and took the picture from her. "He looks intimidating, but he was…ah…*dolce orso*."

"I don't know what that means," Amy said.

"A gentle bear," Isabella said.

"Oh," Amy said. "Like Giovanni the Italian-speaking bear. I've seen those in Barneys." She smacked her hand over her mouth, then put her other hand to her head and shook it gently. "Excuse me. I don't know what I'm talking about." She held out her glass to Isabella. "May I have a refill?"

Isabella looked at Amy as if she had two heads before stomping off to get the wine.

Gabriele sat at the piano and played, "Take Me Out to the Ball Game." He stopped and turned toward her. "You're odd."

Her face heated. "I don't think anyone has ever told me that before."

"I don't mean it as an insult. You remind me of myself when I first came here. You seem confused, but informed. You look at your surroundings with awe, much like I did, yet you're an American.

You're not in a foreign country. I don't want to offend you. But your skin, your hair, your hands…you look like an angel."

"I *know* no one has ever told me that before."

He ducked his head, blushing. "I shouldn't be so forward. I apologize."

"There's no reason to apologize." She rested her elbow on the piano and cupped her chin in her hand. "You're right. I *am* confused, but informed. I'm seeing the city for the first time, yet I'm very familiar with it. I've been blessed with skin and hair like my mother. I'm educated, and I know an awful lot about baseball, but I don't know who the president is. You saved my life today, and I owe you more than I can repay. Sort of like the way you felt about Micky. To give back the way you have would make him proud."

Gabriele played a riff on the piano. "Maria says so as well."

"Well, she's right." Amy sat next to him. "Do you know how to play 'Heart and Soul?'" It's a fun duet."

"No."

Probably because it hasn't been written yet.

"It's the only thing I know how to play on the piano," she said.

Isabella reentered the room with the wine bottle, refilled Amy's glass, then stomped off again.

"I don't think Isabella's happy I'm here."

"Maria is trying to find a suitor for her, but Isabella runs roughshod over every boy Maria finds, and they don't come back."

"I think she wants you to be her suitor."

"It would not be good. She is my *sorellina.*"

"What is that?" Amy asked.

"Baby sister."

Maria came out of the kitchen carrying two big bowls and set them on the table. "Come. *Mangia!*"

Gabriele escorted Amy into the dining room. "You're about to eat the finest Italian food New York City has to offer."

"I heard you, Gabriele, and it's not true. My mother, may she rest in peace, made the best Italian food in the city. My sister is now the greatest cook." Maria put a spoon in the tomato sauce and gave it a swirl. The room was now even thicker with the tantalizing aroma of garlic, peppers, truffles, and fresh parsley. "Gabriele, take Miss Spalding to the restaurant for lunch tomorrow. She will see for herself who is the *meilleur cuisinier.*" Maria put a fork in the bowl of pasta. "Isabella, bring the bread and Parmesan."

Gabriele sat at one end of the table, and Maria at the other, with Amy and Isabella on opposite sides.

"Bless the food, Gabriele," Maria said.

He did, and the only part of the prayer Amy understood was amen. The word was barely out of their mouths before they were reaching for olive oil, bread, pasta, sauce, and cheese, ignoring one of Emily Post's most important rules for eating with others.

Amy spooned sauce onto her pasta and sprinkled cheese on top. Then, using her fork and spoon, she tossed the pasta with the sauce and cheese. "In baseball, when a pitcher records a strikeout with no runners on base, the catcher throws the ball to the third baseman. The third baseman throws to the second baseman, who throws to the shortstop, who throws to the first baseman. It's called 'around the horn'. Passing the food around the table reminded me of that."

"Why do they do it?" Isabella asked.

"There're different opinions."

"What's yours?" Gabriele asked.

"It keeps the infielders engaged in the game, and it gives the pitcher time to walk around the mound and re-focus for the next batter."

"I discovered today Miss Spalding knows baseball like I know the market. We went to the Giants' opening game at the Polo Grounds."

"You hate baseball," Isabella said.

"I don't hate it. I didn't understand it," Gabriele replied.

"And you do now?"

He nodded. "Thanks to Miss Spalding's running commentary today, I do."

"Did you bet?" Isabella asked. "If you were as lucky as you are at the stock market, then you must have had a good day."

"Miss Spalding told me what bets to place, and, yes, I was lucky. We're going back tomorrow."

Isabella jumped to her feet. "Can I go? Please. I've wanted to go for the longest time. Remember I asked you to take me, and you didn't want to go."

"I'm sure we could buy another ticket," Amy said.

"I don't think it's an appropriate place for a young girl," Maria said.

"Why don't you come with us too?" Amy said. "You'll see how much fun it is."

Maria shook her head. "Oh, no. I couldn't."

"*Nonna*, pleeeease?"

Normally, Amy wouldn't interfere in a discussion between a parent and child, but she sensed a mood or passion in Maria she couldn't ignore. "There's a song I sing with a very poignant line. It goes, 'When you get the choice to sit it out or dance, I hope you dance'."

Maria's wisdom was visible in the creases of her face. If there was any on Isabella's, it rolled right off her smooth, creamy complexion.

"If we can go"—Isabella clasped her hands and held them to her chest—"I won't object to eating with the Bianchis after mass on Sunday."

"No stomping feet?" Maria asked.

Isabella shook her head, sighing. "I'll even wear the yellow dress you like so much."

Man, oh, man. Isabella must have learned to manipulate her grandparents at an early age. Had anyone ever told her no? How many times had Amy begged her mom to let her watch one more hour of baseball on TV in exchange for cleaning her room? And it never worked for her. Trudging down memory lane distressed Amy. For now, she dismissed thoughts of her deceased parents, home, Joe, the future…

Maria wagged her finger. "If you don't do as you promised, you won't go again."

Isabella sat back in her chair with her chin tilted slightly upward. A self-satisfied smile lingered at the corners of her pink mouth. Amy knew from the look in Isabella's eyes that she was plotting the perfect way to break her promise and still go to another game.

Gabriele studied Isabella, his face impassive. Then he said in a single, unvaried tone, "The game starts at three-thirty. I will pick you up in front of the library at two-thirty. If you're late, we won't be able to get more tickets, and you'll miss the game. *Capisci?*"

"I won't be late. I promise." Isabella clapped and even gave Amy a warm smile. "Will Christy Mathewson pitch tomorrow? I have one of his baseball cards. He's soooo...handsome."

Amy gasped. "You do? Can I see it? I'd love to have a Mathewson card. Where did you get it?"

Isabella tossed her hands in the air, obviously pleased she was in possession of something Amy wanted. "I found it on campus."

Amy's heart pounded with excitement. "Do you have a Honus Wagner, too?"

"I only have Christy Mathewson. But I know where you can get cards without buying cigarettes."

Amy held on to her seat to keep from leaping to her feet.

Can we go right now?

Finally, Amy asked, "Where can I get one?"

"The boys gather in the Grove, a park on the north end of campus. They throw their empty cigarette packs away. I've seen street urchins going through the trash there. When they find a card, they sneak away."

Maria wagged her finger. "Your *nonno* didn't set up an education trust fund so you could dig through the trash for a cigarette card."

Amy hid a smile behind her fist.

"I wasn't going to dig through the trash, *nonna*. I was telling Miss Spalding *she* could."

The conversation quickly turned into a mishmash of English and Italian. Instead of trying to follow what they were saying, Amy turned her thoughts inward. For the first time since coming through the fog, she could take a breath without worrying about her survival.

She was enjoying the most delicious Italian food she had ever eaten, had a lead on a job, and tomorrow she would have enough money to buy clothes and lease an apartment.

The only question left to settle was where she would sleep tonight.

When Maria looked at her with pitying eyes, Amy knew Gabriele had mentioned her housing needs. "You are welcome to stay here. And," Maria laughed, "you can…ah…*lava i piatti.*"

Amy shrugged an I-don't-understand.

Gabriele laughed. "She said you could wash dishes."

"Oh," Amy chuckled. "But I don't want to impose."

"If you need to stay longer, you can rent the third bedroom." Isabella looked from her grandmother to Amy, then back to her grandmother, as if needing reassurance. "*Nonna* could use the extra money."

Maria patted Amy's hand. "We will talk tomorrow after you conclude your business."

Tears burned Amy's eyes, but she blinked them back. Why had the brooch kidnapped her, then given her everything she needed to fully live life, and put her within touching distance of a Honus Wagner card? Amy put her hands in her lap and pinched herself. She still wasn't dreaming.

She had a master's degree in sports psychology, and had learned athletes in all major sports had a hierarchy of needs. The needs differed from Maslow's hierarchy, but were similar. No single need could be fulfilled without the one ahead being fulfilled first. So far, she could scratch off the first two levels—physiological and safety. If she landed a job at the newspaper, she'd be able to scratch off a couple more.

To say life was good went a giant leap too far. Her life was totally disrupted, she was separated from Joe, and her dream job was in jeopardy. She needed to remember, no matter how well things were going, in the end, nothing good could come of this.

Isabella picked up her plate. "Miss Spalding, while we wash dishes, you can tell me everything you know about baseball."

Amy grabbed her plate and silverware and followed Isabella to the kitchen. "I can tell you the basics, but the sport is complex and very strategic. You'll have to watch lots of games to understand the nuances."

"Like what?" Isabella asked.

"I don't know." Amy thought a minute before saying, "There are unwritten rules, like don't steal a base when you have a large lead. Don't bunt to break up a no-hitter. No intentional distractions while an infield is fielding a pop-up. Things like that."

"What happens when you do one of those?"

Amy filled a dishpan and put the plates in to soak, relieved to know the apartment had hot water. "There's no penalty to be enforced by umpires, but the batter might get hit by a pitch."

"Ouch."

Isabella quickly forgot about the pain of getting hit by a ball and instead asked about the marital status of players she read about in the newspaper. Amy rattled off a list of statistics until Isabella got bored and left Amy to dry the pots and pans. She didn't mind. She used the quiet moments to form a plan. As her father was fond of telling her, if she didn't know where she was going, any road would get her there. She couldn't afford to take any road.

Her brain had been churning for hours with the thought that there must be other brooches like hers. And if so, somehow, she would find her way back home.

10

Present day MacKlenna Farm—Jack

ELLIOTT FRASER WAS the last one to take his seat in the conference room at the farm. If this meeting went the way the family meeting last October had gone, he was in for a fight.

Jack's proposal kept him up all night worrying about repercussions. As Chairman of the Board of MacKlenna Corporation, and President of the recently formed MacKlenna Adventure Company, decisions impacting the companies fell on Elliott's shoulders, and required him to consider the needs of all its members.

Months ago, Jack had committed to go back in time to rescue Amy Spalding. After the death of Carolina Rose Arées, he abandoned the plan, but in the past forty-eight hours, two events occurred to directly impact the Amy Spalding matter. First, the New York City grand jury handed down an indictment against her fiancé, Joe Gilbert. He would now stand trial for Amy's murder. And secondly, Jack found a connection between Amy and Carolina Rose.

Jack's current plan was to go back in time to interview Catherine Lily Sterling about a sister she didn't know existed. To Jack, Amy Spalding was no longer the focus of the mission.

And that was the crux of the matter.

Elliott cleared his voice. "Let's bring this meeting of the MacKlenna Adventure Company to order. And order is the operative word. I'll adjourn the meeting if it gets out of control. I expect an orderly discussion of the proposal under consideration."

He slid a notepad and pen to Meredith, who clicked the pen, ready to write. "As secretary of the corporation, your task is to take minutes of this meeting. Let the minutes reflect the following are in attendance: Elliott Fraser and Meredith Montgomery, Kenzie and David McBain, Kit and Cullen Montgomery, Jack Mallory, JL O'Grady, Kevin Allen, and Pete Parrino, with Charlotte Mallory, Braham McCabe, and Shane, Jeff, Connor, and Pops O'Grady participating by videoconference from various locations around the country. Have I left out anyone?"

"I think Julie called in, too," Jeff said.

"Julie, are you there?" Elliott asked.

"Sure am, boss."

"Let the minutes reflect Julie O'Grady also participated by phone," Elliott said.

Meredith looked up. "I just have one question. What do you intend to do with these minutes? Keep them in a binder on display in my office? If anyone read them, they'd think I was writing fiction."

"Lock them in the safe," Kenzie said. "The minutes aren't to protect us in the event of a lawsuit. It's a record for future generations. I want my children to know what we did, why we did it, and the mistakes we made. Each brooch has its own power, but we've seen what happens when the power is combined. We could change history with a couple of tweaks. We aren't smarter than any other group of people. Our moral compass isn't perfectly aligned, but we don't have evil intentions. We are, however, human. We do screw up. Our children need to learn how to handle the power from both our successes and failures."

Connor sat forward in his chair. "Do you consider our last mission a failure?" He looked from Kenzie to Elliott. "We found a treasure that put money in all our pockets, with enough left over to fund our new company."

"Carolina Rose was killed, and we didn't need the money," Jack said.

"The mission was a clusterfuck from the beginning," Elliott said.

Meredith flipped a page and kept writing. "We lost Carolina Rose, but we saved Kit and Cullen's lives."

Cullen lifted his coffee cup in a salute. "And we certainly appreciate it."

Kit dug a yellow highlighter out of the well-stocked organizer on the table. She highlighted a line on the report Jack distributed earlier. The highlighter squeaked against the paper. She glanced up, blinked once, twice.

"What is it, lass?" Elliott asked.

"She's family."

"Who is?" Meredith asked.

"Jack's report..." Kit's voice squeaked. She stopped, cleared her throat, started over again. "Jack's report says Catherine Lily was adopted in 1855 by a woman from the Highlands—a woman named Alison Morrison Taylor."

"That's all I have right now," Jack said. "I've asked Meredith's team of genealogists to work on it."

"It's not necessary," Kit said. "Alison is, or was, my first cousin. She was the daughter of my aunt Ainsley. Although I didn't grow up in the Highlands around my mother's family, Cullen took me there to meet them. I spent a day with Alison and her daughter, Lily."

"Holy crap." JL pressed her hand to her forehead. "The MacKlenna family tree gives me a headache. All I can remember about my line is I came from the wrong side of the blanket."

"Hey, that's my line, too, you're complaining about," Kevin said.

"And mine," Elliott added dryly.

Meredith waved her hand in JL and Kevin's direction. "Shush." She turned back to Kit. "That would make Catherine Lily your second cousin."

"And Carolina Rose, too," Jack said.

With a bare lift and fall of her shoulders, Kit said, "If they're related, yes."

"Jack," Charlotte said.

Everyone in the room turned to the monitor on the wall showing the faces of the videoconference attendees.

"If Carolina Rose is related to Kit," Charlotte continued, "she's related to us, too."

JL marched over to the credenza. "I need some ibuprofen."

"That's what you get for drinking a bottle of wine all by yourself," Meredith said.

JL popped two pills. "You asked me to try your new label. If I drank only one glass, you would have asked me why I didn't like it."

"You drank a whole bottle just so you wouldn't hurt my feelings?"

Elliott knocked on the table to get their attention. "Let's return to the topic of discussion. Jack, why don't you pick it up from here?"

"I can handle this mission by myself," he said.

"As I told ye yesterday, ye have to have a team." Elliott glanced quickly at David to be sure his second-in-command was on the same page. "Nobody goes it alone. Period. JL and Kevin volunteered last fall to go with you. They're still game."

JL returned to her chair. "We can't stay long, though. The invitations for both Austin's graduation celebration and our wedding have been mailed. We have to get in and get out."

"Elliott," Kit said, tapping her highlighter against the paper. "My aunt Alison had a sister named Gracie. She ran off with a man, left the country, and no one ever heard from her again."

"Is that relevant to this adventure?" Cullen asked.

"I think so," Kit said. "My Aunt Gracie ran off with a Frenchman."

11

Present day MacKlenna Farm—Jack

FOLLOWING KIT'S REVELATION about her aunt, the noise level escalated, bouncing and echoing around the room, so no one could hear what anyone else had to say. When Elliott couldn't get control of the group, he hammered on the table with a stapler, called the meeting to a halt, and strode out of the room.

Fifteen minutes later, he returned to find the buzz had died down to an anxious silence, and JL pouring shots of whisky for those who remained at the table.

Elliott poured himself a cup of coffee and returned to his seat. Meredith patted his hand before picking up the pen to continue her note-taking. Her eyes asked a silent question, and he nodded to reassure her his blood pressure was under control. The medical professionals debated whether the transient ischemic attack he suffered during the last adventure was due to stress or not. But he knew the answer, and so did the family.

David signaled a question, *Are ye okay?*

Elliott answered the non-verbal code they had developed over the years by twitching *okay* with his finger. When Kevin's eyes asked the same question, Elliott said, "I checked my blood pressure. It's normal. If ye're ready to conduct this meeting with only one person talking at a time, we'll continue. What are yer theories?"

Jack tossed back his shot, then pushed his glass toward JL to hit him again. "There's only one as far as I'm concerned. Gracie ran off with Arées and had two daughters. We don't know if they married or not. Carolina Rose told me her mother died when she was a baby, and she was raised by her grandmother. I suspect Arées gave Catherine Lily to his wife's sister to raise. Either he never told the caregivers there were two children, or the caregivers never told the children."

"My money is on the asswipe never telling the caregivers," Pete said. "I have a fondness for grandmothers, and find it hard to believe they would have kept a secret like that."

JL refilled Jack's glass, then her own. "Why'd he do it? How could he be so cruel?"

Elliott lowered his head and threw a hot glance over the top of his reading glasses toward his VP of Global Security. He found JL's question hypocritical, but had no intention of calling her on it. She hid her son's true parentage from him for seventeen years, and was in no position to label someone else cruel for doing the same.

"JL, you did it," Kevin said.

JL hesitated only a moment before replying, and although she looked uncharacteristically embarrassed, she squared her shoulders and said, "I did it to protect him from social stigma. What was Arées' motivation?"

Meredith finished her shot and turned the empty glass upside down on the table so JL wouldn't refill it. "Maybe Arées told his mother he had two children, but she could only care for one."

"I thought they were twins," Kenzie said, putting down her smartphone. "It's hard enough for me to care for two the same age. I can't imagine how difficult it would be for an elderly woman."

"Those two squiggly butts of yours would be too much for Mary Poppins," Kevin said.

Kenzie wagged a finger at him. "I can talk about my kids' squiggly butts, but you can't. Just wait until you have a couple of your own."

Elliott slowly raised his hands up and down. "Cool it, or we'll take another break."

The Diamond Brooch 97

"Until we get the DNA report, this is all hypothetical," David said.

"I'm convinced the results will confirm what David's age progression photographs have already told us," Jack said. "The women were sisters. We just don't know yet if they were twins or not."

"Isn't Amy the reason for this mission?" Connor asked. "It seems to me we're getting sidetracked."

"This is Amy's history, too. Don't you think she'd want to know the truth?" Jack asked.

A message flashed on the face of Kenzie's smartphone. She picked it up and swiped at the screen. Her ability to multi-task was astounding. She rarely sat in on a meeting when she wasn't on her smartphone texting, or on her Mac working either on a document or sending emails. In her office, she did all that and more, often while nursing a baby.

"I agree what happened with Catherine Lily and Carolina Rose should interest Amy," Kenzie said, "but it wouldn't be her number one concern. I know from personal experience, Amy just wants to go home. She's your priority, Jack. And don't forget Joe Gilbert is facing a murder trial. We have to end his nightmare, too. Don't dick around with this."

"I hate to miss out," Connor said, "but I've got deadlines on the Colorado project. I agree with Kenzie. Don't screw it up and make me come after you. I'm tired of cleanup duty."

"My calendar is clear," Pete said. "With JL and Kevin, we'll have a four-person team. JL and I can do recon while Jack and Kevin infiltrate the social scene. If we're going to focus on baseball to find Amy, we've got three teams to check out in New York. The Highlanders in the American League, and the Giants and the Brooklyn Superbas in the National League. The picture Jack found of Ty Cobb sliding into home with Amy in the background presents an additional problem. The picture was taken during a game between the Detroit Tigers and the Philadelphia Athletics. If it's our only lead, we need to go to Detroit and Philadelphia, not New York?"

"We can split up," Jack said. "Pete can go to Philadelphia, Kevin and JL can go to Detroit. I'll go to New York."

"I've got no desire to go to Detroit," JL said. "You go there, Jack. Kevin and I will go to New York. It's a bigger city, and there's two of us."

"Ye're not splitting up," Elliot said. "It was a mistake to do it in California, and we're never doing it again."

"David and I split up when we went back for Kenzie," Jack said.

"And look what happened. We almost lost you *and* Kenzie. I won't approve the mission if that's your plan. You signed the bylaws giving the president the authority to approve or disapprove all missions." Elliott thumped his thumb against his chest. "That means me."

"Okay. Okay. We won't. We'll start in New York. If we don't have any luck there, we'll go to Philadelphia, then Detroit."

"If we're going to run the op that way, we need more people," Pete said. "Connor, can you adjust your schedule?"

"It's not my schedule. It's Elliott's," Connor said.

"Kenzie can move some meetings around and go to Colorado," Elliott said.

"When does Shane get back from Australia?" Meredith asked.

Connor scrolled through messages on his smartphone. "According to his recent message, he has meetings with the representatives of the stud farms we're considering for purchase, plus interviews with potential stallion managers. He's booked an empty leg flight charter back to Lexington next Saturday."

"I told him he could take the jet," Elliott said.

"I wish everyone around here was as cost-aware as Shane. If he can get an empty leg it saves money, so you guys"—Kevin flipped his thumb toward Connor and Jack—"can take the company jet to New York to catch a baseball game."

"I didn't know that. Did I approve it?" Elliott asked.

Jack sneered. "Take it out of my reserve account."

"I will," Elliott said. "It's time for Jeff to retire from the force and get his ass out here. Kenzie needs help."

"He graduates in June, but then he's got the bar to study for.

He'll be out of pocket until fall," Connor said. "Julie doesn't want to move until you decide where you want them to live—Kentucky or Colorado."

"It's not fair to my kids to keep relocating them," Julie said.

"I want you in Kentucky for at least two years," Elliott said. "Which means, Connor, ye'll manage the Colorado project. Shane will manage the property in New South Wales."

"For how long?" Connor asked.

"Until we have people we trust managing the properties," David said.

"What about me?" Pete asked.

"I'm negotiating with the owners of a winery in Tuscany. If we can reach an agreement, I'll need you to take the lead on that project," Meredith said.

Pete whistled. "When do I leave?"

"As soon as you get back, I need you to go with me to Florence. So wrap up the Amy Spalding matter ASAP."

"Okay," Pete said. "We'll take a five-member team and evac Amy from somewhere in the early twentieth-century and be back within… What? Five to seven days?"

"If ye need another member, I'll go," Cullen said.

Everyone at the table turned and stared. "No," Elliott said. "Ye can't disappear in 1881 and show up in 1909."

Cullen let out a discouraged breath and chucked down his pen. "Kit and I want to see our children and grandchildren."

Elliott removed his reading glasses and rubbed his eyes before resettling them. "I understand, but if ye visit yer children, news will get out. Ye wouldn't be able to explain why ye haven't aged. Ye'd only be fifty-seven when ye should be…what…eighty-five?"

Kenzie handed Elliott a tissue. "You've got smudges on your lenses." Then to Cullen she said, "I agree with Elliott, but for a different reason. I enjoy working with you. I don't want you to leave. I've learned more from you in eight months than I learned in law school."

"Thank ye, Kenzie, but Kit and I have to go home soon."

"No! You can't leave until after the wedding. Please, stay," JL said.

Cullen turned twinkling eyes on her. "Don't delay your nuptials just to keep us here."

"Would I do that?" Her words hung in the air while everyone at the table laughed. Even Kevin. She threw shade at him.

"Don't look at me like that, sweetheart," he said.

"And don't sweetheart me."

"We all agree, JL. You've turned into bridezilla." Kevin scooted back in his chair as her elbow shot toward his abdomen. He caught her arm, pulled her to him, and kissed her squarely on the mouth.

"Your mother has turned this into Lexington's social event of the season. I'd rather elope, but we have Austin's graduation party, too," JL said.

Kenzie cleared her throat. "If we can, let's put parties and nuptials aside for now and finish this discussion. I have a question about...hmm...transportation, I guess. Is this a one-brooch mission, or three? Are Jack and Amy"—she pursed her lips—"I can't ask this delicately enough, so I'll just come out with it. Are the two of you meant to be soul mates?"

Jack was in the middle of taking a drink, and instead of swallowing the whisky, spewed it across the table. "What? You can't seriously be asking that after what's taken place. I've sworn off women, and I've never had any interest in dating a jock. The answer is no way. Nohow. Never. Let's move on."

David and Elliott gave him similar looks, both saying, "Ye're crazy."

Kenzie threw the box of tissues at him, and Jack snatched it out of the air. "Sorry I brought it up," she said, "but it was the elephant in the room."

Jack yanked several tissues from the box and cleaned up his mess. "Why ask me? Why not Pete? He's unattached now. Or Connor?" Jack threw the used tissues into the trash can and reclaimed his seat, leaning back and folding his arms. "I don't believe in this soul mate crap."

"How can you say that after what happened to Charlotte and Braham and me and David?"

"It had nothing to do with a stone, and everything to do with two horny guys. No, make that three. I include Kevin. So, as you say, let's move on. What's next?" Jack said.

"I take umbrage at yer comment," David said.

"And I do, too," Braham said.

Kevin looked at JL. "We were both hornier than hell, weren't we?"

She pointed her finger and cocked an imaginary trigger, clicking her tongue. "Still are, sweetheart."

He feigned being shot in the chest. "You had me at, 'Hi, I'm Austin's sister.'"

Elliott knocked on the table again. "This is tension relief for all of ye, but let's wrap it up. It's beginning to feel like part two of our last adventure."

"Feels like part three to me," JL said.

"How so?" Kevin asked.

"Think about it. News of Amy's disappearance broke the night of Austin's kidnapping. Then, after everyone was safe, Jack found the baseball picture with Amy in the background—part one. Meeting Carolina Rose in San Francisco—part two. This adventure will resolve Amy's disappearance and shed light on Carolina Rose's past—part three. The trilogy is over, and three new projects are slated to begin. Let's just hope to God I don't have triplets."

Kevin shot to his feet. "Are you trying to tell us something?"

Everyone around the table seemed to be poised, waiting…

"Like…"

"Triplets? Are you pregnant?"

"Seriously, Kevin. Don't you think you'd know if I was?"

"How would I?" Kevin asked.

David grabbed Kevin's arm and pulled him down until he was once again sitting in his chair. "Shut up. Ye're digging a hole."

JL closed her eyes, groaning softly.

Elliott didn't miss a beat, and covered the awkward silence with a question. "Is this meeting over?"

"Not yet," Connor said. "What about Kenzie's question? If this isn't about soul mates, what does it mean in terms of the brooches?"

Kit, who had been quiet through most of the discussion, said, "Maybe only the ruby, sapphire, and emerald lead to soul mates."

"The broken brooch led me to Kevin," JL said with a small line forming between her brows. "Didn't it?"

Kevin winked. "I thought Austin did."

David held up his hand to stop the babble around the table. "JL, is yer brooch engraved with the Celtic words?"

"I don't know. I've never opened it. Kevin said not to."

"And you listened to him?" Pete asked. "That's a first."

"I beg your pardon. I take the brooches seriously. I'm afraid I'll be carried off to the time of the dinosaurs."

Elliott knocked on the table again. "We're getting far afield. Take the ruby, sapphire, and emerald brooches. Ye should land wherever Amy is—New York, Detroit, or Philadelphia. After ye find her, Jack can interview Catherine Lily. Ye should be able to get in and get out within a week. When do ye want to leave, Jack?"

"I want the DNA results before I go. I told the lab I wanted the rush processing service, so I should have a report within forty-eight hours." He glanced around the table. "Let's travel light. We can each buy one set of period clothing from the costumer downtown. Then buy more clothes when we get where we're going."

"We need weapons and surveillance equipment," JL said. "Connor, Pete, let's meet David in the gun room. What about money?"

"We've collected several thousand dollars in twenties and hundreds from the early 1900s. Plus, I have diamonds and gold nuggets to exchange for cash," Jack said.

JL placed her hands on the table. "Sounds like we've got everything we need: diamonds, gold, guns, and cash. Let's rock and roll."

12

1909 New York City—Amy

Gabriele drove Amy to the Providence Loan Society's office on Park Avenue and 25th Street. The sidewalks were crowded with businessmen, managers, clerks, and messenger boys all waiting for businesses to open for the day.

Amy had spoken the magic words three times before she turned out the light and fell asleep, and three more times when she woke up. The stubborn stone still refused to work. It was time to move on, and use the brooch to secure a loan. If she'd only brought one of the rings in the jewelry box, she wouldn't have to be using the brooch as collateral. But she didn't.

Maybe when she tried again in a few weeks, the blasted diamond would cooperate.

Gabriele stopped the car in front of a four-story building. "I'll leave you to transact business while I go to my office. When you finish, you can find me there. Just ask anyone for directions."

Squinting, Amy glanced up to the top of the white marble building. A high balustrade balanced the tall base of pink granite. "I thought you said your office was on the fourth floor. I only see three."

Gabriele looked up, shading his eyes with his hand to cut the glare. "You can't see the fourth floor. The windows are hidden behind the balustrade."

"Obviously, money wasn't a concern when building this… What would you call it? The biggest private pawnbroking institution in the world?"

"They aren't unscrupulous pawnbrokers. You'll be treated fairly."

She sucked in a deep breath and walked boldly through a bronze door with richly designed grills, the silk of her petticoat swishing about her bare legs.

Inside, the main floor was divided into departments for men and women. The door to the elevator was open, and the attendant was sitting on a stool waiting for the next passenger. Three black-and-white photographs of gray-haired men with mustaches or funny sideburns lined one of the wood-paneled lobby walls. The brass plates attached to the frames identified them as J. P. Morgan, Cornelius Vanderbilt, and Solomon Loeb. With such prestigious names associated with the business, it had to be legit.

She followed the sign to the women's department and was immediately assisted by a dark-haired, lanky man in his forties. He introduced himself as Mr. Carter, and escorted her into his neat but small office at the end of the corridor.

After taking a seat behind a polished oak desk cluttered with only a wooden pen-and-ink set and a sheaf of paper, he plucked the pen from the holder, asking, "How may I be of service, Miss Spalding?"

Something about the guy, maybe his obsessive eye contact, grated against her last nerve. "I need to secure a loan."

"Of course you do." He tsked his tongue. "What is your address? What is your husband's name, and are you employed?"

"One-twenty Riverside Drive. I'm not married, and I'm currently unemployed." Technically, she wasn't. She had a job at ESPN. Or had, or would have. "But it's temporary."

He put on a pair of little round glasses without earpieces that fit snugly on his nose. She'd seen pictures of Teddy Roosevelt wearing the same style glasses. Mr. Carter wrote quickly on a piece of paper. "When is the wedding?"

She tilted her head. Joe hadn't even proposed yet. "What wedding?"

Mr. Carter removed his eyeglasses, and his piercing gray eyes pinged against her last nerve again. "You said temporary. I assumed it meant you were intending to marry."

She focused on his moss-green and white tie instead of his eyes. "I'm temporarily unemployed. I have a job interview at the *New York Herald.*"

His pen scratched across the paper. "What loan amount are you requiring?"

"Depends on the value of my jewelry."

"Under a hundred dollars, I assume."

Something—a strange ripple, like a pebble thrown into a creek—went through her. She had a much larger amount in mind, and was offended because he assumed she couldn't own an expensive piece of jewelry. Was it a sign? Did it mean she should get out of there and cling to the brooch until the door to the future opened to take her home?

She flicked the clasp on the Japanese jade purse Isabella loaned her and wrapped her fingers around her ticket home. The metal might have warmed her skin the day before, but it chilled it now. The door to the next dimension was frozen shut.

"I have a much higher number in mind," she said. "Something in the several-thousand-dollar range."

His head jerked up, his hand shot out. "May I see the piece?"

She put the brooch in his hand and watched his shoulders straighten, and his jaw muscles flex. "Where did you get this? It's exquisite."

"From my cousin."

"I'll have to have this appraised." He stood. "Wait here."

She pushed to her feet. She wasn't about to let her property out of her sight. "No," she said sternly.

His Adam's apple bobbed as he swallowed. "I beg your pardon?"

She tucked back a lock of windblown hair, a result of riding in

Gabriele's car with the windows open. "It's a family heirloom. I'm not letting it out of my sight until we reach an agreement and I have the proceeds in my hand."

His brows drew together, and he paused. Then, appearing to reach a decision he said, "Come with me."

He led the way back down the hall to the lobby, where he pushed the elevator button. The elevator arrived, and Mr. Carter asked the operator to take them to the second floor. The loan officer didn't speak again, but his finger rubbing across the diamond said all that needed to be said. He was drawn to the stone, not to the Celtic silver filigree design she found so breathtaking.

He escorted her to an office, and asked her to wait in the hall while he went in to converse with the occupant who, according to the plate on the door, was an appraiser. She watched the minutes tick away on a wall clock. After fifteen minutes, the door opened, and Mr. Carter asked her to come inside.

"Miss Spalding, please have a seat. I'm Mr. Potter." Mr. Carter stepped to the side, watching. Potter's dark eyes peered over the top of a pair of pince-nez identical in size and shape to Mr. Carter's. "Your brooch is magnificent. Where did it come from?"

"Originally? I don't know. It belonged to my cousin. She left it to me in her will."

"Do you know the carat weight?"

"Several, I imagine."

"It's thirty. We pay a set amount per point. A point is one tenth of a carat."

Thirty frigging carats went beyond her expectations. She knew the stone was large and very valuable. But thirty? She forced herself to remain focused on the speaker, studying him as she would a batter, watching for clues to his thoughts and intentions. And she gritted her teeth to keep from revealing any of her own.

Potter tapped on a Burroughs Adding Machine. Amy wasn't a neophyte when it came to diamonds or calculating values. In fact, she was adept at figuring baseball statistics—ERAs, RBIs, and batting averages. And when it came to diamonds, she had done her share of research, anticipating shopping with Joe one day for a ring. A thirty-carat diamond could easily cost six to eight million dollars in her time. If she used an inflation rate of about three percent a year and worked backwards, she would arrive at a reasonable value. In the absence of a calculator, she would have to resort to using high school algebra to find the unknown.

"May I have paper and pen please?" He handed her a gold-band Waterman fountain pen with a clip cap and a sheet of paper. She pulled her chair to the desk. A few minutes later, she had calculated a reasonable value. She sat back and waited for Mr. Potter to reveal his number first.

"We can go as high as seventy-five dollars at four percent interest."

The number was insulting, but it was the first shot in a highly tactical negotiation. She crossed her arms. "By my calculations, the value of this stone is approximately three hundred thousand dollars."

There was a charged silence, except for the constant din of the horses' iron shoes clop-clopping against the pavement flowing into the room from the open window.

Mr. Potter, with his long neck and overbite, cleared his throat. "How much were you expecting, Miss Spalding?"

Without flinching, she said, "A hundred thousand dollars." She let a beat pass before adding, "At three and a half percent."

Mr. Carter leaned over and whispered in Mr. Potter's ear, and Potter's eyes narrowed in concentration.

She went into the meeting without a preconceived notion of the value or interest rate. She just knew how to haggle, thanks to her dad, once she knew the range. "Look, if I don't repay it, you auction it off and make two hundred grand. I can't imagine Mr. Morgan or Mr. Vanderbilt turning down such a large profit. Can you?"

All she needed was enough to buy a few clothes, pay for rent, food, and incidentals. She would invest the rest and reclaim the brooch within six weeks. Seventy-five dollars was too little. A hundred thousand was too much, but...

Potter's fingers moved along the rim of his desk as if playing trumpet buttons. Then, coming to a decision he pushed back his rolling chair. "I'll have to consult my superior. We'll have an answer for you within an hour." He turned to Mr. Carter and said, "Miss Spalding might enjoy a cup of tea in the conference room while she awaits our decision."

She didn't want tea, and she didn't want to be patronized. "I have a friend who has an office on the top floor. I'll go visit him while I wait. Please call him when you've made a decision."

"Certainly. Who is your friend?" Potter asked.

"Gabriele Moretti."

Potter and Carter exchanged unreadable glances, then Potter tugged on the sleeves of his gray-striped suit jacket, perfectly tailored to his slender form. "When we have a decision, we will telephone Mr. Moretti."

The glance between the two men disconcerted her. Hadn't she already told Carter she didn't want to be separated from her brooch? Then why do it now?

"On second thought," she said. "I'll stay with my diamond. I don't want to be separated from the brooch until we conclude our business. Nothing against you or the company, but it's all I have right now, and I can't afford to lose it. Where did you say we're going next?"

"I assure you, Miss Spalding," Potter said dismissively, "your jewelry is completely safe in my hands."

"I'm sure it is, Mr. Potter, but it's a big, crazy world out there, and if I don't protect my interests, I might not have the outcome I expect."

Using the same exact tone Mr. Carter did a few minutes earlier, Potter said, "Come with me."

She marched after Mr. Potter. From the corner of her eye, she saw her image reflected on the glass door panels, and watched the plume on her tricorn-shaped hat bob on her head in time with her steps, until they reached another corner office on the front side of the building. The door plate indicated it belonged to the president.

Potter knocked and was invited in. "Wait here," he said to her. Five minutes later, the footsteps of a heavyset, balding man pattered hastily down the hall toward her. He knocked on the president's door, too. The door opened, he entered, and the door closed behind him. A couple of minutes later, another man, who could have been the brother of the first, hustled toward her, knocked on the door, and was immediately ushered in.

Fifteen interminable minutes later, the door opened and the last two men who entered departed in the same hurried fashion. Potter invited her into a spacious office with pulled-to-the-side maroon drapes, open windows, the scent of spring in the air, and a gorgeous view of a skyline that didn't exist in her time.

A graying man in his early fifties, with a chiseled jaw and deep-set brown eyes that flicked quickly as he looked her over, stepped out from behind a large mahogany desk, smiling appreciatively. "I'm Mr. Thomson, president of the Providence Loan Society. I'm sorry to have kept you waiting, Miss Spalding, but you have presented us with an unusual request." He gestured toward one of two leather wingback chairs. "Please, have a seat."

"I have an unusual brooch, Mr. Thomson, and I'm sick at heart"—she pressed her hand against her chest—"to have to *temporarily*," she emphasized the word, so he would understand she had every intention of reclaiming her property, "part with my family heirloom." She sat on the edge of the chair and placed her gloved hands in her lap. She crossed her legs at the ankles and lifted her chin slightly. Attitude was everything.

"Are you related to A. G. Spalding?" he asked.

"Distantly," she said. "I haven't met him, but I've read about his baseball exploits…and his business acumen, or, as some might call it, shrewdness."

The corner of Mr. Thomson's mouth tucked in, a small, secret expression, indicating he knew more about Mr. A. G. Spalding than he was willing to say. "Do you follow the sport?"

"I do, and I'll be glad to discuss player stats and team strategy with you as soon as we settle the matter of my loan."

He blinked several times before taking his seat. "Tell me, Miss Spalding, if we loan you a hundred thousand dollars, what would you do with it?"

Sweat trickled down between her breasts, causing the chemise, under the corset Isabella insisted she wear, to stick to her skin. She needed to play to Thomson's interests. He was a banker. Which meant he had one main interest: money. His eyes were fixed on her.

"Invest it. I want my money to work for me, so I can repay the loan within six weeks."

His brows drew together and stayed that way while he tugged on his tear-shaped right earlobe. The ear-grab body language told Amy that he didn't believe her. "You want to borrow money to invest, not to pay debts or living expenses?"

On reflection, it didn't make any sense. If she continued along those lines, he'd say she was crazy and toss her out of his office. "I just arrived in the city. My suitcase was stolen, and the only clothes I have are the ones I'm wearing. Besides purchasing a few items, I also need to eat and rent a room."

"And invest the rest?"

"Exactly."

He swiveled his desk chair and crossed his legs. "What stocks interest you?"

"Transportation and utilities."

He fired back with another question. "Automobiles, railroads, or airships?"

"Commercial flight, and anything built by Henry Ford. He'll revolutionize the automobile industry. I have no interest in purchasing a General Mills bond. I may sound like a reckless lunatic, but I want a portfolio based on profitability, not tangible assets."

Bless Joe's heart. She napped through most of his dry, boring stock market lectures on the history of investing, but was glad this very handy tidbit of knowledge had seeped in through the cracks in her brain.

"I have a different opinion of the advantage of owning corporate bonds, but I would be interested in hearing more of yours."

"A portfolio of common stocks would make me *persona non grata* in affluent circles, but I would be happy to share my opinions, as long as you don't laugh at me."

"I would never be so rude, Miss Spalding."

"My thanks, sir. Since we're talking about investing, do you have a stockbroker you would recommend?"

"As a matter of fact, I do. An excellent one, and if we reach an agreement, I will make an introduction. Now, Mr. Potter has informed me you want to borrow one hundred thousand dollars at three-point-five percent, and use as collateral a thirty-carat diamond valued at three times the loan amount. Is that correct?"

She propped her elbows on the arms of the chair and steepled her fingers. Again. Perceived attitude was everything. "You have summed it up nicely, Mr. Thomson."

"Are you contemplating marriage, Miss Spalding?"

She cocked her head and gave him a coy smile. "Are you allowed to ask that on a loan application?"

A look of surprise was quickly veiled, but a telltale blush crept up his neck.

"Forget it. There's a simple answer. No. And," she continued, "although I'm unemployed today, I intend to get a job as a baseball reporter."

"You are a most unusual woman." His tone conveyed both curiosity and amusement.

"Mr. Thomson," she said, using the same tone of voice, "we're back to where we began this conversation. What's it to be?"

He sat forward and clasped his hands together on top of his desk. "The Providence Loan Society will loan you the sum of seventy-five thousand dollars at a rate of three-point-seven-five percent for a term of one hundred and eighty days. As collateral for the loan, we will accept your thirty-carat diamond, appraised at two hundred seventy-five thousand dollars. We will have the documents ready for you to sign this afternoon."

"That's too late," she said. "I need disbursement of the funds this morning. The Giants play at four o'clock, and I have shopping to do. I can't wear the same dress I wore yesterday and hope to impress the editor of the *New York Herald.*"

Mr. Thomson looked up at Mr. Potter, who was standing nearby, and Potter nodded.

"Give us an hour," Mr. Thomson said. "In the meantime, I recommend you go across the street and open an account at the Bank of New York."

"The bank started by Alexander Hamilton?"

"Yes, in 1784."

"It's a sound institution. Maybe I'll invest in it." After watching *Hamilton: An American Musical,* she read up on the founding father and discovered his bank remained in business until its merger with the Mellon Financial Corporation in 2007. The man was a genius. If the brooch had taken her back to 1804, she would have stopped his duel with Aaron Burr by hitting them both over the head with a rubber bat.

"Would you mind placing a call to your contact at the Bank to let them know I'm coming to open an account?"

"I'd be pleased to." He picked up the handset of a black candlestick telephone on his desk—no dial, no buttons. The call went directly to an operator, who then placed the call. "Jonathan, this is Stephen Thomson. I have a young woman in my office who just arrived in the city." He smiled at Amy. "She wishes to open an account with you. Yes… A young heiress… Amy Spalding… Yes, a relation… She knows quite a bit about investments. I would be *en garde.* Yes… Thank you."

Mr. Thomson replaced the receiver. "There, that's done. Let me jot down his name for you." He opened the desk's top drawer, removed a business card, and wrote on the back. "Ask for this gentleman. He'll provide all the services you need. When the documents are ready for signature, Mr. Potter will bring them to you, along with the proceeds of your loan."

She stared at the brooch, lying on a green velvet jeweler's tray in the middle of the desk. The diamond sparkled in a thin ray of sun beaming through the window. This was her last chance to back out and consider another option, but she knew in her heart she had none. She couldn't live off Maria's charity. And she had the impression Gabriele wanted people to believe he had a healthy bank account when he was probably teetering on the line between operating in the black and drowning in the red. She wasn't sure what gave her that impression—maybe the frayed shirt sleeves. But she would never embarrass him by asking.

She extended her hand to Mr. Thomson. "I appreciate your help. Thank you."

He held on to her hand a beat longer than was proper. "I'd still like to discuss the game of baseball."

"I'll be at the game this afternoon sitting in the second deck, away from the annoying pillars, and as close to home plate as possible."

He smiled a little crookedly. "If possible, I'll adjust my schedule to attend."

An hour later, she took the elevator to the fourth floor of the Providence Loan Society Building with cash in her purse and a ledger sheet showing the deposit of seventy-four-thousand, nine hundred dollars.

She didn't know how much her clothes would cost, but the banker had given her a list of shop owners who would extend store credit for her purchases. After checking in with Gabriele, she was going to shop the Ladies' Mile, then taxi back to the apartment. If the rest of the day was as productive as her morning, by four o'clock she would be sitting in a box seat at the Polo Grounds, watching the Giants play and chatting up an editor. She needed a job, and working for the *New York Herald* was right in her wheelhouse.

13

1909 New York City—Amy

AMY LEFT GABRIELE'S OFFICE and cabbed it to the Ladies' Mile, a trapezoid-shaped shopping mecca from 14th Street and Broadway to 23rd and 6th Avenue. A. T. Stewart's Iron Palace anchored the south end at 10th and Broadway, and the enormous Stern Brothers dry goods store on 23rd, just off 6th Avenue, anchored the north end.

From what she was told at the bank, during the afternoon shopping hours the streets were crowded with broughams and coupes, and the sidewalks were packed with a procession of well-dressed women. Amy intended to arrive early and avoid the crowd.

She experienced a real-life Julia Roberts *Pretty Woman* moment while shopping at the Iron Palace. The side glances and whispers from the salesclerk gave Amy the impression Mr. Thomson, aka Stephen the widower, not only recommended the store, but had also notified the manager she was on her way. Mr. Thomson's moniker—Stephen the widower—came from the clerk, who sized Amy up with a highbrow glower.

"Mr. Thomson is one of our most important clients. I know exactly what he likes." Amy was distracted by the price tags and totally missed the woman's innuendo until she directed Amy toward a rack of silk dressing gowns. "He especially likes silk and lace."

The implication smacked Amy in the face, and she whirled

around to face the woman. "Excuse me?"

The woman flinched. "I'm just saying, if you have questions about appropriate attire, I can make recommendations based on his previous purchases." She fingered the sleeve of a lace gown with chiffon lining, and gave Amy a stiff smile.

Amy didn't know whether to claw out the woman's eyes or kick her in the knee. Words piled up like a traffic jam in her throat, and she ended up just standing there, mouth agape. What gave Mr. Thomson the impression she was available for extracurricular activities? Was he a misogynist? She hadn't flirted with him, or given him any reason to believe she was interested...or had she? Norms were different than in her time. Maybe she had unknowingly given him the wrong impression. Like what? She didn't know, but right now she needed friends, especially ones with influence.

Amy backpedaled like crazy and gave the woman a let's-do-business smile. "My traveling trunk was stolen yesterday, and I need a new wardrobe. If you can make recommendations, I'd be very grateful."

The woman smiled. "I'll be glad to help." She picked up a small journal and pen and began to write. "Mr. Thomson said you intend to work at a newspaper and attend baseball games. Of course you'll need dresses for dinners, theater, a party or two, an ensemble to wear while bicycling in the park, and traveling dresses."

"I'll also need undergarments. I borrowed a corset today, and," Amy leaned in to whisper, "my breasts are smaller than the corset owner's." If Amy wore a thirty-four B, Isabella would wear at least a thirty-six C.

The woman chuckled. "A good corset is a special order, and rarely fits anyone else." She wrote in the journal. "I suggest we start with morning dresses and work our way through the day."

Two hours later, Amy signed the store charge slip to be delivered to the bank for payment, then bundled up her packages and hatboxes. The store seamstress made a few simple alterations to three skirts so Amy would have clothes to wear for the next few days, but the gowns and suits needed major alterations, and would be delivered to Maria's apartment later in the week.

Amy hugged the store owner, the buxom, middle-aged Madam Wallace, on the way out. "I'll come back in a week or so to buy the other pair of shoes."

"I'll send word as soon as I have them in stock. Enjoy the game this afternoon. One of my clients, Mrs. Helen Hay Whitney, is a baseball fanatic, and often takes her children to the games. If you see her, give her my regards. She's a lovely woman. And be sure to thank Mr. Thomson for the referral," Madam Wallace said with a wink.

Amy laughed. "I told you I'm not interested in him."

"He's a good man, Miss Spalding."

He was a good man, Amy discovered. He hadn't shopped at the store for other women, but for his invalid wife.

She hailed one of the yellow-paneled taxis for the ride to the Upper West Side. She had blown her budget and felt guilty, but she truly enjoyed herself, and her outfits were lovely, as well as appropriate to wear to work and to ball games. If she was going to be taken seriously, she couldn't dress like a charwoman.

The taxi driver stopped in front of the apartment building and helped her carry the packages to the elevator, which was now back in service. The operator helped her load the packages for the trip to the top floor, and she tipped him, thanking him profusely.

Isabella opened the apartment door and squealed when she saw Amy loaded down with packages and hatboxes. "What did you buy?"

"Help her with the packages, Isabella, and give her time to take off her jacket and hat." Isabella joined her grandmother on the sofa, and both women sat primly, watching Amy with excited eyes. Their eagerness eased some of the guilt Amy felt for pawning the brooch. Maybe not guilt so much as fear. What if something happened and she lost permanent control of the stone? Her only hope of getting home would be finding another one, and as soon as she landed a job, she'd start looking for evidence others existed.

She plopped into a chair. If she thought living in New York City was hard in the twenty-first century, it was nothing compared to the early twentieth. Plus, riding in a car was dangerous. Well…maybe it wasn't so different, after all.

"Everything worked out fine. I borrowed money for rent, clothes, and emergencies."

Isabella pointed to the hatboxes. "And hats," she said excitedly. "Let's see what you bought. You have such marvelous taste. I love the one you're wearing."

I do too. Thank you, Catherine Lily.

Amy opened a hatbox and carefully lifted out one of three Metropolitan hats. Isabella nearly jumped off the sofa. When her eyes lit up, Amy said, "Here. This one is for you, for being so kind."

Isabella clasped her hands to her chest. "For me? Are you sure?"

Amy held out a dark green one. "Yes, I'm sure. This will look gorgeous with your olive skin and big brown eyes. Try it on." While Isabella primped in front of the walnut mirrored seat and umbrella stand, Amy opened another hatbox and lifted out a blue one. "This one is for you, Maria. It will look sumptuous with your salt and pepper hair."

"For me?" Maria asked, her eyes sparkling.

Amy fitted it on the older woman's head. "We'll need to fiddle a bit to tuck in all your hair, but you look beautiful. Don't you think so, Isabella?"

Isabella hugged her grandmother. "You look beautiful." Then she hugged Amy. "Thank you. The hats are divine. Can we wear them today?"

Amy laughed. "Of course you can, and look," she opened another hatbox, waded through tissue paper, and presented a third one, which featured a medallion and a peacock feather. She and Madam Wallace picked apart two hats and remade them, and the result was a roaring twenties look Amy loved. "It's *au courant*. Don't you think?"

Isabella twitched her nose at the hat and then giggled. "I like mine better."

"Isabella, what an awful thing to say," Maria said. "Amy was so kind to think of us, and you insult her."

"I didn't mean to, *nonna*. It's just that I like yours and mine better. But Amy's is pretty, too." She primped in front of the mirror again and then darted off toward her room. "I have to find a dress to go with this."

Amy sat down next to Maria. "Thank you for letting me stay here. You're a godsend." She took eighty dollars from her loaner purse and gave it to Maria. "Gabriele negotiated eighteen dollars a week for room and board, but it's worth more than that. I don't want to take advantage of you."

"You spent a week's rent on two hats. You can't afford to waste your money."

Amy accepted the chastisement silently, but only for about ten seconds. "I know, but Isabella dressed me this morning, and loaned me a purse, a corset, and a petticoat, without complaint or expectation of a reward. And she wouldn't have enjoyed her hat half as much if you didn't get one, too."

Maria patted the back of Amy's hand. "You understand her well. I've tried to give her a mother's love, but it has never been enough."

"My mother died when I was young, and my father passed away a few years ago. I miss them every day. Isabella is lucky to have you."

"I'm sorry you lost your parents. They raised a *ragazza dolce*."

Amy smiled. "Thank you,"

"Amy," Isabella called from her room. "Will you help me pick out a dress? I don't know which one to choose."

"Isabella is *fortunata* to have you now."

Amy didn't know how *fortunata* Isabella was to have her around, but Amy knew how fortunate she was to have Isabella, Maria, and Gabriele. The next few weeks would be difficult, and having them to depend on would make adjusting to her new life much easier.

And then there was Stephen "the widower" Thomson. How would that play out? She glanced at the clock on the mantel. The game started in three hours. If Mr. Thomson showed up at the game, she'd have to give his attention more thought, but until then, Isabella was calling.

14

1909 New York City—Amy

THE DAY BEFORE, Amy received dozens of wolf whistles as she made her way through the upper deck at the Polo Grounds. Today was much worse. The red tango suit with the skirt styled in the modified-trousers effect drew more reactions than she anticipated. And Isabella, who looked drop-dead gorgeous and glitteringly alive in pale green, amassed dozens more.

The turban framed her olive skin and almond-shaped eyes, and the combination created a seductive yet innocent appeal. If she was looking for a husband, she would easily find one here. Unless they were Italian, though, they might as well not apply. Maria hadn't come right out and said Isabella could only marry an Italian, but the sentiment was implied.

Isabella paused and glanced down at the field several times. Amy couldn't tell if she was curious or just drawing attention to herself.

Either way, Amy didn't wait for her. Instead, she made a beeline for the open seats to secure four in a row. One of the four seats was close to a pillar, but she wasn't going to do any better. She'd give the seat to Isabella. The pillar would give her an excuse to stand up and pose charmingly while she watched the action.

"Miss Spalding," a man said.

She looked up. "Mr. Bennett. What a pleasure." He was sitting two rows behind her, and next to him sat Mr. Thomson from the

Providence Loan Society. Stephen nodded politely, showing little recognition.

Her already-high opinion of him was ratcheted up another notch. He was obviously not going to admit he knew her, so they could keep their business confidential. Or, he had already told Mr. Bennett about her, and they were being coy, not admitting they discussed her. She wasn't going to worry about it. When Isabella's arrival distracted her, she turned her focus on the young woman.

"This is so exciting. Where is Christy Mathewson?" Isabella asked.

"The team will take the field in about fifteen minutes. Why don't you sit on the other side of Gabriele, and Maria can sit next to you?" Amy wanted Gabriele next to her so she could feed him tips. The Giants would win the day, and Amy and Gabriele should make some money, especially with Mathewson pitching. She was giddy with anticipation, not about betting, but about watching Christy pitch.

"What are we betting on today?" Bennett asked.

Amy was so focused on getting her companions seated, she hadn't noticed Bennett and Thomson switched seats and they were now sitting directly behind her. "Giants will win by three," she said low-voiced, "and our All-American boy will be explosive on the mound."

"By three?" Bennett asked. "I'll place a wager on that."

"Who's the All-American boy?" Stephen asked.

Bennett nodded toward Stephen. "This is Mr. Thomson, president of the Providence Loan Society."

Stephen tipped his hat. "Mr. Bennett has spoken highly of you, Miss Spalding. I'm looking forward to your running commentary on today's game."

She extended her hand, just as she did that morning. "Nice to meet you." To her relief, he wasn't as presumptuous about retaining her hand as he was earlier.

"To answer your question," she said, "it's Mathewson, and I'll give you five reasons why he's the All-American boy." She pressed down on her pinky. "He studied analytical chemistry at Bucknell."

Next, she tapped her ring finger. "He writes poetry, is musically inclined, and plays multiple sports." Then she moved to her middle finger. "He's wholesome and a good role model." Then to her index finger. "He's a devoted husband, a loyal son, and a good Christian. And on top of all that"—she held her thumb—"he's one heck of a baseball player, with amazing control. He reads a batter's weakness and lays the ball exactly at their weak point." She signaled with her fingers shot out to the side. "Strike."

The two men laughed. "The lady knows her baseball," Stephen said, the corner of his mouth lifted in a secret smile. "I doubt baseball is the only topic in which she's equally conversant."

With pretend nonchalance Amy said, "Based on my recent experiences, I can also talk about traffic. In five minutes, I can give you a handful of suggestions that will improve traffic flow at little cost to the city, and will also save lives."

"Lady," a man sitting in front of her said, "if you can fix the traffic, the city will erect a statue of you at Columbus Circle."

The man next to him said, "I'm on the city council. If you know traffic as well as you know baseball, I'd be interested in hearing your ideas."

"Anything more than 'Hey, watch out', would be a spectacular improvement," she said. "The main problem is drivers don't understand velocity and centrifugal force, or why they turn turtle when they take corners at high speed." She looked down on the field. "Matty is coming to the plate. Let's watch the game and solve the city's problems later."

Would she be changing history if laws were implemented years before their time? She couldn't sit idly by when easy fixes were available to improve, and even save, the lives of New Yorkers.

"Matty's fastball is a fierce weapon, and requires an expansive wind-up," she said to Maria. "Watch his arms swing like huge pendulums."

The batter hit a short ground ball to Bridwell at shortstop. Bridwell took a gamble and threw to Devlin at third to cut down the lead runner. "No, don't do it! He's not paying attention," she yelled. Too late. Devlin wasn't expecting the toss and muffed the tag. She cupped her hands around her mouth. "Wake up out there! You're getting paid to play ball." She yanked off her hat and gloves and threw them on her seat. "I'd dock his pay."

Gabriele picked up her hat and held it for her. She yanked it out of his hand, and he pulled the hat pin out of his jacket sleeve. "Next time you express your disapproval, remove the pin before you throw the hat."

She clapped her hand over her mouth. "You aren't hurt, are you?"

"No." He reshaped the hat, straightened the feather, and she set it back on her head.

"Does it look okay?"

He angled it slightly and secured it with the pin.

"Thanks. How'd you learn to do that?"

He stared at her, eyes fixed, deep brown, and unblinking above a small, slightly pensive grin. "I have three younger sisters."

She touched his arm lightly. "Still in Italy? I'm sorry. I know you miss them."

"Mr. Moretti, are you placing a wager on Murray?" a man sitting near them yelled.

Amy and Gabriele shot a quick glance at the field. Red Murray left the on-deck circle and approached the plate. "He'll get a hit," Amy said sotto voce.

"Two bits Murray gets a hit," Gabriele announced, orchestrating his next wager. Several men took the bet, and Gabriele got to his feet to watch the action.

Murray connected and sailed a fly ball to left field. The runners held their bases as the ball descended, and shot off as soon as it touched leather. The pitcher's throw to the plate was off-line and the catcher moved to his right to snare it backhanded.

"Two bits he throws to third," Amy said instantly.

Gabriele collected the bets just as the catcher considered his options. There was no chance for him to reach the plate in time to tag the runner speeding home, so he smartly whipped the ball to the third baseman.

Amy was up on her feet yelling, "Slide!"

The third baseman slapped a tag on the surprised Giants runner, who hadn't bothered to listen to Amy, or the third base coach, or "coacher," as they were called early in the century. She reached for her hat again, but Gabriele gestured, hitting the side of his right hand with the palm of his left, which she'd learned meant stop, get out, cut loose. She looked at him with her softball power glare, guaranteed to intimidate.

He shrugged. "You can't afford to ruin your hat."

For Amy, baseball was serious stuff. But he was right. Trashing an easily replaceable ball cap was one thing. A delicate, fashionable hat another.

By the third inning, Gabriele was up twenty dollars, and Amy's throat was sore from yelling. He went to get lemonade for the ladies, a beer for himself, and hot dogs for everyone.

The Giants' fans were so vocal, only those sitting close by could distinguish her voice above the others. Maria and Isabella weren't as loud as Amy, but they were on their feet, wearing a look of righteous indignation while using their outstretched hands in an Italian gesture for—*look at that idiot.*

During a quieter moment while the Giants took the field, a woman sitting in front of Amy said, "My husband wanted me to come with him today. This is my first baseball game, and I didn't know what to expect, but I'm coming back. I know the players' names now, and I've become a Mathewson devotee. Do you know him, by chance? Can you make an introduction?"

"I haven't met him yet," Amy said.

"You should write articles for the newspaper," Stephen said. "You'd have a large readership within weeks."

"I would read your column," the woman said.

Was this a setup? Or had Stephen just figured out what she meant earlier when she said she hoped to work at a newspaper.

"Since meeting with you yesterday, Miss Spalding, I've considered how the *Herald* could interest more women in baseball. I'm now convinced you've identified a need the paper can meet," Bennett said. "I'd consider"—he twirled one side of his President Howard Taft-ish handlebar mustache—"giving you a weekly column to write baseball articles to appeal to our female readership."

Stephen clapped Bennett on the back. "Weekly? That isn't enough to develop a following. Miss Spalding would need at least three articles a week."

"I like your thinking," Amy said. "But I have a question. Would the articles appear on the sports page or the society page?"

"Society page, of course," Bennett said.

Amy didn't respond. Gabriele did. He tapped his fingers against his thumb, mimicking a puppet chatting away to itself, indicating Bennett was talking, but not saying what she wanted to hear. She flicked an eyebrow at him in agreement.

Under his breath he said, "Stand at the plate and guard your ground."

She licked her bottom lip. How could she stand her ground, yet not offend Bennett? It wouldn't do any good to take a stand if she lost the war during the first battle.

She tapped the shoulder of the man who said he was on the city council. "Sir, if I wrote a column for the *New York Herald* about baseball, would you read it?"

"Sure would."

"Would you read it if it was on the society page?"

He shook his head. "Probably not."

"Women won't turn to the sports page to read your column, and that's the readership you want to grow," Bennett said.

"And the men won't go to the society page," Amy said. "But both would read"—she decided to go for it, hoping to land on solid ground—"the front page."

Astonishment briefly blanked Bennett's face. "I'm not offering you a column on the sports page or the front page. I have other writers for that."

She had made it to the men's table in her time, but it wouldn't happen in this one. If she settled on this point, she would end up settling on others. Room and board cost her twenty dollars a week. Her salary needed to cover that, plus interest and principal on her loan, clothing, transportation, and so on. She needed at least fifty dollars a week, which would give her an annual salary of twenty-six hundred. Based on what she knew of players' salaries in 1909, it was probably high for a reporter, but if the paper's readership increased because of her articles, she would pay for herself, and she wasn't opposed to doing some of her own marketing.

When the inning ended, she said to Bennett. "I want a five-day a week column at ten dollars a column."

Bennett shook his head. "Can't do it."

"Readership will increase, so will ad buys. Together they will more than pay my salary."

The discussion was interrupted when Arthur Devlin was called out at the plate for trying to stretch a three-bagger into a home run. He got in the umpire's face—yelling loud enough to hear him from the stands—and told the ump he was blind and needed glasses.

Matty grabbed Devlin's arm. "Forget it. We got a lead without the run."

Devlin walked away, griping. "I wasn't kicking it up over the run. The ump cost me money. I wanted a homer to pay for a new suit."

Amy laughed before sobering and returning to the conversation about a possible job. "Give me a four-week tryout. If your readership and ad buys don't increase enough to pay my salary and add to your bottom line, you can fire me."

"Four weeks, huh?"

"Ten dollars a column, five columns a week, and a byline."

"Nobody gets a byline."

"There's always a first time."

"If I give a byline to you, the other writers will expect one, too."

"What's wrong with giving writers credit for their work?"

"It's not done."

"But it can be."

"If I don't fire you after four weeks, we'll talk about it. I want eleven inches of copy on my desk every morning by nine o'clock.

You've got three New York City baseball teams to cover, and if one of them isn't playing in town, I want special interest stories about the players and their wives."

"How many words is eleven inches?" she asked.

"About three hundred. Can you do it?" Bennett asked.

She didn't know if she could write it or not. But she knew she could speak it. Mentally, she put herself in the broadcasting booth. She stood to have a better view of the field from the upper deck. It was Brooklyn's turn at bat.

"Count my words."

The gestalt of baseball invaded her senses—the smell of peanuts and beer, the whack of the ball hitting leather gloves, the sight of players happy as young boys romping in newly-mown grass, and vulgar language peppering the hum of conversations in the stands.

She opened her mouth and words spilled out. "Mathewson towers over the field like a mighty giant. A deafening, reverberating roar galvanizes the crowd, cheering for the fresh-faced, well-groomed, quintessential turn-of-the-century American male."

She increased the volume and tension in her voice. "Matty pushes off the pitcher's box and drives for the plate with startling power. His follow-through ends with a light kick, and he finishes on his toes, feet apart, hand at his side, ready for a fielding play. Strike two. He took the catcher's return throw and regained the mound in three long strides."

She cupped her fist in her hand, pretending she had a ball and glove. "His broad shoulders taper to a narrow waist. His belt sits low on his hips, and his powerful legs appear taut beneath his uniform's billowing knickers. He tips his cap back on his forehead, revealing a fringe of thick brown hair. He bends for the sign, shakes it off, then rolls into motion and throws a fastball."

She threw an imaginary ball.

"The batter swings, and the ball bounces to first base. The first baseman gloves it and tosses the ball underhanded to Matty, who catches it in full stride and kicks the base for an easy out."

She formed a hammer with a clenched right fist and delivered a quick, sharp blow. "You're out!"

Everyone around her seemed to exhale at once. She glanced over her shoulder. Both Bennett and Thomson were leaning forward, eyes wide, listening intently.

"That's only five inches. Keep going," Bennett said.

She refocused on the field. "Matty stands on the hill, waiting for the catcher to return to position, his left leg slightly bent, his weight on the right. He gloves the toss, and it rests in the pocket of his small, brown glove. He seems as fresh as when he started the game—no heaving breath, no shirtsleeve drawn across his sweating brow.

"He mixes power with guile and throws his famous fadeaway, a right-handed screwball. The batter axes the ball into the hard dirt in front of home plate. It bounces high as Matty glides in beneath it, snatches it with his bare hand, and snaps a throw to second base for the third out."

She turned toward Bennett, hands on hips. "Ten dollars a column, five columns a week, each one eleven inches…and a byline."

She saw something flicker deep in Gabriele's eyes. Otherwise he didn't move, didn't breathe. Isabella's expressive hands seemed to hang in the air, as if paused by a remote control. Maria smiled slyly, unable to mask a look of triumph. Amy's pulse, which had been jumping up and down, settled on a quick, light thump, discernible only in her fingertips.

"I'll give you a month," Bennett said. "If circulation increases, I'll give you another month. If you can't hold on to your readership, I'll let you go."

"Don't forget the byline."

Bennett stared at her, baffled. "Reporters don't have bylines."

She ignored him, but nervously pleated the cloth of her skirt between her fingers. "I'll have the first eleven inches on your desk tomorrow by eight a.m." It might be 1909, a decade before women gained the right to vote, but she wasn't one for quiet grit or backing down. She would work harder than any man on his staff, and whatever he asked of her, she would give him more. Instead of eleven inches, she would write fifteen.

Bennett nodded toward the field. "The next time one of those ball players negotiates a new contract, they'd be smart to take you with them."

Stephen laughed.

"First thing I'd do is challenge the reserve clause. Players should be free to bargain, to be free agents, but don't get me started," she said.

"The reserve clause keeps salary demands in check," Stephen said.

"It might be fair to the owners, but it's not fair to the players." She tapped her finger against her jaw. "Maybe I'll use it as the subject of my first column."

"If it is, it will be your first and last," Bennett said.

A fit of pique would do no good, and offending her editor and publisher would be a huge mistake. She conceded the point with a nod. Besides, the publisher was probably friends with the club owners. If the owners had it in for her, they'd never allow interviews with the players. To write entertaining articles, she needed access.

"It was just a thought," she said.

"A thought you should keep to yourself. The newspaper reports the news. It doesn't make it, and it can't be an advocate for one party's interest over another," Bennett said.

Talk of business deals subsided while they watched the rest of the game. Dusk approached, and the grandstand was only three-quarters full when Matty came out to pitch the ninth. His spikes left a straight track in the dirt as he crossed the infield and climbed the mound. He joked with the players and the front row spectators. The first three batters choked up high on their bats and chipped at the ball with half-swings. This late in the game, trying to hit a pitch off him was like trying to tag sparks as they popped out of a fire pit.

She'd watched pitchers her entire life, and had always known Matty was a power pitcher. Watching him now, though, at the top of the ninth, it was obvious why he remained on the top ten list of all-time major league pitchers. When she interviewed him, and she knew she would, she hoped to God her fan-crush wouldn't tie her tongue into a thousand macramé knots.

The game ended, and Gabriele collected their winnings. At last count, they were closing in on the hundred-dollar mark. He'd made a good business decision moving to the other end of the grandstand to make bets before those closest to them became suspicious.

They agreed before the game started they would split the winnings as well as share the losses equally. Fifty dollars wouldn't put a dent in recouping her shopping expenses, but it would pay rent for two weeks. At the rate she and Gabriele were going, she might be able to repay her loan sooner than she expected.

Bennett said goodbye, and Amy assured him she would have her first column on his desk first thing in the morning, even if it meant staying up all night to write it. She expected Stephen to say his goodbyes, too, but he surprised her with an invitation.

"I'd like to take you and your companions to dinner to celebrate."

"I should be the one extending the invitation," Amy said. "I have a job, thanks to you."

"I was only protecting my investment."

"Do you do that for all your customers?" she asked.

His eyes darkened, but stayed steady on her face. What was he recalling? A long-ago event? Another customer he helped? His late wife?

"No, just you," he said.

"Well... We would love to have dinner with you, but it must be at the finest Italian restaurant in Little Italy."

"I'm not sure I know which one that is."

"Not a problem, because Maria knows the owner. Do you like lasagna?"

"It's one of my favorite dishes."

"Great, because I hear it's one of Maria's sister's specialties, and it's my favorite, too. I ate it in every restaurant from Rome to Venice, and was tempted to turn around and start all over again."

He laughed. "Is there anything you don't do, Miss Spalding?"

"I don't cook."

She could hold back a burst of laughter, but not the twinkle she knew was sparking in her eyes. In the last thirty-six hours, three men had come to her rescue. Three honorable men had taken a chance on her. She had a bed to sleep in, clothes to wear, food to eat, a challenging job opportunity, a side gambling operation, Giants baseball, and, most importantly, friends.

And for now, that was enough.

15

Present day MacKlenna Farm—Jack

JACK LEANED AGAINST the window behind the antique mahogany desk in Elliott's office in MacKlenna Mansion. The view of the paddock had been his favorite since his first visit to the farm over twelve years ago. He had watched all four seasons unfold through these glass panes—beginning with the transitional season of spring, a time of phenomenal renewal. To the longer days of summer, which often dissolved shadows in his life. To nature's last hurrah of autumn, his personal favorite. Then finally to silent winter, a time of contemplation and indwelling.

What the fuck did that mean? This contemplation crap was getting old. That's why he deleted all his notes for a self-help book for men struggling with grief. He didn't have anything to contribute. Grief was hell. Period. You couldn't buy your way out of it. You couldn't skip over it. You couldn't deny it. You just had to fucking live it.

He pushed away from the window and crossed the room to the refreshment bar. Whisky or coffee? Better start with the high-octane stuff. He selected a dark roast K-cup and punched the button on the coffee machine. The aroma perked him up almost as much as a hit of caffeine. He carried the steamy mug over to one of two leather wingback chairs and kicked back to wait for the rest of the team to arrive.

"There ye are. I heard ye came in. Did ye sleep well?"

"I haven't slept well in eight months, Elliott."

Elliott clapped Jack's shoulder. "Ye're like a son to me, lad. I worry about ye, and have since the first day ye and Charlotte came to my door. Ye're a good man. Ye have a good heart. Yer reckless at times, aye. But ye've never intentionally hurt anyone."

Jack pretended to stick his finger in his ear and do a fake cleaning. "Excuse me. I think I have a hearing problem."

"Yer hearing's fine." Elliott popped a pod into the coffee maker. "I wish I had the wisdom of my grandsire to help ye muddle through what aches yer soul. I don't, but I'll tell ye this. Ye'll find what ye're looking for. Maybe not today. Maybe not tomorrow, but it'll come to ye. Have patience, walk with confidence, and have yer hands out ready to grab it when it shows up."

"Master Obi-Wan, you only think you don't have wisdom. Those childhood lies you believe have distorted your view of yourself. It's not true, and the family knows it. So, I'll ask you, what words of wisdom do you have for this mission?"

When Elliott's cup finished brewing, he leaned against the counter, stirring sugar into his mug. "Words of wisdom. Let me think." He took a sip, then another. "Don't rush it. I know ye want to get in and get out, but listen to the rhythm of the story. Let it happen organically. The richness of the adventure will play out if ye give it room to breathe."

"Just the opposite of what I was hoping for," Jack said.

Elliott crossed the room to his desk. "If ye hadn't wanted me to confirm yer intuition, ye wouldn't have asked."

Connor's voice rose above the din of the video game James Cullen was playing in another room in protest for not being allowed to go. "You could have left the rocket launcher behind," Connor said.

"I didn't pack a rocket launcher," Pete said, "But I was tempted."

"Then what the hell do you have in your duffel? It's big enough to carry a dead body."

"It'll come in handy, then, if you shoot somebody and we need to remove—" A loud, clinking thud cut off the rest of Pete's statement.

"So, what's in there?" Connor asked.

"Regular shit. M4 rifle, M9 Beretta, grenade pouches."

"Grenades? You packed grenades? Forget it," Connor said. "I'm not going."

"Just fuckin' with ya," Pete said.

"Connor, you know how Pete is," JL said. "You'll never catch him unprepared."

"Yeah, I know. Pete's a regular boy scout," Connor said. "He's never been unprepared for anything except screwing his first girlfriend."

"You two can be so crude," JL said.

"If you're finished with your laptop, I'll pack it with my gear," Connor said.

"I'm not taking it, but I do have one more email. Then I'll be done," JL said.

Jack had a *déjà vu* moment, recalling when Charlotte told him she'd be ready to go chase down Braham after she wrote one more email. It had been a monumental undertaking for his sister to put her work on hold to rescue history from a rogue time traveler. And then to rescue Jack from certain death.

Connor and Pete strode into the office wearing gray, chalk-striped wool, double-breasted jackets with narrow lapels, buttoned up high, with matching vests and pants, black fedoras canted to the side, and unlit cigars clamped between their teeth.

"Jesus Christ," Jack said. "You two look like 1920s gangsters."

Wagging his eyebrows and flicking a Cuban cigar, Pete quipped a comeback in a croaky voice. "Just make me an offer I can't refuse."

"Who picked out your clothes?" Jack asked.

"I did." JL strolled in with a deadly swagger and a laptop parked under her arm, looking radiant in a metallic brocade and lace dress. A corset turned her sporty, muscular body into a movie-star hourglass figure. If she was carrying a gun under the dress it would have to be the smallest gun ever made.

"You did a much better job with your dress. You look lovely, JL."

"Coming from you, Jack, that says a lot." She set the laptop on Elliott's desk. "Hold on to this, will you?"

"I'll send it over to yer office," Elliott said.

Kevin followed her into the room. "I agree with Jack, sweetheart. You do look lovely."

"Thanks to you for tightening my corset, I now have a twenty-inch waist."

"Your cop clothes do nothing for your curves, JL. I told you that years ago," Pete said.

"That must have been the first time I could have filed a sexual harassment claim against you."

"Come on, *ragazza tosta*. You know I've never hit on you."

"I thought it was because you were gay."

"Ah, jeez."

Kevin paused in front of the mirror over the refreshment bar and adjusted his felt hat. "Looks good on me, don't you think?"

"You got the gangster look going on, like Connor and Pete," Jack said. "Even without machine guns, people will scatter when they see the three of you striding down the street. The costume shop screwed up the era. You should look more like the characters in the *Titanic* film. You can buy period-appropriate clothes when we arrive."

Pete strutted over next to Kevin and studied his reflection, rolling his shoulders as he straightened his tie. "I'm going back to meet my people. I want to make a good impression."

Connor, standing nearby, grabbed Pete's hat and swatted him with it. "You idiot. What makes them your people?"

Pete looked crestfallen. "Over four million Italians immigrated to America before 1920. My great-grandparents were part of that immigration, which makes them my people."

Connor smoothed out the creases in the hat and set it back on Pete's head for him to fiddle with again. "Oh, now I get why you insisted on going. You want to introduce yourself to them, don't you?"

"I've always heard I resemble my great-great-grandfather. He was a New York cop, too. You know? I wouldn't risk having a conversation with him, but I'd like to see him from a distance."

"The O'Gradys were cops, too. Maybe we should look for my *people*, too," Connor said.

"Connor," Jack said. "You're responsible for Pete. Keep him away from his family, and stay away from yours. They'll think he's crazy, and will have him locked up in Bellevue."

"Everybody knows I'm crazy," Pete said, twirling a finger at the side of his head. "But they're not so sure about you. And besides, I'm not the weak link in this mission."

Jack jumped to his feet, almost spilling his coffee. "You got a problem with me, Parrino?"

JL rushed over to stand between them, holding out her arms, the tips of her fingers pressed into the men's chests. "If you've got something to say, say it now. We're not carrying an undercurrent of resentment with us. Spit it out, or swallow it."

Pete backed off. "I got nothing to say."

"Look. I'll admit it. I messed up." The words in Jack's mouth felt like fragments of shattered glass. "I've had eight months to reflect on my mistakes. If you want to lead this mission, go for it."

"I don't want to lead it," Pete said, "but I don't want you to go rogue again, either."

The statement made Jack's throat cinch up tight. "You have my word." He extended his hand to Pete. "It's all I can do. I need you on this trip. But if you can't trust me...stay home."

Pete stared at the extended hand for a moment before slapping it and giving Jack a fist bump, followed by a man hug and claps on the back.

"We're cool," Pete said.

Elliott opened the rosewood box on the desk. "Which brooch do ye want, Jack?"

Jack studied the contents of the box. Using one brooch worked when pursuing a love match, but it wasn't the case here. The four brooches—ruby, sapphire, emerald, amethyst—glimmered, even in the subdued light of the desk lamp. "I'll take the precious stones."

"Nobody ever wants mine." JL rubbed her finger across the amethyst. "Did you guys know that up until the nineteenth-century, amethyst was considered a precious stone too? Whoever made these crazy brooches considered mine to be on par with the big four." The scene around the desk became as still as a photograph. Then she broke the silence. "Just saying…"

"We don't doubt its power," Elliott said. "We all saw the display when the brooch healed itself. It's even possible it has more power than the others."

"Then why not use it?" she asked.

"If you were going into space, JL—" Connor said.

"If? I think space is exactly where I'm headed."

"Bear with me," Connor said. "Would you rather travel on a spaceship used on several successful missions, or a spaceship making its maiden voyage?"

She lowered herself to the corner of the sofa, laid her hand against the base of her neck, and rubbed a spot there with a steady rhythmic motion. "I see your point, but still…"

"Until we get more information, JL, we'll continue to rely on the legend of the three brooches. We know what they can do. Yers hasn't been tested yet," Elliott said.

"What stone does Amy have?" Jack asked. "Has it been confirmed?"

"I had to beat it out of Jeff," Connor said. "Based on Laurette Cooper's estate inventory, the police believe Amy disappeared with a diamond brooch. It's the only piece of jewelry missing. It forms the basis of the state's case against Joe Gilbert. It's an eight and a half million-dollar white diamond."

"When you find her, and if she gives up her brooch, the clan will have control over the four precious stones, and one stone that's fallen from grace," JL said.

"There could be at least seven more semiprecious stones," Kevin said. "The amethyst won't be alone."

"Speaking of alone, Amy's been that way for a while now. Let's go get her," Pete said.

"How's this going to work?" JL asked. "Are we going to tell the brooches to take us to Amy Spalding?"

"It's what we did last time. Let's not mention a city, though, in case she's not in New York," Connor said.

Jack lifted the ruby, sapphire, and emerald brooches from the box. "Elliott, I've updated my will to include Charlotte and Braham's new baby when she's born. I didn't mention it to Charlotte. She's too emotional right now. If anything happens—"

"Stop it, Jack," JL said. "When did you turn into Mr. Doomsday?"

"Eight months ago," he said, dryly.

"If ye don't come back," Elliott said, "I'll give her the message." He rinsed his dirty mug in the sink. "I'm going to leave the room. Based on what happened the last time, the sparks went everywhere, and I don't want to get caught in the fireworks." He gave everyone a hug before heading to the door, looking very misty-eyed. "Please be careful."

"Don't worry about us. We'll find Amy and do a quick turnaround," Jack said.

"I will worry," Elliott said. "Along with everyone else. And I seriously doubt ye'll come right back. Ye had yer final briefing with David at breakfast, so this is it. We'll all be waiting for ye. Be safe."

When the door closed, Jack said, "In case we get separated, everyone go to the Hotel Netherland on 59th Street. And if we end up in another town, we'll meet at City Hall."

JL threw the question at him like a dart. "Why would we get separated?"

"Calm down. There's no reason. It's never happened, but just in case..."

Connor broke in, saying matter-of-factly, "Makes sense to have a rendezvous point."

Jack fingered the three brooches. They warmed in his hand,

revving their engines. "We'll set up the operation center, then split up. Any questions?"

"Yeah. When do we shop?" JL asked. "If I'm going to be running around the city, I want trousers."

"Depends on what time we arrive. Anything else?"

"Nope, let's go," Connor said.

Jack handed out the brooches. The ruby to Kevin, the emerald to Connor, and Jack kept the sapphire. "Pete keep your gun handy. I don't anticipate trouble, but we need to be prepared."

"I'm as good a shot as Pete," JL said.

"I know you are, but you're not dressed for a shootout."

"I won't bitch as long as that's the only reason."

"That, and Meredith made me promise you and Kevin won't get shot again," Jack said.

"Nobody can make that promise," JL said.

"Don't make a liar out of me," Jack said.

JL stepped over to Elliott's desk and wrote on a pad of paper next to the rosewood box. "I forgot to tell Austin his dad is coming to town next week." She tore off the note and left it on top of her computer. "Now, let's get out of here before Meredith acts on her threat to pull the plug on this adventure until after the wedding?"

"Okay. Gather your medical supplies, gear, weapons, link arms, and open your stones," Jack said.

Together they recited the Gaelic words. "*Chan ann le tìm no àite a bhios sinn a' tomhais a' gaol ach 's ann le neart anama.*"

The three stones crackled and popped, and an eruption of fiery golden rain sprayed out in all directions. The rain turned into multicolored stars, and swirled up in a spiral above their heads, spattering and spinning.

"Keep the circle tight!" Jack yelled.

The walls in the room dissolved, creating a sense of infinite space. A roar like a dozen high-speed trains circled them, and they held hands in steely death grips while they were whisked at warp speed in a dizzying ride through time and space.

16

1909 New York City—Jack

THE RIDE THROUGH TIME ended abruptly, slamming Jack backwards onto the ground. He shook his head to clear the muddle. Usually he arrived on the other side unfazed by the stomach-churning loop-the-loop of a ride, but not this trip. A hell of a headache and a hangover stomach landed with him, and he had no over-the-counter meds to help with either one, or a sister-doctor in tow.

A cloak of dense vegetation wrapped him in its ghostly presence, and stones poked him from beneath a prickly bed of decomposing leaves. Before he moved from the miserable spot, he pinned the brooch inside his vest pocket and patted it for reassurance. He had lost a brooch before. Desperate times often call for desperate measures, and he had been desperate, and hoped to God no one else in the family ever had to resort to losing control of a brooch to save it or themselves.

He climbed to his feet, and, warmed by the night air, he removed his jacket and slung it over his shoulder, hanging it there by two fingers.

Where was he? In New York? In Kentucky? There was no way to know. And where were the others? When he and David arrived in London in 1944, they landed almost side by side. Matter of fact, he had always arrived with his traveling companions. Whatever happened this time didn't bode well for the next few days.

He called out, "Kevin." There was no answer, no groan, no cry for help. "Connor." No answer. "Pete? JL?" No answer from them, either. A light breeze sent a shudder of movement through the branches, and a shadow lurched across the serpentine path in front of him. He quickly stilled himself while two large raccoons, locked in a mating embrace, gave him a startled stare.

"Don't mind me. Go on about your business," he said, giving them a wide berth. They ignored him and went back to what they were doing.

Jack followed the path, passing a meandering stream and giant boulders. Except for the bats and rats and horny raccoons, he was alone in the woods.

He crossed a rustic bridge and continued walking along a serpentine path lined with outcrops and thickets, reaching a large slab of rock with a giant balanced boulder perched on top.

A huge sigh of relief whooshed out of him.

He pressed his hand against the rock and said a silent thank-you. He still didn't know where his friends were, but at least he knew where in the northern hemisphere he landed. As New Yorkers, JL knew the park well, as did Connor and Pete. They could find their way to an exit and head in the direction of the hotel, but Kevin might get turned around.

The path was leading Jack through the Ramble in Central Park. He wasn't far from 5th Avenue and the 79th Street Transverse. He ran through the park often, and knew most of the landmarks, including the boulder. He also knew the cross streets, and which areas to avoid at night. And right now he was smack in the middle of one of them. The Ramble was a magnet for bird-watchers and nighttime trysts— both raccoons and humans.

He considered what to do next—search for the others, or head over to 5th Avenue and make his way to the rendezvous point. What would David do?

David would find the others.

If they had all been scattered, JL might be alone. He would never admit it to her, because she'd yell at him and call him sexist, but he was worried about her. If she'd been dressed in twenty-first century garb, he wouldn't be, but she was wearing a dress which would limit her range of motion. It wouldn't be easy for her to defend herself.

Jack called out again, scaring several rodents, who scurried through the underbrush. "JL. Where are you?" For the second time, he was met with stony human silence. The clip-clop from the metal shoes of horses pulling carriages and hacks over the nearby cobblestone streets reminded him he wasn't alone in the city that never slept.

He reached the Black Tupelo, a three-trunk tree considered to be one of the estimated hundred trees dating back to the park's opening in 1862. The tree sat at the southern boundary of a meadow. If he went north, he'd reach the 79th Street Transverse, Belvedere Castle, and the Great Lawn. If he headed south, he would reach the Lake, Bethesda Terrace, and the Mall. Plus, he'd be going in the right direction for the rendezvous point.

"Go south, young man."

The incandescent lights gave an enchanting nighttime glow to the park, giving him a false sense of security at a time when he needed to stay alert. He put his jacket back on, patted his pocket again for reassurance, and followed the Gill, a tumbling stream, as it trickled down a rocky slope before spilling into the lake.

Every fifty feet or so, he called out to his companions. The longer he went without hearing from them, the more he worried.

He approached the esplanade on the shore of the Lake from a long sloping path. From there, he strolled around Bethesda Fountain. The lower terrace was constructed of New Brunswick sandstone and paved with Roman bricks, and his shoes clicked softly against the surface.

When he found no one there, either, he sat on the lip of the fountain and dipped his hands into the cool water. At the last second, he splashed the water on his face instead of sipping it. His stomach was still churning, and he didn't know if the water was safe to drink.

He checked his pocket watch—1:05. Since he hadn't seen anyone, friend or foe, he assumed the park was closed to visitors. In which case, the police wouldn't be too friendly if they found him there. Which presented a dilemma. If he wanted everyone to find him, he needed to be visible. To stay out of trouble, he needed to stick to the shadows.

He climbed up the granite staircase to the upper terrace leading to the Mall. If he followed the walkway, he would arrive at 66th Street.

When he reached the upper terrace, he looked across the lake to the rugged shoreline of the Ramble. The water rippled gently in the moonlight, but nothing else moved. He thumped his fists on the railing. How could fourteen people have travelled back in time together and arrived in the same place at the same time, and on this trip, five people couldn't even land on the same acre of ground? He ripped off his hat and raked his fingers through his hair. Was the separation a fluke, or the result of unstable stones? He didn't know, but staring into the darkness wasn't going to find the others. He had to keep moving.

He slapped the hat back on so hard it bent the tops of his ears. Then he whipped around on his heel and jogged across the terrace, where he paused again, and listened. Whatever he expected to hear, he didn't.

He continued out onto the Mall. The American elm trees were fully leafed out, and a tunnel of green enclosed the wide walkway, blocking out most of the light from the night sky. What light there was came from evenly spaced streetlamps. In a few hours, carriages would bring hundreds of visitors to see the stately staircase and elegant archways overlooking the lake. He had to find his friends long before then.

Keeping to the shadows, as he and his brother-in-law, Braham, did months earlier on the docks in San Francisco, Jack stayed low near the gnarled tree trunks. After moving stealthily for twenty-five to thirty yards, he spotted two men sitting on a park bench. He stopped to study them. Their canted hats and cigars gave them a distinguished gangster look. There might be other men in the city dressed like Pete and Connor, but not in the middle of the night sitting on a park bench.

"Connor. Pete," Jack called softly as he hurried toward them. The two men jumped to their feet, waving. "God, I'm glad to find you. Have you seen JL and Kevin?"

"No. Connor and I just found each other wandering through the elms over there. What's going on? Why'd we get separated?"

"I don't know. It's never happened before. I'm worried about JL, though."

"If she runs into trouble, she'll pull up her dress and fight like hell." There was a wobble in Pete's voice that belied his confidence in his former partner. "I sure hope she and Kevin are together."

"What do you think we should do?" Connor asked.

"JL knows her way around the park. If they're here, they'll come this way," Pete said.

"Let's give them about fifteen minutes, then," Jack said. "If they don't show up, we'll go to the hotel and wait for them there."

"You two stay here," Pete said. "I'm going to walk through the arcade, go up the central staircase, check the fountain, then climb the staircase to the top terrace and circle back. They could be sitting up there looking for us."

"I just came from that direction," Jack said.

"They could have been behind you. Besides, I can't sit still. Drives me nuts to wait. I'll be back in a few minutes." Pete disappeared through the arched walkway, which served as a passageway under 72nd Street.

"I don't get it," Connor said. "Why didn't we land together?"

"We must have broken our holds. When we go home, we better lash ourselves in a huddle, or we might end up in different decades."

Connor's eyes popped a little. "Could that have happened? Could they have landed in a different time?"

"No, I was joking. There's a lot about the brooches we don't understand, but I don't think the stones would drop us like pick-up sticks in different decades."

Jack's mind latched on to what losing Kevin and JL would mean to him personally, to the family, and to the mission. Screw the mission. The loss would devastate Elliott and Pops. They would blame him, and he'd deserve it, just as he deserved all the recriminations from the last disaster he caused. He infused his voice with false confidence and said, "They're here somewhere."

Fifteen minutes later, Pete returned. "The only humanoids I saw were the angel and four cherubs on the fountain."

"Let's go to the hotel and wait," Jack said.

Connor shook his head. "I don't know. Doesn't seem right to leave them behind. What if they're hurt?"

"If they're in trouble, they have the ruby brooch. They can go back, if that's any consolation," Jack said.

"It's not," Connor said. "How will we know what happened to them?"

Decision time. Bad decisions were moderately better than indecision. The travelers were well-resourced, and skilled, and making a small decision would empower them. "One of us needs to go to the hotel to see if Kevin and JL are there. The other two should stay here and search the north side of the park."

"Connor and I will stay. You go check in," Pete said. "If JL and Kevin show up, send them to get us. We'll circle back to this spot every two hours." Pete checked his wristwatch, a twenty-first century watch with bells and whistles, not the wristlet kind men wore in the early 1900s. "I've got one-thirty. We'll be back here around three-thirty."

Jack checked his pocket watch again. "I've got one-thirty, too. I'll take your duffel bags so you won't have to lug them around."

"You can't carry all three," Connor said.

"I'll catch a taxi on 5th Avenue."

Connor and Pete loaded two small packs with canteens, protein bars, extra ammunition, flashlights, and a small trauma kit. "I wish we had communicators," Connor said.

"Just think what Alexander Bell could do if he got his hands on one of those," Jack said. "The telecommunications industry could explode decades before its time. I hate to think what that would do to the value of Elliott's Apple stock. Same for your fancy watch. Keep it hidden."

Jack slung the straps to the bags over his shoulders. "Jesus. These are heavy. You brought the rocket launcher, didn't you?"

"No, but I'd rather be overprepared than underprepared," Pete said.

"Do you have any ibuprofen in here? My head feels like it's splitting open."

"Yeah. In the trauma kit."

"Good. Now, if there's an emergency, find a phone and call the hotel. I don't think coin-operated public telephones will be available for another couple of years. You'll have to ask a policeman or store owner where you can make an emergency call. I'll be back here at five-thirty. Good luck."

Jack left the two former NYPD detectives and made his way through the park toward 5th Avenue and the stone wall bordering the park. Children's Gate was carved into the sandstone at the exit near East 76th Street. He only had to walk a block along the bench-lined, slate sidewalk before he hailed a taxi.

He kept his eyes peeled as the car traveled slowly down 5th Avenue, lined with mansions, toward the Hotel Netherland at 59th Street. But there was no sign of JL and Kevin.

He now had three missing people to find in this city. At least two of them, though, knew where to find him. He suddenly became very concerned about Connor and Pete. Was he doing the right thing leaving them? Now he was overreacting. The plan all along was to separate to cover as much ground as possible in the search for Amy. He was being paranoid.

He settled back in the seat and tried to relax.

Jack had never worried about other people—hell, he never worried about anything until recently—and he wasn't sure he liked it at all.

17

1909 New York City—JL

THE STOMACH-CHURNING EFFECTS of the swirling ride through time spread throughout JL's body. She had barely held on to her breakfast. Now she wondered if she could hold on to her head. For some reason, Humpty-Dumpty came to mind. What had she been doing? And why was she lying on a bed of smelly dead leaves and gnarled tree roots?

She sat up, stifling a groan, and leaned against a tree trunk. She didn't recognize her immediate surroundings, but the stony slope of the ground was strangely familiar. She reached for her tapestry bag and pulled it closer.

"JL, is that you?" Kevin asked.

"No. It's Humpty-Dumpty," she grumped. "I feel like I've been chewed up, spit out, and stomped on. What happened? And where are the others?"

"You felt the same way yesterday, and the day before, and the day before. Is there something you want to tell me?"

"I'll tell you the same thing I've told you the last three days you've asked. There's not a chance in hell I'm pregnant. I've got a stomach virus." She dug through her bag for a canteen and took a long swig before passing the water to Kevin. "Where are the others?"

Kevin called out, "Connor... Pete... Jack... Where are you?"

There was no answer. "No one has ever gotten separated before. This is weird."

"Great," JL said. "We used malfunctioning brooches. Do you have any idea where we are?"

"You're the New Yorker. If you don't know, we're out of luck."

"I don't even know if we're in New York. Nothing looks familiar. If you were dropped on the ground at the farm in the middle of the night, you'd be confused, too."

"Let's walk around. The landscape might look different from another angle."

JL got up, stepped away from the tree, and into a clearing. "Well, I'll be."

He joined her. "What is it?"

She pointed in the direction she was looking. "Either we're in Europe, or the castle over there is Belvedere."

"I hope Belvedere is in New York City."

"Yep, and it has been since the mid-eighteen hundreds. We're north of the Ramble and south of the Great Lawn."

He picked up JL's bag and his duffel and slung the straps over his head, settling one on each shoulder. "That doesn't mean anything to me."

"We're in the middle of Central Park. Let's go east, hit 5th Avenue, and catch a taxi to the hotel."

"Don't you want to look for the others?"

"The park is more than eight hundred acres. We could wander around until dawn and never find them. Let's go to the hotel. They'll probably beat us there."

"I don't like the idea of going off without them."

"I don't either." She studied him for a moment. "If I wasn't wearing this getup, I'd search for them, but I'm not going to hike through the park dressed like this. Here, why don't you take the brooch? I'm afraid I'll lose it."

Kevin pinned it in his jacket pocket. "What about a compromise? Let's go to the hotel. If no one's there, you can stay and wait, and I'll come back."

"I'm not sure I like that idea. Let's think about it."

As they neared the park's exit at 5th Avenue and 76th Street, Kevin dropped the bags and pulled her into his arms. "We have Central Park to ourselves. We should at least make out." He brushed his mouth across her face, not so much kissing as feeling the contours of her cheekbones and brow. Then he settled on her mouth and kissed her with more force, sliding his tongue between her lips. Her nipples went from sweet to wanton, and she sighed his name, moving restlessly in his arms.

He nipped at her neck.

"Ouch. That'll cost you."

"How much?"

"Five dollars."

"I can afford it." He nipped at the other side of her neck.

"Now, that'll really cost you."

"How much?

"More than five dollars."

Someone tugged on her arm, yanking her away from Kevin. She spun around and threw a jab that connected with her assailant's jaw. He bowled over, grunting loudly. She lunged to punch him again, but he grabbed her fist and held it so tightly she was afraid he might crush it. She threw a kick, but he turned and, instead of hitting him square in the balls, she only grazed his leg.

"Bitch," he growled. "You'll pay for that."

JL wiggled her fingers in a come-on motion. "You want to play rough…"

Kevin pushed his way into the middle of the brouhaha, elbowed the man aside, and lightly squeezed JL's shoulder. "Stop. He's a cop." Then to the man he said, "If you hadn't accosted my fiancée, she wouldn't have hit you."

JL shot a wicked glance at the stocky cop nursing his injury. "Why didn't you identify yourself?"

The cop, holding a nightstick in one hand, rubbed his split lip with the back of his other hand. "You're under arrest for soliciting and assaulting a police officer. Put the cuffs on her."

The Diamond Brooch 149

JL jerked around to see who he was talking to. Another cop also dressed in a knee-length, single breasted frock coat, was standing a few feet away, grinning while twirling the ends of a handlebar mustache that wiggled over a mouth missing several teeth. She didn't find anything humorous about the situation, but Mustache Cop probably hadn't seen his partner bested by a woman before. If Kevin let go of her shoulder, she'd show Mustache Cop what she thought of his smirk.

She stepped sideways, adjusting her position to keep Mustache Cop in her peripheral vision. "Look. We have a huge misunderstanding here. My fiancé and I arrived in the city late this evening. We were strolling through the park. Sat down on a bench and dozed off. It's been a long day. We're on our way to our hotel."

"Which one?" Nightstick Cop asked.

She pointed south. "The Netherland. Right down the street."

Nightstick Cop laughed, then quickly stopped and pressed his finger against his cut lip. The reminder of what she'd done to him didn't sit well, and he puffed himself up and gave her a cold, gray stare. "No working girl can pay for a room in that pricy hotel."

"I'm not a working girl. I'm a..." It took more restraint than she knew she possessed to keep from spitting out she was a former NYPD detective.

"Whore is what ya are." He nodded to Mustache Cop. "Get the wagon."

This wasn't going well at all. If they took her in, it could be hours before Kevin found the others and they got her out. If she went to court, she could be convicted of the assault charge. Dealing with her problems would pull the guys away from their search for Amy. The longer it took to find Amy, the longer it would take to return home. She had appointments with the wedding cake designer, musicians, and photographer. A trip to jail would screw up her calendar. And besides, she'd heard about The Tombs, as the city prison was called, and she had no desire to find out whether the old stories were true or not.

"Look. I thought you were a threat. I was defending myself. I didn't know you were a cop. I'm sorry. Can we forget this happened and move on?"

"You assaulted a police officer and solicited this gentleman," Nightstick Cop said.

"I wasn't soliciting!" Adrenaline pumped hard and fast through her blood, a mad mix making her shake. She didn't think she would ever say this, but she needed Jack. He had a host of traits she disliked, but he was a lawyer. Although the only courtroom he'd ever been in was run by a military panel of Union officers who tried to convict him of the assassination of Abraham Lincoln.

Mustache Cop slapped manacles over her wrists. "You were trespassing in a closed park. I clearly heard you say you would charge him five dollars."

"It was a joke," Kevin said. "She's my fiancée, for God's sake. Can't you get that through your thick skull?" Fear flashed in Kevin's eyes. It was a look JL hadn't seen before, not even in the cave when they confronted the drug cartel.

"No respectable lady would be found in a closed park at one-fifteen in the morning. No respectable lady would assault a police officer, and no respectable lady would sell sexual favors." The cop nudged her with his nightstick. "We're taking you downtown. You can tell your story to the judge in court tomorrow. See if he believes you."

Kevin dug into his pocket. It wasn't the pocket with the brooch, which meant he was reaching for money. Corruption in the police department was rampant, and the cops arresting her might be willing to take bribes, but they also might be two of the few good ones, and if so, they could also arrest Kevin and charge him with attempted bribery.

She shook her head, reading his actions as well as his mind. "No. If you go to jail, too, how will we get out?"

Kevin relaxed his hand. "I can't let them take you away."

The cop nudged her with his nightstick again, harder this time, almost pushing her off balance. Kevin rushed to her side, and for an instant, she was terrified of what flashbacks he might have when faced with violence, or what steps he might take to protect her.

Kevin poked the cop in the center of his chest with a two-finger jab. "If you touch her again, you'll have a split lip on both sides of your mouth."

Mustache Cop blew his whistle, and the shrill sound sliced through the quiet night, disturbing the critters scampering in the dry underbrush.

"This has gone far enough," Kevin said. "She is my fiancée, and I'd appreciate it if you would take those cuffs off and let us go on our way."

Mustache Cop, shorter by several inches, moved in close, threatening Kevin. "Move! Or we'll arrest you along with the whore."

"I am not—" She was incensed by the cop's assumption and her inability to make him fully understand the situation.

This was getting old, but instead of escalating the situation further, she needed to defuse the tension. If she mouthed off again, the cops would take her for one of the trashy gutter whores they encountered nightly, which wouldn't get her anything but harsher treatment, and she'd still be thrown into the police wagon.

Kevin fisted his hands and moved into a boxer's stance. "You're not taking her anywhere. Let go of her, now."

"Kevin, stand down," JL said. "Catch a taxi, follow the wagon, and bail me out."

"For a whore, she's making sense. Sounds like she's acquainted with the judicial system," Nightstick Cop said.

An early twentieth-century, van-like vehicle drove up and stopped at the curb under a streetlamp. The front was fitted out with an open-air, two-person bench seat. The back was a square box with a small, rectangular window at the top of the sides. If they transported her in that, they might try to take advantage of her. She had a pocket rocket, a small but powerful handgun, in a high-thigh leg holster. If they threatened her, would she use it? Maybe, but first she needed to get out of the cuffs.

A few months earlier, she and David had a contest to see who could escape from different restraints the fastest. He won every time, but, after the contest, he taught her everything he knew, including how to use the file in his escape ring to open locks. Kevin immediately bought her an identical ring, and she always wore it.

Kevin took a step closer, challenging Nightstick Cop again, hands fisted. "You're not putting her in that box."

The cop tapped the nightstick against Kevin's chest. "This is your last chance. Stand back."

Kevin pushed against it, eyes wild, teeth clenched. "Where my fiancée goes, I go."

The cop pushed harder. "If you want to spend the night in a holding cell at the precinct, suit yourself."

"Kevin, stop!"

Her sense of unease reached a high pitch, and fear surged through her gut at Kevin's obvious distress. His eyes didn't meet hers. Was he having a traumatic reminder of the last time he tried to save her...the gunshot, the pain? He was still, almost panther-like, for at least a ten-count.

"Follow us in a taxi," she reminded him, as calmly as she could, hoping it would neutralize some of his panic. "I'll be okay."

"Where are they taking you?" he asked.

"Jefferson Market Prison," Nightstick Cop said, with an almost feral twitch of his lips.

Kevin's hand shook as he swiped at his sweating face. "Where's that?"

Even calmer this time, she said, as if going out for bagels, "It's on 6th Avenue and West 10th Street."

Mustache Cop snickered. "Guess she's been there before."

JL kicked her skirts aside and, with the cop's assistance, climbed the two narrow steps. The stuffy box reeked of urine and vomit, and her stomach pitched again. Benches were bolted to the floor, and small windows were cut into each side of the wagon close to the ceiling, providing the only light inside the wagon.

Mustache Cop climbed in behind her, huffing, and from the outside the lock clicked into place. Within seconds she had executed her best Harry Houdini trick and had the cuffs unlocked.

Kevin banged on the side of the box. "Why are you being so calm?"

"I don't have to walk. Hurry up. Get a taxi. Follow us."

Mustache Cop pushed on her shoulder. "Sit down and shut up."

She fell backwards, and when the engine started and the vehicle jerked, she slid off the seat and landed sprawled on the floor. Her hands were free of the cuffs, but pinned beneath her. She wiggled backwards until her head banged against the front of the box. She raised up slightly to get her hands free.

Mustache Cop unbuttoned his trousers.

"Don't even think about it," she said, snarling.

He laughed and lunged for her. Her hands came out from behind her back, and in a rapid one-two-three punch, she boxed his ears, rammed his nose with the heel of her palm, and jammed her fingers into his larynx. He rolled over grabbing his face.

She pushed her way free of his body. "I told you not to think about it."

"You'll never get out of jail now," he cried in raspy voice.

"That's where you're wrong." She wasn't done with him yet. This one was for Kevin. She stomped on the cop's balls. He groaned and threw up all over himself. She stepped out of his way while he writhed on the floor, pressed down the front of her dress, and put the cuffs back on. She wouldn't lock them until the door opened and she was sure they were at the police station.

She sat as far away from the cop as possible and worked to control her breathing while ignoring his moans. The only thing echoing around in her brain was the heartbreaking sound of Kevin's distress. She loathed the creep crawling around on the floor for what he had done, not to her, but to the man she loved. She had unleashed a beast of an enemy and fed its hunger. Not her worst, by any means, but a badass enemy nonetheless.

Time seemed to slog—minute to minute—while she agonized over Kevin. A counselor was treating him for his PTSD with talk therapy and antidepressants, but she didn't think he was taking his meds consistently. Coming on this trip was a huge mistake. If they were lucky, they would find Amy tomorrow and go home immediately.

The vehicle stopped. She glanced at the jerk, who was sitting now, holding his bloody nose. The lock on the door clicked, and the door opened in front of a two-story, ornate Gothic Revival-style building. It was the Jefferson Market Prison. She was sure of it. There were pictures of all the old jails at the station house where she had worked. She got to her feet, locked the cuffs, and, with the assistance of Nightstick Cop, who must have ridden up front, climbed down the steps.

"You might want to look in on your partner," she said. "He had a nasty tumble and hit his head. He's not doing so good."

"Bitch. I didn't fall. She hit me," Mustache Cop moaned.

She glanced over her shoulder. "You better see a doctor. You might have a concussion. I'm sorry I couldn't do anything to help you, but my hands were cuffed behind me." She turned toward Nightstick Cop. "See? Locked up tight."

She had no tolerance for bad cops, especially for bad cops who took advantage of women.

She was escorted inside the building and taken to a holding area in the basement, where she waited in line behind two women with pockmarked faces, greasy hair, and dirty dresses, reminding her she'd better look for head lice later. She imagined the bloodsucking insects were already feasting on her scalp.

"Next," a sergeant behind a desk said.

Nightstick Cop had maintained a death grip on her arm and shoved her forward.

"State your name and address," the desk sergeant said.

"Jenny Lynn O'Grady, Old Frankfort Pike, Lexington, Kentucky."

"What's your address in the city?"

"I just arrived in town. I'll be staying at the Hotel Netherland with my fiancé and three other friends."

He recorded the information in the police blotter. "Miss O'Grady, you're being charged with assault, solicitation, and trespassing."

She gave the sergeant an exaggerated sigh and tried to force a smile. "Look. The charges are trumped up, totally fabricated. I was grabbed from behind and defended myself. The man I was kissing is my fiancé, and we were out for an evening stroll and didn't know the park was closed."

"Tell it to the judge in Women's Court tomorrow. He'll decide whether to hold you over for trial." Then to Nightstick Cop he said, "Lock her up in the holding cell. It's too late to take her to the Island tonight. Next…"

"You can't hold me here," she said. "I haven't done anything wrong."

"According to this report, you're charged with three serious offenses. If you're convicted, you'll get a year in state prison."

"This isn't right," she argued.

He gave a small gesture of dismissal. "Take it up with the judge."

She had spent her entire life in a station house. First visiting her father, then her brothers, before joining the force herself. She wasn't intimidated by her surroundings, but she was concerned. At least she was in the United States, where prisoners had rights. She could handle lockup for a couple of hours. Couldn't she? No one knew her identity, so there was no fear of reprisals from other prisoners because she was a former cop.

What a night. She was attacked twice and had beaten up both cops. And if David hadn't taught her how to escape from handcuffs, she would have been raped. Her friends were missing, her fiancé, the only person in their group who wasn't familiar with the city, was doing God knows what trying to rescue her, and she probably had head lice. Gross.

Nightstick Cop unlocked the cell door, then unlocked JL's cuffs and shoved her inside the holding cell. The ten-by-ten-foot bricked room held eight women, and stank of smoke, body odor, urine, puke, and everyday filth. Globs of unidentifiable stains were splattered on the walls and floor. A single bulb hung from the ceiling and lit the room with a freakish yellow light.

The smell didn't bother her. The down-on-their-luck women did. She doubted any of them had ever been given a break. They were fighters. All of them. No one moved to make room for her on one of the short benches. She was a newcomer, and could expect no breaks from them. A horrible, prickly heat crawled over her skin. Turning her back on them could prove fatal.

She needed to send signals she wasn't afraid of them in ways they'd understand. No crouching. No hunching. No sign of fear. She stood tall, with an openly displayed chest and straight back, her chin lifted confidently.

An attack would come—fast, explosive, and out of nowhere. No rules, and bloody.

Which one would come for her first? Which one would throw the punch they all wanted to throw? The large woman on the end who pretended to be asleep...maybe. The droopy-shouldered one in the middle with a lip twitch...maybe. The pock-faced one sitting next to her...maybe. Or the younger woman with a chip on her shoulder, begging to be knocked off...probably.

In January, David had devised a schedule she never deviated from. One hour was spent in mixed martial arts or street fighting. Another hour was spent running, practicing yoga, or weight training; and another hour in meditation. Eight hours of reading and computer work filled the rest of her day. She was in damn good shape, but not good enough to take on eight angry women.

It was only a couple of minutes before one made a move. It was the chip girl—several inches taller than JL, and fifty pounds heavier. She half sauntered, half waddled. "Ya don't look like a whore. Whatcha doin' here, bitch?"

JL pointed with her thumb toward the sergeant. "He thinks I am. So do the cops who brought me in."

Chip Girl moved to within a foot of JL, forcing her to look up. The woman snatched JL's hat off her head. "No whore would wear a hat like this, so it must be true." She threw the hat on the floor and stomped on it.

The other women jumped to their feet and jeered.

JL stared longingly at the crushed felt hat with its broken feathers, which had managed to survive a roller coaster ride through time and an attempted rape. She tsked. "I liked the hat."

Chip Girl glowered, ramping up the threat level, the veins pulsing in her neck. She anchored her hands on her hips and squared her feet. Her heavily lidded eyes, a result of too many punches to her face, raked JL up and down. Although the woman had size on JL, the years of bullying others and being bullied herself gave her an ugly confidence JL could exploit.

Chip Girl's hand whipped out, snake-like, and slapped JL, almost lifting her off her feet. JL had been expecting a punch in the gut, not a blindsiding slap across the face. Her eyes watered and blinked against the sudden pain, which was stinging as if she'd been bitten by hundreds of bumblebees.

"Try that again," JL warned, "and you'll be on the floor in this rat-infested hellhole with my boot squeezing the air out of your throat. Got it?"

Chip Girl threw a tomahawk chop. But JL was ready this time. She grabbed Chip Girl's arm in midflight, twisting it behind her back, and jerking up on it until she dropped to her knees. JL increased the torque until she whimpered. Then JL let go and shoved Chip Girl on her face.

"Touch me again and I'll break your arm." JL slowly turned in a semicircle, making eye contact with every one of the women whose hardened faces were blank with shock at how quickly their cellmate ended up flat on her face.

"That goes for the rest of you, too." She pointed to the end of the bench closest to the jail cell door. "Move over. I want to sit right there." She had asserted her dominance. With luck, it would be enough intimidation to avert additional attacks. The women quieted, and Chip Girl returned to her corner, a boxer in retreat, to nurse her wounds.

The women crowded together, giving JL enough room for two. Time to put herself to rights. Kevin would notice every curl out of place, every smudge, and every wrinkle. To keep him from stressing more, she had to restore her ready-to-go-on-a-picnic air, instead of looking like an abused prisoner.

Curls had fallen loose and hung down the back of her neck. Her face and hands were dirty, and her hat was squashed. Some repairs were beyond her abilities. She volleyed a glance at the desk sergeant, a tired, crinkled-faced cop with a portly belly. She wondered if any of his descendants were currently on the NYPD.

"What's your name?" she asked.

"Officer Sheridan." His mask of expressionlessness slipped away, and he nodded sagely, as if he understood what the hell he'd just witnessed. A lopsided smile flickered across his face, and a powerful sensation crawled along her spine. She had learned years earlier that respect was expressed in different ways, and his lopsided smile said as much as he could say.

She knew a detective in the Midtown North Precinct named Sheridan. She couldn't put the sergeant's face on the detective's muscle-bound body, but there probably was a family connection. Cops were parents of cops who were parents of cops. Same with firefighters.

JL got busy repairing the damage to her hair, face, and pitiful hat, while still watching and listening. The rhythm of the station house was sounded out by its creaky floorboards and squeaky doors. She yawned, and her eyes grew heavy, but she shook off sleep. She didn't trust her cellmates, and doubted the sergeant, even though he acknowledged an ounce of respect, would come to her rescue if she was attacked again.

A lanky cop with hair so blond it was almost white, his face patchy and scarred, ambled in from a back room and rested on the corner of the counter next to the sergeant.

"Close this file," Lanky Cop said. "The detectives have interviewed the porters, diner crew, and lounge car attendants. No one on the train from Washington remembers Miss Amy Spalding or a report of a stolen suitcase. It's been two months, and we've got nothing."

JL jerked upright—Spalding, two months, stolen suitcase. Her detective antenna shot through the ceiling. She got up, yawned, and circled the small cell before leaning against the bars, acting disinterested.

"Was she lying?" the sergeant asked.

Lanky Cop shrugged. "Don't know."

The sergeant dropped the file into a drawer. "Tell Miss Spalding we closed the case. If she can provide additional information, we'll take another look."

Lanky Cop shook his head. "We don't have an address for her."

"Is there a contact?"

Lanky Cop held out his hand. "Give me the file." He flipped through the pages. "A man named Gabriele Moretti brought her to the station to file the complaint. He has an office in the Providence Loan Society Building on Park and 5th Avenue."

"Send someone over there tomorrow. Ask him if he's got an address for her."

Another cop, who was sitting on a bench, glanced up over his newspaper. "If you're looking for Miss Spalding, you can find her at the *New York Herald*." He held up the paper and pointed to an article below the fold. "She has a daily baseball column. If you haven't been reading it, you've missed the city's latest sensation."

JL gasped. With a slow, disbelieving shake of her head, she swallowed a laugh, falling back on her undercover training to help her keep a straight face. She gave another disinterested stretch before casually crossing the room and returning to her place on the bench. She considered the family's brooch stories. The stones always put time travelers in the right place at the right time, although the journeys were never easy. The information she overheard would save them hours of sleuthing and layers of shoe leather. They might even be able to go home this afternoon.

A ruckus in the stairwell had the women in the cell awake and alert. The familiar voices of Jack, Connor, Pete, and Kevin propelled JL to her feet again. She put her head as close to the bars as she could, but she couldn't see the guys.

Jack approached the sergeant. "I'm Miss O'Grady's attorney, and

I demand to see my client."

The sergeant looked up at Jack, deadpan. "Miss O'Grady will appear in Women's Court at nine. You can see her then."

Connor sidled up next to Jack. "She's my sister. Has bail been set?"

"Bail will be set when she goes to court."

Pete rested his arm on the counter and leaned on it. "Here's the thing, Sarge. Miss O'Grady and I are partners. We own a private detective business in Kentucky." He thumped his chest with his thumb. "I used to be a cop. Went private a couple of years ago. You got nothing here. JL's a law-abiding citizen, and one hell of an investigator. She's also the daughter of a retired deputy police commissioner." Pete leaned closer. "Between you and me, her attorney is a vexatious litigator. Do you know what that means?"

The sergeant shook his head.

"He sues everybody, and he'll be filing a wrongful incarceration suit as soon as the courthouse opens. Why don't you save us time and trouble and let my partner go home with us now? We'll come back for court."

"Your partner has been charged with solicitation, assault, and trespassing. I can't let her go."

"Not one of those charges will hold up," Jack said. "Your arresting officers will look like idiots who harassed and terrorized two innocent visitors. The press will have a field day criticizing the department, and the police commissioner will see that heads roll. Do you want one of those heads to be yours?"

The sergeant heaved a long sigh. "Wait here." He left the desk and went into a back room.

"Hey, guys. I'm over here," JL said.

Kevin rushed across the room and covered her hands with his, both gripping the bars, and he kissed her. "Are you okay? What happened to your hat?"

"I'll tell you later."

"Nobody hurt you, did they?"

The sergeant returned. "I'll release her to your custody," he said to Jack. "She's to appear in Women's Court at nine o'clock. If she's not there, a bench warrant will be issued, and she'll be arrested on sight." The sergeant slid a piece a paper across the desk. "Sign this."

Jack signed. "Anything else?"

"No. She's one tough gal. Good luck tomorrow," the sergeant said.

Kevin fell silent, and for a second or two they simply gazed at each other. Something invisible and yet entirely real stretched between them. "I should have fought harder. If…" He stopped, but JL heard what he didn't say. If he had been David or Braham, JL wouldn't have been arrested.

"I'm glad you didn't," JL said. "They wouldn't have been shy about beating you up. It all worked out."

Connor snatched the keys off the counter and, before anyone could stop him, he unlocked the door. "Come on. Let's get the hell out of here." He locked the door back and tossed the keys onto the counter.

No one said anything until they were a block from the jail.

"You're not going to court," Kevin said.

"What?" Jack said. "Don't you trust my legal skills?"

Pete hailed a taxi. "It's not your legal skills. We just don't trust the police or courts in 1909. Let's go."

As soon as they were settled in the taxi, JL asked, "Where did you find each other?"

"I landed by myself in the Ramble," Jack said. "I found Pete and Connor on the Mall about ten minutes later. They decided to stay and look for you and Kevin, while I went to the hotel to see if you were there. Kevin was talking to the clerk at the registration desk."

"I couldn't get a taxi to follow you," Kevin said, "so I ran after the wagon until I reached the hotel, and went in to see if anyone else was there."

"We decided to find Connor and Pete before we came here. We thought they might be able to handle the cops at the station house better than we could," Jack said.

"I don't know why the brooches separated us this time," Kevin said. "But it's been a colossal screw up."

"No, it hasn't," JL said. "You're not going to believe what I found out."

"Don't keep us in suspense, *ragazza tosta*."

She sat back and laced her fingers in her lap. "I think I'll just hold tight to my information and let the three of you suffer a bit to equalize our experiences."

Kevin pounded his thigh with his fist. "If you think this has been easy on us..." The tightness in his face and around his eyes scared her.

"You're right," JL said, reaching for his hand. "That was mean of me. I'm sorry. I know you were all worried."

"Spill it, JL. We aren't in the mood for games," Connor said.

"A man named Gabriele Moretti filed a report for Amy Spalding claiming her suitcase was stolen off a train from Washington, DC. Moretti has an office in the Providence Loan Society building on Park and 5th. And Amy is a sports reporter for the *New York Herald*. Evidently, she's the city's latest sensation."

"A reporter?" Jack asked. "Does she have a byline?"

"She must, or else the cop wouldn't have made the connection between the baseball reporter and the claimant."

Pete gave her a knuckle bump. "Way to go, partner."

"I'm surprised I didn't find any mention of her column during my search of the New York Historical Society archives," Jack said. "But then, I wasn't looking for baseball articles."

"So, what's our plan now?" Connor asked.

"JL and I will have to make an appearance in court. I don't want the NYPD looking for her. Connor, you and Pete find Gabriele Moretti. We need to know how he fits in."

"Do you think they're soul mates?" Connor asked.

"David and I thought Kenzie's pilot friend was her soul mate, but he wasn't. We can't assume Moretti is the *one* just because he's involved with Amy in some way. Approach him cautiously."

"What's our cover?" Connor asked.

"We can assume she made up a story. Whatever you tell him will probably contradict what she told him. Play it by ear. Tell him anything, as long as you get her address."

"He might call her and warn her two men are looking for her," Pete said.

"Shit. You're right. That won't work." Jack drummed his fingers on his thighs. "You'll have to take him with you and hope he doesn't put up a fight."

"What's my assignment?" Kevin asked.

"Go to the *New York Herald* while JL and I go to court," Jack said. "We might be able to wrap this up tomorrow."

"Then why go to court?" Kevin asked.

"As we've already discovered, if something can go wrong, it will. I don't want to be on the police radar. You go to the newspaper, Kevin. JL and I will go to court, and Pete and Connor will go find Moretti."

"It's four-thirty. Let's get a couple of hours of sleep, then head out. If we're at the Providence Loan Society and the *New York Herald* by nine o'clock, we should be able to find her, wrap this up tomorrow, and go home," Connor said.

"Do you want me to tell Amy where I'm from?" Kevin asked.

"Sure. Then take her to the hotel and wait for us there," Jack said.

"But won't JL need me as a witness?" Kevin asked.

"Not for the arraignment. Bail will be set, I'll pay it, and we'll be out of there."

"What if they lock her up again?" Kevin asked. "I should go with you. We should all go."

Connor clapped Kevin's shoulder. "Hey, we live in America. Even in 1909 defendants had rights. Granted, not as many as they do now, but JL doesn't look like a prostitute. No judge is going to believe the soliciting charge, or the trumped-up trespassing charge. Relax."

"Isn't the assault charge more serious than the other two?" Kevin asked.

"If the judge doesn't believe the soliciting and trespassing charges, do you think he'll believe JL assaulted a cop twice her size?" Pete asked. "Not likely."

"I guess you're right, but it doesn't mean I won't worry."

The taxi pulled up in front of the hotel, and they piled out. A couple walked out the other door while JL and Kevin walked in. Jack pulled his hat down low on his forehead and sneaked in behind them, bumping into JL.

"What are you doing?" she asked.

"Don't look now, but that's Lillian Russell."

"Where?" JL turned and stared.

"I told you not to look," Jack hissed. "If she recognizes me, we've got a problem."

JL looked back at Jack, and was shocked to see his face paling beneath a sheen of sweat. "Lillian is getting into a taxi. You're safe."

Jack exhaled a thank-God-for-small-blessings whoosh. "She'll ask about Carolina Rose, and I can't tell Lillian the truth."

"You can tell her Carolina Rose died, can't you?"

A silence followed. He fixed her with his blue eyes, frowning. "No. I can't answer any of her questions."

"You're being evasive. What's the real issue?"

"Drop it, JL. Just drop it." Jack stormed off toward the elevator, leaving them all in the lobby gawking.

"What the hell was that about?" Pete asked.

JL shook her head. For the second or third time in the past few hours, unease swamped her. The mission could easily unravel if anyone pulled on a loose thread. And grief was yanking on the threads of Jack's knitted scarf. He hadn't yet learned grief's favorite trick, how it hides, then jumps out unexpectedly, startles you, and strips away all pretense of a normal life. Maybe a confrontation with Lillian Russell was exactly what he needed.

18

1909 New York City—Jack

THE NEXT MORNING, Jack arranged with the concierge to send a vendeuse and seamstress to JL's room to help her choose and be fitted for a new wardrobe to wear during her stay in New York City, beginning with her court appearance.

His goal for the hearing was to exploit JL's assets—close to a perfect ten body, creamy, flawless skin, and radiant auburn hair. She was a gorgeous woman. Although she downplayed her looks and talents, Jack knew she could star in any award-winning play or musical on Broadway, and he was counting on her acting skills to convince the judge she was incapable of assaulting a police officer. If the judge threw out that charge, the other two—trespassing and soliciting—would follow. To help her stay in character, he'd given instructions to the women assisting her to tie her corset as tightly as possible. He wanted her breathless and weak.

Kevin poured his second cup of coffee, plated a biscuit and berries, and carried them over to the sofa where Jack sat waiting patiently, reading the New York Times.

"Are you sure this is going to work?" Kevin asked.

No, Jack wasn't sure, but he wasn't about to share his doubts with Kevin. He lowered his arms and let the newspaper crinkle in his lap. "You said the cop skimmed just over six feet and was fifty pounds heavier than JL. What judge is going to believe a demure lady could beat up a cop twice her size? Plus"—he nodded toward the bedroom where JL was dressing—"my instructions to the vendeuse were to dress JL in high fashion and accentuate her assets."

Kevin choked on the biscuit, pounding his fist against his chest, coughing hard.

"Are you okay?" Jack asked. "Do you need water?"

Kevin shook his head, cleared his throat. "That's the second time in the past few hours you've made a comment about JL's assets."

Jack looked away deliberately and focused on the American Impressionist painting over the sideboard instead of Kevin's tiff, until Kevin backhanded his arm. "I don't like it," Kevin said.

Jack folded the newspaper and tossed the rag on the table in front of the sofa. "Sorry, but your fiancée will be dressed so the judge will notice. He won't be able to take his eyes off her. If JL plays it right, he'll ask her to dinner, whether he's married or not."

"We should skip the hearing, change hotels, and let JL wear trousers. They'll never find her."

"That's one way to keep other men from looking at her." Jack tapped a light tattoo on his thigh with two fingers. Kevin needed to be on board with the plan. If he lacked confidence in it, so would JL. "I don't want to spend our time here looking over my shoulder. I know what it's like to be in jail in another time and, trust me, after seeing the jail cell, you and I know it would be much harder on JL."

"You're an 'ignoranus.' This isn't 1865, and she won't be charged with murdering a president."

"What did you call me?"

"An ignoranus. It's a made-up word for someone who's both stupid and an asshole."

Jack nodded. "Good one. I'll have to remember that. So, look. I'm not worried about the charges against her. I'm worried about her being incarcerated. She handled herself well this morning, but she'll be harassed by male guards. Do you want her subjected to that?"

Kevin gave a testy sigh. "Come on. You know that's not what I want."

"Anything can happen. I want to be prepared for the unexpected."

"Like you were prepared for your plane to crash in the English Channel?"

Jack shivered at the memory. "Do you have a point?"

"Yeah. You can't be prepared for everything. You train for what might happen, and hope for the best. But you're being too cautious. We're not sticking around here long enough for there to be fallout. JL doesn't need to go to court."

Jack's muscles tightened involuntarily. If he'd been more cautious, he would have been able to save Carolina Rose from her uncle. "I'm leading the mission, Kevin. If you don't like it, you know the way home."

Kevin came to his feet, and Jack saw more than anger in his eyes, something buried deep, something that scared the crap out of him.

Kevin crossed the room to the sideboard and refilled his coffee cup. "Nobody's going home until we all go." Then he leaned against the window frame, drinking coffee and staring out at the row of white-marbled 5th Avenue mansions modeled after Italian palazzos.

"You accused me of dredging up old wounds," Jack said, "but yours are bleeding all over the place. I know it was hard on you when JL went off on her own to rescue Elliott and Meredith, and then when she and Braham came to get me in San Francisco. Her life was in danger both times, and I don't blame you for worrying about her now. But don't you think it would be better if the police aren't looking for her?"

"Worrying about JL is a consequence of loving her. I couldn't do a damn thing to stop them from taking her away in the police wagon this morning. I'm not David. I couldn't swoop in and rescue her." Angry lines formed around Kevin's mouth, and his eyes shone almost black. "Something happened to JL while she was being transported to jail. She said the trip was uneventful, but I can tell when she's lying."

Jack joined him at the window and asked low-voiced. "Why do you think something happened?"

"When we entered the jail this morning, I saw the cop who rode in the police wagon with her, and he was nursing a broken nose. I heard him tell another cop he fell down the stairs."

Jack shrugged. "Maybe he did."

"Then how'd JL's hat get destroyed?"

"Did you ask her?"

"She said one of the women in the cell tried to bully her. After Round One, the woman returned to her corner, and JL didn't have any more trouble."

"But you don't believe her."

"I believe her"—Kevin lowered his voice a decibel—"but I also believe there was an altercation with the cop in the police wagon."

"She would have been charged with assaulting two police officers."

"Not if he didn't report it."

An uneasy feeling slithered up Jack's back. "That doesn't make any sense. Why would he not report it?"

"She was handcuffed when she entered the police wagon, and I assume she was handcuffed when she came out. But I can't guarantee she was cuffed the entire time she was in the wagon."

Jack narrowed his eyes, and a few beats of silence followed. Then he said, "If the cop intended to assault her, he wouldn't have taken off the cuffs. If she broke his nose, she must have escaped the restraints." He and Kevin exchanged nods. "I smell David in this scenario."

"He taught her how to spring handcuffs open," Kevin said. "They made a contest of it. JL could never beat David in a timed test, but she came close. She would never admit it to anyone, but she kneels at the altar of David McBain."

"There are others who drank from the same kettle of Flavor-Aid."

"Including yourself?"

"David saved Charlotte's life, and was instrumental in saving mine. JL is probably the only person, except Kenzie, who could ever measure up to David's exacting standards when it comes to overt and covert operations."

"Then why are you so worried about her?" Kevin asked.

"I'm responsible for her."

"Wait. Rewind. Who am I talking to? You've barely been responsible for yourself. I don't get it. Unless…" Kevin kept his eyes fixed on Jack for several beats before moving on. "She reminds you of Carolina Rose, doesn't she?"

They continued to glare at each other in a bristling silence.

"You're way off base," Jack said. "They don't look or act anything alike."

"For some reason, you've decided you need to protect JL. I'm just trying to figure out why."

"There's nothing to figure out. I only want to find Amy, have a conversation with Catherine Lily Sterling, and go home without having to deal with the police or the court after today."

Kevin's chest inflated around a deep breath that he then expelled in a gust. "Okay, we'll play it your way. I'll go to the newspaper to find Amy while you and JL go to court. We'll meet back here before lunch. And if you're not here, I swear I'll—"

"You can threaten me Kevin, but we both know neither one of us is a fighter. We'd both rather talk our way out of the pickle jars we get into. And we're also far better at doing it than anyone else in this clan, so let's play to our strengths."

"You don't have a fiancée you want to protect."

"And I never will…" Jack's hopes for the future had been scattered on the wind like dandelion fluff. He moved away from Kevin, returning to the sofa and a cold cup of coffee. Time to change the subject. "Have you thought about how you're going to approach Amy?"

Kevin poured another cup of coffee and sat on the sofa with Jack again. "I thought I'd open with, 'How 'bout those Cubs?' Or, 'It took the Cubs a hundred and eight years to win the World Series.'"

Jack almost spit out a mouthful of coffee. "Damn. That's good.

You'll definitely get her attention." He wiped his mouth with a napkin. "Do you think she'll be more shocked about the Cubs winning, or because you're from the future?"

"Knowing her passion for baseball, I'd say the Cubs winning would be more of a shock."

"Wait a minute. Wasn't the World Series over by the time she disappeared?"

"Major League Baseball had a later-than-usual start in 2016, and, combined with the expanded playoffs, it pushed game seven into November. She was gone before the series started. I remember hearing the analysts in the broadcasting booth pleading with anyone who had information about her disappearance to call the NYPD."

"I hope you have more details than who got the win. She'll ask, you know."

"Give me a break. I'm a numbers guy. The Cubs battled back from a three-one deficit to win over the Indians in a classic game seven. It took a tenth-inning rally to get the W."

Jack laughed. "Who scored in the tenth to win the game?"

"Damned if I know. Baseball isn't my sport du jour. The only reason I know anything about the series is because I needed talking points for a telephone conference shortly after game seven ended."

"Did it work?"

"No. I blew it and had to confess I knew more about wine than baseball. The man I was talking to told me if I could prove it, he'd listen to my spiel."

"What happened?"

"I ended the call with a contract to supply Montgomery wines to an upscale restaurant chain located in cities from New York to LA."

"Congratulations." Jack clapped Kevin on the back. "Are we good now?"

Kevin straightened his shoulders, as if adjusting an invisible load, and gave Jack a baleful look. "If JL gets hurt, you better be hurt worse."

The door opened and JL waltzed out.

"Holy shit." Kevin grinned, smiling with mischief. "I take it all back. She's not going anywhere with you. She's not going anywhere with anybody. Matter of fact, she's never leaving this room." He met her halfway across the room, wrapped her in his arms, and kissed her. "You look gorgeous."

"I can't breathe," she gasped. "My waist is seventeen inches now."

"It's not your waist I'm looking at, sweetheart."

Jack almost groaned. His instructions were to make JL appear breathless and weak—not irresistible. But that's exactly what they had done. He second-guessed his decision to make a court appearance, but the result was the same. He knew it was the right thing to do. If it came back and bit him in the ass, everybody could blame him. As usual.

19

1909 New York City—Jack

JL AND JACK left the Hotel Netherland and hailed a yellow-paneled taxi for the trip downtown to the Jefferson Market Courthouse. The tight corset forced JL to sit ramrod straight on the taxi's leather seat.

"My stomach is in my throat. My liver is where my stomach should be, and my lady parts are tickling my funny bone." She wiggled, pushing at her sides and breathing as deeply as she could, which only made her lightheaded. "Get me out of this contraption before I faint."

"Hang in there for a while longer. You look gorgeous, and the judge will be so distracted he'll forget why you're in his courtroom."

"That's not what I asked."

He pressed against the center of her back. "Sit taller."

She swatted at his hand. "Stop it. I'm sitting as tall as I can." She put her hands to her mouth and breathed in and out. "Those dress shop women came at me so fast, it was like the 'dopeler effect.' I bought into it hook, line, and sinker, and now I'm suffering."

"I'm supposed to be the wordsmith, but you and Kevin have both thrown made-up words at me this morning. What's the 'dopeler effect'?"

"It's when stupid ideas seem smarter when they come at you really fast. That's what those saleswomen did. A seventeen-inch waist didn't sound so stupid when they were throwing suggestions at me about stripes and plaids and high and low necklines. You wanted me to appear shorter and vulnerable. I get it, but they didn't. They were interested in framing my face with color, accentuating my long neck, puffing me up with frills and horizontal stripes. I look four-eight now instead of five-two, and probably twenty pounds heavier. Can you tell?"

"You do look shorter." He laughed. "I want the judge to see the difference in height between you and the cop. The shorter you look, the harder it is to imagine you beating him up."

"A prosecutor would want the cop to look shorter, too. It doesn't matter now. I'll pass out before the bailiff calls my case. Seriously, I can't breathe. Unbutton the back of the dress and loosen the ties, or you'll have to carry an unconscious woman into the courthouse."

"If I loosen the corset, will you still fit in the dress?"

"I don't care. Just give me room to breathe."

"Turn around." JL angled slightly so he could reach the buttons, and his hand hovered near her neck. "Kevin won't like this."

"Just do it. If it comes up, I'll tell him you saved my life."

Jack unbuttoned the dress and loosened the corset strings. "Better?"

"No. But it'll do. Close me back up, and let's get this hearing over with."

He deftly rebuttoned the tiny pearl buttons. "There you go. All done."

"You have large hands like Kevin. He can make the smallest stitch and button these tiny buttons. He credits his EMT training, but how'd you learn?"

Jack wiggled his fingers. "As a teenager, I wanted to be able to unbutton, unsnap, or unhook…uh…obstacles. I practiced on Charlotte's Civil War reenactment dresses until I perfected my delicate skills."

"You are such a player."

"I *was*," he said, emphasizing the past tense. "Now it's not worth the effort. Why bother when I know it won't mean anything or last more than a few weeks? I have my work and my family, that's enough."

"Work and family can help fill a void, but it's never enough. Trust me, I know."

Jack stared out the window, his gut tightening with irritation. "It's enough for me. Things I thought were important when I was younger aren't important now."

"You're full of crap, Jack Mallory. You're handsome and virile...a little gray, yeah, but it's sexy. You'll turn heads well into your eighties. Look at Elliott and Pops. They're in their sixties and seventies, and everywhere they go, women notice. It's called magnetism. And you have it in hearts and spades and diamonds, too."

She winked at him. "Part of your magnetism is in your smile, and the crinkles at the corners of your eyes. Your baby-blues aren't diamond-twinkly like they were when I first met you, but they will twinkle again. It'll start here"—she laid her hand on his chest—"as a small flutter at first. Then it will pound and finally explode. I know you don't believe this, but maybe we won't see the old Jack Mallory smile again. Maybe we'll see a new and more honest one."

"You sound like Meredith."

"Probably because I've spent a lot of time with her lately. Planning a wedding is stressful, but she's turned planning Kevin's and my wedding into a fun adventure. We've laughed until we cried, and cried until we laughed. And stayed awake drinking champagne and fallen asleep drinking coffee."

"Isn't it supposed to be the other way around?"

"With Meredith, what's up is down."

"Are you saying she's unpredictable? I've always found her to be just the opposite."

"She's the biggest out-of-the-box thinker I've ever met, and so wise. Wisdom can't be taught, you know. You either have it or you don't. Elliott's wise, too, but he can be so stubborn his wisdom occasionally gets lost in the battle—"

"—wisdom gets lost in the battle," Jack repeated. "Do you mind if I use that? I have a conversation between two characters in my work-in-progress crying out for that expression."

"Sure. Knock yourself out. It's not original. It's something my priest said to me a long time ago."

"I never had a close relationship with, or enough confidence in, a member of the clergy to share my innermost secrets," Jack said.

"It's a double-edged sword. Growing up, I went to confession because I felt better afterwards. On the flip side, because I had a personal relationship with Father Paul, I was hesitant to confess my sins to him, so I avoided doing something that made me feel better."

"You could have gone to another priest."

"God, no. Pops would have found out, and then I'd get into trouble for doing something so bad I couldn't confess it to Father Paul."

"Sounds like Pops."

She pulled off her skin-tight gloves, slowly, one long finger at a time. "Sometimes when I'm with Meredith and Elliott, I feel like I'm being groomed."

Jack raised an eyebrow. "That's a non sequitur, JL. What do you think you're being groomed for?"

"I wish I knew, because I don't like my number one guess."

"Which is?"

"That I'm not good enough for Kevin, and they're tweaking me so I'll measure up."

"You're full of crap, JL. That's ridiculous. Any father would love to have you as a daughter-in-law."

JL put her hand on Jack's forehead. "You feel a little warm. Are you having fever-induced hallucinations? Who are you? And what have you done with Jack Mallory?"

"I don't have a fever, but I am being more conscious of my decisions these days."

"Have you figured out yet if you put your hand on the stove you'll get burned? If that's the case, all you've learned is what not to do. You're acting like you've reached old age and have stopped reading new books. You've given up and resigned yourself to reading only the classics."

She stopped lecturing him and frowned at something outside the window. Then, after a few moments, asked, "Do you plan to spend the rest of your days rummaging through your old shit and never reading anything new?"

"Stop psychoanalyzing me. I've—"

Before he could finish, she held up her hand to stop him. "Learning what not to do is only half of the equation. Living in freedom is the other."

"I already know the other half." He adjusted the knot in his tie, then his shirt cuffs, snapping them sharply so the right amount of shirt showed below the sleeves of his coat. "We're only a few blocks from the courthouse, and we need to talk about what will happen in court."

"I spent a decade as a detective. I know court procedure."

"You're not a witness for the prosecution. You're a defendant. It's a different game, different rules."

"Okay, what do you want me to do?"

"Nothing. Absolutely nothing. Keep your mouth shut unless I ask you to speak. Got it?"

The side of her hand rested on her forehead in an eye-shading salute. "Yes, sir. I got it, but do you?"

While Jack had a law degree from Harvard, he'd never practiced law. And, except for being a defendant in a military trial, the only courtrooms he ever entered were the ones he created in his mind while writing his novels. Did she really want to depend on him? Short of hiring a jailhouse lawyer, what were her options? What would David do?

The answer was easy. David would vanish, and the police would never find him unless he wanted to be found.

20

1909 New York City—Pete

AFTER NEARLY GETTING run over crossing the street, Pete decided New York City needed a modern lesson in traffic control. And if he changed history, so be it.

At 5th Avenue and 34th Street, he finally took a stand. Cars, wagons, carriages, trolleys, men on horseback, and pedestrians were all attempting to cross the mud-caked streets at the same time, so of course nobody could move. There was no method to the madness. There were no right-of-way rules, and no one seemed able to use courtesy or common sense to work out how drivers and pedestrians should behave in an uncontrolled intersection.

Pete scratched his head. "Are these people stupid, or what? They can build a car, but can't write laws to protect the people driving them?"

Connor shrugged. "They have no concept of a controlled intersection."

"Then let's show 'em."

Pete and Connor weaved their way through the congestion until they reached the center of the intersection. "I'll whistle, you direct." Pete stuck his fingers in his mouth and whistled, loud and shrill, while Connor pointed and waved. Everyone ignored him, forcing Connor to approach drivers and ask for their help to clear the intersection.

When they went out of turn, Pete whistled louder. After fifteen minutes, two NYPD cops approached. One of them said, "Whatever you're doing, it's working. What can we do?"

"If we could get one person stopping traffic at each corner, we could take turns. You," Connor pointed at one of the cops. "Go there, and you," he pointed at the other one. "Go there."

"What are the signals?"

Pete held his arm out straight, fingers pointing up. "This means stop." He then waved toward himself. "This means go." He jerked his fingers right. "This means turn right." He did the same with his left fingers. "We'll move in a clockwise direction."

Fifteen minutes became thirty, and thirty became forty-five. After an hour, and the addition of six more policemen, the intersection was clear, and traffic was moving smoothly, except for the occasional spoiled motorist who thought he was too important to wait. Shop owners came out of their stores to watch traffic moving smoothly down the street.

"We've got to go," Pete said to one of the cops.

"I'm going to tell my precinct captain what you two did here."

"Tell him to start a traffic division," Pete said. "Get a big red sign with the word stop on it. A green sign with the word go, and a white sign with the word walk. The signs will be easier for drivers and pedestrians to see."

"Practice your whistling," Connor said. "And before you roll out a traffic plan, let New Yorkers know what to expect. Publish instructions in the newspapers so everyone will know what to do at a controlled intersection. Come on, Pete. We're an hour late."

They hurried down 34th until they reached Park Avenue, then followed Park to 25th, arriving at the white marble, three-story Providence Loan Society building. They walked through tall bronze doors, into the lobby.

"Hey, look at the wall of rich dudes. There's Vanderbilt and J. P. Morgan," Pete said.

"Let's find Moretti's office." A man came out of the elevator, and Connor asked, "Do you work in the building?"

"Yes," he said, extending his hand. "I'm Stephen Thomson, president of the Providence Loan Society."

"I'm Connor O'Grady. This is Pete Parrino. We're looking for Gabriele Moretti. Do you know where we can find him?"

"Moretti Freight Brokerage Firm is on the fourth floor."

"Fourth? But this building only has three," Pete said.

"The top floor is concealed behind a high balustrade." Thomson stepped out of the way so Connor and Pete could enter the elevator.

"Fourth floor, please," Connor said to the operator.

Pete and Connor took a slow ride to the top floor and found Moretti's office in the corner. They entered an empty waiting room—no people, no furniture. A voice came from a room at the end of a short hall. "The *SS New York* leaves Saturday for London. I can get your freight booked on it, and it will be in London by Friday. I can also arrange first class passage for two. I'll telephone you with a quote. Yes, sir."

When the call concluded, Connor knocked on the interior door. "Excuse me. I'm looking for Gabriele Moretti."

A man in his mid-thirties—muscular, Italian, handsome, honest face, dark hair, penetrating eyes—came around the desk, taking several big strides, and gave each of them a firm handshake. "Gabriele Moretti, President of Moretti Brokerage. How may I help you?"

"I'm Connor O'Grady, Amy Spalding's cousin. According to a police report filed two months ago, you were listed as a contact. Are you still?"

Moretti crossed his arms, and gave Connor and Pete a suspicious glare. "Amy said she doesn't have any family."

"She has a large extended one." He nodded toward Pete. "My friend and I are visiting the city, and we'd like to invite her to dinner. Do you have an address for her?"

"I do, but she's out of town. The Giants are playing a three-game series in Pittsburgh, and she won't be home until Sunday."

Connor looked at Pete. "It's a good thing Jack went to the courthouse this morning."

"Ya think?" Pete said, and then to Moretti he said, "How'd you meet Amy?"

Moretti hitched his hip on the front corner of his desk and opened a humidor, offering both former cops a cigar, which they gladly accepted. Moretti held his cigar to his nose for a moment. Then he struck a match and rotated the cigar while he toasted it in the flame. When it began to smolder, he puffed while keeping the flame close until the tip was glowing.

"A couple of months ago, I was paying a call on Mr. Sterling, who owns a residence over on Riverside. I wanted to see if we could do some business. Miss Spalding was there interviewing for a position. Neither Mr. or Mrs. Sterling were home, so Miss Spalding and I ended up going to the Giants game. After the game, I introduced her to Maria Ricci, a dear friend. Maria agreed to rent her a room. It's been a good arrangement for Maria and her granddaughter, Isabella, and for Miss Spalding, too."

"Do you see her often?"

"Maria cooks dinner for us every night. Finest Italian food in the city."

"Are you and Amy an item?" Connor asked. "I mean are you and Amy…"

"Sweet on each other?" Pete finished the question.

Moretti rolled the tip of the cigar along the edge of an ashtray filled with a day's worth of ashes, and tapped it gently to let the gray ash fall into the dish. "It's nothing like that. We're business partners."

"Oh," Connor said. "Has she gone into the freight business, too?"

Moretti laughed. "Not freight. Baseball. If you're her cousin, you already know she has a phenomenal knowledge of the game. We took her knowledge and my hustle and etched out a pretty good betting operation. We've won a lot of money in two months."

"How large?" Pete asked.

"Thousands," Moretti said. "But business has been slower this week."

"How come?" Connor asked.

"We want to be the number one bookmakers in the city, but when you never lose, clients go elsewhere."

Connor rotated the foot of his cigar above the flame, drawing smoke into his mouth as he considered Moretti's business acumen. "What's your marketing plan?"

"Simple." Moretti parked the cigar in the corner of his mouth. "We've got to find a way to lose a little bit to make a hell of a lot more. Got any ideas?"

21

1909 New York City—Kevin

KEVIN TAXIED TO the *New York Herald* building on 6th Avenue between 35th and 36th. He exited the vehicle and paid the fare, and turned to see an Italian palazzo building identical to the Palazzo del Consiglio in Verona. He and Meredith had traveled extensively throughout Italy, sampling wine at dozens of large and small wineries, and he planned to take JL to Italy for their honeymoon.

In addition to romancing his bride, he planned to whittle down the list of wineries in Tuscany he and Meredith had compiled to a manageable number. After studying the financials, they would then visit their top three choices during the fall harvest and make an offer on at least one. Although, he believed Meredith had already picked her favorite and was keeping it under wraps for now. That was fine with him. He could independently evaluate the businesses without being influenced by her preference. At the end of the day, it was her company, and she could buy any winery she wanted, regardless of his opinion.

He hadn't discussed living part of the year in Italy with JL, and wasn't sure how she'd feel about it, but someone needed to spend time there managing the business.

If not him, then who? Certainly not the whisky drinkers in the family.

Thoughts of Italy and wineries were set aside when a clock on a parapet above him sounded the hour. He glanced up to see two aproned bronze typesetters swinging hammers. He watched the swinging clockwork figures until their mallets stopped, wondering where he had seen the clock before. Somewhere in the city. And then he remembered. It was on a monument in Herald Square near Macy's.

Stop stalling. He wasn't. He was just being observant.

He strolled through the graceful arcade along the side of the building, glancing inside the windows at the giant presses in motion. He watched for a while, totally enthralled…and stalling again. But why?

Hadn't he rehearsed what he wanted to say to Amy? Yes, but he was still hesitant about approaching her. Her reaction was unpredictable. It was possible, although unlikely, she was staying in the past by choice. If so, she wouldn't be happy to learn people had arrived to take her home. She might run away, cause a scene, call the police, or call him crazy. He wasn't in the mood to deal with a hysterical woman.

The minutes ticked by as he watched operators type on keyboard-like typewriters that produced perforated bands of paper. The bands were then decoded by machines that cast type from hot metal. The process fascinated Kevin. And he was still stalling.

Why?

He rubbed his shoulder. High humidity affected his muscles and joints.

Was that it? Was he afraid of being shot again? Who wouldn't be? Courage was acting despite fear. He jumped Thoroughbreds over obstacles, and, while there was nothing more exciting than the thrill of horses whooshing through the brush jumps, and the pounding of hooves as they hit the ground, the sport was dangerous. It wasn't that he lacked courage. If anything, he was overly cautious. If he hadn't been so cautious, would he have acted differently in the park? Would he have confronted the cops and protected JL?

God only knows what really happened to her in the police wagon. It made him physically ill to imagine the possibilities. But it annoyed her when he tried to protect her. She was a trained cop, and she considered it her job to protect others. He tried to be sensitive to those needs, but she should be able to understand he had needs, too.

He and James Cullen were Elliott's sons and heirs to the MacKlenna legacy. It was their responsibility to collect and protect the brooches for the family.

It wasn't Jack's responsibility, or David's, or Braham's. It was Kevin's—like it or not—and it was time for him to step out of his comfort zone and be the leader Elliott expected him to be.

Amy had a brooch. Ergo, it was his responsibility to approach her, befriend her, and take her and the brooch home.

He pushed away from the oversized windows overlooking the presses and entered a circular entrance lobby with marble floors, columns, and graceful chandeliers. Teller-type windows at the back of the circle had long lines of customers buying space to advertise everything from elixirs to Prince Albert tobacco. A large directory standing near the staircase listed the offices on the second floor. No names, only positions—publisher, editors, reporters.

Kevin took the wide staircase to the top, then wended his way down a long corridor. He passed a crowded room with two dozen desks or more, where men with shirtsleeves rolled to their elbows pored over stacks of papers. At the end of the hall, a male secretary sat at a desk typing.

Kevin approached the man. "I'd like to see Miss Spalding, but I don't have an appointment. Is she available?"

The man rolled a sheet of paper out of the typewriter and placed it on top of a one-inch stack of loose pages. "The Giants are playing a three-game series in Pittsburgh," he said, smiling at Kevin. "Miss Spalding took the train with John McGraw's and Christy Mathewson's wives on Tuesday. They won't be returning until Sunday."

"When are the games?"

"They're playing game one today. They're off tomorrow, then play Friday and Saturday."

Kevin had no idea who McGraw and Mathewson were but had

the good sense not to let on. "Pittsburgh, huh? What luck," he said. "I'm heading there, too. Do you know where she's staying?"

"The Fort Pitt Hotel," the man said. "She'll be back in her office on Monday."

"Where is that?" Kevin asked.

"In downtown Pittsburgh. I don't have the address."

"I didn't mean the hotel. I meant her office. Is it on this floor?"

The man pointed back down the hall. "Second office on the left."

"How often does her column appear?" Kevin asked.

"Monday through Friday." The man gathered up the papers. "The publisher wants her to write seven, but she said no. She wants to keep her readership wanting more. I heard she's fielding offers from other newspapers." He leaned in and whispered. "The *Herald* will have to pay her more, or she'll leave. I wouldn't blame her. The other reporters wanted to dislike her, but she's..." he scratched his head, then seemed to catch his thought and continued, "...she's a team player. I think that's how she phrased it. The other reporters go to her for advice now." He straightened. "Is there anything else I can help you with, Mister—?"

"Allen," Kevin said quickly, extending his hand. "Kevin Allen. I'm one of the thousands of Giants' fans from San Francisco."

The man shook Kevin's proffered hand. "I'm pleased to meet a fan. Miss Spalding is always looking for interesting stories to connect with her readership. I'm sure she'll be glad to meet a Californian who shares her passion for the Giants." His wide, bright eyes matched his tone of astonishment. "A Giants fan, all the way from California. How did that happen? Oh, never mind. Don't tell me. I'll wait to read Miss Spalding's article about how San Francisco fell in love with the Giants."

"I do have an interesting story to tell. I look forward to her return on Monday." He was deliberately coy. Amy would be curious about him. Curious enough to see him on Monday, he hoped. "You've been very helpful. Thank you."

On the way out, Kevin glanced inside Amy's small office. Autographed, framed pictures of ballplayers lined the walls. An open rolltop desk revealed a neat, organized work space—a dictionary, pen set, and a few sheets of stationery were the only visible items, except for an upside-down ashtray and a handwritten sign saying, no smoking here.

Thirty-seven, unmarried, baseball fanatic, and a sports reporter. In a brief time, she not only turned an ashtray upside down, but she turned the *Herald* upside down, too. He couldn't wait to meet her, and he couldn't wait for Jack to meet her, either.

Kevin could imagine the fireworks.

A writer, a baseball fanatic, and currently in a committed relationship. Oh, well. It was only a thought.

22

1909 New York City—JL

THE TAXI STOPPED in front of the 6th Avenue entrance to the Jefferson Market Courthouse shortly before nine o'clock. Jack held JL's hand as she stepped out of the taxi and onto the cobblestone street, which was muddy from the early morning rain. "Can you breathe?" he asked.

She took a deep breath to test whether her lung capacity was impaired, even though Jack had loosened the strings of her corset. "Barely," she grumbled.

"If you faint, I'll catch you."

"Thanks for caring."

"I do care, but fainting fits well with the image I want you to project."

Humans responded very strongly to visual stimuli, and made snap decisions in less than a few seconds. She learned the lesson very early in her career. Like Jack, she wanted the judge to see her as helpless and fragile. If he saw her as helpless, she was confident he would drop the charges.

She glanced up, shielding her eyes from the sun. It had broken through the clouds and now sank in the notch between two of the few skyscrapers standing tall in Greenwich Village. She hadn't noticed any of the surrounding buildings earlier, but she did now. Small presses, art galleries, and experimental theater thrived in

Greenwich in the twenty-first century, and from looking around at the businesses nearby, the bohemian lifestyle was alive and well in 1909, too.

"I didn't get a chance to take in this complex last night. It's interesting and...opulent," Jack said.

"In the twenty-first century, the jail is gone, but the judicial building is the home of the Jefferson Market Library."

"Library, huh? Maybe I can schedule a book-signing there."

"Do you always think about marketing?"

He rolled his shoulders in a defensive gesture. "Not all the time."

"Your historical novels and the library would be a good fit." She led the way into the Victorian Gothic-style building wedged into the angle of the lot, but scarcely noticed the limestone detailing, walnut doors, and stained-glass windows she usually enjoyed during visits to the library. "Come on. Let's get this over with." She found the building directory on the wall near the wide spiral steps. "Women's Court is down the hall."

Jack took her elbow, gave her a remember-your-role look, and steered her toward the courtroom. The doors were open, but lawyers and defendants remained huddled in the hall for last-minute conferences.

"Let's sit near the front. I want an unobstructed view of the judge." Jack said.

"To see how he runs his courtroom?" she asked.

"Some judges like to look sleepy and distracted, but it's a ruse to catch lawyers off guard."

"Sleepy-eyed old sharks," she said.

Sitting on the last row was a uniformed cop with a handlebar mustache and a bandage across his swollen nose. He looked up and scowled at her from beneath his beetled, Cro-Magnon brows. Bruises covered his face, ears, and throat. It was her handiwork, all right. There was no doubt he was the creep who assaulted her in the wagon. How should she play it? Call him a coward and a bully to his face, or just ignore him?

Jack leaned down and whispered in her ear. "He's not going to hurt you."

"Who?" she asked, without taking her eyes off Mustache Cop.

"Did you break his nose?"

She responded with a one-shoulder shrug.

"He attacked you in the police wagon, didn't he?"

She fired a hot glance at Jack. "Why'd you say that?"

"When we were at the jail earlier this morning, that cop was standing outside the building complaining to another cop about how he fell down the steps. Sounded like a strange thing to happen. I put two and two together—"

"—and came up with sixteen." She tilted her head to the side and looked up at him, narrowing her eyes. "Good try, Mallory. You can't make the leap between a cop's broken nose and me unless you were in the park last night and recognized him as the cop who rode in the wagon. Which means"—she paused a moment, letting her thought hang in the air—"Kevin believes I was assaulted."

"Were you?"

A spurt of anger warmed her face, but she bit her tongue before she smarted off. Whatever Jack believed, he was reflecting Kevin's thoughts, and she needed to be sensitive to that.

"Do you want to talk about it?" Jack asked.

"We are talking about it," she quipped. "The creep tried to hurt me, and, as you can see, I'm not the one sporting a face full of bruises. He is. Kevin doesn't need to know any of this. He's still struggling with the events of last fall."

"He won't hear it from me, but you should discuss it with him. If you don't, what he believes will be worse than what actually occurred."

"If I was still a detective with the NYPD, I wouldn't talk about my job. What took place in the wagon wasn't any worse than what has happened to me while carrying a badge. Let it go."

The bailiff entered the courtroom, and Jack and JL found seats near the front. "Do you think the cop will testify?" she asked.

"No. He doesn't want anyone to know you bested him."

"All rise," the bailiff said.

The judge entered and took his seat behind the bench. "Call the first case," he said to the bailiff.

While they waited for her case to be called, JL prepared an affidavit describing what happened in the park. When she finished, Jack submitted the document to the prosecutor. A few minutes later, Mustache Cop sat down next to the prosecutor and read the document, shaking his head adamantly.

After the judge dispensed with almost twenty cases, the bailiff finally called her name. As she and Jack approached, he said, "Don't say anything unless I give you permission."

The judge looked at her over the top of his glasses.

"Miss O'Grady is charged with assaulting a policeman, trespassing, and soliciting," the prosecutor said.

"How do you plead?" the judge asked.

JL wobbled and leaned into Jack. "Not guilty," she said breathlessly. "The policeman grabbed me and scared me. How can I be charged with soliciting the man who has asked me to be his bride?"

"What were you doing in the park at one o'clock in the morning?"

She sighed and rubbed her forehead lightly, flashing her six-carat emerald-cut diamond, nestled in a platinum setting. "We lost track of time, your honor. We'd been on a long walk and decided to sit on a bench to..." She lowered her head demurely. Then glanced up at the judge, gazing beneath lowered lashes. "We were sparking in the park, your honor. Are you a married man? If you are, then surely you know what it's like to be young and in love."

"Did you strike the policeman?" the judge asked.

"I struck him when he grabbed me from behind and pulled me away from my fiancé. It was late and very dark. I was scared, your honor. My first reaction was to protect myself. I'm not from this city. I didn't know the police could arrest me for kissing my fiancé."

"Where are you from?"

"Kentucky. My fiancé brought me to New York City to shop for my trousseau." She patted the hair around her ear, flashing her ring again. "We're going on a six-week European honeymoon. But I'm so distraught now"—she wobbled again and reached for Jack's arm—"I just want to go home." Her wispy voice barely carried two feet, and the judge pulled his chair closer to hear her.

"I'll ask you again, Miss O'Grady, did you assault a police officer?"

"Your honor, I'm so little I can barely swat a fly, but I did try to protect myself."

"Were you trespassing in Central Park?"

She lowered her face and peeked up at the judge through her eyelashes. "I was in the park after hours with my soon-to-be husband. If we had known we were breaking the law, we certainly wouldn't have been there."

"How long have you been a prostitute?"

JL gasped. "You honor, I'm shocked. I'm sure you've had…prostitutes…in your courtroom before. Do I"—she pressed her hand against her chest—"look like one of those women?"

The judge sat back in his swivel chair, linked his fingers, rested his hands on his stomach, and tapped his thumbs together. He did an eyebrow hike, watching her closely, as if trying to reconcile the woman before him with the charges against her. On cue, JL looked him in the eye and smiled coyly. After thinking for a minute, the judge sat straight in his chair, picked up his gavel, and said, "There's insufficient evidence to hold Miss O'Grady over for trial. Charges dismissed." He hammered his gavel. "Next case."

Under his breath Jack said, "Don't stop. Don't speak. Don't look around." He took her elbow, squeezing it lightly, and guided her out of the courtroom. His long stride forced her to take two steps for every one of his, but she didn't dare ask him to slow down.

As soon as they cleared the door, Mustache Cop blocked her path. "You may have fooled the judge, but you didn't fool me. I heard you soliciting the man you claim was your fiancé. If he was, he'd be here in the flesh to defend you. But he isn't. I don't believe the crock-of-shit affidavit you signed, any more than I believe you. Admit it. The affidavit, just like your performance, was nothing but a pack of lies."

JL had worried the judge might use Kevin's absence against her, but she was more worried about what Kevin would do if he saw the cop who arrested her. Low-voiced she said, "I told him not to come. I was afraid he might beat the shit out of you. Instead of stomping on your balls, he would have cut them off and shoved them into your mouth." She bared her teeth, too defiant to be a smile. "Now get out of my way."

"If you have anything to say to my client," Jack said. "Say it to me. And if you ever approach her again, we'll file assault and attempted rape charges against you."

"You can't prove anything." The cop sneered, thumping his finger into Jack's chest. "As long as you're in the city, keep looking over your shoulder. You wouldn't want anything to happen to you or Miss O'Grady."

A shiver rolled up the length of JL's body from her boots to the top of her head. She clenched her fists until they shook, but kept them hidden in the folds of her dress. Her nails dug into her palms, and she bit her lip to keep herself from putting more marks on the asshat's face.

"You're a bully, a coward, and a disgrace to the NYPD. As long as I'm in the city, keep looking over your shoulder. I have friends, and they'll be looking for you. Trust me."

Mustache Cop's face turned so red she thought for sure he would stroke out.

Jack leaned into the cop and sniffed. "Come on, JL. Let's get out of here. It's starting to stink."

JL kept it together until they were in a taxi heading uptown. "That son of a bitch. I should have filed a complaint against him. Why did I let him get away with what he did to me?"

"If you filed a complaint, he would have lied, and the judge would have looked at your case differently."

"You think the judge would have believed him, not me?"

"Not the way you acted in court. Worthy of an Oscar, even though I told you not to say anything without permission. This could have gone down differently. After all, the cop was the one with the cuts and bruises, not you. I'm just glad we don't have to go back."

"I didn't say thank you. So, thank you."

"A word of advice. Don't let the incident in the police wagon fester. You don't need to carry scars. The cop will carry plenty. You busted his nose, and he probably didn't get medical treatment. He'll have a facial deformity, deviated septum, and breathing problems. He'll curse you the rest of his life, and he only has himself to blame. He tried to rape a woman in restraints."

"A dirty cop. Nothing pisses me off more." She cleared her throat and unclenched her hands. "We can't tell Connor and Pete what happened, either. They'll go looking for him."

"They won't hear it from me. As far as I'm concerned, this case is closed." He looked down, fixing her suddenly with a dark blue stare in which pensiveness and sorrow were mingled with a good many other things she couldn't read.

"Good." She tried to muster a bright, artificial voice. "Where to now?"

"The Providence Loan Society. It's on the way to the hotel. Pete and Connor might still be there."

"Sort of a sorbet to cleanse our palates between the entrée and main course."

Chuckling, he offered her a quick hug. "Great analogy."

"It bothered you more than you anticipated, didn't it? Going to court, I mean," she said.

Jack used his handkerchief to blot perspiration off his forehead. "It's always pissed me off to see men bullying women, but now it's worse." His frustration spilled over in his voice. "I barely kept it together."

"You did well. You weren't overly emotional, even out in the hall."

"I can't put the omelet back in the eggshells," he said. "All I can do is try to control my behavior so no one else ever gets hurt at my expense."

She patted his hand. "You're a good man, Jack Mallory."

He gave a bark of humorless laughter. "Do you mean that?"

"Yes, unless you do something stupid again. Then all bets are off."

23

1909 New York City—Jack

JACK AND JL arrived at the Providence Loan Society thirty minutes after leaving the courthouse. His heart rate had slowly returned to normal. If JL attended court in the twenty-first century, she could have handled the entire messy business by herself. But not this court. It triggered too many emotions for her. If Jack hadn't been there, she would have fought back against the court's bias against women and she would have landed in a very nasty jail.

Jack held open the heavy bronze door, and JL breezed across the threshold and into the lobby. "Let's find this Moretti character and see how he fits into the story."

"The directory is next to the elevator." Jack walked over to the placard attached to the wall and read the list of names. "Moretti's office is on the fourth floor." Jack pushed the up button on the elevator's bronze signal plaque. The door opened, and the operator slid back the Gothic style interior grille. Bowing slightly, Jack said, "Ladies first." Then to the operator he said, "Fourth floor, please."

JL swished her skirts as she entered the small passenger elevator. "Since we're not at home, and some men have problems with aggressive women, I'll let you do the talking."

They remained silent in the elevator. As soon as they stepped off on the fourth floor, Jack said, "If he's a friend of Amy's, don't you think he's used to modern women by now?"

"We don't know how friendly they are with each other," she said, looking at the names on the office doors.

"True," Jack said. "I'll take the lead, then. But I bet Connor and Pete have manipulated Moretti into giving up everything he has on her."

They found Moretti's office at the end of the hall. Jack opened the door and ushered JL inside the foyer. The room was empty, but they could hear Connor and Pete talking in a rear office. Jack and JL wandered in to find the two former cops sitting next to each other on a stripe-patterned loveseat, leaning forward with their forearms resting on their thighs, fingers clasped. They faced two wingback chairs. A man sat in one, his head clearly visible above the chair's upholstered top back rail.

Pete rose to his feet when they entered. "What are you doing here, *ragazza tosta?*"

The man stood and turned, smiling. "Tough girl?"

"Well," JL blushed. "Pete thinks so." She walked toward the man, extending her hand. "I'm Jenny Lynn O'Grady. We're all Amy's cousins." She pointed at Connor. "And he's my older brother."

"Connor told me you're all related, but there's no resemblance between your beauty, signorina, and your brother." The man took JL's hand and kissed it. "I'm Gabriele Moretti."

Jack shook hands with Moretti, and got to the point without wasting time on the niceties. "I'm Jack Mallory. I understand you know Amy Spalding."

"Whoa, Jack," Connor said. "Ease up. First, tell us what happened in court."

"It was a quick in and out," JL said. "No fuss. No muss. No fine. The charges were dropped. And I should get an award for my performance."

"I wasn't needed in court," Jack added. "JL played her part beautifully. Fluttered her eyelashes on cue. Flashed the rock on her finger, and the judge dismissed the charges. As she said, 'No muss. No fuss.'"

"I made an enemy, though," JL said. "One of the cops told me to keep looking over my shoulder."

"I hope you told him to keep looking over his," Pete said.

JL's mouth curved. "Don't worry. I did."

"We'll handle him," Pete said.

"Yeah, like we handled the traffic," Connor said.

"Oh, geez. What'd you do?"

"We'll tell you later," he said. "But what about the cop? Do you think he'll cause any more trouble?"

"If you see anyone suspicious-looking tailing us, the cop's easy to recognize," JL said. "He's the one with the broken nose, bruises, and a handlebar mustache."

Pete tilted his head one way then the other. "And you don't have a mark on you."

She shrugged. "I got lucky."

Jack reached into his pocket for a roll of bills, and then he said to Gabriele, "I'd like to compensate you for any out-of-pocket expenses you've incurred on Amy's behalf."

JL gave him a hard look, like she was tasting something and finding it unpleasant. He ignored her and kept his attention focused on Moretti.

"I don't have any. I mean…Amy paid her own expenses. She borrowed money to replace the clothes she lost. But, between her job and our gambling enterprise, she's made enough money to repay the loan after her next paycheck."

"Who did she borrow money from? If she borrowed from a loan shark, the interest rate would be astronomical," Jack said.

"The Providence Loan Society," Moretti said. "She used a piece of family jewelry for collateral. She got a square deal at a fair interest rate."

A sinking, twisting feeling wrapped around Jack's throat. "Which piece of jewelry did she use?" he asked, although he didn't want to hear the answer.

"I never saw it, but she said it was a diamond brooch. She borrowed seventy-five thousand dollars for six months."

"*For goddam clothes?*" Jack exploded. His rage was like a rock the size of a fist stuck in his throat. After what happened in court, hearing what the cop had done to JL, and now the additional trouble Amy had caused, he'd reached his limit and beyond.

"What the hell is she wearing? A gold-plated corset?" The words were forced out by the bitterness and rancor churning in his gut. He wanted to find Amy Spalding and shake her till her teeth rattled. The brooch could change the world, and she flippantly gave up control of its power for a goddamn corset.

JL turned on Jack, her fine nostrils flaring. She poked him with her finger. "If you've got a bee in your bonnet, you better get a new hat, because this attitude isn't going to get you anywhere. *Capisci?*"

"Fine. You handle it." He crossed the oriental carpet to the love seat, sat next to Connor, and crossed both arms and legs.

"Why did Amy want so much money?" JL asked in a neutral voice.

"To invest," Moretti said. "She's turned her investment broker on his head with her trading recommendations. I've made all the same investments, and have doubled my portfolio in two months. She's a genius."

"I wouldn't say that," Jack mumbled. Connor gave him a warning glance, but Jack ignored him.

"Is there any one in particular I can speak to at Providence who's familiar with Amy's loan?" JL asked.

"Stephen Thomson. He's the president. He handled the loan."

"I'm going to ask this as tactfully as I can," JL said. "Is there a reason the president of the company worked with Amy on her loan? Are they...dating?"

"Dating?" Moretti asked.

Jack launched himself off the couch and paced across the spacious room. "You know... Romantically involved." The mission was going off the rails, slowly but surely.

"Thomson is a widower. Amy has accompanied him to the theater and to dinner parties, but I wouldn't say they are romantically involved," Moretti said. "She confides in Isabella. You might ask her."

"Who is Isabella? And does she have a last name?" JL asked.

"Isabella Ricci. She and Amy live with Isabella's grandmother, Maria Ricci," Connor offered, "in an apartment at one-twenty Riverside Drive."

"Riverside? That's a pricey address," JL said.

"Maria's husband and I made a good deal on two apartments in the building while it was under construction. He died shortly after we moved in. I do what I can for Maria."

"That's kind of you." Jack leaned against the windowsill. "Where is Amy now? At the newspaper?"

"Gabe told us before you arrived that she's in Pittsburgh. The Giants are playing a three-game series. She won't be home until Sunday," Pete said.

"Sunday?" Damn. Could the situation get any worse? Jack needed to get his hands on the brooch, now. Once they had the diamond, they could take the train to Pittsburgh, find Amy, and go home. "I'll go talk to Thomson and pay off the loan. Where's his office?" Jack asked.

"Second floor. But you don't have Amy's money," Moretti said.

"She can pay me back later," Jack said. "I don't like her owing anyone money."

Moretti took a position in front of the door, arms crossed. "Nobody leaves until you explain what the hell is going on. You barge in here, demand information about a woman I befriended, make light about angering a cop, and act like you're her goddamn husband. Who the hell are you?"

Since Jack couldn't explain who they were and why they were there, he had only one choice. He didn't like it, but he was backed into a corner. "I'm not her husband yet, but I intend to be."

"She's never mentioned you. How do I know she wants to marry you?" Moretti asked.

"Why else would we be here? Why else would I go pay off a seventy-five-thousand-dollar loan? The future Mrs. Jack Mallory is going home with me, even if I have to throw her over my shoulder and carry her there. That's who the hell I am."

The room, as well as Jack, vibrated with his anger. Moretti, who was a few inches shorter and forty pounds lighter than Jack, wisely stepped aside.

"What do you want us to do?" Connor asked.

Jack took a calming breath. "Find out what time the next train leaves for Pittsburgh, then call the hotel. Leave a message for Kevin. Since he went to the newspaper, he probably already knows about Amy. Tell him where we are. If he doesn't want to wait for us at the hotel, he can come here."

"I'm going with you, Jack," JL said.

"I can handle it."

"I'm sure you can, but I'm still coming."

"Suit yourself."

Jack and JL left Moretti's office and took the elevator to the second floor. The hall was lined with closed-door offices.

"Don't you think we should ask someone, or let someone know we'd like to see the president?"

"No." Jack led the way down the hall, passing offices for bookkeeping, appraisers, accountants, and corporate officers. The last office belonged to the president, Stephen Thomson.

"This is it." Jack knocked.

A voice inside said, "Come in."

Jack pushed opened the door and stepped aside for JL to enter first. "I'm Jack Mallory. This is Jenny Lynn O'Grady. We're Amy Spalding's cousins, and we'd like to discuss her loan."

The brows, which had lowered severely when the door opened, popped back up. "I'm sorry, Mr. Mallory, Miss O'Grady, but Miss Spalding has never mentioned you, and her relationship with our company is strictly confidential."

Jack pulled a small leather pouch from his pocket and tossed it onto Thomson's desk. It held more than a half million dollars in gold nuggets. "I'm here to pay her loan. We have a family policy about borrowing money. If I had known it was her intent, I would have sent money two months ago."

Thomson opened the pouch and poured the nuggets into his palm. His mouth quirked wryly as he met Jack's eyes.

"There's more than enough to pay her loan, plus interest," Jack said. "If you'll get me a payoff amount, we can settle up."

Thomson swept his arm in the direction of the two chairs arranged in front of his desk. "Please, have a seat. Have you spoken to Miss Spalding about this?"

Jack waited until JL sat before he took a seat. "Miss O'Grady and I just arrived in town, along with her cousin, her brother, and a business associate. I'm a distant cousin to them, as I am to Miss Spalding. We were visiting with Mr. Moretti, and he informed me Amy used her diamond brooch to secure the loan."

"You're correct. She told me recently she had saved enough to pay off the principal and would have the interest in another week or so. I'm very impressed with her investments and frugality."

"I intend to pay off the loan today," Jack said.

Thomson picked up the pouch. "Miss Spalding has money set aside to repay this loan."

"She can pay me back. We're on our way to Pittsburgh, and when I see her, I'd like to give her the brooch, and the promissory note marked paid in full."

"I see." Thomson got to his feet. "Give me a few minutes, Mr. Mallory."

Thomson left the room and Jack considered his resources. He had another pouch of diamonds worth more than the nuggets, plus several thousand dollars in cash.

"I can't believe she gave up possession of the brooch. I would have starved," JL said.

"Kenzie at least had diamond earrings to sell. If she hadn't had them, she might have resorted to pawning the brooch, too."

"I guess we can assume the brooch didn't work when Amy tried to get back to her time, and she's stuck here. She probably figured there was no harm in using it for collateral when it didn't work."

"As we both know, just because it didn't work for her, didn't mean it lost its power."

The clock on the wall ticked and ticked and ticked. When Thomson was gone for fifteen minutes, Jack considered tracking him down. After thirty minutes, Jack got up out of the chair. "I'm going to find Thomson. If he calls Amy, we might have a problem."

Five seconds later, the door opened and Thomson entered. "I'm sorry it took so long." He returned to his chair. "I've discovered a scrivener's error. The original loan officer, Mr. Carter, inserted the wrong date on the note, and instead of a six-month loan, Miss Spalding had a two-month loan, which she defaulted on. The brooch was sold at auction."

Jack shot out of his chair. "How the hell did that happen? Don't you have a loan review committee?" He ran his fingers through his hair as he paced the room. "Call the purchaser, explain the mistake, offer to buy back the brooch for ten percent more than the purchase price."

"The purchaser has given the brooch as a gift, and has no intention of reclaiming it. I'm sorry, Mr. Mallory. We will, of course, reimburse you the full appraised value, less the outstanding loan."

"That won't do at all. The brooch is a family heirloom." Jack rubbed a hand over his face, and shook himself, as if to throw off a nightmare. "Who bought it?" he demanded.

"Since it was a public auction, I can tell you the purchaser was Diamond Jim Brady."

"How much did he pay for it?" JL asked.

Mr. Thomson swallowed visibly. "Three hundred ten thousand dollars, but," he added quickly, "Mr. Brady gave the brooch to—"

"Let me guess," Jack said sarcastically. "Lillian Russell."

"Do you know her?"

Memories of the night Carolina Rose died came back in a landslide of emotions, shaking him to his core. "We met several years ago in California."

"If you intend to negotiate with her, you'll need to move quickly. I just read in today's *Herald* she's leaving Saturday for London on the *SS New York*," Thomson said.

"This is devastating news for our family." Jack glanced down at

JL to find her looking up at him, her eyes round and dark. The consequences of this fuckup clearly rattled her, as it did him. "Come, my dear. Let's advise the others." Then to Mr. Thomson, Jack said, "My lawyers will be in touch."

Mr. Thomson wrung his hands. "Lawyers? There's no need to involve them." He recovered quickly. "If you negotiate a deal with Miss Russell, we will forgive the interest on the loan, and I will personally guarantee the difference between her asking price and the appraised value, up to three hundred ten thousand dollars."

Jack slapped his palms down on the desk, and pressing into them leaned forward. "No, Mr. Thomson, you will pay whatever price she asks."

Mr. Thomson winced briefly—probably imagining the legal entanglements resulting from the company's mistake. "When you see Miss Spalding, please give her my sincere apologies. I'll find a way to make this up to her."

"That's impossible." Jack yanked the pouch of nuggets off the desk. "The brooch is part of a set, and is hundreds of years old. It's irreplaceable."

Jack and JL were quiet as they rode the elevator back to the fourth floor. They entered Moretti's office to find Pete and Connor sitting in the same seats, drinking coffee and laughing.

"I'm glad you found something to laugh about," Jack said.

"Moretti knows a family of Parrinos in Tuscany," Pete said. "I wonder if they're related."

"I need something stronger than coffee." Jack stared at Pete. "I thought your family was from Sicily."

"People migrate. Some of the family could have gone to Tuscany. Who knows?"

"I want something stronger, too," JL said.

Moretti opened the bottom drawer of his desk and pulled out a bottle of whisky and two small tumblers. He filled them and handed one to Jack, one to JL.

"Must have been rough if you're drinking the hard stuff before noon," Connor said.

Jack turned up the glass and emptied it. "The company fucked up. The brooch was sold at auction two weeks ago."

Pete jumped to his feet, spilling his coffee. "Holy shit! How do we get it back?"

"Thomson called the buyer, Diamond Jim Brady, but he gave it to Lillian Russell," Jack said.

"You know Lillian. Go talk to her," Connor said.

Moretti refilled Jack's glass. "You've got a problem."

"Yeah, tell me about it," Jack said, sipping the refill.

"Lillian Russell is leaving Saturday for London," Moretti said.

"Thomson told us," Jack said.

"What do you want me to do?" JL asked.

Jack set his glass on the table, walked over to the window to look out on the city, and considered the most efficient way to use his assets. "You and Kevin go see Lillian and offer to buy the brooch."

"What do you want me to do?" Connor asked.

"Go to Pittsburgh with me to find Amy."

"What's my job?" Pete asked.

"Guard Kevin and JL, watch out for crooked cops, and see what information you can glean about Catherine Lily Sterling."

"I can help with the Sterlings," Moretti said. "I can also arrange transportation to Pittsburgh, recommend hotels. Whatever you need. I'm the one who recommended the company downstairs to Amy. It's my personal responsibility to do everything, by whatever means, to recover her brooch. You can count on me."

Jack clasped Moretti's shoulder, gave it a squeeze. For the first time in twelve hours, he had more than a smidgeon of confidence in the success of the mission. It was a long way from a full cup, but they had a solid plan and capable people to carry it out.

"Is there anything else you need?" Moretti asked. "Anything? I can make it happen."

"Get us first class accommodations for six people on the *SS New York*. If Lillian sails with the brooch, we sail, too."

24

1909 Pittsburgh—Amy

AMY SAT AT the breakfast table in the dining room at the Fort Pitt Hotel waiting for her traveling companions, Jane Mathewson and Blanche McGraw, to join her.

Her interviews with Jane and Blanche had gone well, and she had enough material for several articles. Amy intended to lead with her favorite Jane story. Before Jane and Christy married, they negotiated two significant differences. Matty left the Baptist Church to become a Presbyterian, and Jane gave up her Democratic affiliation and joined the Republican Party. Amy wouldn't give up her membership in the Democratic party for any man, not even the wholesome, handsome, broad-shouldered Christy Mathewson.

She didn't know until she arrived in Pittsburgh the day before that the city was celebrating its sesquicentennial. Although the celebration wasn't scheduled to begin until the 4th of July, there were exhibits already in place. Since there wasn't an afternoon game scheduled, she was joining Jane and Blanche for a tour. The first planned stop was Mount Washington for a view of the city, followed by a long lunch, then on to Carnegie Institute to see the 13th Annual Exhibition, slated to continue until the end of the month.

Amy was enjoying a second cup of coffee when a waiter in a white jacket brought her a copy of the *Pittsburgh Daily Post*.

"Here's the newspaper you requested, Miss Spalding. A report of yesterday's baseball game is on the Sporting Page."

"Thank you." She unfolded the paper. A front-page article about her number one complaint since arriving in 1909 caught her eye.

DOES NEW YORK CITY NEED A TRAFFIC SQUAD?

NEW YORK – The congestion on the streets—especially downtown—is a subject being seriously discussed, and numerous plans have been presented to help relieve the situation.

A bottleneck at 5th Avenue and 34th Street spurred two enterprising visitors to the city to take matters into their own hands. Armed with only the ability to whistle loudly and wave their arms, the men stood in the center of the intersection without fear for their own lives, directing traffic with the skill of orchestra conductors. After an hour, two policemen offered up their batons, and the men continued directing carriages, wagons, trucks, bicyclists, and pedestrians through the intersection in an orderly fashion.

The City Improvement Commission is reviewing several reports of the incident, including interviews with the two industrious men who encouraged drivers to use hand signals. Additionally, the Commission is in talks with the police commissioner to establish a traffic squad to lessen traffic congestion, facilitate progress, and add to the businesslike appearance of the thoroughfare.

Fair play to all will be the fundamental principal of the traffic squad plan. Traffic bound in one direction will get its chance to pass, and then others who have waited for them will be given their turn. The man afoot, too, will be permitted to cross intersections without danger of being run down by an unbroken parade of vehicles, and without being compelled to wait from dawn till darkness. Special attention will be paid to the progress of women and children and to the infirm.

It was later reported to the police department the two men were carrying concealed weapons, which is a felony in New York. If found, they will be arrested.

Amy whistled softly. She had been in that intersection. To stand in the middle of it took either incredible guts or rampant stupidity. Something about the article triggered a memory. What was it? She read it again.

...including interviews with the two industrious men who encouraged drivers to use hand signals...

Hand signals? Impossible. Signals weren't widespread until the 1940s. The only reason she knew was because, as a teenager, she researched who used signals first—baseball or motorists. Baseball beat out motorists by fifty years. She read the article a third time. How did those men know hand signals?

...visitors to the city... without fear for their own lives... carrying concealed weapons...

They sounded like cops. But if they were with the NYPD or another police department, wouldn't they have introduced themselves to the cops who offered up their batons? When she returned to the *Herald* on Monday, she'd ask around.

What if there were other time travelers? What if she could go home?

Would she go? She missed her shampoo and her shower. She missed ibuprofen. She missed running in the park and Saturday yoga classes. She missed wearing jeans. She missed Joe, although not as much as she thought she should.

She missed ESPN, but she loved her job at the *Herald*. She enjoyed her colleagues and adored her new family. Maria was a concerned and loving parent. Isabella, despite her shenanigans, loved to hang out in Amy's room and talk about boys and fashion. And Gabriele was the protective big brother she never had.

Bottom line: she loved her life.

Chills peppered her arms at the thought, but it was true. Home wasn't calling her name. Not yet, anyway. It wasn't by accident that she was stuck in 1909. There was a purpose, and one day it would be revealed.

When had her change of heart taken place? When had her psyche accepted she wasn't going home? She knew the exact day—two weeks after she started working at the paper. Bennett dropped the new readership numbers on her desk and told her to add her byline to her column on the society page. Two weeks later, her column appeared on the sports page.

A week later, an interview with her picture appeared in *Vogue*. She was now recognized wherever she went, and was warmly received at the Polo Grounds, Hilltop Park, and Washington Park. Players never declined an interview, because they knew she would treat them fairly. And the owners appreciated Amy's understanding of the game and its future as a business enterprise. They tolerated her lobbying them to either remove the reserve clause in contracts or deposit a lump sum in an association for the players to divide based on their contributions. She wasn't getting anywhere with it, but it was early in the game.

She pushed away thoughts of time travelers and going home and turned to the sports page. Mathewson had been on the slab for the first game of the three-game series, and the Giants defeated the Buccaneers, ruining Pittsburgh's fourteen-game winning streak. The Giants barely made it out of the stadium after the game.

PITTSBURGH, Mathewson was in good form, although the Pirates hit him freely. But he kept the bingles well scattered and seemed to get better as the game progressed. The Pirates registered one run in the second inning, another in the third. After that they did not score. Sam Leever replaced "Lefty," and the Giants added one off him in the fourth. In the sixth, they pounded the veteran, and during the slaughter, the Goshen boy was taken out of the game.

The Pirates, or Bucs as Amy usually called them, would play their last game in Exposition Park on June 29. When the Giants returned for a two-game series beginning July 30, they would be playing in the new Forbes Field. She had only seen pictures of the ballpark, which closed in 1970, and couldn't wait to take the ten-minute trolley ride from downtown to the field.

How many times had her dad told the story of the 1960 World Series between the Pirates and the Yankees? Too many to count. It was one of his favorite beer-drinking stories. She knew it by heart, but never interrupted. Game seven was played at Forbes Field, and ended with a walk-off home run hit by Pirates second baseman Bill Mazeroski. If her dad only knew she'd be at the field for one of the Pirates' first games, he'd be overcome with emotion.

Memory lane wasn't a place she wanted to travel right now, so she shook off the memories, and returned to reading the newspaper. There was a picture of New York's star twirlers, Christy Mathewson and Hooks Wiltse.

For the first time, she zeroed in on Christy's glove. It resembled a toddler's toy. She had her own little quirks when it came to her game glove, but none of her superstitions were as odd as some MLB players. Infielder Darwin Barney always took five gloves—all the same model and size—to every game, but never used his game glove until he walked out on the field.

She doodled in her notebook, sketching Christy with a ball in his hand. What could he accomplish using a twenty-first century glove with a deep pocket and webbing to hide his grip on the ball? She drew his glove alongside one used by pitchers in the future.

"What's that?" John McGraw asked. The Giants' manager was handsomely dressed in a vested gray suit with a high white collar and a diamond-patterned cravat. At his wrists, a large expanse of white cuff was held by diamond-studded links.

"Good morning, John. Are you trying to read my notes so you'll know what players' wives are saying about their husbands?"

"I read all your columns, Amy. So far, you're the only reporter who hasn't upset my boys."

"I want the Giants to win the pennant this year. I'm not going to mess up their heads." She knew the Giants would finish third in the league behind Chicago and Pittsburgh, but history could be changed. Right?

"What are you drawing? I've never seen a glove like that."

He reached for her journal but she smacked his hand. "Stop it, you hoodlum. It's just an idea. I'd rather not show it to anyone until it's finished."

The jockey-sized, pugnacious McGraw, baseball's premier strategist, sat down beside her. "Give me the drawing."

"You may be 'the real and authentic, most remarkable man in America,' but I don't work for you."

He laughed. "That's what George Bernard Shaw said about me."

"Don't let it go to your head. Oh, my bad," she said. "It already has." She slid her arm over the drawing. "Why don't you go to the races, or find a card game?"

"I'm doing that later." He snapped his fingers, nodding toward her journal, his light blue eyes flashing at her. "You know, I can make your job easy or hard."

She gasped, doing her best impression of being shocked. "Are you blackmailing me, John?"

"I'm Mr. McGraw to you," he said.

"No you're not. I'm the daughter you never had, like Matty is the son you never had." McGraw had a reputation of being an ass on the field, but he was one of the most gentlemanly men she had ever met, and always respectful. He also happened to be extremely competitive, and if a newfangled glove would give his players an advantage, he'd jump on it.

"I'm not opposed to blackmailing you if it will get me what I want."

"I realized something the other day when I was watching you," she said.

"What's that?"

"You were arguing a call so vociferously last week you got tossed out of the game."

"It was a bad call."

Amy shrugged. "Maybe. But you didn't stick around to see how the game ended. You went to the track to bet on the ponies. You know, don't you, the umps are on to your scam?"

He looked down his nose at her. "And...so is the newspaper? Is that what you're saying?"

"Nah, I wouldn't do that to you," she said.

He stretched his neck to look at her journal. "But you'd keep me from gaining an advantage over the rest of the league."

"I'll give you the sketch, but only because I don't believe it's cheating." She ripped out the page and gave it to him.

"It's too big. Players wouldn't be able to get the ball in time to make quick plays."

"It's not too big," she said. "A player just needs to get used to it. Since a pitcher is trying to deceive the batter, the best glove for him is one with a closed web to hide the ball and the hand grip from the batter. This glove gives the pitcher added catching support, and the shallow pocket makes it easier to transfer the ball to the throwing hand to make fast plays."

"I'd like to try it out with Matty. Where can I buy one?"

She shook her head. "It doesn't exist. The one I tried out...uh...got lost."

"How'd you get it?"

"I'm a Spalding." She knew mentioning her last name would intrigue him. "But in a few years, someone will take a similar design to Rawlings Sporting Goods, and they'll start producing the first edition. It'll be a few more years before one this advanced comes out."

He crossed his arm, rested his elbow there and brushed his finger down an imaginary handlebar mustache, the kind he couldn't grow. "You know more about baseball than most managers. You have a good instinct for the game, and a special insight when it comes to the future. If you were a man, you'd be playing for me."

"Thank you." She had an idea on the train coming up, but had been hesitant to mention it to him. In the mood he was in, she'd never find a better time. "I've been thinking about a series I'd like to write to encourage young women to play baseball."

"You're changing the subject."

"I'll circle back to it." She took a deep breath. "I'd like to work out with the team."

"What?"

"Wait." She reached out and touched his arm lightly to calm him. "It'll be a PR puff piece. I want girls to see they can be serious players, and I think the guys would be okay with it. It would last about ten to fifteen minutes. I'll bat, we can toss the ball around, then take pictures."

"No! It'll make my boys look soft."

"It will make them look relatable. We could open practice to women only, and have an autograph session afterwards."

John scratched his head. "I don't know. Let me think about it."

"Talk to Blanche. She thought it was a great idea."

"I should have known you already had her and Jane on your side."

"I do my homework, which brings me back to the glove. If we can get a prototype made, I'll use it during the workout since I'm familiar with how it feels," she said.

"What's a prototype?"

"An early model of something to test to see if it works."

"Let me see if I can get one made. If I can, we'll talk later about how to test it out."

He folded the drawing and put it in his pocket. It would be another ten years before Bill Doak designed a glove with a web and pocket. She was just speeding up the development of the game she loved. Was that wrong? Why put her here with the knowledge she had and not expect her to make a difference? What would a surgeon do if he or she was thrown back into the middle of the Revolutionary War? They would use their knowledge to save lives. Her situation didn't have life or death consequences, but the game was important to the country's collective psyche.

John left her alone with her thoughts, and a waiter came over to refill her coffee. She put her hand over the lip of the cup. "Would you ask the bartender to make me a mimosa?"

The Diamond Brooch

He left and was back in a few minutes. "The bartender has never heard of a mimosa. If you can tell him what's in the drink, he said he might be able to prepare one for you."

"Put three-fourths orange juice and one-fourth champagne in a wine glass. That's all there is to it."

The waiter left with the instructions and Amy sat back and picked up her pencil. She tapped it back and forth between her teeth, thinking about her conversation with John. She doubted anything would come of it, but if he did manage to get a prototype made, what would she do?

She glanced around the room, and her eyes settled on two men sitting a table away, realizing they'd been there for some time. There was something oddly familiar about the handsome, blond-haired man. Had she seen him before? He had perfectly straight white teeth, and his intriguing smile brought out the crow's feet at the corners of his lake-blue eyes. The teeth alone looked out of place in 1909. His textbook-perfect mouth with classically defined lips matched his physically fit physique and expensively tailored chestnut brown suit. He was a walking GQ ad, leaning toward the young, silver-foxy demographic.

His smile connected to her on a gut level in a way she had never experienced before. She quickly looked down and returned to doodling in her journal. Surprisingly, her hand shook. She was tempted to sneak another peak, but shut down the urge.

"There you are." Blanche gave Amy a quick, one-arm hug. "John said you were waiting in here for us. We were in the lobby."

"I'm sorry." Amy smiled at the two inseparable friends, who were both wearing the latest fashion in printed silk day dresses. Earlier they went through Amy's closet and selected a similar dress for her to wear on their outing, knowing she would have worn the same dress she wore the day before if they hadn't insisted. She cared about her appearance, but she was also a light packer, and perfectly willing to re-wear her clothes. She didn't want to re-wear a dress to a game, but she would to go sightseeing.

After reviewing the colored confusion in her closet, Jane and

Blanche insisted she wear the one-piece gray dotted cotton with gray satin trim and a standing lace collar, even though Amy explained it was to be worn to Saturday's game. They compromised. Amy wore the dress, and Blanche loaned her a hat—a large, crowned straw hat with a black velvet band decorated with clusters of cloth roses. On Saturday, she could wear the ensemble again, but with her own hat.

"Are you ready to go?" Jane asked.

"I just ordered an orange juice. Do you mind waiting a minute?"

Blanche sat where John had been sitting, and Jane took the chair across from her, blocking Amy's view of the handsome man with the too-perfect smile. However, she could see his companion—a younger man, cute as he could be, with an angular face, prominent jawline, square chin, high cheekbones, deep brown eyes, tall and muscular. She had observed guys in and out of locker rooms, and could sum up their assets quickly. The blond guy, though, had vulnerability swimming off him in waves, and the vibes she picked up jolted her. There was a sensual lingering in his eyes, like he not only saw her, but saw through her.

And it unnerved her in a way a fast pitch never had.

The waiter brought her mimosa, and she sipped it slowly. "This is delicious. Thank you." She held it out to Blanche. "You have to taste this. It's orange juice and champagne."

"Hmm. Sounds decadent." She took a sip, and sighed before handing it to Jane to taste. To the waiter, Blanche said, "I'll have one, and bring one for my friend, too."

Jane looked at the glass as if it contained something unpleasant. "It's ten o'clock in the morning. I can't drink champagne,"

Blanche nudged Jane's arm to lift the glass to her mouth. "Of course you can. This is ladies' day out."

"I'll have to tell Christy you twisted my arm."

"Tell him Amy threatened you. He won't object if the idea came from her."

"Why do you say that?" Amy asked.

"Christy thinks you're a genius. The talk you had with him on the train about pitching had him icing his arm and shoulder last night. He said he could feel a difference this morning."

"Good. He needs to ice it a few more times today, too."

The waiter returned with two more mimosas, and Amy clinked her glass against theirs. "Here's to ladies' day out."

"Did you make a luncheon reservation?" Jane asked.

"Yes, at the Oyster House, a few blocks from here. And we can buy tickets for the Carnegie exhibit when we get to the museum."

Blanche sipped her drink, then smacked her lips. "This is divine."

"It is luxuriously self-indulgent to drink champagne in the morning," Jane said, smiling.

"I'm glad you like it. I rarely drink, but I could drink another one of these." In the last few weeks, her alcohol consumption had risen dramatically. Maria, Isabella, and Gabriele enjoyed a glass of wine every night with dinner, and it seemed easier to join them than explain why she preferred not to drink. She had seen the destruction alcohol caused, and after years of Al-Anon meetings, had finally come to terms with her late father's disease.

"Are you going to write about our outing today?" Jane asked.

Amy laughed. "I will if you say something witty and clever."

"I'll try to say something clever, but please don't mention the champagne," Blanche said. "John wouldn't care, but the fans would."

Amy picked up her half-full glass and tilted it gently, so the rim touched her lips just as Jane bent to whisper to her and Blanche. Amy met sexy guy's gaze straight on. They both sat still as stone, looking at each other, until her heart hammered in her ears.

"There are two handsome men at the next table," Jane said. "They were staring at you, Amy, when we came in, and probably still are. Do you recognize them? Are they baseball players?"

"They could be," Amy said. "But I think the blond guy is a lawyer type, and the other one is a cop or detective."

"How do you know?" Blanche asked.

"Experience," Amy said. "If y'all are ready. It's time for our ladies' day out to get rolling."

Jane and Blanche laughed and clinked their empty glasses. "Ladies' day already started."

Was giving them mimosas a good idea? Maybe so. Maybe no. They were having fun. Amy picked up her parasol, purse, and journal, and fiddled at the table, hoping to catch one last long look at those sexy eyes. Before she turned toward the door, she risked it. He was looking right at her, his long, thick lashes shadowing his regard of her.

As she swept back the loose curl dangling from the coiled bun at her neck, she had an intuitive flash.

...visitors to the city...without fear for their own lives...carrying concealed weapons...interviews with two men who encouraged drivers to use hand signals...

Of course. She knew him, or she knew *of* him, and he had come to take her home. For a moment, she gawked, blinking in the beam of sunshine from the window. The room was quiet, save for the low murmurs of the wait staff and the clinking of china as the tables were cleared.

I'm not going home.

Her heart leapt in her throat. She turned and darted out of the room, hissing under her breath. He could try, but she wasn't going. She gave a rueful shake of her head. Not today. Not tomorrow. Not next week—even if a life depended on it.

25

1909 Pittsburgh—Jack

AT TWO O'CLOCK the previous afternoon, Jack and Connor caught the last train to Pittsburgh and arrived at the Fort Pitt Hotel late at night. Jack tried to sleep, but after tossing and turning in the lumpy bed, he gave up and went for a long walk through downtown, planning what he was going to say to Amy.

Knowing how much she loved baseball, he ruled out spoiling the World Series for her. Which left Jack Mallory, *New York Times* bestselling author, with the unthinkable—no beguiling line.

Several songs came to mind, like "Homeward Bound" by Simon and Garfunkel, "Country Roads" by John Denver, "Home" by Michael Bublé. He wasn't going to serenade her, but a recognizable and cool song lyric always worked on the spur of the moment as an icebreaker. Not this time, though. All the songs he came up with rang cold, flat, and uninspiring. He couldn't even depend on his book-jacket smile.

No original lines, no song lyrics, no smile, and all his words came back in shades of mediocrity. Thank you, Paul Simon.

Was he living in a nightmare, sitting in a railway station, playing in a bad B-movie…or screwing up someone else's life? If he couldn't come up with a line between now and the moment he confronted her…

Confronted? Didn't he mean approached her? See? He was

totally off his game. The logical approach should be a winning smile followed by, "Hi, I'm Jack Mallory."

Prior to crashing for a couple of hours after his walk, Jack had scribbled a message to Connor and slid it under his door. Jack wanted to catch a couple of hours' sleep before meeting for a late breakfast at ten o'clock.

At ten fifteen, the two men entered the hotel's dining room. Jack had only a few hours to convince Amy to get back on the train to New York City. If they weren't on the afternoon train, the one on Friday would push their return into the late evening. If there were any delays along the way, they could miss departing on the *SS New York* Saturday morning.

But there was another reason Jack had to leave today. He scheduled time on Friday to meet Catherine Lily. After all, this meeting was the compelling reason he agreed to the mission. If he had to choose between leaving the country to chase the diamond brooch or staying in New York to meet Catherine Lily, there wasn't much of a choice.

With luck, JL would persuade Lillian Russell to sell the diamond brooch, or Pete would find a way to steal it. If they didn't succeed— since Lillian was flirtatious when she and Jack last met in San Francisco—maybe he could romance the stone away from her. Nah. Not even for the brooch would that ever happen.

However this went down, the time travelers had less than forty-eight hours to get it done.

He strolled into the dining room behind Connor while reading the front-page headline in the morning copy of the *Pittsburg Daily Post*. Jack followed him to a table in the center of the room, an odd place to sit, considering all the empty tables. The warriors and former police officers in the MacKlenna family always sat with their backs to the wall. But he didn't say anything. Instead, he took a seat opposite Connor and turned over his coffee cup as a signal to the waiter to fill it with his morning jolt.

And that's when he saw her…

His gaze flicked between Amy and Connor, then back to her,

and his hand shook as he returned the cup to the saucer. Dozens of her pictures had come across his desk, and he spent hours watching videotapes of her in the broadcasting booth, but sitting ten feet away, he could see the details cameras were unable to convey—the symmetry of her face, the slight curve of her nose, the quizzical lift of her brow, the turquoise color of her eyes. She was a woman filled with clarity and peace, who carried herself with absolute confidence.

And the vision in front of him pinned him flat against the wall...

Amy Spalding wasn't out of time and place. The diamond brooch had brought her to a world she had dreamed of, a world that captured her heart; a world that wouldn't easily let her go.

In 1865, Jack faced a hangman's noose. In 1944, the B-17 he was flying in ditched in the English Channel. Eight months ago, the most exciting woman he had ever met died in his arms. Why did the brooches put him in such cruel and impossible situations? He had thought this mission was a no-brainer.

A wave of dizziness having nothing to do with hunger or lack of sleep or traveling through time made his head swim. He was in an untenable position. He saw it as coolly as possible, but his heart gave a convulsive leap and tried to burrow out of his chest.

If he pulled Amy out of 1909, it would break her heart...

Connor kicked him under the table, and in a hushed voice said, "You're staring. Stop it." He kicked him again, and Jack made an inarticulate sound in his throat, reminiscent of his Scottish cousins.

Amy's friends left the table, and she hurriedly gathered her belongings, looking at him, brow creased with worry. He tried to smile to ease her concerns, but his stiff lips wouldn't cooperate. He made a move to stand. He wanted to follow her into the hall and explain why he was there, but his legs wouldn't lift him from the chair.

An echo of an odd fear rang in his bones. And then she was gone. He closed his eyes momentarily, hoping when he opened them again she would still be there. He had been holding his breath without realizing it. Now he let it out, forcing himself to breathe slowly.

"That went well," Connor snapped. "Did you see how white her face got when she saw you? She recognized you. You scared the hell out of her. Why? It doesn't make any sense. If she knows we're from the future and came to rescue her, why'd she run?"

Jack's voice was barely audible when he said, "She doesn't want to go home."

"What? Did you say she doesn't want to go home? Why? That's crazy. She just inherited millions of dollars. She has a relationship and a great job. Why stay here? Call me slow, but I don't get it." When Jack didn't answer, Connor reached across the table and poked him. "Explain."

Jack drew a series of deep breaths considering an explanation. Then he said, "Amy's mother died of breast cancer when she was in elementary school. Her father was a college baseball coach and an alcoholic. He died of liver disease a few years ago. She's an Olympian, an heiress, intelligent, beautiful, and is almost engaged to one of New York City's most eligible bachelors. For those of us looking at her life from the outside, she appears to have everything. To Amy, she's missing two important motivators: family and passion. Here in 1909, she has both."

"Sorry about her luck, but Joe Gilbert is on trial for his life. Staying here isn't an option. It's time to suck it up, put her game face on, and do what has to be done. And if you won't tell her that, I will."

"Look at it from her perspective, Connor."

"With a man's life at stake, there is no other perspective."

"You need to understand where she's coming from."

"No, I don't. We need to grab her, get back to New York, recover the diamond brooch, and go home. That's all I need to understand." Connor's tone screamed unease and impatience.

Jack gave him a piercing look. "What's going on with you? Why are you in such a hurry?"

"No reason."

"Bullshit. Fess up."

Connor's face reddened. "There's nothing to confess."

Jack sat back and scratched his jaw, watching his friend shift uncomfortably in the chair. Connor was a trained detective, a veteran of the finest police force in the world. He never shifted uncomfortably anywhere. There was only one reason for this kind of change in his behavior—a woman.

"You've met someone, haven't you?"

"What gave you that idea?" Connor said tersely.

"For starters, you're blushing."

"I'm not blushing."

"Look in the mirror."

Connor didn't look in a mirror. He looked at his coffee as if he could read the future in the muddy sediment at the bottom of the cup.

"A woman is what your soul longs for, coffee is just the excuse."

"You're waxing poetic, Mallory."

"When you spend time in Turkish coffeehouses, you pick up a thing or two. If I were to read the shapes of the coffee sediment in your cup, what would they say? Hmm. You've spent most of the last three months in Colorado working with a real estate agent and a lawyer. At least one is a beautiful, sexy woman." Connor ignored him and drank his coffee. "I'm going with the real estate agent," Jack continued. "You would have spent more time with her, driving around the state, looking at property, having lunch together, maybe dinner, staying in the same hotel." Jack lifted his eyebrows. "What's her name?"

Connor gave an exaggerated sigh even as a smile began to form, small at first and then it broadened. "Olivia Kelly."

Jack sat back and slapped his hands on the table. "Well, I'll be damned. Can't believe you didn't tell me."

"Sorry, buddy. I didn't think you'd want to hear about her."

"I may have sworn off women, but I still want to hear about my friends' happiness. It's nice to know Cupid's bow doesn't need restringing."

Connor chuckled. "We'll talk about it later. Let's get back to Amy."

"Okay, here's my analysis. For the first time in several years, she has created a family with Maria and Isabella Ricci and Gabriele Moretti. She's spending time with her favorite baseball team, and has a job she enjoys."

"And," Connor said, "she's getting city-wide recognition for her reporting. Maybe more than she gets in the broadcasting booth."

"Hard to say." Jack glanced up to see Amy return to the table for a scarf folded over the back of her chair. Before she turned toward the door, their eyes met, and he sat motionless while a spark flared up in his gut like a lit match. She swept a loose curl back into the coiled bun at her neck.

Sunlight kissed her golden hair, a beauty on earth is but so rare, a lass the mother of my heir...

Why was he thinking in iambic pentameter when the most beautiful woman he'd ever seen stood frozen in a beam of morning sun? He pushed to his feet because he didn't know what else to do, and she ran out of the room.

"Come on. Let's go," he said.

"If what we overheard is correct, do you plan to grab her at Mount Washington?" Connor asked.

"We'll skip Mount Washington and catch up with her at the Carnegie Institute."

Connor scooted back from the table. "I was looking forward to lunch at the Oyster House. So your plan now is to grab her at the museum?"

"We won't have to grab her," Jack said with a hint of wry humor. "She'll go voluntarily."

"It sounds like you know her well."

"When she disappeared, I was fascinated by her story and wanted to figure out why she went back to 1909. I read everything I could find."

"You believe she'll do the right thing?" Connor asked.

"She won't let Joe Gilbert be convicted of a murder he didn't commit. She's a very honorable person." Jack rubbed his lower back, a habit developed over the past few months, but not because it hurt, at least physically. "As my sister is fond of saying, sometimes God's

The Diamond Brooch 223

plan isn't at all clear, and all you do is stumble around without any direction until you find your way, and even then, it's not always clear."

"We have a very clear path, Jack. Get Amy on the train. Beg, borrow, or steal the diamond brooch. Get the hell out of here. Bada bing, bada boom."

Jack swiped his jacket aside and linked both hands behind him, under his coattail and stalked out of the room with Connor at his side. "Good luck with that. Don't you know when men plan—"

"—God laughs. I know, but he's not laughing at this plan."

"If this mission gets as fucked up as the last one—"

"I know. You'll be the first one to remind me to listen for who's laughing now."

26

1909 Carnegie Institute, Pittsburgh—Amy

AFTER CHAMPAGNE FOR BREAKFAST, a tour of Mount Washington, and wine with lunch at the Oyster House, Amy, Blanche, and Jane took a taxi from the restaurant to the Carnegie Museums on Forbes Avenue. The taxi pulled into the carriage driveway and stopped in front of the Romanesque-style building.

"Where do we start?" Blanche asked.

If Amy had access to a smartphone, she would have jumped on the museum's website and taken a virtual tour so she would know what to expect. She had visited museums all over Europe and never entered one without a list of specific exhibits to see. To go in unprepared wasted time and energy, and she wasn't a wing-it kind of person.

The taxi driver pointed as he told them, "The entrance to the Museum of Natural History and the Museum of Art is on the left, and the Music Hall entrance is on the right."

"The hotel concierge said to start at the Museum of Natural History," Blanche said.

Amy paid the fare. She also paid the fares to Mount Washington and to the restaurant, and she paid for lunch. When neither of the women offered, Amy realized they thought she was entertaining them in return for interviews. Paying all expenses had been her initial plan, but she was enjoying their company so much, she forgot the outing was work-related. She would add the fares and lunch to her expense report, and the newspaper would reimburse her.

As they walked toward the entrance, Jane said, "This is a massive building. Do you think we can see all the exhibits in one afternoon?"

"If we don't dawdle," Amy said. "Or we can split up. You two want to see the art exhibits, and I want to see the dinosaurs and the sculptures."

"We don't want you to go by yourself," Jane said. "We can hurry through the art exhibits and then go see the dinosaurs."

"I've toured lots of museums by myself, so I'll be perfectly safe looking at dinosaurs. I doubt anyone will accost me there. You two go look at the art, and I'll meet you back here at the entrance in…what?"—she checked the time on the hall clock—"say, two hours?"

She watched Jane and Blanche march off arm in arm to find their way to the upstairs exhibits. They were sweet women, devoted to their husbands, and, as far as Amy could tell, the husbands were devoted to their wives. The Giants equipment manager didn't keep a special cigar box where wedding rings were deposited during road trips.

Amy picked up a museum brochure, perused it quickly, then followed the signs to the Hall of Sculpture. She didn't know exactly what to expect while she walked up several steps, but it certainly wasn't what she found. A gasp, a disbelieving stare, and giddiness, all in one. She intended to stand right there, not move, and take it all in, even if it took her entire allotted two hours.

According to the brochure, the room was inspired by the Parthenon's inner sanctuary, complete with a double tier of columns. Directly below the skylight was a plaster reproduction of the carved frieze that originally graced the exterior of the Parthenon's inner sanctuary. The room was constructed with brilliant white marble from the same quarries in Greece that provided the stone for the Parthenon. Sixty-nine plaster-cast reproductions of Egyptian, Near Eastern, Greek, and Roman sculptures occupied the ground floor. The balcony had a decorative iron railing to allow viewing from the second floor.

She moved from one reproduction to the next, reading descriptions, and had almost circled around to the entrance when a man's voice said, "Excuse me."

She spun around and, without thinking, responded the same way she did at the Polo Grounds, where she'd been given carte blanche access to the field, clubhouse, and grandstands, "May I help you? Are you lost?"

"Probably," a man said.

Her hand flew to her chest, she gasped. "It's...you." She had thought his vulnerability swam off him in waves, but up close, his raw sexuality was a full-blown tsunami. She stepped back to create space between them, wondering how this man, out of hundreds she had met, could trigger this sort of upheaval in her. The waves swept away her sass. When the sass found its way back, she said, "You were in the restaurant at the hotel."

"I'm Jack Mallory."

"Of course, you are, and I'm Danielle Steele."

"I know Danielle, and she has thirty years on you."

"Then I'm Nora Roberts."

"Nora has at least twenty-five, and so does Diana Gabaldon. Anybody else you want to try?"

"No. I've run out of authors. Ask me about baseball players—"

"—then you'll outrun me by a mile."

Amy glanced at the doorway to see if Blanche and Jane were on their way to rescue her. They weren't. "I recognized you in the restaurant from the jacket on a book in Laurette's sitting room. It must have been a much earlier book." She scratched at her temples. "You have more gray now."

"Thanks for reminding me."

She cocked her head to study him more closely, and found herself wondering if he could throw a curve ball...from a reclining position...while on top of her...kissing her with his Cupid's bow lip...

Her face heated. "I haven't read anything you've written. Are you any good?"

"That's a loaded question."

"I'll load the baseball feeder and see how many you can hit out of the park."

"I can throw a pretty mean curve ball, but I'm not a home run hitter."

The conversation verged on the surreal. "Whichever genie bottle you popped out of, you can get back in."

"I can't," he said.

His presence would ruin everything for her, and his presence right now dominated the gallery. She wanted to snap her fingers and poof—make him disappear. "Why are you here?" she demanded.

"I've come to take you home."

"I would have gone with you two months ago, but now it's too late." She walked toward the doorway. "I'm going upstairs." He followed her. "Go away."

"I can't."

"Trust me. You can."

"Amy, stop."

She turned, glaring, and punched her hands on her hips. Maybe she could annihilate him with a death ray stare. "You're too late, Mallory. I have a life, friends, and a job I love. I'm not going back with you."

He threw up his left hand in a stop position, "Okay. No pressure." He had long, slim fingers, buffed, short nails, and veins and muscles leading up to muscular forearms.

A baseball would fit perfectly in his hand…

She would fit perfectly in his hand…

She intensified her death-ray glare. Why was he being agreeable? Better yet, why was she reacting so strongly to him? Now was not the time to have inappropriate thoughts about a man she didn't know—a man she found to be unpretentious, and his humor rushed into all the gaps in their conversation.

"May I walk with you?" He didn't break eye contact, which unnerved her.

"Where's your friend, the cop?"

"What makes you think he's a cop?"

"Because he looks like one."

"His name is Connor O'Grady. He's a friend and, yes, a former NYPD detective." Jack glanced over his shoulder then shrugged. "He's around here somewhere."

"Guarding the door so I can't leave?"

Mallory's eyes crinkled at the corners. "You're not a prisoner. You can leave any time."

"But if I do, he'll follow me?"

Mallory didn't answer. He didn't have to.

She took hold of the fabric of her dress and lifted it slightly above her ankles, then, with more confidence than she felt, lifted her chin and climbed regally up the stairs, hoping to lose him along the way. No such luck. His bootheels clacked on the marble floor right behind her. She crossed over to the railing and looked down.

"How'd you know I was here?"

He leaned against the white column and crossed his arms. He was built like a pitcher—tall, a lanky lefty, handsome—an athletic phenom.

"I heard you and the other ladies discuss your plans."

Her hands wrapped the railing so tightly her fingers turned white. "You know that's not what I meant."

"There's an iconic picture of Ty Cobb sliding into home plate. You're standing on the baseline."

She pushed back and forth against the railing, as if building up enough momentum to launch herself to the other side. "I don't believe you."

"Then how do you think I found you?"

"You're Oz, hiding behind the curtain, turning knobs and sending unsuspected travelers to God knows where."

"Oz might exist, but I'm not him."

"Then how...?"

"The picture was on the cover of a new baseball book released last year. I was browsing at a bookstore, saw it, picked it up, and spotted you right away. I don't know if I would have made the connection if it hadn't been just a week since your disappearance."

"A week?" Fear hardened in her chest. "I left in October. It's now June. What took you so bloody long?" If he had come right away, she would gladly have gone home.

"But it was April when you arrived. Right? You've only been here two months."

"The first hour dragged on long enough to be a month. Tack one more onto your total."

He was quiet. So was she. They both had a lot to ask but no segue to the big questions. Finally, she went first. "I guess you have a diamond brooch, too."

"There's only one diamond, as far as we know. But the MacKlenna family has possession of four brooches: a ruby, sapphire, emerald, and amethyst."

A shiver passed over her, leaving her head spinning in its wake. She considered there might be more. But four? "If you want mine to add to your collection, it's not for sale."

"We discovered yesterday that, due to a scrivener's error, your brooch was sold at auction two weeks ago."

She gasped. "That's impossible. Stephen wouldn't have sold it without discussing it with me first."

"He claims he didn't know."

She moved away from the railing before she went with the kill-the-messenger option and shoved Jack over, head-first. "Are you always the bearer of such good news?"

"Once I had to pass along some bad news, but I did it quickly and ran away. I don't know how it was received."

"Do you make a joke out of everything?"

"Me? I'm not the jokester in the family."

"Oh, no? Then what are you?"

Something dark skittered through his eyes, but he recovered quickly, and it faded. "I'm the problem child."

Although she didn't want to find him charming, she did, and her mouth quirked in a tight smile. "They sent the problem child to get me. Terrific." She let her study of him travel over his smooth, too-handsome face, searching for a clue to his real intentions. "I disappeared in October. I arrived here in April. It's now June. How long have I been gone?"

"Eight months."

Her legs wobbled. "Oh God," she groaned, and grabbed the railing again. "Joe has to be heartsick."

Mallory tipped her face up with his finger, which put them barely a finger-width apart, and she held her breath, because he smelled like sin and salvation. A host of things unsaid passed between them, most of them indecipherable. If he wanted to scramble her, he did. He was about to say something, but instead backed away from her.

She took a breath, pulse hammering. She stared him down, praying he couldn't see her fear. "What is it you're not telling me?"

"Connor was a former NYPD detective, and his brother is still on the force."

She twirled her finger. "Speed it up. Get to it."

"The police opened an investigation into your disappearance within hours of when Joe reported you missing. Because of your relationship, he came under suspicion. They searched his car and found your blood in the trunk."

"Oh, that's easy to explain. A few months ago, I tripped, hit my head on the open trunk lid, and fell into the trunk. I wasn't seriously hurt. I just cut my head. I could have gotten a stitch or two, but I didn't want them to shave any part of my hair. In hindsight, I should have gone to the hospital. There would have been a record of the accident."

"He told them, but they didn't believe him. He's been charged with your murder."

"Murder?" She covered her face with her hands. "Oh, God." She shook her head. "Oh, God. Oh, God. Oh, God. How's that possible?" She looked at Jack, battling back the burn of tears. "Is he in jail?"

"He surrendered his passport, but the judge said he was still a flight risk. He locked Gilbert up and won't let him out. He's been there since Christmas."

Her stomach roiled. She put her hand to her mouth, bent over, gagging.

Jack put his hand on her back. "There's a spittoon by the door if you're going to be sick."

She held her hand out to be left alone until her stomach settled. She had to be practically at death's door to throw up. The queasiness would pass. It took a couple of minutes, but finally she straightened and leaned against the cool marble wall, resting the side of her face there.

He handed her a handkerchief with an interesting pineapple motif, and she dotted it against her face.

"Do you know who bought my brooch?" she asked.

"A businessman named Diamond Jim Brady."

She unbuttoned her top button and wiped away the perspiration at her neck. "I met him at Delmonico's. He's a friend of John McGraw's. If Diamond Jim knows how important it is to me, he'll sell it back."

"He gave it to Lillian Russell."

"The actress? She was with Diamond Jim when I met him. I'll ask John to invite her to a game so I can interview her."

Jack shook his head.

"Why are you shaking your head? It's a good idea."

"Lillian Russell leaves Saturday morning for an extended vacation in London."

"London?" Amy's throat went dry as her body clenched with abrupt, intense pain. An old, old wound ripped open, and out poured memories of the hopelessness that had consumed her life during her mother's final days.

The cosmos was conspiring against her, against Joe. He had been cooped up for months because of her, because of the damn brooch. The thought intensified her roiling stomach. This time she bolted across the room and threw up in the spittoon.

The weight of Jack's hand pressed softly against her back and remained there until her stomach emptied. "Wait here. I'll go find you a glass of water."

She wiped her mouth with his handkerchief, slid down the wall, and sat on the floor. She didn't care about the stares from other visitors. She didn't care about anything.

"Ma'am. Ma'am," a woman shook Amy's shoulder lightly. "Do you need assistance?"

Amy opened her eyes to see a woman's face pinched with concern. "No. There's nothing you can do."

Jack came up just then with a glass of water, and knelt beside Amy. "Here, darling. Drink this." He glanced up at the woman and said, "We just found out we'll be parents by winter."

"Oh, I see." The woman patted Amy's shoulder and took her leave.

Amy sipped the water, swished her mouth, and spit. Then repeated the sequence until the glass was empty. She wiped her mouth, wishing she had a toothbrush. "I can't believe you said that."

"Instead of visitors talking about a sick woman, they'll be smiling and snickering behind their hands. And you won't be harassed by the staff wondering if you need medical attention."

"Thank you, then. You're very thoughtful."

She made a move to stand, but before she could, Jack swooped her up, cradling her in his arms. She didn't have the energy to object, and rested her head against the hard muscle of his shoulder. As he walked, she had the impression of great physical power beneath the fabric of his suit. His arms didn't quiver from the burden of her weight. He carried her down the stairs and into an alcove where a sofa, deeply and richly upholstered with silky embroidery, was arranged with a side table and a vase of yellow roses.

Jack set her down on the sofa and slowly withdrew his powerful arms. She closed her eyes, hoping to hide her overwhelming visceral reaction to him, but doubted that would cover up the heated flush on her face, the heart palpitations, or the rapid breathing.

The light, purposeful approach of footsteps on the marble had her eyes popping open to see who was coming their way. It was the cop.

"What happened?" he asked.

"The oyster lunch didn't sit well. We're ready to go. Do you know where the other two women are?"

"They were at the last art exhibit a few minutes ago. They should be down shortly."

Amy recovered sufficiently to speak and extended her hand. "Hi, I'm Danielle Steele."

He shook it firmly. "Nice to meet you, Ms. Steel. I'm Connor O'Grady." He winked and one corner of his mouth crooked up. "My sister-in-law, Julie, reads all your books. You'll have to autograph one for me."

She gave him a thumbs-up. "I'll do what I can." She wasn't sure what to think of Mallory, but virile Connor O'Grady was an absolute heartthrob. There had to be a hospital for broken hearts in New York City. She needed space from these two men. Their testosterone levels were off the chart.

She unpinned her straw hat and fanned it in front of her face. "I need to go back to the hotel."

"I'll get the other women," Connor said. "Why don't you take Ms. Steel outside and flag our driver? I'll get a car for the others."

"I can't leave them," Amy said. "As cute as you are, you'll make them nervous. And I don't want to upset their husbands. Baseball players are so superstitious. They don't need anything else to worry about."

"Stay here, then. You can see them when they come down the stairs. Connor and I will go arrange transportation," Jack said.

"No, you stay with Ms. Steele," Connor said to Jack. "I can manage."

She scooted to make room on the small sofa. Jack squeezed in beside her, and she gave him a wistful smile. "I should tell Connor I'm not Danielle Steele."

"I wouldn't spoil it for him." Jack gave her a wicked grin. "Connor's a good man. Dependable and fiercely loyal. If you've got him on your side, you've got a friend for life."

"I guess that means you've got a friend for life."

Jack shrugged. "Connor's still thinking about it."

She sensed there was a chasm beneath Jack's easy shrug, but it was none of her business. "I was thinking about Lillian Russell," Amy said. "If she wants more than what Providence appraised the brooch for, then I won't have enough money to buy it back right now. Maybe I should wait and approach her when she returns from her trip."

"The Providence Loan Society is legally responsible. If she offers to sell it back, Providence will come up with the money, or we'll sue them."

"I don't want to do that. They've been good to me."

"You mean Thomson's been good to you."

She forced a smile to show she wasn't at all affected by his tone or cleverly directed innuendo. "I have a boyfriend. Remember?"

"You don't seem to be in a hurry to return to him."

And there was a question without a question mark. What Jack really wanted to know was why she wasn't in a hurry to return home to Joe. She heard it in Jack's voice. But why did he care?

"Joe hasn't even been born yet. What does it matter if I go home today, tomorrow, or next week?"

"I'm not sure it does. To be honest, Amy, we don't fully understand why or how the brooches work, or why they send travelers to particular time periods."

"Can I go back to the moment I opened the brooch?"

Jack raked his fingers through his thick hair, revealing more gray underneath. "I don't know. That would be ideal, though. We can try."

She leaned her head against the curve of the high-back sofa, closed her eyes, and continued fanning her face. "Have you been here before?"

"To 1909? No. I've traveled back to 1865, 1881, and 1944."

"Do you go home, or just travel around and write books?"

"We go home, live our lives. When we discover another person has disappeared with a brooch, we get involved."

"We? You and Connor?"

"The MacKlenna Family."

"Who are they?"

"It's complicated, but the short answer is your six-times great-grandfather was James Thomas MacKlenna, and we can all trace our lineage back to him."

"We're all related?"

"Distantly."

"Connor, too?"

"Connor, too. His sister JL, her fiancé Kevin, and her former partner Pete are also in New York City working on the brooch angle. There are several more people, but I don't want to confuse you right now. You'll meet them all eventually."

"I've been confused for two months. Do you know why I'm here?"

"To get baseball cards."

She opened her eyes and glared at him. "Seriously?"

"Other than your passion for the Giants, I don't know."

"Why wouldn't the brooch take me home?"

He gazed at her, and the look was almost a physical touch. "We don't know. Kit MacKlenna's brooch worked whenever she needed it to. My sister and I used the sapphire brooch to come and go. Kenzie Wallis-Manning was given the emerald brooch and got a one-way ticket to London the week before D-Day. Fourteen of us used the ruby, sapphire, and emerald to go on a reunion trip to San Francisco in 1881. When the brooch doesn't work, at least in our experience, it's because there's another person involved. Someone you wouldn't have met without the brooch interfering in your life."

"I've met so many people I never would have met, and my life is richer for it, but why did you come? Did the MacKlenna Family draw straws and you got the short one? Oh, no, wait. You're the problem child."

"That's true, but in the spirit of full disclosure, I discovered Catherine Lily, the woman in the portrait hanging in your new mansion, is possibly the twin sister of a woman I met in San Francisco in 1881."

"And you want to ask Catherine Lily about the woman you met?"

"I don't believe she knows anything, but I want to know what her adoptive mother knows. She might have told Catherine Lily about her birth parents."

"I don't know if I can face her. I stole her clothes."

Jack laughed. "You inherited everything in the house. Including her clothes."

"That's one way to look at it," Amy said. "But I did it with intent. Which makes me really guilty." She was quiet for a moment, and then she asked. "Do you think ESPN will give me my job back?"

"I don't know. Do you want it?"

She stopped fanning her hat for a moment and thought. "I loved my job there, but I've discovered I have a knack for connecting with readers. I want to write, maybe in a Sunday section, or a blog, or *Sports Illustrated*. We'll see what happens when I get home."

"If we can go back to the twenty-first century and arrive the moment before you said the words, nothing will have changed in your life."

"Will I remember what happened here?"

"You should remember everything."

She fanned the hat faster, trying to dry her tears before they trickled down her face. "I don't want to forget the people I've met or the things I've done."

"I don't blame you. It sounds like you've done well here." He pulled out his pocket watch and opened it. "We have to catch the afternoon train to New York, and it leaves in two hours."

A swish of skirts and briskly clicking heels announced Blanche before she called out to Amy. "There you are," she said entering the alcove.

Jack sprang to his feet with surprising agility for a man his size who wasn't a professional athlete, and he bowed politely. "Mrs. McGraw, Mrs. Mathewson. I'm Jack Mallory. I'm afraid Miss Spalding isn't feeling well."

Jane sat in the place Jack vacated and took over the hat-waving task. "My, dear, you do look dreadfully pale. We must take you back to the hotel."

"I'll go find us a taxi," Blanche said.

"That's not necessary, Mrs. McGraw."

Blanche turned to look at Jack, then pointed at him like an ump calling a strike. "You're the man from the restaurant this morning. What are you doing here?" Then with hands on her hips, said accusingly, "You followed us?"

Amy spread her arms like an ump calling a runner safe, and almost groaned when she realized both she and Blanche were using baseball signals. "He's a friend. There's been a tragedy, and I have to return to New York and make plans to go home."

Jane's bewildered gaze bounced from Blanche to Amy and back again. "To South Carolina? For how long?"

"I don't know yet," Amy said. "It's possible I'll have to stay. I won't know until I get there."

"That's just dreadful. John will be heartbroken," Blanche said.

"The entire team will be heartbroken," Jane added. "Not to mention the rest of New York City, when they wake up and can't start their day reading your entertaining prose."

Connor entered the alcove. "The taxis are waiting."

Amy retrieved the hat from Jane. "I might not see you again before I leave. Please tell John and Christy I said goodbye. Oh, and tell John to do whatever he thinks is appropriate with the glove."

Blanche tilted her head curiously. "What glove?"

"He'll know," Amy said, returning Blanche's hat to her.

Connor took Blanche's arm and escorted her out of the building while Amy and Jane followed, huddled in conversation. "Listen to me carefully," Amy said. "A war is coming in a few years. Don't let Matty join the Chemical Service. It will make him sick, but don't mention it to him until the time is right. He's a brilliant ballplayer, and will always be remembered, as will John."

Jane's head jerked back. "How do you know this?"

"I can't explain it other than to say I have a gift. I'm not wrong about this. If Matty does join the Chemical Service, tell him to be very careful in France. Accidents happen."

Jane, a bit pale now, hugged Amy. "I won't forget."

Next, Amy hugged Blanche. "Thank you so much for everything, and for befriending me. You and John and Jane and Matty have been dear friends, and I'll never forget you."

"Travel safely, my dear."

Connor helped both women into the taxi and paid the fare back to the hotel, then joined Jack and Amy in the car they hired for the day.

"Nice ladies," Connor said. "They're very upset."

"Yes, they are, but they'll hide it well from their husbands, at least until after the games. This was supposed to be a fun baseball weekend, and now my life has been turned upside down again."

"I think it's been turned right side up," Connor said. "You'll be going home soon."

"It doesn't feel very right side up at the moment." She rubbed her forehead, shaking her head, trying to understand it all, but she couldn't. "I need to go to the hotel and pack my clothes."

"We…uh…did that for you," Jack said. "To save time."

She was aghast and turned on him. "You what? Went through my personal things?"

"You're very neat and tidy," Jack said. "Connor and I both have sisters, nieces, and have—or had—girlfriends. We know all about female undies and feminine products."

Her face heated, and she wanted to smack them for invading her privacy.

"We were very respectful," Connor said, wearing a serious cop face, but she was pretty sure there was a grin beneath it.

She swallowed hard, thinking back to how she left her guest room. Soiled clothes were packed in a dirty clothes bag. Toiletries were in their proper place in her small travel case. Corsets, drawers, chemises, petticoats were folded neatly in the dresser, and could easily be transferred to her suitcase. There was nothing there to embarrass her. However, if they had packed her lacy, modern-day silky bras and thongs, she would have been mortified.

Her temper simmered while the taxi drove through Pittsburgh, and by the time they arrived at the train station, it had cooled. They were on a tight schedule, and Jack and Connor's actions had saved thirty to forty-five minutes. She couldn't fault their efficiency.

Two hours later and emotionally drained, Amy relaxed in the sleeping compartment of the private railroad car Jack rented for their return trip to New York City. As she closed her eyes, thrilled she didn't have to nap sitting up, she breathed deeply, unable, once again, to find fault with Jack and Connor's efficiency.

She was obviously traveling with pros, boys who knew how to play the game.

27

1909 New York City—Jack

THE TRAIN FROM PITTSBURGH approached Grand Central Station in New York City around midnight. Jack's butt was dragging from weeks of little sleep. A lumpy mattress was a reasonable excuse to stay awake the night before, but if the constant clacking of the wheels and the gentle sway of a railroad car couldn't put him to sleep, then he had to admit he was the textbook definition of an insomniac.

He stretched his arms over his head, then groaned at the stabbing pain in his shoulders. He lowered them slowly, wincing, then clapped a sleeping Connor on the arm. "We're approaching the station."

Connor rolled over on the sofa and sat up, scratching his balls. "Did you get any sleep?"

"Several hours. How about you?"

"You're a lying son of a bitch. You got up six times to piss, refilled your whisky glass three times, read a folder full of memos, and scribbled out ten pages of notes on your legal pad."

"I assume I didn't burp, or you'd have mentioned that, too."

Subtle tension creased Connor's brow. "I'm only doing my job."

A catch in the middle of Jack's chest caused a light gasp. "And what job is that, exactly?"

"Elliott asked us to keep an eye on you."

Jack harrumphed, looked off into the distance to a place far outside the walls of the train. "He doesn't trust me."

"He trusts you to do what has to be done, but he's worried over you for months, and just wanted to be sure someone would be with you if—"

"If what? If I broke down again? I did that for weeks after Carolina Rose died. I've dealt with it, and moved on."

Connor got up and hitched his hip against the side of a chair. "The thing about grief, which I discovered when mom died, is you can't predict how long it will last, or when it will show up again and smack you in the face. You know, like it's mad because you forgot about it for an hour or a day or a week. It's all part of the process. It sucks."

He paused, looked off to the side briefly, took a breath, then continued, "Mom was the center of life at home. We were devastated. We had little Austin to care for, and that kept us going, but watching Pops mourn nearly killed us. Elliott understands grief, and he wanted to be sure we'd take care of you."

Jack had trouble swallowing past the lump in his throat.

"Father Paul told us that everyone who lives long enough to love will experience a great loss sometime in their life. But you can't let fear of losing again take away the joy of living."

One of the hardest lessons Jack learned over recent months was to accept compassion from his friends. It wasn't easy for him, but when he took a risk and accepted what they offered, he always walked away a few pounds lighter.

"You're right. It comes out of nowhere and hammers you to your knees." He gave Connor a bro hug. "Thanks, man. I appreciate it." He punched Connor lightly in the arm. "I'm going to wake Amy. Be right back."

Connor sipped from a cold cup of coffee and grimaced. "We're only a few minutes away from the station."

"Huh?"

"I don't know about you," Connor said, "but when I wake my lady friends, it always takes a while, if you get my drift."

"I get it, O'Grady, but it's drifting up the wrong bank. She's off-limits. No dice."

Connor made a fist, blew on it, then flung his hand open like he was throwing dice. "Of course she is." He returned to the sofa and closed his eyes, chuckling.

The former cop was professional to the nth degree. He rarely slipped out of character unless he was with one of his brothers, Pete, or Austin. Jack liked him, trusted him, and relied on his judgment, and was even learning to read his deadpan delivery style. The sneak peek into Connor's love life, and the exchange they just shared told Jack he was close to being accepted into the tight-knit O'Grady circle. And their acceptance was more important to his state of mind than he previously realized.

Jack steered toward the rear of the private railroad car and knocked on the door of the sleeping compartment. "Amy." He knocked again. "Amy. The train's coming into the station. We're almost back in New York."

She opened the door, yawning. Short strands of hair fell free of a ribbon-wrapped ponytail and created a wavy golden frame around her face. A crumpled white shift, revealing every luscious curve, skimmed her body. He blinked, and his thoughts went to a toasty blanket on a cold winter's night. His stomach betrayed him, turning over and over, as if he was on a roller coaster, plunging down a dangerous length of track.

"What?" she demanded, in a voice both deep and sultry.

"We're here. Time to"—his eyes lingered too long on the swell of her breasts. Instead of looking into her eyes, he looked at his feet so he wouldn't telegraph every lascivious thought in his pea-sized man-brain—"get dressed."

"What if I don't?"

The mind of his sixteen-year-old-self didn't rise to her challenge, but his body did. He ignored his quickly developing problem. Modern jeans wouldn't have been as forgiving as loose-fitting trousers.

"You'll end up back in Pittsburgh."

"Oh, okay. Will you help me with my corset?"

What was it with Edwardian women? Why couldn't they wear clothes they could put on themselves? And why did women *assume* he could handle a corset?

"I don't have enough energy to go through the motions." She picked the garment up off the chair, placed the busk in the center of her midriff, and snapped the metal loops and studs.

"You should be well rested. You slept for ten hours."

"Really? It only feels like a couple."

Jack adjusted the modesty panel behind the laces and pulled the lacing, snugging her into the corset.

"A little bit tighter," she said.

"JL asked me to loosen her laces yesterday, and you asked me to tighten yours today. Maybe I should get a job as a ladies' maid."

She turned, and her keen eyes challenged him. "Is JL your"—she glanced down at his hand—"significant other? You're not wearing a wedding ring."

"Oh, God, no. JL's my cousin. She's engaged to Kevin, another cousin."

"I didn't think cousins could marry."

He made an audible sigh. "You're joking, right?"

She squinted, a thinking expression he had noticed before. "I thought you were quicker than that, Mallory. You mentioned JL. Don't you remember?"

"Yes, but I didn't expect you to."

She puffed out her cheeks, looked up, and blew softly. The resulting gust of air caused wisps of hair to momentarily float up off her forehead before settling back down in front of her turquoise eyes. He had a sudden urge to gently push the strands of hair away from her face, but he stopped—he was already pushing the limits of his self-control.

"Catherine Lily is the great-granddaughter of James Thomas MacKlenna," she said. "Connor O'Grady has a sister, JL, who has a fiancé, Kevin. If you'll give me the rest of the family names, I'll remember them, too."

Without losing a step, he said, "Elliott Fraser is the Chairman of the Board for MacKlenna Corporation. His wife, Meredith Montgomery, is the president of Montgomery Wineries."

"The winery in California? That's impressive."

"They have a son, James Cullen. Elliott has another son, Kevin, who is engaged to—"

"JL," she said. "What's her real name?"

"Jenny Lynn."

"I'd go by JL, too."

"Kenzie Wallis-Manning McBain is married to David McBain, and they have three children. Kenzie is the corporation's legal counsel, and David is president. They are both former military. My sister, Charlotte, is a surgeon in Virginia. She's married to Braham McCabe, who was born in 1824. He was a lawyer, but now he's a horse breeder and vintner. They have two children, and another on the way. And lastly, Kit MacKlenna Montgomery is James MacKlenna's granddaughter. She's married to Cullen Montgomery. Kit is Elliott's goddaughter."

"So she's a traveler, too?"

"She was born in 1826, but spent her first twenty-five years in the future before going back to the mid-1800s. It's another long story. Anyway, she and her husband are Meredith's six-times great-grandparents. They started the winery in Napa, and are currently in Lexington visiting."

"They left the nineteenth-century to come visit for a while? Really?" Amy asked.

"They came home for health reasons, and will eventually go back to the winery in the 1880s."

Amy stretched and twisted, then idly picked up the dress she folded over the arm of the chair hours earlier and shimmied it over her head. Without asking, Jack set about buttoning the tiny buttons.

"People really can come and go," she said. "That means I should be able to use my brooch whenever I want."

He shrugged. "I'm not sure why you would want to live in two different worlds."

"I don't know if I do, but I'd like to have the option." She patted her hair, then her face. He expected her to pat her nose, chin, and arms, too, as if signaling a base runner. "I think I've got it now."

"What?"

"The names. Elliott is married to Meredith, and they have two children named James Cullen and Kevin. Meredith's ancestors, Kit and Cullen, started her winery. Kenzie is married to David. They were both soldiers. Your surgeon sister, Charlotte, is married to Braham, who is from the nineteenth-century. JL is engaged to Kevin, Elliott's older son, and she has a brother named Connor and another brother who is a current cop—"

"She has four brothers," Jack said. "Connor, Jeff, Patrick, and Shane, along with a son named Austin, and their father, Pops, and a former partner, Pete."

"Okay. JL has four brothers, a son, a father, and a former partner named Pete. And there are also seven and a half other children."

"There's one more child I haven't mentioned, Emily, who is Kit's ward. We'll save her story for later." Jack crossed his arms and leaned against the doorframe. "You're impressive, though. How do you keep all those facts straight in your mind? I've got sticky notes posted on sticky notes."

She opened a small travel case and grabbed a handful of pins and a hairbrush. He stretched to see what was inside, since he hadn't looked when they packed up her guest room at the hotel. He was being nosy, but he was curious. There was a toothbrush, Colgate toothpaste, talcum powder, a bottle of Everdry antiperspirant, a bar of Pears soap, pins, hair combs, an extra set of laces, and half-dozen ribbons in assorted colors.

She snapped the box shut. "When I was little, I wanted to remember the players on my dad's teams so I could call them by name. But they changed every year, and it frustrated me. I was determined to find a way to remember them, so I did a little research, and came up with a system that works for me. It's how I remembered everything about the 1909 Giants."

"Will you teach me?"

"I've been doing this for thirty years. It might take a while. Do you have that much time?" She untied her hair and ran the brush through the tangles.

He took the brush from her. "Since I'm your lady's maid today, let me." He brushed every silky strand from her crown to her shoulders, even the wispy strands falling into her eyes.

She rolled her head back and moaned. "You're hired. I hope you don't charge much. How'd you learn to do that?"

"Grooming horses, but manes and tails pale in comparison to women's hair."

And horses don't moan in ecstasy.

But he refrained from mentioning it. He didn't want her to stop the sensual moans.

He replaced the brush with his fingers and gently raked them through the strands, letting them fall to her shoulders. "The tangles are gone."

My hard-on is not.

A mesmerizing lemon, ginger, and lime scent wafted around her. He would never again smell lemon and ginger without thinking of her.

She pulled her hair back into a tight bun, and Jack handed her pins to secure it neatly at her nape. "Next time we're stuck on a plane, train, or automobile, since you don't need lady's-maid training, I'll introduce you to a memory technique devised in ancient Rome and Greece called—"

"—loci. I've heard of it, but never tried it."

"I don't know what I'd do now without it. Baseball is a slow game, so we have a lot of air time to fill while we're in the broadcasting booth. My job is to share details and statistics. My ability to remember information makes me good at my job."

"I've watched films of you in the booth. You're fantastic. You always have an interesting fact to contribute, whether a guy played in the 40's, the 90's, or is currently playing. You make it sound natural, like an everyday conversation. I haven't read your columns yet, but I can see why you're a hit."

"And you're telling me I have to quit while I'm at the top of my game."

"If it wasn't for Joe's situation…"

"I know and I understand. If I had listened to Joe, gone to the hospital, and gotten a stitch or two, he wouldn't have been arrested. I'll never let my stubborn streak get in the way of doing something good for me ever again." She opened a door to a small closet then closed it. "Do we have access to a bathroom?"

He pointed over his shoulder. "It's at the other end of the car."

"Thanks. I'll only be a few minutes."

Jack watched her walk away with her little traveling case, and had a vision of her disappearing into a cloud. He reached out to catch it, but it vanished between his fingers, and floated inside his chest, squeezing his heart so hard it could hardly beat. He shook his head at how overwrought he sounded, but it was how he felt, and it conjured memories he didn't want on the surface of his brain right now.

Instead, he gazed out the window, watched the train pull into the station, and thought about baseball. The four years he spent as a scholarship baseball player at the University of Virginia were probably the happiest of his life. But he gave up baseball, said no to the Yankees, and packed his bags to attend Harvard Law School.

Would he have met Amy sooner if he'd been a ballplayer? He rubbed his shoulder, thinking about the hours of icing after he pitched a game. If she remembered him at all, it would have been as a promising young pitcher who retired early with a bad arm. And who would want such a legacy? He moved away from the window, picked up his files and notes, and stowed them in his briefcase.

Bad decisions were better than indecision. Right? And trying to take the edge off with a well-timed wrist flick—a perfect curve ball—wouldn't create a better version of himself.

28

1909 New York City—Amy

BEFORE AMY LEFT the train, she wanted to be clear about the plan going forward. "Where are you staying tonight? And what have you planned for tomorrow...or rather, later today?"

Jack picked up his duffel and briefcase. "We have suites at the Hotel Netherland on 59th Street, and we'll have to talk to the others before we decide what's next."

"Is JL at the hotel?"

Connor slung the strap of his duffel over one of his shoulders, then took Amy's suitcase. "Should be. If she gets arrested again, she can just stay in jail."

Amy shivered. "She was arrested?" Amy had talked with the newshounds who reported on crime in the city. From the stories she'd heard, she couldn't imagine the dreadful conditions in The Tombs. She never had a run-in with the cops, not even a traffic ticket, and being around a former cop now, while it brought some sense of security, caused just as much unease.

They exited the train and climbed the steps to the main concourse.

"JL's arrest is a long story—" Connor said.

"All your stories are long. So are Jack's. Do you have a short one?"

"I'll see what I can do," Connor said, laughing. "Back to JL's

The Diamond Brooch

arrest... Jack has a license to practice law, but he doesn't practice. His grand idea for JL's court appearance was to dress her up like a frail heiress. He had her corset tied so tight she couldn't breathe, in hopes the judge would see a breathless *ingénue* and not a hard-ass former detective who beat up a cop while handcuffed in a police wagon."

"Whoa. That's not a short story. That's a tome." Amy laughed. "I take it the ruse worked."

"Almost suffocated her, but yeah, it did."

They entered the cavernous concourse, and Amy was struck by how quiet it was without the bustling crowds. "Look," she said. "I didn't notice the other day when we left the city, but doesn't it look weird without the September 11 flag hanging between the columns?"

"Yeah, you're right, and there're no ticket vending machines, and no golden clock," Connor said.

"If I tell you to meet me under the clock, you'd meet where it will be one day, right?" Amy asked.

"Right there," Connor said, pointing to where the information booth would stand.

Jack glanced in the direction Connor was pointing, and he shrugged in a disinterested manner. "Come on. Let's get out of here."

"Hold up," Amy said. "You've never been here before, have you? I mean"—she lowered her voice—"in our time."

Jack shook his head. "Yesterday was my first visit."

Connor chucked Jack on the arm. "Mallory flies around on private jets. He's too good for public transportation."

Jack pushed opened the door leading to 42nd Street, and they walked out into the muggy night air. "I take taxis."

"That's bullshit. You always have a car service."

Amy laughed. "You bicker like a couple of old ladies."

Jack raised his arm and hailed the taxi at the taxi stand on the corner of Park Avenue. "Do you see a car service waiting for us? Because I don't."

A four-person yellow taxi pulled up, and the driver exited the vehicle to help with the luggage.

"I was thinking about where I should go tonight," Amy said, climbing into the taxi. "Maria and Isabella aren't expecting me back until late Sunday night. If I walk in now, I'll scare them to death."

Connor sat in the front passenger seat next to the driver. "You can go with us and stay with JL."

"I don't want to impose."

"She won't mind," Connor said. "JL grew up in a small house with her son, four brothers, and very little personal space. You'd think she'd hoard whatever space she could get now, but she doesn't. And you're not the first woman we've pawned off on her."

Jack groaned.

Amy patted Connor on the back of his shoulder. "You must be the youngest in the family. You sure know how to make a woman feel welcome."

He jerked his head around. "I'm sorry. I didn't mean it the way it came out. I mean—"

"Connor," Jack said, "shut up."

Connor couldn't let Jack have the last word, so he added, "JL's the baby of the family. With three older brothers, she had more protection than she wanted."

Since meeting Jack and Connor, Amy felt like she'd been dropped into the middle of the third season of the MacKlenna Family TV series, with a wonderfully nuanced plot, and a massive, quirky cast of characters, and she'd never catch up with the rest of the fans.

At this hour of the night, while the streets weren't empty, they weren't congested, either. During the mile drive to the neo-Romanesque, seventeen-story luxury Hotel Netherland, she sensed a stillness in the men, not because they were tired, but because they were mentally preparing for what was to come.

The taxi pulled up in front of the hotel across the street from Grand Army Plaza and the Cornelius Vanderbilt II house, one of 5th Avenue's grandest Gilded Age mansions. From what she could see in the limited light of the streetlamps, the only structure still standing in the twenty-first century besides the hotel was the General Sherman statue.

Amy walked between Jack and Connor through the hotel's lobby. It wasn't unusual for a woman to be seen at the Hotel Netherland late at night with an escort, since the hotel was one of the see-and-be-seen spots in the city.

Jack approached the desk for the room key.

"Good evening, Mr. Mallory," the clerk said.

"Good evening, Charles. My cousin, Miss Spalding, and I just arrived from Pittsburgh. Since it's so late, she'll be staying with her cousin Jenny Lynn O'Grady in room 1720, instead of traveling uptown to her apartment."

Charles, a middle-aged man crisply dressed in hotel livery with a striped cravat and a comb-over slicked down with pomade, said, "We're delighted to have Miss Spalding with us this evening. My wife is looking forward to reading your interviews with the Giants' wives." He blushed. "I have to admit, I am, too. And she thoroughly enjoyed your interview and seeing your photograph in *Vogue*."

Amy tilted her head slightly, smiling. "The first interview will be in the paper tomorrow. I hope you both enjoy the article."

"I'll be sure to tell her." The clerk spun around and faced a wall lined with small mailboxes, turning his head side to side until he found box 1720. He withdrew a room key. "Is there anything else I can do for you, Mr. Mallory?" he asked, handing both to Jack.

"Is the restaurant still open? Miss Spalding would like to order a light dinner," Jack said.

"Until three," Charles said. "A copy of the menu is in your suite. You can telephone the operator, and she will connect you with the dining room."

"Marvelous." Amy turned to Jack. "I can't wait to see Cousin Jenny Lynn again. How long has it been? Three years?"

Jack picked up on the question she pitched him and answered as if he'd memorized a script, complete with appropriate Southern inflection. "She thought it had been four years, my dear, since you both visited me in Virginia."

"Four? Well, I'll be. She has a better memory than I do, then."

"No one has a better memory than you, Miss Spalding," Charles said. "You remember every pitch Matty threw last season."

Amy touched his arm lightly. "How kind of you to say so, but I think I missed a couple." She put her finger against her lips. "Shh. Don't tell anyone."

He puffed up and tugged on the ends of his vest to straighten it, even though it didn't need straightening. "No, ma'am. They won't hear it from me."

"Good night, Charles," Amy said.

Jack took her arm and ushered her toward the elevator. "That went well, Cousin Amy."

"Thanks for playing along. I think my reputation remains intact." She looked up at him and studied his face. "In fact, it's the second time you've done that. It's like you can read my mind. You can't, can you? I mean, if you could, all you'd read are baseball statistics. Unless you love baseball, you'd find my mind rather boring."

"I read all the box scores. I don't have your memory for statistics, but I remember game-changing plays. And I seriously doubt any information you've got stored up there"—he tapped her forehead with the tip of his finger—"would be boring."

Connor met them at the elevator. "Did you protect Amy's reputation while you were chatting up the desk clerk? We wouldn't want anyone to get the wrong impression."

"It's intact for now," she said. "Mallory always knows what to say. It's like he's reading from a script. I'm going to catch him dropping a line before this is all over. But where did you disappear to?" she asked Connor.

"I looked inside the bar area to see if Pete was there. He's not."

"Pete? As in JL's former partner?"

"Right," Connor said. "You should probably stay away from him. He's a great cop, but has a terrible reputation with women." Although Connor disparaged his friend, he said it with a small smile playing around his mouth and eyes.

Amy nodded slowly. "I'll remember the advice."

The elevator operator delivered them to the seventeenth floor. When they stepped off, Connor pointed to the right. "The rooms are that way." They walked down an empty hall until he stopped and knocked. When no one answered, he said, "JL must be asleep."

"Or else they're all in my suite." Jack went to the next door and inserted a key.

As he unlocked the door, Amy quickly glanced up and down the hall, trying to hide her unease. Her reputation wasn't impugned yet, but it didn't mean she'd be free of gossip if anyone saw her entering a hotel room with two men, even if they were her cousins. By early twentieth-century standards, the corset-tying and hair-brushing incident on the train was scandalous enough. If word of that got out, she'd never write another article for the paper.

Why was she so concerned, when she was on her way back to the future? Because, dang it, her reputation was all she owned, and if she had to return to the future, she wanted to be remembered as an honorable woman. An honorable woman who believed any man sensitive enough to stand by her side while she threw up could be trusted with a hairbrush.

On reflection though, she might trust Jack, but she wasn't so sure about herself. She shivered, aware of him as a virile, living, breathing man, and the heat of his energy left a sensory memory of his hands in her hair. How long would it last? A day, a week, the rest of her life?

Jack pushed open the door to the suite. The aroma of cheese, garlic, tomatoes, onions, peppers, and yeasty bread wafted over them.

"Smells delicious," Amy said.

Two men and a woman sat at a table eating pizza. "There's plenty. Come join us," the woman said. She was striking and petite, in her mid-thirties, with auburn hair and green eyes.

"Where'd it come from?" Jack asked.

"Lombardi's, the original pizzeria in Little Italy. Pete was out late doing reconnaissance and brought it back." The woman brushed bread crumbs off slim-fitting trousers and a silk blouse, and crossed the room, sidestepping Jack with the lithe grace of a ballerina. The outline of a gun in a waist holster was visible beneath her white blouse.

She extended her hand. "Hi, I'm JL, and this guy"—She pointed to an unnervingly handsome man walking toward her with dark-brown hair and deep-set brown eyes—"is my fiancé, Kevin Allen." She pointed to the second man. "And the guy stuffing his face is Pete Parrino."

Pete rose to his feet and hustled over to shake Amy's hand. If Kevin was unnervingly handsome, Pete, a few inches shorter than Kevin, was a hunk, dark and swarthy. Rolled-up shirtsleeves revealed ropy arms lightly dusted with dark hair. He was too hot to touch. No. Correction. Too hot to handle. And when he smiled, Amy heard the bubbling of hearts melting around the world.

There was enough testosterone in the room to supply an entire baseball team for a season. Where did these guys come from? They were handsome, sexy, gorgeous men, but they had something else, a deep substance to them, a purpose beyond a mission. And while she hadn't seen them fight, she sensed that beneath their gentle demeanor, they were invincible warriors.

Connor yanked off his jacket, slung it on a chair, and commandeered JL's seat before he quickly dove in for a large bite of the pizza on her plate. "Hey, stop that," she said. "That's mine. Get your own."

Pete shoveled a piece of pizza onto a plate and handed it to Amy, along with a beer. "I'm assuming anyone who lives and breathes baseball loves beer."

"Beer and baseball go together like hot dogs and mustard," she said.

"Mantle liked to start his day with a shot or more of brandy, and some Kahlua and cream," Jack said. "But he ruined his liver."

"Thank goodness we don't drink much." Pete dragged a chair to the table and cleared a space next to him, then bowed slightly. "Madam, your chair."

"Don't forget I warned you, Amy," Connor said.

She laughed. "He looks harmless."

"Pete? Harmless?" JL said. "God, he's got a trail of pissed-off women from Brooklyn to the Bronx. Stay away from him unless you need your life protected or want the last beer. He'll save your life and give you the beer."

"Then he'll show up at your door with his tongue lolling out the side of his mouth, hoping you'll invite him in and love on him," Connor added.

Pete smacked Connor's upper arm with the back of his hand. "Ignore him, Amy. He's just jealous."

Amy changed her mind. It wasn't the third season of the MacKlenna Family TV series. It was the tenth, and she'd never in a hundred lifetimes understand the nuances and the quirky characters. But she was already addicted to their antics and their larger-than-life hearts.

"How'd everything go in Pittsburgh?" Kevin asked.

"I'm here," Amy said, dusting pizza crumbs off her hands. "The shock hasn't worn off, and I'm still confused, but I'm ready to do what needs to be done to clear Joe's name."

"She slept all the way back," Jack said.

"Gabe said he rented a private railroad car for the three of you. Was it really necessary?" Kevin asked in a surly tone.

It seemed excessive to her, too, but she wasn't complaining. The trip to Pittsburgh was cramped and lacked privacy, so returning in a private car with a sleeping compartment and a clean bathroom was a welcomed luxury.

"Someone has to worry about expenses, Kevin, and I'm glad it's you, not me, but had I known Amy would sleep through the entire trip, I would have gone another route. I thought she'd want to talk, and I didn't want to risk people overhearing our conversation."

"I should have warned you. I fall asleep in planes, trains, and automobiles," she said to Jack. Then to Kevin she asked, "You mentioned Gabe. Are you talking about Gabriele Moretti, or is there another member of the team I haven't heard about?"

"Gabe Moretti," Kevin said. "JL got a lead on him while she was in jail, which is how we found you so quickly."

"It's part of the abridged version of the story," Connor said. "The police report you filed led us to him. He's been an immense help with logistics. Nice guy."

"Does Gabriele know what's going on here? Where we're from?" Amy asked.

Kevin gave the iffy sign, waggling his hand. "He suspects something unusual, but he hasn't asked any questions. In fact, he reminds me of our cousin, David McBain. David makes things happen, so does Gabe. He's slick about it, too. You think he's working over here"—Kevin pointed to the side—"but he's really working back here"—Kevin aimed his thumb. "You give him an idea of what you want, and he puts a plan together."

"What plan has Gabe put together?" Jack asked.

"Last night, Kevin and JL went to the theater and sat next to Diamond Jim and Lillian. While they were at the theater, I searched Lillian's brownstone on West 77th near West End Avenue and found a safe, but couldn't open it. Gabe said he could handle it, so we're going back in about an hour. JL and Kevin are going to meet Diamond Jim and Lillian for a late dinner at Delmonico's. Hopefully she won't be wearing the brooch."

"Are you considering stealing it?" Amy asked. "I can't condone that."

"We have to get it back, and if she won't sell it, we don't have a choice," Pete said.

"There's got to be another way. Do they know it was mine?"

"They only know the owner wants to buy it back," Pete said.

"Amy and I could go with you to dinner," Jack said.

"You can't go, Jack," JL said. "How would you explain why you haven't aged in twenty-eight years? And do you really want to get into a discussion with Lillian about Carolina Rose? Stay away from her."

There was a cold stillness in the room, as if a spray of Arctic air blitzed through and hosed them all down. The men at the table studied their plates. JL didn't take her eyes off Jack, and he didn't take his eyes off her. There was another massive tome behind the remark, and Amy wasn't sure she wanted to listen to the audio version.

All the wonder and warmth seemed to vanish from Jack's eyes. "I'll introduce myself as William Mallory, Jack's younger brother, and avoid any discussion about Carolina Rose. Twenty-eight years is a long time, and our acquaintance was so short, I doubt she'll remember me."

A heavy knock on the door startled Amy. But not the cops. They were on their feet. Pete put his finger to his lips as he, Connor, and JL drew their weapons. Pete pointed to JL, then to Amy, and motioned for them to leave the room. JL tugged on Amy's arm, and they rushed toward the bedroom. As soon as the door closed they put their ears to the wall and eavesdropped.

Pete said, "Who's there?"

A muffled sound came from the hall.

Amy reached for the doorknob to open the door. "It's Gabriele."

"Don't open the door until Pete says it's clear," JL said.

Amy froze in place at JL's strident tone.

"JL, come on out," Pete said. "It's Gabe."

"I told you," Amy said.

JL set her back to the door, holstered her weapon, and her guarded eyes briefly narrowed. "We're coming off a clusterfucked mission. People got hurt, and we're all a bit sensitive right now. We're going to play this one by the book, so bear with us. We're only trying to protect you and get us all home safely."

Amy hugged herself, feeling a chill ripple through her. Was Carolina Rose one of the people who got hurt?

Before JL opened the door, Gabriele's disembodied voice asked, "Is Amy back?"

Amy hurried into the room, arms wide. "I'm so glad to see you. Thanks for helping these guys out."

She hugged him and he whispered, "They said they're your cousins. I don't believe them. But I don't believe they'll hurt you, either."

"They've come to take me home."

Gabriele gave a small, quick nod and his eyes softened. "I could have done that."

She squeezed his arm. "We'll talk more later."

Gabriele turned to face the men. "I got a telephone call from Delmonico's. Diamond Jim cancelled his reservation for tonight. Miss Russell is going to Washington in the morning, so she went home after the theatre. If you want to travel on the same train, I need to make arrangements now."

"Is she still leaving Saturday for London?" Connor asked.

"Those plans haven't changed."

"Let's widen the lens," Jack said. "With Lillian leaving town tomorrow, it looks like we'll be leaving on Saturday on the *SS New York*. Have arrangements been made for first-class cabins?"

"I have three suites for you, and I purchased two," Gabriele said. "I promised Isabella I would take her abroad. When she heard Amy was traveling to London, she begged to go, too."

"Three for us?" Kevin asked. "It sounds like JL and I won't be together."

"You're the one who's managing the purse strings," Jack said.

Kevin cast a glance at JL.

"We'll survive, Kev. It will only be a few days," she said.

"Tonight's surveillance has to be cancelled," Connor said. "If Lillian is going out of town tomorrow, maybe we can get into her apartment after she leaves, and try to steal it then."

Jack heaved a heavy sigh, shoved a hand through the blond hair, and he studied Pete in the room's half-light. "I agree. We don't have a choice."

Gabriele picked through what was left of the pizza on the table. "You might not get into her apartment tomorrow. Her daughter is there."

"If we can't get in, we'll have to wait until we're on the ship," Connor said.

"What if she doesn't take it with her?" JL asked.

Jack fixed JL with a serious look. "Then it'll be a wasted trip."

"Five days over, five days back. What if someone stays behind?" she asked.

"We separated before, and you know how it turned out," Jack said.

JL sat down on the sofa and pulled her feet up under her hip. "You and Connor went to Pittsburgh, and that worked out okay."

Jack remained motionless in tense silence, staring at her. "We can't sail to London and leave anyone behind."

Amy piped up. "I'll stay. It'll give me two more weeks to work at the paper."

Jack's reply was a simple eyebrow arch.

Amy kicked off her shoes and, mimicking JL, sat on the sofa and pulled her feet up under her hip. "Just saying. If you need someone to stay, I will."

Jack poured a glass of whisky and drank it slowly. "Here's what we're going to do. Pete and Connor will surveil Lillian's apartment. If there's an opportunity to get inside and open the safe, take it. Amy and I are going to the Sterlings' mansion to meet Catherine Lily. Afterwards, I'll take her to her apartment. The rest of us will meet back here for dinner and prepare for embarking Saturday morning. Any questions?"

"What are Kevin and I supposed to do?"

"Stay out of trouble," Connor said.

"Gee, thanks. No, seriously," JL said. "Give us something. I've done all the shopping, and the clothes and steamer trunks for the voyage are being delivered today."

"Do we need to go in for final fittings?" Jack asked.

"The measurements were so specific, the tailor said he didn't need you and Connor."

"Then you have a free day."

"If you go to the park, be careful. Those cops you tangled with won't need an excuse to harass you," Pete said.

"Gabe, hire a couple of street boys to watch JL and Kevin. If anyone shows too much interest in them, JL needs to know,"

Connor said.

"We don't need babysitters. I know how to spot a tail."

"Done," Gabriele said, ignoring JL. "Anything else?"

"Amy, can you think of anything we left out?" Jack asked.

"I need to go to work in the morning to turn in my columns for the next two weeks, and tell Mr. Bennett I'm leaving for a while. After that, I want to see Stephen Thomson. What time do you want to visit the Sterlings?"

"According to the calling hours on the card the housekeeper gave me," Gabriele said, "Mrs. Sterling is at home on Fridays from twelve o'clock till four. Assuming she isn't traveling."

"We'll go at two o'clock," Jack said. "Better yet, since the tailor doesn't need me for a fitting, I'll also escort you to the newspaper, then to Thomson's office." Then to Gabriele he asked, "Can you arrange for a car and driver for our use today?"

"To quote JL, I don't need a babysitter," Amy said.

"This isn't about having babysitters, Amy," Pete said. "Everyone needs to be accounted for, and since we don't have communicators, working in teams is the only way to keep track of everyone."

"What's a communicator?" Gabriele asked.

Jack looked at Amy. Amy looked at Pete. Pete looked at Connor. Connor looked at JL. JL shrugged and mouthed, "Why me?"

Jack dug into his briefcase, pulled out a smartphone, and showed Gabriele. "This is a communicator, but it doesn't work here. If it did, we could punch a button and talk to each other."

Gabriele's face tightened as he tried to comprehend what Jack was telling him, but his puzzled expression said he didn't get it and it frustrated him. He shot a hard look at Amy. "*Non capisci.*"

"Let's get my brooch back. Then I'll explain everything. I promise."

"It's…" Gabriele's voice broke off, and she watched his eyes and his internal struggle to grasp new concepts. Should she tell him everything now? Or wait until time wasn't as pressing. She glanced at Jack, but could read nothing in his expression.

Before she could offer up an explanation, Gabriele said, "*È complicato.*"

After all the time they spent together in the last two months, she knew his rhythms and inflections. Gabriele was brilliant, and nothing got past him, but he had never pushed for more than she could give, either on a personal level or an intellectual one. He knew she was different. He knew the other men and JL were different, too, but he accepted them as he had accepted her. He would wait for an explanation, but he wouldn't wait forever.

"How many times have I said that to you?" she asked.

Gabriele held her hand and kissed it. "You're a *ragazza dolce,* but very odd. I will wait for your full explanation. But," he added, squeezing her hand, "when the time comes, and I need to know the truth, you will tell me whether you are ready to or not."

Without pausing to consider what he was demanding, she said, "Agreed."

The people in the room breathed a collective sigh of relief.

"Good," Jack said. "Then if we're all on the same page, let's get some rest. It's going to be a long day."

JL pointed to the room where she and Amy were hiding. "We're bunking in there. I'm going to bed. Good night."

"Guess I'm bunking with you, Jack," Kevin said. "Good night, Amy."

"Connor and I will be up and out early," Pete said. "We'll meet you back here by five. If anything comes up, we'll leave a message with Charles or his crony at the front desk."

Gabriele gave Amy a tight hug, as if to reinforce their promises to each other. "I'll have a car and driver here by seven-thirty, and will see you at Maria's tonight for dinner."

"Oh, one more thing," Amy said. "My crystal ball predicts the Giants won't play well today or tomorrow. Both games will be low-scoring, and we'll fall to the Pirates by one run each game."

"Does your crystal ball have final score predictions?"

There was a grinding ache in her throat. Gambling on a sure thing had always been cheating, but she rationalized it because she needed money to pay off her loan. That was no longer the case. She would take the win, but not the small bets on the score.

"Sorry, the crystal ball was silent when I asked the final scores."

Gabriele nodded his understanding and acceptance that the ride might be over. "I'll make the bets. See you tonight."

The room became suddenly quiet and very warm. Jack was pouring a glass of water from a pitcher. "I think I just heard someone's conscience getting the best of them."

"Yeah, well. It seemed okay when I needed money."

"We've all been put in similar situations. You do what you have to do, and hope your decisions don't impact history adversely."

There was a tome behind that statement, too. Before this adventure was over, she would likely have an ample collection of giant books.

"I told Jane Mathewson not to let her husband do something. If she listens to me, Matty might live a longer life."

"He'll probably die anyway, and all you've done is change the timing and given her false hope," Jack said.

A hot numbness swept over Amy's face, and she tried to swallow, but a knot was lodged there. "Did...did you really have to tell me that?"

"We can change history in small ways, but the people we try to save die anyway. Maybe not the way they would have died without our interference, but they die just the same."

"Why did you say that? I'll live with the guilt for the rest of my life. What if Matty dies at the Western Front instead, and Jane can't be with him? God." Amy covered her face and groaned. "What have I done?"

When Jack didn't answer, she hurried into JL's room and caught herself before she slammed the door, letting the latch click firmly instead.

"What's the matter?" JL asked.

Amy pulled pins from her hair and dropped them carelessly on the dresser. "Jack was being a jerk."

JL rolled over in bed and propped herself up on her elbow. "Yeah, well, he can be, but we love him anyway."

"Christy Mathewson is a pitcher for the Giants. During World War I, he'll accidentally get gassed and subsequently develop TB. He'll spend the rest of this short life fighting the illness. I told his wife to stop him from going into the Chemical Service. And Jack said—"

"Let me guess," JL said. "If we interfere with someone's life and they die or don't die, we haven't changed anything. We've only changed the timing, and by telling Christy's wife to do something, you've given her false hope."

"That's pretty much it. How'd you know?"

"Because I know Jack."

Amy unbuttoned as many of the buttons as she could reach before tugging the dress over her head. "I feel just awful now." She hung the dress in the wardrobe, then collapsed on the bed. "I don't know what to do. Should I send Jane a note and tell her she and Christy will need to make their own decisions when the time comes?"

"Look. We don't know how interacting with people from the past impacts the future. Braham tried to save Abraham Lincoln. Kit saved an entire wagon train from a cholera epidemic. Jack met a woman last fall who was killed. He believes he's responsible for her death. If he hadn't interfered, he believes, she would have survived—"

"To die another day," Amy said.

"Who's to know? You could call a friend at home and delay her so long, she misses a massive crash that would have killed her. We aren't God, and don't know what the next minute will bring. We do what we can with what's in our toolbox."

Amy slumped from the weight of it all. "That's insightful."

"It's not original. Elliott shared it with me a few months ago," JL said. "As much as he denies it, he's the insightful one. Before he met Meredith, he was a famous womanizer. He's still got the charm, but he loves his wife more than anything in the world. He's a wise old owl. But don't tell him I called him old."

There was a knock on the door. "Amy. Can I talk to you?" Jack asked.

"Go talk to him," JL said, but Amy shook her head. When Amy didn't budge, JL uncovered her foot and pushed Amy's butt with her toes. "Go talk to him. He's a good guy. He didn't mean to hurt your feelings."

Amy looked around for something to put on. JL's silk paisley wrapper hung on a hook. "Can I wear your robe?"

"It's all yours."

Amy left the bedroom to find Jack on the sofa, legs stretched out, crossed at the ankles. He rose to his feet and gestured for her to join him. She did, and tucked her legs up under her hips again.

"I'm sorry. I was out of line." He sat, rested one bent leg on the cushion, leaned forward, and laid his arm across the back of the sofa. "I would have done the same thing you did, without hesitation. It's in our DNA to try to make life better. It wasn't fair to unload my doubts and fears on top of the ones you're already carrying. You've made a difference in the lives of people you've met here. We don't know and can't predict what will result from our influence. I'm sorry I upset you."

"JL mentioned you feel responsible for the death of a woman you met a few months ago. Do you really believe she would have died anyway?"

"Carolina Rose died in my arms. I'll always believe her death was my fault. If she hadn't died then, would she have died the next day, or the next? I don't know. I haven't been able to get beyond my own guilt to seriously consider it."

"That's a heavy weight to carry. Are you sure you want to?"

"Do you want to carry the guilt of when and how Christy Mathewson dies?"

"Touché."

Jack took her hand and held it for a moment, and then relinquished it to stroke the back of his fingers down her arm. "You, Kit, Charlotte, and Kenzie have all had unique experiences. Kit walked across the Oregon Trail, fighting buffalo stampedes and renegades. Charlotte was dropped into the middle of a Civil War battle. Kenzie was stalked by England's secret service. But you're working with people you've admired all your life. You found a job that inspires you, and have made friends you don't want to leave behind. Coming here disrupted your life, but leaving it will disrupt it just as much."

"I don't want to leave, Jack. I love it here. Kit stayed in the past. That's what I want to do, too. I mean, after I go home and fix things for Joe."

"Kit was born in 1826. She belonged in the past. You're a woman of the future. This isn't your home."

"The more I think about it, the more I know it's what I want. And if I'm coming back, I need to be mindful of the way I leave. I can't disappear without a reasonable explanation, and I can't sully my reputation."

He gave her nape a squeeze with one hand. "I don't know how this will work out, but I promise you it will. If your goal is to come back and pick up your life before we intruded, I'll help you manage it."

They got up and stared at each other for a moment. She wanted to hug him, but sensed if she fell into his arms she might never want to leave.

She cleared her throat. "Thanks. I'm glad we got that settled. I'll see you in a few hours." She crossed over the oriental rug to the bedroom door.

"Amy." She turned to look at him, and he continued, "You might think it's settled. But it's not. One day we'll have to deal with what's between us."

"I thought we had an understanding."

"I'm not talking about where and when you live."

"I know we're not, Jack. Good night."

29

1909 New York City—Amy

As Jack and Amy left the Hotel Netherland at seven-thirty in the morning, she inhaled moisture-ladened air. Amy associated rain with rainouts. Mother Nature had the potential to change the dynamics of a game, and although the meetings she had today would be conducted inside, her psyche was already considering how a spate of rain or a crash of thunder could affect the outcomes of potentially intense sessions with Stephen, Mr. Bennett, and Catherine Lily.

That was silly. But after a lifetime of playing games outside, she couldn't help but associate weather with her performance. Would she be at her best? Would she think quickly, respond appropriately, remain cool under pressure?

To their right was a taxi with its lamp turned off and a street urchin leaning against the rear of the car. His posture—arms crossed, hat tipped low on his forehead, and sour expression—conveyed both boredom and bad attitude to everyone who passed him on the street. When the boy saw them, he straightened and said something to the hack man, who nodded in response.

"Is that our car?" Amy asked.

"Looks like they're waiting for us," Jack said.

The boy, who was probably twelve or thirteen, opened the door and stepped aside while Amy climbed into the vehicle. Jack flipped him a coin. "Why don't you sit up front? I'll have errands for you later."

The boy shrugged half-heartedly, like it was no big deal whether he worked or not. But his big blue eyes betrayed him, and surprise flashed across his face before the studied neutrality returned. "Mr. Moretti didn't say anything about running errands." The boy's stare wandered momentarily. "I suppose I could help you out for a while."

Jack gave the lad a congenial fist bump to his arm. "Appreciate it. What's your name?"

"Patrick," the boy said, jumping into the open-sided front seat of the cab.

To the hack man Jack said, "First stop is the *New York Herald* on 6th Avenue between 35th and 36th Streets." He then slid in beside Amy. "Traffic should be light," he told her. "We'll be there before eight."

She wasn't thinking about what time they would arrive. She was more concerned about her game face, especially with Jack sitting so close beside her, their shoulders rubbing when the car dipped and swerved. His parting words to her earlier and her reply played a loop recording in her brain.

Yes, she was attracted to him. She couldn't deny it. And she believed he was attracted to her. When she returned to the future, though, Joe would be there. Whether she stayed in the twenty-first century or not, she would never see Jack again, except on a bookrack in the airport.

While she appreciated him escorting her about town, she didn't want him to interfere with what she needed to do. She'd done well negotiating her loan with Providence, and her salary requirements at the newspaper. She didn't need a man stepping in now to help negotiate her exit.

She cleared her throat. "I appreciate you going with me today, but would you mind…"

"Staying out of your way?"

"You're astute, Mallory."

"I've been accused of many things, but being thickheaded isn't one of them." He glanced down at his hands and absentmindedly picked at his thumb, which was perfectly manicured and buffed. "You've accomplished so much by yourself, it would be rude of me to butt in now."

"I don't want you to hover. Hoverers drive me nuts. If you're in the meetings, both Bennett and Thomson will direct their comments to you. Not me. I can't stand to be talked over. It makes me feel like a child."

"I'll wait in the car," he said. "And, Amy, I would never talk over you. These meetings are about your exit strategy. I want it to be as uncomplicated as possible."

They rode in silence down 5th Avenue to 36th Street, where the hack man crossed over to 6th Avenue. He stopped and parked in front of the *New York Herald*.

"This building looks exactly like—"

"The Palazzo del Consiglio in Verona. I know. Have you been there?"

"I met Meredith and Kevin in Venice while they were touring Italy, looking for a winery to buy. We took a day trip to Verona."

"Were you looking for a winery, too?"

"I'd been in the Himalayas and was on my way to London. When I heard they were in Italy, I changed my flight and hung out with them for a couple of days."

"I thought you always flew on a corporate jet."

"Not always, despite what Connor said. I enjoy using the MacKlenna Corporation jets when I'm on company business, but when it's personal, I fly commercial." Jack glanced out the window toward the newspaper building. "You realize you're stalling, don't you?"

"Yeah, but I was hoping you didn't."

He squeezed her hand. "You're in full-throated action mode. You'll be fine."

"What makes you say that?"

"Your game-time aura is glowing." He got out of the vehicle and came around to her side to open the door and help her out, holding her hand firmly in his. "I'll be here waiting when you get through. If

I'm not, I'll be close by, and Patrick will find me."

"Since you don't have a working smartphone, you can either stroll along the side of the building through the arcade and watch the giant presses, or get a newspaper and enjoy another cup of coffee at the café across the street."

"Don't worry. I'll be fine. I don't mind waiting."

"Most men do, you know."

"My sister is a surgeon. Years ago, I learned the art of actively waiting."

Amy clutched her leather portfolio to her chest. "I shouldn't be longer than an hour."

"Take as long as you need."

He wasn't intentionally flashing strength and patience, but she saw those qualities in him. She couldn't deny the sexual tension between them, and doubted he could either. But she was convinced, even with a strong sexual pull, they could stay within their boundaries. Because of that, neither of them had any fear of being themselves. When you could be yourself and not worry about what another person might think of you, a friendship had the perfect soil in which to grow.

She placed her gloved hand tenderly on his face. "You're a good man. I'm glad to have you in my corner."

He covered hers with his. "You're a good woman. Now, go kill it."

She thought back to the first time she'd walked through the *Herald's* doors, armed with only a business card and the promise of a possible collaboration. Since then she'd created a highly successful five-times-weekly column, which brought enjoyment to her fans and money to the paper's coffers. Would it all come crashing down on her head today?

She went inside and spoke to the staff and visitors as she made her way to her office, where she left her purse, hat, and gloves. Then she walked down to Mr. Bennett's office. "Good morning, Smithers."

Bennett's gangly secretary sat at a desk outside the door, typing on a manual typewriter. Shock registered on his face when he saw her, and he jumped to his feet, knocking over a stack of papers. "What are you doing here? You're not supposed to be back until Sunday."

"I know, but I had to return early."

The secretary leaned in and said confidentially, "There was a man here Wednesday looking for you."

"My cousin Kevin. He found me. Thank you for letting him know where I was. Is Mr. Bennett in?"

"Yes, and he'll be surprised to see you, too."

Amy steeled herself for the next conversation before knocking on the door.

"Come in." Bennett looked up when the door opened. "Miss Spalding, I thought you were in Pittsburgh." He stood and invited her to sit in the chair near his desk.

"I had to return for a...family emergency."

"I hope it's not too serious."

"I'm afraid it is," she said, taking a seat in the chair offered. "I need to leave town, and I may be gone for a few weeks. I don't expect you to hold my job open, but I do hope when I return you'll give me a chance to earn it back."

Bennett sat, leaned back in his chair, and crossed his hands over his stomach. "This is both sudden and inconvenient. I don't have another reporter to take over your column. Fans are used to seeing you at the games and reading your spot daily. The paper will lose the gains it's made. Where are you going?"

"Where? Ah... South Carolina?"

"When are you returning?"

"I'm not sure. My father is ailing, and I'm needed at home to care for him." Lies were flying off her tongue as fast as balls could shoot from an Iron Mike Pitching Machine.

"I'm disappointed. I obviously made a mistake giving a woman a column on the front page. Granted, readership increased, but we'll lose them now if your articles aren't there. Women belong at home, not at a newspaper."

She looked away for a moment, knowing her eyes were blazing, and if she looked at him with her death-ray glare he might spontaneously combust, or more likely, fire her on the spot. "That's not fair. I've done an excellent job here."

"But you're not dependable."

His comment froze the breath in her lungs. "H-how can you say that?"

"A man wouldn't pack up and move to South Carolina to care for an ailing father. He would bring his father here."

She replied first with an eyebrow arch, and then she said, "He would bring his father here for his *wife* to care for."

"I won't argue with that. Taking care of her father-in-law would be her responsibility, while his would be to provide for his family."

Never in her life had she encountered this kind of sexism. She sat straighter, pressing her back against the slats of the ladderback chair. Her mouth opened, but no words came out. What could she say to change his opinion?

Nothing.

She opened her portfolio and placed a stack of papers on his desk. She had been writing her players' wives' series over the past ten days, and had stayed up after leaving Jack to write the last one from her interviews with Jane and Blanche.

"Here are ten columns from interviews with players' wives. This will give you two weeks to come up with a plan to replace me."

"When are you leaving?"

"Tomorrow."

"If you're taking the train to South Carolina, I'll come down to see you off."

"That's not necessary."

"Yes, it is. I intend to bring a photographer to take a photograph of me sending you off to care for your father. I want the readership to know we're concerned about you and hope you'll return to New York as soon as possible to resume your responsibilities. But in the meantime, I'll have to find another reporter to write your column."

"So, I'll get it back when I return?"

"I didn't say that," Bennett said.

"Then what did you say?" she asked.

"I'll hire another reporter to write your column."

She had given the suffragettes a wide berth since coming to the city, but she now realized what a huge disservice she had done to them and herself. She began to speak, her voice unnaturally loud and angry. "You can come to the train station in the morning, but I won't be there. I'm sailing to London with my fiancé for a European honeymoon."

He jumped to his feet. "You're getting married. Why didn't you say so?" He paced the room, thinking. "I'm sending a reporter to sail with you. He'll file daily columns about the engaged couple. The readership will follow you throughout Europe. We'll sell thousands of newspapers."

"You don't need to send a reporter. I can write them."

"It's your honeymoon. Our women readers would be offended if you had to work during your trip."

She forced down rising panic, and shaking her head ruefully said, "What if I decide before the ceremony not to go through with it?"

Bennett threw up his hands. "Don't be ridiculous. Of course you'll go through with it. Now, who's the lucky man?"

She responded with the first name that came to mind, "Jack Mallory." She shuddered in anticipation of what Jack would say when she told him how well she'd "killed it."

"Jack Mallory, huh? Where's he from?"

"Virginia."

"How old is he?"

She really didn't know, but offered a guess, "Late forties."

"Good. Then he can't be the Jack Mallory charged as one the co-conspirators in President Lincoln's assassination. His attorney proved he'd been framed, but the public had a tough time accepting it. If you marry Mr. Mallory, you'll be giving up one of the most well-respected names in America for a name many still connect with the president's death."

"How could anyone blame Jack for something done by a man

The Diamond Brooch 273

with a similar name who was framed and exonerated?"

"If Mallory had stayed in town and done interviews, he could have salvaged his reputation. But he chose to disappear. I heard he showed up in California in '81, but he still didn't give any interviews."

She tapped her fingers against her portfolio, thinking how best to respond to Bennett's unreasonableness. "Jack will do an interview for me, and I'll write an article to rehabilitate the Mallory name."

"If you marry him, I'll take away your byline."

A rock the size of a fist stuck in her throat. She couldn't believe his attitude. "You can't be serious?"

"I can't put Mrs. Jack Mallory on my front page."

"But you could put Mrs. Amy Spalding Mallory."

"Or nothing at all," Bennett said.

Amy snapped her portfolio closed at the same moment a thunderbolt rattled the glass panes in the window. "We'll continue this discussion when I return. And when I do, I may have a Pulitzer-worthy article on living life to its fullest after being wrongfully accused of a conspiracy for my first column."

"What's a Pulitzer?"

"You haven't heard of it? Well, you will." She skated out of Bennett's office, bumping into Smithers who'd been listening with his ear to the door. "Did you get all that?" she asked.

He pulled Bennett's door closed. "Everybody likes you, Miss Spalding. I'll do what I can to calm the boss and smooth the road for your return."

She squeezed his arm. "Thank you."

Smithers reached for an imaginary hat and doffed it in a grandiose flourish. "Anything for you, ma'am."

She walked back down the familiar corridor to her office. The world hadn't ended. Breath was still moving in and out of her lungs. But oh, my God, what will Jack say?

She put the thought aside while she made a pit stop to collect her hat, purse, gloves, and autographed pictures. The pictures were too valuable to leave behind, even though she intended to return.

274   *Katherine Lowry Logan*

Armed with her collectibles, she left the *Herald* to confess her latest sin.

Jack was walking across the street when she exited the building, and when he saw her, he waved. She waited beside the car while she focused on the next pitch instead of the last one.

"How'd it go?"

She glanced up at the dark clouds. Rain was coming, and soon. "Do you want the play-by-play or the box score?"

He opened the car door and she slid across the seat to make room for him. "Give me the box score, and then we'll do the play-by-play."

She folded her hands in her lap, squeezing them tightly. "Besides being the most sexist conversation of all time, Bennett said if I got married, he won't let me—"

Jack quickly formed the letter T with his hands. "Time out! You told him you were getting married? Who's the lucky groom?"

"You." She didn't stop to give him time to react, and continued, saying, "Bennett won't let me use my married name as a byline because it will remind readers of Lincoln's assassination."

"Ouch," Jack said. "My mind is still tripping on the married part. Start from the beginning. Forget the box score. I'm almost certain nothing was mentioned about marriage before you went in to meet with Bennett. I write fiction, but I can't connect any threads to what I know of the plot. Help me out, will you?"

Amy told the hack man to take them to the Providence Loan Society on Park Avenue and 25th Street. Then she sat back and rested her head against the rear window.

"The conversation got out of control, and I spun one whopper after another until I got tangled in a web of lies."

"That's a typical problem for time travelers. You just have to keep the lies as close to the truth as possible."

"I learned that lesson weeks ago, but this… Oh my, God." She scrubbed her face with her hands. "I'm so sorry I dragged you into this."

"Amy, sweetheart. You didn't drag me in." His pursed lips

curved in what might have been a shadow of a smile. "I doubt it's so bad."

The term of endearment calmed her momentarily, but couldn't completely ease her fear. "Oh, but it is."

He pulled a flask from his inside jacket pocket. "Drink. It's from home, and it's the finest whisky you'll ever taste."

"I don't drink whisky."

"You do now."

She put her nose to the flask, and a blast of strong whiskiness rushed out. She didn't know much about whisky, but she knew what was in the flask, and if she hadn't been sitting down, it would have knocked her on her butt. "Smells like rocket fuel. Although I've never smelled rocket fuel before…"

"That's from the barrels it was aged in. It should smell sweet, too. Just drink it."

She took a hesitant sip. It was salty, mildly smoky, spicy, and very smooth. The alcohol imparted a mysterious warmth to her tongue, throat, and eventually her tummy. She took a second sip. Before she could take a third, Jack tugged the flask out of her hand.

"You have more meetings. It wouldn't do to go in drunk."

She licked her lips. "You're right. Okay, here's the deal. I told him I was going to South Carolina for a family emergency. His response surprised me. He said he would bring a photographer to the train station to take my picture so my readership would know I was leaving and why. Well, his threat scared me, because I wasn't going to the train station. So I had to come up with another lie. I then told him I wouldn't be at the train station because I was sailing to London for a European honeymoon before I traveled to South Carolina."

"So what's the problem?"

"He's sending a reporter to follow us around Europe and write daily articles about our trip."

"Okay. That's a problem," Jack said. "But maybe we can use it to our advantage. If the reporter is interested in us, we could be the distraction for the others to search for the brooch."

"Except now I don't know if he's going to send a reporter or not. When he learned your name—"

"—hell broke loose," Jack said.

"That's exactly what happened. So I told him if I married you, I would write a Pulitzer-worthy article to restore your good name. Then he asked what a Pulitzer was."

"Pulitzer's were first awarded in 1917. Did he ask how you could give up a time-honored name like Spalding for a cursed name like Mallory?"

"Matter of fact, he did. He also said, because you disappeared after the trial and didn't give any interviews, this mystery still hangs over Jack Mallory's head."

"After I was exonerated, I just wanted to get out of there."

"He said you were last seen in San Francisco in 1881."

"I met a few newspapermen while I was there. They wanted to do an interview. I wasn't interested. I want to erase the whole incident from history."

"Can you do that?"

"I would have to go back to the time before I was arrested, and I wouldn't put Charlotte or Braham through the pain again."

"I should have told him I was marrying Connor O'Grady."

"Connor and JL's family were New York City cops in the early 1900s. No telling what kind of hornet's nest entangling him would have stirred up."

"You're right. It could have caused problems for them," Amy said. "This just keeps getting more complicated, doesn't it?"

"Was the conversation with Bennett resolved?"

"I guess we'll find out tomorrow when a reporter either shows up or doesn't."

Jack scratched thoughtfully at his jaw. "When are we supposed to get married?"

The question hit her like a wet noodle. "Married... Yeah... Well..."

"It's a simple question, Amy."

"I didn't exactly say when, only that we were going on a European honeymoon. I thought I was getting myself out of something, but instead I made a bigger mess."

Jack laughed, and the sound was deep and rich and sensual. He tapped on the glass between the enclosed part of the taxi and the open-air front seat, and said loud enough for the hack man to hear, "Take us to 5th Avenue and 57th Street."

"That's just a couple of blocks from the hotel. Where are we going?"

"If we're getting married, you need a ring."

Something twisted and tightened in her chest. This wasn't the right thing to do. "I don't need a ring for a fake wedding."

"If you intend to use my name, you'll wear a ring."

"You're not mad about this, are you?"

"A beautiful woman wants to pretend to be my bride during a luxury sailing adventure across the ocean? Every night there will be promenading in the moonlight and champagne dinners. Why would I be mad about that?"

"The operative word, Mallory, is pretend."

He gave her a snappy comeback without saying a word. He just grinned, and a slight dimple appeared. She was too much of a coward to ask what he was thinking.

The hack man stopped the car at the corner of 5th Avenue and 57th Street. Jack hopped out, but Amy didn't budge. "I can't go in there."

"You started this. If we're getting on the ship tomorrow, we're going as an engaged couple. If you want to break it off after a day, fine, but my fiancée isn't going to announce her engagement and not have a ring to show for it."

"I still can't go in there."

"Why not?"

Her good sense splattered all over the sidewalk like a melon dropped from a second story window. How could she explain what she was feeling without looking like an idiot? "It's like this. I've been waiting for years, it seems, for Joe to propose. I've been looking at rings in magazines, in store windows, and on women's fingers. I've fantasized shopping with him, and where we'll be when he proposes. It's special, Jack. I don't want to shop in Tiffany's for a pretend ring when I've waited so long for a real one."

"I get it," he said. "A girl should get only one engagement ring, and only one proposal, in her lifetime. I'm going into Tiffany's to get a pretend ring for a pretend engagement, and if you don't want to pick out a pretend ring, I'll do it myself, but my pretend fiancée *will* have a ring." He lifted the hem of his vest and pulled on a thread until he had a two-inch piece. Then he wrapped the thread around her ring finger to mark the diameter. "Sit here. I'll go get something suitable."

After fifteen minutes, Amy sent Patrick in to see what Jack was doing. Five minutes later, the boy returned. "Mr. Mallory is leaning over a counter covered with rings, looking at each one through a jeweler's loop."

She closed her eyes and waited. When Jack still didn't come out, she sent Patrick to the ice cream parlor on the corner. She had just finished eating her cone when Jack finally returned.

"Drive up to 59th Street and let us out at the park," he told the hack man before climbing into the cab beside her. He was quiet, looking at her, then licked his finger and wiped above her lip. "Ice cream? Was it good?"

She licked her lip. "Delicious. I didn't save you any."

"We're even, then. I didn't share any of the croissant I ate at the café while you were meeting with Bennett."

The cab stopped at the corner of 5th Avenue and 59th, and Jack hopped out. "Park close by. We won't be long," he told the hack man. Then to Amy, he said, "Come, my dear." He reached for her hand. "You can't say no this time."

"Where are we going?"

"We're going to walk off the croissant and ice cream before you go meet with Thomson." Jack linked his arm with hers. They entered Central Park and strolled along the path, past a row of nannies and mothers pushing wicker strollers, until they reached the pond.

"What are we doing here?"

"Patience, sweetheart." He studied the area. "There," he said, pointing. He pulled Amy over to a park bench shaded by a clump of trees.

And that's when it hit her. "Are you going to make a pretend proposal?"

"Shhh," he said. "I'll never do this for real, so I want to do it right."

He dropped to one knee, pulled a small box from his pocket, and opened it. Amy gasped and swayed slightly. The ring—an emerald cut sapphire surrounded by diamonds—was the reverse of a ring that had haunted her dreams for more than a decade, a ring she had never seen in a store or magazine or on anyone's finger.

Jack took her hand, slid the ring on her finger, and regarded her with a heart-melting gaze, the clear blue of his eyes in stark contrast to the sky bruised with a brewing storm.

"I can't imagine my life without you in it, without your smile to grace my mornings, without your sigh to still my nights. I long for the sound of home that pours unbidden from your voice, and the silky touch of your lips against mine. We are two behind one vision, one flesh, one bone, one heart. Make me the happiest man in the world. Say yes, and be my bride today and always."

He left her speechless—no facts, no statistics, no observations— nothing percolated on the tip of her tongue. There was only dead air, impossible to fill. She dropped to her knees, tears welling in her eyes, a sob tightening her throat. The proposal she had fantasized about for years had just been delivered by the wrong man, a man whose pain darkened his shimmering eyes, a man whose soul lay bare for her to see, a man so loving and giving he had kindly and gently shattered her illusions.

She placed her hands on the sides of his face and had to swallow a throat full of tears before kissing him tenderly at the side of his mouth. "Thank you for coming to get me. Thank you for the sacrifices you're willing to make. Thank you for protecting my reputation, and for knowing it's all I really have. I am touched by your giving heart, by your thoughtful words, and by the pain you're surrendering to me. I embrace it all, Jack, and I will cherish your friendship for the rest of my life."

Neither of them moved until sprinkles splattered around them. "We need to go." He helped her up, then returned the ring box to his pocket. "You have a ring and a story now."

She gave him a watery, grateful smile. "A beautiful ring and a beautiful story, like characters in a movie, a script written just for us."

"After you visit Thomson, we'll enjoy a celebratory lunch."

She shimmied the ring around her finger. "Before we say goodbye, I'll give this back."

He surprised her with a soft kiss on her temple. His breath was scented with butter and jam. But she was wrong. The kiss wasn't soft at all. It was hot and charged and erotic.

"It's yours." His whispered words were a caress against her ear and the sensitive side of her neck. "Sell it, wear it, or give it away, but please don't give it back."

She didn't answer right away. "I can't make that promise right now. Can we hold it for later?"

"No. This isn't a for-later decision. I don't want it back."

And she didn't want to keep it. The ring would always be a reminder of what seldom happens in life and in baseball—a perfect game.

She pointed to the low, gray clouds, ominous against the dark blue of the sky. "It's going to pour. We should go."

They trekked back through the park and spotted Patrick waiting at the entrance. When he saw them, he ran off, and by the time they reached the corner, their taxi was waiting.

"Twenty-fifth and Park Avenue," Jack said.

Amy tucked up next to him, feeling an unexpected warmth toward the man who had invaded her dreams and bought her the ring of her heart. "I can't believe what you've done to protect my reputation, and set plans in motion for my return."

"Only the lucky ones find their heart's desire. If you've found yours, I'll do everything within my limited power to help you succeed," he said.

Her heart tightened a bit. "I couldn't ask for anything more."

30

1909 New York City—Amy

THE TAXI PULLED to the curb in front of the Providence Loan Society building at Park Avenue and 25th Street. The rain had held off a little bit longer, but it was coming.

To say Amy had lost her bearings was an understatement. She had entrusted Jack's proposal to memory and locked it in her heart. There had to be some way she could keep it safe, yet forget it, too. Joe's proposal, if it ever came, would never compare. She was so conflicted. Did she want Joe to propose, or did she want to eventually return to the life she had created in 1909?

And what was she going to tell Stephen? They had developed a special relationship and she depended on his advice and counsel. In recent weeks, she'd sensed he was growing very fond of her, and hinting at a deeper relationship. But she hadn't encouraged him.

Often, when they went out to dinner, she was approached by a fan or ballplayer. Stephen resented the intrusions, and was often rude to the person. She had called him on it more than once, but he brushed aside her censure, saying, "I don't like to share you."

She tolerated his behavior because he was a member of the highest echelons of New York society, and he opened those doors for her. But baseball was what provided the entrée to soliciting investment advice. And she used the advice to develop a short-term investment strategy, which had paid off magnificently. In less than eight weeks, she made enough money to repay her loan, although now it didn't matter.

"Are you sure you don't need me?" Jack asked.

Amy's hands were tightly clasped in her lap. She was trying very hard to restrain her emotions about the proposal, and about confronting Stephen. She wanted Jack to go with her, but she didn't need him to go. It was more appropriate if she talked to Stephen alone.

"I'm sure."

Jack opened her door and escorted her to the front of the building. "I'll be here waiting."

"I won't be long."

She needed to bullet-point the meeting before she went in. What were her objectives? Berating Stephen for the loss of her brooch was pointless. But she wanted to know what he intended to do about it.

She crossed the lobby and paused at the elevator to take a few breaths, and to prepare mentally for a possible confrontation she didn't want, but from which she wouldn't back away.

The elevator door opened, she stepped in, and the operator took her to the second floor. The silk of her skirts swished about her ankles as she marched down the long hall toward his office. When she reached his door, she pulled her white cotton gloves from her purse and slipped them on. If she did return to 1909, it would be without a husband, so why interject the subject of marriage into what would be a tense discussion? Bennett knew her plans, though, and he might tell Stephen. Did it really matter? If Bennett sent a reporter to follow her and Jack, Stephen would read the stories. This was a lose-lose situation, and one she'd have to play by ear.

Her heart pounded like a dryer full of sneakers. She grinned and wondered, if she did return, would her mind eventually stop thinking in terms of the twenty-first century? Could she ever truly be at home in the early 1900s?

She put steel in her spine and knocked on the door.

"Come in," Stephen said.

She peeked in before she opened the door wide enough to walk through. "Are you too busy to see me right now?"

He pushed back his chair and leapt to his feet. "I'm never too busy for you. Please, come in." He crossed the room to take her hand. "I thought you were in Pittsburgh."

"I was, but my cousin brought upsetting news. So here I am."

He led her to the chair in front of the desk, where she took a seat, while Stephen drew up a chair to sit beside her. He sighed heavily. "I'm so sorry this happened. It's a first for the company. We initiated an investigation immediately."

"My cousin told me, but unfortunately it doesn't help recover my property."

"Let me explain. Mr. Carter, the bank officer you met with the day you came in, changed the date on the loan agreement you signed. Then he waited until he knew I was out of the office and arranged for the brooch to be sold at auction. He then notified Diamond Jim Brady that a diamond he would be interested in was slated for auction the next day."

"So, my brooch was basically stolen. Is that what you're telling me?"

Stephen nodded. "Diamond Jim paid Mr. Carter a commission."

"Where is Carter now?"

"He quit his job and left town. We've notified the police, and a warrant has been issued for his arrest. The police are confident they will find him."

"Which doesn't get my brooch back."

"I've telephoned both Diamond Jim and Miss Russell. Neither expressed interest in reselling the piece of jewelry. I told your cousin we would pay you the full appraised value, less the loan amount, and we'll forgive the interest. If Miss Russell changes her mind and agrees to sell, we will pay her a reasonable price for the brooch."

"Stephen, I intend to hire a lawyer. A mistake is one thing, but this was intentional. I can't imagine the sale of stolen property would be upheld in a court of law. If I can have the sale voided, Diamond Jim would have to return the brooch. I have the names of several attorneys who would be willing to take my case, and I have appointments this afternoon." She was bluffing, of course, but time was of the essence. If she exerted pressure on Stephen, maybe he would exert more pressure on Diamond Jim. "I'll instruct my attorneys to proceed immediately."

"Give me a few more days," Stephen pleaded. "Let me try again to work this out."

"I'm sailing to Europe tomorrow. By the time I return, this must be resolved."

"This is sudden. Why are you going to Europe?"

"It's a personal trip. So, you see, this must come to a quick resolution. I have to recover my family heirloom."

"Miss Spalding…Amy, please. Don't leave like this. I had hoped, after we spend more time together…" He moved his thick, purple-veined hand off the arm of the chair and covered hers, which were folded in her lap. His finger twitched against her ring, and a confused expression crossed his face. "You're wearing a ring you haven't worn before."

She didn't want him to see the irritation she knew was growing in her eyes and the tightness around her mouth. Looking away momentarily, she said softly, "It's new."

"Are you…engaged?" The words were roughly spoken.

She hadn't wanted this to happen, but now it had, Stephen needed to understand they could never be more than friends. She enjoyed his company, and while she had no romantic interest in him, she hated lying to him, dashing his hopes, and hurting his feelings.

Their eyes held as she forced herself to say the words he knew were coming. "Jack Mallory and I are engaged."

He continued to glare at her unmoving. "Who?"

"You met him the other day."

There was a heartbreaking loneliness about Stephen he couldn't disguise, and while it touched her deeply, she couldn't let it influence her decisions.

"The man I met the other day said he was your cousin."

"Six or seven times removed. We're not closely related."

He dropped her hand, and walked over to the window to stare

out at the darkening New York City skyline. The dampness in the air made the residual cigar smoke in the room more pervasive, and tickled her throat, making her cough. She scooted closer to the edge of the chair. If Jack ever offered to go somewhere with her again, she wouldn't say no.

Stephen turned to face her. His brown eyes and graying hair both seemed darker when shadowed by the dim light from outside the window. "When will you return to the city?"

"I don't know."

"What about your column?"

"Bennett is giving it to another reporter."

"You worked hard to develop your readership. Do you intend to give up on it now?"

She answered swiftly, almost sharply. "When I return, I intend to earn it back."

"On what ship are you sailing, and what is your destination?"

"The *SS New York*. London."

As if the sun had popped out and brightened the day, he smiled, took her arm, and guided her toward the door. "You must have a dozen things to do to prepare for your journey. I will bid you goodbye for now, and look forward to our reunion." He squeezed her hand. "Until we meet again, my dear."

He ushered her out of his office and quietly closed the door. Amy rotated her neck, hoping for a quick recovery from the whiplash Stephen's changing mood had caused. She'd have to look at her mental replay to figure out what just happened, but she'd do it later. Two meetings down and one to go. She was very curious about Catherine Lily Sterling, and what, if anything, Mrs. Sterling knew about the brooches and the MacKlennas.

31

1909 New York City—Jack

WHEN AMY WALKED out of the Providence Loan Society building, her face showed signs of strain, and while she wasn't shaking, she did keep her hands clasped tightly together, as if she didn't trust them not to shake. As soon as she was ensconced in the back seat of the taxi, she tugged off her gloves and demanded, "Give me your flask."

After she took a quick sip, Jack reached for the whisky, but she held on to it with a white-knuckled grip.

"What happened?" he asked. She took another swig, and when she went in for the third, he slipped the flask out of her hands. "I should have gone with you."

She shook her head. "I saw a side of Stephen I hadn't seen before, a side I needed to see. I'm fine now. I did tell him, though, that I intend to hire an attorney to review the illegal auction of my property. Should we find someone before we leave town?"

"We already have."

"Good. Who is it? I should have a name if anyone asks."

"It would be...me."

She made a surprised O with her mouth. "Grrreat. But don't you think I need a real lawyer, not an author who writes legal thrillers?"

"You have me confused with Scott Turow. He writes legal thrillers. I write historical thrillers, and, while I don't practice law, I do have a law degree."

"Oh yeah? From where?"

"Your buddy Scott and I both graduated from Harvard." Jack then hastened to add, "Not at the same time. He's much older."

She stifled a chuckle. "If it wasn't for your crow's feet and the touch of gray at your temples, I would say we were close to the same age. But I know you're older."

"But not any wiser." He turned and rested his arm on the back of the seat, his thumb innocently teasing the tip of her jacket collar. "You arrived here with nothing but your brains and determination—"

"And a brooch valued at three hundred thousand dollars."

"Which gave you a sense of security, but you would have gotten to the same place without the loan."

"Your brutal honesty is really brutal, Mallory. You need to work on that. You're telling me I lost my brooch and didn't have to because I have the brains to solve my problems without having any money. Thanks a lot. It makes me feel like I got credit for a home run I didn't hit."

"You're not the only one who's tossed a brooch out the window, and probably won't be the last."

She looked at him, trying to puzzle out what he meant.

"That's not a figure of speech. I actually did it."

"Out the window?"

"It was the only option at the time."

"I hope you weren't in a castle surrounded by a moat."

He attempted a smile, but knew it didn't work. "I was in a room surrounded by Union soldiers determined to arrest me. I couldn't let them take the brooch too."

She gave him a dark sideways look. "Have the stones done any good for anybody?"

"The diamond worked for you. You don't want to leave here. That hasn't happened before."

"You said Kit stayed in the past."

"It's where she was born, where she belonged. She wanted to live the life she was destined to live, not the alternate one given to her by a brooch."

Amy sat back, and, although she appeared unruffled, the tic in her jaw as she gritted her teeth was a dead giveaway he had pissed her off again. He fell into a silent study of her, of himself. Was he living up to his reputation as a jerk without intending to? If so, he wasn't proud to find out he could still slide so easily into his old persona.

The hack man stopped at a café on the Upper West Side, the Silver Palate, which served Greek Mezes and Moroccan chicken pies.

"Are you ready for our celebratory luncheon?" Jack asked.

She looked out the window. "I haven't eaten here before. I love Greek food—hot or cold, spicy or savory. Yum."

"Patrick made the recommendation," Jack said.

"Oh, he did?" She winked at the boy, whose wary eyes were watching for her reaction. "Then we should definitely give it a try."

Patrick's face brightened before he jumped out of the car to open her door. Jack gave both Patrick and the driver coins to buy their lunch. "This should be enough to buy hot potatoes and baked apples from a street vendor. Give us an hour to eat, and then we'll go to our next stop," Jack said.

He and Amy entered the stuffy diner, buzzing with a busy lunch crowd speaking in a melting pot of languages. The pungent scents of garlic and lamb sizzling on the grill had Jack's stomach growling. They were quickly seated, and a waiter brought servings of crisp sliced cucumbers, olives, and feta cheese to their table.

After Amy answered his first two questions about her meeting with Thomson with a simple yes or no without elaborating, he postponed trying to draw her out, and while she sampled the meze spread, he decided to meditate in preparation for the upcoming meeting with Catherine Lily Sterling.

Was he ready to meet the woman he believed was Carolina Rose's twin sister? Could meditating prepare him to come face-to-face with a woman who would conjure bitter memories of shattered dreams amid bloody shards of glass.

It would have to...

"...Jack. Jack." Amy shook his arm. "Are you ready to go? It's one-thirty."

He drifted back to the diner, mostly empty now, aware that her voice sounded soft, concerned, a little desperate. He touched her hand, chilly beneath his. "I'm sorry. I disappeared for a while, didn't I?"

"The only way I knew you were still alive was the slight pulse in your carotid. You must meditate often to go so deeply and quickly into a trance."

"How long was I out?"

She shrugged. "About twenty minutes. When you didn't answer me, I decided to let you be. I've meditated for years, and do a lot of visualization, but I've never gone as deep as you were. The café could have burned down around you."

"It saved my life once, but let's talk about something else," he said, finally sampling some of the dishes on the table.

She gave him a small, quick nod. "Okay. What's your plan for meeting Catherine Lily?"

"Believe it or not, I don't have one. It's like writing. I'm flying by the seat of my pants, just going where the story takes me."

"I've heard of writers who do that. I don't get it. When I wrote my thesis, I had every paragraph outlined. I have to know exactly where I'm going, so I can structure the path to get there."

"You miss out on the fun of the adventure if you only focus on the destination."

"It might work for you, but it doesn't work for me."

"I'm a pantser, you're a plotter. If you were a writer, you'd probably write your last line, last paragraph, last page first. I don't know what they'll be until I get there."

"That would drive me nuts."

"Hmm." He thought a minute. "To keep your sanity, then, I'll give you my opening salvo."

She cupped her hands at the sides of her head. "I'm all ears."

"I plan to tell Catherine Lily I saw a picture of her in a newspaper, and it reminded me of a woman I met in San Francisco two decades ago."

"That's it?" Amy asked.

"Yeah. Then I'll see what loose needles shake off the tree."

"Did you actually see a picture of her in a newspaper?"

"No. Hopefully, she won't ask."

"What if she does?"

"I'll tell her I can't remember. Then I'll ask her if she's traveled lately. When she mentions a trip, I'll say that must be it, and distract her with questions about what she did there. After she's comfortable talking to me, I'll work my way back to the questions I want answers to."

"Are you always so conniving?"

He slapped his hand over his heart. "How cruel. It's called research, sweetheart. It's an interview technique."

"You have to get the interviewee to trust you before you can get the information you want. Is that it?"

"That's it."

"Is that what you were doing when you were so attentive when I got sick at the museum? Trying to get me to trust you?"

He tried hard not to blanch. If he'd been standing, he would have stumbled back. "A legitimate question. My sister is pregnant for the third time. With every pregnancy, her stomach has gotten more sensitive. When she gets sick, I run off and call for help. When my niece and nephew are with me and get sick, I usually throw up, too. To take care of you, I had to focus on my turn at bat."

She laughed. "It's impossible to stay mad at you."

He pulled money out of his pocket to pay their check and signaled the server. "You just don't know me well enough."

Patrick was waiting at the door when they exited the restaurant. "The hack man is parked around the corner," he said, leading the way.

"Did you get enough to eat?" Amy asked.

"Yes, ma'am. Even saved a bit for tonight."

Jack studied Patrick closely, or rather looked through the dirt on his face closely. With his slender frame, dark blond, wavy hair, and blue eyes, Patrick could have been a teenage version of himself.

"Is that the only supper you'll have?" Jack asked.

"It's enough," Patrick said.

"Where do you sleep?" Amy asked.

He looked down, kicked at a rock on the sidewalk. "Here. There. I get by."

"What about your parents?" she asked.

"I'm too poor to have any, ma'am," Patrick said.

Amy laughed. "That's a joke, right?"

He smiled.

She tugged on his cap. "You're a cutie. Do you like baseball?"

His blue eyes lit up. "Yes, ma'am. All boys like baseball."

They reached the car, but before they climbed in, Jack asked, "Patrick, what are you going to do after today?"

"I guess I'll look for someone else to run errands for. Do you want to hire me again?"

"I might. Do you know how to swim?"

He shook his head. "I went to Coney Island once. Didn't like it much."

"Have you ever been on a ship?" Jack asked.

Patrick scrunched his face and shook his head. "No, sir. Don't think I'd like that, either."

"Are you interested in trying it out?"

"I don't know. What's the deal?"

"You've been very resourceful today. If you're interested, we'd like to take you with us to London."

Amy's eyebrows flashed.

"London! England?" Patrick asked.

"Interested?"

Patrick took off his cap and scratched his head. "I don't know, sir. How would I get back to America?"

"With us in two to three weeks. We'll pay all of your expenses, plus clothes to wear."

"What would you want me to do?"

Jack shrugged. "Stuff like what you're doing today. Keep your eyes open. Carry messages."

"Where would I eat, sleep?"

"In a cabin on board ship, and you'll eat in the dining room."

"I can sleep on the floor. I don't need a bed, and I don't want to eat at a fancy table. And, well… Will you pay me every day, or will my room and board be my pay?"

"I'll pay you a daily rate, plus room and board. Do we have a deal?" Jack extended his hand.

Patrick shook it. "Deal." He then opened the cab's door, and Amy slid into the back seat smiling up at Jack.

"Riverside and 107th," Jack said to the hack man.

He didn't know what possessed him to offer the boy a job, other than he had shown initiative today, and having an errand boy on board would be helpful, since their means of communication were so limited.

But what would Jack do with him when the brooch was recovered? He couldn't abandon Patrick at sea. Did that mean he'd have to take him to the twenty-first century? And if so, what would he do with him there?

He considered the question during the short drive to the Sterling's residence on Riverside Drive. The hack man stopped in front of the sprawling mansion. Patrick jumped out and opened Amy's door while Jack walked around from the other side and met them on the sidewalk.

"We'll be about an hour," Jack said. He took Amy's arm and escorted her along the walk, passing the lions. "If you keep this house, I hope you get rid of these."

She stared at him for a long three-count. "You don't like the king of the jungle?"

"Not a good welcoming symbol, but it might scare solicitors away."

She patted one of the lion's paws. "If I get rid of the lions, I'd put pineapples there."

"That's a good Southern tradition."

"I'll probably sell the house anyway. Let someone else deal with the lions, the leaky roof, peeling wallpaper, and rusty pipes."

As Jack mounted the steps to the portico, he thought about what she said. If she intended to sell the house, the MacKlenna Corporation might be interested in buying it. As often as Meredith, JL, and her brothers visited New York, having a residence in the city would be convenient. Was that it? Was that what Jack wanted? Use of the house whenever he came to the city? Or did he want possession of Catherine Lily's portrait?

They reached the front door and his finger hovered over the doorbell. "Are you ready?"

"I'm just along for the ride. The question is, are you?"

This might be a huge mistake, but meeting Catherine Lily was something he needed to do. He pushed the button, and a houseman dressed in livery opened the door.

"May I help you?"

Jack handed the houseman a business card he'd had printed in advance of the trip, identifying him as C. Jackson Mallory, Attorney at Law. "I'm Mr. Mallory. This is my fiancée, Miss Spalding. We'd like to see Mrs. Sterling if she's receiving company this afternoon."

The houseman read Jack's card. "Mrs. Sterling is traveling."

The news was like having a ship sail in front of him, blocking his wind. He lost speed and his sails flapped uselessly. How could this have happened? He would never meet Catherine Lily now. The sense of loss triggered a flashback to the night Carolina Rose died in his arms. And before he could control himself, his breathing hitched, and a cold sweat streamed between his shoulder blades.

Amy must have sensed his distress. She immediately picked up the conversation and, gesturing toward Jack said, "My fiancé is Mrs. Sterling's cousin from out of state. He's only in the city overnight, and was hoping to pay her a visit. If she isn't available, perhaps Mr. Sterling is?" Amy leaned forward in a confidential way, and continued, "At least he could tell his mother when he goes home that he visited with his cousin's husband. You know how mothers can be. Would it be possible...?"

Although Jack didn't see her do it, if he were asked, he would swear Amy batted her eyelashes. With his explosive emotions back under control, he gave her an amused smile. She was all business, with her adorable chin tilted upward, flashing her moxie.

"Come in. I'll see if Mr. Sterling is available."

Jack and Amy were shown into the drawing room. As soon as the houseman was gone, Amy asked, "Are you okay? You went pale and then broke out in a sweat."

"I have flashbacks. They knock me down. It takes a few minutes to recover. Then I'm fine. Thanks for picking up the ball." He moved across the room to stand at the window overlooking Riverside Drive toward the Hudson River. If possible, the clouds were darker than they were when they walked in the park. He turned to watch Amy pace the room. She had a great strut that added drama and intrigue to her personality. It wasn't a catwalk swagger, or a swaggering flash. It was natural and confident, and he enjoyed watching her.

She picked up a book off a nearby table and thumbed through it. "This is a first edition of *The Wonderful Wizard of Oz*."

"First edition? Really? Do you think it's still in the house? If so, it could be worth a hundred thousand dollars."

"I didn't make it through the entire inventory. I'll have to look. But a hundred grand? Seriously?"

"How much was the Christy Mathewson baseball card you wanted to buy?"

She looked at him with a raised eyebrow that would have made any true daughter of the South justly proud. "Sixty-five thousand. But how did you know?"

"The police followed up on calls and text messages you made and received prior to your disappearance."

She shivered. "I guess the police went through my whole life, searched my apartment, read my emails, talked to my doctors, co-workers..." She shivered again. "I feel violated."

He reached out and touched her gently, the backs of his fingers drifting over the slope of her shoulders. "They were doing every-thing they could to find you."

She reached up to her shoulder, placing her hand on his.

The soft click of shoes crossing the foyer's marble floor echoed through the mansion. The houseman entered the drawing room. "Mr. Sterling has a few minutes and will see you now. Follow me."

They followed the man through the wide foyer and into the library. Mr. Sterling rose from behind a large oak desk. "Mr. Mallory, Miss Spalding. Please have a seat."

Jack and Amy sat on a sofa while Mr. Sterling sat in a leather chair opposite them. He crossed his legs, coughed lightly, and looked inquiringly at them. "You're Miss Spalding, the reporter."

A glint sparkled briefly in her eyes. "Yes, sir. I am."

"I've seen you at the Polo Grounds. My wife and I both enjoy your morning column in the *Herald*. Your writing is"—he rubbed his fingertips with his thumb—"fresh and spirited."

"Thank you."

Mr. Sterling removed his spectacles and rubbed the red crease across the bridge of his nose. "I understand you want to see my wife, and you're related somehow. How may I help you?"

Jack leaned forward and propped his forearms on his thighs. "Your wife and I share a complicated family tree."

"I've met my wife's parents, and a few of her aunts and uncles, but I doubt I can be of much assistance."

"You may have heard something during your marriage that might be helpful," Jack said. "Are you familiar with your wife's great-grandfather, James Thomas MacKlenna?"

"He died in America a few years before we were born. That's about all I know."

"My family's line comes through Thomas's great-aunt Lorna MacKlenna Mallory. But I have a dear friend who also happens to be a distant cousin. Her name is Kit MacKlenna Montgomery, and she is Thomas's granddaughter, which makes Kit and your wife's mother first cousins."

Mr. Sterling listened, nodding, eyebrows alternately rising and falling at each fresh piece of information. "I might need to write this down."

"It will become clearer in a moment." Jack paused and took a breath.

"Twenty-seven years ago, I visited Kit and her husband at their winery in Napa, California. During the visit, I also traveled to San Francisco. While I was there, I met a Frenchwoman named Carolina Rose Arées."

Mr. Sterling's face paled.

Jack made the instant decision not to stop and query Mr. Sterling, but to continue. "Miss Arées was an artist who had been employed at the Metropolitan Museum of Art. She died shortly after I met her, as did her Uncle Edmond."

Mr. Sterling rose to his feet. "I've neglected my responsibilities as a host. May I offer you refreshment? A glass of whisky perhaps?"

"I'd love one," Amy said.

Jack glanced at her, eyebrows raised, and his unvoiced question was answered with a shrug. He had spoken with several of Amy's friends, and they all said she rarely drank. When she did, they told him, it was never more than a beer. Then Jack discovered her father died of alcoholism-related liver failure. Jack figured she didn't drink for fear of ending up like her dad. From what he knew about her so far, if she had an addiction, it was to the game of baseball.

Mr. Sterling crossed over to a nearby table with a silver tray holding a corked bottle of Dewar's whisky. He poured the alcohol into three crystal glasses. "Continue with your tale, Mr. Mallory." He handed a glass to Amy, to Jack, and then Mr. Sterling returned to his chair, carrying one for himself.

Jack continued, "Recently I saw your wife's picture, and was struck by how much she resembles Carolina Rose. The resemblance is so remarkable, in fact, they could have been twins. I contacted friends in the Highlands and discovered your wife was adopted by Thomas's granddaughter Alison and her husband Brian Taylor. I also discovered Alison had a sister Gracie, who ran off with a Frenchman."

"I'm vaguely aware of Gracie's story. I believe she died a young woman," Mr. Sterling said. "But how did you find out about the adoption? It's not widely known."

"Kit Montgomery lives in California, but she has remained in close contact with her family in the Highlands." Jack promised himself he would apologize to Kit for implicating her in a lie. "Families rarely keep secrets among themselves."

"That's a secret they should carry to their graves." Mr. Sterling didn't conceal his growing irritation. Jack needed to press for answers in case Sterling was getting ready to toss him out of the house.

"Carolina Rose told me she was raised by her French grandmother following her mother's early death. Was Gracie Morrison Carolina Rose's mother?"

Mr. Sterling shifted, and the chair uttered a groan, as if the leather wanted to speak for the man. "I don't know."

"Did Gracie run off with Jules Arées?"

"I don't know."

"Did she have twin daughters Catherine Lily and Carolina Rose?"

"I don't know."

"Were the babies split up and raised in different countries?"

"I don't know."

"If I'm right," Jack hammered in to make his main point, "Gracie Morrison is your wife's mother, not her aunt."

Mr. Sterling tilted his head back to let the whisky slide down his throat. Then he rose to refill his glass. "Do you have a picture of Carolina Rose?" Sterling carried the bottle back to his chair.

Jack unclipped the chain to his pocket watch and offered the timepiece to Mr. Sterling. "The painting inside is dated 1881, when Carolina Rose was in her mid-twenties."

Sterling traded the bottle for the watch and Jack poured a dram into his glass, but didn't offer any to Amy.

Mr. Sterling replaced his spectacles on his nose, and leveled a steady gaze at the picture. "I carry a picture of my wife on our wedding day in 1878." He opened his watch and handed both watches to Jack with a shaking hand. "These women look identical."

The picture of Catherine Lily confirmed what Jack already knew.

Mr. Sterling sat and refilled his glass. "What is it you want, Mr. Mallory?"

Jack had considered the question a dozen times or more. "I want the truth."

"There's only one person who can give you that—Alison Morrison Taylor—my mother-in-law. And she's dying. My wife is sailing to London, hoping she'll arrive in Inverness in time to see her before she passes."

Amy handed Jack her glass. If she expected him to refill it, she could just keep on expecting. His tender heart was out of the supporting-you-while-you-throw-up business. "Did you have any idea your wife might have a sister?" he asked Mr. Sterling. "Or did she?"

A frown rippled over Mr. Sterling's face, like a stone thrown into dark water. "More than twenty-five years ago, a colleague mentioned he saw a woman at the Metropolitan who resembled my wife. I was curious and hired an investigator to find her. He followed her to California, but before he could interview her, she disappeared. The authorities believed she might have died in a fire that killed her uncle. I continued to pay the investigator for another year while he followed leads throughout California, even to Napa, but he never found her. I put the entire matter out of my mind."

"Did Mrs. Sterling know about the look-alike woman or the investigator?" Amy asked.

"I never told her."

"Did she ever wonder about the identity of her birth parents?" she asked.

Mr. Sterling looked confused.

"She was adopted. Was she curious about where she came from?"

"My wife was never told she was adopted. That's why news of the family gossiping about it is very disconcerting."

"But you knew?" Jack asked.

"Her father told me before we married. He thought I should

know the truth, but they didn't want Catherine Lily to know."

"It might be time to tell her, so she can ask her mother what she knows before it's too late," Jack said.

"I still don't understand why this matters to you, Mr. Mallory."

Jack's hands trembled slightly; he took a deep breath and clasped his knees to still them. "Dr. Edmond Arées killed his niece, Carolina Rose. She died in my arms in October of 1881. If Catherine Lily is her sister, Carolina Rose would have wanted her to know."

32

1909 New York City—Amy

JACK AND AMY left the Sterling residence in silence. The rain had come and gone, and the heavy clouds had lifted, leaving behind a refreshing, clean scent in the air.

Amy didn't bother to raise the hem of her skirt or dodge puddles as she crossed the brick path from the house to the street, passing the lions. This time, though, she didn't pat their paws. They could have growled to their hearts' content, or lifted her up in a Simba moment. She didn't care. She was trying to wrap her mind around Jack's revelation about Carolina Rose. If Amy was reading between the lines correctly, he had been and probably still was very much in love with her. Amy couldn't help but feel sad for him.

Her watery eyes clouded her vision, but not her insights. On second thought, it wasn't sorrow she felt for Jack. It was empathy. She knew firsthand what it was like to be at a loved one's side when they died. She had been there for her parents. While she had turned her grief into anger at the diseases that killed them, Jack turned his into guilt for the role he played in Carolina Rose's death. Both were destructive emotions. Thankfully, her anger mellowed, but Jack's guilt was still sharp-edged and raw.

Patrick was waiting on the curb, his hand on the open car door. He had scrubbed his face and finger-combed his over-the-collar hair. His high cheekbones, strong jaw, and full bottom lip combined to create a striking profile, but it was his deep blue eyes that caused a visceral reaction. They were too wise for his age. Amy couldn't begin to imagine the evil he'd seen in his dozen years. But he had adapted and survived despite the conditions. If anyone deserved a chance, he did.

When they reached the car, Jack said, "I don't want to get in yet. Will you walk with me?"

A walk in the clean air was exactly what she needed, too, especially since the sun was peeking through the clouds now, and the humidity had dropped considerably. She smiled at Patrick, wanting him to know she appreciated his efforts to clean himself up, but she didn't want to embarrass him. "Thank you for taking your job so seriously," she said. "Will you meet us at 84th Street and Riverside? Mr. Mallory and I are going to walk in the park."

"Yes, ma'am." He closed the back door of the cab and hopped into the front seat.

Amy took Jack's proffered arm, and when it was safe to cross, he led her to the crowded path on the opposite side of the divided drive. The shade-dappled path was bordered by a low, castle-like retaining wall on the river side and a hurdle fence on the other side. Below the wall the ground sloped down to another path meandering along the river and the landscaped park. The path led to the Little Red Lighthouse, where the George Washington Bridge would stand one day.

They walked a half block in silence before Jack said, "I owe you an explanation."

She waved her hand, brushing away his perceived obligation. "No you don't."

"I dragged you in there. You should know what it was about."

"You didn't drag me. We were paying a visit to my three-times great-grandmother. But I'd be lying if I said I wasn't curious. If you want to tell me, I'm all ears."

He cleared his throat, as if preparing to give a speech, and wiped his forehead with a handkerchief. "How about I give you the synopsis? Then you'll understand Connor, Pete, Kevin, and JL's nuanced conversations and comments about me."

"I noticed something was going on, but really, it's none of my business. I'm a short-timer in this group."

He directed her out of the line of pedestrians and toward the wall, where he leaned on his forearms and looked out over the river. He didn't speak for several moments and then he said, "A self-portrait of Kit MacKlenna has hung in the winery's welcome center in Napa for more than a century. Last fall, Elliott's younger son, James Cullen, was studying Morse code, and found a hidden message in the painting no one had noticed before. It said, 'bring insulin'. After a few heated discussions, eleven adults and five children traveled back to 1881 for a visit with Kit and Cullen at Montgomery Winery."

Amy leaned against the wall too, but instead of looking out toward the water—while she breathed in the fragrant, honeyed scent of daylilies planted near the wall—she watched Jack's bland mask fade away until it was replaced by a tight, pained grimace.

"Taking five children along was very brave," she said.

He chuckled. "The kids refused to stay behind, and they actually handled it very well. In fact, they all want to go on another adventure."

She barked a laugh. "They're welcome to any spots with my name on them."

He gave her an easy smile. "Before this last trip, they thought adventures were like playing parts in a movie. Now they know they're serious business, even Kenzie and David's wild twin boys."

"Are they wild because they're not yours?"

"They're wild because they know their parents, Kenzie and David, are dragon slayers."

"I didn't have dragon slayer parents, did you?"

"My mother was one."

"Really? What'd she do?"

"She was a United States Senator. When my dad died, she was appointed to fill the rest of his term, and then she ran for reelection and won." Jack took Amy's arm, and they began walking again.

"Thanks for the distraction."

"I'm sorry. I didn't mean to do that."

"It's not a criticism. I'm glad you did. It's too big a story to tell cold. You need to"—he did a snake arm—"glide into it."

"You didn't say who needed insulin. Was it Kit?"

"No. It was the thirteen-year-old granddaughter of her dearest friend. Kit knew if help came, it would only be temporary. If the child was going to survive, she'd have to live in the future."

"How'd the child feel about it?"

"She accepted it. She's an exceptional young woman. She's been in the twenty-first century for eight months now, and you'd never know she was born in the 1800s."

The bustle of the Upper West Side seemed to fade away, leaving Amy in an echo chamber with Jack, unaware of anything outside their bubble.

"After we got there," Jack continued, "everyone pursued their own interests: painting, horses, wine, exploring."

"What was yours?"

"Seeing San Francisco before the Golden Gate Bridge was built and the 1906 earthquake destroyed so much of the city. I sneaked off and caught the train. When I got there, my first random stop was the Conservatory of Flowers. That's where I met Carolina Rose."

Amy tugged him over to an empty bench, where they sat facing each other. "With her name, it seems an appropriate place to be. What was she doing?"

"Sketching flowers. We talked until the museum closed. I arranged transportation for us back to her hotel."

"Had you planned to stay overnight?"

"I intended to go back to the winery."

"Didn't you think they would worry about you being gone so long?"

"The winery's manager knew I took the train to the city. I figured I had twenty-four hours before someone showed up to drag me back, and I planned to return to Napa by then."

"I'm guessing you didn't make it."

His face paled beneath a sheen of sweat.

She touched his arm gently. "You don't have to talk about this."

"I'm okay," he said, wiping his face again.

"So you went to the hotel. What happened then?"

"Carolina Rose had a prearranged meeting with her uncle, but he didn't show up. She decided to go to her studio to work instead. I offered to walk with her."

Jack turned away from Amy, eyes half-lidded, fingers tented in his lap, and took a long, slow breath before continuing. "On the way out of the hotel, we ran into Lillian Russell and her entourage. Lillian knew Carolina Rose from New York City. We talked for a few minutes, then before we left, she invited us to come to her show."

"She's vivacious, isn't she?"

"Lillian? Yes, and beautiful. At least she was almost three decades ago, and what a voice."

"She still is beautiful." Another heavy silence fell between them. Then Amy said, "I find it strange that you met Lillian while traveling back in time, and here she is again involved in another—as you call it—adventure."

"It is rather strange, and makes me wonder if I triggered something that caused this mess."

Amy leaned closer, hoping to reassure him. "How could your meeting then affect me now? It happened almost three decades ago. And besides, you weren't even here when the mess-up with my brooch occurred."

"You're right."

She laughed, quite softly. "I've been right more times in the last two months than I've ever been in my life. It's weird. Go on. What happened next?"

Jack crossed his leg, and looking very distracted, flicked his finger back and forth over the steamed crease in his trousers, as if the sharp point mirrored the vividness of his recollection.

"We walked to Carolina Rose's nearby studio, where I met her Uncle Edmond. He was meeting with a man I recognized—General Albert Pike—and I was immediately alarmed and suspicious."

"Why?"

"Because the general was a founding member of the Knights of the Golden Circle."

"Never heard of the Knights," Amy said.

"You've heard of the Confederate gold that supposedly disappeared the night Richmond burned at the end of the Civil War?"

"Sure, who hasn't?"

"Braham and I were in Richmond the night of the fire, and tried to stop the train from leaving the city with the Confederate treasury. We failed. We both became obsessed with finding it, and spent countless hours tracking down rumors."

"How do the Knights of the Golden Circle fit in?"

"If the rumors were true, the KGC buried it."

"What was your plan? To ask the general for a map?"

"Let's just say I was curious."

"Compared to the rest of you, my adventure has been risk-free. I made friends. I got a job. I have money and a place to live. I even started an early version of Little League on the Upper West Side with some kids I met. There hasn't been a war or a missing Confederate treasury."

"But the difference is, we all knew within a week we'd go home again. You thought you'd spend the rest of your life here."

"You were stuck in a prison. Did you think you'd go home?"

"That was different. It wasn't my brooch. It wasn't given to me."

"A brooch wasn't given to me, either. I inherited one. But let's get back to your story. You met this general guy, who might know something about the gold. What happened then?"

"Carolina Rose and I had dinner, and if it's possible to fall in love in a few hours, I did." His reply seemed casual, but there was something very odd in his voice, as if he were struggling to mask his emotions. "After dinner," he continued, "we went to a party given in Lillian's honor. That's where I met the newspaper reporter who wanted to interview me."

"Oh, yes, the press contact Mr. Bennett mentioned. What'd you do?"

The Diamond Brooch   307

"I told him I wasn't interested. But the encounter with the press wasn't the highlight of the party. Carolina Rose's uncle was there, too. I followed him and overheard him planning to move the treasure."

"Wow. You kept showing up at the right time and place."

"Everything was going great until Braham and JL crashed the party."

"They literally crashed it?"

He shook his head.

"You'd only been gone a few hours. Why'd they come so soon?"

"Kit had fallen off a horse, and my sister…you remember she's a surgeon…was afraid Kit might have a spinal or brain injury and needed to go to a modern hospital for possible surgery."

"But they couldn't leave without you."

"Right. But Braham told Charlotte if Kit's life was in danger, then to leave immediately."

"Then how were you, Braham, and JL supposed to get back?"

"Kit's care trumped the rest of us. Then, when Kit's husband had a heart attack, and Elliott had a mini-stroke, Charlotte had no choice but to leave, and take Emily, too."

"Holy cow."

"Since we were stuck in the past, Braham and I decided to pursue the gold, and were captured by Uncle Edmond's men. He also sent his soldiers to collect his niece, who we had left in JL's care."

"So now the bad guys have you, Braham, JL, and Carolina Rose. Where was Kevin?"

"Kevin refused to go home without JL. As soon as the others left, he caught the train to San Francisco, and arrived about the same time as Connor, Pete, and Braham's son, Lincoln."

She held her hand out in a stop gesture. "Whoa, wait a minute. Charlotte took everyone home, then Pete and Connor used the brooches to come right back?"

"Correct. Along with Braham's son."

"So now," Amy scratched her head, visualizing people and places, "there are four captured people and four rescuers. Dang, I need a score card to keep all this straight."

"Everyone but Lincoln was eventually captured. The seven of us were tied up, and Carolina Rose was being held at gunpoint by her uncle. He was convinced there were more people coming for the gold, and threatened to shoot Carolina Rose unless we told him who else was involved."

"But there isn't...wasn't...anybody else."

"Right. But he didn't believe us."

"So...what happened?"

"Lincoln sneaked into the building where we were being held and communicated with his dad through this secret signal they have, and Lincoln shot through the connector attaching the chandelier to the ceiling."

"He's how old?"

"Ten, and an excellent shot. Better than I am. The moment the gun discharged, Carolina Rose fought her uncle for control of his gun, but he pushed her into the path of the chandelier as it crashed to the floor."

"He pushed her? Why?"

"I don't know. Maybe he thought she betrayed him."

"Did the chandelier fall on her?"

"Shards of glass peppered her body, and a chunk stabbed her in the neck.

Jack held his hand to the side of his neck while he spoke conversationally, but he had a faraway look in his eyes. Amy wanted to reach out to touch him, but she held back, not sure he'd appreciate her comforting him right now.

"We went home immediately," Jack continued, "but Carolina Rose...she didn't survive."

Amy decided to keep him talking, hoping he wouldn't fall head first into the pain of the memory. "What happened to Edmond?"

"He died, too. When the chandelier crashed, it started a fire. We only had a couple of minutes to get out before the building blew up."

"Two dead and no gold."

"Two dead, but we eventually found the gold. When I met Carolina Rose, she was painting a collection of flowers for a botanical book her uncle was writing. After her funeral, Kenzie was looking at Carolina Rose's sketchbook and found hidden pictures in several of them. They were clues to the gold's location."

"Carolina Rose was part of the KGC?"

"I don't know if she was part of the organization or not, but she knew where the treasure was buried, and she knew the real reason why she was painting the flowers."

"That had to hurt."

"Everyone was pissed at me for going off to San Francisco, and pissed at Carolina Rose for betraying us." He jumped up and paced unsteadily in front of her.

"Let's walk." Amy hoped moving forward would break the hold the memory had on him. "How did it feel to find a treasure you'd spent years searching for?"

"I didn't go on the hunt. I went to the Himalayas for several weeks."

Amy stopped walking and turned to face him. "I appreciate you telling me the cold facts, but I don't think it's the cold facts you wanted me to know."

"That's it. That's all of it. I wanted you to know in case you picked up on some old hostility between me and the others."

She crossed her arms. "I can read between the lines. I learned how to do it as a kid, when people talked about my dad and alcohol. And I can read between the lines of the story you just told me. You fell head over heels in love with Carolina Rose in only a few hours. Her death, for which you feel responsible, broke your heart, and it's still mending."

His eyes stayed steady on her face for a moment before he looked away.

"The romantic marriage proposal in the park," Amy said, "was for her. Wasn't it?"

He didn't say anything.

"I knew it wasn't for me. I thought it might be for a character in an upcoming book, but it was for Carolina Rose. It was the proposal you never got to make. That's why you postponed coming after me, isn't it? You probably wouldn't have come at all if you hadn't made the connection between the love of your life and Catherine Lily."

"It's not like that," he said.

"Save the denials. Look, I like you. I have fun with you. You're a great guy, and one of the most interesting people I've ever met. But we're not on the same path. I love my life here. I want to stay, but I'm going home to clear Joe. I don't know if I'll come back or not. If I don't, Joe and I will get married in a few months. I'll have a couple of kids who'll play Little League baseball, and I'll get to coach them. There are so many roads we can take in our lives, and they all have potholes. The best we can hope for is to have a life partner who knows where the holes are and how to fix them. Joe knows mine. I know his. The hole you're carrying, Jack, is deep, but not impossible to fix…if you'll allow those closest to you to help."

"Mr. Mallory."

Jack and Amy turned quickly at the sound of his name and the sweep of boots through the grass.

"Patrick. What's the matter, lad?" Jack asked.

The boy came striding swiftly down the path. "Mr. Moretti is looking for you. Should I tell him to come here?"

"What's the closest cross street?" Amy asked.

Patrick pointed. "If you take the path to the right, it'll come out at 86th."

"Tell Mr. Moretti we'll meet him at the apartment," she said.

"What's the apartment's address?" he asked.

"One-oh-seven and Riverside." Amy watched Patrick run off. "He needs new boots, too. There're more holes than leather in the ones he's wearing."

Jack was still for a moment, frowning. Then, "I guess his holes can be fixed."

She merely smiled, not bothered by his tone. "I'm not saying you can't be fixed, Mallory. Matter of fact, I think you're further along than you give yourself credit for. I doubt you could have told your story several months ago. Maybe not even one month ago. You're healing. It doesn't mean you'll forget her. It means you'll learn to live with the loss of her. And besides, I wouldn't be turning you on if you weren't getting your life back on track."

He pulled her into his side, hugging her, and kissed the top of her head. "Since you've put sex on the table, and we are engaged..."

She elbowed him in the ribs. "Forget it, Mallory."

"Haven't you heard of pity sex?"

"You're not a pity sex kind of guy, plus I have a boyfriend I'm faithful to, but good try. Come on. Let's go see what Gabriele wants."

As they followed the path up the hill Amy said, "You know, it all fits together now."

"What does?"

"Running off to San Francisco, and being a writer who flies or writes by the seat of his pants. You don't like structure. You're afraid it will kill your creativity. If you told everyone where you were going, you would have had to explain why. You didn't know why. It was an organic trip. Your muse is entirely too sensitive. You're like a baseball player. You know what's worked for you before, so you set up rituals. If you don't operate the same way every time, you believe your muse won't respond. And if your muse won't show up, you're facing writer's block."

"You sound like my therapist."

"If that's the case, you know the way out. You just aren't ready to take it." Amy waved at Gabriele, who was standing on the corner with Patrick.

Jack took out his pocket watch. "It's almost four. I know you have a lot to do to get ready for tomorrow, but would you like to have dinner tonight?"

She shook her head. "I've been gone since early Tuesday morning. I'll stay home and pack. If we get the brooch, we won't come back here, will we?"

"There's no reason. We can leave from London, or from the ship. It doesn't matter."

They crossed the divided boulevard at a much busier intersection than they had crossed earlier, and reached the corner where Gabriele and Patrick were waiting, "What's up?" Jack asked.

"I just left Pete and Connor at the hotel," Gabriele said. "They struck out. Someone was in the apartment all day."

Jack grimaced.

"I can get in anywhere," Patrick said. "Do you want me to try?"

Jack tugged on his cap. "No, I don't. Where are Kevin and JL?"

"They're still shopping. What about tonight? Do you want theater tickets or dinner reservations? Maybe at Delmonico's? They're probably booked for the evening, but I can make a few calls and work it out."

"I'd rather go someplace simple," Jack said.

"Lilla's Restaurant in Little Italy. It's good food. Good service," Gabriele said.

Amy made a brief gesture of frustration. "Darn. If you're going to Lilla's, I'll have to go, too. I can't pass up her lasagna. What if I bring Maria and Isabella and meet you there?"

"What time?" Jack asked.

"I don't know. Maybe eight," Amy said.

"I'll drive Amy, Isabella, and Maria and meet you there," Gabriele said. "What about the others?"

"They'll go, too. In the meantime, I'll take Patrick shopping."

"What for?" Gabriele asked.

Patrick's face split into a grin. "Mr. Mallory hired me to go on the ship tomorrow."

"He's been very resourceful today," Jack said, clapping the boy's shoulder. "I anticipate we'll need him to relay messages and run errands."

Gabriele gave Jack a slightly worried look. "Are you sure?"

"If he misbehaves, I'll toss him overboard."

Patrick's eyes were huge, and his jaw dropped. "I won't be any trouble. I promise. I'll do whatever you want."

Amy knew Jack was kidding, but it didn't hurt to instill a bit of discipline in case Patrick decided he didn't want to work. Amy put her arm around his shoulder. "You'll be fine as long as you do what you're asked." Then she whispered, "He might make you eat carrots and Brussels sprouts, but he won't throw you in the water."

Patrick visibly relaxed.

"Come on, lad," Jack said. "Let's go buy you some new threads, but first you're getting a bath and haircut."

"A bath?" Patrick's voice squeaked.

"And a haircut."

Patrick opened the cab door, but before Jack slid into the back seat, he gave Amy a hug. "Thanks for listening and not passing judgment. In the past few months, everyone has cast aspersions. I've had enough for a lifetime."

She gently patted his chest, then let her palm rest over his heart for a moment. "I'm glad you told me. I'll see you later." Then she stepped back, lifting a hand in farewell as the engine started and the car drove away. After they disappeared around the corner, she turned to Gabriele. "Are Maria and Isabella packing for tomorrow?"

"I took them shopping for a few things, but Isabella is as you say, over the moon."

Amy did a ballet third position with her arm over her head, adding a flip of the wrist, which flashed her ring. "I'm over the moon, too."

He snatched her hand out of the air and inspected the ring. "What's this?"

"It's an engagement ring."

Gabriele looked at her, wide-eyed and interested. "Who are you marrying? Jack Mallory?"

"I'm not marrying anybody. I had to tell a lie, and Jack was honorable enough to play along."

"Who'd you lie to?"

"Mr. Bennett got mad when I told him I was leaving town on a family emergency. He said he was coming to the train station to see me off and bringing a photographer to take our picture. I had to tell him I was going to London first on a European honeymoon."

"Are you going to marry Jack?"

"Heavens, no. I just said it so it would make sense to Mr. Bennett, and he wouldn't give my column to someone else, but he probably will anyway."

"Taking your column away would be bad for business. Another newspaper would offer you a job, and he'd lose subscribers."

"Why didn't I think of that?"

"You were too busy explaining your other lies."

She would never get used to telling lies, and almost always ended up covering them up and forgetting who she told. Keeping them straight was a full-time job.

They walked into the apartment building and he pushed the elevator call button. "Do you get to keep the ring?"

She glanced at the diamonds and sapphire and twisted the ring back and forth absent-mindedly on her finger. "Jack said he doesn't want it back."

Gabriele opened the elevator's cage door, and she entered first. "You can sell it," he said, closing both doors, "and invest the proceeds. As savvy as you are, you'll double your investment in a month."

A week ago, the idea would have thrilled her. But not today. And not this ring. She would never sell it, or use it as collateral for a loan. And even though Jack's proposal wasn't meant for her, she would never forget it…

I can't imagine my life without you in it, without your smile to grace my mornings, without your sigh to still my nights…

33

1909 New York City—JL

SHORTLY BEFORE EIGHT O'CLOCK, JL led the way into Lilla's Restaurant on Mulberry Street in Little Italy. The hairs on the back of her neck, which had been twitching since early afternoon weren't as strong as they had been earlier, but were still irritatingly present.

She had pulled Kevin aside several times during their shopping expedition to look in windows, hoping the reflection would reveal someone suspicious-looking, but she never spotted a tail. The feeling she was being watched, though, persisted.

Too bad she hadn't found an opportunity to mention the feeling privately to Connor or Pete. They would take her seriously. Kevin would tell her she was worrying unnecessarily. He lived in the world of numbers, facts, and bottom lines. The world she lived in depended on facts, too. But gut feelings had solved cases and saved her life more than once. She never ignored them.

"We're with the Moretti party," she told a woman with slightly graying hair and sparkling gray eyes stationed near the door. JL put her spidey senses on hold while she studied the woman and thought about her dad. It was time for her and her brothers to find Pops a companion. He was happy with his new life at Montgomery Winery, but he was lonely. And he needed a vivacious woman his age to enjoy the California grapes he spent his days protecting.

"I'm Lilla. I've been expecting you. Gabriele told me all about Amy's family. Welcome to my restaurant. I have tables ready for you. Come."

JL, Kevin, Connor, Pete, and Jack followed Lilla to the back corner, out of the way of other diners and customers drinking at the bar. Three tables covered with white tablecloths were pushed together, providing seating for ten.

JL laced fingers with Kevin and steered him toward the end to sit as far from Jack as she could. She was still pissed at him. He had shown up at the hotel earlier with a street kid, and announced he was taking the child to London, like a souvenir he bought at a store. What in the hell did he plan to do with a preteen? Abandon him in England to fend for himself?

The situation was like San Francisco all over again, and gave JL a headache. Regardless of how helpful Jack was during her court appearance, she considered him a selfish son of a bitch, who saw himself through the distorted prism of an all-consuming ego.

Kevin whispered in her ear. "You need to calm down. Have you even stopped seething at Jack long enough to smell this place? I've traveled all over Italy, eaten in dozens of restaurants, but this place is a gold mine."

JL sniffed.

Kevin gave her tense shoulders a quick rub. "What's the strongest scent?"

She sniffed. "Bread. No, garlic." She sniffed again. "Bread, onion, and peppers." She sniffed again. "Tomato sauce and bread."

"I get that you like the bread. What else?"

"Onions, and a slightly earthy, almost narcotic smell. What is it?"

"Truffles," Kevin said. "Sliced over plates of springy spaghetti, they're to die for."

She laughed, waving her hands toward her face, trying to fan all the delicious smells straight into her nose. "You'll have to carry me out of here."

A waiter placed a basket of bread and two bottles of vino on the table. Neither bottle had a label. Kevin picked one up, sniffed, then poured a couple of ounces into his and JL's glasses. She swirled the red wine to intensify the aroma, smelling as she swirled. Kevin had taken great pains to teach her to appreciate the wine instead of gulping it down like beer. She took a small sip, swished it around her mouth, then, after a couple of seconds swallowed.

"It's good," she said.

"It's from the Chianti region. Somewhere south of Florence," Kevin said.

"How do you know?"

"Because I've immersed myself in the history of Italian wines. This is exceptional. I've got to get the name of the winery."

"I don't care where it's from. Just pour."

She picked up a loaf of bread from the basket. "Yum. Still warm." She split off a chunk between her fingers, and steam escaped, along with more of the familiar, yeasty aroma.

With a glass of wine and a chunk of bread, she settled back with her glass and tried to clear her mind and enjoy a delicious Italian meal with the man she loved and would marry in a few weeks. But first they needed to recover the diamond brooch and get home. Austin's high school graduation and relocating him to Lexington had taken up most of May. And, according to Meredith, the acting Mother of the Bride, JL should have tackled more of her to-do list before going on this adventure. The family matriarch had not approved of JL joining the team, but David intervened on JL's behalf to let her go.

In hindsight, she wished David had intervened and kept Jack at home.

As if reading her mind, Kevin said, "You can't stay mad at him."

"Why not? He deserves it."

"I think Patrick will be helpful."

"What's Jack going to do with him afterwards? Has he thought about that? No. Because it would require him to consider someone else's well-being."

"Gabe can bring him home."

"Why should Gabe have to be responsible for him?"

Kevin nodded toward the door. "There's Gabe now. Ask him how he feels about it. If he's not on board, I'll insist the issue be put to a group vote."

"Why put it to a vote? Why not just tell Jack he can't drag a kid away from his home and dump him in England?"

"He's a street kid, JL," Kevin said sharply. "He doesn't have a home."

She wasn't going to back down. Not to Kevin. Not to Jack. "The streets of New York are his home. He doesn't know his way around London, and that could be fatal. Do you want to be responsible for his death? I don't."

For the past several weeks, Kevin would suddenly become more reserved with her, more professional than personal, more perfunctory than passionate. Then, after an hour or a day, he would revert to himself. Right now, he was in a weird mood. It could last for minutes or hours, and she missed him like crazy when he withdrew from her.

Gabe escorted Amy and two other women to the table. Jack, Kevin, Connor, and Pete pushed to their feet for the introductions. "Gentlemen...and lady...it is my pleasure to introduce you to... Isabella and Maria Ricci."

After Gabe introduced her and moved on to the rest of their group, JL studied the women. Maria could have been the identical twin of the restaurant owner, and Isabella was one of the most striking young women JL had ever seen. She was model-beautiful, with long black hair and big brown eyes, and Pete was mesmerized. JL knew more about Pete's love life than she ever wanted to know, and had seen him with dozens of women, but she had never seen him completely overawed, as he was right now.

At the other end of the table, something equally interesting was happening. Amy's eyes lit up at seeing Jack, and Jack's old smile brightened his face at seeing Amy. He leaned down, put his mouth to her ear, and whatever he whispered made her smile, and then he kissed her cheek, barely missing her mouth.

JL grabbed the edge of the table to keep it from rocking. The dynamite blast Jack and Amy set off topped the Richter scale. Everyone else was drawn to Isabella, and missed what JL considered to be far more newsworthy. She didn't think Amy and Jack had slept together, but if they didn't soon, they might simply burst into flames. What the hell was going on?

Then JL's eyes almost bugged out of their sockets when Amy flashed a diamond and sapphire ring; a ring that hadn't been on her left-hand ring finger when she and Jack left the hotel that morning.

To quote James Cullen: *Hashtag WTF*

JL nudged Kevin. "Amy is wearing a very expensive diamond and sapphire ring. Where'd it come from? And if she had it with her, why didn't she use it as collateral for her loan instead of the brooch?"

Kevin leaned past her to look at the ring. "It's beautiful."

"Ask Jack when you get a chance."

Everyone took their seats, with Jack sitting between Kevin and Amy. As several conversations began at once, Kevin spoke low-voiced to Jack, and Jack replied in the same tone. Kevin nodded. Then whispered to JL. "He's going to make an announcement."

A minute later, Jack tapped his wine glass with a knife. "May I have your attention?" He glanced around the room, then smiled down at Amy. "This morning I asked Amy Spalding to marry me, and she accepted."

There was a murmur of voices around the restaurant, "Amy Spalding. The columnist at the *Herald*."

There was stunned silence at their table, except for Isabella and Maria, who clapped and chattered excitedly in Italian. JL clapped, but she was rendered speechless. This had to be a charade, but why hadn't Jack warned them?

An older woman came to their table. "Miss Spalding, I read your column every morning. Saturdays and Sundays are simply dreadful because you're not in the weekend paper. Now you're getting married, I hope you don't quit writing."

Amy laced her fingers with Jack's. "My fiancé is very supportive of my career. I'll continue to write as long as the public buys the newspaper."

"You have a devoted fan in me, and congratulations on your upcoming nuptials. Do you have a date set yet?"

"Next week," Amy said.

The woman smiled and returned to her companions, leaving JL even more confused. Amy and Jack glowed with an intoxicating prenuptial bliss, almost making JL gag. Maria, Isabella, and Pete spoke in animated Italian, and Connor and Kevin drank another glass of wine. JL's head was spinning, but then her keen eye noticed Gabe was calmly dipping his bread in olive oil.

She leaned over to her brother. "Look at Gabe."

"Okay, why?"

"Why is he so calm about the news?"

"Guess he knew," Connor said. "Or, maybe he has feelings for Amy and isn't happy about it."

"Unrequited love?"

"Something like that."

"Nah," JL said. "He'd be drowning his unrequited love in another glass of wine. It's something else." She leaned back and considered possibilities. She had to think in terms of 1909, and not the twenty-first century. Jack had mentioned Amy was considering returning to the past once she cleared Joe Gilbert's name. If she returned, she would want to resume her life. She couldn't afford to have her reputation sullied. She leaned over to Connor again.

"It's a sham," she said. "He's doing it to protect Amy's reputation, but what's in it for Jack?"

"How do you know it's a sham?"

"Just call me Sherlock."

"Honestly, JL…" Concern in Connor's voice softened his words. "I, for one, would like to see him happy. I hope it's for real. And your snarkiness is driving us all nuts. Lighten up, will you?"

She scratched the side of her face, staring at her brother. "I'm that bad? Really?"

"I know you've got a lot on your mind with the new job, Austin's graduation, pressure from Elliott, and the wedding, but you're acting weird as shit. So give it a rest, okay."

If her behavior was bothering easygoing Connor, then she needed to lighten up.

Two waiters arrived with plates of ravioli, spaghettini, capellini, fettuccine alfredo, lasagna, calamari, antipasto and more, covering the table with some of the most deliciously scented food JL had ever smelled.

"Can we take Maria's sister home with us?"

"If it's as good as it smells, you got my vote to kidnap her," Connor said.

Gabe cupped his hand next to his mouth and directed his voice in JL's direction. "Maria is a better cook, but don't tell her sister, Lilla."

"Then I vote we kidnap Maria."

"And Isabella," Pete added.

"As long as we're kidnapping people," Connor said quietly to JL. "I vote for Gabe. If you dropped David and Gabe in the woods without anything but the clothes on their back. David would make weapons out of sticks and stones to hunt for food, but Gabe would find a tribe to feed him and provide transportation out of the woods."

"That's impressive," JL whispered back.

"He's got a knack for logistics." Then, as an aside, Connor added, "He might have a gambling problem."

"What makes you think he has a problem?" she asked.

"Didn't you notice he was driving a different car today?"

"I did. But I didn't say anything."

"He lost the other one in a card game last night. He borrowed the one he's driving now," Connor said.

"It was probably a bad bet?" JL said.

"He needs his car for business. If he didn't have a gambling problem, he wouldn't have risked it."

"Elliott tolerates a lot of things," she said, "but he wouldn't tolerate high-stakes gambling."

Connor laughed. "What the hell is thoroughbred racing?"

More dishes were brought to the table: sautéed mushrooms, crispy pizza, more lasagna, grilled fish with artichoke caponata, and wine and more wine. The conversation grew louder, and the family stories, while heavily censored, were funny and entertaining. JL couldn't remember the last time she laughed so hard. She and Connor teased Pete relentlessly, and the more they teased him, the more notice Isabella gave him.

"Gotta watch that girl," JL said to Connor.

"Gotta watch Pete," Connor said. "He's too old for her."

After about two hours of shoveling food, JL pushed back her plate and said, "Enough. If I eat one more bite, I'll explode."

Kevin refilled her wine glass. "Then drink, because this is delicious."

The dishes were cleared, more wine was brought out, and the now-empty tables at the front of the restaurant were pushed back against the wall.

"It's time to dance," Isabella said.

JL jumped up excitedly. "Are we going to do the tarantella?"

"Do you know how?" Isabella asked.

JL emptied her wine glass again, and Kevin refilled it. "Yes, thanks to Pete."

A parade of musicians carrying a mandolin, guitar, accordion, tambourines, flute, and a fiddle came through the front door to the rousing applause of the other diners. Lilla called for all the women to join her.

"Come on, Amy." JL hurried to the dance floor, latching on to Amy's arm. "Be my partner." Maria and Isabella followed behind them. As JL made her way through the diners, she did her fourth or fifth radar sweep of the night, but while nothing pinged on her screen, her senses remained alert.

"Do you know the tarantella?" Amy asked JL.

"Yes, do you?"

"Isabella taught me. I love it, but you're Irish. How'd you learn?"

"When I joined the NYPD, Pete asked to partner with me. He was determined to prove the Irish and Italians could work together.

The whole love-hate thing drove him nuts. We were letting off steam one night, and he taught me how to do the tarantella." JL waved her arms above her head. "Woohoo! Let's dance."

Maria, Amy, Isabella, and JL formed a foursome. When the music started, they moved up and back with one hand on their hips, the other holding a tambourine, bouncing and kicking, crossing their right foot in front of the left, and the left in front of the right. Nothing else mattered to JL when she was dancing, not even the constant prickling sensation on her neck, and her blood was pumping to the tempo of the music. She tapped the tambourine to her left shoulder, left hip, right hip, then repeated the triangle across her body, smiling at the other three women.

She was tipsy, but, man, oh man, music and dancing touched her soul as nothing else could.

JL placed her right hand in the center of the foursome, and the others joined hers to form a star shape. Then, with their left hands holding their tambourines, she and the others performed the tarantella steps simultaneously while rotating in a clockwise circle.

The tempo increased into a frenzied dance. She laughed. Amy laughed, Isabella and her grandmother laughed, and when JL looked out over the heads of the other women, she saw Kevin laughing, too. He must have some Italian in his blood, because he loved everything about the country—the food, the music, and especially the wine.

The frenzied dance continued until she could barely catch her breath. When the dance ended, Kevin swept her into his arms and kissed her. It was clear he intended only a brief kiss, but his mouth was soft and warm, and she moved instinctively toward him as the music started up again for the teasing, flirtatious couples dance.

"Hey, cut that out, *ragazza tosta*," Pete said to JL as he knelt on his right knee, tapping the tambourine over his head while Isabella performed the tarantella steps in a counterclockwise circle around him.

"God, you looked sexy dancing," Kevin said. "If they hadn't invited the men, I would have crashed the party." He knelt so JL could dance in a circle around him. Then Pete and Isabella and Kevin and JL stood opposite each other, held their right hands in the center, forming a star shape, as the women had done in their dance, and while their left hands shook the tambourines, they rotated clockwise.

She'd been out clubbing with Kevin, and they danced everything from disco fever to the funky chicken, and the Village People's YMCA to the macarena, but they had never done the tarantella before now.

"Let's do this at our wedding," she said.

Kevin grabbed a cloth napkin off the counter and patted the sweat off JL's forehead. "We'll have to invite more Italians, or we'll be the only ones on the dance floor."

"We'll have Jack. He knows the tarantella. Look at him." She'd never seen Jack on the dance floor before, and was surprised by his natural rhythm and the ease with which he moved with the music. He and Kevin were both natural athletes, but Jack had something else—an innate dancer's grace.

When the music stopped, JL's head didn't. She needed air and a bathroom. Kevin pulled her into a hug. "Where's the bathroom?" she asked.

"Right out the back door. I asked, knowing you would need to go. I'll go with you."

"Don't you think I can potty by myself?"

"No."

They headed toward the back door, but Connor stopped them. "What do you think of this kid Jack wants to take with us?"

"I'd tell you exactly what I think, but I've got to pee. You tell him, Kevin."

He kissed her again. "I'll meet you at the table. Do you want more wine, or something else?"

"How about a glass of water?"

"No. It's wine or something else. We're going to make crazy love later, and I don't want you to sober up yet."

"Okay, that's too much information," Connor said.

"Kevin, sweetheart, you can have your way with me anytime."

"Go to the outhouse, JL. Connor and I need to talk."

Who flipped Kevin's switch? The Kevin who just said he wanted to make love with her was the Kevin she loved and wanted to marry. The one who snapped at her was not.

JL stepped out of the restaurant into the moonlit alley. Indoor plumbing had taken huge leaps by 1909, but it hadn't reached Little Italy yet. Before using the facilities, she did a radar scan. Nothing pinged, but her neck continued to itch. She slipped her hand into the slits Kevin had cut into all her dresses and silk underpinnings—since he knew how to sew and she didn't—until she reached her thigh. She was carrying her Glock tonight, and it was there, secure in its holster.

If she'd been wearing pants, it would have taken less than sixty seconds to get in, pee, and get out, but with all the layers she wore, it took several minutes.

When she exited the outhouse, she was still straightening her clothes when—wham!

She was body-slammed. But instead of throwing her on the ground, her assailant pinned her against the wall of the restaurant, knocking the breath out of her.

Her mind yelled, "Watch out! He's big. He'll hit hard."

She was smart. She was trained. She was tipsy, but not drunk. She screamed.

He twisted her arms sharply over her head, and she grunted at the intense pain. A large hand slapped over her mouth, and a heavy man, reeking of body odor, alcohol and onions, pressed like a one-ton boulder against her, further restricting her breath.

If possible, more alcohol than blood flowed in her veins. Her reflexes might be slow, but her muscle memory wasn't. She wrenched a hand free and went in for a palm strike to the chin. He caught her hand before impact, and gave her a quick clout to the side of her head, rattling her teeth. Her body jerked, quivered. He hit her again. The body shot landed right below her rib cage, like the teeth of a buzz saw—piercing, pulsing primal pain.

He shoved a wad of cloth deep into her mouth. She tried to spit it out, pushed it with her tongue, but it wouldn't budge. Didn't matter if she couldn't breathe around the wad, though. If her attacker kept her mashed against the wall, she'd suffocate anyway. She had to get her hand free again. But he held both of her hands in one giant paw with a vise-like iron grip.

"I've been watching ya from across the street. Knew sooner or later, you'd come out. We got business to settle."

The heavy wrinkles on the man's face deepened as he growled. Her adrenaline went haywire, her body's response to what her mind didn't want to accept. Mustache Cop was back for revenge. There would be no mercy, not from him.

Now she understood why her neck had been prickling all day. He had been watching, waiting for a chance to grab her, and she walked right into his snare. If she could get to his broken nose, she could do more damage. Where else had she hit him? Flashes of the attack in the police wagon blurred in her brain. She couldn't sober up fast enough to pull a memory through the thick, cloudy haze.

He flipped her around, scraping the side of her face against the rough wood of the wall and holding it there. Hairpins popped out and curls cascaded over her shoulder. She couldn't defend herself against a hair-pull attack. But it didn't matter now. He already had control of her head.

He rummaged through her skirts, tearing the satin, scratching her skin. She squirmed, pulled on her arms, and tried for a donkey kick, but the layers of petticoats and silk made them ineffective.

He had to weigh a hundred pounds more than she. He had her pinned against the wall and she had no room to maneuver.

If she didn't stop him, he would find the gun strapped to her leg. He slid his hand up her thigh, and his touch on her skin make her sick. This wasn't about sex. This was about domination, humiliation, retaliation, and he intended to hurt her…and hurt her bad.

And then he found what terrified her more than being assaulted—her gun—a weapon he could use to shoot her, hit her, kill her.

He tugged on the holster strapped to her leg with Velcro and scratched her thigh viciously, yanking at the holster until the gun came free. She couldn't stop him now. Did he need an excuse to accelerate the violence? If she were passive and endured him, would he stop short of killing her?

Thwack!

JL shuddered as his heavy body fell away and thumped to the ground. She yanked the cloth out of her mouth and moved into a defensive stance. She wouldn't be caught off guard again.

"Come on, ma'am. Hurry."

"You're...you're Jack's friend, Patrick."

"Yes, ma'am. We have to get out of here." He pulled her toward the door leading to the restaurant. "More cops are out front. When he doesn't come back, they'll come looking for him."

"I can't leave my gun. Help me find it." She squatted, searching the ground.

A disembodied voice from around the corner of the building said, "He went this way."

Patrick tugged on her arm. "We have to go. Now!"

JL couldn't risk being caught with an injured cop. Patrick helped her stand, then opened the door wide enough for her to squeeze through without lighting up the alley. She ducked in quickly, and he rushed in behind her. Her head throbbed, and the scratches on her face hurt like hell.

They waited in the storeroom off the kitchen and listened for voices in the alley. None came. They must have dragged the cop off, but what about her gun? She hugged Patrick close and kissed the top of his head. "Thank you. You're my new hero."

He stepped out of her embrace. "Where's Mr. Mallory?"

JL leaned against the wall, breathing deeply. "Inside dancing."

"I'll go get him."

JL squeezed Patrick's shoulder. "No, wait. I don't want anyone to see me like this. Help me brush off the dirt and fix my hair." Several hairpins had fallen out, but many of them still dangled in what was left of her bun.

He brushed her hands away. "I'll do it." He pulled out the pins, tucked the loose hair back into the bun, and pinned it securely.

She patted her hair. "How'd you learn to do that?"

"I know lots of stuff," he said.

"Do you know what I can put on my face? This scrape burns."

A bulb about the size of a lit match dangled from the ceiling, emitting a hazy, yellow light. Barrels and crates were stacked against the wall. Sausages hung from the ceiling. Jugs of olive oil and baskets of fresh fruit filled one long row of shelves. Jars of canned vegetables filled another.

Patrick moved jars around, clinking them together. "Here, this is good," he said, handing her a small jar.

"What is it?" she asked.

"Raw honey. Spread some on your face. It'll keep it from getting infected. Garlic is good, too, but not for the skin."

She found a knife and spread honey on her cheek. "Do you remember meeting Connor?"

"Not the Italian," Patrick said, "but the other man?"

JL nodded. "See if you can get him to come back here without causing a disturbance."

"You're not getting rid of me so you can go back out there and look for your gun, are you?"

"No, I'll wait right here."

He nodded, then disappeared. JL put her ear to the door and listened. There were still no voices or commotion coming from the alley. The men had to have found Mustache Cop by now. Did they find her gun, too? She had to find out. She turned the doorknob but stopped short of opening the door to look out. She couldn't take the risk of being caught, not without backup.

She'd been in dozens of altercations during her career. She'd been attacked, beaten up, and shot twice, but what just happened to her probably scared her the most. She rubbed her wrists. They were both tender and bruised. She glanced at the shelf. What would Patrick recommend for her wrists? She moved jars around but didn't know what she was looking for.

The clicking bootheels announced her brother's effortless cowboy strut. "What happened to you?" he asked.

"Mustache Cop was just here."

His fingers settled gently on her chin and he turned her face toward him. "The bastard hurt you?"

"Only my pride. But he took my Glock before Patrick knocked him out. I haven't looked outside, but his friends probably carted him off. I'm sure they took my gun, too."

"Pete and I will go after them."

Patrick came up behind Connor. "I know where to find him."

"Good. Tell me, then stay here with JL," Connor said.

"You don't know what he looks like," Patrick said. "I got a good look at him."

JL eyed him suspiciously. "In a dark alley?"

Patrick gave her a sidelong look. "I saw him well enough."

"The bandage across his nose is a dead giveaway," she said. "But what are you doing here? I thought you were at the hotel."

He looked down at the floor while his shiny new boots kicked through some sawdust. "Mr. Mallory told me to stay put, but I decided to keep watch while he was having dinner. He probably was checking to see if I could obey orders. If he was, looks like I failed."

"You didn't obey his orders, but you saved me from getting beat up. If he gets mad, I'll stand up for you, but next time, if he tells you to do something, you better do it."

"I will." Patrick tucked his hands into the pockets of his jacket, elbows out, and puffed up his chest, looking bigger, older. "I know where cops go to drink after work. Bet the cop who hurt you went there."

"Probably the same bar they go to—" Connor said.

JL punched Connor's arm before he could make a reference to hangouts in the future.

The purposeful approach of footsteps on the tiles belonged to Kevin. When he saw her, anger radiated off him like heat rising from a volcano. "What's going on? What happened to you?"

She composed herself quickly, approaching him with a just-another-day as-a-cop smile. She endured his stare and held her ground.

Connor slapped Kevin on the back. "I'm going to get Pete. Watch her. Don't let her go back outside."

"JL," Kevin said her name in a hybrid tone of fear and anger. "What happened? And don't you dare tell me nothing."

JL couldn't lie to him again. "The cop came back and wanted to finish what he started last night. Patrick smacked him in the back with…" She looked at Patrick. "What was it? A bat."

"A piece of wood I picked up in the alley."

Kevin put his hand on her neck and brought her close. Her eyes fluttered closed as his lips hovered a breath away from hers. The tension in him was palpable, barely controlled. "Why didn't you tell me?"

"I was—"

"Don't you dare say you were trying to protect me," Kevin said. "That's crap. You emasculate me every time you do it. Is that what you want?"

"God, no. I realize now I didn't handle the situation well."

"If you want our marriage to work, you can't keep shutting me out and treating me like a goddamn eunuch."

"That's not my intention. I'm a cop. I've lived in a cop's world my entire life. My job is to protect people. Not for people to protect me."

"I'm not a fighter, JL. You know that. I hate guns. I hate violence. Hell, I won't even watch violent movies, but it doesn't mean I wouldn't do everything in the world to protect you. I would stand between you and a bullet."

"You did. You saved my life."

"And since then, you've treated me like I'm less than a man. 'Kevin, don't do this you're going to hurt your arm. Kevin, don't do that, you're not fully recovered. Kevin, don't do this… Kevin, don't do that… JL, you have to stop! I don't want a mother. I want a wife."

"I'm so sorry," she said.

"I'm sure you are." Kevin snorted in disgust before turning and stomping away.

"Don't walk away." She ran after him. "We can fix this." She pointed to herself. "I can fix this. We'll go see your counselor together. I don't want to be your mother. I want to be your lover, your partner, and the mother of your children. You've got to give me a chance to fix this."

"If you can't change, we don't have a future." Kevin shook off her arm.

JL saw her life with the man of her heart passing like a brisk wind. It seemed more surreal than what occurred in the alley.

And that was Kevin's point, wasn't it? She lived in the world of violence. And he didn't want to be a part of it. He might have jumped in front of a bullet for her, but she was the one who had meddled in another police department's case, and caused the gun to be fired in the first place.

"Kevin, wait." He didn't turn around. Her head throbbed, her face burned, and the dampness on her leg told her the scratches on her thigh were bleeding. "Don't shut me out."

"We're not going to talk about it tonight." Kevin disappeared down the hall.

Pete and Connor passed him on their way in. "What'd you do to Kevin?" Pete asked.

"What'd Kevin do to you?" Connor asked.

JL accepted a hug from her brother and laid her head on his shoulder. "I'm a cop. He's not."

"I warned you," Pete said. "Civilians don't understand us."

"I'll talk to him," Connor said.

"No, don't. Give me a chance to work it out. If I don't get anywhere, you can try."

"We can all walk away from the MacKlenna clan. They don't own us," Pete said. "The NYPD would take us back."

JL straightened. "We're getting out over our skis. It won't come to that. We'll work it out."

Patrick cleared his throat. "Those cops might not stay at the bar all night. We should go."

Pete nodded toward Patrick. "Smart kid."

"Take care of him," JL said. "If you have a choice between the cop or the gun, get the Glock," JL said. "We can't afford to leave it behind."

"Maybe the bastard will blow his brains out," Pete said.

Patrick opened the door. "No one's out there."

"Let's look for the gun," JL said.

"We'll look," Connor said. "You need to go back in and talk to Kevin."

She'd rather go with Connor and Pete and face a vicious cop who was psychologically off his chain and almost raped her twice, than go back into the restaurant and face Kevin.

Lilla met her coming in and gave her a hug. "I heard what happened. I'm so sorry. We've never had any problems before."

"I had a run-in with that cop yesterday, and he was waiting for me. It had nothing to do with you or the restaurant," JL said.

"Let me get you a glass of wine," Lilla said.

"I'd rather have something stronger, like a double shot of whisky." She wanted her buzz back. She wanted to wipe away the past fifteen minutes. She wanted a mulligan. But there was no do-over for her.

Lilla handed JL a glass packed with the aromas of decadently ripe fruit. On her tongue, the taste was full and rich. Just what she needed—liquid sunshine. She looked around the room for Kevin. He sat at the table talking to Isabella and Maria. JL knew exactly what they were talking about—Italy. She returned to the table, and Kevin pulled out her chair.

Maria reached for JL, but didn't touch her. "Your face..."

"It's just a scrape. I'll be fine. Patrick put honey on it. It's sticky."

"Honey's good," Maria said. "And your wrists... Are you hurt anywhere else?"

JL shook her head. "I'm fine. Really, I'm fine."

Kevin put his arm around her, but he didn't pull her close. What he didn't do said more about his state of mind than his mildly affectionate gesture. She took a big gulp of whisky, hoping it would warm the chill in her heart and dull the sharp edges of everything wrong in her world.

Kevin picked up the thread of the conversation from before her interruption. "I'm familiar with most of the Tuscany wineries started in the 1700s. Which one belongs to your family?"

Gabe returned to the table. "We have to be at the ship before nine o'clock in the morning. We should go."

"What time is it now?" Kevin asked.

"Eleven-thirty," Gabe said.

"We should go, too," Kevin said, before turning back to Maria, "We'll continue this conversation on board the ship."

"I'm happy to tell you everything about my home country, but you're already well informed." Then to JL, Maria said, "Wash your face good before you go to bed. Be sure to get out all the dirt."

"I will," JL said.

"I have medicine to help her face heal," Kevin said to Maria, not to JL.

"Amy, are you coming with us?" Isabella asked.

Amy broke away from a conversation with Jack. "Yes. I still have packing to do." Then she looked at Jack again. "We'll talk more tomorrow."

Jack's voice was as stirring as the way he smiled at Amy, eyes crinkling. "Yes, we will." He reached for a strand of hair that had come loose from her bun and tucked it behind her ear. "Sleep well."

JL had enough problems of her own without trying to decipher what the hell was going on between Amy and Jack. She took a deep, shaky breath and let it out. If they were faking a relationship, then they were beginning to believe their own PR. From what JL could see, a powerful, earth-shaking desire connected them, hot and wet and hazardous to their emotional well-being.

JL needed to get back to the hotel quickly. This was the last night she and Kevin would share a bed for the next few nights, and they needed to have mind-blowing makeup sex. Sure, they needed to resolve their issues, but it would be easier to talk about what needed to change when they weren't fighting or drinking. Kevin once accused her of being an adrenaline junkie, and maybe she was. But honestly, she needed the high she got when she fell into the ecstasy of orgasm.

She learned in her first marriage, though, she couldn't depend on sex to save her relationship. They couldn't just cuddle up and go to sleep. She needed to confront her demons, and Kevin needed to be honest with her and confront his own. Was she really the kind of woman he wanted to spend the rest of his life with? If he couldn't answer that with a resounding yes, then they had bigger issues than makeup sex could ever hope to resolve.

34

1909 SS New York—Amy

WHEN AMY WOKE on Saturday morning, she found her clothes laid out like the first day of school, thanks to Isabella. A straw hat with white flowers and a sapphire blue ribbon matched the color of a blue silk traveling suit. Amy rested her hand on the fabric, and was surprised at how well the sapphire in her ring matched the blue of the dress.

Obviously, Isabella selected the outfit to showcase the ring. What a sweetheart.

Getting dressed, Amy buttoned her blouse, only to realize she was one button off and had to start over. She put her stockings on backwards, and then she stuck her head with the pearl-tip hat pin while trying to perch the hat correctly atop her head. To say she was distracted was an understatement.

She couldn't stop thinking about Jack. When was the last time she had so much fun? Never? Jack was an incredible dancer, and more than once his moves on the dance floor led her mind astray. She stayed up all night, visualizing strolling arm-in-arm with him by moonlight on the promenade deck.

But strolling with Jack wasn't the only visualizing she had done.

No one asked if she had issues with traveling by ship, and if she had been asked, she wouldn't have fessed up to her fears anyway. As a teenager, she was diagnosed with thalassophobia—a compulsive fear of the sea. Counseling hadn't helped. She was afraid of the creatures who lived there, and of the vast abyss itself. To her, the ocean was the most terrifying place on the planet. She should have told Jack, but in the core of her heart she'd believed the brooch would be recovered long before the ship sailed.

In hindsight, she should have had a backup plan.

The only thing visualization did for her was keep her awake all night with alternating fantasies of moonlight strolls with Jack and coping with white-knuckled fear. Now she had dark circles under her eyes, tremors, and slight nausea.

When Gabriele arrived to pick them up, she was pacing the living room, trying to cope with her fear and wondering if it was too late to cancel the trip.

"Are you ready?" he asked.

No!

"I'm coming." Isabella dashed into the room carrying a small traveling case. "I'm on time, too."

Gabriele opened his pocket watch. "You're two minutes early."

Maria walked out of the kitchen. "Everything is turned off, and I left instructions for Lilla in case something happens and we don't return."

Oh, God! Amy hugged herself. The only reason Maria wouldn't return home was if the ship sank in the middle of the ocean.

Gabriele opened the door. "Good. Then let's be off."

Amy was the last one to leave the apartment, dragging her feet.

The trip by taxi through the first shafts of buttery morning light to the docks in lower Manhattan took almost an hour. Horse-drawn cabs and sputtering automobiles converged simultaneously, and their taxi let them off in a sea of top hats and glamorously hatted ladies. The congestion created a hot, swirling crowd of buffeting shoulders and jostling elbows, and Amy, holding tightly to the brim of her hat, was poked repeatedly.

Gabriele had prearranged for their trunks to be picked up at the apartment and stowed in their staterooms on board ship, which made the sidewalk-to-ship boarding time only a few minutes. He

The Diamond Brooch 337

ushered them toward the gangway, and she followed reluctantly into the belly of the behemoth, which dwarfed every other craft in sight.

"Oh, Amy. Isn't this wonderful?" Isabella's voice climbed several notches with her growing excitement. Her face popped with a fresh, rosy color and her brown eyes were wide, taking in all the activity on the dock. She had an air of self-possession today, and it suited her well. It was as if she'd matured from a flighty girl to an elegant young woman overnight.

For the first time in Amy's life, instead of simply avoiding situations that caused her anxiety disorder to flare up, she resented the fact she couldn't enjoy an experience due to a dumb, irrational fear. She couldn't put the kibosh on her friend's enthusiasm. She had to do something besides throwing up, or hiding in a closet, shaking like a wagging finger at an unruly child.

This wasn't any different from playing ball with an injury. Playing with sprains and bruises was nothing new to her. Couldn't she pretend her phobia was an ankle sprain? She could try it. Sure, and horses might fly, and confidence might cover her phobia the way the soot from the smokestack was starting to cover her linen suit.

The breeze took hold of Isabella's hair and swept it lightly around her face. "Doesn't it smell divine?"

Amy inhaled the briny scent. "It smells like the ocean." What she didn't say to Isabella was that it smelled like the sea where giant creatures lived, feeding off the remains of rotting fish, and where ships sank...

Instead of thinking about the vastness of the ocean, she watched the seagulls soar above the colorful fishing boats to catch fresh scraps thrown their way.

"Where are Mr. Parrino and the others? Have they already boarded?" Isabella asked.

"We're to meet in the Reception Room before the ship leaves port," Gabriele said.

He then spoke with the chief steward who gave him a flower for his buttonhole before thumbing through pages of a log book. The steward then signaled a man with brilliantined hair who appeared to be in his mid-twenties.

Handing over a set of keys, the chief steward said, "Take the women in the Moretti party to Rooms 52, 54, and 56. Mr. Moretti and the other men in their party will occupy Rooms 58, 60, 62, and 64."

"We have three rooms?" Isabella whispered.

"I think one is a sitting room," Amy said. "You and Maria will take one room, JL and I will be in the other, and we'll share the sitting room."

"Do we have a bathroom of our own?" Isabella asked.

Amy shrugged. "I hope so."

The steward clasped the keys in his right hand. Then he addressed Amy, Isabella, and Maria properly, "Miss Spalding, Miss Ricci, Mrs. Ricci, your first-class parlor suites are on the B Deck, port side. We're on B Deck, starboard side. The Boat Deck is above, and it's the only open space on the ship. If you'll follow me, I'll take you to your suite."

"I'd rather wait with you, Gabriele," Maria said, beaming with excitement. "This reminds me of Carnivale in Naples when I was a little girl. I don't want to miss anything."

Amy and Isabella handed over their valises, which the steward accepted. Then he led them through the double doors to the B Deck near the Grand Staircase.

"The cafés are on B Deck," he said." The Reading and Writing Room for the ladies is on A Deck. The Reception Room and First-Class Dining Room are on D Deck. If you have any questions, at any time, please ask."

"I'm interested in the Turkish baths and the gym. Where are they?" Amy asked.

"They are on the F Deck and Boat Deck. The women are allowed in the baths in the morning."

"What about the gym?" she asked.

"For a fee, you can visit the gymnasium any time of the day," he said.

When they reached the Grand Staircase, both Amy and Isabella stopped and gawked. The wide, sweeping staircase was simply breathtaking. It was an intricate work of art, decorated with oak paneling and gilded balustrades, and crowned with a magnificent glass dome.

"What's the distance from the lower landing to the skylight dome? About sixty feet?" Amy asked.

"Exactly," he said politely. "The style is seventeenth-century William and Mary, made of polished oak, wrought iron, and boutique glass. The dome allows in natural light at any hour of the day."

"Look at the cherub at the bottom of the steps," Isabella said.

"Cute." Amy had to admit the atmosphere was intoxicating. The inside of the ship smelled of fresh paint and wood polish and baked goods. Her stomach rumbled, an encouraging sound. She couldn't be hungry and scared at the same time. Maybe this wouldn't be as bad as she anticipated. If she stayed inside, her psyche might forget she was in a floating city.

"Your suite is this way, through the first-class entry foyer," he said. "It has the only enclosed promenade on the ship. The men's first-class accommodations don't have access to your private promenade."

Was he letting them know the enclosed, private promenade couldn't be used for a midnight rendezvous? Amy rolled her eyes behind the steward's back, to which Isabella giggled. Amy put her finger to her lips. The steward turned around and, for a split second, he dropped his professional mask, and Amy got an inkling of the man beneath the job.

Curious about him now, she asked, "What's your name?"

"Chester," he said, without inflection, but his eyes were wide and anxious, as if anticipating a reprimand.

First-class passengers expected stewards to serve their needs and anticipate their wants, and, when not needed, to remain out of sight but close by. If this was done with tact and diligence, a steward might be worth a tip at the end of the voyage. At least that was the gist of the brochure Gabriele left for her to read. But no one usually took the time to even learn their steward's name, and that didn't sit well with Amy. While she appreciated good service, she wasn't any better than anyone else on the ship, and she should treat everyone from the boiler room to the bridge with the respect they deserved.

She softened her voice. "Where's home?"

He stopped walking and was looking at her now, one eyebrow slightly raised. Obviously, she puzzled him. "New Jersey," he said.

Amy racked her brain for another line of questioning and gratefully pounced on it, wondering why it took even a moment to think of it. "You live close by, then. Have you seen the Giants play this year?"

He broke into a smile, and she knew she had him. "I was there for opening day."

"Can you believe that game?" she asked. "Red Ames pitched a no-hitter and they lost."

"I haven't met many female passengers interested in baseball."

Isabella pointed her thumb at Amy. "She's Amy Spalding, and she knows more about the game than most men. She even writes about it in the *Herald*."

A pinkish tinge rolled up his face. "You're *that* Amy Spalding? My mother reads your column every day. I mean…I mean I read it too, when I'm home. Golly."

Another steward passed them in the narrow corridor with cabin doors on both sides, and Chester sobered. "Your rooms are here. There's a separate door for each room, with interconnecting doors, and another door leading from each room to the enclosed promenade."

Amy liked the idea of an enclosed promenade. She might be able to enjoy the sea breeze without looking out over the ocean.

"I'm sure you and Mr. Mallory will enjoy the private promenade"—Isabella winked—"but I intend to enjoy my moonlight walks on the A Deck."

"And who do you intend to go strolling with?" Amy teased.

Isabella whispered, "Don't you think Mr. Parrino is the handsomest man you've ever seen?"

"He is pretty cute," Amy agreed.

Chester stopped. "This is your suite." He pointed to a sign above the door. "All rooms have a plaque indicating the style of furniture. This particular room is decorated in the style of Queen Anne." He inserted the key and unlocked the door. Then he stepped smartly back out of the way so Isabella could sashay into the room to appraise her accommodations. Amy followed her into a parlor and pirouetted, looking around the whole cabin. It was a palatial room, with woven carpets, embroidered curtains, a mahogany-paneled wall, and rose silk damask wallpaper.

There was a round table and four chairs in the center of the room. A sofa was arranged along one wall, and two upholstered chairs sat on either side of a non-wood-burning fireplace with an electric heater installed in the hearth. In the corner, a writing desk was positioned below a square, curtained window. And a chandelier and two lamps cast muted light across the room.

Isabella swept into the adjoining bedroom. "Do you want this room or the next, Amy?"

"You and Jack will stay up late talking. JL will probably be with Kevin. So…" Isabella puzzled through her decision with her hands clasped and held close to her chest. "You can have this one."

"Whatever," Amy said, and then she remembered Chester. "Thank you for your help." She dug into her purse and found coins to tip him. "I appreciate your assistance." She pressed the coins into his hand as she walked him to the door.

He removed the key from the lock and handed it to her. "Anything you need, press the call button. There's one next to each bed."

If there was anything she needed, she should tell him now. It might take a while to get his attention once everyone was on board, making demands on his time. She wasn't hungry, but she was thirsty, and a diet coke would be nice. She could forget that. "Save me the trouble of looking for the button and bring a bottle of champagne, an ice bucket, and three glasses."

"If… I don't mean to be presumptuous, but if you suffer from seasickness, many of our guests find Mothersill's Remedy in gelatin capsules a sure cure. I could bring some."

"Is it obvious?" She fanned her face. "I guess it is. Thank you. The capsules will be greatly appreciated."

Chester flushed, bowed slightly, and withdrew, saying, "I'll be back shortly."

Amy closed the door gently behind him, then walked into the bedroom and sat on a bed decorated with a quilted valance and headboard. She bounced up and down, and gave a nod of approval. "Not bad."

Isabella studied herself in the gilt-framed mirror and removed her straw hat to reveal her lustrous hair parted in the middle and gathered into a small bun at her nape. "I'm going to stand at the railing and watch the ship leave the harbor. Do you want to come along?"

"Not me. Go. Enjoy yourself."

Someone knocked. It couldn't be Chester back already unless, he stocked champagne in a nearby closet. "Who is it?"

"JL."

Amy opened the door wide, and JL breezed in, kicked off her shoes, and collapsed on the sofa. "Don't wake me up until we get to London."

"That bad, huh?" Amy said.

"God, you wouldn't believe it. Kevin and I had a huge fight last night. I wanted to have makeup sex, but he turned me down—again. I tried to talk to him, but he just shut me out." JL swiped at her eyes. "I'm not going to cry. I refuse to cry, even if he wants to break our engagement."

Amy's chest shuddered with her next breath. "Oh, no. Are you sure?" She sat on the arm of the sofa. She didn't know JL well enough to hug her, so she rubbed her shoulder and arm instead. "Was the fight with Kevin about what happened in the alley? The altercation wasn't your fault."

"I'm a cop. I protect people. People don't protect me. He doesn't want a cop for a bride."

A tight sensation formed around Amy's eyes. She was tagging

her own distraught state of mind to the tail end of JL's emotional state, and was near tears herself. She reached for the handkerchief in her pocket and handed it to JL to wipe her face.

"Weren't you a cop when you met him?" Amy asked.

JL dabbed at the corners of her eyes before handing it back. "A damn good one, too."

Amy shoved the handkerchief back into her pocket. "But you're not a cop anymore, right?"

"I'm the vice president of global security, but to Kevin that's still a cop."

"Do you want Jack to talk to him?"

"Jack? No!" JL said. "That'd be a huge mistake."

Isabella entered the parlor through the promenade door, concluding her circular tour of the suite. "Hi, JL. Do you know where Pete is?"

"Isabella..." JL slid to a sitting position on the sofa, straightened her shoulders, her back, her posture, and patted the cushion. "Sit. Let me tell you something important."

Isabella sat next to JL and folded her hands in her lap.

"I've known Pete for years. I love him like a brother. He's the first person I would call in an emergency. He's Italian, from a fantastic family. He's charming, considerate, handsome, sexy, funny, and a great dancer, but he's terrible boyfriend material."

Isabella's face pinched. "I don't understand. What's a boyfriend, and what does sexy mean?"

JL looked at Amy for help, but Amy made a hands-off gesture that said to leave her out of it.

"Thanks a bunch." JL frowned at her, then answered Isabella. "Sexy is spelled P E T E. He has everything a girl would notice in a man. Dreamy, dark eyes, a kissable mouth, a lightning-bolt, irresistible smile, a muscular body, expressive hands, great sense of humor, thick and luscious hair. He can make you feel like you're the most important person in the world. That's what sexy means. And a boyfriend is a *fidanzato*. A beau, sweetheart. Got it?"

Isabella nodded.

"Well, see. Pete's not good at the sweetheart part of the business. He's so charming, you'd never know he was really a wolf. You've got to trust me on this," JL said. "You don't want to mess with him. He's a short-timer. And you're too sweet for him."

"Maybe we should swear off boys for the week," Amy said. "You and Kevin are fighting. Jack and I are getting a little too close. Pete is chasing a girl half his age—"

Isabella shook her head. "He's not that much older, and *nonna* didn't object."

"*Nonna* saw a nice Italian boy who you happen to like," Amy said. "The age difference doesn't bother her because you're happy."

"But she doesn't know Pete," JL said. "If she knew what a cad he can be, she wouldn't like him."

"He's your friend. Why are you saying such bad things about him?"

"That's a good question," JL said. "Basically, because you're too innocent for him."

"He likes that I'm so innocent."

JL held up her hands in a don't-you-see-the-obvious gesture, and said in a tone dripping with sarcasm, "I'm sure he does."

"If we're swearing off boys, we can't include Gabriele in the "out" group. He's like one of the girls, we can trust him," Amy said.

"We can't trust Connor. He tells Pete everything," JL said. "We need to make a pledge to spend the day without Kevin, Jack, or Pete."

"One day? How about the week?" Amy asked.

"One day at a time. We'll worry about tomorrow, tomorrow." JL held out her hand, palm down and Amy put her hand on top. Then she nodded to Isabella.

"Does this mean I can't talk to Pete at all?"

"Not today. We'll reevaluate tomorrow," JL said.

Isabella sighed deeply and placed her hand on top of Amy's.

"On the count of three we'll say, 'A day without Kevin-Jack-Pete.' Ready, one, two, three," JL said.

"A day without Kevin-Jack-Pete," they shouted in unison, and

The Diamond Brooch 345

then fell back on the sofa, howling with laughter.

It wasn't thirty seconds before someone knocked on the door. "What do we do?" Isabella asked.

"Answer it," JL said. "If It's Kevin or Jack, tell them we're in the bathroom."

"What if it's Pete?" Isabella asked.

"It won't be Pete. But if it is, I'll come out and tell him you're in the bathroom."

Isabella thoughtfully gnawed on her lower lip. "If I answer the door, he won't believe you."

"Well, that's probably true," JL said, whispering, "but I promise you it's not Pete knocking." JL shoved Amy into the next room and closed the door. They both put an ear to the keyhole and listened.

"Coming," Isabella said. Then: "Hi, Jack."

"Is Amy here?"

"She's…in the bathroom."

"Do you mind if I come in and wait for her?"

"Ah, she'll be a while. She's…ah…taking a bath," Isabella said.

Amy and JL looked at each other, covered their mouths, and barely contained their laughter.

"Maybe you should go wait with Kevin and Pete," Isabella said.

"Why is she taking a bath now?" Jack asked.

"I don't know. *Nonna* said it's good for a queasy stomach."

"Is her stomach upset?" Jack asked.

"Yes… No… She…ah…takes her bath in the morning, but she didn't have time before she left the apartment. Can I give her a message?"

"Tell her if she'd like to have brunch, I'll be waiting in the Reception Room. Oh, wait, while I'm here, I have a question for JL."

"She's in the—"

"Bathroom, too," Jack said. "I see. Well, tell the ladies if they want company to send a message. Kevin and I will go to the Smoking Room while they're…detained."

JL glowered.

Amy mouthed, "What's wrong?"

The door closed, and Isabella plowed through the connecting door, almost knocking JL and Amy on their butts. "We can't do this. I'm taking my pledge back. You made me lie to Mr. Mallory. Urg!" She snagged her purse and hat from the table in the parlor. "I'm going to the Reception Room." The door closed behind her in a swirl of silk.

"Urg?" JL said.

Amy shrugged. "She might have gotten the expression from me."

The door had only been closed a few seconds when someone else knocked.

"Urg. It's a damn revolving door." JL flung it open to a startled Chester.

"I have your champagne and Mothersill's Remedy," he said.

Amy crossed the room to the enclosed promenade deck and waved over her shoulder for Chester to follow. "Thank you. We'll drink the champagne out here."

He carried the ice bucket, bottle, and flutes out to the promenade deck, setting the bucket and glasses on the table. "Do you want me to open it now?"

"Please," JL said. "I'm going to sit here and drink until I pass out."

Chester popped the cork, poured two glasses. "Will there be anything else?"

"Another bottle." JL said.

"Should I bring more glasses? Will the rest of your party be joining you?"

"Maybe," Amy said. "Why don't you bring two more glasses?"

Chester gave Amy the package of medicine, bowed slightly, and left the room.

JL handed a glass to Amy. "Cheers." They clinked glasses and then stretched out on the teak furniture to enjoy the bubbly and the breeze blowing in through the windows.

Amy sipped, trying to remember the last time she drank champagne. It was one of those slap the forehead moments—mimosa time in Pittsburgh—and seeing Jack for the first time in person. How could she forget?

"What do you think champagne tastes like? How would you describe it?"

JL laughed, and Amy was surprised by how lyrical her voice sounded. "I'm the wrong person to ask. Champagne needs to taste like whatever champagne tastes like. The flavor is irrelevant. It's champagne." JL emptied her glass and poured another.

"That doesn't make any sense."

"What can I say? My preference is beer," JL said.

Amy held up her hand to high-five JL. "Bud Light."

JL slapped her palm. "You go, girl." Then she looked at her glass, studying the contents. "This is probably the hair of the dog. Don't you think? You had as much to drink last night as I did."

"I wasn't counting your drinks and forgot to count mine, but I did go home a little woozy."

They sat quietly drinking for a few minutes, while the buzz of voices from the upper and lower decks filtered in through the windows.

"Do you enjoy working for MacKlenna Corporation?" Amy asked.

"I do," JL said. "Kevin's bio dad, Elliott Fraser, is the most demanding boss I've ever had, but he's fair, and he's smart. The thing about Elliott is, if you're part of the family, he has your back. It's a sure thing."

"What happens if you and Kevin break up? If Elliott is his dad, won't he side with Kevin?"

"My job isn't contingent on our marriage. I'm as much of a MacKlenna as they are, and I have a brooch. Elliott doesn't have one, and neither does Kevin."

"Who does?"

"The women have control of the family jewels in this operation. Kit MacKlenna Montgomery has the ruby. Charlotte, Jack's sister, has the sapphire. Kenzie McBain has the emerald. I have the amethyst. You have the diamond."

Amy cracked up. "We have our hands on the family jewels. That's too funny."

They both laughed long and hard.

"I wonder which one is the hardest?" JL asked, giggling.

Amy wiped laughing tears from her face with the heel of her palm. "The diamond by far."

If, at some point in the future, Amy ever wondered about the moment she bonded with JL, it would be right then—a moment in time when two hungover, confused women who both worked in a man's world needed an understanding ear, a strong shoulder to cry on, and a drinking buddy to either laugh with, or give a middle-finger to whoever, in their opinion, deserved it. Cupid might be a good start.

"What happens to you if you don't get married? Where will you live?" Amy asked.

"I haven't really thought about it. I guess I'd stay in California. That's where Pops lives now. He's my dad. Kevin wants to buy a winery in Italy. I could see him living there."

Amy emptied her glass and held it out for a refill. JL poured and topped off her own. "You don't really think it will come to that, do you?"

"Kevin and I fell in love or lust within an hour of meeting. My son, Austin, worked for Kevin."

"As what? A ball catcher? He can't be ten years old."

"Actually, Austin is eighteen. He moved to Napa to attend an elite high school basketball program. He got an internship at the winery his senior year. That's how he met Kevin. The MacKlennas sort of adopted him. Watched over him, since he was so far from home."

"Oh, you started young, then?"

"I got pregnant in high school. It nearly killed my mom. She had hoped I'd follow her to Broadway."

"Your mom was on Broadway? How cool."

"Yeah, it was pretty neat going to rehearsals with her when I was a kid. But it was a long time ago."

"What does Austin's dad do. Is he a cop, too?"

"Nope. His name is Chris Dalton. He's a—"

"—power forward for the Golden State Warriors. I know who he is. I've met him. Dalton must be so proud of his son."

"He is, but it's a long story, and right now I don't want to be reminded of all my relationship failures. The current one is bad enough."

"I'm sorry I brought it up."

"It's okay. Chris and I get along great, and he and Austin hang out when they can. Everything's good there, but... Oh, well, never mind."

The ship's whistle echoed through their private promenade, and Amy shuddered as a cold chill surged through her, reminding her of the ocean, the sea creatures, and all the horror that lay beneath the surface.

"Oh, my God, Amy." JL swiveled in her chair and scrambled to her feet, reaching for Amy's arm and spilling her drink at the same time. "Your face is stark white. Are you sick? What's wrong?"

Amy pulled her legs to her chest and hugged them tightly. "We're getting ready to leave." Her voice, high and piercing, cut through the echo of the ship's whistle.

JL blew out a breath of relief, and, using the cloth covering the bottle of champagne, wiped the spill off her skirt before returning to her reclining position. "Did you think we were going to just sit at the dock...of the bay...watching the ships roll in?" JL slapped her hand over her mouth. "I'm sorry. I didn't mean to laugh."

Amy grimaced. Since the ship was leaving the harbor, she couldn't pretend any longer they were on a stationary boat. "I don't like the ocean very much."

"From the look on your face, it's not a mild dislike. It's more like terror."

Amy turned her glass up and drank it all, hoping it would numb her fear quickly. "I'm terrified of the sea. I have thalassophobia."

"That sounds fatal. What is it?"

"Unless I get so scared I have a heart attack, it's not fatal, but it is a fear of the sea. I know it's irrational, but I can't help it. I've had it for as long as I can remember."

JL emptied the rest of the bottle into Amy's glass. "Drink up. You need this more than I do." JL turned the bottle upside down in the bucket. "If you don't look at the water, will you be okay?"

Amy drew in a deep, ragged breath and dropped her chin on her knees, which she'd pulled up tightly to her chest. "I don't know. I've never been on a ship before. Chester gave me some seasickness medicine. But it's not nausea or anxiety. It's irrational terror."

JL looked at her with warm and empathetic eyes, as if she'd once been on a first-name basis with absolute terror and had punched it in the face. "Does Jack know?"

Amy shook her head forcefully. "No! And please don't tell him. I don't want anyone to know. They'll think I'm weird."

JL made a shooing motion with her hand. "You're already weird. Finding out you have a phobia isn't going to make you more so."

Amy closed her eyes and groaned softly. "Thanks, JL. I was just thinking about how empathetic you seem to be."

JL clicked her glass against Amy's tightly gripped one. "I'm on your side, kiddo. I was just trying to dilute a fear cocktail with an ounce of humor." She sipped her drink. "Let's talk about something else. What do you do for fun? Do you like to go to the beach?"

Amy glared at her.

"Oh, guess not. Well... How about the mountains? They're Jack's favorite hideout. He has a cabin somewhere in the Smokies. When he has a deadline, he goes there so no one will bother him. I think he has a cabin in Colorado, too."

"I love the mountains. Love winter sports. Does Jack ski?"

"He and Kevin ski, run, work out in the gym, and even do yoga. When they're not watching ESPN, they'll get out on the basketball court with the kids, but they both have a bad shoulder. If they take enough ibuprofen, they can get through a tennis game or a round of golf."

"If I could watch ESPN all week, I'd stay right here and do just that, and never know I was on a ship."

"Maybe Jack can put you into a trance."

"I've seen him do that on himself."

Someone knocked again, startling Amy, and she jumped slightly.

"I hope it's the champagne and not one of the guys."

"I'll flip you to see who answers." Although Amy offered, she didn't really want to move from her chair for fear of catching a glimpse of the water.

"That's okay. I'll get it. Kevin's not going to come looking for me." JL's voice was raspy, neither deep nor high, just rough. "Not today, anyway."

JL opened the door, and Chester entered with another bucket and bottle. "I'll take it," she said.

"Do you need anything else?"

"How about sandwiches and fruit? Can we have it brought to the room?"

"The staff will prepare and deliver anything you want to eat," Chester said.

"Fantastic. Will you bring another bottle of champagne, a couple of roast beef sandwiches, strawberries, apples, whatever you have?"

"I'll be back in about thirty minutes," Chester said.

JL put the new bottle and bucket on the table on the promenade deck. "I didn't get any sleep last night. This is going to knock me out."

"I didn't sleep either. Between fantasizing about Jack and worrying about getting on this boat, I was up all night. If we finish off the second bottle, I'll sleep the rest of the day."

"I should have asked Chester to open this."

"Do you know how to do it?"

"Yes, but I'm not an expert."

"What does that mean? Are you going to whip out your six-shooter to dispose of the cork?"

"I hope not. It could get messy, and draw unwanted attention." JL popped the cork and ducked. The cork hit the ceiling, bounced, and knocked over one of the potted palms. She stared at the dirt on the floor. "Oops. I wasn't expecting that. Do you think Chester can arrange to have it cleaned up, or should I do it?"

"As much as we're paying for this room, twenty-four-hour cleaning service should be included. Next time he comes to the room, be sure to tip him again. We might have to pay extra for his discretion. We don't want him tattling on us."

"Oh, yeah, right. Good idea. He would likely fold under Jack or Kevin's glare." JL poured another glass and stretched out again on the teak chaise lounge. Then sat back up and looked pointedly at Amy. "I do have a question. Inquiring minds want to know. You and Jack acted like lovers last night, what with all the touching and gooey-eyed smiles. Was it real or a ruse?"

"It was supposed to be a show for my readers, in case any were there, but I think I went overboard. Now I'm baffled. I like him a lot, but we're on different trajectories. I've got a committed relationship to go back to. I love Joe. I plan to marry him unless I come back here. So either way, spending time with Jack will only mess with my head."

"And your heart," JL said.

"Your heart and my heart are in jeopardy right now, aren't they?"

JL swiped at her face again. "I should have seen this coming, but I guess I was too close."

"You couldn't see the forest for the trees."

"Something like that." JL released a sigh, her shoulders sagging. "To quote Robin Williams, 'Reality: What a concept.'" She drank the rest of the champagne in her glass and twirled it, staring at its emptiness. "You know, don't you, that Jack's a pain in the ass. I'm not sure what you see in him."

"Thanks a lot. Are you questioning my judgment?"

"Nope, just your sanity."

"He's a great guy. He's handsome, sexy, considerate, intelligent, funny…"

"He's still an asshat," JL said.

"He told me what happened in San Francisco."

"That's a surprise."

"He wanted me to know so I'd understand the subtle and not-so-subtle nuances in the group. He blames himself for everything that happened."

JL refilled her glass and guzzled it like a glass of water on a steamy day. "He should. It was all his fault. Did he tell you what his sister did to Kevin?"

Amy shook her head.

"She told him they were all returning to the future and leaving me, Braham, and Jack behind."

"He told me—"

"—she didn't give Kevin a choice," JL said, talking over Amy, slurring her words. "He was furious. And what made it even worse... Kevin was dealing with PS...PD...PST..."

"PTSD."

"Right. He was dealing with that. He got shot, you know. He almost died. If Charlotte hadn't been there..."

"Maybe you should go to gouples counseling. I mean couples...couples counseling."

JL shook her head in a slow, exaggerated way. "We went. He gave up. He said, 'Fooey.'" She swatted at the air. "Fooey."

Amy laughed. "Nobody says fooey anymore. They don't say Dewey or Louie, either."

JL laughed, too. "Well, Kevin did. So fooey on him. He doesn't love me. I've picked all..." She held the all as one musical note, stringing it out in perfect pitch. It went on and on and on. Finally, she ended it with a definitive, "All...the petals off the daisy. All thirty-four."

Amy clapped. "Bravo. You have a beautiful voice. Maybe you should serenade him. Sing his favorite songs. And get a daisy with more petals."

"A serenade would be the same as a one-way conversation."

Amy had a vision of a pitcher-umpire chest-bump during a confrontation, but JL was so much shorter than Kevin, it wouldn't work. "Seduce him. Give him a—"

"— I tried last night. He even turned that down."

Amy divided the remaining champagne between their glasses, then turned the bottle upside down in the bucket with the other one. "Well, it looks like there's only one thing to do. Ignore him."

"Isn't that how this conversation started?" JL emptied her glass. "Absence makes the heart grow fonder." Her eyelids drifted shut. "Wake me up when the food gets here."

Amy tossed a pretend basketball into a pretend basket. "Swish." She finished her drink. Rolled over and closed her eyes, too, but the ship's rocking motion reminded her of where she was. She sat up, choking back terror. Then her mind went wonky and she got a mental picture of Jack floating facedown in the ocean. Terrified, she ran into her bedroom and crawled under the covers, shaking.

Getting on the ship was a big mistake. She might not survive the next few days. She dug deeper into the covers and prayed either the alcohol or a miracle would put her out of her misery.

And sooner rather than later.

35

1909 SS New York—Jack

AFTER THE SHIP sailed, Jack decided to head to the first-class Smoking Room on A Deck to smoke a cigar, a luxury he enjoyed, but couldn't partake of at home in the twenty-first century. The women in the family would ream him out.

Kevin had disappeared, and Jack suspected what happened at the restaurant the night before made the situation between the engaged couple much worse. He was staying out of it, but would make himself available if either of them wanted to talk.

Isabella had sought him out to apologize for lying to him, then found her grandmother, and the two women ventured up to the Boat Deck to bask in the warmth of the sun and breathe the fresh ocean air.

Gabe was playing cards, and Pete, Connor, and Patrick had donned their deerstalker hats—figuratively—and set out to mingle with other first-class passengers. Patrick was a trooper, and Jack was pleased with himself for inviting the youngster along. He still wasn't clear about what would happen with the boy at the end of the voyage, but felt certain an answer would present itself.

With Kevin off sulking, the Three Stooges playing Sherlock Holmes, and JL and Amy enjoying some good clean fun in their bathtubs—or, as Chester volunteered, drinking champagne on the promenade deck, and the Italian women off taking in the view from the Boat Deck, Jack could enjoy a cigar in peace.

He didn't recognize any of the men there, but unless they were historical characters, he wouldn't have recognized them anyway. Nobody pointed an accusatory finger at him, claiming he was a Lincoln conspirator. But, just in case, he had a story ready if anyone asked, or commented, or threatened to throw him overboard.

He hadn't seen the reporter or photographer Mr. Bennett threatened to send on the voyage, either. The publisher probably quashed the idea after learning the name of Amy's fiancé, which suited Jack just fine. The one picture of him in the late nineteenth-century archives was already one too many. There didn't need to be one from the early twentieth-century, too.

With everyone accounted for, he could purloin an hour to enjoy a cigar, a cup of strong coffee, and quiet reflection, starting with what happened last night.

JL was pissed they didn't find her gun, but they found no trace of the cop at the bar Patrick guided them to, and no one had seen a man with a bandage across his nose. Connor and Pete even staked out the police station, but the cop never showed up. Now a pistol that wouldn't be designed for another seventy years was floating around Manhattan. At least the creep wouldn't be able to use it again after he emptied the seventeen-round magazine.

After a short draw on the cigar, Jack removed it from his mouth and studied it as if the tobacco was the real question on his mind. It wasn't.

When Isabella delivered the news that Amy and JL had decided to stay in their cabin for the day, he'd been confused. It didn't make any sense. He and Amy spent an enjoyable evening in Little Italy, and had ended the evening in high spirits. So why was she avoiding him?

His pondering came to a halt the moment Jack saw Kevin enter the Smoking Room from the Verandah & Palm Court entrance. He quickly crossed the red and blue carpet to join Jack at his round card table.

"Where'd you get the cigar?" Kevin asked.

"They have several brands for sale at the bar. Ask the bartender."

Kevin returned a few minutes later with a shot of whisky, a Cuban cigar, and three different New York papers.

"Where have you been?" Jack asked.

Kevin shrugged. "Checking out the ship. It's huge. A floating city. I made an appointment at the Turkish baths. I'm hoping for a complete detox." He glanced around. "This is a beautiful room."

"Be sure to look at the ancient ships and mythological figures in the painted glass windows. If I could, I'd take a couple of them home."

"The mahogany paneling is extraordinary. They didn't spare a dime on this room."

"Millionaires have high expectations, even when they travel, regardless of the century." Jack rolled the tip of the cigar along the edge of an ashtray and tapped it gently to let the ash fall. "Did you see Amy and JL?"

"Nope. Did you?"

"I think one or both are pissed."

"Ya think...Sherlock?" Kevin said sarcastically.

"You have me confused with your bride-to-be. I'm Philip Marlowe. JL is Sherlock."

"Whatever." Kevin removed the label from his cigar and ran the tightly rolled bundle of dried and fermented tobacco leaf under his nose, sniffing. "Patrick said three bottles of champagne and sandwiches were delivered to their suite."

"I guess they're having a party without us."

Jack's words hung in the air while Kevin frowned behind a flaring match and a cloud of cigar smoke. "No, they're getting drunk."

"Their state of sobriety doesn't answer my question. What's wrong with them?"

"Isabella said Amy didn't sleep last night, and Gabe says she has dark circles under her eyes. She's tired."

"What's JL's excuse?" Jack asked.

"She didn't sleep either."

"I don't buy it. If they were tired, why drink three bottles of champagne? Which brings us back to my original question. What's wrong with them?"

"Understanding women is above my paygrade. You'll have to figure it out on your own time." Kevin sipped whisky while rolling the cigar between his fingers. "I'm only interested in finding the brooch and getting the hell out of here."

"Connor and Pete are watching for Lillian. Patrick is tasked with locating her suite and connecting with her assigned steward. There's nothing we can do right now except wait."

"Waiting is not my forte."

"I don't know why not. As many years as you worked for Elliott, I would have thought you perfected the art."

"I did. I'm just frustrated right now."

"Frustrated is an understatement. Your joint is rolled so tight you're not getting any air at all. What's this funk you're in all about? What's eating at you?"

Kevin crossed one leg over the other and fiddled with the cuff of his trousers. "I'm tired of JL acting like my mother."

Jack lowered his head and looked at Kevin over the rim of a pair of invisible glasses. "You're kidding, right? I've stayed in the room next to yours more than once. I don't know your mother, but I seriously doubt she sounds like JL."

Jack was pretty sure he knew what was eating at Kevin. JL's arrest was bugging the hell out of him, and he needed to talk about it, but it wouldn't do any good for Jack to bring it up if Kevin wasn't ready.

"Did she tell you what happened in the police wagon?"

Jack hesitated. He needed to tread softly to keep Kevin talking. "What happened in the wagon when she was alone with that creep?"

Kevin rolled his eyes. "I've had counseling, Jack. Don't reflect. Just answer the question."

Jack leaned back, balancing on the chair's rear legs, the cigar clamped at a jaunty angle between his teeth. He'd never make a living as a counselor, but he was technically JL's attorney. What would she want him to tell Kevin? Jack puffed on the cigar, sending the rich tobacco's fragrance into the air between them.

"I told her I had to know everything from the time she was arrested until she was released."

"She thinks I'm a wuss."

"Nobody thinks that, Kevin. There aren't many men who would take a bullet for someone else. You have more courage than I have. If anyone is a wuss, it's me."

"If we're going to compare traumatic experiences, Jack, you'll come out on top. So let's skip it and talk about why she didn't tell me."

"She's worried about you. You're struggling with PTSD. You have relapses. Look…" He dropped his chair to the floor and leaned forward, elbows on his knees. "I've never told anyone this, and if you repeat it, I'll deny it. Some nights I wake up in a cold sweat. I have two different nightmares. One, I'm in prison with a hood over my head, and the other I'm holding Carolina Rose, who's covered in blood."

Jack took a deep breath and continued, "Some nights the terror dreams get mixed up, and I have a bloody hand on my head, and my arms are tied up in canvas. I can't go back to sleep. Meditating doesn't work. I'll go out and run intervals around the plantation at three o'clock in the morning until I'm exhausted, but even then, I still can't sleep. I don't take drugs, and I try to limit my alcohol consumption.

"I'm sorry I put you and everyone else through the trauma in San Francisco. I fucked up big time, and I'll carry the scars for the rest of my life." Jack stubbed out the cigar. "Let me carry the scars, buddy. Don't take it out on JL. My jaw has never been the same since David slugged me. I deserved his punch." Jack turned his face away from Kevin and pointed to his jaw. "Hit me. Let me carry the scars, because you don't deserve them."

Kevin squeezed his eyes shut and pinched the bridge of his nose. He seemed to be in a battle with himself. His shoulders and arms shook. He finally straightened and looked at Jack, eyes red and glistening. "I know I'm not myself. The shooting, followed by what happened in San Francisco, was a double whammy. Now, with the wedding coming up, buying a ranch in Colorado, and a winery in Italy, plus building our house and starting the winery there, it's too much. Too many decisions to make, and too many demands on my limited time. I can't handle it."

"You don't have to, pal," Jack said. "Put the Italy winery on the back burner. Hire a new CPA for the Colorado project. Take Gabe and Maria back with you, and give them the winery at the farm to develop. From what little I heard of your conversation with her, there's not much about growing grapes she doesn't know. As for your wedding, you have to answer one important question."

"What?"

"Do you love her?"

"Honestly, I don't know."

"Then figure it out. You're on a five-star luxury liner without the distractions of loud music, TVs, computers, and cell phones. Take the time to reacquaint yourself with her. Enjoy candlelight dinners and strolls in the moonlight. If you do that, you'll have your answer by the end of the week."

"I don't know if she's the right woman for me."

"Well..." Jack scratched his head. "She's gorgeous, talented, loving, has guts of steel, and the damn woman drives me insane. But I'll tell you what, as pissed as she is with me, she'd still risk her life to save me." Jack scrunched his face. "Matter of fact, she did. And she'd do it again, because that's the kind of person she is. If I needed to pick people for a team, I'd pick her in a heartbeat. Matter of fact, I did." He leaned back on the chair's rear legs again. "If you're not getting the message, let me spell it out. She's one hell of a woman. And you're lucky she picked you."

"If I'm so damned lucky, then why do I feel so miserable?"

"If you figure out the answer to that question, my friend, be sure to let me know."

36

1909 SS New York—Jack

AT EIGHT O'CLOCK, the ship's bugler sounded the traditional shipping line's meal call, signaling the passengers should make their way to the respective dining rooms. Jack, Kevin, Connor, and Pete entered the First-Class Dining Room on D Deck wearing evening jackets with matching waistcoats and white bowties. All four men, standing six feet tall or taller, made a rock-star entrance. But Kevin, wearing the MacKlenna plaid, turned heads, and a buzz of voices followed them through the massive, elegant room decorated in the seventeenth-century Jacobean style. The oak walls, leaded windows, alcoves, and recessed bays couldn't compete with the four men striding through the room, or the crisp pleats of Kevin's swaying kilt.

"Why, exactly, are we making a statement?" Connor asked Pete.

"It was Jack's idea. It has something to do with Amy. I don't get it, though."

Jack would rather have Amy at his side than Kevin, but for a prelude to what Amy's readers could expect when they learned she left the paper for a romantic European honeymoon, this was almost a "greatest hits." If their charade proceeded as Jack planned, news would circulate in New York that Amy and her betrothed celebrated their nuptials and honeymooned in grand style in Europe. If it took her six months to return to the past as a grieving widow, her readership would welcome her with open arms.

The maître d' led them to a four-top oak table in the center of the room, exactly where Jack had requested they be seated after Gabe, Patrick, Isabella, and Maria altered their plans and dined earlier in the À la Carte Restaurant.

Pete set his menu aside and asked, "If passengers get curious about us, what are we supposed to say?"

"Didn't you get the briefing notes?" Connor asked.

Pete drew his jacket together with a tug and swore under his breath. "It's bad enough I'm forced to eat in this monkey suit, but I didn't even rate notes."

"There aren't any," Jack said. "We're winging it. I told a man in the Smoking Room earlier today that we're a group of businessmen from Lexington, Kentucky, traveling with our Scottish cousin on our way to Europe to consider investment opportunities in aviation and armaments. Anything more, deflect, unless it's about Amy, then pour it on."

"Since you're wearing a kilt, are you going to do your Elliott impersonation?" Pete asked.

"I had to pay the New York tailor a premium price to get this kilt made in time. So, aye, I'll do my impersonation of the clan chief. James Cullen, now, the lad, he does a better one," Kevin said in a heavily accented voice, then he switched back to his regular voice. "Elliott caught us making fun of him years ago, so we don't do it if he's close by. Meredith does a pretty good impersonation, too. But don't tell Elliott."

"Why does he care?"

"When he went to vet school at Auburn in the nineteen-seventies, he was laughed at. It reminds him of being an immigrant, an outsider," Kevin said.

"You sound like you're from Scotland," Connor said.

"Since my early twenties, I've spent long stretches of time in the Highlands. I picked up the rhythm of the language."

"So, on this trip you're a Scottish arms dealer?" Pete asked, chuckling.

"Why armaments and not Thoroughbreds?" Connor asked.

"Because there's an arms race in Europe," Jack said, "and it's accelerating. It makes sense for American investors to look at opportunities."

"I didn't get European history in high school or college. Who's racing?" Pete asked. "England and Germany?"

"Along with other countries," Kevin said.

A waiter came to their table to take their orders. They revisited their menus, made their dinner selections, then continued the conversation, keeping their voices low.

"The Triple Alliance of Germany, Austria-Hungary, and Italy are squaring off against the Triple Entente of France, Russia and Britain," Jack explained. "They think the alliance system will act as a deterrent to war, but instead it ties the countries together, so if one country goes to war, they all go."

"Like NATO today?" Pete asked.

"Yes," Jack said. "I researched this for a World War I book idea I had a couple of years ago, and might still write if I can find the right hook."

"The bottom line is," Kevin said, "Germany is afraid of the armament increases in Russia, and the Brits are afraid of the German naval buildup."

The waiter brought a tray with four glasses of whisky.

Connor took a sip. "Okay, back to this story. So, the arms race leads to World War I."

"It was part of it," Jack said. "Right now, all European nations are militaristic. They see war as a valid means of foreign policy. Germany and Austria-Hungary are the worst."

Pete twirled the amber liquid in his glass and sniffed. "Since we're here, isn't there something we can do to stop it?"

"Like what?" Connor said. "Tell the Archduke Ferdinand not to go to the museum? That didn't work for Braham."

"If that's supposed to be an inside joke, I don't get it," Pete said. "Guess I'm not on the inside."

"It's a reference to Abraham Lincoln going to Ford's Theatre,"

Kevin said.

"Conflict is deeply rooted in European history," Jack said. "They've had only a couple hundred years of peace out of three strife-torn millennia, stretching back to antiquity."

"In other words, there's nothing we can do," Pete said.

"In a few years," Jack said, "Churchill will say, 'the world is arming as it has never armed before.'"

"If he could only see what was happening today," Connor said, staring over Jack's shoulder. "The more…things change…the more they stay… Jack, take a long drink, now. Don't ask questions. Just do it."

Jack picked up his glass and sipped.

"Drink it," Connor said. "Drink all of it."

Jack had never questioned Connor's judgment, and wouldn't now. He emptied his glass. Then he looked at his friend, waiting for an explanation.

"Don't react to what I'm about to tell you. And don't anybody turn around. Keep looking at me." He paused for a moment, then said casually, "Catherine Lily Sterling just sat down at a table about twenty feet from us."

The floor fell away beneath Jack's chair, and he sank deep, deep within himself. Everything around him disappeared in a thick fog. The kettle drumbeat of his heart sounded—and felt—like distant thunder and tumbling avalanches rolled into one bloody big drum. He couldn't move, he couldn't think. He was immersed in the booming heartbeat of a universe that held him with tenacious desperation against its breast.

"Jack's in my line of vision," Pete said.

Kevin, sitting next to Jack said, "Are you sure, Connor?"

"I saw Carolina Rose in person, and I've seen Catherine Lily's portrait in the mansion. I'm a cop. I'm trained to recognize people. The woman sitting behind Jack *is* Catherine Lily Sterling, or there's another sister we don't know about."

The drum beat slowed, quieted, but didn't completely go away. "It's impossible," Jack said. "She sailed yesterday."

Connor sipped from his glass, but kept his eyes focused on the woman the others couldn't see. "Mr. Sterling lied to you. What does he look like?"

"Tall, gray hair, sharp features, distinguished, but I wouldn't call him handsome. Why?" Jack asked.

"A man fitting that description just sat down next to her. There are four other people at their table, two men, two women."

"How does she look? Like the portrait?" Jack asked.

Connor shook his head. "No..."

Jack sighed. He didn't want to see Carolina Rose's twin sister as an older, wrinkled woman. When the waiter passed their table, he held up his glass for a refill. The waiter set the glass on his tray and walked away.

"... no, she doesn't," Connor continued. "The woman I'm looking at is gorgeous, almost regal."

The statement packed a punch, and Jack did a short, quick head shake. He couldn't turn in his seat and look at her until he had his emotions back under control. "She is? Really?"

"The artist didn't capture the woman I'm looking at. You called Carolina Rose ethereal. Catherine Lily is that, and more. The years have been extremely kind to her."

"I have to see her."

"You can't turn around. Her husband is looking in this direction."

Remaining at the table through a ten-course dinner...each with an accompanying wine, and lasting for hours...without looking at her was out of the question. He needed to leave the room for several minutes and then return, walking slowly and steadily so he could gaze at her.

The waiter returned with Jack's drink. He sipped it. He could have gulped it, but it wouldn't have made any difference. It wouldn't have numbed the pain, the memory, the absence of Carolina Rose in his life.

"I'm going to walk out for a few minutes. When I come back in, I'll look at her," Jack said.

"You can't go by yourself," Kevin said. "I'll go with you."

"You attracted enough attention parading in here wearing a kilt. I'll go," Connor said. "But I don't like this. Sterling won't be happy to see you again. Didn't you say he asked you not to tell his wife about the adoption? Bet it's why he lied to you about her departure. If he knows you're on this ship, he'll do whatever he can to protect her. Although I don't understand why she would care now."

"Trust me," Kevin said, his face red, his dark eyes intently focused. "Doesn't matter how old you are when the truth is dumped on you. The fact you were lied to hurts like hell. It strikes at your core, your identity, your self-worth. Catherine Lily will be devastated. If I was Sterling, I wouldn't want her to know." Kevin upturned his glass, slammed it down on the table. "She's on her way to see her dying mother, for God's sake. Why put that pressure on her? If you tell her, you'll open a Pandora's box, and you have no idea what will fly out and smack you in the face."

Jack regarded Kevin, who was almost the spitting image of Elliott. His pain was visible in the furrows between his eyebrows, the tightening of the muscles around his eyes, and the deepening of the creases at the sides of his nose. Jack had been so absorbed in his own pain, he'd been oblivious to the hurt Kevin had spent months trying to hide.

"I'll respect her privacy, but I have to see her, even if it's from a distance."

"Then come on," Connor said. "We'll walk out the way we came in. When we come back, you can get a look at her. Just don't stare, or her husband might call you out, and I don't want to be your second when Sterling challenges you to a duel to defend his wife's honor."

"If I stare, just shoot me and get it over with," Jack said to Connor, then to Kevin he said, "If the waiter comes back, order me another drink."

"Me too," Connor said.

Jack and Connor walked out into the Reception Room, where several dozen first-class passengers, also dressed in evening attire, waited in a spacious area with dusty color carpet and floral-patterned Victorian easy chairs. A trio of musicians playing violin, piano, and cello entertained them. Jack crossed the room to stand by the Grand Staircase with an unobstructed view of the door. If Sterling or Catherine Lily followed him out, he wanted to know before they had a chance to surprise him. Connor snagged two glasses of champagne from a waiter serving the passengers gathering to go into dinner.

Jack had just taken a sip when a woman called his name.

"Jack Mallory? Is that you?"

He almost spit out the champagne. His hand went to his mouth as his brain instantly put the voice and name together—Lillian Russell. The timing couldn't be worse.

He glanced up to see the famous actress gliding down the stairs as if onstage. She was twenty-eight years older, and had added several pounds, but she was still beautiful. He reached out to take her hand as she approached the last two steps.

"I can't believe it's you." She bussed his cheeks. "You're as devilishly handsome as you were then. You haven't aged a year. What's your secret?"

He spotted the brooch immediately, nestled between her large breasts. "I fell asleep beside Rip Van Winkle, and just woke up to see you again."

She laughed. "You're such a charmer."

"How long has it been? Ten years?" he asked, hoping she had forgotten the year they met.

Lillian's voice climbed a notch. "Heavens no. It's been twenty-eight."

"That's impossible," Jack said. "Are you sure?"

She tapped a finger to her temple. "Yes, it was definitely 1881. I played *Babes in the Woods* at the Bush Street Theater."

"You have a better memory than I."

Lillian looked around him. "No beautiful lady by your side this time?"

He struggled to keep the smile on his face. "Not tonight." He pointed at Connor. "Only Connor O'Grady."

Lillian smiled at Connor, and then to Jack she said, "I never got a chance to tell you how sorry I was to hear about Carolina Rose Arées and her uncle. Such a tragedy."

He swallowed as nausea crawled the walls of his gut, and he strove for control. "Yes, it was a tragedy."

She squeezed his arm affectionately. "I'm traveling with a companion, but we have room at our table. Join us for dinner."

Grief, his powerful enemy, was suffocating him in its triumphant embrace. He had to break its hold. But how? Lillian and Catherine Lily both reminded him of what he had lost. Lillian wanted to embrace him. Catherine Lily would be frightened of him.

"I'm dining with a group of investors tonight. Can we meet later, perhaps? For drinks? I noticed a Steinway Crown Jewel on the other side of the room. It's a mahogany grand piano. I heard that music played on it will carry throughout the ship. Maybe you will entertain us with a song or two."

She tapped Jack's shoulder with her folded fan. "I would love to sing for you. Shall we meet at midnight?"

"Midnight. Under the dome." He bowed slightly, and then he and Connor reentered the peanut-white room. "At least we don't have to spend another minute wondering if Lillian has the brooch with her," Jack said under his breath.

"It looked underwhelming on her," Connor replied.

"We're one step closer to home." Lillian and the brooch had distracted him. Now he steeled himself, breathed through his mouth, and relaxed the focus of his eyes just as they settled softly on Catherine Lily. His step faltered, and a crushing pain landed on his chest as the vision of loveliness registered in his brain. His heart stopped…and maybe time itself.

Catherine Lily was a slightly older version of his Rose, but just as beautiful and exotic.

"I need help," Jack whispered.

"Sure, partner," Connor said. "Put your hand on my shoulder. We'll get through this. Go slow."

Jack couldn't take his eyes off the elegant movement of her

hands as she conversed with the people at the table, or the bright light in her violet-colored eyes, or the defined peak of her cupid-bow lip.

Anger shredded his guts, and jealousy, an emotion previously unknown to him, set off the primordial lizard part of his brain, and he wanted to beat the crap out of Sterling.

"Here's our table," Connor said. "Sit."

Jack dropped into his chair and picked up his drink with a shaky hand. The whisky slipped across his tongue, followed by a warm burn.

"If your ghostly face is any indication of what you just saw, I guess it's her," Kevin said.

Jack nodded. It was all he could do. Thank God, Amy stayed in her room tonight. Amy—her face, her voice, her eyes—came to mind, and slowly stilled the turmoil within. And the shaking ceased. First in his torso, then his arms, finally his hands.

"We saw Lillian in the Reception Room," Connor said. "She was wearing the diamond brooch."

Pete did a fist pump. "Yes! Then what's the plan?"

"I'm meeting her at midnight in the Reception Room," Jack said. "She mentioned a companion. We need to find out if they're sharing a cabin. We also need to know where she's storing her jewelry, in the purser's safe or in her room."

"Pete and I will see what we can find out while you meet with her," Connor said.

"If we can get our hands on the brooch tonight, we can go home," Pete said.

"I don't think we can take possession tonight, since she's wearing it," Jack said.

"She won't take it to the safe tonight. It'll be too late after she meets you. If she's sleeping alone, we might be able to slip in and steal it. But, if there are two people in the room, I wouldn't risk it," Connor said.

"The sooner we get out of here, the better for all of us," Kevin said.

"If we're going to steal the brooch, it has to be planned. We need to be ready to leave immediately," Connor said.

"What about Gabe, Maria, Isabella, and Patrick? We can't leave without telling them. They deserve an explanation," Pete said.

"Let's meet in the women's sitting room tomorrow morning. We'll tell them who we are and where we're from," Jack said.

"And invite them to go home with us?" Pete asked.

Jack pressed his palms together, his index fingers resting against his lips. "If they want to come, they'll be welcome, at least as far as I'm concerned."

What would Elliott say if he returned with four new people? What would Charlotte and Braham say when they discovered he intended to adopt a boy he brought back from 1909? Adopt? Where did that thought come from? Had it been his plan all along, but unacknowledged until now?

Patrick looked up at him with adoration and faith. How could Jack not take him home? And if he took him home, he would raise him as his own. He wasn't completely heartless.

37

1909 SS New York—Jack

AT MIDNIGHT, JACK entered the Reception Room on D Deck to find Kevin standing sentinel next to the fireplace, stance solidly balanced, pronounced jaw, mouth clamped, eyes staring, arms crossed. Between the scowl, the kilt, and the body language, he screamed fierce-eyed Highlander warrior, don't mess with me.

If Jack didn't love Kevin like a brother, he would have kept his distance like the other passengers gathered in the room. Jack shook his head at the snippets of conversations he overheard. A loud and clear warning was going out from the men to their wives—stay clear of the dangerous Scot.

Jack clapped him on the back. "Are you intentionally trying to scare everyone, or are you in such a crappy mood you don't care if you look like a Scottish brute?"

"I don't care," Kevin said.

Jack studied Kevin for a moment. "Did anything in particular set you off, more than you already were, or is it a culmination of the past few months?"

The twining tendons in the back of Kevin's hands pulsed as he squeezed his crossed arms, his fingers digging into the fabric of his jacket. "I stopped by to see JL. Nobody answered the door. I saw Patrick. He said both JL and Amy have been asleep for hours."

"After drinking three bottles of champagne, we might not see them until dinner tomorrow night."

"Four bottles."

"Jesus. Amy's not a big drinker, either." Jack crossed his arms and rocked back on his heels. "I'm glad you went by there and made the effort. Patrick will tell her you stopped by."

Kevin's unhappiness and confusion radiated off him like a breaking fever. "If he does, he does. I don't know if it matters."

Jack tilted his head in a why gesture.

"I went by there out of a sense of obligation. I'm glad she was asleep."

Jack stared, unable to speak. Then finally he said, "You've descended farther into the pit of despair since this afternoon."

"I took a long walk on the Boat Deck, sat in the sun, and listened to the waves. When I closed my eyes, all I could see were miles of vineyards in Tuscany. As soon as we get home, that's where I'm headed. If Gabe, Maria, Isabella, and Patrick want to go with me, I could use their help with the winery we buy. Plus, it will give JL the freedom to stay in Lexington and be there for Austin without having me around."

"I think she would rather have you there, and so would Austin."

"Not until I get my head together." Kevin's dark complexion lost a bit of color, and his eyes seemed unfocused, as if all he could see were the problems lurking in the dark places of his mind, not what was going on in his heart or what was taking place around him.

"Do you really think running away will help you get your head together?"

"You're a fine one to talk." Kevin grabbed a glass of champagne off a waiter's tray. "You keep running away to the monastery."

Jack lifted his hand to signal the waiter to give him a moment. During the intervening seconds, he grew very still, then spoke with acidic sharpness. "I don't run away from things. I run toward them."

He took a glass from the waiter's tray, nodding to indicate to the waiter he could move on, then calmed himself with a sip of champagne. "The monastery is a place of solace, a place to put life in perspective. It eliminates the white noise so I can hear my heart.

When I'm still and reflective and prepared to hear what it wants to say, I can heal. I'm not completely healed, yet, but I'm not full of knotholes, either."

Someone tapped on Jack's shoulder. He jerked his head around to find Patrick at his side. "What are you doing here? I told you to go to bed." The boy was still dressed in evening clothes, looking like Jack's mini-me.

Patrick cupped one side of his mouth, and Jack leaned down to hear him as he whispered, "Miss Russell was attacked. She's on B Deck in the first-class passengers' corridor, port side."

Jack raised his eyebrow in a silent question.

Patrick shook his head, answering Jack's unasked question. "She's not bleeding. Hurt her head and arm. He didn't beat her up or anything. Do you want me to take you to her?"

Jack tousled Patrick's hair. Then to Kevin, he said, "Lillian's been attacked. She's not seriously hurt, but I bet she's badly shaken. She's in the first-class passenger's corridor on B Deck. Get JL, and let her know where we are."

"Let me go to Lillian. I might be able to help her. You get JL," Kevin said.

"There's a ship's doctor to handle medical emergencies. You get JL. If we don't tell her what happened, all hell will break loose."

"You didn't wake her up to tell her about Catherine Lily."

"That doesn't have anything to do with the brooch. Lillian does. Let JL know. I'm going to see if I can help Lillian." Then to Patrick he said, "Lead the way, but go slowly. We don't want to draw unnecessary attention."

Patrick pointed with his chin. "With Kevin in that dress, you got all the attention in this room. Look at the people staring at you."

"It's not a dress," Kevin said with a hiss. "It's a statement."

"Don't mind him. He's in a foul mood," Jack said.

"JL isn't in a foul mood, but she hurts"—Patrick pointed to his chest—"pretty bad."

Jack was astonished by how quickly Patrick picked up on names, relationships, and nuances of the mismatched group of adventurers.

374   *Katherine Lowry Logan*

But Jack was mostly surprised by how quickly he had become attached to the former street urchin.

"Do you want to take the lift or the stairs?" Patrick asked.

"Stairs," Jack said.

When they reached the landing on B Deck, Patrick said, "Port side."

He darted in front of Jack, and pushed through the door into the narrow corridor leading to the first-class cabins. Halfway down the hall, a small group—the Master at Arms, a steward, and a woman—huddled around Lillian, who was sitting on the floor. Her unpinned hair draped her shoulders like a golden shawl. When she saw Jack, she shifted her position and pushed her hair over her shoulders, revealing the real damage done to her.

And to him... And to the family...

The attacker had ripped her décolletage and stolen the brooch.

Anger froze the breath in his lungs. He clenched his jaw, fisted his hands. With hundreds of women sporting jewels just as exquisite, why target Lillian? Could Connor or Pete have done this? Could JL? Or even Gabe? No. He refused to believe any of his team members could have committed such a heartless crime.

While the plan had been to steal the brooch, it never included the option of assaulting Lillian. His team was not responsible, but, whoever was, just made their task much harder. With two thousand passengers, how could three former NYPD detectives identify the culprit and find the brooch in five days?

"Go find Pete and Connor. Tell them to hurry," Jack said to Patrick. "Then go to bed." He knelt at Lillian's other side. "I heard you were hurt. What can I do?"

"Oh, Jack," she cried. "It was simply horrible."

"Are you bleeding anywhere?"

"I don't think so," she said. "My head hurts, though. I hit it on the brass railing. See if I'm bleeding."

"The ship's doctor has been notified," the Master at Arms said. "We'll transfer Miss Russell to his care. Thank you for your assistance."

Jack wasn't about to let the man push him aside. "I'm a friend of Miss Russell's, and will see to her care." Jack parted her hair with his fingertips, gently moving his fingers around her head, looking for blood. "You have a small cut. It might require a stitch. What about your shoulder, arm, hand? An ankle, maybe?"

She rubbed her shoulder. "I hit the wall here, then fell and hit my head."

"Your dress is ripped in the back and in the front," Jack said. "Are you sure you're not hurt anywhere else?"

"I don't think so."

"We need to move Miss Russell to the hospital," the Master at Arms said, his bushy eyebrows raised in question. "Did you see the man who attacked you?"

"He wore a mask," Lillian said. "I didn't see his face." Lillian licked her lips and took a deep breath. "I was unlocking my door. He rushed up to me, grabbed at my bosom, pushed me down, and ran off. I didn't see anything, it happened so fast. She patted her chest. "He stole my brooch." Her voice broke.

The Master at Arms removed a leather notebook and a stub of a pencil from his jacket pocket. "What kind of brooch was it?"

"A diamond." Her voice shook a little, and her mouth shaped the words with nervous jerkiness. "V-very valuable... You must find it."

"I assure you, we will search the entire ship until we find the culprit and your jewelry," the Master at Arms said, jotting in his notebook. "And what is your name, sir?"

"Jack Mallory. I'm an old friend of Miss Russell's." He took in all the details: the locations of the hall lights, the nearest doors, the exits, and the spot of blood on the brass railing attached to the wall. He filed the information away for later. "Do you think you can stand?" he asked her.

She looked up at him in a panic. "Not on my own. You'll have to help me."

He put his arm around her and pulled her to a standing position. She swayed slightly, and he automatically hugged her closer, steadying her. "Lean on me, sweetheart. I won't let you fall." Then to the Master at Arms, he said, "Where's the hospital?"

"Starboard, aft, D Deck."

Jack repeated the directions while drawing a mental map. "Starboard, aft, D Deck. Got it." The hospital wasn't far from the Reception Room.

The woman at Lillian's side asked, "I'll get a change of clothes and bring them to the hospital. Would you like a glass of sherry?"

"First she needs a compress for her head and a shawl to cover up the rips in her dress." Jack said.

"Certainly, and let me make repairs to her hair. It will only take a minute or two."

"Rosemary, bring the mink when you bring the sherry," Lillian said.

Rosemary hurried into the room and returned with a mink stole, a glass of sherry, a folded cloth, and a brush and hairpins. Jack held the mink while Rosemary pressed the cloth to the wound, and Lillian emptied the glass.

"Can you hold the compress against the cut while I pin up your hair?" Rosemary asked. She quickly made the repairs while Jack helped Lillian into the mink. After giving Lillian one final pat and adjustment, she said, "I'll get a change of clothes and meet you at the hospital."

The Master at Arms said to the steward, "Place a call to the hospital and advise them Miss Russell is coming in with a small head wound, then knock on all the doors in this corridor. Most first-class passengers are either still at dinner or in the Reception Room. Their servants, however, might have noticed something. Inform them of the robbery. Ask them to check their possessions to see if anything is missing. Also ask if they heard or saw any suspicious activity in the last hour."

"I'll take Miss Russell to the hospital," Jack told the Master at Arms, "which will relieve you to go search for the thief." Jack wanted Pete and Connor to interview Lillian about the attacker without the Master at Arms hanging around. Based on his experience, if she was questioned by cops skilled in the art of interviewing and interrogation, they would likely get a better description than the one she gave the Master at Arms.

Jack escorted Lillian into the first of three electric lifts directly across from the grand staircase. Lillian sat on the sofa built into the back wall. Before the lift attendant could close the door, Pete hopped in. Jack gave the detective a quick shake of his head then flicked his eyes toward the lift attendant.

Pete faced the front and held his conversation to some mundane chit-chat about the shiny brass elevator. When it stopped on D Deck, he casually walked out.

"This is where we get off." Jack helped her stand. She was still wobbly, so he held her tightly to him. As they walked away from the elevator, Pete joined them. Jack said to Lillian, "This is my friend, Pete Parrino. He's a detective. What can you tell him about the assailant?"

"Not any more than what I told the Master at Arms. He wore a mask and he shoved me. That's all I remember." They turned to walk through the Reception Room, but Lillian stopped. "I don't want to walk through there. Let's go out on the promenade deck."

"It'll be chilly," Jack said.

"I'd rather get a chill than walk through the First-Class Dining Room and have people see me in a state of dishabille."

Jack escorted her through the double doors and onto the lighted promenade deck. The salty sea breeze hit them immediately, and she tugged her fur tightly around her. When she shivered, he snugged her closer to share his body warmth.

"Was the man who attacked you taller or shorter than you?" Pete asked. "Was he my height?"

She glanced up and studied Pete. "No. Closer to mine."

"Can I see your shoes?" Pete asked. "I need to know how high a heel you're wearing."

She stopped and lifted her foot slightly off the floor so he could see the heel of her shoe. "You are about five-five with two-inch heels. That would make him five seven, five-eight. Was he bigger, smaller, or the same size as you?"

"The same, I think?"

Pete studied her. "I'd say the man who attacked you is about five-eight and weighs approximately two hundred pounds. Does that sound right?"

Jack saw several men early in the day who would fit the description. It would take the entire team performing a round-the-clock investigation to whittle the male passenger list down to a handful of possible suspects.

The three-piece orchestra was playing in the First-Class Dining Room. "I promised you a song," Lillian said. "Do you know the one they're playing?"

"I haven't heard it before," he said. "But there will be plenty of time to sing later."

"I'm in a nice bit of trouble, I confess. Somebody with me has had a game. I should by now be a proud and happy bride, but I've still got to keep my single name."

Jack laughed.

"There was I, waiting at the church, waiting at the church, waiting at the church. When I found he'd left me in the lurch, Lor, how it did upset me!"

"How would you describe the man's voice?" Pete asked.

She thought a minute, humming. "He didn't say anything."

Pete pulled a small notebook, identical to the one carried by the Master at Arms, from his inside jacket pocket along with a pencil, and jotted down notes. "Did he grunt or moan?"

"He moaned."

"Like he was in pain, or did the effort to knock you down make him groan?"

"It was a pained moan," she said.

Jack guided her toward another set of double doors. "The hospital is this way."

"What did the mask look like?" Pete asked, following behind her. "Black, white, cotton, canvas, holes for the eyes?"

"Canvas, with holes for the eyes, nose, and mouth."

"Did you see his hands?"

"His hands?" she asked. "It happened so fast."

"Were they fat, thin, long fingers, short fingers?"

Lillian pressed her hand to her breasts as if recalling the moment. "They were fat, with stubby fingers, dirty fingernails, no wedding ring. Does that help?"

"Excellent," Pete said. "What about his clothes?"

"Dark navy sack suit, white shirt, matching high-cut vest."

"Did you smell anything? Hear anything? Was he breathing heavily?"

She thought a minute. "He was breathing loudly through his mouth."

They reached the hospital, and Jack held the door for her. An attendant was sitting nearby. "This is Miss Lillian Russell. She was attacked and pushed to the floor. She has a cut on her head, which might require stitches, and she probably has bruises on her right shoulder."

Lillian's companion, Rosemary, came in after them, carrying a dress over her arm.

"I received a call to expect you," the attendant said. "If you'll follow me, I'll take you to an examination room."

Lillian kissed Jack's cheek. "Thank you. I'll be fine now. Rosemary will help me get back to our rooms. Let's have brunch tomorrow."

"Wait and see how you feel," he said.

"Nonsense. I'm a trouper. I've treaded the boards for over thirty years and never missed a performance. I will meet you for brunch. Say eleven o'clock in the À la Carte Restaurant, and I will sing a full song for you."

"I'll look forward to it," he said.

Jack and Pete returned to the promenade deck instead of walking through the First-Class Dining Room. Jack wanted to hear Pete's opinion. "What do you think?"

"I thought we'd have a couple hundred men to interview until Miss Russell said her attacker was a groaning mouth breather," Pete said. "Then my dashboard warning light came on."

"What causes mouth breathing? An obstructed nasal airway?" Jack said. "And how do you get one of those?"

"Allergies, sinus infection, enlarged adenoids...broken nose," Pete said. "And who do we know has a broken nose?"

Jack could see where Pete was going, but he was skeptical that JL's Mustache Cop would go to such extremes for revenge. Then, wham, it made sense. "Un-fuckin'-believable."

"You're the fiction writer. It sounds like the kind of story you would write."

"A mentally unbalanced cop unmanned by a female twice," Jack said. "But how could he afford a ticket to London? Surely the department isn't paying for it. And how in the hell did he make the connection between JL and Lillian's brooch?"

"Those lines are easy to connect," Pete said. "He followed JL to Little Italy, where he saw her attorney, you, with Amy Spalding, the owner of a diamond brooch auctioned in a fraudulent scheme instigated by an employee of the Providence Loan Society. Thomson probably told the cops who bought the brooch, and that the company was trying to buy it back. When JL's cop discovered Lillian was sailing to London, and then witnessed our bon voyage party last night, he put the pieces together. As for who paid for his ticket, I doubt the department knows what he's doing. My guess is he borrowed the money."

"If I was writing this story, the cop would plot to kill the heroine, steal the brooch, sell it in London, and retire in Europe a millionaire."

"I wouldn't be at all surprised if you're right," Pete said.

They went back through the Reception Room and crossed to the Grand Staircase. Jack ignored his inclination to hang around there hoping Catherine Lily would appear. She could wait. He had to get the team working on the theft of the diamond brooch. Catherine Lily wasn't going anywhere.

They reached the B Deck just as JL and Kevin rushed through the first-class corridor door. Lillian, even after being attacked, seemed more put together than JL. Her hair was loose and disorderly, her eyes were red and glassy, and her dress was one big ball of wrinkles.

"Where's Lillian?" JL demanded. "How is she?"

"Let's go to your suite. I don't want to talk out here."

JL unlocked her door, and Jack stepped into the room, smelling the unique scents of the women occupying it, layered between alcohol and the salty breeze. He glanced toward the closed door to the bedroom where Amy slept. When he realized how strongly his eyes were drawn there, he refocused them on the people with him and the problem at hand. He crossed over to the sofa and sank onto one of its cushions.

JL and Kevin paced on opposite sides of the room, like boxers moving around the ring, preparing to come out swinging when the bell rang at the start of the next round.

Pete sat in an easy chair and looked from JL to Kevin. "What is wrong with you two? Sit the fuck down."

Testily, JL said, "Nothing," before dropping lightly on the sofa next to Jack. Her thick lashes covered her downcast eyes. Kevin eased into a chair at the table, crossed his legs, and swiveled an empty champagne flute in slow circles on the tablecloth.

Pete sat forward, elbows on the chair's arms, tapping his fingertips together. His glare switched from JL to Kevin and back again. Then he shook his head slowly.

"Stop with the theatrics, Pete, and tell us what's going on," JL said.

"No need to get your panties in a wad. Lillian Russell was attacked, and the assailant ripped the brooch off her dress."

JL jumped to her feet. "Damn it!" She started pacing again. "This complicates everything." She stopped pacing, her face scrunched in thought. "We have four days to find a thief. If we don't catch him by the time we reach London, we'll never get the brooch back. There could be four thousand suspects on this ship."

"We have a lead," Jack said.

"You do? Well, why didn't you say so?"

"We were waiting for you to stop the theatrics. Sit down, and I'll tell you," Pete said.

Glaring at Pete, she sat across from Kevin and mirrored his fidgeting, whirling another champagne flute in geometric shapes on the tabletop.

"The attacker is five-seven, five-eight, two hundred pounds, and has a mouth-breathing issue," Pete said.

Jack watched JL absorb the information. Like Pete, he wanted JL's analysis independent of theirs. After a few moments, her mouth twitched, exhibiting the tiniest and briefest of smiles.

"That jerk followed us on board."

Kevin arched his eyebrows at her. "What jerk?"

"Mustache Cop."

"It doesn't make sense," Kevin said.

"It does to me, and obviously to Pete, too," JL said. "Mustache Cop could easily have known about the auction of Amy's brooch and the charges filed against the Providence Loan Society's employee. He could also have learned who bought the brooch. Once he connected Amy, me, and the brooch, all he had to do was follow the diamond."

"He'll set another trap for you, JL," Pete said.

"But we'll have an advantage, because he won't know we know he's on board. We'll have to set a trap for him."

"JL, he's had two shots at you," Kevin said. "You can't use yourself as bait. It could backfire. He could—"

JL reached out and touched Kevin's hand. "I promise I won't take any risks. I'll play this by the book, and won't leave this room without having someone with me."

He put his other hand on top of hers, sandwiching it between his, and squeezed. "I'll hold you to that promise." He withdrew his hand and glanced around the cabin. "Got anything to drink in here?"

"There's some champagne left out on the deck."

Kevin walked out onto their private promenade deck and Pete glared at her again, and said low-voiced, "What the hell's going on with you two?"

JL shook her head. "We'll talk later."

Kevin reentered the room carrying three bottles upside down and a fourth partially emptied. He filled the flute he'd been twirling. "The cop thinks he's invisible to us. That mistake will get him killed."

Someone knocked on the door and Kevin opened it to find Connor and Patrick, carrying trays with coffee and Danishes. "I figured we wouldn't get any sleep tonight," Connor said, setting down his tray. "Bring me up to speed. All I know is Lillian was attacked."

"She's at the hospital now. She's shook up, has a cut on her head, and a sore arm, but her spirits are high," Jack said. "Her health isn't our problem."

"What is?" Connor asked.

"We believe the cop who attacked JL twice also attacked Lillian and stole the brooch," Pete said.

Connor picked up an apple Danish and bit into it, then his eyes bored into his sister. He put down the Danish and marched over to the sofa, where he towered over her. "I'll say this once." He pointed his finger at her. "You're the best cop in the family. I need you to promise right now you'll use your head. Don't go out alone, day or night. Stay alert and in crowded areas. If the asshole drags you into the belly of this ship, we'll never find you in time."

Pete added sternly, "That's not hyperbole, *ragazza tosta. Capisci cosa intendo?*"

What color remained on JL's face after hearing Mustache Cop was on the ship ebbed, her lips fading to white. She got the message.

"Where are Maria, Isabella, and Gabe?" Jack asked.

"Maria and Isabella are in their room asleep, and Gabe is either playing cards or romancing the woman he met in third class," Pete said.

Kevin sat down again, moving almost painfully, as if the news had aged him in just these few minutes, and he looked closer in age to Elliott's mid-sixties than to his own early forties.

Kevin's eyes were fixed on JL.

Jack drew in a deep breath, as deep as he could manage, and held it. He used his inflated lungs to massage his heart and force it to slow down, way down. If Kevin abandoned JL now, it would shake up the fragile bonds of this hapless group of time-travelers, and the diamond brooch wouldn't be the only thing lost to the clan forever.

38

1909 SS New York—Amy

AMY WAS CAUGHT at low tide in the unsteady flow of a rip current. Surging waves pulled her farther from shore, now only a distant line on the horizon. Salt water went up her nose, and shapeless, slimy creatures nibbled on her toes.

Flailing her arms and legs, she tried to escape the swift-moving waves, but she couldn't escape the current. It was too strong, and forced her down, down into the angry sea.

She didn't take a breath. Would never inhale the salty water. Never.

Darkness closed in from all sides.

Panic locked in her throat.

She wasn't supposed to die like this. Her life couldn't possibly end when there was so much more living to do.

She screamed, "Help!"

39

1909 SS New York—Jack

AMY'S SCREAM EMPTIED JACK'S head of everything but the essential: get to Amy, now! He leapt to his feet and rushed toward the bedroom door, Patrick on his heels.

Several things happened at once in a well-choreographed sequence. Connor and Pete drew their weapons and blocked Jack's path. JL drew a gun from a valise on the floor. Kevin snatched a parasol from an umbrella stand.

Connor grabbed Jack's arm. "Wait. I'll go first. Pete, take the key and go through the corridor door. JL, take the door on the promenade deck. Patrick, sit on the sofa and don't move."

Amy screamed again.

Pete rushed out into the hall. JL and Kevin hurried to the porch.

Jack tried to sidestep Connor to get to Amy, but Connor shoved him back.

"Stay out of the way." Connor threw open the door. Simultaneously, Pete kicked open the corridor door.

Behind him, people were gathering in their nightclothes. Two stewards, in the process of putting on their jackets, hurried into the suite's parlor.

Back-shadowed by the lamps on the promenade deck, JL appeared at the entrance.

Connor turned on the bedside lamp and studied the room.

So did Jack.

No one other than Amy was there.

None of the furniture was overturned or out of place. The other bed was rumpled, but the dresser drawers were closed, and the personal items on top were neatly placed.

Amy was sitting in the bed with her hands covering her face, her hair in wild tangles. The sheet was twisted around her, blankets and pillows were strewn about on the floor.

Amy was rocking back and forth, trembling. "I can't breathe. I c-can't breathe."

Isabella and Maria, rushed to Amy's bed in their nightclothes. Maria cradled and rocked Amy like she was a child. "Shhh. Shhh, *mia dolce figlia. Non piangere.*"

"All clear," Connor said, stepping aside to let Jack into the room.

When Maria saw Jack, she said, "*La tua fidanzato è qui adesso.*"

Hearing himself referred to as Amy's fiancé sounded strange, but somehow also normal. He exchanged places with Maria, holding Amy as her surrogate grandmother had. "You're safe now. You had a nightmare. We're here. You're safe."

Sweat soaked her cotton sleeping gown. Her white face matched the bedsheet she clutched in her hands. The top of one foot, poking out from under the sheet, was scratched and bleeding.

Jack took her hands and cupped them over her mouth. "Breathe slowly. There's nothing here to scare you. Shhh. Breathe in through your mouth, out through your nose. Breathe in. Breathe out."

Pete turned to the gathered crowd, holstering his weapon. "It was a nightmare. Go back to your rooms."

Connor spoke to the stewards, "Report to the Master at Arms. Tell him one of the passengers had a nightmare, and her screams woke several people. She's awake now, and is being comforted."

"Should I bring tea?" one of the stewards asked.

"Peppermint, if it's available," Jack said. "I also need a cool cloth."

"I'll get one," Isabella said.

JL and Kevin entered the room. "I have medication," he said, "but with all the alcohol she consumed earlier, I wouldn't recommend a sedative."

"The tea might help."

Isabella handed Jack a damp cloth, and he wiped Amy's face, cooing while he washed away the sweat. She gasped in short, rapid breaths while continuing to whimper and tremble. "She needs a fresh gown. She's sweated through this one, she'll get chilled if she doesn't get dry."

"I'll help her change," Maria said.

"I don't want to leave her." Jack said.

"You can come back in as soon as she has a fresh gown." Then to Isabella, Maria said, "Get one from the drawer, *per favore, nipotina.*"

Jack didn't want to leave, but Maria wasn't going to budge. "Do it quickly." He closed the door behind him, and Connor handed Jack a cup of coffee. "I don't know how many nights I've woken like that. It's a horrible feeling."

"After the traumatic events you and Kevin have been through, I'm not surprised either of you have them, but what happened to Amy? Did coming here cause that?" Connor asked.

"Coming on the ship? Or back in time?" Jack took a big gulp of the lukewarm coffee.

"Either," Connor said.

The steward returned with a pot of tea. "The pantry is stocked with several flavors. If you need anything else, please ring. I hope the lady recovers quickly." Jack tipped the steward with one of the coins stacked like poker chips on a small mahogany side table, then ushered him out and shut the door.

JL was standing in the doorway leading out onto the promenade deck, her back to the rest of them, her gun still in her hand, finger off the trigger. Tension radiated off her, and she was unusually quiet.

"JL, you know what scared her, don't you?" Jack asked.

She turned slowly and looked at him, nodding. "She's scared of the ocean. She has thalassophobia, and didn't want anyone to know. She confessed the fear to me while under the influence. I don't think she would have told me otherwise."

"What is that?" Pete asked. "Sounds fatal."

"A fear of the ocean," Kevin said. "In any given year, four to five percent of the US population has one or more clinically significant phobias. The one Amy has is hard to determine, because it's often misdiagnosed as ADHD or bipolar disorders. But I don't think she has either one of those. I could have given her anxiety meds. Why didn't she tell us?"

JL packed her gun away in her travel bag and reached for a cup of coffee. "She was embarrassed. She thought if she stayed inside she'd be okay. It didn't occur to me her fear would manifest in this way." JL glanced at Kevin. "I wake up with night sweats. I should have anticipated this."

Isabella opened the door to Amy's room. "She'd like to see you, Jack. If you need us, knock on our door. We'll sit with her. Otherwise, *nonna* and I are going back to bed."

"Thanks, Isabella." Jack picked up the tray with the teapot and headed toward the bedroom, but stopped and looked around. "Where's Patrick?"

"He ran out in the hall after me," Pete said.

"I'll go look for him," Connor said. "I bet he's gone looking for the cop. The warning I gave JL applies to all of us, especially the most vulnerable, and don't you dare take offense at that, sis. But dressed like you are, you're at a disadvantage, as you learned last night."

Jack pulled a key out of his pocket and tossed it to JL. "Here's the key to my room. I'm going to sit up with Amy. After she falls asleep, I'll lie down in your bed for a while."

Kevin shot him a confused look, and a cold gust blew across Jack's heart. He knew in his gut where this was going to end up. Kevin and JL were perfect for each other, but maybe not perfect for each other right now.

"Wake me if you need anything," JL said.

Jack entered the bedroom. Amy was curled up on her side, eyes open. The covers and pillows had been picked up off the floor, straightened and fluffed. "How about a cup of tea? It's peppermint, and will help relieve your anxiety." He set it on the table and poured a cup.

"I'm sorry."

"There's nothing to be sorry for."

"Did JL tell you about my phobia? I should have told you."

Jack sat on the bed. "I won't disagree with you there. Kevin has anti-anxiety meds, and I have a few meditation techniques that might help, too."

Amy sat up, and Jack propped pillows behind her back. When she was settled, he gave her the cup, but it rattled in her hands and tea sloshed onto the saucer.

"Take this. I can't hold it."

He put the cup to her lips and tipped it forward for her to drink. She took a couple of swallows then pushed the cup away. "That's enough."

He set down the cup, took her hand, and rubbed her wrist and palm in a soothing pattern. "Do you know what caused your phobia?"

"No. I just know it has something to do with the beach and the ocean. If I avoid both, I'm fine. I'm not afraid of swimming pools, bathtubs, water, swimming. Only the ocean. I brought it up in counseling once, but nothing ever came of it. I haven't had a nightmare since I was a teenager."

"Did you go to the beach when you were little?"

"After my mom died, Dad got a coaching job at a college in California. We lived a few blocks from the ocean, and went there on weekends and after games. I don't want to talk about it."

He ignored her. "Did something happen to you at the beach?"

"I don't know," she said, her voice high with tension. "I just remember not wanting to go to the beach anymore." She reached for the teacup. "I think I can hold it now." She sipped slowly. "This is good, refreshing."

"How old were you?"

"I don't know. Can we talk about something else?"

"Were you five? Ten, maybe?"

She huffed and looked at him with a lifted brow. "Nine. Ten. I don't remember. Where's JL? I'm sure she's tired and wants to go to bed."

"I gave her the key to my room. If she gets sleepy, she'll go there. What did you do when you were ten? Did you go to parties? Did you have lots of girlfriends, or only a few very close ones?"

"I had lots of friends and there were always parties."

He stroked her arms. "Were they at friends' homes, party rooms, the beach?"

"A friend had a beach party. I didn't want to go, but my dad insisted. He left me there. It was awful. I spent the entire party sitting in the parking lot with my back to the beach."

"You were afraid of going to a party at the beach, but your dad didn't know you were afraid, did he?"

"I never told him." She winced as if it was a new realization.

"What didn't you tell him?" Jack asked softly.

She shook her head, and her breathing and trembling accelerated again.

"Did you believe he would be mad at you?"

"I don't know. I don't remember. It was a long time ago." She set the cup and saucer on the table and pulled the sheet up to her chin.

"Do you want to know what happened to you? What your fear stems from?"

"Do you know a psychiatrist who can cure my phobia?"

"My sister probably does, but I can help you go back there and try to pull out the memory buried in your subconscious. It's concealed what happened to you for a long time."

"I don't want to remember."

"But if you do remember, you'll be able to deal with it. Something happened to you as a child, Amy. You were traumatized, and afterwards you believed something bad would happen to you if you went to the beach or sailed on the ocean. It's a lie you've believed for years. You don't have to believe it anymore. You don't have to let it control you."

She crossed her arms and held them close to her body. "I don't want to know."

He couldn't coerce her. If she didn't want to remember, her mind would never release the memory. "Your subconscious is holding you captive. Every now and then it sends you hints, and you react viscerally. If you decide, *when* you decide to be set free, I'll help you."

She ran a shaking hand over her hair and curled the ends around a finger. She tried to give him a tight-lipped smile, but from the twitching around her mouth, even that was too much of an effort. "You'll think less of me if I don't face my fears?"

The woman before him now was vulnerable and insecure, almost childlike. Someone or something had hurt her badly, and it pissed him off. He pulled her in for a hug and kissed the top of her head.

"I'll never think less of you. Try to get some sleep. If you like, I'll take you to the First-Class Dining Room for brunch. We can try a short outing and see how you do."

There was a small and nearly imperceptible flinch in her eyes. "No. I don't want to go out. I'll stay here."

"If you stay here, you won't get to meet Catherine Lily."

Amy sat straight up, eyes wide, rounded, not blinking. "She's on this ship? How's that possible?"

"Her husband lied to us."

Amy's chest hitched when she gasped a short breath. Jack debated whether to press or not. If he did press, was it for his benefit, or hers? He considered the question. It was for her benefit. He had nothing to gain. If she spent the week inside the cabin, he would stay with her. Having her to himself would be a very pleasant way to spend the next few days.

"I want to meet her, but what if I…I don't know…have a panic attack or something while I'm talking to her?"

He leaned forward and gave her nape a squeeze, then brushed her face with his knuckles. "We'll deal with it then." He considered telling her about Lillian and the brooch, but decided the news was too stressful to share right now.

"I'll think about it in the morning," she said.

"Do you want to leave the light on?"

"Yes," she said, and then after a beat or two, asked, "If I wanted to remember, how would you help me do it?"

Jack took a slow breath while he considered his approach. "I'd put you in a deep relaxation state and then ask you a few questions. You'll be totally aware of what you're saying. I'll ask you to tell me exactly what you're seeing, hearing, thinking. You'll be in control."

"And I can stop at any time?"

"Any time. It isn't much different from the relaxation and visualization techniques athletes are taught."

"I want to meet Catherine Lily," Amy said, twirling the ends of her hair. "I just don't want to freak out in front of her." Amy closed her eyes, and Jack watched for signs of distress. Her jaw tightened and the tension in her neck and shoulders increased. "It won't hurt, right?"

"That's subjective. It won't hurt physically, but it might be emotionally painful. If it is, and you don't want to talk about it anymore, we don't have to. We'll talk about the Giants instead."

"I want a safe signal. Like a word or sign."

"I'm not hypnotizing you, sweetheart, or tying you up. I'm going to put you in a relaxed state and ask a few questions. I want you to tell me what comes immediately to mind, no matter how frivolous it seems."

She licked her lips, still twirling her hair. "I'm willing to try it, but if I get scared—"

"—you just stop talking."

40

1909 SS New York—Amy

AMY SCOOTED DOWN the bed in her cabin, her heart beating a frantic staccato, drumming against her ribs. She squeezed her eyes shut and swallowed back a knot in her throat, nodding slightly, signaling she was ready.

"I want you to focus on relaxing each toe, Amy," Jack began in his smooth, Southern drawl, speaking her name like a kiss. "Relax the top of your feet. Just let them go. Don't try to hold them up, just relax them completely."

Her feet flopped to the sides and the tightness trickled out of her feet. The frantic staccato beat of her heart slowed to a walking pace.

"Relax your ankles. Listen to the sound of my voice."

His voice, resonating through her, was mesmerizing, and the sound of it, the sound of the South, the sound of home, relaxed her.

"Relax the muscles connected to your shins... Relax your knees... Relax deep into your muscles, all the way down to your bones... Relax your thighs, your pelvis... Relax your stomach muscles... Let all your muscles soften... Slow your breathing while you listen to my voice... Let the relaxation spread into your lungs... Focus on each breath. Soften each breath, so it becomes easier, more comfortable... Relax," he said on a single breath, stretching it out.

"Let the relaxation move into your shoulders, down your arms, into your fingers. Relax, Amy."

Her jaw dropped slightly.

"Let the relaxation return to your shoulders, up your neck to your jaw. Relax your jaw... your mouth... Let the relaxation move into your eyes."

She no longer squeezed her eyes shut. She relaxed them, and her eyelashes stopped fluttering.

"Relax your eyebrows, your forehead. Let the relaxation wash over your entire face."

It was as if a warm cloth moved across her skin, washing away the tension, the fear, but not the sound of Jack's sensuous voice. His voice breathed with hers, as if making love to her.

"Let the relaxation spread to the top of your head, down the back of your head to your spine... Let it go, one vertebra at a time until it reaches the base of your spine."

Even the base of her spine tingled.

"Relax. Let the relaxation travel down your hamstrings to your calves... to the bottoms of your feet... to the backs of your toes. Your body is completely relaxed now, isn't it?"

She nodded. Her body felt like overcooked spaghetti. If he put her on her feet, she couldn't have stood on her own.

"Tell me about the dream. Do you remember? Do you see it? Tell me the first thing that pops into your head. Stay relaxed... Let your toes relax... your legs... your arms... relax. Tell me what you see while you stay relaxed. Talk to me. What do you see? What do you hear? Relax and breathe softly. What do you smell? What do you taste?"

"I'm riding in the back seat of my dad's car. It's cluttered with muddy cleats, sports magazines, food wrappers, empty beer bottles, ball caps, smelly towels. He's pounding the steering wheel with his fists," she said in a breathy, childlike voice.

"Do you know why?"

She shook her head.

"Does he say anything?"

"Damn. He says damn over and over. I hate it when he cusses."

"Why?"

"He only does it when he's mad."

"And he's mad now. Look closely, Amy. Why is he mad?"

"I don't know."

"Look. Look deep into the picture in your mind. What do you see?"

"Gin spilled all over the kitchen floor."

"How did it get there?"

"The bottle slipped out of his hand and it all spilled on the floor." She sniffed. "It smells like Christmas trees. I don't want to smell Christmas trees in the summer. My dad gets mean when he drinks. I don't like him then."

"How does he get mean? Does he hurt you?"

She shook her head. "No, he doesn't hurt me. He gives me the mean face he gives to umpires."

"What did he do after he spilled the gin?"

She brought the mental picture back to her mind. She could see it all clearly. "He grabs his keys. He tells me to get in the car. I don't want to," she added quickly. "I don't like to ride in the car when he drinks. He scares me."

"What did you do? What do you see?"

"I get in the back seat, the dirty back seat. He drives funny, going from one side of the road to the other." She rolls back and forth on the bed. "*Bang!* He hits a neighbor's trashcan, and it rattles down the street, garbage all over the place. That makes him mad, too. He cusses the neighbor for leaving the trashcan in his way. He drives off without picking it up. I want to pick up the mess, but he won't stop."

"Where are you going?"

"To buy more gin." She shivered, remembering the fear.

"What are you remembering that makes you shiver?"

"I hope he doesn't crash. He makes it to the store and goes inside. I go, too, but he doesn't have enough cash. Now he's really mad. He tells me it's all my fault."

"Why?"

"He spent his cash on a baseball card for my collection. I didn't ask him to do it. I save my money and buy my own cards. But he has to use his credit card to buy the gin. He wants to go to the beach, but I don't want to go. My friends are all on vacation. There won't be anyone to play with. He ignores me."

"Where's the beach?" Jack asked.

"Close to our house. It's down this road tourists don't know about. It's quiet. Out of the way. He likes it. I don't. I like to go where the people are."

"Were you scared?"

She shook her head. "I'm not scared. I'm mad. We're both mad."

"What happens when you get to the beach?"

"I jump out of the car as fast as I can. I want to get away from him. I slam the door. He yells at me. I don't care. I grab a blanket from the trunk and spread it out on the sand. He sets up his chair. The fold-up kind, you know, with drink holders. He put his new bottle of gin in one holder, his cup in the other. Then he waves at me like I'm a fly bothering him. He tells me to go play, but there's no one to play with. He doesn't care. He has his gin for company."

"Had he ever told you to go away before?" Jack asked.

"After my mom died, he told me to leave him alone. I know he didn't want me around. I think he blamed me for her death."

"Why blame you?"

Amy's breath hitched. "I didn't give her cancer, but he blames me anyway. He cries and drinks, except for when he's around his ballplayers. He never drinks around them. Just me."

"After he sends you away, where do you go? What do you do?"

"I go for a walk along the beach. I remember the sun being in my eyes. I didn't bring my ball cap, and I don't have any sunglasses. It's hot and I walk and walk. I take my shoes off and walk in water up to my ankles. I'm looking down at the shells and dead critters the tide brings in." Her voice quavered.

"I walk for a long time, until I can't see my dad. If I keep walking, he'll never find me."

"How do you feel about that?"

"Where would I live? He's all I've got. For good or bad, he's it for me."

"What happens next?"

"I keep walking, looking in the shallow water. And then I see something farther out in the water, and I walk toward it. The water almost comes to my knees. Hair, almost as bright as the Pringles chips can, floats around a woman's head. Her arms are outstretched. She's just floating in the water, like a mermaid in the current. I can't take my eyes off her."

Amy could feel her heart thumping hard. "I can't stop watching her. The sun...the sun is shining on her hair. It's so red, so bright. And then...and then she floats into me and I see her face." Amy was gasping now.

"I see her face. Her eyes...her eyes are open. She...she...she's looking at the sky. But her eyes aren't moving. And she has...she has this"—Amy poked at her forehead with her finger—"she has a hole in her head. I scream and push her away. There are sea creatures eating her feet, and her face is all fat and funny, and she looks ugly. I scream and scream, and then I try to run through the water, but it's like syrup and my legs won't move fast enough to get away from her. She bumps into me again, and I scream and scream. I finally get out of the water, and I run, yelling for my dad, but I've gone too far, and he can't hear me. I run. That's all I can think to do. Run... Run... Run... I run until I can't breathe and have to stop."

She panted as if she had been running, gasping, struggling for her next breath.

"I finally find my dad, but he's asleep. I shake him and shake him and shake him, but he won't wake up. The bottle of gin is empty. I have to find someone else to help the woman. I run back to the place where I saw her, screaming for someone, anyone to help."

Amy turned on her side and pulled into the fetal position. "I run back to the spot where I saw her, but she's gone. Maybe I'm in the wrong place. I must be. I keep running and running, but I can't find her. The waves must have carried her away. She's gone, and I can't help her now. I fall on the beach, breathing fast, and I lie there, hoping the waves will bring her back so I can help her, but the sun is going down, and I have to leave. I can't wait anymore. My dad's too drunk to save her, and I'm too little."

Amy exploded into a paroxysm of tears. Jack wiped her forehead with a damp towel and, in a soft voice, asked, "What does the adult Amy believe?"

Her breath hitched again and again. "I couldn't have done anything to save her."

"Was there anything your dad could have done?"

"He could have pulled her body out of the water."

"Would it have saved her?"

Amy didn't answer. Jack cupped her face and, with utmost tenderness, brushed a kiss on her forehead. Finally, she rolled over on her back and wiped her face with the sheet. "He couldn't have saved her either. She had a bullet hole between her eyes." Amy covered her face with her hands and wept, deep, racking sobs. "How could I forget that? How could I be thirty-seven and not remember something so significant?"

Jack wiped her face again with the towel. "Your mind tucked it away to protect you."

"I was angry with my dad for years, and never knew why. I blamed it on the alcohol. I blamed it on how distant he was. I blamed it on his diet. I blamed it on dozens of things, but I never blamed him for what happened that day."

"If you knew why you were angry with him," Jack said, "then you'd remember what happened, but you didn't want to remember. All you knew was you didn't want to go back to the ocean and you were mad at your dad. Since you didn't remember the reason, you needed to come up with a new one, and any reason would do. The memory has always been there, waiting for you. You just needed the right triggers to bring it back."

She curled on her side again, facing Jack. Weak and shaky, she felt completely drained, physically, mentally, and emotionally.

"Will you hold me?" She knew she was asking a lot, but she

needed to be held. She needed to be touched, if only to reassure herself another person was there with her, and not a figment of her memories.

Jack lay down behind her and snuggled her to him. The smell of the ocean in his hair and on his skin, was almost erotic and powerfully seductive. She wanted to hold the scent in her lungs and never let it go.

"Will you wake me before sunrise? I want to watch the sun come up over the ocean. When I was little, it was my favorite time of day."

"I'll wake you. And I hope it's the most beautiful sunrise you've ever seen."

41

1909 SS New York—Jack

JACK HELD AMY in his arms until dawn, numb with grief for the child who suffered so much from her mother's death and her father's alcoholism. If Joe Gilbert couldn't find a way to make up for what Amy lost, Jack would.

Stand aside, man. I'll give her the world.

He and Amy were wrapped in each other's arms on the private promenade deck at sunrise. Her blue eyes were soft with sleep, and her hair tousled. The eastern sky unveiled a celestial show rivaling any fireworks he had ever seen. The last stars reluctantly gave way to the growing blush of dawn, leaving one lone star, the morning star.

When the sun's rays burst over the horizon she oohed, and when the dark skies began to welcome splashes of color, she was awed. Streaks of pink and orange and yellow painted the eastern sky before the star of the show peeked over the water and began its ascent, signaling a brand-new day.

"I've never seen anything so beautiful," Amy said.

Jack gazed down at her while her voice whispered over his skin like cool morning air. "I haven't either."

JL walked out onto the deck with a cup of steaming coffee. "What's going on out here?"

"Watching the sun come up," Amy said. "Come join us."

JL stepped over to the window. Jack wrapped his other arm

around her, and she leaned against his shoulder.

"It's the most beautiful sunrise I've ever seen," Amy said, widening her eyes a little for emphasis.

"It is beautiful, but I'm confused," JL said. "Yesterday you wouldn't come anywhere near this window. What happened between the time I left the bedroom and right this minute?" She frowned up at Jack, and then at Amy. "If you tell me you had sex, I'll scream, and then I'll be furious with both of you."

Jack took JL's cup for a sip of hot coffee. Most members of the family doctored it in some way, but JL drank hers thick and black, and would even drink the last dregs in a morning pot. "We didn't have sex. Although it's fine with me if Amy wants to."

Amy elbowed him in the side. "I'm committed. Remember?"

JL took her cup back. "Just be sure you remember. Jack can be persuasive."

"I've discovered that," Amy said. "Don't worry. I won't forget."

"Okay, if you didn't have sex, what changed?" JL asked.

"A childhood memory gone awry. I'll tell you all about it later, but right now I'm starving. I want to take a long bath before I go to the dining room for a huge brunch, where I hope somebody will bring me up to speed on everything that's happened in the last twenty-four hours."

"You mean you haven't heard any of the news?" JL asked.

"Jack told me Catherine Lily is on the ship, and we're meeting Lillian Russell for brunch. That's all."

"Go get your bath," JL said. "We've got a lot to talk about."

Amy kissed Jack's cheek. "Thank you."

He watched her walk away, surprised by how effortlessly, how lightly she moved. She might be high on the kind of relief and release that follows unearthing old memory blocks. If he spent the next four days cementing his position as a trusted confidante, maybe she would call on him if she found her feelings for Gilbert somewhat shaken when she saw him again. Jack would gladly calm those feelings, giving her a warmhearted perspective from someone who genuinely cared for her.

JL backed away from Jack and looked him over. "Are you sure you didn't have sex? You both have the familiarity lovers have, but friends don't."

He threw JL a crooked grin. "Trust me." He made a cross over his heart. "I never touched her."

"I'm still not sure I believe you."

He turned to face her, put his hands on her shoulders, and looked her in the eye. "I walked her through deep relaxation, and asked her to tell me the first thing that came to mind. She told me a childhood story about going to the beach and finding a woman with a bullet hole between her eyes floating in the water. Her father was too drunk to help, and the woman floated away. Amy had blocked it all out of her mind."

JL opened her mouth to speak then closed it. Swallowed, then said, "Wow. Okay, I believe you now. Did she ever find out anything about the woman?"

He shook her shoulders. "Amazing. All I need to do is put a police matter in front of you, and everything else takes second chair. In answer to your question, no, or if she did, she blocked it all out."

"If she'll give me specifics, I'll check into it. The body was probably recovered."

"JL," Jack said, sharply. "Stop with the body ID. Think about what it did to a ten-year-old."

"I don't want to think about what it did to a ten-year-old. It's easier for me to focus on what I can solve, and that's to ID the body. I can't fix Amy's mind. But obviously you can, Dr. Mallory. How did you get her to spill the beans?"

"The triggers were all there. Her mind was ready to open and spit it out. I was just the vehicle to help her get through it."

"Can you do it for Kevin?" For an instant, JL's eyes were dark, naked with feeling, and Jack was caught up in what he saw there, tangled in her pain. Before Carolina Rose, he would have run from what he saw in JL's eyes. He couldn't run anymore. Carolina Rose had humanized him, and for the first time in his life he connected on a deeper level with the people he cared for. It wasn't easy, but if he was going to love people, he needed to expose his own vulnerability.

"I don't think Kevin is ready," he said.

"Tell me about it. I'm going to break our engagement."

Her non-sequitur almost knocked him off his feet. "What? Have you thought this through?"

"No, I'm just throwing it out there." She paused for a six count. "Of course, I've thought it through."

"Is it what you really want?"

"No! It's not what I want. But I can't live with the illusion anymore. I can't fix him. I can't fix us. I can't fix what happened. I regret the part I played in putting him through so much trauma. And I couldn't bear to hear him say he wants to break our engagement. I'd turn into a puddle and remain on the floor until someone mopped me up. Trust me. It'll be easier if I call off the wedding and give him time away from me to figure out what he wants."

"Regrets expand," Jack said. "They gather strength like a late summer storm that starts out over the ocean and heads toward land. They're living organisms. We have to let go of them before they cannibalize us."

"That's hard to do when they keep coming at us like paintballs. Splat!"

"What happened to you in New York City was like another paintball, wasn't it?"

"Yep, and it made the situation worse, or brought it to a head. I'm sorry it happened, yet glad it did. Does that make any sense?"

"A pile-on is never a good thing. But I understand."

"Kevin can't shake the traumas he experienced in October and November. And he definitely can't shake Elliott's lie. I don't know if one is worse than the other."

"It's cumulative. He's going through a rough patch, and he doesn't know what he wants, except to feel better. With all that's going on with the brooch and the danger surrounding us, he's being triggered right and left."

"If we break the engagement, he won't have to worry about me."

"You're kidding, right? Just because you give him the ring back doesn't mean he'll stop loving or worrying about you."

"What?" She socked Jack's arm. "Do you think I'm crazy? I'm not giving this ring back. This nugget was a gift. I'll wear it on my right hand until he decides to put it back on my left."

"What if he doesn't?"

"God, you sure know how to make a girl feel better. It won't be the first time some guy has jerked me around."

"Is that how you feel?"

She threw up her hands in obvious exasperation. "No. It's not how I feel. I know being in love with me complicates Kevin's life. So I'll offer him one less complication. If he wants to make it permanent…." She sighed. "I'm tired of talking about it."

Jack pulled her in for a hug. "Break the engagement and step out of his way. He'll come to his senses or he won't. There's not much else you can do. It might take him a few months, though. How long are you prepared to wait?"

JL sounded a bit weary when she said, "I'll give him six months…or a year…or eighteen months. Then I'll have to move on."

"You'll leave the family?"

"No, it's my family, too. If he wants to date other women, I might not like it, but I'll deal with it."

"Look, I've known Kevin for years. I've met dozens of the women he's dated. They've been beautiful, professional women, even a doctor or two, but not one of them would have fit into the family the way you did from day one."

JL's eyes flashed, reflecting the rising sun. "It may not be important to Kevin. But it is to you. It's the one condition that will make or break any future relationships you have."

"You're right, kiddo. And we've come a long way, haven't we?"

"If you're expecting me to give you a break the next time you fuck up, forget it. I'll be the same hard-ass, but it won't mean I love you any less."

He laughed. "I wouldn't expect anything less from the toughest O'Grady I know."

42

1909 SS New York—Jack

JACK AND AMY entered the À la Carte Restaurant shortly before eleven o'clock. Jack gave the maître d' his name, and they followed him across the carpet to one of the half dozen walnut-paneled alcoves with candle-style lamps and gilt bronze wall sconces. Curtains were neatly tucked to the sides and could easily be pulled if he wanted privacy. The room was designed for elegance, intimacy, and romance.

A table for six with damask chairs was set, as requested, with the Panel Reed pattern of cutlery. Its deeply fluted handles were glitteringly polished, without a speck of tarnish in the relief. Since stepping onto the ship, Jack had been taking copious notes, cataloguing everything his senses could absorb: fixtures, furnishings, staff, music, clothing, smells, tastes. Not one detail escaped his notice. Not even the cutlery, or the exuberant, large-scale arrangements of pink roses and white daisies arranged in glazed iron, urn-shaped vases. He had spoiled his readers previously with historical minutia in the settings he created, and he couldn't stop imagining his characters walking the decks of the *SS New York*.

"Who else is joining us?" Amy asked.

She looked gorgeous this morning, dressed in a navy tailor-made suit with a straight-line skirt, jacket, and a crisp white blouse with a high collar, ruffles, and exquisite hand beading. He much preferred knee-length skirts over ankle length, but the suit looked sexy on her, and he enjoyed watching the sway of her hips as she walked in the tightly-fitted skirt.

He made note of that, too. He could try using his next novel as justification for watching the sway of her hips, but it wouldn't fly far. He'd done enough book research for the day. He slammed his mental notebook shut and smiled at her.

"JL, Connor, and Pete. However, it could change, depending on what Gabe learned during his all-night poker game."

"What's he looking for?"

"Something out of the ordinary, something useful."

The maître d' seated Amy on the side of the table with a full view of the dining room and the ocean beyond the open windows, and Jack took a seat next to her. A waiter came immediately to the table with a silver carafe and filled their coffee cups.

"Where exactly are we on the ship, and what's close by?" she asked.

Jack glanced around to get his bearings. Along with Pete, Connor, and Gabe, they had divided the ship into quadrants to map and explore, then merged their findings. Jack had the B Deck's layout memorized. "We're on the other side of the bulkhead from the Second-Class Smoking Room, close to the promenade, and down the corridor from our rooms."

"Thanks, but it doesn't help much. I need a map. I'm a visual learner."

"I'll draw you one later." He spread a cloth napkin in his lap and tried not to catalogue the starched thickness of the fabric or the sharply-ironed creases. "How does it feel to be out of your cabin?"

"Kevin gave me a concoction that guaranteed I'll be ready for a glass of champagne during brunch. Although the thought of it makes my stomach churn."

"Well, you haven't eaten in twenty-four hours."

"Longer than that. I didn't eat breakfast yesterday." She beamed a smile right at his heart. "I feel weightless today, like I'm walking on air. It probably doesn't make sense, but a heavy weight has been lifted, and I can't thank you enough."

"I was only the facilitator. You did all the heavy lifting." He decided to change the subject so she wouldn't focus on her recovered memory. She needed to wear it for a while before she disassembled it to analyze all the parts and pieces, which she was bound to do when the fuzziness of time and distance cleared the path to total recall. "What I want to know," he said, "is how you and JL drank three and a half bottles of champagne."

"It was easy. We were both in a mood, and quenching it with alcohol seemed the right thing to do. I'm not a fortune-teller and can't see the future, so I don't know what's going to come of JL and Kevin's engagement. Sadly, I don't think they're going to work it out right now. She seems determined to break the engagement before he does."

"She wants to protect him," Jack said, his coffee cup halfway to his mouth.

"I think you're right. If she breaks it off, he won't have to be the bad guy."

"She can't stop playing the protector role, even when it's not in her best interest."

Amy poured cream into her cup and leisurely stirred. "Bless her heart. Well, I'm staying out of it, at least until we open another bottle of champagne. It was delicious, by the way. I hope it wasn't too expensive."

"Compared to twenty-first century prices, it was cheap."

"Who's paying for this trip, by the way?"

"The company."

"Our three-room suite is the most expensive one on the ship. JL said it costs twenty-five-hundred dollars, the equivalent of sixty-one-thousand dollars in the twenty-first century. That's insane."

"But you need to remember, darlin', we're not paying twenty-first century prices. A twenty-five-hundred-dollar suite for five days is a bargain in my travel itinerary."

"When we get back, I'll reimburse the company for all the expenses."

"You can try, but Elliott won't accept it."

Amy pointed. "Look. Here come JL, Connor, Pete, and Lillian Russell."

Jack rose when Lillian reached the table. "How do you feel this morning? You look lovely. You'd never know you suffered an upsetting incident last night."

"JL gave me a little white pill she promised would take my dreadful headache and toss it in the ocean. If you see it floating by, you'll know the pill is working."

"If it came from JL, I guarantee it will work," Jack said. "I know you met her at the theater with Kevin, and you met Pete last night and now you've met Connor."

"I've met everyone, darling," Lillian said patting Jack's arm. "Even this lovely creature sitting next to you." She extended her hand to Amy. "You were with Stephen Thomson at Delmonico's. It's wonderful to see you again."

Amy smiled warmly. "I'm so sorry to hear about what happened to you last night. I hope you didn't suffer any significant injuries."

Lillian did a little wrist flip. "The doctor put me back together and sent me to my room. I'm sufficiently recovered. But, I'd rather talk about you. I thoroughly enjoy your column. You write like a man. I never trust interviews written by women. They're more interested in my toilette than what I have to say." Then, as if performing on stage she said, "'The fair Lillian is in town, fortified against the ravages of age. Away from the lights, it does not take an experienced eye to see the fine lines above the haggard orbs of the actress…' It enrages me," she said. "A man wouldn't write that, and neither would you."

Amy laughed. "I'm not interested in the fine lines above your orbs, only your voice and acting skills."

"See?" Lillian glanced at Jack. "This woman has a head on her shoulders." Then to Amy she said, "If you decide to interview actresses instead of ballplayers, I'll give you a marvelous interview guaranteed to sell papers."

Amy laughed again. The sound was pure magic, and Jack's heart capered around like a kid on Christmas morning.

"I'll remember that," Amy said.

Jack turned back to Lillian. "Are you sure you're well enough to be out of your cabin?"

"Yes, but I want to know if Pete has made any progress in the investigation."

"We're making a list of possible suspects to interview, but so far nothing," Pete said.

"I can't tell you how much I appreciate your support last night. I couldn't have gotten through the ordeal without you, and I never would have come up with a description of the assailant without Pete's prodding." She looked closely at Jack. "Seeing you in the daylight, I'm even more amazed at how you haven't aged. You must tell me your secret."

"I stay out of the sun. I don't smoke. I get at least eight hours of sleep a night, and I drink gallons of water. That's it," Jack said with a tiny shrug.

Lillian eyed him suspiciously, but thankfully a waiter stopped by to serve coffee, and the conversation turned to music.

"I spoke with the violinist this morning and told him I'd like to perform this evening in the First-Class Dining Room. He said he would have the full orchestra there by nine o'clock for a concert."

JL clapped her hands. "I'm delighted. I haven't had a chance to hear you perform before. This will be amazing."

"My sister is a performer, too." Connor said.

JL tilted her head to one side, eyes narrowing, as she glared at her brother. "And Connor never grew out of his tattletale stage."

"Then I shall tell the violinist to expect two performers. The passengers will be delightfully entertained." Lillian patted Jack's hand. "Darling, look at that woman."

"Where?" Jack asked.

"Walking in our direction. I hate to dredge up painful memories, but doesn't she look like Carolina Rose Arées? Older, perhaps, but still a remarkable resemblance. As I recall, you were quite smitten with her, and she with you. Of course, we were all very fond of her.

I must find out who this lookalike is. She might even be related. Maybe she knows the real story of what happened to Carolina Rose and her uncle."

A gust of chilly air touched the back of Jack's neck, and the hairs rose silent on his skin. This wouldn't turn out well. He stood, as did Pete and Connor, while Lillian left the alcove and approached Catherine Lily.

"What are we going to do?" Amy whispered.

"I don't see her husband." Jack said. "We'll have to play it by ear."

Lillian stopped Catherine Lily a few feet from the table. "I'm Lillian Russell, and you look exactly like a woman I knew almost thirty years ago. So much so you could be her twin sister."

"Oh, no," Jack groaned.

"Miss Russell, I so enjoyed yer performance last year when ye appeared as Henrietta Barrington in the play, *Wildfire*. Ye were marvelous. I didn't know ye were sailing on the *SS New York*. What a wonderful surprise to meet ye. Tell me about yer friend. What's her name? Maybe I've heard of her."

"Carolina Rose Arées. I met her in New York City in 1879, I think. Join us and meet my friends. We can have another chair added to our table."

"I would be delighted. My husband and I were dining alone, but who wants to dine alone when there are so many interesting people to converse with?"

Jack signaled the maître d'. "Two more place settings." Within moments, two additional settings were added to their round table. Jack couldn't take his eyes off Catherine Lily. Her violet eyes matched Carolina Rose's, as did her silky hair. His heart pounded suddenly, for no reason, as though he had run miles. Something was not quite right, and then he knew.

Her voice. The Scottish accent was all wrong. It grated against his memories.

Had Carolina Rose's accent influenced his thinking? Would he have been less enthralled if she hadn't been French? Her beauty, her talent, her French accent and Parisian mystique created an irresistible radiance Catherine Lily simply didn't have.

Catherine Lily sat in the chair next to Lillian, who made the introductions. A strange ripple, like one caused by a stone thrown into the water, spread in concentric circles, each one an unasked question. The time travelers shared looks of bafflement. Sterling had asked Jack to respect the family's request not to tell Catherine Lily the truth. Could Jack honor the request now?

"Where was yer friend born?" Catherine Lily asked.

"France, I believe," Lillian said. "She was a French artist. Such a lovely girl. She and her uncle were killed in 1881 in a horrible accident in San Francisco."

"What did she paint? Have I seen any of her work?"

"She was working on a collection of flowers at the Conservatory of Flowers in San Francisco when she died," Jack said. "I believe the complete collection was purchased by a single collector."

"What a shame. I would have liked to have seen her work. Do ye know where in France she was from? I've traveled widely. Maybe our paths crossed."

JL's eyes went wide for a moment, then narrowed in calculation. "We don't know. But..." She paused for a moment and looked at her brother, but not Jack. Connor nodded, giving her the go-ahead.

Jack cleared his throat, darted a glance at JL, but she ignored him.

"We believe her mother was from the Scottish Highlands," JL said.

"I'm from the Highlands, too," Catherine Lily said. "Near Inverness. Where was she from exactly?"

"We're not sure, but we believe she was related to the MacKlennas."

Catherine Lily raised her brow. "My grandmother was Ainsley MacKlenna. Her other daughter, my aunt Gracie, ran off with a Frenchman. No one ever saw her again. If Aunt Gracie was your friend's mother, it would make us first cousins."

"My dear, there you are." Jack's head jerked around to see Edward Sterling walking toward their table. He reached his wife and rested his hand on her shoulder. "I've been looking for you."

She glanced up at him. "Darling, let me introduce my new friends. This is Miss Lillian Russell, and her friend Mr. Jack Mallory. Miss Amy Spalding, a columnist at the *Herald*. Brother and sister Miss Jenny Lynn and Mr. Connor O'Grady, and Mr. Pete Parrino. They've been telling me about a woman who might be a cousin I've never heard of."

"You'll have to excuse us," Sterling said, glaring icily at Jack. "I've made luncheon arrangements in the First-Class Dining Room. Come, my dear."

Catherine Lily darted glances over her shoulder, as though she was afraid of her husband. "I understood we were dining alone."

Jack looked at Amy. He wasn't sure what she would do. If her skin crawled with the same revulsion his did, she wouldn't let it pass, and neither would JL.

Sterling blew out his breath in frustration. His expression didn't change, but something unsettling flowed through the depths of his eyes. "Our plans changed. Please excuse us." He put his hands on the back of his wife's chair.

"Mr. Sterling, join us. We're enjoying your wife's company," JL said.

Jack sipped cautiously at his coffee, hyper-aware of it gently searing his throat and running hot down into his stomach. JL was intentionally antagonizing Sterling, trying to force the issue, and by doing so, she would arouse Catherine Lily's curiosity even more.

Catherine Lily stood. "I would like to continue our discussion. Would it be convenient to meet for afternoon tea in the Café Parisien?"

"That won't be possible," Sterling said. "We've already accepted an invitation."

"This evening, perhaps. In the Reception Room at eight-thirty before Miss Russell's performance at nine o'clock in the First-Class Dining Room," Amy said.

"A free Lillian Russell concert is unheard of," JL said. "This will be a treat for all first-class passengers. You won't want to miss it."

"How divine." Catherine Lily turned to her husband. "We'll certainly attend. Won't we, darling?"

"We'll discuss it." He took his wife's arm and escorted her out of the restaurant.

"What strange behavior. We must plot to get Mrs. Sterling away from that domineering man long enough to continue our conversation. Now," Lillian said, studying the menu. "What shall we eat?"

"Caviar, lobster, quail from Egypt, plover's eggs, hothouse grapes and fresh peaches, green turtle soup, and prime rib. I've heard it's all superb," Jack said.

"Haute cuisine, not merely good food," Amy said.

"I'll have a bit of everything," Lillian said to the waiter who appeared at her side. "Then I'll probably start over."

A few minutes later, a trio of immaculately well-groomed musicians began playing music from Puccini, and the time travelers sat back and listened to Lillian tell the story of songwriter John Stromberg writing the prettiest song she ever sang. "He kept delaying delivery of the song, insisting it wasn't ready. Then," she said dramatically, "he took a fatal dose of insecticide and the completed manuscript for the sentimental ballad, 'Come Down Ma Evenin' Star' was found in his coat pocket. On *Twirly Whirly's* opening night, the papers reported I burst into tears while I sang it."

"I heard that story," JL said. "Is it true?"

"Well," Lillian said, "Who can argue with a press agent's publicity? The song has since become my trademark number."

"Will you sing it tonight?" JL asked.

"For you, my dear, of course."

A cold prickle on Jack's neck had him glancing around the room. His stomach clenched when he saw Sterling standing at the entrance to the restaurant with the Master at Arms. Sterling was pointing straight at Jack. Jack caught Connor's eye and flicked a nod. Connor's face tightened when he saw Sterling, then the taut lines in his face relaxed, and he focused on the heaping plates of food delivered to their table.

If Connor could register a problem and switch gears so quickly, Jack could, too. He clasped Amy's hand and winked, and the smile she gave him whetted his appetite as no other woman ever had. Ever.

A red stain spilled across her face, but she didn't back down or look away. Her hand warmed in his, and he smiled, too. He kissed the backs of her fingers, and her gaze traveled over his face. Was she searching for a clue to his intentions? He didn't have any. She was the one with the commitment. She would have to make the move.

Then something bold and electric passed between them. Her energy swept across him and prickled his skin, unnerving him for a moment. He released her hand, and picked up his fork. God help him, but he would resist even a good night kiss, unless she told him she intended to end her relationship with Gilbert. Jack's heart was too fragile to lose another woman.

Too fragile to love again unless he knew it would last forever.

43

1909 SS New York—Kevin

KEVIN WANDERED INTO the Smoking Room at two o'clock, searching for Jack. While Jack was enjoying brunch with JL, Amy, and Lillian Russell, Kevin had been working out in the gymnasium on the Boat Deck. The shipping lines' idea of a gym and his were a century apart. He found the mechanical saddle mildly entertaining. The punching bag, however, gave him an aerobic workout but used up only a fistful of his pent-up frustration.

When he didn't find Jack, Kevin ordered a whisky and purchased a Cuban cigar from the bartender, a twenty-something freckled man wearing the white tunic worn by the first-class stewards. Kevin lit the cigar and tossed the match into an ashtray. Next to the ashtray was a pack of Piedmont cigarettes. Curious, he picked it up and read the packaging. On the flip side was a picture of a Pittsburgh baseball player—Honus Wagner. Didn't he hear Amy was a baseball card collector? Was she interested in all players, or just the Giants? He tossed the cigarettes aside and picked up his whisky.

The bartender wiped the bar with a cloth, emptied the ashtray, and picked up the cigarette package.

"I noticed the baseball card," Kevin said, easily falling into his Scottish persona. "Do people collect them?"

The bartender studied the Wagner card. "Boys collect players from their favorite teams. I collect them for my nephew. He trades the ones he doesn't want. Since we sailed, I've found four in discarded cigarette packs like this one." He flashed the back of the pack to make his point. "This will be number five."

Kevin leaned against the mahogany bar's brass railing, rolling the cigar between his thumb and fingers, not saying anything while the bartender continued to wipe the top of the bar. Then: "May I see yer collection?"

A grin spread slowly across the bartender's face, rearranging his freckles. "Sure." From underneath the bar, he produced a two-by-three-inch green Adams House Lilliputians cigar box, about the same size as the Wagner card. He tugged on the tassel and the inside slid out, revealing the four cards.

Amy had probably collected all the cards she wanted, but, like the bartender's nephew, she could trade the ones she didn't want. "How much do ye want for the box and the four cards?"

The bartender's observation of Kevin narrowed, sharpening, as he tried to figure out how much Kevin was willing to pay, and how much he might have had to drink in one of the other bars on board the ship, without pricing himself too high and missing the sale. Finally, he said, "Five dollars."

Kevin dug into his pocket and pulled out several bills. But before he handed them over, he harrumphed and scratched his jaw, faking indecision. After a few beats, he slapped the bills on the bar. He would have paid any price the man asked. The bartender added the Honus Wagner to the box and handed it over.

"Check back before we dock. I might have more."

"Sure thing. Nice doing business with ye." Kevin tucked the green box into his jacket pocket and patted it. He wasn't much of a hero these days, but at least he'd given freckle-face a story to tell and a few bucks in his pocket.

Kevin pushed away from the bar to find a chair, keeping his distance from the others in the room. Apparently, his Scottish warrior pose the previous evening accomplished his objective, because no one approached him. No one extended an invitation to join a conversation. No one even nodded hello.

He chomped down on his cigar and strode through the room with his whisky until he found a vacant chair in an empty corner. The leather was still warm from its previous occupant, a portly gentleman with a New Jersey accent who was now engrossed in a conversation with a group of investors Kevin had avoided.

Every hour he stayed aboard ship, he was more and more dogged by the problems he couldn't solve. He had always been lucky. His parents had doted on their only child and given him opportunities that fueled the dreams of his friends. Then he met Elliott, and the doors Elliott opened for Kevin surpassed even his own expectations.

Where had luck, destiny, karma been for the past eight months, while his world spun out of control? Were they all just illusions? Something to hang your hat on when no other explanation seemed viable? Yes, they were. His life had nothing to do with fate or luck or karma—which was often fickle—and everything to do with his own fucking stupidity.

He felt boxed in, trapped, entombed, and it was time to break out. But how? When? He couldn't make a phone call and order a helicopter like a limo service to pick him up at sea. He frowned angrily behind a cloud of smoke and took a deep swig of whisky.

"Mr. Fraser. Mr. Kevin Fraser. Mr. Fraser," a steward moving through the room was calling quietly. At first Kevin ignored him and then remembered it was the name he was using.

Kevin raised his hand, holding the cigar loosely between two fingers. "Here. I'm Kevin Fraser."

The steward presented a silver tray with a white envelope addressed to him. The shipping lines' logo appeared on the flap. He broke the seal and read the card:

Please, come by my suite. We need to talk, JL.

"Is there a reply?" the steward asked.

Kevin put a coin on the tray. "No reply. Thank ye." He emptied his whisky glass and stubbed out his cigar. JL was a woman of action. If he didn't show up, she'd come looking for him. If the men disliked him now, they'd like him even less if his fiancée barged into a men's-only Smoking Room.

He took the Grand Staircase down to B Deck, looking for Jack, but didn't see him in the Reception Room either. After he talked to JL, Kevin would search the Boat Deck. There wasn't anyone else he could talk to who would understand what he was going through—nightmares, performance anxiety, fear. If Kevin couldn't satisfy his fiancée, what good was he to anyone? JL had been attacked twice, and what had he done to help her? Nothing.

He paused in front of the door to her suite with his hand poised to knock. He felt like a high school kid summoned to the principal's office. Whatever happened inside JL's room, detention hall would seem like a day at Coney Island. He took several deep breaths to steady his shaking hand then knocked.

The door opened, and he took another deep, steadying breath. JL looked as beautiful as he had ever seen her, dressed in a cream silk tea gown with forest green details. Her auburn hair had grown over the past few months, now falling well below her shoulders. The green of her eyes was deeper, darker than he had ever seen them, and he had spent countless hours gazing into their depths. He knew the number of flecks in each eye, and how the corners crinkled when she laughed. They weren't crinkling now.

He waited for some signal from her. A touch, a kiss…something…but she gave him nothing, only gazed into his eyes and remained silent, which was a signal of sorts. Apparently, confusion had hit her as hard as it had hit him.

"I was afraid you might stand me up," she said.

"I wouldn't do that."

He closed the door and pulled her into his arms. He didn't kiss her, though. It would have been too easy to respond to the need they shared for each other. And it would have delayed the long overdue conversation. He breathed in the water lily fragrance of her shampoo, and was nearly undone by the image of the bottle in their shower, with its purple cap, and the little sticker that said it was paraben and gluten free. A bottle he might never see in his shower again.

She pulled away. "Let's sit out on the promenade deck."

"Do you have champagne?" he asked, going for a laugh, unsuccessfully.

"Not today."

JL was almost a stranger to him now. She wasn't the woman he'd shared a bed with for eight months. Or, more likely, he just wasn't the man she'd shared her bed with.

They sat in rattan chairs opposite each other, their knees almost touching. The chairs must have been moved so she could use one to sit in and the other to stretch out her legs. "How was your workout?"

"If you could call an electrical saddle a workout, it was interesting." He smirked. "I did work my arm and shoulder. So that was good. How about you? How was brunch?"

"We were having an interesting conversation with Catherine Lily Sterling until her husband all but yanked her out of her chair. Before he did, though, we told her about Carolina Rose and that her mother was from Scotland.

"What'd you think of her? Catherine Lily, I mean?"

"She's a beautiful woman, but she's not anything like Carolina Rose. Carolina Roses' Frenchness made her unique—to me anyway. I haven't talked to Jack about her."

Kevin's lips were rubbery and thick, and he caught himself holding his breath. How was he going to start this conversation? Before he could find the words, JL said. "I can't go on like this."

He gasped at the suddenness, boldness, and directness of her statement. "Like what?" He squeezed his eyes shut for only a moment, then reopened them, but glanced away. He was such a damn coward. He forced himself to stop hiding and look at her. "I can't either, but I don't know what the answer is."

She shot him a look so intense, so deadly serious it would likely leave a bruise. In fact, he was sure it had.

"Do you love me?" she asked.

Taken aback by the question, he responded without thought, "Of course I do."

"Kevin," there was a new tone in her voice. Not just uncertainty. Fear. "The time for honesty is now. I love you. I want to marry you. I want to have your children. You're struggling. I understand that. The past few days have been difficult, as have the last several months. They haven't been a holiday for me, either, but they've been especially difficult for you."

Kevin laced his fingers to keep his hands from shaking. "I can't stop thinking about last fall and how close we came to dying or what happened to you in New York. I can't live like that every day. I'm not a crime fighter. I'm not used to this violence. We shouldn't have come on this adventure."

"But we're here, and we have to deal with it. I'm going to ask you again, and I want you to think hard before you reply this time. Do you love me?"

While her voice was stretched tight like a rubber band at its limit, her scent was bleeding through his senses, but he couldn't let it disrupt his thinking—if, in fact, he was thinking at all. He took another deep breath, hoping it would prop up his courage, but it wasn't working so far. He blew it out.

"I don't know," he said. "Right now, I want to take you to bed and make love, but it won't change what I feel in here," he said, poking at his chest.

"And what is it you feel...?"

He saw the same recognition in her expressive eyes. Their physical connection had been so strong from the moment they met, it transcended flesh and bone. But the kind of forever love Elliott had with Meredith was born of trust, and right now Kevin didn't trust JL.

"You want me but you don't love me. You love me, but you don't trust me. You don't... What? Tell me, Kevin."

"I'm afraid you're going to get one of us killed."

She jerked, gasped, and wrapped her arms tightly around her.

"Oh, God. I've spent most of my life trying to protect others, and you're afraid I'll…" Her eyes misted and her voice quavered.

He was frozen to his chair. He couldn't comfort her. He couldn't speak words that would give her any hope. He remained frozen, not only to the chair, but to his fear. He handed her a handkerchief.

She swatted it away. "I don't want it." Then she pulled a handkerchief from her sleeve and blotted at her eyes and nose. She also removed her ring. "Take this."

"I'm not asking you to end our engagement."

"We aren't any good for each other right now. And we certainly don't need the pressure of planning a wedding neither of us is sure we want."

He closed his fingers around the diamond ring, still warm from her finger.

She reached into her pocket, and when she opened her hand, the amethyst brooch glistened in the light of the afternoon sun. "Take this brooch and go home. Let Elliott and Meredith know what's going on here. Decide what you want to do. Go to Italy. Go to New South Wales, stay at the farm…" She shivered. "We don't need to be in the same century right now. It breaks my heart to say this, but go home, Kevin."

He stared at the brooch. "Where did you get this?"

"I took it out of the box on Elliott's desk when I wrote Austin a note. I had a premonition I would need it."

"I can't leave you like this."

"You left me some time ago."

Her words were like bullets, wounding him. "Where will you go?" he asked.

"If you stay at the farm, I'll go to Napa."

"No. You should stay at the farm while Austin is playing basketball at UK. Finish the house. I'll go to Napa or Italy."

"I don't… I don't care. You do what makes you happy." Her soft sobs were about to shred his self-control. She gripped the lacy handkerchief fiercely, squeezing it tightly into a knot, as if the fabric could wick away her pain. But he knew the only thing that would ease her pain was time and separation from him.

She took a deep breath. "I don't know what's hurting you more, PTSD or Elliott's betrayal, but whatever it is, it's eating you alive."

"That's not it, JL. It's all the drama, and your belief that I can't take care of you because I'm a pencil-pusher and not a cop or a soldier."

"God, Kevin. Is that what you believe? You saved my life. You jumped in front of a bullet without thinking of yourself or the consequences. There is no more noble or courageous thing anyone can do than lay down his life for another person."

"But you're breaking our engagement."

"Didn't you come here to break up with me?"

He didn't say anything because she was right. He did come to break up with her.

"I gave you back the ring so you won't feel guilty about breaking the engagement."

He snorted in disgust. "There you go again. Trying to protect me." He pushed to his feet and kicked the chair. The rattan chair's leg broke off and rolled across the wood floor. "Don't you understand? I don't want your protection."

"I'm a cop. That's my job."

"But it's not your job to protect me."

She slapped the brooch into his palm and it turned warm against his skin. Her eyes were downcast. "You should leave before one of us says something that will end any hope of a reconciliation." She pressed her fist against her mouth, and he wondered what other words she wanted to say but was trying to hold inside.

She didn't walk him to the door. It was the loneliest thirty feet he had traveled in his life. He couldn't feel any worse if he'd taken another bullet. He opened the door and closed it quietly behind him. He slowly banged his head against the wood.

"You goddamned idiot."

He made his way to his room and dug through a few things in his duffel bag. He'd leave the medical kit for Jack in case they had an emergency. Then he sat on his bed. Maybe if he stayed in his room, he'd feel better tomorrow and they could talk again, iron out their differences.

But he knew in his heart even an industrial-size iron couldn't manage it. The wrinkles were too firmly set.

The door opened and closed in the adjoining room, and foot-steps tracked across the floor. He listened for a minute and heard drawers open and close. Either Jack was back, or a thief was searching the room.

Kevin knocked on the connecting door.

"Come in," Jack said.

Kevin stood in the doorway and watched Jack change his shirt.

"You look like hell." Jack tossed the shirt on top of a dirty clothes pile in the corner. "I guess that means you talked to JL. How'd it go?"

Kevin sat at the nearby desk and fiddled with a heavy glass pa-perweight. "I was going to leave you a note."

"I'm here now, so you don't have to. What's up?"

"I'm going home."

Jack tucked in his shirttail then stood in front of the mirror and tied his cravat. "Are you going to jump overboard and hope Saint Peter welcomes you into Heaven?"

"JL gave this to me and told me to go home." Kevin opened his hand revealing the amethyst brooch."

Jack's face paled, and there was a moment of utter stillness. He shook his head. "I didn't know she had it with her."

"I didn't either." Kevin unclenched his other hand." She gave me this, too." The diamond ring glinted in his shaking hand.

Jack opened his mouth, but must have thought better about what he was going to say because he shut it quickly.

"You don't look surprised. You knew she was going to return it."

"She said she was going to keep it." Jack nodded toward his other hand. "Right now. I'm more concerned about the brooch. We haven't traveled with that stone before."

Kevin narrowed his eyes, studying it closely. "If you didn't know it was broken, you couldn't tell now. As soon as JL put it in my hand, it warmed. I think she's right about the amethyst. It's as strong as, if not stronger, than, the others."

"What are you going to tell Elliott?"

"I'll bring him up to speed, let him know you're on this floating palace, that JL and I have called off the wedding for now, and that I'm going to Italy to buy a winery."

"I think going home is the right thing to do. And after last night's angry Scot performance, I doubt anyone will miss you."

"An angry Scot who picks up a parasol to defend a screaming woman while the rest of the men and JL draw guns," Kevin said.

"You didn't see me with a gun."

"You intended to barge in and confront an attacker with only fists and guts."

"Okay, so I'm stupid. You don't have to point it out to me," Jack said.

"That's the thing, Jack. You're not stupid. You're not a coward. You're not—"

"Whoa. Is that what this is about? You believe you're a coward? You'll never see me jump in front of a bullet. I don't know what lie you're believing, but it's a whopper. And it's spilling all over your life, making one hell of a mess." Jack let out an exasperated sigh. "Do me a favor, stop believing such crap and find a therapist who specializes in PTSD. If you need a referral, call Charlotte."

"I don't need a referral, but I do need to talk to Connor and Pete before I leave."

Jack gave him a dark, scowling look. "No, you don't. Connor is JL's brother, and Pete is her protector. They might throw you overboard. I'll explain to them what happened. But JL will probably get to them first."

"God knows what she'll say."

"She'll be honest about it, and tell them it was a mutual decision. If they ask me, I'll confirm whatever she tells them."

"You're more accepting of her than you've been before," Kevin said.

"JL and I reached an understanding. We've each seen a different side of the other. She's an amazing woman who will make a wonderful wife and mother. So get your act together and work things out."

"Look in on her after I'm gone. She shouldn't be left alone."

"I'll go right there."

Kevin reached into his pocket and pulled out the box of baseball cards. "I bought these off the bartender in the Smoking Room. They're baseball cards. You might want to give them to Amy."

"I'll tell her they're from you."

"Whatever." He gave Jack a bro hug. "Thanks for understanding." They slapped each other on the back and then bumped fists.

"I don't know if I'm doing you any favors. But traveling across the ocean with a woman when your differences are wider than the water you can see is probably not conducive to finding a middle ground." Jack's eyes glistened. "Go home, buddy, and find a way to bridge the divide, or lose the most wonderful thing that ever happened to you."

"She asked me if I loved her, and I couldn't answer, not honestly, anyway."

"Well, here's the thing, Kev. Meredith and Elliott love you. James Cullen loves you. I love you, and so does everyone else. But all the pressure is getting to you. It's getting to JL, too. You both need a break to figure out what you really want. Use this time to do that. We'll take care of JL. You take care of you."

Jack grabbed his jacket and left the room hurriedly, leaving Kevin alone with his thoughts. If he stayed, he and JL couldn't patch up their differences. Not right now. He needed to go home and figure out what he wanted.

He picked up his duffel bag, opened the brooch, thought about where and when he wanted to end up, and spoke the ancient words. Something was different, though. But when the fog and the scent of peat engulfed him, he didn't give it a second thought.

44

1909 SS New York—Amy

WEARING A HAT with an ostrich feather around the brim and a coat trimmed with fox fur, Amy strolled along the Boat Deck with Jack, holding hands, enjoying the warmth of his strong fingers, and the wind and sun in her face. For miles in all directions, all she could see was water.

Jack's intervention had scooped out her fear, thrown it overboard, and showered her with security. To be outside enjoying the sun and sea breeze was indeed a miracle. And to find the source of the anger at her father was a life-changing revelation. Even if he had been sober that day at the beach, he couldn't have saved the woman. It didn't excuse his drinking, and she would never condone his behavior, but, coming on the heels of her mother's death, it was at least understandable.

"I don't feel tension in your hand," Jack said. "You must be okay with being out here. But let me know if it changes, and we'll go inside immediately."

"Free at last. Thank God Almighty—"

"—I'm free at last," he finished her take on the famous Martin Luther King, Jr. quote. His tone was lightly teasing, his smile a hundred-proof testosterone, spiked with endearing nonchalance.

She tucked both hands around his arm while they strolled, leaning into him flirtatiously. She was more comfortable with Jack than she was with Joe, and that concerned her, but it didn't stop her from wanting to get closer emotionally. She would have Jack to herself for a few more days, and then she would return to her life in New York City...although in which century remained a big, unanswered question.

"Have you used the meditation technique you used on me on yourself, or allowed someone else to do it to you?" she asked.

"Several times," he said. "I get almost there, but I'm never fully redeemed."

"Doesn't almost count?"

"It does in horseshoes and hand grenades."

"Amy!"

Amy heard her name, turned and waved. "Isabella."

The young woman was hurrying toward her, holding tightly to a wool cloche hat, a fitting hat to wear on the Boat Deck, but rushing into the wind tempted even the ones as securely pinned as the one Amy wore, which had almost blown off twice.

Isabella came to a stop, breathing heavily. "I rushed up two flights of stairs. The lifts all had long lines." She paused to take a breath. "JL's in the cabin crying, and they're not crocodile tears, either. Kevin has upset her, and Pete can't find him, and I hope he doesn't. He said he might punch Kevin and throw him overboard. But Pete wouldn't do that, would he?"

Jack glared at Isabella. "What are you doing up here by yourself, young lady? You had orders not to go anywhere unaccompanied."

Isabella had a habit of closing her eyes to avoid serious stuff, as if it would make it all go away. Her eyelids fluttered. "Oh, oh, I didn't...I'm not." She opened her eyes, her face flushed. "I came up with Pete. I wouldn't disobey you, Mr. Mallory. Pete's back there," she pointed behind her. "He stopped to speak to a man, and told me as long as I stay where he can see me, I could catch up to you and Amy. But if I shouldn't even do that..."

Jack glanced back, as did Amy, to see Pete talking with a man who looked oddly familiar.

"He looks familiar. Who is he?" Amy asked.

"I don't know." Jack then said to Isabella, "I apologize. I should have known you would take my request to heart."

"*Nonna* and I won't leave our rooms unless we're together or accompanied by someone else." Isabella leaned closer so a couple walking near them couldn't hear. "You don't think Pete will harm Kevin, do you?"

"Pete's like a brother, but I don't think he'd go *that* far." JL had mentioned Pete's temper. He might act aggressively toward Kevin, but hit him? Amy considered the men she knew. Mostly baseball players. When they got mad, some were known to throw punches.

"*Nonna* is trying to comfort her, but JL won't stop crying. Will you please come and see if you can help?" Isabella pressed her hands together and held them under her chin. "Please. She's so sad."

"Jack and I both looked in on her earlier. She asked us to leave her alone, but I'll go back." Amy looked at Jack. "Will you come with me?"

He smiled at Amy in his slow, Southern way, and touched her in a place she didn't need his smiles to go—her heart. "Your wish is my desire, darlin'."

"Do you want to come with us, Isabella, or are you going to walk with Pete?" Amy asked.

"*Nonna* told me to return as soon as I found you. She wants me to dress for afternoon tea. She's meeting a couple of ladies she dined with earlier. I don't want to go, but she said the ladies have sons who want to meet me. I can't complain. I promised to do whatever she asked if we came on this trip. I don't mind meeting those boys, as long as I get to walk with Pete."

"Just curious. How did you find him?" Jack asked.

"We called our steward and told him we were looking for any of the men in our party. He said Pete was in his room. The steward knocked on Pete's door for me. I was afraid Pete might hear JL crying, so I asked him to take me to find you."

"How clever of you," Amy said. "Come on, let's go see her."

Pete nodded when he saw Jack escorting Amy and Isabella off the Boat Deck and through the first-class entrance. "Grand Staircase

430   *Katherine Lowry Logan*

or elevator?" Jack asked.

"Staircase," Amy and Isabella said at the same time, laughing.

They passed several young men on the way down to B Deck. They all gave Isabella big smiles, and she batted her eyelashes at them in return. One of the men turned to stare at her and almost tripped and fell. Isabella giggled behind her hand.

"You're enjoying yourself, aren't you?" Amy asked.

"I've never had so much fun."

"What do the young men talk about?" Jack asked.

"College life, and what they intend to do when they graduate. Most are going into banking, or their fathers' businesses. A few are considering political careers. A few of the boys think it's admirable that I want an education. But when I tell them I want to be a doctor..." Isabella laughed. "They're appalled."

"You really want to be a doctor?" Jack asked. "It will take several years to get through medical school."

"I don't plan to marry right away. I want to get an education and start a career before I consider a marriage proposal."

Amy winked at Jack.

"I believe I detect a bit of Amy's influence, here."

"I've considered the idea of medical school since last year, but I didn't believe it was possible until I met Amy. She keeps saying, 'You can do whatever you want to do.' And I believe her."

"She can do it," Amy said. "I've talked to several of Isabella's professors. They're very encouraging. She's the top student in her freshman class."

"I'm very impressed," Jack said.

Amy had a vision of Isabella going to medical school, but in her vision, Isabella wasn't wearing long dresses, but short ones. She shook off the thought of taking Isabella to the future, and nearly stumbled when she saw Stephen Thomson standing at the bottom of the steps.

She gripped the railing and murmured to Jack, "Looks like Stephen Thomson is sailing to London, too."

"What's he doing here? He didn't mention a trip to you, did he?"

"No. It must have come up suddenly."

"Like the moment you told him you were sailing on Saturday. You don't have to reward his rudeness by talking to him," Jack said.

"Yes, I do," she said. "He's been a good friend, and I'll need his friendship if I return."

Jack tightened his grip on her arm. "I don't like him."

"I know you don't, but please be nice."

When they reached the bottom step, Stephen bowed slightly. "I'm so pleased to see you, Miss Spalding." He shook Jack's hand. "And Mr. Mallory."

"What are you doing here?" Amy asked. "You didn't mention traveling."

"The trip came up suddenly." Stephen reached for Isabella's hand. "Haven't I seen you at the Polo Grounds? We've never been properly introduced. I'm Mr. Stephen Thomson, President of the Providence Loan Society. And you are...?"

"Isabella Ricci, a friend of Amy's."

Jack put his hand on Amy's back. "If you'll excuse us, we have a family matter to attend to." His voice was tight and overcontrolled. Isabella had been wondering if Pete would punch Kevin, but now was a good time to wonder if Jack intended to punch Stephen.

"Obviously, it doesn't concern Miss Spalding. I've never seen her look more beautiful. Don't let me keep you, Mr. Mallory," Stephen said. "I'll entertain her in your absence. I'm on my way to the Café Parisien for tea." He watched Amy narrowly, offered his arm, elbow bent. "Please, my dear. Join me?"

Amy couldn't turn down the invitation. Neither could she allow Stephen to believe she preferred his company to Jack's. She went up on tiptoe and kissed Jack's cheek, intentionally lingering, breathing in the sweet, woody—and not at all overpowering—scent of him. "Darling, take Isabella with you. Then join us for tea as soon as you can."

"Give me a few minutes," Jack said.

As Stephen escorted her away she said, "You've mentioned your travel plans to me before, but not this time. Why?"

"I thought I would surprise you. Vice President Owens intended to make the trip, but became suddenly ill. I had only a few appointments on my calendar, and those could easily be postponed."

Amy noticed a nervous flick of his eyes and a slight quiver at the corners of his mouth. Was he lying? Until their recent exchange in his office, Amy believed Stephen had a tight grip on his emotions, but the exchange proved her wrong. What was he up to?

"I volunteered to go in his place," Stephen continued. "It would give me more time to press my case before your nuptials."

So that was it; a direct attack. "My mind is made up, and so is my heart."

"Until you exchange vows, I still have a chance, especially after you hear what I have to say."

"I doubt it, but I'll listen. And you press your case once, I expect you to respect my decision." What could he possibly have to tell her? The thought of listening to him left a hollow pit in her stomach and an unnamable dread in her mind.

They entered the Café Parisien. Amy was surprised by the restaurant's casual elegance. They were seated in rattan chairs at a wicker table surrounded by ivy-covered trellises. A romantic setting, but because she was with Stephen instead of Jack, the company detracted from the ambiance.

They served themselves at the buffet-style table set with dainty sandwiches, scones, and sweets, and the waiter brought teapots and tea to the table, along with a box of small silk pouches. Amy took one of the pouches, put it into her cup and poured hot water over it. Stephen eyed her curiously.

"Aren't you going to strain your leaves?"

"What leaves?"

"In the tea bag."

"No," she said, with a quick shake of her head.

Stephen opened a silk pouch, poured the leaves into a strainer, then poured in hot water, letting it sit for a moment or two before removing the strainer and setting it aside. Amy removed the tea bag and left it on the edge of the saucer.

"Milk? Sugar?" he asked.

"Nothing. Thank you."

He added both to his cup. "I've never seen anyone pour hot water over the bag before. Does the tea taste the same?"

"I don't know why it wouldn't." Curious about his question, she asked. "Are these silk bags new?"

"I heard an American tea importer was shipping his tea in small silk pouches, but I didn't know the pouch was intended to be infused with hot water."

"I think gauze would work better than silk, but I'm not a tea importer," she said.

Stephen bit into a cucumber sandwich and chewed, then dabbed his napkin at his mouth. "Have you been to London before?"

Was this a trick question? If she admitted to going there, would he ask where she stayed, where she went, what attractions she enjoyed? Instead of admitting she'd been to London a dozen times, she said, "No, I've never had the opportunity."

"I'd like to show you a few of the city's treasures, if you have time."

"I don't know what our plans are, yet, but I doubt I'll want to leave Jack's side to go sightseeing with another man. Besides, I wouldn't want to monopolize your time by taking you away from your business meetings." She tried to say it in a teasing manner, but she didn't think he took it that way.

He pushed his plate aside, tossed his napkin on the table. "Did your fiancé tell you he was accused of conspiring to assassinate Abraham Lincoln?"

She couldn't resist teasing him again. She put her hand to her mouth, gasping. "Seriously?"

Stephen said smugly, "So he didn't."

She sipped her tea. "Of course Jack told me. And Mr. Bennett enjoyed retelling it."

Stephen's glaring eyes became little slits, and his jaw clenched and unclenched. "My dear, you don't understand the stigma attached to the Mallory name. You will lose your readership."

"This stigma discussion is ridiculous."

"But the stigma exists. I'm your friend, and if you intend to continue writing for the newspaper, you cannot marry him. If you do, I'm sure no newspaper in New York City will offer you a position."

She struggled to keep her face neutral to show she wasn't affected by his cleverly directed threat. Her eyes fixed on him unwaveringly. "This is a nonissue. If New Yorkers don't want to read my columns, we'll simply move to California."

He shook his head, but there was weariness in the gesture, as if he knew he was losing the argument. But he wasn't ready to give up. "Mallory's name and association with the assassination will follow you no matter where you go."

"You've been a good friend, Stephen." She patted his hand, which was resting on the table next to his teacup. "I would hate to see our friendship dissolve over this, but if you can't respect my decision, then I have nothing more to say." She scooted back her chair, but he held tightly to the arm.

"Let's forget this and drink our tea. Where are you staying in London?"

"At the Savoy. What about you?"

"The Carlton."

She sipped her tea then said, "Did you hear what happened to Lillian Russell last night?"

"No," he said.

"She was attacked, and the thief stole my brooch."

"I'm sorry. I know you have your heart set on recovering your family heirloom." His voice was tight, as if his throat was closing around it. "Are there any leads?"

She debated what to tell him. He had a financial interest in recovering the brooch, but unless she cleared it with Jack or JL, she couldn't tell him who they suspected of the crime. "Not yet."

In her periphery, she spotted Jack entering the restaurant. He stopped near the entrance while he scanned the room. His body language didn't change immediately, but something in his blue eyes…or some insignificant movement in the corner of his mouth—betrayed his awareness of her.

He sauntered across the room. "There you are, darling." He kissed her on the mouth, taking her breath away. She licked her bottom lip, surprised by her reaction. She'd been kissed hundreds of times, but the effects of the tender touch of their mouths tingled on her lips. He pulled out a chair, sat next to her, and signaled to the waiter. "I'll have a cup of tea." Then to Amy he said, "What have I missed?"

"I was just telling Stephen about how Lillian Russell was attacked last night and the thief stole my diamond brooch."

"I'm sorry to hear there are no leads," Stephen said, tugging on his right earlobe.

"I'm sure the Master at Arms will apprehend the culprit before the day's out." Jack stroked the side of Amy's face. "When he does, we'll negotiate with Lillian. You'll have your brooch back. I promise. I know it means the world to you."

"When you make a promise, darling, you always deliver."

The waiter brought Jack's tea, and he steeped his teabag exactly the way she did. Stephen watched with interest.

"Stephen was warning me about taking your name. He believes your association with the Lincoln conspirators will offend my readers."

Jack added sugar to his tea and stirred the hot liquid, watching the sugar melt. He set down the spoon, sipped, then calmly returned the cup to the saucer. Amy watched Jack's artful deliberation, assuming it was a tactic he used to unbalance an opponent or interviewee. And she waited patiently for his response.

"I think, sweetheart," he said, smiling, "that your readers would be more interested in what happened to your family heirloom under Stephen's leadership at the Providence Loan Society, than what happened to an innocent reporter forty-four years ago, but," Jack shrugged, "maybe not."

Stephen's hands smoothed over the lapel of his coat, the dark tie, the white shirt collar. Then he did it again—coat, tie, shirt. She had never noticed the odd, nervous dance before. He glanced at his watch. "Time has gotten away from me. I have an engagement. Miss Spalding. Mr. Mallory. I hope I'll see you again." He darted away, barely missing a waiter carrying a tray with a teapot.

"Well." Amy blotted her lips with her napkin. "I don't think Stephen will ever bring that topic up again. Well played, Mallory."

"Maybe not. I don't think I did you any favors. I may have turned a friend into a foe."

"We'll see how he acts the next time I see him."

"Are you sure you want to?"

"I can't avoid him. It's not like we're in the city. We're both first-class passengers. We're bound to run into each other."

"We could settle this quickly by getting the captain to marry us. Then he'd have to accept defeat." Jack got to his feet and held her chair, then he tucked her hand into his elbow, and they worked their way toward the door. "I'm sorry about the mouth kiss, but—"

"You were only marking your territory. I've got you figured out."

He slapped his chest. "You enjoy busting my balls, don't you?"

She laughed. "You have me confused with JL."

"Trust me. I'll never confuse you with JL."

Jack might not be confused, but confusion was swirling inside Amy's head, and in her heart. His suggestion they have a pretend wedding might unwind her issues with Stephen, but promising Jack she'd be his loving and faithful wife in plenty and in want, in joy and in sorrow, in sickness and in health—unless it was the real thing— was simply out of the question.

"In answer to your suggestion that we get married, I can't do it. I'm only getting married once. And when I do, it will be for a lifetime."

"Darn, a pretend wedding would be my once-in-a-lifetime wedding. There you go, busting my balls again. But I do have a question. Did you ever give Stephen the impression there could be a deeper relationship with him?"

Jack cocked his head, waiting for her answer, and his gaze—all hot, warm, and sexy—traveled over her. And it made her wonder if she had given him the impression they could have a deeper relationship.

"I enjoyed my time with him. I won't deny that. If he interpreted my enjoyment to mean more than I intended, I'm sorry."

On their way through the Reception Room, Amy spotted the bald man Pete had been talking to on the Boat Deck. But it wasn't the bald man who interested her. It was the man he was talking to. "Jack, there's a man over there, talking to the bald man we saw with Pete. Do you see him? He's a vice president at the Providence Loan Society. I went to one of the company's dinner parties as Stephen's guest, and he was there. His name is Mr. Owens."

"Which means Stephen lied to you about his reason for this trip."

"Obviously, but why?"

"His purpose is clear to me. He intends to stop your wedding."

"Whatever," she said. "I can't worry about it. JL's used up my worry quota right now. Which reminds me, do you really think sending Kevin home without her was the right thing to do?"

"JL's the one who told him to go home. I just told him goodbye. But if you want to bust my balls over that, too, go ahead. They're all yours, darlin."

45

Present day MacKlenna Farm—Kevin

KEVIN CAME THROUGH the fog and immediately regretted his decision to leave JL behind. He should have brought her home with him. How could they work out their differences when they were a century apart?

He glanced at the cold stone in his hand and reconsidered, but the click of Elliott's boots on the hall's hardwood floor told him the door to that option would close in seconds. He knew the sound of Elliott's walk as well as he knew the sound of his own breathing.

Elliott opened the door to his office, stopped short, and did a quick double take. Then in a sonorous voice asked, "What are ye doing here, lad? Didn't you go with the others?"

"How long have I been gone?"

Elliott glanced at his watch. "Just long enough for me to pick up the mail from the front door mail slot. It's 1:05 now." He crossed over to his desk and tossed the first-class mail there.

"That's weird. We landed at one in the morning. JL was right about her brooch." Kevin handed the stone to Elliott. "Will you put this away?"

"I will if ye tell me what the hell is going on." Elliott put the brooch in the rosewood box and closed the lid.

"In a nutshell, the prodigal son has returned from four days in 1909."

"But ye were only gone a few minutes. The brooches haven't worked like that before."

"This brooch is different. More powerful. I told it to take me to MacKlenna Farm as close to the time I left as possible. Plus, the words written on the stone are different. The ride is shorter, not as twisty, twirly. It was more like a Star Trek beam-me-up-Scotty kind of trip. I disappeared and reappeared. Boom-bam-boom."

Elliott opened the desk's secret compartment and put the box away. "How different are the words?"

Kevin shrugged. "I don't know. Jack's the polyglot. He could tell you, but I'm not opening any of the brooches ever again. And I wouldn't advise you to open one either, unless you want to end up on the Titanic."

"When ye left, ye were going to 1909. The Titanic disaster was in 1912. Where did you go?"

"The ship we were on reminded me of the Titanic. That's all."

"Different words on the stone. The Titanic. Home alone. Nothing is adding up," Elliott said. "Now! Where. Are. The. Others?"

Kevin sighed with ill-concealed impatience. "In the middle of the Atlantic."

"I hope they're on a luxury liner and not at the bottom of the sea." If possible, Elliott's deep voice resounded an octave lower. He picked up the desk phone, dialed. "Kevin's back. Better come to the office." Without saying anything else, Elliott crossed the room to the refreshment bar and brewed a cup of coffee. By the time it finished, Meredith waltzed in.

Her eyes widened. "Kevin. I thought you left." She glanced around the room. "Where are JL and the others?"

Elliott handed Meredith a cup of coffee and brewed another cup for himself. "He left her and the others in the middle of the Atlantic."

Meredith made a sudden hissing sound as she sucked a breath between her closed teeth. "I can't think of any reason for that to happen, unless they're at the bottom of the sea." She looked down at the mug of coffee in her hand. Then said to Elliott, "I may need something stronger than this."

"If I were you," Kevin said. "I'd start with coffee. Work up to whisky. You'll need to take in this story incrementally." He sprawled at one end of the sofa facing the fireplace, stretched out his long legs, crossed his ankles, and absent-mindedly picked at the pleats on his trousers.

Meredith sat at the other end, turned to face him. "Cate is clearing my calendar. I have all morning for you, and all afternoon if necessary." She sipped her coffee. "I know you well. I love you to the moon and back, and I can read your body language, because you're exactly like Elliott. You're pretending to be relaxed, but it's a big, fat lie. You're so tied up in knots you remind me of a macramé planter I made in the seventies. What's going on?"

Elliott sat across from them in one of the leather wingback chairs and neatly crossed his leg. "Do we need to bring David in on this?"

Kevin shrugged. "There's nothing he can do."

"What can I do?" Elliott asked.

"Stay calm. Don't overreact."

"I'll do what I can."

Kevin dug into his pocket, pulled out JL's engagement ring, and twirled it between his fingers. The brilliant emerald-cut diamond winked in a stream of light from the recessed lighting.

Meredith sighed, reached out and rubbed his arm affectionately. "JL shared some of her concerns with me last week. She wasn't checking items off her checklist with her usual efficiency. I literally backed her into a corner and forced her to tell me what was going on. But I doubt her concerns are the same as yours."

"If you force me to take sides, I'm on yers, of course," Elliott said. "We both are. But we won't like it."

"JL's like a daughter to me. I love her dearly. I'll give you both my love and my honesty. JL and her family will always have a home at the winery."

"I agree with Meredith about the O'Gradys," Elliott said. "Regardless of what happens between you two, they are part of the family. It'll be awkward for a while, but we'll adjust."

"What happened to bring it to a head?" Meredith asked.

"The drama. I can't take it anymore. There's always drama."

"It may seem that way, but she's level-headed, honest, and loyal to a fault, which occasionally puts her perpendicular to the square. But I value her opinion," Elliott said.

"You need to start at the beginning," Meredith said, "and tell us everything that happened once you arrived in New York City, and how you jumped ship in the middle of the Atlantic."

Kevin pulled up his legs, curled them on the cushion, propped his arm on the back of the sofa, and combed his fingers through his hair. "We landed somewhere in the middle of Central Park very late at night…"

An hour later, Elliott and Meredith were both wiping away tears.

"So, you see, I couldn't handle it another day. When JL handed me the amethyst brooch, I took it and didn't look back."

Elliott returned to the bar, poured three shots of whisky, handing one glass to Meredith, another to Kevin. "*Slainte*"

"*Slainte*," said Kevin, clinking glasses with Elliott and Meredith.

"*Slainte*," said Meredith.

They all drank their shots, and Elliott refilled their glasses before returning to his seat. "What do ye plan to do now?"

"I want JL to finish the house and live there while Austin is playing basketball. He'll probably get drafted after his freshman year. Then she'll want to be close to whatever franchise grabs him up. I'm going to buy a winery in Tuscany, live there, and work for the company remotely."

"I'm asking this out of curiosity, but everyone will want to know. Is the wedding postponed indefinitely, or called off permanently?" Meredith asked.

"Is there a difference?" Kevin asked.

"A big one. Indefinitely implies it will eventually take place."

"It's called off."

"I hate that, Kevin. I know it's selfish, but the thought of you two marrying and having a houseful of children has kept me busy planning my retirement so I can be a full-time grandmother."

"I don't see it ever happening, regardless of who I marry. If I ever do. But JL will probably find someone else. She's beautiful, talented, and very wealthy. You'll eventually get to plan her wedding."

Meredith slammed down her glass. "Stop it, right now. Don't you dare take that defeatist attitude with me. I'll give you two a few months to sort this out. You might give up on her, but I know she'll never give up on you." Meredith jumped to her feet and paced the room, sniffing quietly.

Tater Tot pushed open the door and trotted in. The dog went immediately to Kevin and nosed his leg. "Hi, boy."

"We can't start making phone calls until JL comes home and tells Pops. She wouldn't want anyone else to tell him."

"He's going to find out Kevin's here, and he'll need an explanation for why JL isn't," Elliott said.

"Then we can't let anyone know Kevin came home."

Kevin mirrored Meredith and slammed his glass down on the coffee table. "Damn it. I'm in the room. You don't have to talk about me like I'm not here."

"Then what's yer suggestion, lad?"

"Hold your thought," Meredith said. "I have an idea. We'll all go to Italy."

"Today?" Elliott asked.

"The owners of the winery I'm most interested in buying have lowered their price. I want one last visit before I make an offer."

"Is this close to the one Kevin wants to buy?" Elliott asked.

"I don't have one in mind," Kevin said. "We've looked at several."

Elliott slapped his thighs. "Well, I need to pack. What about James Cullen?"

"He leaves tomorrow to spend two weeks with Lincoln. Braham is taking them on a camp out. He won't cancel his outing for a trip to Italy with us to visit wineries," Meredith said.

"I need to talk to David. Let him know we're leaving."

"Are you going to tell him about Kevin?" Meredith asked.

"I'd rather not, but he should know what's going on."

"What about Charlotte and Braham?"

"I trust David to keep this to himself, but I don't trust anyone else. For JL's sake, I'll limit it to David," Elliott said.

"But he'll tell Kenzie," Meredith said.

"I know it's hard to believe, but there are some secrets even David doesn't share with his bride."

"I don't want to know that, Elliott. It implies there are secrets you keep from me," Meredith said.

"We already know Elliott keeps secrets from me." Kevin stomped over to the door and yanked it open. "I'm going upstairs to my old room to take a shower. I'd appreciate it if someone would get me a change of clothes and my passport from the guest house. Even if there wasn't a risk someone would see me, I couldn't go into the room JL and I shared. There's too much of her there."

"I'll take care of it, but, Kevin—"

"I can't listen to any buts right now, Meredith." Tater Tot trotted over to Kevin and sat, looking up at him. Kevin rubbed his head. "Do you remember when Elliott was in the hospital and you left, crying, because you couldn't take it anymore? That's how I feel. So, don't try to defend Elliott's lies. They're indefensible."

"Don't be rude to Meredith. Ye know I don't tolerate anyone talking back to her."

"I'm your son, Elliott. We've lived under the same roof for more than twenty years. I walk like you. I can, but I don't, talk like you. I have a similar temper, although I don't show it as often as you do. I've loved women as passionately as you have, but I hope to God I'm never the hypocrite you are."

Kevin stormed out of the room, took the stairs two at a time with Tater Tot running after him. When he reached his old room, he threw off his twentieth-century clothes, and for the next hour cried in the shower until the water turned cold.

46

1909 SS New York—JL

AFTER KEVIN RETURNED to the future, JL spent forty-eight hours wandering aimlessly in her room, moping about on the promenade deck, or crying in her bed. Maria, Isabella, Amy, Jack, Connor, and Pete set up a rotation schedule to sit with her, but she refused to talk or eat anything other than chicken soup. The broth did nothing to soften the pain, but it did keep her hydrated.

Maria believed JL was going to die of a broken heart. JL thought so too. She had survived an unplanned pregnancy, her mother's death, and a failed marriage. But sending Kevin away was worse than all three of those combined into one huge wallop of regret, loneliness, and gut-wrenching grief. A profound feeling of emptiness lodged painfully in her chest.

Did Kevin hurt like this, too? Was he hiding from it, or reaching out to Elliott or Meredith or James Cullen for comfort? They all loved him dearly, and would offer him a shoulder to cry on, but would he accept it?

Kevin said she came with too much drama. Was he right? If they reconciled, could she give up her job to stay home, keep house, and raise their children? Was it even in her DNA to play the happy homemaker role?

Could JL give up her career for love and never look back? Whatever he wanted her to be, could she be? Whatever he wanted her to do, could she do? Could she lose herself in love?

A five-alarm warning went off in her mind. She couldn't give up herself for Kevin or any man. If she found her way there by making choices for herself, then great. But she couldn't, and shouldn't, sacrifice who she was for him.

If this journey was about her changing, then the changes couldn't be made for him. If she did, she would eventually resent the hell out of him. If she made changes for herself, to improve her life, whether she ended up with Kevin or another man, she could embrace them.

So, that was it. She would try on a new JL, like a new pair of jeans, and see how they fit. Too big, too small, too tight, too loose, too blue, too black, until she found a just-right pair. And it might mean they were close to the ones she already wore, or they might be a brand-new style.

On their last evening aboard the *SS New York*, JL decided to join her friends for dinner. Her emotions were still raw, and she might not last through the entire evening, but she would attempt an appearance. Lillian was giving another concert, and if JL missed the chance to hear and see one of Broadway's earliest stars, live and in person, she would regret it forever.

She ordered tea bags for her swollen eyes and soaked in the tub, washing away days of grunge from self-absorption and grief.

After drying off, she spent thirty minutes in the wardrobe room considering her dresses, finally deciding on a blue and gold velvet, Princess-line, one-piece gown with a long train. Depending on the light, the metal lace worked into the bodice, the pale blue tulle over her breasts and sleeves, and the gold cord around her neck would shimmer like the moon on a lake.

Kevin had picked out the dress she was wearing tonight during their Friday afternoon shopping excursion in the city. He thought the texture of the fabric and the blue-gray color looked gorgeous with her hair and eyes. Would he think the dress looked gorgeous with her eyes now—puffy from heartbreak?

When she was ready to go, she rang the steward's call button.

Chester arrived within minutes. When she opened the door, he smiled. "I'm glad to see you're feeling better, ma'am."

"Thank you, Chester. Would you mind escorting me to the First-Class Dining Room? Mr. Mallory has insisted I not walk around the ship alone."

Chester proudly offered his arm. "We've all been worried about you, Miss O'Grady. When Mrs. Ricci said you received sad news, we knew your heart was broken."

When they reached the entrance to the dining room, Chester asked, "Do you want to go the rest of the way by yourself? If you don't mind me saying you look lovely tonight, you do. When you walk into the room, even the darkness will tremble." He stepped aside, bowing slightly.

"Thank you, Chester." JL sucked in a deep breath of control, kicked aside her waning confidence, and waltzed into a dining room full of five hundred diners, chin up and smiling. Heads turned, men and women alike. She owned it. She needed it, and she reveled in the obvious male appreciation.

Maybe her high school boyfriend who impregnated her, her ex-husband who cheated on her, and her ex-fiancé who thought she was addicted to drama hadn't appreciated her, but the men in this room obviously did. For now, that was enough. Their appreciation would get her through the next few hours.

When she reached the large table Jack reserved for them, the men stood. Connor and Pete both hugged her, and Jack pulled out a chair next to him. "I'm glad to see you, but how'd you get here?"

She rustled up a flimsy smile. "Don't worry. Chester, our steward, escorted me."

"Good," he said, giving her fingers a gentle squeeze.

"What have I missed?" JL asked.

"Not much. We've had no luck finding the brooch," Jack said.

Someone patted her shoulder, and she jerked her head around. The men at the table were all on their feet again. "Miss Russell, how good to see you."

Lillian's eyes held a quiet understanding. "I'm happy to see you here tonight, dear. I heard you've been ill." She glanced around the table. "Where's that handsome fiancé of yours?"

"Ah…" What could JL say? "He's…not feeling well."

"I'm sorry to hear that. Did he catch what you had?"

Heartbreak? The question hit JL like a physical blow. Her reaction when seeing Kevin for the first time at the winery—hearing his deep, smoky voice, and watching the cheeky little quirk at the corner of his mouth—was to stay clear of the heartbreaker. What happened to the look of mischief dancing in his eyes that day? Had she destroyed it?

She took a breath and said to Lillian, "I think so."

Lillian patted JL's shoulder lightly, and the warmth and strength the touch conveyed reminded JL of her mother doing the very same thing, letting JL know she wasn't alone.

"I'm giving another concert tonight, and you should perform."

JL shook her head. "I haven't rehearsed with the orchestra. I wouldn't want to ruin your show."

"Nonsense. You'll do fine. The musicians have a repertoire of over three hundred songs. I'm sure you can find one to suit your voice. Have you looked at the song book?"

JL put her hand to her throat. Crying made vocal cords and sinuses swell and they wouldn't work effectively. If she tried to sing, she would sound nasal, like she had a cold. "I haven't seen it. But even if I find one that's appropriate, my voice isn't up to it tonight."

Connor held up the songbook. "'Londonderry Air is number 255. You can sing 'Danny Boy.'" You probably haven't sung it since Mom's funeral. Tonight it could be cathartic."

"No. I couldn't get through it."

"I'll make a deal with you. You sing it, and if you struggle, I'll sing with you," Connor said.

"Seriously? You have one of the most beautiful tenor voices I've ever heard, but you've always hated to sing in public. Why tonight?"

"Because you need to sing," Connor said.

Pete threw his napkin on the table. "Jesus Christ, man. The song is about lovers parting. Are you torturing her on purpose?"

Connor held up his hands in surrender.

"The song is about saying goodbye." Amy glanced momentarily at Jack. "If giving that reality a voice, then I have to agree with Connor. It will be cathartic. And besides, I would love to hear you sing. Your speaking voice is so musical."

Jack looked at her and said in a for-your-ears-only soft tone, "I can still hear you singing at Carolina Rose's funeral. It will be hard for me to listen to you again, but if I can listen, you can sing." His eyes were somber, even a little misty. "I have a feeling this performance will go down in family history."

She nodded and her eyes misted over, although she was quick to blink the moisture away. Then she turned to Connor. "Warm up your vocal chords. You got me into this, so, you're singing with me."

"Marvelous." Lillian tapped her palm lightly with her fan. "I'm not familiar with the song, but I'm sure you'll sing it beautifully."

Jack pointed at Lillian's hand-painted silk fan. "May I see that?"

"Not only may you see it, darling, you may have it. I brought it tonight intentionally, to see if you would remember where you saw it last. I didn't want to offer it to you otherwise."

"Carolina Rose left it at the Hopkins' Mansion. I wondered what became of it." He gestured nonchalantly. "You've had it all these years. Please keep it."

Lillian slid the attached gold velvet ribbon off her hand. "She would want you to have it."

JL's senses quickened while she watched Jack to see how he would react. He digested Lillian's offering with no change in facial expression, but the muscles in his neck tensed. After what she had gone through the last few days, JL knew Jack's memory of the fan must be like a knife filleting his insides. He tucked the fan into his jacket pocket.

"Thank you," he said, patting his chest. "Your impulsive generosity is legendary."

"I've been blessed," she said. "I do what I can."

JL flinched at the pain she now saw in Jack's eyes, pain that found a home in her heart. And then, like the good detective she was, she wondered why—if Lillian's generosity was so legendary—she hadn't returned the brooch to Amy? JL glanced at her naked finger. Because girls should never return diamonds…or was there another reason?

"If you'll excuse me," Lillian said. "I'll let the conductor know you'll be singing to 'Londonderry Air'.

The waiters brought the first course to the table, *hors d'oeuvres* and oysters. JL passed up the oysters. She did manage to swallow the second-course offering of Consommé Olga, then nibbled at the third course of poached salmon. She picked at the fourth course of filet mignon, and pushed around the green peas and carrots presented with lamb for the fifth course. When the sixth course arrived, she drank all the rum-spiked shaved-ice Punch Romaine. She ignored the seventh course of roast squab, and the eighth course of cold asparagus, but she did eat the celery served with the ninth course, and all the chocolate eclair served with the tenth.

Wine was served between all courses. She limited her consumption, however, to only a few sips to taste each selection, making mental notes of the look, smell, and taste to share her conclusions of each pairing with Kevin later. When she realized what she was doing, she paused, thought about erasing them, but couldn't. Even if she and Kevin didn't have a future, he would be interested in the pairings. She could put the info in an email. He would appreciate that.

Finally, the men settled back in their chairs with cigars and port, the women with fruit and coffee. JL wanted a glass of port instead, but passed it up for a cup of tea with honey. The eight-member orchestra began playing classical compositions by Camille Saint-Saens and Sir Edward Elgar, then moved into a blend of schmaltzy popular songs of the early 1900s and highbrow music.

JL reviewed the songbook, trying to find another song that wouldn't be as difficult to get through. "This is like karaoke," she muttered. "Find a number, play a song."

"Did you see 'Nearer My God to Thee,' and 'Somewhere A Voice is Calling'?" Pete asked. "You like both of those."

"I'll wait and see what Lillian sings and how the crowd reacts. They might like a song with more pizzazz."

"You're not getting out of this, sis."

"We'll see," she said.

The conductor introduced Lillian, and for the next ninety minutes, she sang one hit after another: "I've Got Rings on My Fingers and Bells on My Toes," "I Don't Care," from the Zigfield Follies, "Shine on Harvest Moon," "Oh London is Really a Wonderful Town," "Ti Ra La La," "What Can We Do Without a Man" from *The Chocolate Soldier*, and a dozen other songs, each to rousing applause.

When she finished, Lillian said, "I have a new singer I'd like to introduce tonight. Please welcome to the stage Miss Jenny Lynn O'Grady."

A tepid reception welcomed JL. The audience obviously wasn't ready to give Lillian up. JL spoke quietly to the conductor. "Would you play song 255, 'Londonderry Air'?" Her mother made it through a Broadway performance the night JL told her about her pregnancy. She gave one of the primo performances of her career while brokenhearted over her daughter's situation. If her mother could perform under those conditions, JL could perform under these. Or try to.

The conductor announced number 255 to the orchestra, and the violinist entered, playing the first three and half measures. She hit her first note of the soaring ballad, and it could well seal the tone for the night.

"Oh Danny Boy, the pipes, the pipes are calling, from glen to glen, and down the mountain side. The summer's gone, and all the roses falling. It's you, it's you, must go, and I must bide."

JL held tightly to the tears threatening to erupt, yet at the same time she wanted to let them go.

"But come ye back when summer's in the meadow, or when the valley's hushed and white with snow. 'Tis I'll be here in sunshine or in shadow, oh Danny Boy, oh Danny Boy, I love you so."

In her mind, she replaced the words with the ones in her heart.

"Oh, Kevin, I love you so."

The tightness from her tears of sadness and loss finally overwhelmed her, and she couldn't hold them back. She signaled the conductor to stop. Then the most gorgeous tenor voice picked up the song, singing flawlessly, without stage effects or accompaniment...

"But when ye come, and all the flowers are dying, and I am dead, as dead I well may be. Ye'll come and find the place where I am lying, and kneel and say an 'Ave' there for me."

Connor's contagious charm enraptured listeners in an instant. JL joined him in a well-matched, harmonizing duet, singing with heart and skill in equal measure. There was nothing scripted, nothing choreographed, only their honest voices.

"And I shall hear, though soft you tread above me, and all my grave will warmer, sweeter be. For you will bend and tell me that you love me, and I shall rest in peace until you come to me."

The dining room's acoustic environment held the last note for one very long moment in time.

Connor pulled out his handkerchief and wiped her face. "Beautiful. Mom would be so proud."

The audience was on its feet, applauding. Connor and JL took their bows, and he escorted her off the stage, where Lillian was waiting. She pulled JL to her and hugged her tightly. "That was the most beautiful song I've ever heard. You have an extraordinary range, balanced and structured, without vocal flaws. Your voice is golden. We'll talk more when we're in London, but I want to do a show with you."

JL sniffed. "I can't think of anything I'd enjoy more." And while it couldn't possibly happen, to be asked by Lillian meant the world to JL.

"Encore!" the audience shouted.

"Hear that?" Connor asked. "You have to give them one more."

"I can't do it by myself. Not tonight. Not after that. You'll have to sing with me."

"I'll sing one, but then you're on your own."

Connor and JL took to the stage again, and she gave the conductor the number for "Amazing Grace." But the audience shouted above the music. "Danny Boy. Danny Boy. Danny Boy."

"Do you want to sing with or without accompaniment?" the conductor asked.

JL looked at Connor, and he gave her an understanding smile loaded with reassurance. "Let's go without music again." It was the purest way to sing the song.

The conductor nodded. "Who wrote the lyrics?"

"Frederic Weatherly," Connor said. Then to JL he said, "This time will be easier."

"I don't think so, but let's give it a go, and then I'm done."

By the time they finished the first verse, a few of the audience members were humming along. Connor stepped back and slowly moved off stage, leaving JL to finish the song by herself. When she reached the last line, the entire room was singing, "...*and I shall sleep in peace until you come to me.*"

"Encore. Encore. Encore." The audience demanded again.

Lillian gently ushered JL off stage. "The first rule of theater is to always leave the audience wanting."

"That's credited to P.T. Barnum, I think. But now I know who really said it."

JL and Connor returned to the table. "Why aren't you singing professionally?" Amy asked. "You have a phenomenal voice, and it was a brilliant duet."

JL puffed out a breath, and allowed herself a semblance of a smile. "I couldn't have gotten through it without Connor."

"And I didn't even know *he* could sing," Jack said.

"I only sing in the shower."

"*Meraviglioso*," Gabe said.

"*Brava*," Maria and Isabella said.

Thinking about the song and the words of loss, JL just sank lower. She swallowed hard. She needed to step out before she started crying again.

"I've got to go to the restroom and powder my nose. It's up

there by the door. I saw it when I came in. I'll be right back," she said to Connor.

"I'll go with you."

"No you won't. You can watch me from here."

Connor smirked at the suggestion, but relaxed a little when he saw where the restroom was located. "Don't go anywhere else."

For once she could think of no quick response, so she turned and hurried away.

Two other women were in the restroom, sitting in chaise lounges while attendants repaired their hair and fluffed their clothes. JL didn't want to get caught in a discussion with them, so she hurried into the stall, used the toilet, washed her hands, and hurried out.

She hesitated in an alcove, engaging herself in silent debate—go back to bed and cry, or go back to the table and pretend to be sociable. While the debate continued, the muzzle of a gun pressed forcefully into her back. A nauseating odor assaulted her nose and triggered her memories.

She knew without hearing a voice—it was Mustache Cop. He grabbed her in a rear naked choke hold, and she immediately dropped her chin to protect her throat, stepped to the side, and tried to strike his groin, but her dress severely restricted her, and her punches missed their mark. He dragged her farther back into the alcove.

"We're leaving here," he hissed into her ear. "If you cause a scene, I'll kill you with your own fancy gun." She tugged on his arm with both hands, tried to reach his nose, but he pulled his head back and squeezed her tighter. He was out for vengeance, making him a deadly opponent.

With the orchestra playing in the First-Class Dining Room, a pianist playing in the Reception Room, and the buzz of over five hundred people, no one would hear her if she screamed. "There's no escape from here," she said. "Everyone will see us."

"While you've been crying in your cabin, I've been searching escape routes. We're going through a hatch. No one will rescue you. And no one will find you."

Connor's words came back in a rush of terror. *"The asshole will drag you into the belly of this ship, we'll never find you in time."*

She had to stall. Connor would come looking for her if she didn't come right back.

"Where's the brooch? Show it to me, and I'll go with you."

"I don't have it. I left it in a safe place in case I need a bargaining chip." There was a thread of steel in his voice. He couldn't be deflected.

"Then I'm not going with you." If she died, she would never see Kevin again. They would never have a chance to reconcile, and he would never know how hopeful she was that they could reset their relationship.

"If you think I won't shoot you, think again. I've got fifteen bullets in this gun. I might not survive, but I can take a lot of people with me. The first bullet will be for you."

She managed a hollow laugh. "You're crazy." A bullet in the back with her gun would kill her, but if she went with him, he would kill her anyway, and it wouldn't be an easy death.

"We're leaving. Back up, and don't make any moves to draw attention. I will shoot."

She took a breath against the pain of the gun pressed roughly into her kidneys. "If you hurt me, my brother will kill you."

He squeezed his arm around her throat again. "Connor O'Grady. Mr. 'Danny Boy.' Do you think I'm afraid of him?"

"You should be. I am." Her backup gun was in her pocket, and she was itching to blow this fucking son of a bitch into a gazillion tiny pieces.

When he cocked the gun, she knew he didn't have her Glock. She would have a chance now. She kicked his shin, elbowed him in the gut, and opened her mouth to scream, but her defensive moves were cut short when he delivered a hammer blow to her head.

47

1909 SS New York—Amy

WHEN JL DIDN'T return from the restroom after a few minutes, Amy was afraid she was in there alone and crying. "I'm going to check on JL. If she's upset, I'll take her back to the room and call it a night."

Jack was puffing on his cigar, blowing rings, which seemed to entertain him. "I'll walk with you."

Amy patted his arm affectionately. "Enjoy your smoke rings. I'll be right back to let you know what we're going to do."

He held her chair. "Don't leave under any conditions."

"Not even if we hit an iceberg?"

"If a disaster happens, get out as fast as you can." He bussed her forehead, his lips lingering against her skin. "Remind me to tell you what this week has meant to me," he whispered.

"Whatever you have to say is exactly what I would say. We probably should keep our thoughts to ourselves."

She was ambivalent about Jack clueing her in to his feelings. To use her favorite life metaphor, baseball, she sensed they were in the top of the ninth. The game was almost over, and if she was completely honest with herself, she was praying for a rain delay. Parting with Jack and the rest of the family would be difficult. She'd formed important attachments, and she didn't want to break them.

Once she got her brooch back, she'd also be a member of the

family, but how would Joe feel about it, especially since he never heard of them before? And if he accepted her newfound relationships, how would he get along with Jack? Something tightened inside her. It would never work. The guys would be civil, but they could never be friends.

Amy entered the crowded ladies' room, weaved her way through to the other side, and immediately left. JL wasn't there.

Outside the ladies' room, to the right, were two other rooms…an alcove and a coat closet, and a short hall with a hatch-type door at the end. All were empty. JL wasn't herself, but she wouldn't leave the dining room on her own. Amy hurried back to the table.

Anxiety tightened her shoulders and neck, and swirled up in Amy's stomach, starting a very bitter churn. "JL's gone, and I don't think she would have returned to the cabin by herself."

"You're right. She walked here earlier with the steward," Connor said.

"Maybe she went with a group, or found an escort," Jack said.

"Or an escort found her," Connor said.

Pete's hand went to his hip. His automatic response to check for his weapon frightened Amy.

"I'll go check the cabin," Connor said.

"Someone had to see her leave," Pete said. "I'll ask around."

Jack signaled to Patrick. "Take Maria and Isabella back to their room and guard them. Don't let anyone come in the room, and don't leave Maria and Isabella under any condition."

Patrick frowned, and his entire body seemed to get into it. "I want to go with you."

"Not this time, buddy," Jack said. "Next time you will, but only if you do exactly as I've directed. I need to know I can depend on you."

Patrick pulled his cap from inside his jacket and tugged it tight over his head, as if the cap alone poured confidence over him. "You can. I'll take fine care of the women. How long will you be gone?"

"As long as it takes. Go on with Connor. Keep the ladies safe.

You're the only one who can."

"I'm going down to third class," Gabriele said. "There's a card game going on, and if there's anything nefarious happening aboard ship, they'll know."

"Have you learned anything from those boys you keep losing money to?" Amy asked.

"I lose on purpose. I told Connor a woman and her two children have been missing for two days, and a man with a busted-up nose is a third-class passenger. I haven't seen him yet, so I don't know if he's the cop who arrested JL. I'll leave word with Patrick if I get any news."

"Be careful," Jack said. Then to Pete and Amy he said, "Let's go to the Reception Room and wait for Connor."

Amy swallowed back the lump in her throat. "What can I do?"

"It depends on what Connor finds out."

They made their way through the crowd to wait in the Reception Room near the door to the first-class suites. It didn't take long for Connor to come barging through the door. "She's not there. Any news here?"

Pete joined them, huffing. "Several people saw a man carrying a woman down the stairs, saying he was taking his wife to the hospital."

"What'd he look like—?" Connor asked.

"What'd she look like?" Jack asked over the top of Connor's question.

"They didn't remember the man, and couldn't see the woman's face, but one of the women I talked to said the color of the dress was similar to the dress worn by the woman singer."

"Let's start at the hospital." A blend of impatience and fear threaded through Connor's tone. "I doubt it's a good lead. Whoever took JL wouldn't carry her through the ship. It's too risky."

Pete glanced around, running fingers through his thick black hair. "Where'd Gabe go?"

"To a card game in third class," Jack said.

Connor nodded approval. "That's his source for the scuttlebutt he's passed along. I picked up our maps when I checked to see if JL was in her cabin. Gabe's marked areas that might be good hiding places. We'll start on those after we go to the hospital."

"He said he'd leave word with Patrick if he picks up any more information." Amy glanced away, then winced. "Here comes Stephen. I can't deal with him right now."

Jack turned to see the banker walking hurriedly toward them, his face tense with what looked like excitement. "I've been looking for you." He took a heavy breath. "I want to apologize for my behavior this afternoon. Will you walk with me?"

Amy feigned a smile to hide her irritation. "Not right now. I'm sorry."

Jack pulled her aside. "You were upset with the way things were left the other day. Stay here in the Reception Room. Work things out with Stephen. I know his friendship has been important to you, plus you're not dressed to crawl around the ship's nooks and crannies, and you'll be safe here with him." Jack pulled her in for a hug. "Don't go anywhere else. I'll be back soon."

"But..." Jack was out of earshot or intentionally didn't respond. She was now stuck with Stephen while everyone else searched for JL. It was the same as being sent to the locker room for the remainder of the game, and it sucked. Intellectually, she knew they could move faster without her, and if there was trouble, she didn't want to be in their way. But still...

Stephen took her arm. His hands seemed clammy, and his long, thin, cold fingers reminded her of icicles. "I met some people this afternoon, and they're having a gathering near the squash court on G Deck. Will you go with me?"

"I don't think so. Let's stay up here. I thought you wanted to talk."

"We can still talk, but I need to make an appearance. They're investors looking for opportunities, and I have opportunities looking for investors. We'll come right back."

The tension from the last few days was taking its toll on her, and worry over JL had Amy's heart pounding. If she was forced to sit and wait without news for an hour or two, or more, she'd go crazy. She didn't want to leave, but Jack had made it very clear she was never to be alone. It wouldn't hurt to go with Stephen for a few minutes. Then they could come back, listen to piano music, and wait indefinitely.

"Okay, but I can't stay."

He looked at her with the same eagerness she saw before, and for some reason she remembered what the saleswoman, Madam Wallace, said about him. "He especially likes silk and lace." And he had taken care of his invalid wife. Then Amy remembered something Mr. Bennett mentioned once in passing, about how awful it had been for Stephen following his wife's accident. The accident must have been what turned his wife into an invalid prior to her death.

Amy and Stephen took the elevator down to the F Deck, then crossed over to the stairs and climbed down a flight to G Deck. Her heels clicked on the metal steps, joining the rising din of the engines driving through the water and the grinding propellers. The hull radiated all the noises from the internal mechanics of the ship, and the deeper they descended into its belly, the louder and scarier the sounds became.

"There's not a party going on down here," she said. "It must be over. We would have heard something, seen someone."

"Let's go this way," Stephen said. "I'm sure they said F Deck." She paused while he made a careful inspection of one room after another. "Maybe I was wrong." They wandered down one hall, then another, but didn't find a party. Matter of fact, there weren't any people anywhere—no passengers, no ship's officers, no crew.

"Let's go down one more floor," he said.

Amy had enough. She wasn't scared of Stephen, but being down this far was spooking her. If Jack came looking for her, and she wasn't in the Reception Room, he would think she'd been abducted, too.

"No. I want to go back."

Stephen's face creased with irritation. "One more flight of stairs.

If we don't see anyone at the bottom, we'll come back up."

She chewed her bottom lip. "There's nothing down there."

"I could be missing a huge opportunity. The Society will be hurting after we pay your claim, and if I can bring in new business, it will help recoup some of the losses."

She bristled at the suggestion his problem was because of her. "That wasn't my fault."

"I'm not saying it was, but I don't want to miss the party completely. Let's go down one more flight, then we'll turn around if no one is there."

If she didn't trust him, she'd feel like one of those idiot women in a horror movie who walked into a haunted house by herself, and then was surprised when something bad happened to her.

They climbed down another set of steps. "What is this deck?"

"I think it's the Orlop Deck."

"What's that?"

"The lowest deck on a ship."

Her stomach did a few flips of fear. "Okay, I've had enough, Stephen. We're going back. The treasure hunt is over."

She turned around. In that singular moment, his congenial mask fell away, and she saw the icy coldness of a man she didn't know. Stephen pointed a gun at her. The belly of the ship became utterly still and so did she, except for the wild beating of her heart.

She realized too late that she was the stupid woman in the horror movie.

"I don't want to hurt you."

She took a deep, steadying breath, then another, trying to suppress the rustle of terror. "You already have. Is this about Jack? Do you think you'll lure him here to rescue me? To do what? Beat him up?"

Stephen clucked disapprovingly. "Keep walking, Amy."

"I'm not going any farther."

He pressed the gun to her head. "Keep your hands up where I can see them."

Both hands went up, both shaking. How many times in her life had she found herself at the plate, bottom of the ninth, bases loaded, two outs, and a full count? She'd never choked, and she wouldn't now. She'd wait for the right pitch, a four-seam fastball, then she'd hit it out of the park. Patience. Keep him talking.

"You really don't want to do this, Stephen. We can work it out. I can postpone my wedding. Would you like that?" She could scream, but no one would hear her. She could try to run. In workout clothes, she could outrun him, but not in these crazy shoes and tight dress.

She needed a bat. When she got her hands on one, she'd start at his knees and work her way up.

They walked down a narrow hall until they reached a hatch. "Open it," he demanded.

"No," she said.

He pressed the gun against the back of her head. "Open it."

She hesitated, chewing her lower lip. He cocked the gun, and she shuddered. She turned the wheel, and it squeaked a bit as the hatch opened. The cavernous space, the size of a large hotel conference room, was lit with battery-powered yellow lamps, and the room was full of cars. Dozens of cars. Some crated. Some not.

And a rancid smell of sweat and fear and other bodily fluids. The stench climbed into her nostrils and hung tight. She breathed through her mouth.

"Go on." Stephen's voice was unnaturally loud and angry as he prodded her with the gun.

If she could climb through and pull the door closed, maybe it would give her a second or two to run and hide behind one of the cars. She lifted her skirt, took her time, and climbed through, Then, she jerked on the wheel, yanked it shut behind her, and gave the wheel a quick spin.

Fear crunched in her veins. Which way? *Go right.* She ducked and ran until she was thirty to forty yards away from the door, then she stopped, and removed her shoes.

The hatch eked open again, and she swallowed hard, knowing he was coming after her. "There's nowhere to go, Amy," Stephen said.

She crept alongside the car, listening for his heavy footsteps. She needed a way to defend herself. What could she use? *Think!* She was surrounded by cars. Cars had tires. Tires needed jacks and tire irons.

She opened a wood storage box strapped to the running board of a Model T Ford. Holding her breath—afraid the lid would squeak—she slowly and quietly lifted the lid.

Inside, were gloves, a hat, a robe for warmth, plus goggles, a jack, tire tools, a full tire repair kit, a two-foot-long piece of wood with a flat edge, and two four-foot strips of rope. She had no idea what the piece of wood was for, but she knew how she could use it.

Swallowing against the urge to gag at the sickening smell, she pulled her dress up to her knees and tied one piece of rope around her hips to hold it up.

If she was on first base, from the sound of Stephen's voice, she put him somewhere in center field. If she could get him to move to left field, she could run back to the hatch. She grabbed a wrench from the toolbox.

"You can't get away from me," Stephen said. "You'll only make me mad, and you don't want to do that. My wife made me mad. I didn't make enough money to suit her. I didn't socialize with the right people. She was disgusted by her wifely duty. But she learned to submit. And so will you."

Amy's heart was skewered with fear. "I don't think so," she muttered.

The distance from home plate to second base, and first base to third base, was eighty-four feet. The cargo hold, to her best estimation, was about the distance from home plate to center field. She couldn't throw the wrench to the other side, but she could shake things up a bit.

"On three," she said under her breath. "Ready. One. Two. Three." She threw the wrench and ran back toward the hatch, carrying the flat edge piece of wood. The wrench hit the top of a car with a clank and bounced onto the wooden floor with a thwack.

"Good try, Amy. Do anything that stupid again, and I'll shoot your friend."

She ducked behind a car and froze in place. *Oh, God. He kid-*

napped JL, too? But why? To get to me? If she surrendered, he would kill them both.

"Your friend is beat up pretty bad. She's barely alive, and she needs medical help, or she might end up dead. Come out. Let's talk. You agree to come with me, and we can send a letter telling the Master at Arms where to find her."

"Yeah right," Amy whispered.

"Come out," he said, cold as steel.

He cocked the pistol, and the sound echoed through the cargo hold.

"I'm going to put a bullet in her head. Is that what you want?" He counted. "One. Two. Three. Four. Five."

He fired, and the sound of a thousand fireworks exploding at the same time reverberated through the room. Her heart raced, sending a burst of fear to her chest that quickly dissipated throughout her body. Could he really have shot JL? She couldn't believe the man she'd shared meals with, and enjoyed lengthy intellectual discussions about baseball and finance with, could be that cruel. That insane.

Maybe he didn't really have JL down here. She could ask him to prove it before she came out of hiding. No. She couldn't reveal herself. If she and JL were to have any chance of getting out of there alive, she couldn't surrender. She had to resist.

She tensed, readying herself to fight to the end. She would not submit to him. Never. She crawled closer to where she had heard his voice. And then she saw him, and gasped.

He was holding JL under his arm, dragging her like a rag doll.

Her eyes were closed, and her head lolled to the side, her hair falling forward in a red cascade.

Amy crept closer.

When she was within five feet, she took a breath, jumped up, and darted toward him, swinging the piece of wood at his upper back, but he turned, his face a mask of fury, and she missed.

She swung again and hit his head, which cracked like a split watermelon. Blood splattered. She swallowed bile and grabbed JL before she hit the floor with him.

Amy laid her down gently and checked her injuries. There was no active bleeding. He hadn't shot her. Her breathing was shallow, but she *was* breathing. Her left forearm was turned in an unnatural position, probably broken. Her fingernails were cracked and bleeding. The left side of her head had an egg-sized knot. Her dress was shredded. Her throat and chest had multiple scratches and small cuts. Amy lifted JL's skirt. Her thighs were scratched and bleeding, but she had on all her undergarments.

"Hold on. I'll get you out of here."

She went back to Stephen and checked his carotid. There wasn't even a weak pulse.

She had killed him. *What do I do now?*

Her number one priority was getting JL out of there. She couldn't carry her. What she needed was a cart or a wheelbarrow, anything small with wheels. She circled the car and stopped suddenly, gripping the fender as she stared at a man with a bullet hole in the center of his forehead. His face was swollen, and his nose looked like it had been broken.

Was he JL's cop?

Amy gritted her teeth and searched his pockets. He didn't have her brooch. But it didn't matter right now. She checked the man for a pulse just to be sure he was dead. He was.

She walked over to the other side of the vehicle, hoping to find a cart of some kind, and her legs buckled and her stomach heaved at the sight of what awaited her. *Oh, God. This is the smell.* A woman and two small girls lay in a tidy row on the cold wood floor. They were dead, and from the condition of their bodies, she knew they hadn't died easily.

Amy gagged and threw up.

It took a moment to compose herself before she returned to JL. They were leaving this horror house now, before she found another dead body. She glanced at Stephen. How could she have been so wrong about him?

Wait. She hadn't checked his pockets. Maybe he had her brooch. She rummaged through the inside jackets, finding money, business cards, and…a diamond brooch. Did he have it earlier, when they had tea? She wanted to kick him, or better yet, pick up the piece of wood and bash his head again.

No. She wasn't going to waste another minute of her time or one more ounce of energy on him.

She ran back over to the car where she found the wrench, and grabbed her shoes and the thick lap robe. Getting JL out of the hold wasn't going to be easy, but Amy was determined to do it.

Carefully, she wrapped JL in the robe, tied her with a strip of rope, and dragged her to the hatch.

"Okay." Amy rubbed her hands together. "How am I going to do this?" She needed help, but she refused to leave JL behind. She would never leave another injured woman. She glanced over her shoulder.

What about the woman and children? Amy shook her head. *They're dead.*

She unwrapped the lap robe. Ripped her underskirt and made a sling for JL's arm, tying it tightly to her body. JL weighed about hundred twelve pounds. Amy could dead lift that much. She put on her shoes, then squatted, picked JL up, and straightened, grunting. Then she straddled the hatch and climbed through, breathing heavily.

Now what? She couldn't climb the steps with JL.

Well, certainly not all of them, but maybe one at a time.

She put JL on the floor, reached in and grabbed the lap robe, and wrapped her up again. Then she dragged her to the stairs. If she held JL in her lap, Amy could butt-climb one step at a time. She wouldn't think about how many flights she had to climb.

"How are you doing, drinking buddy?" Amy asked JL. "When we get out of this, we're celebrating with the most expensive champagne Jack can afford."

She pushed JL's hair out of her face. "What I'm about to do might hurt, so I'm apologizing up front. Hang on."

She watched JL's face closely. No reaction. "Your expression is impossible to read. Can you blink or something?"

Nothing. "Well, okay. Since you're not going to talk, I'm moving forward with my plan."

Amy dead-lifted JL again, her thighs quaking under the weight. Then she eased down on the bottom step. Stopping wasn't an option. JL was depending on her. Amy cradled JL in her lap, then grabbed the railing and climbed up on her butt one step at a time. She almost reached the top step when she heard footsteps.

"JL, I don't know how I'm going to explain what happened to us, but I've got to get you to the hospital. We don't have a choice." If she called for help, the authorities would find the dead bodies, and she might be arrested for murdering Stephen. The footsteps were moving away from her. If she didn't cry out, they wouldn't find her. Her heart was pounding, her legs were drained.

She had no choice.

"Help! Somebody help!"

The footsteps stopped. Then: "Amy. Is that you?"

She shuddered with relief, deep and absolute. "Jack! We're over here. Hurry."

Amy reached the top step just as three men came barging around the corner.

"Oh, thank God."

"Here, let me take her," Connor said.

"No, wait," Amy said. "There's a mess in the cargo hold. I think Stephen killed the cop. I killed Stephen, but one of the men beat up JL and murdered...a woman...and two children. It's a grisly scene."

Jack squatted beside her. "You carried her up the steps?"

"I couldn't leave her." Amy sniffed. "I couldn't run for help and leave her behind. I couldn't do that again."

He pulled Amy close, and held her there. "Shh. We're here now. Let me take JL."

Amy pointed down the steps. "There's a lap robe at the bottom. I need to wrap it around her."

"I'll get it," Pete said.

Connor sat on his heels next to Amy and lovingly stroked JL's face. "How bad is she hurt?"

"She's beat up. I don't think he raped her. I can't say the same for the others down there. Look at her fingers. JL fought him."

"You did, too," Jack said.

Amy was finally struck dumb by what she'd done. All she could do was shake her head. Finally, she found her voice and said, "I didn't fight him. I killed him."

Pete returned with the robe. "Connor, let's clean up what we can. People saw Amy with Stephen, so we can't let there be any connection between her and his death."

"What do you suggest?" Connor asked.

"Throw him overboard," Pete said.

Connor raised his eyebrows and gasped in mock astonishment. "And let the sharks eat him? Great idea."

Jack lifted JL up in his arms. "You two do whatever you have to do. I'm taking JL and Amy back to their cabin to treat what we can. Check the bodies for the brooch."

Amy swallowed, her throat painfully dry. "I found it in Stephen's pocket." The image in her mind of Stephen's bashed-in head would stay with her for a very long time.

"Good. I'm glad we don't have to keep looking for it," Connor said.

"We'll take care of this mess and meet you back at the room. It won't take me five minutes to get ready to leave," Pete said.

"Me, neither," Connor said. "But we have to find Gabe. That might take a while."

Amy wrapped JL in the robe again, and untied her hiked-up skirt, letting it flow to the floor. "Don't you think she needs to go to the hospital?"

"Too many questions," Jack said. "We'll be home in a couple of hours." He positioned JL's head so the big knot was against his chest. Amy tugged on the robe to cover most of the scratches and torn dress. Then they climbed the stairs to D Deck, where they caught the elevator to B Deck.

"Do you need the hospital?" the lift attendant asked.

"No. She fell asleep out on the promenade deck. Too much

champagne," Amy said.

They exited the elevator on B Deck, and walked through the moderately crowded Reception Room on the way to the first-class corridor, Amy joked about JL having too much champagne. Passengers stepped aside to give them room to pass, but some gave Amy a nasty look.

"Not one of those women could have survived what JL went through. I want to smack them," Amy murmured to Jack.

They finally reached Amy's suite. She knocked softly, and whispered, "Patrick. It's Amy and Jack. Open the door."

Patrick cracked it open, and his sleepy blue eyes peeked around the edge of the door. When he was sure who they were, he opened it wider. He looked at JL, then cleared his throat. "Did the man…you know…hurt her bad?"

Amy knew what he was asking. "I don't think so. Will you get me a bowl of hot water and a washcloth?"

"And the red medical bag out of my closet," Jack added.

Jack gingerly placed JL on her bed. "Based on what little I know of him, and the question he just asked, Patrick's seen more than any child should ever see."

"He's smart and sensitive," Amy said.

Jack rubbed her shoulder. "You're operating under delayed shock, and it's probably going to hit you shortly. Why don't you go take a bath? I'll take care of JL."

"She would appreciate the offer, I'm sure, but I'll do it. I'm worried, though. She might have a concussion. We can't stay much longer." Panic threatened to envelop Amy, but she couldn't let it. Not now. Not when JL needed her.

Patrick came back with a washbowl of hot water and the medical bag. "We need to take her clothes off and wash the dirt out of her cuts so she won't get an infection."

"Are you sure you don't need me?" Jack asked.

Patrick opened the medical bag and sorted through the tubes, studying each one. "What's antibiotic?" he asked.

"It's special cream to put on cuts so you won't get an infection,"

Jack said. "I'll leave the door partially open. Call me if you need help."

"I've never seen this ointment before, or these," he said, holding up packages of sterile pads and elastic bandages.

"We'll use the elastic bandage on her arm." Amy dug through the bag and found a pair of scissors. "We need to cut the dress off." Her hands shook so badly she couldn't hold them.

Patrick took the scissors and cut down the front of the dress. "Were you with her?"

"Not when this happened." Amy fisted her hands, remembering the feel of the rough wood, the grip, the swing, and the splat. She shivered. "I've lost track of time. I'm having trouble processing it all."

Patrick stopped cutting and gently put his hand on Amy's arm. "I can do this. You need to go sit with Mr. Mallory."

Amy shook her head. "Not right now."

Patrick cut the dress down the middle, and his deft fingers unhooked the corset. "She won't want to keep any of these clothes, will she?"

"No." White-hot anger boiled up inside Amy. "She'll want everything burned or dumped in the ocean." Where Amy hoped Pete and Connor would dispose of the bodies. She couldn't stop thinking about the woman and children. Their mutilated bodies flashed before her eyes. She gagged and dashed off to the bathroom to throw up again. The sound of her retching brought Jack into the room.

She scooped water from the faucet and rinsed her mouth, then washed her face with a washcloth. "I don't know what part Stephen played in the deaths of the woman and her children, and I don't want to know. But I'll never forget it. It makes me sick. And what that cop did to JL... I should have bashed his head in, too."

"Connor and Pete won't be gentle with the bodies."

"She's lucky to have them, and I'm lucky to have you here with me." Despite his comfort, she felt heartsick. The pain and sorrow and even guilt overwhelmed her, and she wept.

When she regained composure, she said, "There will be time for crying later." She wiped her nose with a tissue. "I need to get back to JL."

She returned to the bedroom to find JL covered with a sheet and her dress neatly folded on the floor. Patrick was sitting on the corner of the mattress squeezing liquid antibacterial soap on a washcloth.

"I don't know what antibacterial means, but I know what soap does. JL's got red bruises up and down her arms, neck, and on her legs. Her arm is the only part that looks broken. Did the cop do this?"

"I think so." Amy pulled one of the laces out of the corset and used it to tie JL's hair into a ponytail. "How did you learn so much about injuries?"

"We lived in a tenement downtown. There was a doctor's office on the block. I ran errands for him, picked up medicine, cleaned his office, whatever he needed. When he wasn't busy, he would teach me to read. I paid attention to everything he said and did. Then he died."

Amy dipped a cloth into a washbowl and gently cleaned JL's face and chest. "What happened to your parents?"

"My mom got sick. I tried to do what I saw the doctor do, but there was no money for medicine. She died a year ago. I couldn't pay the rent, so I got kicked out." Patrick spread antibiotic ointment on JL's scratches and small cuts, using it sparingly, as if it were a priceless and irreplaceable gift of the Magi.

"What about your dad?"

Patrick shrugged. "I don't remember, him. He and my ma came from Scotland before I was born. Ma said he died when I was two or so." Patrick's legs were crossed, the top leg pulsed to a measured beat, regular as a metronome, his blond hair combed off his face— Jack's mini-me.

For a moment, Amy wondered if Jack had time-traveled back to the late 1890s and somehow fathered this boy.

"What's your last name?"

"Wilson. My pa was baptized William, and my ma was baptized

Mary Agnes."

"I know you miss your mom. I lost mine when I was a bit younger than you."

Amy washed JL's broken arm and wrapped it with an elastic bandage for now. "I wonder how her arm got broken. It's not a compound fracture, thank goodness. She should be okay until we can get her to the hospital."

"From the looks of her ripped dress, she was probably dragged across the floor by her arm. Why don't you take her to the ship's hospital? The doctors can fix it, can't they?"

"They'll ask too many questions. We can wait an hour or so," Amy added, while doubts and hopes and fears tumbled around in her head. Time was running out. Jack would have to tell Patrick, Gabriele, Isabella, and Maria where he and the others came from. Where she came from, too.

"But we won't be in London for several more hours." Patrick fell silent, his leg stilled. "That's where we're going, isn't it?"

Amy stepped over to the dresser and dug through a drawer until she found a short-sleeve nightgown. "That's where the ship is going, yes." She pulled a gown over JL's head and carefully slipped her injured arm through the wide arm hole. Except for the knot on her head and a couple of scratches on her face, you'd think she just fell asleep.

"I'll stay with her," Patrick said. "You need a bath to wash off the blood." He pointed at her burgundy evening gown. "It won't clean. Throw it away."

Patrick took it all so matter-of-factly, his eyes open to every detail. But while she could tell he tried to be reassuring, he wasn't very successful. Sorrow bled through.

She hugged him, and he wrapped his arms around her, then quickly pulled away, sniffing. He refused to meet her eyes as a resolute silence seemed to grip him. Amy lifted his face with her index finger. His eyes were veiled, but on his face, she read a layer of emotion he couldn't hide.

"You're an intelligent and exceptional young man. Don't worry.

Jack, JL, and I will take care of you. Wherever we go, you'll go, too. You'll have food to eat, a bed to sleep in, warm clothes, an education, and lots of love."

He flung his arms around her waist and hugged her tightly. Then he let go again. "Go on, now. Get your bath."

Amy left him sitting on the end of JL's bed and returned to the bathroom. Her tear-streaked face didn't begin to tell the story of their night. She had none of JL's bruises, scratches, or breaks, and she wouldn't be haunted by the memory of abuse, but she had killed a man. A man who had taken care of her, advised her, helped her adjust to her new life in New York City. And she killed him.

She should have bunted, knocked him out, but when she saw him hauling JL along like a bag of trash, she lost it. Yes, she should have bunted, and for the rest of her life she would wonder why she didn't.

She filled the tub, stripped out of her clothes, then sank deep into the warmth and closed her eyes.

"Amy," Jack said, knocking on the door. "Are you okay?"

"I'm not sure I'll ever be okay."

He came in, and she covered her breasts with a washcloth. She was soaking in the bathtub and Jack was there, but right now she really didn't care whether it would be construed as cheating on Joe or not. When she didn't object, he must have taken her silence as permission.

He sat on the edge of the tub. "Sit up and I'll wash your back. If you want to talk, I'm here to listen." He took the washcloth out of her hand and dipped it into the water. Then, sweeping her hair aside, he laid the cloth on her shoulder and washed in careful circles, moving down her back.

"I like the tat." His voice was as stirring as the way he had looked at her in the restaurant in Pittsburgh. "How long have you had it?"

The hot water, his voice, the memory of a more pleasant time in her life, eased her away from the horror of the night. "I was playing in a softball tournament in China ten years ago. I saw the design on another player and wanted one just like it. It's called—"

"A unalome," Jack said.

"I thought a Buddhist symbol for the journey to enlightenment was fitting. Joe wants me to have it removed."

"What do you want?"

"I like it," she said. "It has meaning for me."

Jack's fingers traced the spiral along her spine, sweeping up and down in short strokes, as if he was using a paintbrush. "Have you found enlightenment?" His voice was oddly thick.

"I am more enlightened now than I was when I first climbed aboard this ship, but my struggle with life will continue for some time, I think."

"Because of what happened tonight?"

She swallowed the knot in her throat. She wanted to turn around, pull Jack into the water with her and make love, but she couldn't. Life was so short, but to give in to the moment, to find comfort and ease in his arms, would only add another layer of guilt to her already heavily laden heart.

"Yes," she said on an uneven breath. "Because of what happened tonight."

48

1909 SS New York—Jack

A SOFT KNOCK on the door woke Jack. He had a crick in his neck and something heavy on his chest. He opened his eyes to find a blond woman asleep on his chest. After Amy's bath, he laid down beside her and held her until she fell asleep, and after she did, he continued to hold her. The memory of her scream the other night was still fresh in his mind, and if she had a nightmare about what happened in the cargo hold, he wanted to be able to calm her immediately and reassure her that she was safe.

He didn't want to leave JL, either. She awakened once, asked for water, and went right back to sleep. Patrick continued to sit vigil at the foot of her bed.

"I'll get the door," Patrick said.

Jack gently lifted Amy's arms and slid out from under her. He pulled the covers up, watched her chest rise and fall, then left her to sleep in the dimly-lit room. JL slept with her good arm cradling the broken one. He put his hand on her forehead, checking for a fever. She didn't have one. "Take these broken wings and learn to fly—again," he said softly. He kissed his finger and touched her forehead.

Connor and Pete entered the room. "Hey, buddy. Where's Jack?" Connor asked.

"He's in the bedroom with Amy and JL," Patrick said.

Connor entered the bedroom, and immediately the atmosphere

in the room changed. As he looked down on his sister, his frame tensed and his face went rigid. Jack gestured to Connor to step out into the parlor.

"She woke up about an hour ago," Jack said. "Patrick gave her a few sips of water, and she went right back to sleep."

Pete peeked into the bedroom, then pulled the door shut. "I'm glad Amy got some sleep, too. I still can't believe she got JL out of the cargo hold and up one flight of stairs. No wonder she's an Olympian."

"Amy was in the Olympics?" Patrick asked in a reverent hush. "What sport?"

"Softball. I'll explain later," Jack said to Patrick. Then to Pete and Connor he said, "Amy and Patrick took care of JL. Then Amy broke down. It's going to take both a while to recover emotionally."

Connor chucked Patrick under the chin. "Thanks for taking care of my sister. I owe ya."

"The piece of wood Amy used was embedded in the creep's skull." Pete shivered his shoulders. "She hammered him hard. Regardless of who hurt JL, the woman, and the little girls, both of those men deserved what they got. It was a gruesome crime scene."

"What'd you do with the bodies?" Jack asked.

"We threw everything overboard. Then we poured oil all over the floor. If anyone strikes a match, the ship might go up in flames, but they'll never find any blood." Pete sat down at the table and rested his head on top of his folded arms.

Connor sat down across from Pete. "What are the extent of JL's injuries?"

"She's bruised and scratched," Patrick said. "There's a big knot on the side of her head. The worst injury is a broken arm."

Connor crossed himself. His eyes bespoke a deep weariness. "She's been hurt worse. She'll be okay."

Jack had come across written accounts of several gruesome crime scenes in his research, but fortunately he had never crossed the police tape to see one in person. He couldn't imagine the things Connor, Pete, and JL had seen in their careers. And while he accused

JL of being too cynical, she really wasn't. It was only her tough girl persona.

Pete lifted his head. "Let's get the hell out of here. I'm ready to go home. This adventure business is worse than being an NYPD detective, and this kind of thing isn't what I signed up for."

"You two go get baths," Jack said. "I'll stay here until you come back. Then I'll take mine. Have you seen Gabe?"

"We found him at a card game on D Deck. He said the woman and her two daughters were returning to her parents' home in London. Her husband had abused her, and she was running away. She told another passenger she'd met a policeman and felt safe with him," Pete said.

"I doubt her husband did half of what that creep did to her before he finally strangled her," Connor said.

"Gabe helped us clean up the mess," Pete said. "He found a garbage chute in the hold, and we threw…everything…overboard. Then he opened oil valves in a few cars and let the oil leak out to cover the bloodstains."

"How'd you stay so clean?" Jack asked.

"We tied lap robes around us. Gabe sees solutions before problems even come up. I've never seen anything like it," Connor said.

"Go get cleaned and packed. As soon as everyone's ready, we'll have a group meeting," Jack said.

Before Pete and Connor left, they looked in on JL again. Patrick let them out and locked the door behind them.

Jack walked out onto the promenade deck and gazed out the window. As the sun came up, he called out to Patrick. "Come here, buddy."

Jack wrapped his arm around the boy's shoulders. "I don't want you to worry about what's going to happen to you. You're staying with me. Where I go, you go."

"Amy told me you, JL, and her would take care of me. I don't need anybody to take care of me. I'm old enough to get by."

Jack squeezed Patrick tight. "You are old enough, but Amy, JL, and I are going to do much more than just take care of you. We're a family now." Patrick looked up at Jack. "We're going to love you. Why don't you go get cleaned up, too? We're going to have a busy day."

Jack gave Patrick the room key and locked the door behind him. Then Jack rang the steward's bell. When the steward arrived, he ordered coffee and a large bowl of fruit. While he waited, he sat at the table and spread the four brooches out in a diamond shape. Ruby, sapphire, emerald, diamond. In a way, the circle had closed for him. This would be his last adventure. He should have known shit would happen. Carolina Rose died on the last adventure. JL and Amy almost died on this one. Enough was enough.

Someone knocked on the door. He put the brooches in his pockets. The smell of coffee perked him up instantly. The steward set a tray on the table, and Jack tipped him on the way out.

A minute later, Amy walked in, tying the sash around her robe. "I smell coffee."

"So do I," JL said, cradling her arm while following Amy into the room.

"How do you feel?" Jack asked.

"Like crap," Amy said.

"Like shit," JL said. "What'd that asshole do to me?"

"You don't remember?" Jack asked.

"Not much," JL said. "Will you pour me some of that heavenly-smelling java?"

"Let's sit out on the promenade deck. The sun's coming up."

JL and Amy stretched out on two of the teak chaise lounges after Amy warned JL to be careful of her broken arm.

Jack served coffee, then sat down between them, holding the tray with his cup and the bowl of fruit. Amy and JL both ate strawberries with their fingers.

"What do you remember?" Amy asked.

"Mustache Cop grabbed me outside the restroom and hit me over the head after I gave him lip. After that, all I remember is being dragged around by my arm. A man kept yelling, 'Wake up, bitch. Wake up.' I remember a gunshot, another gunshot. That's about it.

There isn't a part of me that doesn't hurt, though."

Amy selected another strawberry and bit into it. Strawberry juice trickled down her chin. Jack handed her a napkin instead of licking the juice off her face, which was his first inclination.

"Your dress was shredded," Amy said. "I guess he was trying to wake you up by dragging you across the floor."

JL turned and looked at Amy. "You were there, weren't you? You said something about champagne. I remember Jack and champagne."

Amy chuckled. "I was dead-lifting you to get you out of the cargo hold. I knew I had to be hurting your arm, so I told you as soon as we got out of there, Jack was buying us the most expensive bottle of champagne he could afford."

JL looked around. "Well, where is it?" she asked, giving her tone just the right amount of sass.

"As soon as you've been cleared by a team of doctors at home, I'll buy you the most expensive bottle I can find," Jack said.

"You might have a concussion," Amy said. "You were hit pretty hard."

"Okay, I'll wait, but not for long. But tell me this, did Mustache Cop grab you after he grabbed me?"

"Stephen tricked me, confessed to murdering his wife, threatened to kill you, and would have killed both of us. I used his head for batting practice."

"Ouch." JL leaned her head back and closed her eyes. "I remember the first man I killed in a shoot-out. I went straight to confession, then went back every day for six weeks. Then four times a week, three times, and eventually, I was back to once a week. It's not easy to live with. I don't know how you go to counseling when you can't tell your counselor what you've done, but you need to talk to a professional.

The door to the suite opened and Pete, Connor, Gabe, and Patrick entered the parlor to join them on the promenade deck.

"Connor, will you ring for the steward and order breakfast for everyone? We probably won't get to the dining room this morning.

I'm going to take a bath. Everybody needs to stay here. We've got some planning to do when I come back," Jack said. "And somebody wake Maria and Isabella and get them to join us for breakfast."

He walked back into the parlor, stopped, and then glanced back at his friends. The men had pulled chairs up to form a semicircle around JL and Amy. Patrick sat next to JL and rested his hand on her shoulder. Connor might be her brother, and Pete might be her partner, but Patrick was her new protector.

Kevin's decision to leave the ship had been a smart one. His stress would have added a layer a tension none of them could have coped with right now. Jack took a deep, shivery breath, then another.

In moments like this, his jaw hurt where David hit him—a constant reminder of how he had fucked up. And he just did it again. He never should have let JL go off by herself, or let Amy out of his sight.

He knew the right thing to do, but failed to do it. And now he was planning to take Patrick home and raise him. But how could he possibly do that? He was incapable of taking care of anyone. Least of all himself.

He quickly bathed and dressed, then walked down to the Reception Room for a cup of coffee. Even if breakfast had arrived, the coffee hogs would have emptied the pot by now.

Catherine Lily and her husband were sitting together on one of the sofas. Sterling was reading a book, and Catherine Lily was writing in a journal, probably the one David recovered from her dresser. Jack passed up the buffet table and went straight to the coffee.

He didn't have the energy to deal with the Sterlings. Whatever questions he had about Carolina Rose would go unanswered. He took his cup and turned back to the first-class corridor.

He'd walked halfway down the hall when pages of her journal flashed in his mind. With his photographic memory, he could see every page, read every word. There was an entry for May 21: *Attended a charity luncheon at the Metropolitan Museum*... June 1: *Attended a charity auction at the Ritz Hotel...* The next page was dated July 20: *Attended a soiree in Riverside Park...*

Jack returned to the Reception Room. She was writing in the middle of the journal. Maybe it wasn't the same one David found. No, wait. It had to be. This was the middle of June.

The journal had entries for May and July. Then what happened to the pages with today's entry? Also, there was no mention of going to Scotland, or even her mother's death.

Why? Those were notable events. Why leave them out?

Jack walked back down the first-class hall, puzzling through scenarios, looking for plot holes. Why would she not write down her recollections? Because she didn't want to be reminded of them. Why wouldn't she want to be reminded of a possible cousin, a trip to Scotland, her mother's death?

He snapped his fingers, like a light bulb had just gone off in his head with a blinding flash. He turned around again and returned to the Reception Room. This time he didn't stop at the buffet table, but went straight to the Sterlings and sat down opposite them.

"Mr. Mallory, I told you to stay away from us." Sterling loomed over Jack, his face contorted with rage. "Come, Catherine Lily."

Jack ignored him and leveled a steady gaze, eyes boring into Catherine Lily. "You knew all along. Didn't you? When did you meet Carolina Rose? Was it an accidental meeting, or did someone tell you a woman who resembled you worked at the Metropolitan?" Jack sat back, crossed his legs, steepled his hands. "You saw her as a threat, didn't you?"

Catherine Lily passed her palm across the suddenly sweaty surface of her forehead. "I don't know what ye're talking about."

"You don't? Well, let me make myself clearer."

"That's not necessary, Mr. Mallory," Sterling said.

"Oh, but I think it is," Jack said, making sure his voice was saturated with disgust. "I'm talking about your identical twin sister, Carolina Rose Arées. You hated her the moment you saw her, didn't you?"

"I n-never met her," Catherine Lily said.

"I'm mistaken," Jack said. "You didn't hate her the moment you saw her. You hated her the moment you heard her speak."

"If this woman was my twin, she would have a brogue like me. Why would I hate the way she sounded?"

"Because she didn't sound like you. She sounded like an angel. Any woman would have been jealous of her. She was French. And her voice was elegant and rich and romantic. She didn't have a heavy brogue like you."

Their eyes held for a moment before Catherine Lily looked away.

"You hated her because you were sent to Scotland to grow up while she remained in France, where your mother lived. Did Grandmother Arées not want both of you? Was your father forced to find another home for you? Did he have to beg your mother's family to take you off his hands? Is that what happened?"

"Enough, Mr. Mallory. You don't have to listen to him, darling. I'll call the Master at Arms," Sterling said.

"Ye don't know what ye're talking about," Catherine Lily said, ignoring her husband. "I was always wanted. My parents could have taken Carolina Rose, too, and I'm glad they didn't."

"How'd you get rid of her?" Jack asked. "How'd you get her out of New York City?" Another light bulb went off. "Did you pay Uncle Edmond to take her to California? That's it, isn't it?"

Catherine Lily put her writing instrument and journal into a satchel and rose. "I'm tired of this conversation. Shall we go in to breakfast, darling?" she asked, glancing at her husband, who took her arm to escort her away.

"I asked Carolina Rose why she was painting for her uncle, and you know what she said?"

Catherine Lily looked back at him. "I dinna really care."

"'He's the only family I have.' That's what she said. And she was right. Her mother died. Her father gave her up. Her grandmother sent her to Paris to live. Her sister sent her away out of jealousy. Her uncle killed her. A beautiful, innocent woman. And everybody betrayed her."

Jack pushed to his feet. "You were right to send her away. She would have outshone you every day of the week. When God made the two of you, He made only one heart. And Carolina Rose won that deal. She died in my arms, and I will never forget her. But you, Catherine Lily Sterling, I will forget as soon as I leave this room."

49

1909 SS New York—Jack

JACK STRODE DOWN the first-class corridor, his thoughts seething with contempt for the Sterlings. How could any woman be as cold and heartless as Catherine Lily? Granted, Carolina Rose lied, but in the end, she risked her life to save him. She had a heart full of passion for life and art and beauty. She was as delicate as the rose for which she was named.

As he considered all he had learned from knowing her, and how his heart had expanded, he knew he would always be grateful to her. Life lived with love encounters thorns and heartaches, but a life without love has no sweet fragrance and indelible friendships.

It was his love for her that brought him back to 1909, more so than the search for Amy, and it was in her memory that he was returning home, at peace with his past and hopeful for his future.

His time with Amy was ending. He knew that he loved her, but, in this still-evolving version of himself, his heart wasn't broken over losing her. It was full of hope from knowing her.

He smiled, not at something, but because of something. Call it wisdom. Call it personal growth. Call it moving on. He was no longer Jack Mallory with the book jacket smile. He was just plain Jack, and he was ready to go home.

There was a small skip in his step as he strode the last twenty yards to Amy's cabin. He paused at the door, knowing once he walked through to the other side, his life would never be the same. He was taking Patrick home with him. And he would be the one having to call Charlotte, looking for his son, instead of Charlotte calling him to look for hers.

He took a deep breath of new air, and then he knocked.

"Who is it?" Patrick asked.

"It's Jack, buddy. Open the door." He stepped inside the room to find JL, Maria, and Isabella on the sofa. Connor, Pete, and Gabe sat at the table drinking coffee. Patrick obviously had been sitting there, too. Next to the empty chair was Kevin's medical bag and Jack's valise. The clothes trunks were stacked by the door. "Where's Amy?" Jack asked.

"She's in the other room, dressing. But where's Kevin?" Gabe asked.

"I'll explain in a minute," Jack said.

Amy walked into the room dressed in black pants, a white silk blouse, and a short black jacket, her hair hanging loose, falling just below her shoulders. "I'm ready to go."

Isabella gasped, pressing her hand to her mouth. "You can't go anywhere dressed like that."

Amy looked at her and said softly, "Where I'm going, this is appropriate attire. They're the clothes I was wearing when I arrived in your time." Amy sat on the arm of the sofa.

Isabella fingered the fabric of Amy's jacket. "What is this called? I've never felt anything like it?"

"It's viscose, and you will love wearing it."

"Do they have it in London?" Isabella asked.

"They do. And you can shop to your heart's content. Now, I have a story to tell you." Amy glanced at Jack, and he nodded approval. It was going to be hard to explain who they were, and since Amy was closest to these two, she should be the one to broach the notion of time travel.

"I know this is going to be difficult to understand, so bear with me. I know both of you," Amy glanced at Gabe, "and Gabriele have often wondered why I've said and done so many strange things.

There's a good reason. You see... I'm... I'm from the twenty-first century."

Isabella and Maria said nothing, although there was a strange gleam in Maria's eyes.

"I am too," Jack said.

Pete gestured with his head toward Jack. "I'm with him."

Connor added, "JL and I are with them, too. We're all from the twenty-first century."

Maria said something in Italian and crossed herself.

Jack put his arm around Patrick's shoulder. "We want all of you to go home with us."

Gabe shook his head, a lock of his black brilliantine hair falling over his forehead. "No! I've been an immigrant before. I don't want to start over. Maria, Isabella, and I"—he slapped his palm on the table—"will stay here."

Isabella jumped to her feet, flinging her arms wide. "You can stay, Gabriele! But I'm going with Amy." She looked pleadingly at her grandmother. "*Nonna*, come with me."

Maria reached up for Isabella's hand and tugged her granddaughter to her side. To Amy she said, "I've known since you arrived that you were different. I found your clothes, the clothes you're wearing, deep in your closet. I took them out one day when you were away on a trip with the baseball team. I read the labels and knew the clothes weren't bought in New York City. I put the garments back where I found them."

"I never suspected anything," Amy said. "If you were suspicious of me, you hid it well."

"I knew you weren't who you said you were. But there was such gentleness about you, a passion for your baseball team, and your love for Isabella, that I knew you were a gift from God. I've loved you as a daughter."

"And I love you, too," Amy said.

Maria patted Amy's leg. "I had a dream many, many years ago about a child coming to me, a child in need, and I took that child and loved her as my own. I always thought it was Isabella, but it was also you. If you want me to go with you to your time, wherever it is, I will go."

Gabe's chest heaved, his eyes darted from Amy to Jack to Pete to Connor, then back to Amy, while he shook his head. His indecision hung in the air, heavy above them all, and they waited, scarcely breathing, for him, for his eyes to clear—for him to buy in. Finally, after a great, heaving breath he said, "I swore to Micky I would always protect you. If this is what you want, I will take you. But where will we live?"

"There are several places, but you won't have to decide right away. You can live on a horse farm in Kentucky, a winery in Napa or in Italy, a ranch in Colorado or in New South Wales, Australia, Amy's house in New York City, or even Jack's plantation in Virginia. You'll have lots of choices," JL said.

Isabella slapped her hands against her cheeks. "Australia? With the kangaroos?"

"They have bears in Colorado." Patrick said. "I saw that in a book. I don't want to go to Colorado."

Jack laughed. "My brother-in-law will teach you how to fight bears."

Patrick's face paled, and he shook his head. "No, sir. I'd rather stay in New York City. There aren't bears there."

"I would like all of you to stay with me in my house on a farm in Kentucky," JL said. "It's not finished, but it's livable. I'm starting a winery there, and I need help. And I have a son your age, Isabella. He's going to college this fall, and you can go there, too."

"But you are so young to have a *bambino in un'università*," Maria said.

"Not so young," JL said.

Jack watched Patrick absorb the news. His eyes changed, like he was looking at something beyond the room. "What about you, Amy? Where will you live?"

She tilted her head sideways, obviously curious in what Patrick was asking. "I have a house in New York City, and my father's house in South Carolina. In our time, I work in baseball as a…speaker, not a reporter. I travel a lot, reporting on baseball games around the country. The man I'm in love with lives in New York City, so I spend most of my time there."

Patrick dragged the fingers of one hand through his hair in lieu of a comb. His head was down, in a thinking pose. Then he jerked his head up and looked hard at Amy. "I thought you and Mr. Mallory—"

Jack hurriedly interrupted Patrick. "Buddy, it's time you started calling me Jack." He glanced at Amy. "Amy and I are friends, and we'll continue to be friends. That's all we are."

"But you're engaged. I saw you in Tiffany's, buying her ring, and then I saw you in the park proposing to her." Patrick frowned and sighed, clearly agitated. "You're not getting married?"

"We've been pretending," Jack said. "We were trying to protect Amy's reputation."

"I don't understand," Patrick said.

"I knew I was leaving the city to chase Lillian and the brooch to London," Amy said. "And at the time, I thought I wanted to come back to your time, to New York City, and continue doing my job. There was no way to explain a sudden trip to London, other than to say it was my honeymoon. It was a crazy idea, but I thought it would protect my reputation. It made sense at the time."

"You want to come back? Here? To 1909?" Gabe asked.

"I did, yes." Amy glanced away, her bottom lip quivering. Then she looked back at Gabe. "It wouldn't be the same without you, Maria, and Isabella, though. And maybe that's why I wanted to come back, to be with the three of you. But if you're not here, I'm not sure I have a reason to return."

Gabe crossed his arms and tapped his foot. Then he asked, "Does New York City in your time look like it does now?"

"There are more buildings, taller buildings, more automobiles. It's bigger, brighter, busier. Your apartment building is still there," Amy said. "The trees in Riverside Park have grown, and you can't see the river from the street like you can now. The Providence Loan Society building is still there. Central Park is still a park."

"Where is your house in the city?" Gabe asked.

Jack had seen a variety of Amy's smiles—uncomfortable, happy, seductive, sarcastic, and even a fake one—but the one she gave Gabe in response to his question could only be classified as the coolest version of a devilish grin. "Would you believe I inherited the Sterlings' house?"

Gabe regarded her with wide eyes. "On Riverside Drive?"

"Catherine Lily is my three-times great-grandmother. Her daughter, Rebecca, married Duncan Spalding, my two times great-grandfather."

"So you weren't there looking for a job," Gabe said, shaking his head.

"I was stealing clothes from Catherine Lily's closet." Amy chuckled, fanning her hands down to her clothes. "I couldn't go around looking like this."

"I don't understand," Gabe said. "But I didn't understand Americans when I first got off the boat from Italy, either." He paused a moment, shaking his head. Then he said, "I have a good business in the city. If I don't go back, my lawyer has instructions to sell everything I own and give the money to the church. If this is what Maria wants, I'm willing to try it."

"I signed a document at the bank listing Maria as my beneficiary. If you're not there," Amy said, looking at Maria. "I don't know what will happen to the money in my account."

"The funds will go to her beneficiaries," Jack said.

"Everything I own goes to Isabella, then to Lilla," Maria said.

"Then the money in your account, Amy, will go to Lilla, too," Jack said.

"She'll be able to afford indoor plumbing," JL said with a hint of sarcasm.

"I have a question," Isabella said. "How do we get there? To your time? Do we take a boat, a car, walk? Or do we click our magical silver shoes like Dorothy?"

"In our time, Dorothy has ruby shoes. But yes, the way we travel back and forth is sort of like that."

Jack withdrew the brooches from his pocket and gave Amy the diamond. "These brooches have powers we don't fully understand. But when we're ready to go, they will take us home."

Amy tossed her brooch from one hand to the other, like a hot potato. "I'm ready, but I have a question. When I go back, what will the date be? The day I left? A week later? When?"

"We'll all go back to June," Jack said.

Amy leapt off the arm of the sofa. "I can't do that! How would I explain my absence? I have to return to October. It's the only way I can stop Joe from being charged with my murder—"

"Murder? *Madre di Dios!* Who is this Joe?" Maria asked.

"The police have been looking for me since I left. They believe the man I love is responsible for my death. I have to go back to clear his name," Amy explained, and then turning to Jack she said, "I can't lose my job. I worked too hard to get where I am. An eight-month absence would ruin my career. I have to go back to October if it's at all possible."

"She's right, Jack," Connor said. "Amy needs to return as close as possible to the day and time she left. There's no explanation I can think of that the police would believe. They certainly won't believe her if she tries to pawn off an amnesia narrative."

"We can't go back to October. None of us want to re-live what happened in October and November," Pete said.

"My brooch doesn't work, anyway," Amy said as she continued tossing it back and forth.

"Kenzie's brooch wouldn't return her to the future right away, either," Jack said. "Your brooch should work now. It's getting hotter, isn't it?"

"Yes," she said. "It's even warmer than it was before."

"It's gaining power," Jack said.

"I don't get it," she said in an uncertain tone. "Why was I here?"

"Supposedly, the brooches bring—" Connor said.

"—We don't know," Jack interrupted, "all the ins and outs of brooch lore, but one day we will."

Amy looked at Connor, her eyebrows furrowing. "What were

you going to say about the brooches?"

"Ah," he glanced at Jack, then back at Amy. "They bring new people into our lives. That's all."

"It would be nice if you arrived home at an earlier date," JL said. "You could send me an anonymous letter and tell me to cancel my trip to Napa. But I was already in the air by the time you vanished. You could warn Jack, though. Tell him not to go to San Francisco."

Amy looked at him. "Do you want me to do that?"

The hair lifted on his neck and arms. Amy was offering him a do-over. How could he say no? How could he say yes? If he saved Carolina Rose, would she eventually have outlived her usefulness and been murdered by her uncle the next day, or the next? There was no way to know. If he could save her, didn't he have to try?

"Send me an anonymous letter in mid-November, warning me not to go to San Francisco because my life will be in danger," Jack said.

"Are you sure?" Amy asked.

He nodded. "I'm sure." Then he added. "When you go home, go back to your life, to Joe, and put this all behind you."

"But I'll want to talk to you, to JL, to Patrick, to Isabella, to all of you."

"You can't," Jack said. "Isabella, Maria, Gabe, and Patrick won't be there until June. They can call you once they get settled."

Amy sat at the desk and scribbled on a piece of paper, then put a note in Isabella's hand. "Here's my phone number. Call me as soon as you can."

Isabella hugged her. "I will."

Amy stared at her brooch. "I'm scared."

JL put her good arm around Amy's waist. "This is only my second trip, but traveling back and forth isn't scary. Be safe. And I'll see you soon." They hugged each other. "Remember, Jack owes us a bottle of champagne."

"I hope I don't forget any of this," Amy said.

"You'll remember everything, and so will we," JL said.

Jack pulled Amy into his arms. "I'm so glad I got to meet you."

"Kiss her, Mallory," Pete said. "And let's go home."

Jack kissed her forehead. "Be safe, Amy. Be happy." He wanted to pull her into his arms, and kiss her on the mouth, and keep kissing her all the way to her toes. He loved this woman, but he needed to let her go. She wasn't his.

She touched his face with her warm hand. "I've loved every minute of our time together. Be safe, Jack. Be happy." She stepped away from him. "What do I do now?"

"Step into the other room, open your brooch, focus on the time and day you left, read the words, and we'll see you on the other side."

"It's going to be a long wait. But I'll see you all again." She walked slowly toward the door, leaving behind a roomful of choked up friends.

"Wait," Jack said, reaching into his pocket. "Kevin gave me some baseball cards for you." He handed her the little green box. "He thought you might like to have them."

She dumped the cards into her hand. "My God, there's a Ty Cobb, a white-border Honus Wagner, Eddie Plank, and Joe Doyle, and a Christy Mathewson. This is a dream collection." She held the cards against her breasts, and kissed Jack on the mouth. "These cards are worth thousands of dollars. I hope I can personally thank Kevin one day." She took a deep breath and kissed Jack again, then she opened the door to the bedroom and closed it behind her.

The sound of Pete cracking his knuckles was also the sound of Jack's heart cracking. He rested his hand on the closed door. JL came to him, and he hugged her.

"If I'd never met Carolina Rose, I would never have known how to love Amy. If I don't go to San Francisco—"

"You've come so far, Jack. The changes in your heart won't be lost," JL said. "If you don't remember, I will. And I'll find a way to get you back to this place in your heart and in your mind. I'll beat it into you until you get it again. You and Pete are my best friends. I won't let you forget how to love."

"I need to believe that."

"Then believe it," JL said. "I won't let you forget."

Jack pushed open the bedroom door and breathed deeply of the lingering fragrance of Amy's essence.

"Let's go," Pete said.

Patrick picked up the medical bag and the valise. "I'm ready."

Jack handed the ruby brooch to Connor, the emerald to Pete, and he kept the sapphire.

"Wait. Where's Kevin?" Gabe asked.

"He went home already," JL said. "We'll see him on the other side."

"Put the trunks in a circle," Connor said. "We'll sit on them and link arms. We'll read the inscriptions on the stones, fireworks will go off, then we'll go on a curvy, twisty, journey. When the ride is over, we'll be on MacKlenna Farm in Kentucky. If we get separated, stay where you are. We'll find you."

Maria and Gabe's faces grew guarded, almost frightened, and they held tightly to each other. Isabella's face flushed, and she looked wide-eyed at Pete.

"There's nothing to be afraid of," Pete said.

Patrick beamed with anticipation and curiosity. "What about JL? She can't hold on," he said.

"I'll hold on to her," Connor said.

When they were all in place, the men opened the brooches. Jack glanced back one last time toward the bedroom. She was gone from his life now. He loved her, and he would carry that love, along with the love he had for Carolina Rose, for the rest of his life. He might not remember once his trip to San Francisco was cancelled, but he now knew the love he felt for both women would remain in his heart forever.

He tousled Patrick's hair. "Let's go home, son."

50

Present day MacKlenna Farm—JL

WHEN THE WILD RIDE through time ended, JL's knees buckled, and she reached out for Connor's arm for support. It took a moment for the dizziness to pass, but then she loosened her grip. Home, she was home.

Her head pounded, her arm throbbed, but she was incredibly glad to be there, even though she wasn't the same person who left on the adventure days or weeks earlier. Physically and emotionally, she was broken and hurting. Was Kevin anywhere on the farm, or had he left for parts unknown?

A ripple of tension flowed through her as she crossed the room to look at the display on the desk phone for the time and date. "It's one o'clock, June 29. We've been gone two weeks." As much trauma as she'd been through, it seemed like two months. She dialed David's cell phone number and put him on speaker.

"McBain."

Her heart lifted at hearing David's voice, and she took a deep calming breath. David instilled confidence in others because he had confidence in himself. And he wasn't afraid of anything, except losing his family. She had absolute faith in his ability to solve problems, and she wanted him to solve hers. But not even David McBain could put her and Kevin back together again. The fall had been too far and the landing surface had been too hard.

"It's JL. We're back."

"Where are ye?" David asked.

"In Elliott's office in the mansion. Where are you?"

"In my office at the farm. I'll be right there."

Patrick sat down in the desk chair next to where she was standing. He stared at the computer monitor, poking the touch screen with his index finger while the screen saver switched from one picture of the Scottish Highlands to another.

"We brought four friends home with us," she said.

"Maria, Isabella, Gabe, and Patrick. Right?" David asked. "We thought they might come back with ye."

"Do you know where Kit is?"

"In her studio. She's been expecting Maria and Isabella. She'll help them get acclimated," David said.

Maria and Isabella were sitting on the sofa flipping through the photo album on the coffee table. An album JL had looked through dozens of times. It was full of family photos from the famous Hogmanay Celebrations, starting the year Elliott and Meredith met, and up through the most recent family gathering at Austin's graduation.

"Where's Austin?" JL asked.

Over Patrick's shoulder, she logged into the computer system using one hand, and the extra-large monitor instantly divided into squares, each square showing a different view of the farm from the security cameras mounted on utility poles.

"He and James Cullen are playing basketball at the guest house."

She pointed the mouse to the guest house, tapped a couple of keys and the camera switched to the basketball court. Patrick looked closer and closer until his nose was almost on the screen.

"Where's Kevin?"

"In Tuscany."

She flinched. Although she'd hoped he would be gone, having it confirmed made everything that hurt ache ten times worse, especially the pains shooting up and down her arm.

Elliott had four pictures on his desk. One of Kit as a young girl at an equestrian event, one of James Cullen at a similar age, one of JL and Kevin at Meredith's end-of-harvest gala, and a picture of Elliott and Meredith on their wedding day. Looking at Kevin smiling, she rubbed her hand against the fabric of her silk skirt, remembering the feel of his skin, the play of muscles in his shoulders and arms, and the warmth of his hands on her. Whether gentle or rough, rushed or patient, they were always either highly erotic or quietly romantic.

She forced herself to look away. "Good. I don't want to run into him right now." She spoke in a matter-of-fact tone, but knew David's intuition would hear the truth in her voice and the hurt and longing beneath her denial.

"Kevin moved out of the room you shared at the guest house. But the good news is you can move into your new home. The building inspector is coming this afternoon for the final inspection."

The thought of moving into Kevin's new house without him scraped at the top layer of her guilt with the skill of a painter's knife. "That's good news...I guess. Would you let Elliott know we're back?"

"Stay put. We'll be there in five minutes."

"Oh, one more thing. Does Austin know Kevin and I cancelled the wedding?"

"Kenzie and I, Meredith, and Elliott are the only people who know. We figured ye'd want to tell Pops first, so we've kept it secret. Kevin hasn't even told his parents."

After what happened last fall when Austin uncovered a secret she had kept from him, she swore never to conceal anything from him again. "Thanks. I'll tell him right away."

JL disconnected the call and looked at Jack. His hip was hitched on the corner of the desk, one booted foot firmly planted on the hardwood floor, while he scrolled through his cell phone.

"You okay?" he asked.

"It's going to be difficult. But how about you?"

"I've been staring at my phone, scared to Google Amy. If she married Joe, I'm taking a bottle of whisky out to the lake to get drunk. Kenzie says it's the preeminent place on the farm to go if you're looking for a quiet retreat to feel sorry for yourself, but to be wary of stray animals."

"Give me the phone. I'll look," JL said.

"No. I'm not ready."

JL studied him closely, touched his shoulder. "What happened to Carolina Rose?"

"She died after the chandelier crashed to the floor in the saloon in San Francisco. Why?"

"That means Amy didn't send you an anonymous letter warning you to cancel your San Francisco trip."

"I did cancel it," he said. "I had a trip scheduled to go to San Francisco to spend a couple of days researching what happened in the city in 1881. I also scheduled a book-signing at my favorite bookstore. Then I got a letter warning me not to go. I cancelled the flight and the signing."

JL was incredulous. "Research? Book-signing? And you chose not to tell Amy there were two trips?"

He just nodded an affirmative, the muscle jumping in the side of his jaw. "I forgot."

"You're like an elephant," JL said. "You never forget anything."

He was quiet, looking at her, the hint of some unreadable emotion in his eyes. She honestly didn't know if he forgot or not, but she knew she would never ask again.

"Gabe and I are going over to the security center," Pete said. "Then I'll get him settled in at the guest house."

"Thanks," JL said.

Patrick moved away from the computer and looked out the window. "Horses look better now. I wonder what they eat?"

Jack laughed. "Kentucky Bluegrass."

"Doesn't look blue to me," Patrick said.

"In the spring, when you look at the large fields, the grass has a blue cast to it."

"Oh," Patrick said. "I guess I'll have to wait awhile to see that."

Connor opened the refrigerator at the refreshment bar. "Anybody want something to drink? Coke? Water? Coffee?"

"Coffee," Jack said.

"Coca-Cola?" Patrick asked. "I'd like to have one. I had a taste once."

Connor handed him a Coke and showed him how to pop the can's top. Patrick drank it slowly, smiling. Then he looked in the refrigerator and stuck his hand inside. "It's cold. Is this an icebox? There are lots of different colored cans."

"Yes, and you can try them all."

"I need to go to the hospital," JL said. "Will you take me, Connor?"

Elliott and David entered the room. "I'll take you," Elliott said. "Where are we going?"

JL hugged him. "Hi, boss. My arm is broken. I need to have it looked at."

"Your arm is broken?" Meredith asked. "Come with me. I'll take you to the hospital right now."

"I need to change clothes first."

"No you don't. We'll tell them you were trying on clothes for a stage production and fell off a stool. And you've got more than a broken arm. I don't think I've ever seen a knot that big, and you've got scratches on your face and neck. What happened to you?"

"I don't remember, but it hurts like hell, so can we go?"

"I'll grab my purse," Meredith said. "I might have to tell the hospital staff you fell out of a tree."

"I have to see Austin," JL said.

"He's playing basketball with James Cullen. If you're not in that much pain..."

"It hurts like hell," JL said. "But Austin comes first."

"We'll stop by there on the way out." Meredith's voice faded as she disappeared down the hall.

JL turned to glance back into Elliott's office. A wave of dizziness hit her, she grabbed the doorframe. "Patrick."

He crossed the room, drinking his Coke. "Meredith has a son your age. His name is James Cullen. You just saw him on the monitor playing basketball. If you come with me, I'll introduce you to him and my son, Austin. You can talk to them about anything. Ask questions. Whatever."

Patrick's eyes darted back and forth, and he licked his lips. "What about Jack?"

JL took Patrick's hand and squeezed it. "He's not going anywhere." Then to Jack she said, "Meredith and I are taking Patrick to meet JC and Austin."

"Good." Jack lounged at the refreshment bar, nursing a cup of coffee and massaging his temples while he chatted with Elliott and David. "They'll help you get settled. I'll see you at supper. If you need me, ask James Cullen to call my cell."

"Call your what?" Patrick asked.

Patrick still sounded a little wobbly about all the changes, and Jack must have sensed it. He put down his cup, walked over to Patrick and hugged him. "A cell is a communication device. And one more thing…" Jack leaned in and acted like what he was telling Patrick was extremely confidential. "A beautiful young girl your age lives here, too. Her name is Emily, and she came from 1881."

That got a big smile out of Patrick. "She's like me?"

Jack laughed. "No, she's a girl. But, yes, she's a time traveler, too."

Patrick looked up at JL. "Do you know Emily? Does James Cullen? Can I meet her too?" Then he lowered his voice and whispered, "I want to take a bath and brush my teeth before I meet her. Jack said girls like boys who smell good."

"You took a bath last night, son."

"I know, Jack, but that was a hundred years ago. Right?"

JL laughed. "You're absolutely right. James Cullen and Austin will help you with personal hygiene. Austin will probably encourage you to shave the fuzz off your face, but don't do it until Jack tells you. We don't need to rush you to the hospital for a blood transfusion."

Patrick nodded sagely, as if he understood what JL just said.

"Never mind," she muttered.

Meredith returned with her purse and keys, and JL and Patrick followed her through the utility room out into the garage. "We'll take the sedan," Meredith said.

JL pointed to the back door of the Mercedes. "Hop in, Patrick."

When he struggled with the handle, she showed him how to lift it to open the door. He gasped quietly when the door opened from the back instead of the front. "Jeepers!" He swung the door back and forth, watching the hinges move. "I've never seen anything like this."

"Dozens of things will amaze you," JL said. "Try not to get overwhelmed. You'll catch on."

He climbed into the back seat, and sniffed the inside of the car while rubbing his hands over the leather seats. "This had to cost a lot of money."

"More than I can afford," JL said.

Meredith laughed. "This is Elliott's car. Mine isn't this clean."

Right now, Patrick was like a toddler learning to walk, or opening a kitchen drawer and finding a world of possibilities. By tonight, he would be adjusting well. He was a sharp kid, and processed information quickly. She would have to buy eye drops on the way home. If he kept his eyes that wide open for the rest of the day, he'd end up with eye strain.

Meredith explained to Patrick how to put on his seatbelt, then drove out of the garage and followed the road through the farm, arriving a few minutes later at the guest house.

"JL," Austin yelled, waving. She eased out of the car and waited there for him. "What happened?" he asked.

"I broke my arm. It's just a little break. Meredith is taking me to the hospital."

"I'll go, too," Austin said.

"There's no reason for that. I'll be fine, but there is something I need to talk to you about." She opened the door to the back seat, and Patrick climbed out. "This is Patrick Wilson." Then to Patrick, JL said, "This is my son, Austin, and his cousin, James Cullen. Patrick is from 1909. He's going to need some guidance."

"Sure. No problem," Austin said.

Meredith got out of the car and walked over to the boys. "James Cullen and I will entertain Patrick while you talk to Austin. Take your time."

JL gestured with her head. "Let's sit on the porch." She mounted the steps and sat in one of the wicker rockers. While she rocked back and forth, she tried to push away the pain in her head, her arm, her heart, so Austin wouldn't worry about her. "You know Kevin's gone through a rough patch lately," she finally said.

"Yeah, we've talked a little, but mostly we just sit and flip channels, watch games. He's got a lot on his mind. Where is he now?"

JL wondered where to start and how to soften the blow. The last thing she wanted to do was damage the relationship between Austin and Kevin. "We decided to postpone the wedding, and give him time to work through issues that have been bothering him."

Austin leaned against the porch post and rested his hand on the top rail. "That's okay. Everybody thinks you're already married. An official ceremony only matters to Pops."

It mattered to her, too, but now wasn't the time to mention it. "Kevin bought a winery in Tuscany—"

Austin drew a sudden, deep breath. "Italy?"

JL stopped rocking, held out her hand in a stop gesture. "Calm down. Look…" She needed to take this slowly. Austin depended on Kevin, and the separation wouldn't be easy on him. "Kevin needs a break."

"But not from me," Austin said.

"From all of us. He's wanted his own winery for a long time. You know that."

"But he was supposed to start a winery here. Not buy one in Italy. And besides, he'll miss my games."

"Austin, stop it. Listen to yourself. You're an adult, and you're sounding like a kid. Life doesn't always go as we planned. I need you—" She stopped and cleared the logjam in her throat. If she lost it now, so would her son. "I need you to be calm about this and accept the fact Kevin is struggling and needs our support."

"Where is he? I want to talk to him."

"He came back early from our adventure and went on to Italy. He's there now."

Austin crossed his arms. "He should have told me."

JL got up and laid her hand on his arm. "Kevin didn't want anyone to know he was back, because he couldn't explain why he was here and I wasn't."

"I would have understood. I want to go see him."

"When? You're going to Cairo for the FIBA U19 Basketball World Cup. You don't have time before school starts."

"You're right, but I'd still like to see him. Maybe we can Facetime. I know Kev's got a lot on his mind," Austin said, "but he'll work it out. I bet there'll be a wedding before Christmas."

"I appreciate your confidence, but a little realism would be helpful."

"Are we done here? I'm starting to cool off, and I have a hundred free throws to shoot."

JL rolled her eyes. "Sure. We're done."

They walked back to the car. James Cullen and Patrick were throwing sticks for Tater Tot.

"Do you play basketball, Patrick?" Austin asked.

He shook his head. "No, but I want to learn. Looks like fun."

"We'll teach you," Austin said. "I know all of JC's moves. He's not much of a challenge anymore."

"Hey, man. I resemble that remark." James Cullen laughed at his own joke. "Don't listen to him, Patrick. Just listen to me. Austin's a big college boy now, and has girls calling him all the time. His head is getting bigger than the ball in his hands."

Patrick's focused stare went from the basketball to Austin's head and back again. "That's a joke. Right?"

Austin gave Patrick a light punch to his upper arm. "Yeah, it's a joke. See? You're catching on already."

"I've got lots of questions. Jack and JL said you'd answer them. I'm not dumb... I just—"

"Hey, man. We're cool. No judgments. We'll get you settled in, show you the ropes," Austin said. "You'll feel more comfortable about being here after you meet Emily."

Patrick's face lit up. "I heard about her. Can I meet her today?"

"She's at the hospital for tests. She'll be back later," James Cullen said.

"Is she sick?" Patrick asked.

James Cullen threw the stick for Tater Tot again, and the dog ran after it. "Emily's got diabetes. Do you know what that is?"

"A disease that kills people. Is she going to die?"

Tater Tot returned with the stick, and James Cullen threw it again. "No, there's medicine now. If she was here, she'd be playing basketball with us. She's cool."

JL would prefer to stay and spend time with the kids, but she had to get her arm fixed. "I'll see you guys at dinner. Take care of Patrick, and, James Cullen, will you ask David for one of the spare phones? Show Patrick how to use it. His first call can be to me." She hugged Austin goodbye and climbed back into the car.

As Meredith drove through the security gate, she said, "Kevin told us what happened. He's not happy about the way things were left, but he didn't know what else to do. We went to Italy with him and stayed a week. The company bought a winery, and he bought a small adjoining one. Before Elliott and I left to come home, I got a referral for a psychologist in Florence. Kevin made an appointment. There's not much else any of us can do right now."

"When did he get back from the adventure?"

"He traveled with your brooch, and returned a few minutes after he left. It was like he was never gone. Elliott walked out of his office to get the mail, walked back in, and there he was. You were right about the amethyst. It's more powerful than the other stones."

"Have you heard anything from him since you left him in Italy?" JL asked, and then mentally kicked herself. It wasn't that she didn't want to know how he was doing. But she needed to back off and give him space.

"He said he wants as little contact as possible. He's still working for the company, but he only communicates through email or text messages. No video-conferencing or FaceTiming. Definitely no phone calls."

"Austin wants to go over there for a visit, but he doesn't have time right now."

Meredith turned onto Old Frankfort Pike, and the car picked up speed. "Even if Austin had time to go, Kevin won't let him come for a visit right now."

JL closed her eyes and leaned her head against the head rest. "I'm glad Austin won't have to deal with rejection."

"All we can do now is pray for patience, and wait for Kevin to come around," Meredith said.

Sighing, JL said, "You know…everything happened so fast with us. We didn't take the time to grow into a relationship."

"Elliott and I started out fast, too, but my cancer and the pregnancy forced us to slow down and talk about what we wanted individually, as a couple, and as parents. You don't have cancer or a pregnancy to deal with, but you still need to know what you want out of the relationship, and out of your life, too. So, what do you want?" Meredith asked.

"I'm going to resign as Global VP."

"Whoa. Elliott won't like it."

"I know, but Connor can step right into my position."

"Are you sure?"

"Yeah, I'm sure. After I transition the job over to Connor, I want to decorate the house and turn it into a home. See if I can get Pops to spend more time here. He'll enjoy watching Austin play college ball. Plus, I want to travel to locations other than Napa and Scotland. I want to take time to read, start the new vineyards, and do more horseback riding. I've been a workaholic who eats coffee for lunch for way too long. It's time to stop and do all the things I've wanted to do, but never had the time."

"Are you going to send Kevin an email and tell him you're home?"

"No, I'll leave that to someone else. I spent days crying over him. I love him more than anything in the world, but this situation has broken my heart."

Meredith put on the signal and turned onto New Circle Road.

"In three months, I'm going to Tuscany for the harvest. So, starting tomorrow, Ted will spend at least two hours a day with you doing limited exercises until your arm is healed. You'll have weekly counseling sessions and riding lessons, and you'll learn Italian with me. You're going to get into the most fantastic shape of your life."

If JL wasn't already used to Meredith's take-charge attitude, she might be pissed, but she knew where Meredith's heart was. She also knew Meredith always had a plan and a purpose.

"I've been working with Ted since the first of the year. I'm already in good shape, but I'd like to get my pace down, and I'd like to learn Italian. You'd think after all these years of being around Pete, more would have rubbed off. So, I'm game. What's the plan? Do you want a marathon training partner?

"No. I want a traveling partner. You're going to Tuscany with me."

"I don't think so," JL said.

"The week before we leave for Italy," Meredith said, ignoring JL's protest, "we're going to spend four days at a spa in Sonoma. Then off to LA to stay at the Beverly Wilshire and spend a day shopping on Rodeo Drive."

"If you can get hair appointments at Christophe's, I'll go."

"Good. I'll make all the arrangements."

"And… If you think this will win Kevin over, forget it. He won't be impressed."

"I'm not doing this hoping Kevin will see you, realize his mistake, and marry you on the spot. I'm doing this so you'll feel the best you've ever felt, and if you decide it's over, you'll do it with your head held high."

"Okay," JL said. "I'm on board."

Meredith shimmied her shoulders. "I knew you would be. You're just as competitive as I am. You want to go out on top. And you know what else?"

"No, what?"

"You're the daughter I never had, and nobody, not even Kevin, is going to back my baby girl into a corner."

51

Present day MacKlenna Farm—Jack

JACK SAT NEXT to Patrick at dinner in the kitchen at MacKlenna Mansion, but the boy was so involved in a conversation with Emily and James Cullen that Jack didn't want to intrude in what looked like the beginnings of the three musketeers. Make it four. When Lincoln heard the news from James Cullen, he had insisted on coming to the farm. Braham rearranged his schedule, and was bringing his son late to the party. They were arriving before lunchtime the next day, and plans were stacking up like building blocks.

Once the twins arrived the day after with Kenzie, Jack felt certain Patrick would seek him out. The wonders of technology were one thing. The McBain twins...

Enough said.

Braham warned Jack that he expected the full story and wasn't leaving until he heard every salacious detail. Since Charlotte was seven months pregnant, Jack wasn't surprised his brother-in-law was so interested in Jack's sex life. Braham would be disappointed, though...not only because Jack didn't have one, but even if he had, this time he wouldn't have shared it.

Braham would read between every unspoken line. They had a bond, forged in the fires of Richmond during the Civil War. And they shared the love of an amazing woman, Jack's sister.

There was an ache in Jack's gut because Braham would never meet Amy, would never watch them walk hand in hand along the promenade deck, share a glass of wine, or laugh at a hat blown overboard. Braham would never see Jack and Amy gazing into each other's eyes, or sharing a touch, or a kiss. Not only would Braham never see it, but Jack didn't think Braham would ever hear about it, either.

At least not now. Some stories were just too painful, too raw, to share.

The howl of laughter brought Jack's mind back to the dinner table. Maria's beef Bolognese with linguine, spaghetti with roasted red pepper sauce, Italian baked chicken, and garlic tomato bruschetta were hits that just kept coming. The woman was an incredible cook. Mrs. Collins, Elliott's longtime housekeeper-cook, welcomed Maria to her kitchen and watched over her shoulder, taking notes. Mrs. Collins was a great cook, but she couldn't hold all the candles in Wal-Mart next to Maria's magical culinary skills.

Jack would invest in a restaurant if she wanted to open one.

"Where are Isabella and Austin?" Jack asked.

"They went to the hospital to see JL," James Cullen said. "We're going up at ten to get Isabella, because Austin's spending the night. They want to keep JL overnight for observation."

"How're you getting there? Surely Kentucky doesn't allow fourteen-year-olds to drive. Or does your Mensa brain qualify you for a special license?"

James Cullen blushed. "We don't talk about that anymore, Uncle Jack."

"Oh," Jack said. "I didn't get the memo."

James Cullen rolled his eyes, then leaned in to Patrick. "Ye gotta watch him closely. He's sly," James Cullen said, sounding just like his dad.

Patrick gave Jack a confused look.

"JC," Cullen said. "When I met yer Cousin Kit, I didn't get her sense of humor. She would say things that went"—Cullen sailed a flat hand over his head—"zoom over my head. Patrick's the same way. He takes what you say literally. If you see that expression on his face, when his eyes widen and his jaw drops, ye'll know he's not getting what ye're saying. So, back up, laddie."

James Cullen elbowed Patrick in the arm. "I just mean Uncle Jack likes to tease. There wasn't really a memorandum."

Kit brought her plate to the table and sat next to Cullen. "When you match a woman from the early twenty-first century with a man from the mid-1800s, there's bound to be some misunderstandings, and we had our share."

Patrick scratched his head. "You and Mr. Montgomery and Emily are from another time, but you still talk like Jack and James Cullen." Then he whispered, "Mrs. Collins sounds different. What year is she from?"

"She's from a different part of Kentucky," James Cullen whispered. "She's never"—he made air quotes—"traveled."

Kit tousled Patrick's hair. "In a week or two you'll fit right in."

Patrick patted the hair James Cullen had meticulously styled to match his own. "Why does everyone mess with my hair?"

"Because it's beautiful." Kit cocked her head and studied him. "Well, it was until JC put stuff on it to make it spike. But it's soft and thick." She winked. "Girls like that."

"I heard you quoting Shakespeare this afternoon," Cullen said. "He's my favorite writer. Elliott has a wonderful collection in the library. If ye need help picking out a book, I'll be happy to make recommendations."

"My mom had two books. *Romeo and Juliet* and the *Bible*. She read to me every night."

Jack made a mental note to pick up copies of both books from Joseph-Beth Booksellers in the morning, when he took Patrick clothes shopping.

Cullen excused himself, and along with his pipe and a book about the Federal Reserve, retired to the screened in porch. Kit and Maria took cups of coffee to the sitting room off the kitchen to gossip. Jack heard Pops' name mentioned several times. Was Kit planning to introduce the two? If so, Jack felt certain JL would approve.

Pete, Connor, and Gabe swept through the kitchen long enough to fill their plates before disappearing to the finished basement, and as soon as their plates were emptied, the kids ran off to the TV room on the second floor.

Jack was left alone with the dishes. He thought someone would hear him rattling pots and pans and come to his rescue, but for a solid hour no one entered the kitchen. As soon as he pushed the start button on the dishwasher, the kids came down for dessert, Maria and Kit put their coffee cups in the sink, Gabe, Pete, and Connor returned with their dirty dishes, and Cullen, with the aroma of apple-scented tobacco clinging to his shirt, came back for a cup of tea.

Jack swatted a couple of kids' butts with a wet towel, and left the room laughing. He spent most of his adult life eating out, warming up leftovers, or making protein shakes. He couldn't remember a meal for more than two people being cooked in his plantation's kitchen since he was a child.

With Patrick around, that would change. Tonight was good practice.

As he had done dozens of times since returning, he checked his phone for a missed call, text, or email from Amy. Nothing. But in her defense, there was no way she could know he was back. He still hadn't Googled her or attempted a call. Isabella had given him Amy's note with her phone number, telling him, "*Nonna* said you should talk to her first."

He, David, and Elliott had talked at length about what happened during the adventure. Elliott and David knew most of the story from Kevin, but even David was shocked by what had taken place their final night aboard the ship.

Now, as Jack read through an email from his editor, he walked aimlessly through the mansion. A nightcap might help him get through what he anticipated would be another sleepless night.

He walked into Elliott's office and was surprised to find him there. "I thought you went upstairs a while ago."

"I did," Elliott said, "but Meredith kicked me out when I couldn't stop tossing and turning."

"What's keeping you awake? It certainly isn't a stomach full of the most delicious Italian food I've ever eaten, because you didn't have any."

"Oh, but I did. Maria made me *agliatelle al tartufo*—pasta covered in a truffle sauce. It's definitely a dish not to pass up."

"I'm sorry I didn't get a bite."

"I don't know how I'm going to keep her a secret. Mrs. Collins seems to have given up the keys to her kitchen, but I don't know for how long."

Jack poured a whisky. "By this weekend, she'll be in JL's kitchen, so you won't have a problem." He crossed the room, sat in a wingback chair, and put his feet up on the ottoman.

"We'll be over there eating every night, then. Which might cause a bigger problem." Elliott moved from the chair at his desk to the chair opposite Jack. "Ye didn't warn me about JL's plan to resign from the corporation."

"That's between you and JL. I'm not getting in the middle."

"JL didn't tell me. She told Meredith, and Meredith told me."

Jack sipped his whisky, wishing he had a cigar. Smoking wasn't allowed in the house, and after Elliott's health scare, he was forbidden to smoke or be around second-hand smoke, including Cullen's pipe.

"I'm not disappointed she's quitting her job, but I am disappointed she's giving up on Kevin."

"I wouldn't exactly say she's giving up on him. He's the one who left the country."

"This is all my fault."

A soft groan rose from deep in Jack's chest. "Sack cloth and ashes aren't a good look for you, Elliott. JL and Kevin are carrying enough guilt for the entire family. You don't need to heap yours on top of the pile."

"I should have told him I was his father years ago."

"I won't disagree with you there. Keeping the secret was a bad idea, but it's not too late to make up for it."

"I've revised my will to make Kevin and James Cullen equal beneficiaries."

"I'm not talking about your estate. I'm talking about your love. Why are you here? Why aren't you in Italy with him?"

Elliott let out a discouraged breath. "He doesn't want my help."

"Maybe not your financial help, but how about your emotional support for his new venture?"

"He knows I don't like wine."

With an inkling of annoyance at Elliott's stubbornness, Jack walked to the bar to pour another drink. "It's time you acquired a taste for it. My God, your wife owns a winery, and now your son does, too."

"Pour me one, will you?"

Jack handed him a glass. "*Slainte.*"

"*Slainte.*" Elliott took a sip and then said, "Have ye decided what ye're going to do about Amy?"

The change in topics didn't go unnoticed. But Jack would circle back around to Kevin quickly, because he didn't want to talk about Amy. "There's nothing I can do. I assume she's still with Joe Gilbert."

"They're not married," Elliott said. "There's been no application for a marriage license, no wedding showers, no bachelorette parties. At least not any that have made the social columns in the New York papers, or her hometown in South Carolina. She and Joe are high-profile enough that something would have shown up."

"I wonder what she did with the diamond brooch." Jack gestured with his thumb toward Elliott's desk. "It should be in the box with the others."

"She's a smart girl. It's probably in a safety deposit box."

"Are you guessing, or do you know?"

"We know where the brooch is. The real question is, where are ye?"

"What do you mean?"

"The last conversation we had in this room, I told ye I wished I had the wisdom of my grandsire to help you muddle through what ached yer soul."

"You also told me," Jack said, "I'd find what I was looking for."

"Maybe not today. Maybe not tomorrow, but it will come to ye."

Jack cupped his glass between his hands and bowed his head. "Master Obi-Wan, you also told me not to rush it, to listen to the rhythm of the story, to let it happen organically."

"And the richness of the adventure would play out if ye gave it room to breathe."

"We're getting older," Jack said. "Our memories are fading, but we seem to remember sage advice quite well. We don't always take it, though, do we?"

"Ye've taken it, Jackson," Elliott said. "There's a peace about ye. It wasn't there before. Ye're still a wee bit unsettled, but ye've moved on from Carolina Rose's death."

"Peace is a daily process of changing opinions, eroding old obstacles, and quietly building new ones."

"If ye say so," Elliott said.

"I've knocked down the beliefs that allowed me to put myself first. I thought I deserved it. I don't. I'll never chase a dream at the expense of someone else ever again. I've been on the path toward enlightenment for several decades. But the path has had more figure eights than straight lines. Right now, I'm on a straight line. I might veer off into another figure eight, but if I do, I have a feeling I'll autocorrect quickly enough."

Elliott pulled a handkerchief out of his pants pocket, wiped his nose, folded it meticulously so his initial was on the top corner, then put it away. The ritual was both familiar and comforting. He was a man of many emotions, and had never shied away from revealing them.

"Ye're no longer broken, are ye?"

Jack's heart stuttered and shoved his emotions to the surface. "I can laugh. I can smile with feeling. I can love. I never would have started on the journey if I hadn't met Carolina Rose. And I never would have continued the journey if I hadn't met Amy. In a couple of days, Patrick and I are going to the plantation. He's going to school, and I'm going back to work on my latest novel. Life is good, Master Obi-Wan, and it will continue to get better."

Jack finished his drink and put his glass in the sink. "You know, you've never stopped loving me, even when I deserved your censure. Your advice has always been spot on. So, I'm going to give you some first-rate counseling. Go to Kevin. Love him like you've never loved anyone before. Don't give up on him. JL needs him back, and so do I."

52

Three months later Tuscany, Italy—JL

JL DIDN'T DISCOVER until the plane headed out over the Atlantic that Meredith had no intention of going to the harvest and every intention of sending JL by herself. Short of parachuting out of the plane, she was on her way to Tuscany and a reunion with Kevin.

She had dropped a few pounds, toned every muscle in her body, and, for the first time in her life, was running a seven-and-a-half-minute mile. Her sculpted body looked different in and out of clothes. Last week, she showcased her svelte figure in a to-die-for champagne-colored silk satin dress at a cocktail reception fundraiser at the farm. The evening ended with a dinner invitation from a Lexington attorney.

Of course, the next day she called and cancelled, but she was pleased she'd been asked.

She looked better, felt better, ate better than she ever had in her life. Her semi-permanent vacation fit with her new exercise regime. Even if Kevin turned her away at the door, while she would be disappointed, she wouldn't be too heartbroken. The latest version of Jenny Lynn O'Grady was the one she had always strived to be, and had always fallen short.

Before she disembarked the plane in Florence, she sent Jack a text: *Wish me luck. Hugs, JL*

He wrote back: *You know exactly what to do. Now go kill it. Hugs back, J*

She and Jack had spent hours talking about the trip. He put himself in Kevin's shoes and told her what Kevin needed from her, what he would expect from a visit, and what would make him happy. Then he told JL exactly what she could do and what she couldn't. Flirt, yes. Short kisses were permissible, but no inappropriate touching, and absolutely no sex. Jack's list of dos and don'ts didn't include any ifs or maybes. The goal was to finish every encounter with Kevin wanting more.

Sex wasn't the problem with JL and Kevin. The problem was they didn't know how to laugh together, or how to eat ice cream, or how to dance in the moonlight. The plan was simple. Kevin needed to court her, and she needed to let herself be courted. If she didn't, she would never know if they had a relationship worth saving.

The car service was waiting on the tarmac when the plane landed. She deplaned with confidence, but it slowly ebbed with each mile.

She sent Jack a text: *I'm scared. What if he won't see me?*

Jack responded: *Where are you?*

She replied: *In the driveway.*

He responded: *Then he already knows you're there. Relax. Hugs, J*

Surprise visits like this never worked out, and she had low expectations, but she was going through with it, because...well, why not? She looked like a million bucks dressed in this tan leather skirt suit with a wide matching belt by a Belgian designer. The suit and shoes cost a small fortune, but she looked like a runway model.

The driver guided the limo up the long driveway to an estate villa surrounded by sun-soaked hilltops and vibrant vineyards rolling to infinity, and dotted with red poppies and hot pink sweet peas.

He stopped the car on the cobblestone drive in front of an oversized oak door, darkened, as JL had learned, with the patina of four hundred years.

She gathered her poise with a deep breath and positive thoughts, then knocked.

A beautiful dark-haired woman opened the door. *"Ciao*

benvenuto."

"*Ciao, qui è Kevin?*" JL asked.

"*È al piano di sopra. Lo farò.*"

JL muddled through the translation, and thought the woman said Kevin was upstairs, but she wasn't positive. The woman left her in a warm and welcoming foyer with brick arches, wood-beamed ceilings and terracotta tiled floors. After five minutes, JL sat in the living room decorated with neutral-toned sofas and glass-topped side tables. After ten minutes, she got up and paced.

After fifteen minutes, she sent Jack a text: *15 minutes and he hasn't come down.*

Jack responded: *He's taking a shower. Relax.*

She put her phone away and stared out the window overlooking the red and yellow vineyards. She was too nervous to really appreciate the beauty.

"Hi, JL."

She wasn't prepared for the sound of Kevin's voice—the voice which had whispered *I love you* hundreds of times—nor was she prepared for what it would do to her insides. Her heart stilled. Butterflies took flight in her stomach. Her toes tingled. Oh, and her breath got lost along the way.

She still couldn't look at him.

"I'm sorry I kept you waiting. I'd been out in the field, and had to jump in the shower."

Turn around. Turn around and look at him.

She did, and instantly reached out for the chair, hoping the ladderback would support her when her own legs couldn't. He had lost at least fifteen pounds. He was lean, tanned, and mouth-wateringly gorgeous. His brown hair was streaked with gold, and her fingers itched to tunnel them through the soft, damp waves. He wore a short, recently barbered beard, the same golden color as his hair, and the muscles in his arms rippled as he moved toward her.

She couldn't walk. She couldn't talk. And she could barely breathe.

Was he real? Or was he the dream that had haunted her nights and most of her days? She reached out to him, and he took her hand. It wasn't the hand she remembered. This one was rough, as if he spent days in the fields, and calloused by the tools of his new trade.

The look he gave her settled on her in a most unsettling way. "You look beautiful, JL. You've always been beautiful, but there is something different about you. Your hair is longer. Your makeup is perfect, but it's more than that." He stroked her face with the tips of his fingers. "Your eyes are bright and shining. I don't see any pain there now. There's no strain on your face, and your mouth and jaw aren't tensed." He ran his fingertip along the seam of her lips. "You look so damn kissable."

He leaned down and gently fitted his mouth over hers. It wasn't a hungry kiss, a devouring kiss, but slow and still, and she lost herself in the touch of his skin, the tickle of his beard, and in the need to be close and closer still. She gathered her senses and stepped back before it went beyond a hello kiss.

"You look amazing. I love the beard." She rubbed her upper lip. "It tickles."

"So I've been told."

She immediately bristled and flashed him a look, afraid of what he meant.

He gave her fingers a gentle squeeze. "No, no. It's not what you're thinking. My barber told me women say that. I haven't had any personal experience until I kissed you."

"I'd have no right to complain if you did."

"Maybe you see it that way, but I don't."

"I haven't kissed anybody either, with or without a beard…if it matters."

"It matters a lot to me."

"Okay, we got that out of the way," she said. "You haven't slept with anyone, and neither have I. And since, for you, kissing is a big part of sex, if we have sex again, we won't need to have a bunch of tests."

He laughed, and the quick smile that followed set off an explosion of warmth in her midsection.

"You always do cut to the chase."

She wondered what to do now. It was a dance requiring artful steps until they both found their equilibrium. Kevin must have sensed it, and took the lead.

"Come on, I'll show you around." He put his hand on her lower back, and she almost threw him on the sofa and jumped his frigging bones. She had never wanted him more than she did right now, and although she tried not to look, the bulge in his khakis told her his desire was as strong as hers.

"The house is extraordinary," Kevin said, "but the view from the back is what sold me on the property."

They walked out onto a pergola-covered brick terrace, enclosed by balustrades, and filled with large terra-cotta pottery planted with lemon trees, red and white flowers, and luscious vines and ferns. Red and yellow vineyard-covered hills stretched out even further than what she had seen in the front of the house, and the fields were utterly breathtaking.

"Who does all the work?" she asked.

"I've lost count of the regular employees. It seems I add someone daily. The woman who answered the door is the wine-tasting manager. She also books luncheons and tours. I have two cooks, a wait staff, a housekeeper, a groundskeeper, plus a dozen full-time employees directly related to the production of wine: the winemaking director, winemaker, the cellar master, operations director, and others."

"Are you a hands-on manager?"

"I've wanted to learn everyone's job, so I've been all over, doing a little bit of everything." He looked at his hands. "I'm sorry they're so calloused."

She took his hand and kissed his palm. "You've earned every callous you have."

He pulled out a chair at the table and JL sat, looking at the view.

"Enough about me. Tell me what you're doing. How's Austin?"

"I quit the company," she said. "Or, rather I resigned my position. I'm on the board and attend meetings, but I'm not doing much. Connor stepped into my job."

Kevin sat beside her and leaned forward, putting their heads close together. "That must have been a difficult decision."

She closed her eyes for a moment and let the sun beat down on her face. "Actually, it was very easy."

"I'll admit to checking you out in the skin-tight suit you're wearing. If you've got a gun strapped on you, it's a wee one."

"I gave up my gun."

"That surprises me."

"It surprised me too. But after what happened on the ship, I had to make some changes." She didn't want to talk about what happened any more than Kevin wanted to hear about it. One day, if they got back together, they would have to, but it wasn't important now. "Has Elliott been here?" she asked, changing the subject.

"You didn't know?"

"Know what?"

"He was here when I bought the place, went home, and then came right back. He just left last week."

"Elliott's been here for three months?"

Kevin nodded. "Pretty much. He missed Meredith too much to stay the whole time, but he was back within a week after every visit. He's still not completely sold on wine, but he's drinking more of it, and he's learning the business. You would have thought he knew more about the industry than he does. The sales figures have surprised him."

"He's a man of many talents, and hiding his whereabouts is one of them. That stinker. I thought he was in Scotland."

She thought back to the day Elliott confessed to being Kevin's bio dad. The surprise announcement triggered a host of unresolved issues, and while he and Kevin had tried to work through them during the first few months, the distance between them only widened.

"Did you talk to him about the big secret?"

Kevin sat back in his chair and stroked his beard. His expression was soft, eyes unguarded. "We talked a lot, yelled a lot, and cried even more. I aired the grievances I'd been holding in for twenty years. He told me that after James Cullen was born, he resented the agreement he made with my mother to keep her secret, but he couldn't undo it without hurting her."

"Elliot was caught in the middle and wanted to do what was best for you, too."

"Except it wasn't. He should have told me. My anger and resentment have been eating at me for months, and that, coupled with what happened last fall, and the pressure of the wedding, pushed me over the edge."

"But you're good now? I mean…the two of you? You've worked it out?"

"If we could have had just one knock-down-drag-out screaming match and resolved our issues, we would have hugged, and Elliott would have gone home. But one tearful conversation couldn't heal a decades-old fracture. I got pissed and walked away a few times, and so did he. Some days we completely ignored each other, and other days we talked incessantly."

"What was the breakthrough?"

"We were having dinner at a restaurant on the outskirts of Florence a couple of weeks ago when this ninety-year-old woman, all gray-haired and hunchbacked, came up and said to Elliott, 'The love you have for your son, and the love your son has for you, is so beautifully expressed in the way you mirror each other. When son moves back, father moves forward. When father moves back, son moves forward, in a dance as old as time, and as dependable as the tides.'"

"How prophetic," JL said.

"Yeah, well, we thought so, too. We looked at the woman. We looked at each other. And then, as if on cue, we burst out laughing, finally realizing we were the two biggest dumbasses in the world. Our past did not have to be our prologue. Elliott ordered the most expensive bottle of wine in the wine cellar. When the glasses were poured, he made a toast, 'To my son, Kevin Fraser, a man I love and respect.'"

JL's eyes misted, and she blinked to clear the dampness on her lashes. "That couldn't have happened without all the conversations that took place before that night. You wouldn't have been doing the dance if healing hadn't already taken place. You just needed that final punch in the gut to accept it. I'm so happy for you."

Kevin turned away from her to look out across the vineyards and reflexively whisked away the bead of sweat trickling down his temple. Then, giving her a bittersweet smile that easily broke the tension of the last few minutes, he said, "Are you hungry? How about lunch?"

Her stomach—unless she was rolled up in the fetal position crying her heart out—had a built-in response when food was mentioned, so she didn't have to think whether she was hungry or not. It automatically growled.

"You know me. I can always eat."

"From the looks of you, you haven't eaten much lately."

She instantly forgave Ted for every hour he tortured her in the gym. Kevin's appreciative gaze made it all worthwhile. "It's just shuffled around."

"I can see Ted's training fingerprints all over you. He put you through your paces. I bet you can lift fifty pounds more than you were lifting. I've done rehab with him. He can be brutal." Kevin looked off in the distance again, and she knew he was trying as hard as she was to control his emotions. The mention of his rehab following the shooting was painful for them both.

"How about a glass of wine? Red or white?"

"You choose."

"Don't go anywhere. I mean, feel free to walk around. I just don't want you to leave."

Did he not want her to ever leave, or just not leave today? If she asked him, he wouldn't be able to answer, and if he asked her to stay beyond the weekend, she wouldn't be able to answer that, either. Not yet, anyway.

Kevin returned to the house, and while she studied the landscape, she backtracked in her mind. They met a year ago in Napa, and the man who just walked off to get a bottle of wine was not the same man she met then. There was a new maturity about him, and he was more comfortable in his skin.

Kevin returned with a bottle of white wine and two glasses. "I hope this one suits you. It's a *Vernaccia di San Gimignano*, one of Italy's finest white wines. It's characteristically dry, with crisp acidity, and a slightly bitter finish. Here we use oak aging to give the wine another layer of complexity and roundness." He poured an ounce in her glass and handed it to her.

She studied the wine. "Straw yellow color." She swirled and sniffed. "Gentle floral and citrus, with undertones of fruits and fresh herbs, lemon zest, sage, hints of anise and almonds, with a crisp finish. On a day like today, I would pair it with…I don't know… Maybe chicken scallopini."

He poured more into her glass and filled one for himself. "You're in luck. That's exactly what's on the menu."

He joined her at the table and sipped his wine. "I have a picture of us taken at the gala last year. I keep it by my bed. You looked beautiful that night, but today you look amazing."

"Are you hitting on me?"

"No. I just want you to know." He took another sip. "Did you fly in this morning?"

"I just arrived."

"You're welcome to stay here. I have a guest room…several, actually."

"I don't think that's a good idea. I booked a room in Florence at the Helvetia & Bristol."

Their conversation was interrupted by the woman who answered the door. "Do you want salad?" Her English was as perfect as her smile.

"No, thank you," JL said.

The woman left, and returned immediately with bread, followed by their entrée. JL dug into the dish. Maria had spoiled her for most Italian food, but Kevin's chef did an excellent job with the dish.

"Tell me what you've been doing the past three months besides working out," he said.

"Reading, decorating the house, learning to cook Italian."

His eyebrow lifted. "How's that going?"

"You knew Isabella and Maria came back with us, right?"

"And Gabe and Patrick."

"Isabella and Maria live with me, and Pops has been spending more time in Kentucky. I think he and Maria are interested in each other."

"Really? She's a beautiful woman. If she can cook half as well as her sister, Lilla, she'll win Pops' heart."

"Isabella is going to the University of Kentucky. I had her working with tutors this summer before she enrolled as a freshman. Most of the classes are way too easy, but she's still getting adjusted. Austin has taken it upon himself to show her around and introduce her to people, mostly basketball players."

"What about Patrick?"

"He's living with Jack, and comes to the farm once a month to spend time with James Cullen and Emily. He's doing well, especially since he hasn't had a formal education. I'm really proud of him."

"And Jack…"

"He's writing, working in his garden, but mostly he's taking care of Patrick. We go to dinner when he comes to the farm, and talk or text almost every day."

Kevin put his fork down, leaned back in his chair, and stroked his beard again. "You've never been a member of Jack's fan club. Is something going on between you two?"

"He's in love with someone else, and, honestly, so am I."

"Oh." Kevin smiled at her, his bright eyes squinting against the sunlight. "Anybody I know?"

She pointed with her fork. "You aren't really that dumb, are you?"

"Are you saying you're in love with me?"

"I guess I am," she said.

He leaned close and kissed her, and the feel of his lips against hers stole her breath. "There's so much that's different about you, but the taste of you is exactly as I remembered."

"It's the chicken scallopini." She pushed her plate aside, refilled her glass. Then she sat back and twirled the stem of the goblet. "I didn't come here for weekend sex."

"Why'd you come?"

"I want to know if there's anything left of us. If there's not, then—"

He put a finger against her lips. "I don't want weekend sex, either. I mean, honestly, I'd love to take you to bed right now, but it wouldn't answer the question we both need answered. Is it just sex between us, or do we have something special? Something more?"

"Where do we go from here?"

"I didn't know you were coming. I don't have a plan. You always have one. So you tell me," Kevin said.

She took a sip, wiped her mouth. "I've never been to Italy. Show me your adoptive country. Let's drink good wine, eat good food, and see what happens."

"May I kiss you?"

"You can kiss me good night when you drop me at the hotel."

"I can't talk you into staying here?"

She shook her head. "If you talked me into staying here, how long do you suppose it would take you to talk me into sharing your bed?"

"If you're as hot as I am right now, probably less than thirty seconds," he said.

She could easily tell how turned on he was, and she knew how wet she was. He knew it, too. She leaned into him and whispered, "Less than five."

The tenderness in his fingers as he raised her chin, and the hot, deep wonder of his kiss when his lips found hers, was a touch at first, molding shape against shape, and then a sudden burst of hunger as his tongue slid deep within her mouth. She inhaled his virile scent, heavy with arousing male musk. He pulled her onto his lap, and her breasts pressed against him as they continued the kiss.

Her nipples hardened, as did Kevin.

And then she came to her senses.

"I can't do this." She scooted off his lap and reclaimed her chair. "See how easy it is? We could go to bed and spend the next forty-eight hours making love, raiding the refrigerator at midnight, and everything would be great, but nothing would be resolved. Emotionally, I can't handle that. If we can't set boundaries and abide by them, then I'm going home."

"You've turned me on from the moment I met you in the Welcome Center at the winery, but right now, I've never wanted you more. We're not kids, JL. We can be responsible."

"The problem is, Kevin, when it comes to sex, we *are* like kids. We're opposites that attract with a powerful magnetic force. It's our chemistry. We can't resist each other. I have to know if there's more than great sex between us. And honestly, I'm not sure there is. Your depression affected your sex drive, and when we weren't having sex every day, things got worse between us. I'm convinced if we had been a stronger couple, we would have been able to work through it. But we couldn't. So maybe I've had the answer to my question within me all along."

He walked over to the balustrades, rested his foot on the top rail, and gazed out over the vibrant vineyards. He didn't say anything for several minutes. JL just sat there, still as stone, and watched him struggle with his thoughts. She wasn't going to give him an out or try to protect him. He was on his own, wrestling with his soul.

Finally, he turned around and said, "Have you already checked into your hotel?"

"No, I showered on the plane."

"Give me fifteen minutes. Then we'll go to your hotel. You can change into more comfortable touring clothes. We'll see as much of Florence as we can this afternoon, have dinner, and then I'll take you back to the hotel. Tomorrow, we'll tour Tuscany."

"Are you sure?"

There was another heavy silence, and then he said. "Yes, I'm sure. How long are you staying?"

"The plane will be here on Monday."

He nodded. "There's a bathroom right off the foyer, if you want to freshen up. I need to make a couple of phone calls. Can you entertain yourself for fifteen to twenty minutes?"

"Go, do what you have to do. I'll have another glass of wine."

He pulled her to her feet for a hug, and then claimed her mouth in a kiss so deeply passionate, so uniquely him that she almost lost the grip on her resolve. And then he walked away.

She carried her glass of wine with her and walked the length of the terrace, down a set of steps, and out onto the manicured lawn with an extraordinary panoramic view of the countryside. The path followed the curve of the hilltop, past a patio shaded by a rose-covered gazebo. Farther along the path she reached a vegetable garden with cucumbers, tomatoes, strawberries, and more. As she circled around to the other side, she found a bench swing, where she sat and finished her wine, basking in a breeze scented with wildflowers.

She returned to the terrace just as Kevin came out of the house.

"Are you ready to go?" he asked. "I called in a few favors and arranged for tickets to the Uffizi Gallery, the Duomo and the Baptistery, and the Accademia Gallery to see Michelangelo's *David*. We'll have five hours to see what would normally take two days."

"I'm ready."

"I thought we'd stop at Vivoli, one of the most famous gelaterias in Florence, between the Duomo and the Accademia Gallery. I also made dinner reservations at the *La Bottega del Buon Caffe*. Then after dinner we'll stroll across the Ponte Vecchio. I also called a car service. I don't want to drink and drive."

"Yeah, right. I know you well. You want to make out in the back seat."

He tossed his head back and laughed—a welcoming, almost musical sound. "Come on, O'Grady. Let's go sightseeing."

53

Present day Florence, Italy—JL

AT TEN O'CLOCK that evening, Kevin walked JL to the registration desk at the Helvetia & Bristol, a luxury five-star hotel a stone's throw from the Piazza degli Strozzi, the Duomo, and high-end boutiques, located in the heart of the city's historical center.

"May I have the key to Room 206, please?" she asked, laughing because Kevin was tickling her.

The clerk pivoted and faced a decorative panel on the wall with eighty mail slots and hooks for keys. Kevin's hand slipped down her hip and he gave her a gentle squeeze. She squiggled. The clerk found box 206 and lifted the key and its attached gold fob off the hook. "Is there anything else I can do for you, Ms. O'Grady?" he asked, handing her the key.

She had been there less than a day and the staff already knew her name. "What time is breakfast?"

"Seven to nine," he said.

"Great. Thanks." She took Kevin's hand that had been teasing her, and led him down the corridor toward the stairs. "We're taking the steps." The elevator was less than ten feet from the registration desk, and she didn't want Kevin kissing her goodnight in front of the clerk.

He leaned down close to her ear, his breath stirring her hair, and said, "You're afraid to get into a little mirrored elevator with me, aren't you?"

She pretended to ponder, rubbing her chin. This was one of the reasons they'd had such a delightful day—sassy humor, easy dialogue, and potent attraction. "Yes, I am."

They climbed to the second floor and she led him down the hall to her room. "Here I am." She unlocked the door and invited him in.

"Nice…" he said, looking around the king size bedroom with its plush sofa, Art Nouveau wall lamps, and a view of the Palazzo Strozzi.

JL tossed her purse on the bed and kicked off her shoes. "When I arrived, I found a bowl of fruit and a handwritten welcoming note. I was impressed. The staff is awesome."

His gaze drifted and settled on her mouth. "Can I kiss you now?" He didn't move beyond the closed door, didn't touch her at all, but she felt the look he gave her in all the places his kisses had warmed her in the past. Then he reached out and put his hand on the back of her neck and brought her close. Her eyes fluttered shut as his mouth hovered a breath away from hers.

"I want you, but I'll walk away, if that's what you want."

He captured her mouth in a scorching kiss laden with months of pent-up desire and longing. She moved against him, searching for the perfect alignment of their bodies, but she was too short. She raised her leg, rubbed it against him, a signal for him to pick her up. He did. She wrapped her legs around him, and a burst of heat jolted through her.

Every time she tried to finish the kiss, he pressed harder, coaxing her to stay open for him, tasting slowly, with wild, fresh erotic kisses, confusing her senses. She groped his shoulders, her fingers curving over the hard muscles of his neck. He put his hands under her butt, moving her against his erection.

The full-on pressure of him was extraordinary. He was unbelievably hard—everywhere. He kissed her until the sensations flowed in directions she couldn't go tonight. The desperate ache clamored low in her body, and she knew if she slept with him, all the defenses she had built in the last few months would be shattered, with no guarantees they had a tomorrow.

The tension in his arms, taut and powerful, vibrated against her, and the wild beat of his heart thundered in her ear. "I love you, Kevin, but I can't do this."

He groaned, and held her without moving, her head resting in the crook of his neck, and then he squeezed her tightly. "I know, lass."

He had never called her that before, and she was surprised by how much it delighted her. She wasn't sure why at first, and then she knew. It was Kevin's way of acknowledging who he was—Elliott's son, a Scotsman.

Kevin carried her to the bed, put her down, and sat beside her. "I had so much fun today. Why didn't we ever spend an afternoon like this before?"

She tilted her head, studied him, and his gaze was steady as he looked back at her. "We took what we had for granted, didn't we? We thought we had everything we needed, but we didn't. We never learned how to laugh together, or how to sit quietly and watch the world go by, like we did when we ate those silly gelatos. I want another day like today."

"I'll give you another day, and another, if that's what you want. Then we'll talk." He stroked her face and down the side of her neck. Then his hand dropped and he sat there, sighing deeply. "Okay. I have an idea. Be ready at six-forty-five, and dress in running gear."

"Run? You want to run with me? Are you sure you're up for it?" She gave him a teasing grin. "I'm a lot faster than I was the last time we ran together."

He laughed. "So am I. Let's sprint the last ten meters. Winner buys the next gelatos."

She kissed him. "Deal."

He got up off the bed, pulled his shirt down, adjusted himself. "You're killing me, JL."

"Right back at ya, kiddo. I'm hurting, too."

He shook his head as he walked out the door. "I hope you sleep well. I sure as hell won't."

Laughing, she locked the door behind him. Their perfect day was everything she wanted, but was it possible to have another and another?

She sent Jack a text: *Wonderful day. We laughed. We danced. We laughed. We drank wine. We ate gelato. We laughed. We ate. We flirted. We kissed. No sex. Hugs, JL*

Jack wrote back: *Good. Don't give in. Keep laughing. You know what he needs. If you have sex, all bets are off. Stay strong. Hugs, J*

54

Present day Florence, Italy—JL

JL DIDN'T SLEEP well, even though the hotel's king size bed and linens were comfortable and luscious. She kept rolling over and hugging her pillow, wishing it was Kevin. Finally, at five-thirty she gave up and ordered coffee, returned emails to Meredith and Austin, and stretched. Then at six-thirty, dressed to run, she went downstairs to wait for Kevin. She was sitting in the lobby when he came through the hotel's main door—gorgeous, muscular, tanned, and hotter than hell.

She jumped up and rushed to meet him. "I've already stretched. Let's go."

He laughed. "You don't trust me."

"Nope. Fool me once…"

"Come here."

She stepped over to him and he patted her hips. "You really aren't carrying, are you?"

"Are you serious? You just wanted to touch me. You knew I didn't have a gun."

"I couldn't sleep last night, because I couldn't stop thinking about you. The only consolation I had was I might get to stretch you out before our run."

She laughed and smacked him in the arm. "You're pitiful. Let's go."

The city was almost deserted. They ran past the facades of some of Florence's most breathtaking buildings, now more breathtaking while illuminated by the first rays of Tuscan sun. The city's piazzas were bathed in early morning light, and JL fell in love with Florence. She kept pace with him through the entire run. She pointed out shops she wanted to return to later, and after an hour they stopped at a restaurant on one of the tiny cobblestone streets near the Duomo for breakfast.

JL enjoyed a cup of yogurt with berries, a muffin, and coffee. "This is the perfect way to start the day."

"I like the way we used to start our day better," he said, teasingly.

"I think we should get you a gelato so you'll get sex off your mind."

"Sex is on my mind every morning when I wake up and see your picture on my bedside table."

She made a T with her hands. "Look. You're horny. I'm horny. But I'm not having sex with you. Let's have fun and try not to think about it. Where are we going today?"

"You can't blame a man for trying, can you?"

"No, but I'm beginning to feel like a stubborn nail jutting out of a piece of plywood."

"Because I keep hitting on you?" He laughed, and then he said, "We're going to Pisa. I've got a Segway tour scheduled."

"Segway? Really?"

"I brought my clothes. Do you mind if I shower in your room? We'll save time. Our reservation is at eleven."

"Okay, but…"

"I promise to behave and not put any more stress on the stubborn nail."

They walked back to the hotel, and Kevin took the first shower. While he was in the bathroom, she sent Jack a text: *"Went for a run. Kevin is here taking a shower. We're going to Pisa for a Segway tour."*

Jack responded: *Stay strong. You know what he needs. Don't give in. Hugs, J*

She replied: *It's getting harder to stay strong.*

She checked her emails and responded to several. Kevin came out wearing khakis and a polo shirt, his hair still damp.

"Your turn. I'll be downstairs. Take your time."

Her phone dinged with a message. Kevin glanced at the screen. "You've got a message from Jack. Is that your daily text or is he responding to yours?" Kevin's voice held a note of uncertainty.

She unlaced her running shoes. "He's responding to me. No big deal."

"Tell him I said hello." Kevin opened the door. But before he left he said, "Tell me again there's nothing going on between you two."

She tugged off her socks and tossed them into the dirty clothes pile. "There's nothing going on between us. He's in love with Amy…" She smiled at Kevin. "And I'm in love with you."

He smiled back, but it wasn't a full-throttled one. "I'll meet you downstairs."

She picked up her phone and read the text. *You can do it.*

She sent a reply: *Kevin saw your message. I think he's jealous.*

Jack responded: *Nip it in the bud. NOW! Reassure him. Take flirting to the next level. No sex. Hugs, J*

If she stopped to think about it, she would probably laugh hysterically that Jack Mallory, serial dater, was giving her dating advice.

She took a quick shower and was downstairs in under thirty minutes. "I'm ready." She was dressed in a short rugby sweater dress and white sneakers, with her hair pulled up in a fashionably messy bun, exposing her neck, in hopes he would kiss it.

He did, nibbling gently around her ear, and he smelled like butter and jam. "That's a different look for you."

"Do you like it?"

"Hmm. I like everything about you, but you look sixteen."

"Is sixteen good or bad?"

He gave her earlobe a little tweak. "It's good as long as people don't think I'm your father."

She put her arm around his waist and pulled him to her. "Come on, old man. Let's go Segway riding."

Ninety minutes later they arrived in Pisa, and were soon zipping around the maze of medieval streets. They stopped at the Piazza dei Miracoli to see the Duomo, Baptistery, the iconic Leaning Tower, and the Sapienza Palace where Galileo once studied. Then they raced through the upscale shopping district of the Borgo Stretto until they reached the Arno River, where they savored another gelato before returning to the starting point of the tour.

They turned in their Segways, then headed back to the shopping district where JL bought gifts for all the kids, as well as Maria and Isabella.

On the drive back to Florence, Kevin asked, "Do you have any interest in stopping at the American Cemetery? I've never been there before. It's a little out of the way, but we can go there."

"I'd love to. A great uncle of mine fought in the landings at Anzio Beach and the expansion of the beachhead during World War II. He died there. Would he be buried here?"

"I think that's the Sicily-Rome American Cemetery, but we can ask."

Kevin pulled into the parking lot of the small, relatively hidden American World War II cemetery at four-forty-five. When JL got out of the car, she heard a recording of a bugle playing "Taps" over a public-address system.

She grabbed Kevin's hand. "They're lowering the flag. Let's go watch."

They walked to the entrance, which led to the center of the cemetery where the flagpole stood. White crosses marked hundreds of graves spanning out from the flag pole in evenly spaced straight lines. "Taps" finished playing, and an eerie silence pervaded the beautiful cemetery.

"If you have your phone, will you take pictures?" she asked.

Kevin snapped pics of the flag, the grounds, a few selfies of them together, and JL standing frozen, mesmerized, while the flag flowed into the waiting hands of a staff member.

When the man saw them, he asked, "Would one of you like to

help me fold the flag?"

"Really?" JL asked.

"If we have visitors at the end of the day, we always ask for help."

"Go ahead. You do it," Kevin said. "I'll video you."

"Pops will love this." She gingerly took hold of one end of the flag, and together JL and the staff member folded it lengthwise, and in half, and half again, before making triangular folds until the entire length of the flag was folded. She released the flag into the man's hands.

"Thank you for allowing me this honor," she said.

She and Kevin strolled away holding hands. She picked up a brochure from a box near the Memorial Center, and perused it. "You're right. Most of those buried here are from the Fifth Army who died in the fighting that followed the capture of Rome in June 1944, and others who fell in the heavy fighting in the Apennines between then and May 2, 1945. The whole time I was folding the flag, I kept thinking about Pops' uncle, and all the other young men who lost their lives in Italy. I'm so glad we stopped."

Kevin opened the car door, and she slid into the passenger seat, reading more of the brochure.

"Will you come back to the winery tonight?" he asked.

"That's not a good idea, Kevin."

"What if we agree we'll just hold each other?"

She put the brochure in her purse, turned in the seat to find him watching her, a smile softening the crows' feet at the corners of his eyes. God, he was sexy—and doubly so when he smiled like that. She point-blanked it with a directness he had always appreciated. "I'm not strong enough to stop at just holding you. One kiss will lead to a deeper one, and in ten more seconds I'll have all my clothes off, and you'll be inside me."

"What if I promise to be strong enough for both of us?"

She reached up to push his hair back from his face, and he closed his eyes at her touch. "Can you do that?"

His eyes popped open. "You don't trust me."

"I trust you completely, but I don't trust myself, and I don't want to beg you to make love to me. We've had a wonderful weekend. We've laughed more than we've laughed since we met. We've been silly and teasing, and I've adored every minute I've been with you. Neither of us has ever been this relaxed and vulnerable. That's what I want to take home."

He leaned on the open car door, and together they looked beyond the base of the hillside, toward the summit topped by the carving of a woman clutching an olive branch while flying on the back of an eagle—a symbol of peace soaring over the gravesites.

"Will you at least have dinner at the winery? I'll grill steaks. We can eat on the terrace, and then I'll take you back to the hotel."

She considered the offer along with Jack's sage advice.

"You need to understand what he wants as a man," Jack said. "Listen to him and hear what he's not saying. Most of the time guys talk in a different language, and women misinterpret. If he offers to cook or grill out, jump on it. He'll feel like he's taking care of you. It's a macho thing. It harkens back to prairie fires and roasted rabbits over spits."

"That sounds lovely," she said.

55

Present day Tuscany, Italy—JL

KEVIN DROVE BACK to the winery, and JL took a quick shower in his bathroom while he started the grill. She hated putting her dirty clothes back on, so she slipped on one of his long sleeve button-down shirts and rolled the sleeves to the elbows. After she found the washer and tossed her clothes in for a quick wash, she made her way to the kitchen.

An open bottle of wine and a glass were waiting for her there. Kevin had set out the ingredients for a pasta salad, one of her specialties. While the water boiled, she mixed the other ingredients. When the water hit the right temperature, she placed the penne into the boiling water and set the timer. When the timer went off, she poured the pasta into a strainer to cool, and took her wine glass out onto the candlelit terrace.

He whistled when he saw her. "You can dress up to look like a million bucks, but I've always thought you looked your sexiest when you're wearing my shirt." He pulled her into his arms and she looked up at him, at the deep brown of his eyes, the straight line of his nose, the beard that held the lingering scents of ginseng, eucalyptus and rosemary, and his mouth, so quick to curve up in amusement—a mouth that kissed her so exquisitely last night, a mouth she wanted desperately to kiss her now.

"Can you see yourself living here?" he asked.

"I'll live anywhere in the world with you, if..."

"If we work out our relationship?" He released her gently, flipped the steaks, and picked up his wine glass. "Okay then, what's the next step? When can you come back?"

She sat and crossed her legs. The tail of his shirt hit her mid-thigh, and his eyes stayed on her legs. "I don't know."

She turned slightly so her crossed legs fit under the table. "I'm splitting the month of October between the races at Keeneland and the harvest in Napa. Connor wants me to go to Colorado to see the new ranch. Shane wants me to go to New South Wales to see the property he's recommending the board purchase. Basketball starts in November, and it will go through March. I don't know when I can get back here."

"I thought you quit the company. Why are you looking at new property?"

"I'm still on the board. And we're trying to find a place for me that's not in security."

Kevin didn't respond further to her overbooked calendar, and the silence lengthened between them until the sizzling steaks intruded. Kevin removed them from the flame, transferring them to a platter.

Finally, he asked, "How do we work on a relationship if we can't be together?"

"FaceTime, email, text messages. We've gone three months without seeing each other or speaking."

"And you want to go three more?"

"I didn't say that."

"That's what it sounded like."

"We're all gathering in Scotland for Christmas. Will you come there?"

He laid the tongs on the cultured stone grilling island, crossed his arms, his ankles, and through the short distance between them she felt his heartbeat.

Even in the torchlight, he looked like a man evaluating his life and coming to terms with who he was and what he wanted.

She had seen the expression several times during the day, but it faded quickly, as if he tried it on and it didn't fit right. This time, though, it didn't fade away. She knew the moment the puzzle pieces snapped together, and he became fully aware.

He pulled her into his arms, they closed around her, and all she knew was the heat and textures of his kiss. He was spicy and hot, salty and sweet, rough and slick and alive, so alive. He picked her up and she straddled him. She wanted to consume him, to crawl inside his skin and know him again and again, the flesh and blood and heat of him.

He carried her over to the sofa in front of the roaring fire pit. "I'm not letting you leave here without the scent of you on my skin, in my hair, in my heart. I love you, JL. And I'll never leave you again, not even if you tell me to go."

He held out her diamond. "Will you take this back?"

"Are you sure? Is it really what you want, or do you just want my body?"

He sat on the edge of the sofa and took her hand. "It may seem like sex is our only bond, but making love cements us as a couple. It's the way we truly share ourselves. It reflects both our vulnerability and strengths. Sex energizes us, and we were addicted to the energy boost. It's why we got into the habit of finding time throughout the day for quickies. Being in each other's arms makes us happy. It inspires our creativity. Sex is an essential part of our lives, but it isn't all we have.

"We jumped into bed within hours of meeting last October— like crazy rabbits. We couldn't keep our hands off each other, even though we were in the middle of a major crisis involving people we loved. That sexual passion was the fuel that kept fear from consuming us. It's a strength, JL, not a weakness. What we have can't be bought. It's the biggest boost of happiness there is, and we need to celebrate it, not deny it.

"I love you with all my heart. And, yes, damn it. I want to be inside you and never, ever come out. I want my son growing inside you. I want to love you, protect you, cherish you every day for the rest of my life." He squeezed her hand. "Will you take me back? Will you marry me, Jen?"

She couldn't speak, she could only hold out her hand, and he slipped the ring back on her finger. It was warm from his touch, and the diamond gleamed in the firelight. Her finger tingled, welcoming the ring back where it belonged.

He kissed her hand. "I don't want a big wedding. I just want the family to come here for a private ceremony. Will that work for you?"

"I love you, Kevin. And I'll marry you on the moon if it's where you want our wedding to be. Come here and kiss me."

He stripped out of his clothes and ripped the buttons off the shirt she was wearing. After months of therapy, of long dark nights of the soul, he entered her, and in that moment, she knew they had both finally found their way back home.

Later that night, she sent Jack a text: *We had sex. It was everything we wanted. I'm wearing my ring. Kevin wants you to be best man.*

Jack responded: *Did you wear his shirt? It gets a man every time. Congrats! Yes, I'd be honored. Hugs, J*

She responded: *Thanks for opening my eyes. I never would have understood what he needs from me. Hugs, JL*

56

Present day (October) New York City—Amy

AMY CROSSED THE LOBBY of her apartment building on Central Park West, flipping through her mail. One item resembled a wedding invitation, and had a Florence, Italy, return address. Her mind scrolled through her mental contact list. She didn't know anyone who lived there.

She dropped the mail into her oversized bag and took the elevator to the tenth floor. As she exited, her cell rang. She glanced at the display and was surprised to see her boss's number. He rarely called, except to complain.

"Amy, I'm benching you."

"What? I'm fired?"

"Not today. I've rearranged the schedule. You have six days off, but you'll have to either work or travel for the next three weeks."

She unlocked her apartment door. "Thanks a lot," she said sarcastically. "I wasn't planning to take any time off until after the World Series. Apparently, though, you think I need it."

"You do. You've been in the booth or in the office blogging and tweeting every day and most nights for six straight weeks. Get out. Relax. Enjoy yourself. You've earned it."

"Wow. I'm sort of at a loss. I don't have anything planned. I guess I could sleep, veg out, and binge watch the fall season premieres I missed."

"There you go. See you next week."

She kicked off her shoes and fell back on the sofa, staring at the ceiling. What the heck was she going to do? No answer flashed across her apartment in neon lights. She needed a break, no argument there. But a planned break would have made more sense. She could have made reservations for a getaway.

She closed her eyes, turned onto her side, and Jack's face appeared. "Oh, go away." It was embarrassing to admit, even to herself, her moments of yearning were so bad at times she would take all his novels off the shelf and line them up just to stare at his book jackets. She rolled her eyes—how sick.

She switched tracks and considered vacation possibilities.

Why not take the Hampton Jitney to Amagansett for the weekend? Now that would be fun. Or she could rent a car for a crisp day's drive through the Hudson Valley. She'd seen an ad this morning for a tour through America's oldest winemaking and grape-growing region. The tour promised exquisite views of fall colors and tastings of award-winning wines. Sounded like fun.

She didn't consider herself a wine connoisseur, but during her adventure she developed an appreciation for wine, especially champagne. But not the expensive kind. She was holding out for one promised bottle, but every day, when she didn't hear from Jack...

She yanked the afghan off the back of the couch and screamed into it. Well, it was more like a loud groan, muffled by a red Pottery Barn cable knit throw. There was no point in crying over lost loves. Was there?

As soon as she returned last October—only moments after she had disappeared—she jumped right into the playoffs and the World Series and pushed Jack out of her mind, or tried to. She didn't Google him, she didn't stalk him, and she didn't ask anyone about him. She focused on Joe.

Following game seven, Joe had invited her on a weekend trip to the mountains. Thrilled, she packed a bag, convinced he arranged the mini-vacation so he could propose. Sadly, she returned home two days later without a ring.

At that point, she seriously considered breaking up with him. But he promised exciting getaways for Thanksgiving and Christmas. How could she not wait to see if he would deliver the goods?

The holidays rolled by and she still wasn't engaged. That was it. She was through waiting. But the eternal optimist in her gave him another deadline. If he didn't propose by Valentine's Day, it was over.

The day passed uneventfully, too.

After four years of waiting, she gathered up enough courage to quietly end what had dissolved months earlier. Removing what few items they kept at each other's apartments and saying goodbye ended up being a nonevent.

They agreed to keep it under wraps for a while, and she even agreed to attend a few social engagements to protect his image. He was involved in a merger and couldn't afford the kind of negative press a breakup with her would have generated.

How sad their time together ended without either of them caring. Maybe he had sensed her ambivalence. Good for him, if he had.

Jack had captured her heart, but she never reached out to him, other than to send the anonymous letter he requested. She read in the newspaper that his wife, Carolina Rose, died. The paparazzi reported shortly after her funeral that Jack was devastated and left the country.

She regularly scanned the gossip columns for news of him. She didn't find much, and when she did, she didn't know what to believe. He was either pining away at his Virginia plantation or partying with socialites in New York City and LA. She was holding out hope that in June he would call.

When June came and went and he hadn't called, she gave Jack until the end of July. Well, July passed quickly, and when she woke up on August 1, she decided it was time to stop waiting. She hadn't seen him in ten months. It was almost as if their time together never happened.

She did research Stephen, though, and found a few articles about him. One article reported a thorough search for his body was conducted on the *SS New York*. The authorities concluded he had jumped overboard due to depression caused by financial reversals threatening to bankrupt him. An additional article revealed an audit of Providence Loan Society's books found he had altered loan documents, resulting in the sale of several pieces of expensive jewelry from which he had personally profited. A third article, written months later, reported evidence was uncovered implicating him in the death of a former employee who was initially charged with fraud.

She found two articles about herself. The *Herald* reported Amy Spalding, her fiancé, and members of their traveling party disappeared under mysterious circumstances. Another article reported the shipping company claimed there was a mistake in the manifest, and Miss Spalding's party never boarded the *SS New York*, and their whereabouts remained unknown.

Amy did find a rather humorous comment from Lillian Russell about Jack's disappearance. "If you're looking for Jack Mallory, wait thirty years. He'll be back."

As for the woman, her two children, and Mustache Cop, Amy never found any mention at all.

As evil as Stephen turned out to be, she still felt guilty for killing him. So her daytime mind convinced her that he actually had jumped, as the investigation concluded. But her nighttime mind reminded her of the truth, and she often woke up in a cold sweat.

She tried talk therapy, more intensive exercise, and visualization, but what helped the most were anonymous group counseling sessions with other women who had caused someone's death either accidentally or intentionally. She could at least make it through an entire day without thinking about Stephen. But she couldn't say the same about Jack, JL, and the others.

She finally had to let them all go and move on. Their lives changed because of their adventure to rescue her, and they probably didn't want to be reminded of everything they'd endured. So, eventually, Jack, JL, Kevin, Isabella, Maria, Patrick, Gabriele, Connor, and Pete were relegated to her subconscious, while she turned her undivided attention to baseball.

Which brought Amy to where she was now. At loose ends.

She scrolled through the contacts on her cellphone and clicked on her travel agent's number. The call went straight to voice mail. She left a message. "Hey, Bill. This is Amy. I'm looking for a place in Amagansett for a few days—Wednesday to Monday. If you know of any rentals, give me a call."

Her phone rang ten minutes later.

"It's Bill. Sorry. Everything is booked."

"That sucks," she said.

"But, I can get you a good deal if you're interested in Napa. It's fall harvest, and a peak time to visit. I know a singles group with an opening in their charter. They're all professional people—investment broker-lawyer types. Interested? The spot will probably be snatched up by early afternoon."

"Send me an itinerary with the costs. I'll look at it and let you know ASAP."

"Great. You'll have an email in five minutes. Call me back."

She put the phone down, went to the kitchen, and poured a glass of juice. Did she really want to spend her vacation with a group of strangers at a Napa winery? What if they all hated baseball? Nah. Not in New York City. She could find something in common with a tour group full of lawyers and investment bankers. But was it really what she wanted to do with six days off?

Her inner voice said, *At least review the itinerary before you totally nix the idea.*

She carried the glass of juice back to the sofa, took a sip, then set it aside to read her mail and find out who sent her an invitation from Italy. She opened the seal with her thumbnail and tugged out the enclosed card. It was a wedding announcement for… JL and Kevin.

Amy jumped to her feet. "They got back together!" She danced around like an idiot, then plopped back down on the couch. JL and Kevin were getting married, and she couldn't believe it. If she'd known JL's number, she would have called right then. Amy looked at the announcement again. The wedding was on Saturday in Italy.

Saturday? And today was Tuesday.

What was the deal? A call from her boss giving her six days off and a wedding announcement from JL on the same day? Weird coincidence.

Had inviting her been an afterthought? Nobody sent an invitation the week before an event. She turned the card over and found a handwritten note from JL, along with a phone number.

Kevin and I just decided to get married. All the family is available this weekend. We hope you will come. I want you to be my maid of honor. If you're no longer a maid, I hope you'll be my matron of honor. Call me,
JL

Amy immediately sent Bill a text: *Forget Napa. I'm going to Florence, Italy. See what flights are available leaving tomorrow.* Then she called JL.

"Hello."

Hearing JL's voice, Amy saw with remarkable clarity what their friendship meant to her and how the absence of it had truly diminished her life. "It's Amy! Congratulations. I just got the announcement. I'm so happy for you."

"I know it's sudden," JL said, "but can you come?"

"Of course I can. I wouldn't miss it for the world. I just sent my travel agent a text to find a flight."

"Cancel it. I'll make all the arrangements."

"Where are you?" Amy asked.

"Kevin bought a winery in Tuscany. I came for a visit two weeks ago and haven't gone home yet. We're so happy. I can't wait to tell you everything. Hurry up and get here."

Amy walked over to the window and looked out over Central Park, now draped in the vibrant hues of a Joseph's coat. Had the riot of color happened overnight? Or had she been oblivious to the beauty, and the cooler air with its essence of earthiness? As she gazed out over the city below, she could see the red berries covering the hawthorn trees, the various shades of yellow dressing the famous tupelo tree, and the leaves of the European beech trees, dazzling in warm shades of orangey-red.

Amy's world had opened miraculously, and with it came hints of cozy evenings with friends, and warm soups, and long walks through the leaves crunching beneath her feet or pirouetting in an invisible, spiraling breeze, the last visible dance before winter's embrace would claim them all.

She was waxing poetic.

She laughed. Yes, she was. She was alive now, filled with wonder and excitement. Her creative juices were flowing for the first time in months, and she wanted to write down every thought. She had been inspired just by hearing JL's voice—a connection her heart made to Jack.

"You sound like you couldn't be happier," Amy said.

"I sound happy? You sound fantastic. I can't wait to catch up," JL said. "I'll tell you everything when I see you. Let me make some calls, and I'll call you back to confirm. I'm pretty sure I can reroute the girls' plane, and the corporate jet will pick you up on Wednesday, and return you Monday afternoon. Will that schedule work?"

"Sounds perfect. Who's on the girls' plane? Friends from college?"

"No, only family."

"I'm not family," Amy said.

"If you're not, I don't know who is," JL said. "On the plane, you'll meet Meredith, Kit, Kenzie, and her daughter Laurie Wallis; plus Charlotte and her two daughters Kitherina and Amelia Rose; and you'll see Isabella and Maria, and meet my sister-in-law Julie, too. My niece Susan and Kit's ward Emily balked at an all-girl flight, though. The two girls and Kevin's mom are flying over with the boys. Mrs. Allen didn't want to fly for hours listening to crying babies. I'll send flight times as soon as I have them. Joe's welcome to come, but he can't fly on the girls' plane."

"Joe won't be coming," Amy said. "What should I wear?"

"Don't worry about clothes. Meredith has it all figured out. She'll call you later. I've got to run. The priest is here. Call me if you have any questions. I can't wait to catch up. *Ciao.*"

The Diamond Brooch 547

JL didn't sound completely bridezilla-ish, but she was close.

Amy disconnected the call and remained at the window, replaying the conversation. JL had been rushed, as if she didn't want a lengthy conversation, or she was afraid Amy would bring up a topic JL didn't want to discuss. Was Amy reading too much into the call?

Her phone rang, and the screen displayed a 707 area code. Who was calling her from Northern California? She clicked accept and said, "This is Amy."

"Hi, Amy. This is Meredith Montgomery. JL just told me you're going to the wedding. I'm so glad. I can't wait to meet you. I assume your calendar's clear from Wednesday to Monday. Right?"

"Funny you should ask. I just received a call from my boss, informing me I have the weekend off. Very serendipitous."

"Oh, sweetie. Nothing is serendipitous when Elliott Fraser is involved."

"He called my boss?" It was beginning to look like this wedding party had more than one bridezilla.

"Elliott has connections all over the world, and if he doesn't know someone, David does. I wouldn't be surprised, but I have no evidence anyone intervened on your behalf."

"That makes me uncomfortable," Amy said.

"It shouldn't. If Elliott asked for a favor, the network got something of value in return."

"Still…"

"Amy," Meredith said tersely. "Don't spend another minute worrying about it. Focus on what you need to do between now and eight o'clock tomorrow evening. That's what time the Montgomery jet will be at Teterboro to pick you up."

"JL said you would tell me what to wear for the wedding."

"I'll tell you on Thursday. The plane is stopping in Milan so we can shop. Pack your running gear and toiletries, and don't forget your passport. I know you have a wisely invested inheritance, but don't worry about the expense. Elliott is picking up the tab for his son's wedding."

Wisely invested inheritance? How did Meredith know that?

"You mentioned running gear," Amy said. "Will there be a group run? I'm not as fast as I used to be."

"Don't worry about that, either. Charlotte had a baby a few weeks ago and will be pushing a double stroller. We won't go far."

Amy had a sneaking suspicion Meredith's idea of far and her idea of far were several miles apart. "One last question," Amy said. "Where are we staying in Florence? Do I need to make a reservation?"

"We're all staying at the villa, but Elliott has booked several rooms at the Helvetia & Bristol for anyone who's overwhelmed by the children and confusion."

Amy raised her hand—although Meredith couldn't see her—to add her name to the hotel list. Amy couldn't remember anyone ever bulldozing her the way Meredith was doing right now, but if she wanted to be part of the weekend, Amy would have to surrender to the MacKlenna clan matriarch and acting MOB.

"I'll see you tomorrow." Amy disconnected the call, reflecting on the fact Meredith and JL had both avoided mentioning the men, except Elliott. What were they hiding? No sense worrying about it. Amy would know soon enough.

57

Present day en route to Tuscany, Italy—Amy

AT EIGHT O'CLOCK the next evening, Amy was waiting nervously on the tarmac at Teterboro Airport. It would be a crowded flight with eight adults and three children. But as excited as she was to see Isabella and Maria, Amy would gladly give up Delta Comfort's extra elbow and leg room just to be with them again.

A jet landed and taxied over to where she'd been told to wait. It was a huge Falcon 7X with Montgomery Winery painted on the side. The stairs lowered, and Isabella was the first one to appear at the door, waving madly.

"Amy!" Isabella tore down the steps and ran toward her. She looked like any other young American woman, dressed in ripped jeans and a University of Kentucky T-shirt, her hair tied in a funky bun on top of her head.

Amy gave her a tight hug. "I'm so glad to see you. I've missed you so much, and I can't wait to hear all your news. Are you in school?"

Isabella took Amy's hand. "I'm a freshman at UK, and we're going to have so much fun. You'll love Meredith and Kit, and Charlotte and Kenzie. They're our family now. Come on. I'll introduce you."

Amy followed her up the steps and into the cabin. She had flown in small corporate jets, but this one was the biggest and most elegant plane she'd ever seen. White leather seats, beige carpet, deep brown veneer trim, patterned fabric on the divan, cream fabric window panels. But the most striking difference was this plane was packed with beautiful women, and not gray-haired owners of baseball teams.

A woman in her mid-fifties with shoulder-length black hair, gorgeous skin without a wrinkle, and tanned, toned, and friendly, approached her to shake hands. "Welcome. I'm Meredith Montgomery. Come with me. I'll introduce you. Maria, you know."

Amy hugged her. "You look marvelous."

Maria beamed with the kind of look women in love usually have. What was the story there? Amy couldn't wait to hear. "I'm so happy to see you. We have a lot to talk about."

Meredith continued with the introductions. "This is Julie O'Grady, JL's sister-in-law. Over here are Kit Montgomery and Charlotte Mallory."

Amy couldn't take her eyes off Charlotte. She saw Jack in the blue of her eyes, in the way her mouth curled when she smiled, in the exact shade of her blond hair, and the shape of her face. She was as beautiful as he was handsome, and Amy was staring. She quickly pictured herself at the plate with a full count, and instantly regained her composure.

Thank God for baseball.

"And that's Amelia Rose in the infant carrier," Meredith continued, "and Wee Kit is in the bathroom."

A gorgeous woman with red hair and bright hazel eyes, holding a toddler, stuck out her hand and said, "Hi, I'm Kenzie McBain, and this little one is Laurie Wallis. Welcome aboard."

Meredith pointed to one of two empty seats. "The one next to the window is yours. The bathroom is next to the galley. We have a flight attendant, but you're welcome to get up and get whatever you want."

Meredith placed Amy in the chair next to her and across from Charlotte. Intentional? Or accidental? Amy doubted Meredith did anything without thought and planning. Amy began to wonder if this trip was a job interview.

But for what job?

The flight attendant, a young woman in her late twenties, walked through the cabin serving champagne, and within twenty minutes of boarding the plane, they were wheels up and on their way to Italy. Kenzie had everyone in stiches. Amy never heard anyone other than a professional comedian rattle off as many jokes, and most of them were about family members.

Wee Kit came up to her mom and said, "What did the baseball glove say to the ball?"

"I don't know, sweetie, what did it say? I'm stumped."

Amy mouthed, "Catch ya later" just as wee Kit said, "Catch ya later." Then she ran to Isabella, laughing hysterically. "Mamma didn't know the answer. Tell me another one."

"Come here, and we'll find one." Isabella's fingers moved around the laptop keyboard as if she'd been born to it.

Charlotte was nursing her baby, something new for Amy. She couldn't recall ever being around a nursing mother. "You're missing a big playoff weekend."

Amy glanced up from the bundle in Charlotte's arms to make eye contact. "Yes, I am. But I'm glad to have a break. Do you follow baseball?"

"My son is playing Little League, so I'm getting back into it."

"Back into it?" Amy asked.

Charlotte switched the baby to her other breast seamlessly, leaving Amy awed. "I went to as many of Jack's games as I could," Charlotte said.

"Little League and Babe Ruth, I guess. Those are fun games to watch."

"Those and his games at the University of Virginia."

Amy was stunned. "He played at UVA?"

"Star pitcher for four years. Then he was a first-round draft pick."

Amy wasn't just stunned, she was flabbergasted. "Jack Mallory was a first-round draft pick?"

"By the Yankees," Charlotte said.

Amy cleared her throat and readjusted in her seat. "I've heard of Jack Mallory the *New York Times* best-selling author. Is he the same Jack Mallory you're talking about?"

Charlotte laughed, and amusement filled her robin's egg blue eyes. Amy had to glance away for a moment to remind herself they weren't Jack's. "He was on his way to play for the Yankees," Charlotte continued, "but Harvard Law won out. He turned the team down and never looked back."

Amy put her elbow on the chair's arm, intending to prop her chin on her fist, but her arm wobbled and she had to put her hands in her lap. "I had no idea."

"If you Google him," Kenzie said, "you'll find almost as many articles about his passion for sports as you do his books."

"He doesn't talk about his baseball career. At the time, people thought he was nuts for turning down the Yankees, but he had his heart set on going to Harvard, and not even baseball was going to stop him," Charlotte said.

Amy was incredulous. Jack had never, not once, mentioned his baseball career. Why wouldn't he have told her?

Later, while Charlotte napped, Amy held the baby and fell in love with her the instant she had the sweet bundle in her arms. She saw traces of Jack in Amelia Rose's face, and especially in her eyes.

Amy made a point of spending one-on-one time with each of the women, especially Isabella. The diva Amy met a year ago had disappeared, and in her place was a thoughtful, intelligent, caring young woman. Isabella and Charlotte talked about medicine, and Amy had no doubt Isabella would make it into medical school, if for no other reason than Charlotte saw Isabella's admission as a personal challenge.

By eleven o'clock, they had all changed into pajamas, lowered their seats, and covered up with blankets. There were three beds, and everyone agreed Meredith and the two moms should sleep in them. Amy went to the galley for a bottle of water and overheard Charlotte talking quietly on her speaker phone while her baby made sucking noises.

"I love her. She's sweet, and caring, and has such a gentle heart. You should see her with the girls. Wee Kit is already attached to her. Would you believe Jack never told Amy he played baseball?"

"I'm not surprised," a man with a Scottish accent said. "Baseball is everything to Amy. She would think Jack was an idiot for turning down the draft. I'm glad ye like her, though. If we play this right, by Christmas, she'll be our sister-in-law."

Sister-in-law? Play this right?

What in the world was going on? Was Jack dating someone they didn't like? If that was the case, she would turn around and go right back home. They weren't going to use her to break up a relationship they didn't approve of. But wait. No, she couldn't bear to hurt JL. Amy had promised to be her maid of honor. She just had to be sure to stay away from Jack. Was that even possible?

She brought her water back to her seat, where she slipped on an eye mask, put in earbuds to listen to soothing music, and quickly fell asleep.

At eight o'clock, they were awakened. They each were allocated five minutes in the shower, and then they pored over tour books to map their shopping excursion in Milan.

Hours later, they returned to the plane loaded down with packages and fussy babies. Amy couldn't remember ever laughing as hard as she had at Kenzie. So hard, in fact, she almost peed her pants. She'd never felt so welcome anywhere in her life.

An hour outside of Florence, Amy asked Kenzie, "Was the shopping excursion in lieu of a bachelorette party?"

"Heavens, no," Kenzie said. "The dads are keeping the kids tonight. Kit arranged for a car service, and we're going to party big-time."

"I think Kenzie, Isabella, Amy, JL, and Julie are going out to party," Meredith said.

"You're going, too, Meredith. Don't try to get out of it," Kenzie said.

"We'll see," Meredith said. "Somebody has to keep an eye on the men, or someone will sneak Elliott a cigar, and he'll be too intoxicated to turn it down."

Kenzie dug through one of the shopping bags.

"What are you looking for?" Meredith asked.

"We need to pick out something special for Amy to wear to the villa. What do you think of this outfit?" Kenzie held up a fitted leather Herve Pierre skirt and white blouse.

"I think it's perfect. What do you think, Amy?"

"I love it." *That's why I picked it out at the store.*

"Good, put it on. You'll look stunning," Meredith said.

Amy went to the back of the plane, wondering if Meredith was always so controlling, or if this was a wedding weekend thing. Amy stripped out of her jeans and shimmied into the tight skirt. She primped in front of the mirror and had to agree. The outfit was perfect. She looked stunning. But who was she dressing for?

When the plane landed in Florence, two limos were waiting on the tarmac. Amy rode with Charlotte and Meredith and most of the packages.

Except for her father's funeral, the drive to the winery was the most stressful limo ride she'd ever taken. She fidgeted. She checked emails. She checked her makeup. She fidgeted some more.

"Are you nervous, Amy?" Meredith asked.

"Excited, I think. I can't wait to see..." She gasped. "Oh, my God. That's Kevin's winery? It's gorgeous." The villa could be seen from the base of a long, tree-lined drive. The limos pulled up slowly and stopped in a cobblestone courtyard. The front door banged open, and a half-dozen kids ran out, yelling "Hi, Mom," while they raced across the courtyard and disappeared behind a stone wall.

"Lincoln," Charlotte called. The boy ducked his head around the side of the wall and waved again, and then he was gone. "I hope his father has control of the situation and isn't out stomping around in the vineyards."

"You're talking about Braham McCabe," Kit said. "What do you really think he's doing?"

"Sitting out under a tree drinking whisky and smoking a cigar

The Diamond Brooch   555

with your husband."

Kit laughed. "That's exactly what I was thinking."

Amy was loading her arms with packages when she spotted two men racing up the drive, hot and sweaty and grunting. The sun glinted off Jack's blond hair, and her heart leapt to her throat. She dropped the packages on the limo's back seat.

"I'm going to beat your ass."

She recognized Kevin's voice, but she didn't recognize the much leaner Kevin, sporting a full beard.

Jack stopped, put his hands on his hips, and leaned forward to catch his breath. When he could breathe, he kissed his sister on the cheek, then Meredith, and then he spotted Amy on the other side of the car.

His eyebrows shot up, and the evidence of surprise gave her a little thrill she wasn't at all ashamed to revel in for a moment. "Amy? My God. Amy!" He rushed toward her, but she backed up, holding her hands out to keep him at arm's length.

"Slow down, cowboy. It's good to see you, too, and I'd love to give you a hug, but you're pouring sweat, and you'll ruin this outfit your sister insisted I wear." She reached into Charlotte's diaper bag, pulled out a burp cloth, and tossed it to him. "At least dry off your face before you kiss me."

He sniffed it. "This smells like spit-up. Even I don't smell that bad." He glared at Kevin. "Why didn't you tell me she was coming? I wouldn't have gone for a run."

Jack tried again to hug her, but Amy backed up farther. "Go take a shower. I'll wait right here."

Charlotte laughed. "After a year, Jack, Amy deserves a decent hello. Not a hot, sweaty hug."

Amy had never seen him befuddled—angry, sad, horny, funny, loving, tender, sensitive, romantic—but she'd never seen him befuddled. And it tickled her.

"You're right," he said, dejectedly. He pointed to the cobblestone. "Don't move. Stay right where you are. I'll be back in five minutes. Charlotte, make sure she doesn't move from that exact spot." He blew into the house, leaving the door to bang against the wall.

Kevin stretched to kiss her, keeping his sweaty body a safe distance away. His damp beard tickled her face. "I'm glad you came. I guess you saw Jack wasn't expecting you. We intentionally didn't tell him."

She opened her mouth, closed it again. She was stymied, but recovered quickly and asked, "Did you think he would back out?"

Kevin snorted and inclined his head with a mischievous smile. "Are you serious? Until yesterday, we thought you were still with Joe. If Jack had known you were single, he would have called you the day he got back. If we told him you were coming, he would have bombarded us with questions. Do you think Amy this? Do you think Amy that? And we didn't want to listen to him go through a litany of doubts. So we voted not to tell him."

"What kind of doubts?" she asked.

Kevin shrugged. "He was afraid things would be different between you two after all this time? But mostly he had doubts about his age, which bothers him a lot."

"I don't even know how old he is, but his age doesn't matter to me. Oh, by the way, thank you for the baseball cards. The ones you gave me are impossible to find. They were the most awesome gifts I've ever been given."

"I'm not sure what that says about a woman."

Amy laughed. "I don't know either."

"Where's Braham?" Charlotte asked.

"He and Cullen are on the terrace with Elliott and David. I don't know what they're cooking up, but I think it's trouble."

"Where's JL?" Amy asked.

"She's in the kitchen talking to the caterer," Kevin said.

"Everyone can come inside, then," Charlotte said, "except for Amy. Since I promised Jack, she has to wait right there. Grab the packages, Kevin."

"Do I really have to wait out here?" Amy asked, folding her arms.

"Yes, you do," Kevin said. "Besides, Jack will want to show you how glad he is to see you without the rest of us around to watch." Kevin loaded his arms with packages and hanging bags, and they all went inside, leaving Amy alone and waiting.

She crossed the courtyard to sit on a wrought-iron bench surrounded by terra-cotta pots and brilliantly leafed trees. Finally, the door opened and Jack walked out, his wet hair combed back, a white dress shirt untucked and rolled to the elbows, faded jeans, and Birkenstocks. He had taken her breath away a dozen times before, but not like this. She couldn't move from her spot on the bench. If he hadn't stolen her heart already, it would be gone now for sure.

She found the strength to stand and walked toward him. He kissed her brow, lingering there for a long moment. A kiss that said to her, *You're mine. Don't ever leave my side.*

Then he said, "I have one question. Are you still with Joe?" He looked at her with intensity and focus, waiting for her answer.

"We broke up in February."

"I was told you were still together."

She swallowed, but the knot in her throat got bigger. "I heard your wife died."

"We were never married. I lied to the hospital so I could cover her medical expenses. I should have called you."

"I should have called you," she said.

His hands ran soothingly up and down her arms, stopping to squeeze her shoulders. He had yet to kiss her, but if he felt the same way she did, one kiss wouldn't be enough.

"Let's get out of here. I want to hold you without the world watching."

Amy experienced a full-body shiver. "I can't—"

He gave her a scorching look. "I'm waiting for the day when you say 'I can.'"

"I haven't even seen JL. This weekend belongs to her and Kevin."

"She won't care," Jack said.

"But I do. I haven't seen you in a year. We can't just pick right up, as if time hasn't passed since I closed the bedroom door."

Now, he iced her with a cool gaze, another look Amy hadn't seen before. "Why not?"

"Because I'm not made that way," she said. "I'm a slow starter, but once I get to first base, watch out."

"I like the way you're made."

"Jack, you're trying too hard. Slow down. Be the man I met in New York."

His lips quirked in a subtle smile. "Then may I kiss you? A real kiss. Not one of those chaste kisses I gave you before."

He touched her cheek with one finger, then skimmed it up to her temple to push back a tendril of hair. How was it this man could make her feel so desirable with just a look and a touch of his fingertips? He traced a line over her face and down to her lips before pulling her into his arms. His heart pounded against her face as his lightly shaking arms enveloped her.

"I want you, Amy. I can't deny what I feel for you."

And part of what he felt for her was pressing against her hip, hard and insistent.

He kissed her with slow, sun-dusty lips and sandpaper whiskers. He was warm, firm, and thoroughly sexy. His mouth slanting over hers, moving in such a way that she never knew the precise instant her lips opened to the light pressure of his tongue. No kiss had ever made her go hot and hotter and shaky all over. And she almost didn't recognize the husky sound of need as hers.

"I want you, Jack. I can't deny what I feel for you, either."

"Amy!" Patrick yelled. He plowed into both of them at the same time. "I just heard you were here. I'm so happy to see you. Looks like Jack is, too."

Jack tousled his hair. "You're right, son. I sure am."

Patrick fingered his hair to restyle his spikes. "You're not still seeing that Joe guy, are you? You can marry Jack now, right?"

"I'm not still seeing Joe." She quickly changed the subject. "How's school?"

"I'm being schooled at home with special tutors, but I'm playing soccer, so I've made lots of friends." He stopped and glanced around like he wanted to share news but didn't want others to hear. "Have you met Emily? She makes my heart flutter."

Amy laughed. "Flutter? Really? Who's coaching you about girls?"

He glanced up at Jack and pointed with his thumb. "Should I not listen to him?"

Amy laughed again, amazed at how easily Patrick acclimated, and how much he obviously loved Jack. "You should be okay. His advice is probably pretty harmless."

"JL said he should write a Dear Jack column in the local paper."

Jack shrugged, grinning, and her pulse quickened. He didn't give her his book jacket smile, the polished airbrushed one. Nope. This one was a brilliant smile, directly connected to his eyes and heart.

Patrick gave her a hug. "Catch ya later, Amy." And off he went.

Jack took her hand. "Come on. I know a few men who are chomping at the bit to meet you. Knowing their wives, the men have been sent hourly reports. If you snore, they even know that by now."

"How charming," she said. "Honestly, I've never been around so many women, for that long, when someone wasn't complaining about something or someone. But there were no complaints. No snide comments. Nothing. They are all loving and positive women. Women, by the way, who are used to being in total control."

He pulled her in for another hug, and the rumble in his chest tickled her. "That pretty much sums them up. They're all control freaks. Meredith and Charlotte tie for the number one position, though. Come on. Let's go inside."

They walked through the mansion until they reached the kitchen. Maria was in the thick of the commotion, directing six women in Italian.

"Look at her," Amy said. "You didn't include Maria in the group of control freaks."

"When it comes to the kitchen, you either listen to her or you're out of here," Jack said. Raising his voice, he asked, "Has anybody seen JL?"

"She and Kevin went to the little villa," Maria said. "They needed"—she made air quotes—"personal time."

Jack threw back his head and howled.

"Does that mean what I think it means?" Amy asked.

"From the first moment they met, except for a few weeks before they broke up, they've been like that. They were making out within an hour or two of saying hello."

"Within an hour of meeting me, you were comforting me while I threw up. I hope you don't feel cheated." She was relearning Jack's rhythms, quirks, and inflections, and she was pretty sure he was envious of Kevin and JL's mating habits. And who wouldn't be?

"Come on. Let's go outside. I need to warn you, though, David, Elliott, Cullen, and Braham are all Scotsmen. They can be intimidating one on one, but together, all the testosterone can be overpowering."

"You forget. I work in a sport where the average player's age is twenty-six, and each team has a twenty-five-player roster. The average height-weight is six feet, a hundred and ninety pounds, and I spend time in the locker rooms interviewing these guys. In other words, testosterone by the barrel doesn't intimidate me."

Amy and Jack left the house and crossed the terrace, where four men stood to greet her. She picked Elliott out immediately. Not because of his gray hair, but because he was the Alpha of the Alphas. She immediately saw their slight, subtle deference to him, probably an unconscious awareness, and the other three men shifted slightly to protect his flanks.

She tagged the man with the short military haircut as Kenzie's husband, David. But Braham and Cullen looked like bookends. She couldn't figure out which was which until she remembered Braham and Kit were real first cousins. She stopped in front of them and said, "You're Elliott, you're David, you're Braham, and you're Cullen."

"And ye're Amy," Elliott said. "And ye figured out who we were in the few steps it took to get here. I'm interested in yer analysis. What gave us away?"

"You're the Alpha of the Alphas, David has a military haircut, and Braham and Kit have the same hair and eye color, which made Cullen the one with dark hair."

"The odd man out had to be Cullen. Clever girl." Elliott kissed her cheek. "We're glad ye're here, lass."

"Amy!"

She spun around to see JL and Kevin walking briskly toward her. "You look wonderful, JL." Amy hugged her. "I would ask your secret, but I think I already know."

JL whispered, "Great sex, right?" She put her arm around Amy. "I'm taking her with me. You can have her later, Jack."

Amy waved goodbye as they turned back toward the house. "You look so happy."

"I am, but tell me," JL said. "How'd it feel to see Jack again?"

Amy's face heated. "I can't deny it. I love the guy." She opened the door, but stopped when she spotted a ball and glove on a nearby table. "Hold on a minute," she said to JL. "I want to do something." Amy closed the door and picked up the ball.

"Mallory! Catch." She threw one of the best pitches she'd ever thrown, and it landed right in his hands. "You've still got it. You're not too old."

"For what?" Jack asked.

"You should have told me you were a pitcher. You would have gotten to first base."

A chorus of howls followed her into the house, and Jack yelled, "Even though I turned down the Yankees?"

She stuck her head out the door. "I forgive you for that, but if it had been the Giants, you never would have gotten a turn at bat."

"I still haven't," he yelled. "How do I get into the starting lineup?"

Amy thought a minute, then yelled back, "Keep swinging."

58

Present day Tuscany, Italy—Amy

THE BACHELORETTE PARTY IDEA fizzled out. The babies were cranky, and Kenzie and Charlotte didn't want to leave them. After fixing the children's favorite meals for lunch, Maria booted aside Kevin's chef once again, and prepared dinner for her new family. She even included a couple of Scottish dishes she had mastered that only four men would even taste—Braham, Cullen, David, and Elliott. According to Maria, Elliott was the only one who really mattered, even though it was Kevin's winery and Kevin's wedding weekend.

Amy learned from JL that Elliott and Meredith, Mr. and Mrs. Allen, Kevin, and JL had a sit-down meeting where Kevin explained to his parents the wedding would be a Fraser affair, complete with bagpipes. He also announced he was taking the Fraser name. It had been difficult for Mr. Allen, but he acknowledged he'd basically given his son—at age seventeen—to Elliott to raise when Mr. Allen discovered Elliott was Kevin's biological father.

Mr. and Mrs. Allen were just glad to be there.

At eight o'clock in the evening, twenty-one adults, nine kids, and two sleepy infants—attached to their mothers—sat down at a large table on the terrace, where two roaring fire pits kept the evening chill at bay. The meal blended the traditions of the Irish, the Italians, and the Scots. The music was eclectic, and the stories were hot and spicy, mellow and bittersweet, funny and at times raunchy, but always loving, which became the theme of the evening.

Elliott sang his favorite tunes by Robbie Burns, Cullen quoted Shakespeare, and Kenzie told jokes. When calls for JL to sing became too loud to ignore, she, Pops, and her three brothers agreed to sing Irish songs, if the Scottish lads—Braham, Cullen, David, Kevin, and Elliott—sang songs from the Highlands.

And a quintet sing-off began.

The kids made voting paddles, and everyone who wasn't singing became a celebrity judge. They all, including Mr. and Mrs. Allen, laughed hysterically at the antics of both the performers and the kids, who took on personalities of judges they saw on TV. Austin insisted, since he was the oldest, he should be the one to imperson-ate Simon Cowell.

Amy and Jack held hands, kissed, and touched each other on the arm, shoulder, face, legs, and, as the evening progressed and more alcohol was consumed, the touches under the table became more intimate.

She was as hot as the fire in the fire pit.

Jack mentioned JL's performance on the *SS New York* would go down in family history. And it would, but tonight's entertainment would top every one of the stories Amy had heard during her time in the past and the long flight to Italy.

At one point, Meredith said to Amy, "This even tops Elliott's performance at Louise's B&B when he first serenaded me."

At midnight, with the score tied, Elliott made a unilateral deci-sion to end the competition with one final song from each side. The Scottish quintet would sing "Auld Lang Syne" and the Irish quintet would sing "Danny Boy."

"I haven't heard Cullen and Braham sing 'Auld Lang Syne' since they sang James Thomas MacKlenna right into Heaven," Kit said. "I'm not sure I can listen to them sing without crying."

Austin cued up the music. The five Scotsman cleared their throats, downed shots of whisky, and sang...

"Should auld acquaintance be forgot, and never brought to mind? Should

auld acquaintance be forgot, and auld lang syne. For auld lang syne, my jo, for auld lang syne, we'll tak' a cup o' kindness yet, for auld lang syne."

On the final note, it was as if all regret and fear, anger and guilt, grief and longing had been wrung from Amy's soul and consigned to the glowing hot firepit. She couldn't promise herself guilt would never rear its head again, but she had Jack to help her carry it, and he would never leave her alone with its ugliness.

Jack whispered in her ear, "I didn't think I'd ever see you again, or if I did, I would have to pretend I don't love you. Now I want the world to know how I feel."

Amy looked at him, her heart melting, and, sailing on a wave of euphoria, she kissed him. "I love you, too."

Pops joined his children while Austin cued up the music again, and then he took his place next to his mom for the Irish quintet's—plus one—final performance. JL sang the first stanza solo.

"Oh Danny Boy, the pipes, the pipes are calling, from glen to glen, and down the mountain side. The summer's gone, and all the roses falling. It's you, it's you, must go, and I must bide."

The men, like the Scotsmen had done, tossed back shots of whisky before joining in…

"But come ye back when summer's in the meadow. Or when the valley's hushed and white with snow. I'll be here in sunshine or in shadow, Oh Danny Boy, oh Danny Boy, I love you so!"

Kevin abandoned his compatriots and joined the O'Gradys, blending his baritone voice with theirs. And then, to everyone's surprise, Henry and Robbie carried David's sax out of the house. "Play this song, Daddy. Make Mommy happy-cry." They hung onto David's legs and swayed while he added his personal musicality to the recorded music.

With a signal from Pops, Austin cut the music, and the O'Grady men and Kevin sat down, letting JL and David finish the song with a vocal-sax duet.

JL then stepped aside to let David's virtuosity and warm tonal glow glide through the cool, crisp evening, leaving everyone still as air without a breeze, including happy-crying Kenzie.

59

Present day Tuscany, Italy—Amy

WHEN THE ECHO of the final note of the quintet sing-off faded, Jack took Amy's hand and said, "Come with me."

"Where are we going?" she asked.

"To the cottage. Kevin hasn't officially opened it, yet, but he gave me this…" Jack held up a key, and stopped to kiss her. His tongue was soft and coaxing as it slipped into her mouth. He stroked her hair, her face, enfolded her in his arms, and held her so close against him she could feel the beat of his heart.

They strolled entwined through a verdant fall garden of sweet and wild flowers until they reached a two-story, square-shaped villa, framed by vineyards and olive groves. Jack unlocked the door, and they entered a house made of travertine and brick, beamed ceilings and frescoes, a house of simple elegance, with stone walls and terracotta-tiled floors. The furniture was earthy and natural and warm, and the Italian art collection was impressive.

Jack led her into the kitchen, where a bottle of champagne sat chilling in an ice bucket. "This is an Armand de Brignac Brut Gold. The most expensive bottle I could find on short notice. I hope it will do."

"It depends on how much it costs," she said smiling. "A hundred-dollar bottle isn't going to cut it."

"How about sixty-five hundred?"

"Wow. I didn't mean that expensive. We should save it for a special occasion."

"If this isn't a special occasion, I don't know what would qualify." He popped the cork and filled two fluted goblets. "It's the label's flagship *cuveé*, pressed from a perfectly balanced blend of Chardonnay, Pinot Noir, and Pinot Meunier wine. It's lively and full-bodied, with a deliciously creamy texture and a long, silky finish. Let me know what you think."

She sipped. "Much better than what JL and I had on the ship."

He returned the bottle to the ice bucket and cradled the bucket in one arm. "There's a fire in the other room. Let's go in there."

He had created the perfect setting, with a deep-seated, cushioned sofa, low lights, a fire, laid-back jazz, and candles. "You've set a very romantic scene," she said. "Has everything been burning since dinner?"

"Austin and Isabella sneaked over during a break in the entertainment. I had to be creative. I don't write romance, so I had to Google what women like in a romantic setting. I found a helpful article in *Cosmopolitan.*"

"I've read about you—Jack Mallory, serial seducer. You don't have to Google anything when it comes to wine, women, and music."

He gave a remorseful shrug. "I wish I'd been a monk my entire life, and you were the first woman I've ever kissed. I can't undo my past, but I can start a new future with you. I want to make love with you all night. I want it to be perfect, to be a night we'll remember the rest of our lives. I want to touch and kiss you in places to make you tingle and scream, and watch the expression on your face when you reach your climax."

He touched his mouth to hers, and the contact was both sensuous and compelling. His full, firm lips sipped at hers gently, drew away for a breath, and came back for a firmer, more possessive kiss. The tip of her tongue tasted the long, cool finish of the champagne on his lips and in his mouth. Her hands gripped the fabric of his shirt near his spine and held him fast against her.

They shifted the angle of their heads several times, but didn't break the kiss until he pulled away and pressed his lips against her neck, just beneath her ear, his hand resting there, his thumb caressing her cheek while their breaths mingled.

She moaned, a husky sound of greed and unsated desire, desperate longings, and the pulse-pounding ache building within her. Time stopped for a heartbeat, and she found herself lost in the hard planes of his body. She pressed her breasts intimately against his chest, while his hands stroked her back, searing her with his touch.

He kissed her again, and his erotically swirling tongue ignited sparks of intense desire. He groaned, loud and erotic. She would never forget the sound, and the way it vibrated against her lips, echoing into her mouth. Blood coursed through her, hot and thick, and her skin burned under his caresses. She had never been so frantic for anything as she was at the moment. Delirious for him— to make love to him. Right here. Right now.

He must have sensed the urgency building within her. He picked her up. "Once I carry you into the bedroom, I won't let you go." The rough timbre of his voice both aroused and electrified her even more.

"Don't ever let me go again."

He carried her to the bedroom and laid her on a king size bed covered with a down comforter. And she watched transfixed as he unbuttoned his shirt, shed his jeans and boxer briefs. Then he stood there naked, perfectly proportioned, with muscular arms and legs and chest dusted with crisp, light brown hair. His erection was long, proud, and utterly magnificent.

And he was perfect. Absolutely perfect.

He unbuttoned her jeans and slid them down over her hips, then slowly, inch by inch—as if opening a Christmas present he wanted to savor—pulled her sweater over her head, leaving her wearing only her panties and bra.

"God, you're beautiful. I've had all sorts of fantasies, but you've surpassed them all." His hand shook when he stroked her face.

"Are you nervous?" she asked.

"I want it to be perfect. I don't want to rush. I've waited too long for this, and I don't want it to end. But, I'm not twenty-five, Amy."

"This isn't a contest. There aren't any judges. Just two people who love each other." She glided her hands over his chest, and his muscles twitched and flexed while her slow, curious fingers danced over his perfect, almond-shaped nipples. "I don't have any contraception."

He lay down next to her, and the bed dipped slightly beneath his weight. "I have condoms."

She dove headlong into the one question that had to be asked, and she knew he would tell her the truth. "Are you safe? I've only had two partners, and they always used condoms."

"I've always worn one, but you should know..." He stopped, looked away for a moment. "I have to be honest..."

She didn't like the way this was going. Was there someone else in his life? "I always want you to be honest with me," she said, feeling somewhat ambivalent.

"Here it is." He took a deep breath. "I had a vasectomy eight years ago."

Her heart dropped to her stomach. She had always wanted children, and now the man of her dreams, the man she wanted to father those children, was telling her he was sterile. What kind of twist of fate was this? "Is it reversible?"

His blue eyes deepened in intensity. "The success rate depends on several factors."

Shivering, dumbfounded over his confession, all she could say was, "Oh." His palm grazed the side of her arm, as if he thought she might be chilled, but the cold seeping into her went too deep to be warmed.

"There is a bright spot." His fingers skated a path back up her arms, to her face, to her scalp, where he used long, sweeping strokes, massaging down to the base of her head, kneading the area with his thumb.

"Adoption?" she asked.

"My wise sister insisted, when I decided to have a vasectomy, I had to freeze my sperm."

"And you did?" she asked, hopefully.

"I stored enough to populate a small country. If the reversal doesn't work, we have options, but..."

She placed her finger against his lips, overjoyed, but not wanting to dwell on the subject right now. "Thank you for telling me, but can we table it for later? There are other things I'm more interested in."

"Oh? Like what?" he asked, indulging himself by running his fingers through her silky hair.

"Like what's happening right now."

She unsnapped the front closure of her bra and arched her back, lifting her breasts up to him. He pulled a nipple into his hot, wet mouth, teasing her with his swirling tongue, and his warm, strong hand cupped her other breast, tweaking her nipple. The exquisite sensations he invoked were so intense she quivered, her breath catching in her throat, as he continued to stroke her until her nipples were hard. She flattened her palms against the hard muscles of his abdomen, and they flexed beneath her touch.

He kissed her mouth, and the kiss moved like a burning light to inhabit the center of her heart. She had an insatiable craving to taste him and experience every sensual pleasure to be had in his arms. The months of longing were burned away by the heat of his touch, leaving her with a desperate ache clamoring low in her body.

"I've fantasized about this hundreds of times," she said in a breathy voice.

"I hope this is better." He pulled her on top of him and peeled off her bra, throwing it on the floor. His fingers traced the ladder of her spine, raising gooseflesh as he climbed her back. His mouth roamed hers at will with an insatiable kiss, no longer gentle, as he devoured her. He tugged her even closer, consuming her.

"Oh...much better," she moaned against his mouth as she straddled him, and his erection pulsed against her. She was unable to resist the pull urging her to him. She rocked slowly against his hardness. She was burning now, and her breathing came at a fevered pace.

Her senses were heightened as he kissed the curve of her throat and behind and below her ear—an oversensitive area of her body. "Don't make me wait much longer."

With a guttural groan and powerful arms, he flipped her over and grabbed a condom from the bedside table. "I won't. I can't."

She took the condom away from him. "I want to feel your skin against mine. I don't want any barriers between us."

"Are you sure?"

She threw it on the floor. "I trust you. With my body, with my life, with my love."

He peeled away her panties and positioned himself between her legs. She took hold of his erection. She wanted him with an instinctual hunger. Gazing into his blue eyes, she guided him to her with trembling fingers. All the dazzling wonder and tantalizing warmth she identified with him were in his embrace as he thrust into her, and she welcomed him into the depths of her body.

She cried out as she gripped her legs high around the middle of his back, encouraging him to push deeper. And she kissed him with all the urgency charging through her.

Making low, almost-inaudible moans, he pumped harder, faster, his breathing labored, his neck strained. They cleaved to each other, and the taste of his voracious appetite turned tangy and tart, spicy and salty, tasty and ripe all at the same time.

Never had a man so delighted and thrilled her. She rocked against him, enjoying the play of the muscles of his legs and arms and chest beneath her palms and sliding against her skin. She closed her eyes, panting with desperate, quickening breaths, until a tempest rose within her, building to an ever-tightening crescendo. She clawed at his back, clutching him, and then her breathing unraveled as she swept headlong into her climax.

Jack's orgasm hit simultaneously, surrounding her, enveloping her in his heat, more powerful than anything she'd ever experienced, and a savage roar tore from him while their releases merged in a fevered rapture.

And then…

The second time, her orgasm was a supernova explosion.

And the third time… There were simply no words.

The frenzy slowly ebbed, and everything stopped except the wild beats of their hearts and their ragged breathing, leaving Amy in a state of euphoria, wondering what in the world just happened between them.

Yes, it was real. Not a fantasy. Not a dream. Not a wish upon a star. It was real and powerful and forever.

"We just made love, didn't we? It really happened."

"I'm still inside of you, darlin'. It's real."

"Don't move. Stay right where you are."

"I'm not going anywhere. Neither are you. You may never have any privacy again. I'll always be afraid when you close a door you'll disappear, and all I'll have left of you is the lingering scent of your hair."

They spooned for some time, languishing in the sexual afterglow, until Amy made a move to get up.

"Where are you going?" He pulled her tighter to his chest. "Unless you have to pee, you're not going anywhere."

"I want to get the champagne. We need to make a toast, and I'm thirsty."

"Stay put. I'll get it." He rolled over, and slipped on his boxer briefs.

She grinned. "Don't get dressed on my account."

"In case you haven't noticed, there aren't any blinds on the windows."

She reached for the sheet and covered herself. "You mean we could have had an audience?"

"Not the way the bed is positioned in the room. I made sure of it."

"How thoughtful. Hurry. I miss you already." She watched him walk away, and when he turned his back to her, she gasped.

He turned on his heel and faced her. "What's wrong?"

"Your back. When did you get the tattoo?"

"Oh, that. Well…" He sat on the edge of the bed and gently pushed her damp hair off her face. "Not long after the vasectomy. The decision was a turning point in my life, acknowledging the fact I would never have a family. Like you, I was in China. The design spoke to me."

She sighed, and her sigh was a hybrid of sadness and regret. "Why didn't you say something when you saw mine?"

His shoulders slumped slightly, as if the memory was almost too heavy to bear. "It was hard enough knowing we were destined to be together. I didn't want to burden you with the additional knowledge, too. If we were going to have a future, you had to come to the realization independent of me."

She rubbed his temple, stroked his jaw.

"In the back of my mind, I've known since you disappeared and I discovered where you were that we were meant for each other. Everyone else in the family had found their soul mate, and I figured it was my turn. Then I met Carolina Rose and thought she might be mine, but she died."

"Wait. Back up and explain the soul mate part."

"There's a legend about the three brooches—the ruby, sapphire, and emerald. They were given to three brothers as a thank-you for rescuing their laird's wife. It was believed those three brooches had the power to bring soul mates together. The amethyst brought JL and Kevin together, so it may be the purpose of all the brooches."

"And you think the diamond brought us together?"

"I wanted to believe that until Kevin told me the amethyst brooch has a different inscription, and the trip was different. It wasn't a roller coaster ride like the ones he's taken with the ruby, sapphire, and emerald, and it returned him within moments of leaving."

"That's what happened to me," Amy said. "I was right back in my cousin's bedroom, as if I never left, and only five minutes had passed. What's different in the inscription?"

"Kevin didn't know. Maybe David knows by now, but Kevin doesn't speak Gaelic. He only knew some of the words looked different."

"And you think my brooch is different, too?"

"It might be."

She chewed on her lips, remembering how the brooch heated in her hand. The thought of going through time again terrified her. "I don't want to open it, and I don't want to touch it, ever again. I wore thick gloves, put the diamond in a small lead box, and took it to a bank in New York City."

"I don't blame you, but we need to know. David speaks Gaelic. You can give it to him."

"He can lock it up with the others, wherever they are."

"In a secure location at MacKlenna Farm."

"He can go to the bank with me and get it out of the safe deposit box." She raked her eyes over Jack. "I don't want to sound indelicate, but when do you think we could make love again?"

Jack laughed. "I finally get my turn at bat, and the coach is convinced I'll strike out."

She covered her face with the pillow. "That's not what I meant."

He took the pillow away and kissed her. "Try again, darling, and if you can't think of a good comeback, I'll tell you I was ready to play again as soon as I finished."

"Are you saying you're a rookie with the stamina of a veteran?"

"No, it means I'm a man in love, and the object of my affection is the sexiest and most beautiful woman I've ever known. And I'll walk around with a perpetual hard-on so I'll be ready the moment she calls."

"I don't have your phone number," she teased.

"That's all right. I have yours." He kissed her brow, letting his lips linger just as he had done earlier. "I'll be right back."

He returned a moment later with refilled glasses of chilled champagne. He handed one to her, clinking it softly. "To love you as deeply as I love you gives me strength. Being loved so deeply by you gives me courage. May that strength and courage lift us up in times of need, encourage us in moments of weakness, fill us with wisdom in our times of doubt, and fill our hearts with eternal joy.

"I love you, Amy."

"And I love you, Jack."

60

Present day Chiesa di San Martino in Maiano—Amy

THE DAYS BEFORE the wedding were hectic, but it all came together, thanks to Maria, Meredith, and Amy. At JL's request, and unbeknownst to the rest of the family, Jeff had searched Pops' house and found Great-Grandmother O'Grady's handmade Irish lace wedding dress—last worn by her mother the day she married Pops—and shipped it to JL. The high-neck, princess-shaped dress with a short train was made prior to World War I, and, although the top had been too big for JL, Maria gently altered the silk and lace to fit JL's smaller frame.

"Why didn't you wear this to your first wedding?" Amy asked. "It's absolutely gorgeous."

"I told Ryan I wanted to wear it, but he nixed the idea. He wanted me in something sexy, not old lace."

"I'm glad he nixed it, because it's perfect for your wedding today. It doesn't show cleavage, but it's very romantic, and knowing your mother wore it, too, must make it even more special. Will Pops recognize it?"

"Oh, yeah," JL said. "He has their wedding day picture next to his bed. I don't know what he'll do with the picture if he and Maria get more involved."

Amy chuckled. "They'll have matching pictures. Maria has Micky's next to her side of the bed."

"Pops seems so happy around her."

"She's an incredible woman. Even Meredith defers to her."

Jack knocked on the door, opening it at the same time. "Girls, it's time to go."

"Five minutes, Jack," JL said. "Is Kevin going with you?"

"Yes, and we're leaving right now with Father Paul. See you there."

Amy rushed over and kissed Jack, finding his lips soft and welcoming. She tasted a slight hint of whisky on his breath. "You look very handsome, and you and Kevin have been doing shots."

Jack grinned, running his fingertip along the edge of her dress's scooped neckline resting just above the slope of her breasts. "Only a couple, and you look good enough to eat."

She traced her finger around his mouth, and he snatched the digit between his teeth, sucking on the fingertip. "If that's where your mind is, darling, you've had more than a couple."

He released her finger with an even bigger grin. "Can you show a little more cleavage? I forget what your nipples look like."

"I heard that, Jack," JL said. "Now go away and leave us alone, and try to control your lust for the next hour."

Jack closed the door, then opened it again. "The dress still looks great, JL. You're a beautiful bride."

"Still?" Amy asked. "When did you see her dress?"

"She sent me a text yesterday that said, 'I need your advice. Please come.' I didn't know what she wanted."

Amy put her hands on her hips, glaring. "Where was I?"

He kissed her forehead. "Walking in the garden, deep in conversation with David."

"Oh, that's right. You're forgiven, then." She shooed Jack away. "We'll see you at the church."

He closed the door, and his laughter echoed in the hall.

Amy sighed, leaning back against the door. "I'm still in shock over all of this."

JL added one more spritz of hairspray and slipped on a pair of four-inch heels that would still make her half a foot shorter than

Kevin. "I'm still in shock, too. But tell me. Inquiring minds are dying to know, and you've been so hush-hush. Is Jack as good as he's always led women to believe?"

"I don't kiss and tell," Amy said.

"Of course you do." JL linked arms with her, and they left the bedroom, unable to stop laughing. "As silly as we are, you'd think we'd been drinking, too."

"We're drunk on love," Amy said. "And as for Jack… If you've ever watched movies from the fifties and sixties," Amy lowered her voice to a hush. "Jack is Clark Gable and Gregory Peck, with a little James Dean bad boy mixed in. He puts my wants and needs first. He's charming and caring and considerate, highly erotic and adventuresome—"

"Whoa," JL said, stopping at the top of the stairs. "Jack's changed a lot, but are you sure we're talking about the same man?"

Amy was taken aback. "What part doesn't sound like him?"

JL grabbed the stair railing and lifted her skirt, while Amy picked up the short train. "The wants and needs first part."

"When we make love, it's all about me. What I want, what makes me feel good. His erection can last for hours. The second time we made love, I teased him about taking a little blue pill."

"No, not Jack!" JL laughed. "Tell me it's not true."

"It's not true, but honestly, I don't really know, and I don't care. He's a wonderful, caring lover, and he gives me total control—sometimes."

JL laughed again. "You two are perfect for each other. So, has he talked about marriage, kids anything?"

The topic of kids panicked Amy, and she was quiet until they reached the bottom step. "He had a vasectomy."

"He what? Seriously? Say it ain't so, Sam. What was he thinking?" Then JL answered her own question. "Obviously, he wasn't."

"I think he gave it a great deal of thought."

"Can he have a reversal?"

"Charlotte made him bank his sperm. He says there's enough to populate a small country."

"A country filled with only Jack Mallory mini-me's. What a frightening thought."

Amy and JL entered the front room, where Pops was waiting. When he saw JL, he grabbed the back of a chair for support with one hand and with the other he grabbed his chest. JL rushed to him. "Are you okay, Pops?"

"Yes, darlin'. Just surprised. That's all. At first, I thought you were your mother coming back to marry me again. You look beautiful. You honor her by wearing her dress, and you honor me with her memory. Thank you." He kissed her forehead.

Amy handed JL her bouquet of Calla lilies wrapped with her mother's rosary, and then led the way to the courtyard, where the limo waited to drive them to the *Chiesa di San Martino*, an eleventh-century Medieval church situated near the hillside town of Fiesole just outside of Florence.

Once they were settled in the car, JL said, "Remind me of the order of the processional."

"For the third time in the past hour?" Amy asked.

JL squeezed Amy's hand. "I haven't forgotten. I just find your voice very calming. Will you tell me again?"

"If I talk to my audience the way I talk to you, they'd all be asleep."

"Since this isn't a baseball game, how about, as Kenzie says to the twins, 'use your inside voice.'"

Calmly, with more than the usual South Carolinian in her voice, Amy said, "Meredith is inside the church putting everyone in order. The piper will play 'Pachelbel's Canon' for the processional. Elliott, with Kevin and James Cullen, David, Braham, and big Cullen, all handsomely dressed in the agreed-upon MacKlenna plaid will enter first, and will stand on the right side of the predella.

"They'll be followed by Connor, Shane, Jeff, and Austin, all handsomely dressed in white tie and tails, who will stand on the left side of the predella. They'll be followed by Father Paul, Jack, and me. Then the piper will play 'Trumpet Voluntary' for you and Pops."

"What about the twins? Where will they be?"

"With their mom, sitting in the pews with everyone else."

"Having just the men on the predella was a good compromise," JL said. "There isn't room for everybody, although I still think it seems like my family will be standing at the ready to defend my honor if Kevin backs out."

"And Kevin's family will be standing at the ready too," Amy said.

"Well, let's get this over with so we can drink champagne."

When the car arrived at the church, Jack was standing outside the door waiting for Amy. He'd never looked more handsome. Of course, she thought the same thing hours earlier, while she watched him sleep. The tender quivers in her heart had grown stronger during the last forty-eight hours, and she knew they would continue unabated for the rest of her life.

She hugged JL. "See you inside." Amy climbed out of the car and went to Jack.

He kissed her, warmly and softly, on the lips. "You look beautiful…almost as beautiful as you looked this morning in my white shirt, sleeves dangling like Dopey."

"How charming," she said sarcastically. "The dress I'm wearing costs as much as the bottle of champagne we drank the other night, and you're telling me I looked better in your shirt?"

He winked. "The shirt was unbuttoned, and I could see all of you…" His eyes drifted to her décolletage. "Not just the slope of your breasts."

"Well…" She gave him a saucy smile. "Shall we go in? The sooner we get JL and Kevin hitched, the sooner we can get back to the shirt."

"I love you," he whispered in her ear.

He took her arm, and they followed Father Paul down the single nave in the warm and intimate church. As Amy strolled with the love of her life, she realized how unbelievably lucky she was to have found this family of such loving and caring people. Would Jack propose? As much as they'd talked the past two days, he had never mentioned marriage. Would he tonight?

When she and Jack reached the platform where the men waited, she let go of thoughts of marrying Jack and focused on JL. The second piper appeared, playing "Trumpet Voluntary," and proceeded down the aisle. Meredith, the acting MOB, rose and turned to watch the bride.

Amy couldn't see JL's brothers when they glimpsed their sister wearing their mother's dress, but she heard their audible gasps. If JL's expression was any indication, their faces beamed with both surprise and approval. But Amy could see Kevin gazing at his bride while she proceeded regally down the aisle toward her prince. For anyone hoping JL and Kevin would have a fairy-tale wedding, they were not disappointed—least of all the bride and groom.

The ceremony was beautiful in its simplicity, and Amy floated through the prayers, the vows, and the exchange of rings, remembering only snippets of Kevin's promise to cherish, honor and love JL, and her promise to love him in return.

Kitherina was adorable as the ring bearer. It was decided the twins couldn't be trusted, not only to deliver the rings, but to keep their squiggly, kilt-covered bums appropriately covered. They both cried when they were told they had no role to play in the service, and huddled together in a corner, inconsolable, until a compromise was reached.

When the ceremony ended, and the piper began to play "Scotland the Brave," the twins left the pew where they'd been sitting, heads high, and solemnly strutted out of the church behind the piper, their kilts swinging to and fro in time to their swaggering strides.

Yep, the little McBains found a way to steal the show.

61

Present day Tuscany, Italy—Amy

THE MAGICAL WEDDING EVENING ended around midnight, after a scrumptious wedding feast, first dances with moms and dads, the cake cutting, a dozen champagne toasts, and the required participation in the tarantella. Even Elliott danced, and, to everyone's surprise, the man had some Fred Astaire moves. Hundreds of pictures were taken, and everyone with a Facebook page and an Instagram account loaded up their feeds with pictures and videos, even Meredith.

It was the most beautiful, romantic, perfect wedding and reception Amy ever attended.

When the kids were hustled off to bed, and the men turned to cigars and whisky, Amy and Jack returned to the little villa for their last night together.

After they made love, Jack said, "I'm coming to New York in two to three weeks. What's your schedule?"

Amy rose on her elbow and rested her head in her hand, the sheet slipping beneath her breasts. "If the Yankees are in the playoffs, I'll be in the booth for those games. If they're not, I don't know where they'll send me."

"Let me know the schedule, and I'll come up. Can I stay with you, or should I make a reservation at the Plaza?"

"Hey, big spender," she said seductively. "If you're staying at the

Plaza, I'll stay with you."

He rolled over and used the side of his thumb to caress her nipple, smiling as if he'd performed an amazing feat when it hardened. "Can I ask you something?"

She finger-combed through the touch of gray she loved at his temples. "You can ask me anything."

"Where's the sapphire and diamond ring?"

Her breath hitched. "Why? Do you want it back?"

His lips twitched in what might have been a faint grin. "No, I gave it to you. I was just wondering where it was, why you don't wear it."

"It's in the safe deposit box with the diamond brooch. I didn't feel right wearing it. It's a very special ring, with a lot of meaning, and without you in my life, it was too painful to put it on my finger."

"If you don't want to wear it on your finger now, you can have earrings made from the stones."

"David is coming up next week to get the brooch. I'll take the ring to Tiffany's then to see what they suggest." What she wanted was for him to put it back on her left-hand ring finger, but it didn't seem to be an option. She snuggled up next to him. "I'll miss you when I leave tomorrow."

"Not as much as I'll miss you. I'd love to go back to New York City, but I have several commitments in Virginia before I can leave town again."

She nuzzled his chest. There was nothing scent neutral about Jack. He not only did sex well, but he smelled like it, too. "What about Patrick?" she asked.

"He'll stay at Charlotte's. I don't think he has any interest in going back to New York City right now, and he and Lincoln are inseparable. They FaceTime with James Cullen and Emily every day."

"They were so cute at the wedding, even the twins. Did you see Austin teaching Isabella how to dance? She's learned very quickly how to move those hips."

"I like the way you move yours," Jack said, kissing up and down her neck.

His kisses tickled, and she squirmed. "Yes, darling, I know you do, now stop tickling me."

"No, I didn't see Austin and Isabella, but I saw Emily, a head taller than Patrick as they danced together, while James Cullen glared from the sidelines."

"It's going to be interesting to watch those kids grow up and see how it all shakes out."

His fingers were strong and slightly cool as they clasped her nape. "Have you ever thought about how many children you want?"

"That's a strange question for you to ask."

"Why?"

"Obviously you never wanted any."

He sat up, looked at her. "Amy, that's not why I had a vasectomy. I didn't want to have a child with a woman I didn't love, and I didn't think I would ever love a woman the way I love you." He kissed her soundly. "I want children with you. I want an entire baseball team, but... I wonder." He gave her a big Jack Mallory smile. "Who would our children go to for baseball advice?"

"Hmm," she said, thinking about the question for a moment. "I'd say both of us. Our children will want to know we have their backs, and will jump out of the dugout if they ever charge the mound."

"God, I love you, woman. Come here. I'm going to start with your head and kiss you all the way to your toes."

"Why don't you do it differently this time, and start at my toes and work up?"

He kissed the tip of her nose. "I'm on to your tricks, lady. You don't want your toes or your head kissed, and you're too embarrassed to tell me you want my head between your legs."

She cocked her head. "Am I so obvious?"

"Amy, darling, you were giving off vibes the moment I saw you at the restaurant in Pittsburgh. You don't have any idea how you looked at me, do you?"

"I just thought you looked familiar, that's all."

"You thought I looked sexy as hell, and you wanted to jump my bones." He tickled her sides. "Admit it."

She squealed. "No! I'll never admit it."

He tickled her again, and within minutes, he had turned her squeals into cries of pleasure.

62

Present day New York City—Amy

SPORTS FANS PEG OCTOBER as the most exciting month of the calendar year—the perfect restaurant sampler appetizer. Just about every sport is available for rabid fans to enjoy, but baseball, during the World Series, is the *crème de la crème*.

That certainly was Amy's opinion, and one she had espoused for years. This year was no exception. She put the World Series above the Kentucky Derby, the Preakness, the Belmont, the NCAA Basketball Championship, the World Cup, the Stanley Cup, the Super Bowl, and even baseball's opening day.

Tonight the New York Yankees were hosting the Arizona Diamondbacks in Game One of the Fall Classic, and she was jumping-up-and-down excited to be in the broadcasting booth as the fourth member of ESPN's team.

As she looked out over the sea of white and blue Yankee shirts with the smell of hot dogs and popcorn wafting around her, vendors hawking beers, and recorded organ music, she was struck by how much she missed Jack, and even more surprised his absence put an unusual dent in her enthusiasm for the upcoming game. She needed to get a plunger and pop the dent right out, or else fans would hear disappointment in her voice.

Jack sent only one text all day: *Good morning, sunshine. Busy today. Have fun tonight at the game. Chat afterwards. Love u, J*

What kind of text was that? He could have called. Even if he was meeting with agents or publishers, he could have found five minutes. But, as he was fond of saying, "Communication's a two-way process, Amy, so talk to me."

Other than FaceTiming, they hadn't laid eyes on each other since the plane dropped her off at Teterboro on the Monday following JL and Kevin's wedding—over two weeks ago. She knew she wouldn't be able to get to Virginia, but she had hoped he could come to New York, or wherever she happened to be. So far he hadn't been able to work it out. She didn't want to be pissed at him tonight, but she was.

With the start of the game only minutes away and a few notes still to review, there wasn't enough time to call him but she could send a text: *Miss you. Wish you were here. Love, A*

She sat back with her cheat sheets and a highlighter to mark the salient stats.

Jack responded: *Can't chat. Love, J*

Her heart sank in her stomach. How many times had Joe sent her similar texts? Did she read more into her fabulous weekend with Jack than he intended to convey?

The PA announcer came on saying, "Tonight, we have a special guest coming to the mound."

She glanced up, thankful for the distraction. She couldn't do anything about Jack tonight.

"Who is it?" she asked Aaron, another analyst sitting next to her. "I've got the marketing department's press release listing tonight's dignitaries, but there's no mention of anyone throwing out a first pitch."

"Don't know," he said. "He must have been added at the last minute."

Amy grabbed the binoculars and scanned the entrances to the field located next to the dugouts. A man shrugged off his jacket, set his shoulders, and climbed the steps to the field, his thin, elongated shadow gliding over the infield grass toward the pitcher's mound. A rush of tingly sensations powered through her—and not particularly pleasant ones, at that. "Oh, God," she said under her breath. This couldn't possibly be happening.

The PA announcer said, "Please welcome *New York Times* bestselling author Jack Mallory to the mound to throw out tonight's first pitch."

Amy's heart leapt to her throat. If possible, she scooted deeper into her chair, but she didn't drop the binoculars.

"Isn't he the guy you're dating?" Aaron asked.

Was there any room under the table to hide? She checked. If she curled into a tight ball, possibly, but her blue plaid TOMS shoes would poke out.

This had to be a publicity stunt for his new book. His agent must have sent out a press release to everyone but her. He should have warned her. Permission wasn't necessary, but a heads-up would have been nice. Was this the old Jack JL had warned her about? The one who didn't consider the feelings of others?

The eyes of dozens of print reporters and TV announcers turned toward her, as news of her boyfriend heading to the mound spread like news of a shutout through the press box. How did people even know she and Jack were together? It made no sense to her. If he didn't throw a decent pitch, she would never live it down. But, how in the world had he pulled this off? Fame? Fortune? Connections?

And then she knew—Elliott Fraser was from Lexington, Kentucky, and so was the Yankees' GM. No. That wasn't it. Or wasn't all of it. The connection wasn't just Elliott. Amy's research into the MacKlenna clan had uncovered several interesting tidbits. One of which was Kevin and the GM both attended Lexington Catholic High School. Go, Knights!

Serendipitous? Nope. Nothing the MacKlennas, et al, ever did was left to chance. It was methodical, choreographed, and well played to the bottom of the ninth.

"Looks like he's trying hard to impress you. Hope he can pitch," Aaron said.

Oh, yeah. Jack could pitch, and he had just thrown her a curveball. It was veering to the left, hard and fast. She gritted her teeth and smiled sweetly. If she couldn't pull herself together, she'd look like a double-eyed lackwit for the cameras.

"Mallory," she said because she was too pissed to call him Jack, "was a first-round draft pick—twentieth overall—but went to law school instead of playing in the Yankees farm system. He had a good enough arm then, but I don't know about now. He's got good hands, though." She cringed, mortally embarrassed. She really didn't just say that, did she?

Aaron gave her a sideways glance. "Does he, now?"

She ducked her head, pretending to look at the rosters spread out in front of her with notes on the players. "You know what I meant."

He waved his hand like it was sizzling hot, whistling. "I'm a man. I know exactly what you meant."

Amy ignored him, or tried to. "The scouting reports at the time said the six-three, one-hundred-ninety-pound southpaw had a very low-effort delivery, with a clean and easy arm action coming through. Between the projection of his body and the ease with which his arms worked, it seemed inevitable he would add velocity as he matured physically. His fastball topped out at ninety-four mph and worked consistently in the nineties."

Aaron sat back and crossed his arms. "You didn't just pick out facts to remember. You memorized the whole article."

"It was worth remembering." Pride echoed in her voice. But pride did little to counterbalance the other emotions playing havoc with her heart and dreams.

"Impressive," Aaron said. "What a waste, though. He should have played in the big leagues."

She thought so too. What she found, not only when she Googled him, but also the reports she read about his college career, both surprised and delighted her. Since she returned from Italy, she was making time to read all his books, not just look at the book jackets. No wonder he was a NYT best-selling author. He was a prolific writer, with beautifully written prose that brought history deliciously alive on pages that practically turned themselves. She found none of the cockiness in his writing she had originally expected. If she hadn't already been in love with him, she would be by now. His descriptions alone dragged her into the stories and kept her there.

She turned her attention back to the man on the pitcher's mound.

The Yankees' catcher took his place behind the plate, forearm low on his knee, ready for the pitch. If Jack threw wild and hurt the team's starting catcher, she would die of embarrassment.

He squared off to the plate, his long, athletic body... She shook her head to stay focused on the pitch, not on his long, athletic body walking naked through the bedroom.

She gripped the binoculars tightly. The beat of her heart boomed in her ears. She'd been through college championships and the Olympics, but she had never been this nervous about one pitch, on one crisp October night, in the one and only Yankee Stadium.

Jack's hand and wrist were held deep inside the glove, hiding his grip. He began with a full hand raise overhead, into a large leg lift that stayed tight to his body, and the pitch exploded out of his hand...

But there was no ball...

Her heart sank to her stomach. "What happened?"

"Where's the ball?" Aaron asked.

"What's he doing, Spalding?" another reporter asked.

She buried her face in her hands, and reconsidered crawling under the table. "Grrr. He's losing a girlfriend, that's what he's doing."

The announcer said, "Ladies and gentlemen, Jack Mallory needs encouragement on the mound. How about giving him a hand?"

The audience rose in waves, whistling, applauding, and stomping. "Jack! Jack! Jack!"

He rubbed the bottoms of his shoes across the orange cleat-cleaner, picked up the rosin bag—a small, sanitary sock with the ends tied off, used to dry sweat from pitcher's hands, then removed his ball cap to wipe his forehead. After going through a ritual, he set up for his next pitch.

But, he stopped suddenly and threw up his hands.

The PA announcer said, "Ladies and gentlemen, Jack needs even more encouragement."

Amy set down the glasses, scrubbed her face, raked her fingers through her hair, then picked up the glasses again. She would watch this disaster unfold to the very end, and then she would send him a text telling him to never text, call, or FaceTime her again—ever.

The announcer said, "Amy Spalding, come on down from the press box and help him out."

She gasped. "I'm not going down there. I'm not." This was the final straw. Hiding under the table was her only way out. How could he do this to her?

The audience chanted, "A-my! A-my! A-my!"

"I'm not going," she said. "It's bad enough he's embarrassing himself, but now he wants to embarrass me, too."

"Go now. Do not pass go," Aaron said. "Run as fast as you can, or this stunt will cut into the start of the game, and we go live in five minutes."

Reporters, commentators, and analysts in the press box all laughed and cackled when she dashed out of the broadcasting booth. She hurried through Sheppard's Place—the media dining room named after Bob Sheppard, the voice of Yankee Stadium for half a century—to reach the bank of elevators.

The elevator door opened. She pushed the button to the triple zero floor in the basement—not once, not twice, but three times, as if repeating the action would make the elevator move faster. If it stopped on another floor, she'd scream at whoever delayed her. While the elevator descended, she paced, and, as cliché as it sounded, she paced exactly like a caged animal—back and forth, back and forth. If the elevator had bars, she would have climbed them.

It came to a smooth stop, and the door opened, displaying triple zeros on the LED panel.

Triple zero. Her floor. The exit to the field. It was time to conclude this embarrassing charade. She would never forgive Jack for doing this to her. She barged out without looking, focused only on charging the plate, and ran smack into a barrel-chested security guard.

He grabbed her shoulders to keep her from tumbling backwards. "Miss Spalding? Right? If you'll follow me, I'll get you out to the mound."

"How'd you know I was coming down the elevator?" she asked.

"Uh…uh… I heard your name over the PA system. I figured you'd be coming this way. Stay close. It's crowded." Then to the people in the hall he said, "Let us through. Let us through."

"There's Amy," she heard someone say. Followed by additional comments about Jack. "Mallory was a first-round draft pick years ago." And, "I didn't know he played ball. I thought he was just a writer."

Amy couldn't resist a quick retort. "If there's anything else you want to know, ask me now. Mallory might not be alive in five minutes."

A roar of laughter followed in her wake. This was so embarrassing. She put on her game face and trudged ahead. After all her hard work to be accepted in a male-dominated world, this stupid stunt would set her career back years.

The tunnel ended next to the Yankees dugout. The guard opened the door for her, and she stepped out into the glare of the lights. "Good luck, Miss Spalding."

Why couldn't she be a mole and burrow her way to the mound? She hopped over the foul line—bad luck to step on one—and jogged to the pitcher's mound. She might as well be running the New York City Marathon. That's how far the distance seemed from the dugout to the mound where Jack stood staring into his glove, likely puzzling through what happened and why he'd frozen up and couldn't throw the pitch.

After this, he'd probably need six months in therapy to recover. She'd need at least a year.

The fans cheered, "A-my! A-my! A-my!"

If her reputation was on the line, at least she'd be a good sport about it all. She waved, which only stirred the crowd to stomp and yell louder.

A camera linked to the centerfield LED scoreboard that filled a quarter of the entire outfield façade, followed her. Another camera was trained on Jack. The two feeds provided the audience with a split screen—Jack contemplating his glove, and her progress to the mound.

The league was forbidden to show anything that would incite either team or fans. Well, here was one fan who was incited to violence—she was as pissed off as a hive of hornets. After the game, she was breaking up with him. Any man who could be so insensitive was a man who didn't deserve her.

"What the hell are you doing?" she demanded, while still maintaining a smile for the LED scoreboard and the roaring fans.

He kissed her on the mouth, and the crowd went wild. He pointed to the grass outside the pitcher's circle. "Stand right there." After a quick signal to the catcher, he regained the hill. Then he pushed off the pitcher's slab with his right foot and drove at the plate, right into the groove, with startling power. His follow-through ended in a light skip, and he finished on his toes, throwing a perfect strike.

The fans jumped to their feet, rocking the stadium as if he'd won the game with a single pitch. But she wasn't happy. She punched her hands to her hips. This was all a ploy, but why? He doffed his cap and dropped his glove.

And while she was barely holding on to her composure, Jack knelt on one knee.

The roar of the crowd turned silent and still—and so did Amy's heart.

From his back pocket, Jack pulled out a small box and opened it, revealing a dazzling emerald cut diamond surrounded by sapphires. The ring was the reverse of the one he gave her before.

Her heart leapt to her throat. This couldn't be happening. Not only were they on the LED display, but Jack had a mic clipped to his shirt.

"Today our love is new and frantic, tomorrow old and sure. Be my wife, Amy. Marry me, and make me the happiest Yankees' fan on the planet."

After two beautiful proposals—one in Central Park, and a champagne toast after they made love—Jack went for an uncharacteristically dumb proposal.

And the crowd loved it. "Say yes! Say yes! Say yes!"

She held out her hand, nodding.

"Is that a yes?" he asked.

"Yes! That's a yes."

Jack slipped the ring on her finger, picked her up, and spun her around the pitcher's mound, kissing her. The fans exploded in a dizzying wave of noise that nearly brought the bleachers crashing down.

What had begun on the rolling seas of the Atlantic came to fruition under the glaring lights of a baseball stadium. The Yankees charged the mound and escorted them off the field to the continuing cheers of fifty-four thousand fans.

The PA announcer said, "Congratulations, Amy and Jack. Now, *let's play ball!*"

63

Present day (Christmas Eve) Scotland, Christmas Eve—Elliott

MEREDITH PUSHED THE BEDROOM door closed, staggered to the bed, and fell backwards, fanning her arms like a snow angel. Elliott was reclining on the king size bed reading Jack's latest book about the Confederate gold. Elliott removed his glasses and laid them in the middle of the open book. "Ye look tired, my dear. Did the wee ones wear ye out?"

She shook her head, making imprints in the comforter. "Robbie and Henry are brilliant, but having a conversation with them is like having a conversation with David in a miniature body and in stereo. They've developed their own finger signals. David doesn't even know what they mean."

"That's scary," Elliott said. "The lads could be saying, 'Let's take the castle.' And who would know until they locked us all in the dungeon?"

Meredith laughed as she sat up and stripped off her slacks and sweater. "I'd worry if they didn't have such good hearts." She walked into the bathroom, turned on the water, and brushed her teeth while Elliott returned to his book. A few minutes later, she reappeared wearing a green silk gown cut low at the top and slit high at the bottom, topped by a red Santa hat.

His wife excited him as much today as she did when they first met. She might be a bit gray, but she was toned and beautiful and sexy, and he still thought of making love to her at least once every hour of every day, and, no matter how busy she was, she rarely sent him away.

"If there was only one of them..." she said.

"What are ye talking about? I lost track of the conversation. I can only see my Christmas gift. Come here and let me unwrap the package."

She drew back the covers and climbed into bed. "I can manage Henry or Robbie, but not both. Earlier, I had to hand over the Keebler elves cookie baking to Alice while I gave Amelia Rose and Laurie Wallis baths."

"She loves the babies, but she has a special fondness for those boys. I don't remember David when he was a wee lad, but from the stories she's told, he was exactly like the twins."

"Then there's hope yet," Meredith turned out her light and rolled over to Elliott's side. She closed his book and stretched to place it on the bedside table. "What's this?" she asked, holding up a nine-by-twelve white envelope.

"The cost overruns for the renovations of the Riverside Drive house. Ye don't want to see it. Amy was wise to sell the money pit."

"I'm glad we bought it. As many trips as we make to New York City every year, it will be nice to have a home there."

"An apartment on Park Avenue would have been cheaper."

"Probably, but the mansion has more personality." She tossed the envelope on the floor and turned her attention back to him, which is exactly where he wanted it.

"I went looking for ye earlier, but couldn't find ye."

"I was hiding in Charlotte's bedroom. What'd you want?"

He removed his glasses before snuggling under the covers with her. The silk of her gown was cool against his bare skin. "I finally got Jack and Amy, JL and Kevin, and David in one room. I wanted ye there, too."

"About the brooches?"

"Aye," Elliott said, tugging her close to him so he could nibble on her ear. "And areas of responsibility"—he paused for another ear-nibble—"although we didn't get very far."

Meredith ran her fingers through the graying hair on his chest, teasing him. "I assume nothing's changed from what you and I discussed yesterday."

He gave her a tender, lingering kiss, caressing her lips lightly with his tongue. "Ye were right. Kevin intends to come back full time as VP of Finance. His business manager in Italy is very capable, so Kevin doesn't need to be there full time. He and JL miss Austin and want to be in Lexington while he's playing at UK, and they want to be there for Isabella, too."

"You did get season basketball tickets, didn't you?"

"It's easier to get in to see the Pope than get tickets to UK basketball games. I had to donate a new hospital wing, but I got them. Kevin also wants to get the Lexington vineyards producing within three years. Do ye think he can?"

"He's well financed, so he shouldn't have a problem. I'm so proud of him. After your time together in Italy, everything changed. There's no daylight between you now in temperament, looks, physique, or even voice. He's been totally transformed."

"When I retire, he'll be ready to step into my shoes."

"As much as you two resemble each other, most people will just think you had plastic surgery, and Kevin is really you. Yesterday I walked into the library and saw you talking to David. Your back was to me, so I sneaked up, wrapped my arms around you, and kissed your neck. You squeezed my hands, and David cracked up, laughing. 'If Elliott sees ye two, I dinna think he's gonna like it,'" Meredith said, imitating David's brogue. "Well, I immediately realized my mistake, apologized profusely, and quickly left the room."

Elliott laughed. "Kev told me. 'He said, 'Da, if she'd grabbed my ballocks, I'd have died on the spot.'"

"Oh, he did not, and I've never walked up and grabbed you like that."

"Ye did just this morning, lass, when ye tried to get me back into bed to make love to ye."

Meredith swept her tongue against Elliott's, stroking it in an irresistible rhythm. "It would have worked, too, if Robbie hadn't barged in demanding you take him to the barn."

"He heard the cat was ready to deliver and didn't want to miss the birthing. He asked Maria to make him a white doctor's coat to wear. He told her he intends to deliver the next baby in the family, too."

"I don't know where they come up with some of their ideas. If JL hears it, she'll postpone getting pregnant."

"If ye hadn't been so busy with Amelia Rose, ye would have noticed JL didn't have wine at dinner. What does that tell ye?"

"That we should mind our own business. If they have news, they'll share it." Meredith rubbed up against Elliott, purring. "Did Jack and Amy tell you their wedding plans? It was important to them to get your approval, which I thought was sweet."

"For a summer wedding at the plantation? They don't need my approval. I appreciate the thought, though."

"You are the family patriarch. When Amy told me, I had to promise not to tell you."

"I don't know why they try that ploy. It never works. Ye always tell me everything."

"Just like you tell me."

He pulled back and quirked an eyebrow at her. "I don't keep secrets from ye, but I know ye keep some from me."

Meredith rolled out of his arms and fumbled through the portfolio on the bedside table. "You do too keep secrets from me."

She passed a sheet of paper to him with worry wrinkling the bridge of her nose. If he could pack up her worries every morning so she didn't have to bear them, he would. They were both guilty of hiding the thing they feared the most.

The Big C.

He didn't have to read what was on the paper. He already knew. He stacked his pillows and sat up, leaning against them. "I was going to wait until after Christmas."

"We're talking about cancer, Elliott. You can't leave me out of this."

"The PSA is only slightly elevated."

"It was already elevated. It's not just slightly elevated. It's slightly *more* elevated."

"I'll have another test done when we get home. We always knew we might have to move from active surveillance to active treatment. If I need surgery, we'll deal with it. But let's not talk about it tonight."

"I'll agree to put off the discussion for another week, but as soon as we get back to Kentucky, we're seeing your urologist. In fact, I'll call and make an appointment for after the holidays, so you can get right in."

He knew not to argue with her. Cancer scared her more than it did him.

"What was all the commotion in the library while I was helping with bath time?"

"David and Braham were drinking shots before they opened the diamond and amethyst brooches. They wouldn't let anyone else in the room."

Meredith laid her head on Elliott's chest, and slid one leg sensuously over his. "Jack and Kevin should have been there, and why the library?"

"Braham and David both speak the Gaelic, and the library is the coldest room in the castle. If the stones heated, they'd know immediately, drop the damn brooches, and run like hell."

She laughed, and when Elliott did, too, his chest rumbled beneath her face. "What was the result, besides giving them an excuse to drink an entire bottle of whisky?"

"The inscriptions aren't very different. Instead of *capacity of the soul*, the diamond and the amethyst say the *soul's love for humanity*."

"Sounds like instead of leading someone to their soul mate, the stones are more interested in humanitarian causes. Then what did Amy's journey do to improve humanity?" Meredith asked.

"We probably won't know for a while. The more time I spend with Isabella and Patrick, the more possibilities I see. They are both exceptional young people. I haven't had their IQs tested yet, but based on what their tutors are saying, they both have well above average intelligence. Their complex thinking skills show a sophisticated understanding of concepts, critical thought, and logic. If Isabella continues with her progress, she should be accepted into the premed program, and Patrick, while he's a few grades behind James Cullen, should advance quickly."

Elliott removed the Santa hat and threaded his fingers through her hair, silky and cool against his skin. "I saw you in the kitchen with Gabe this morning. I hope you weren't too rough on the lad."

"Connor shuffled him off to Colorado so soon after they returned from the adventure that I never had a chance to spend one-on-one time with him. He's a charmer, and those eyes… Wow. The girls need to watch out."

"Should I be jealous?" Elliott asked, teasingly.

"Gabe's much too young for me, but…"

Elliott tickled her. "Should I call ye Mrs. Robinson?"

She tickled him back, laughing. "Not me, sweetheart."

"Good. I'm glad we've got that settled."

Meredith's phone dinged with a text message. She rolled out of his arms and grabbed her phone off the nightstand. "It's from Cate. She just wanted to wish us Merry Christmas." Meredith typed a returned message then set the phone aside. "Which reminds me. Cate forwarded a report from Gabe's tutors. They seemed pleased with his progress."

"I read that, too. He hasn't had much formal education, but he's well read and a quick learner."

Meredith returned to her snuggling position, and he wrapped his arms around her. "And he's well-mannered, considerate, and thoughtful. I spied on him this morning while he was chasing the kids around the yard. They've all fallen in love with him, especially the twins."

"He's very compassionate. I saw that immediately in the way he talked about Maria, Isabella, and Amy. The only red flag that's been raised is Pete and Connor's concern about his gambling."

Meredith looked up at Elliott, eyebrows raised. "No one mentioned that to me. Are you concerned?"

He rubbed her brow to relax the tight muscles. "No, I'm not, and I didn't want to worry ye. I talked to Gabe about it. He said he's always used gambling to work deals and gather information. He loses sometimes, wins sometimes, but he always seals a deal, making far more money than he would have won or lost on the game. He lost his automobile in a card game before they left on the boat to London, but he signed a contract to ship all the vehicles produced by an automobile manufacturer in upstate New York. It was worth three times what his car was worth."

"And you believe him?"

"I'm a good judge of character, and I have to say the man fascinates me. He'll be a real asset to the company, especially as we do more business in Italy."

"Did he say whether he would go on another adventure?"

"He said yes, as have Pete and Connor. But Jack and Kevin are done."

"And there are at least seven more brooches," Meredith said.

"Speaking of the brooches, Cullen's internet sleuthing found a newspaper article in the archives. Lillian's brooch was insured, and she was eventually paid the full value of the stolen diamond. But here's the interesting part. Neither she nor Diamond Jim were ever informed about the fraudulent sale of the brooch."

"Why?" Meredith asked.

"Cullen surmised Thomson didn't want to buy the brooch back, and that he needed the funds to cover up other fraudulent transactions."

"I bet Jack and JL went bonkers when they heard that," Meredith said.

Elliott slipped her gown off her shoulders while his fingers meandered across the landscape of her breasts. "A massive understatement. It seems Lillian Russell's generosity was legendary. If she had known Amy wanted it back, she would simply have returned it."

"So Jack is kicking himself in the ass for not asking Lillian. If he had, then none of the crap that went down on the boat would have happened. Hindsight is always twenty-twenty. They can't let guilt eat them up over this." Meredith kissed Elliott's neck, his shoulders. "For whatever reason, they did what they had to do. Now don't you think it's time for you to do what you have to do?"

"Lass, making love to ye is never something I have to do. It's something I want to do—as often as I can." He rolled over on top of her and kissed her soundly.

She gave a pleasurable little hum against his lips. "Hopefully we'll have a few years before the next brooch shows up. Personally, I'm not ready to believe the theory the stones aren't meant to bring soul mates together. The amethyst brought JL and Kevin together, and the diamond brought Amy and Jack together."

"Did they?" he asked, focusing more on what his fingers were doing than on the thoughts he was trying to convey. "I thought Austin brought JL and Kevin together. And Jack went back because of Carolina Rose, not Amy."

"Well, that's something to think about, but not tonight. Did you lock our door? I overheard Henry and Robbie say they intended to wake us up to take them downstairs early to see if Santa had come. But I think what they really meant to say was they would come tell us Santa had come and gone."

"I'll lock it after I look in on the kids." He rolled off her and put on his robe. "Keep the bed warm. I'll only be a few minutes."

"Elliott."

He stopped at the door and looked at her.

"Tell me not to worry about your PSA. I can't live without you."

Her stare was a heavy weight on his chest. He returned to the bed and pulled her into his arms, holding her tightly to him. "I pray every day that I go before ye, because I'd be useless without ye. Ye're stronger than I am, Mer. Ye'd hurt for a while, but ye'd go on, because ye would have to. Too many depend on ye. They think it's me, but it's all smoke and mirrors. Ye're the source of the advice I give, the wisdom I convey, and the love I share. Without ye, I'm nothing."

"If you believe that, Elliott Fraser, you're an idiot. It's not smoke and mirrors. You're the real deal, and knowing and loving you has blessed my life beyond my imagination. Now," she said, "go tell the kids good night so you can make love to me."

He kissed her forehead, patted her hand warmly, and left the room for his evening ritual, strolling down the long, familiar corridor covered with oriental runners, and walls lined with paintings of Highland scenes.

David and Kenzie's door was cracked so they could hear Laurie Wallis if she cried. Kevin and JL's door was closed, and no light appeared beneath the door. Cullen and Kit's door was closed, but a streak of light was visible beneath it. Jack and Amy's door was closed, and their room was dark. Braham and Charlotte's door was cracked so they could hear Amelia Rose.

Maria was in the master bedroom on the first floor, because she wanted to be close to the kitchen, which was fine with Elliott, considering the specialties she prepared for him. Connor, Pete, Shane, Gabe, and Pops were bunking in the cottage. Jeff and his crew had returned to New York to spend the holidays with Julie's family.

Elliott opened the door to the kids' room and breathed in the scent of soap and wet dogs. He stepped over bodies in sleeping bags and counted heads as he pressed light kisses on their foreheads: Austin, Isabella, James Cullen, Emily, Patrick, Lincoln, Robbie, Henry, and Kitherina.

A few snickers came from the boys' side of the room, although they all pretended to be asleep for the ritual. The babies in the cribs—Laurie Wallis and Amelia Rose—were the last to receive their good-night kisses.

Elliott paused at the door, gazing into the room full of sleeping children. An arm slipped around his waist, and Kit snuggled close to him.

"A beautiful family, Elliott. We're so blessed."

"Aye, that we are. I hope ye'll be here next year, too."

"We've got to return home eventually, but I'm not ready to leave Emily yet." Kit hugged him. "I love you, Elliott. Good night."

"Love ye, too." He watched her return to her room, and then he reached for the doorknob, closing the door softly. "Good night, lads and lassies. May God hold each of ye in the palm of His hand."

THE END

ABOUT THE AUTHOR

Katherine graduated from Rowan University in New Jersey, where she earned a BA in Psychology with a minor in Criminal Justice. Following college, she attended the Philadelphia Institute for Paralegal Training before returning to Central Kentucky, where she worked as a real estate and tax paralegal.

Katherine is a marathoner and lives in Lexington, Kentucky. When she's not running or writing romance, she's enjoying her five grandchildren: Charlotte, Lincoln Thomas, James Cullen, Henry Patrick, and Meredith Lyle.

Please stop by and visit Katherine on her social media sites, or drop her an email. She loves to hear from readers.

Website
www.katherinellogan.com

Blog
www.katherinelowrylogan.com

Facebook
facebook.com/katherine.l.logan

Twitter
twitter.com/KathyLLogan

LinkedIn
linkedin.com/in/katherinellogan

Pinterest
pinterest.com/kllogan50

Goodreads
goodreads.com/author/show/5806657.Katherine_Lowry_Logan

Google+
plus.google.com/+KatherineLowryLogan/posts

I'm A Runner (Runner's World Magazine Interview)
www.runnersworld.com/celebrity-runners/im-a-runner-katherine-lowry-logan

Email:
KatherineLLogan@gmail.com

Family trees are available on Katherine's website
www.katherinellogan.com/books/the-celtic-brooch-family-trees

* * *

THE CELTIC BROOCH SERIES

THE RUBY BROOCH (Book 1)
Kitherina MacKlenna and Cullen Montgomery's love story

THE LAST MACKLENNA (Book 2 – not a time travel story)
Meredith Montgomery and Elliott Fraser's love story

THE SAPPHIRE BROOCH (Book 3)
Charlotte Mallory and Braham McCabe's love story

THE EMERALD BROOCH (Book 4)
Kenzie Wallis-Manning and David McBain's love story

THE BROKEN BROOCH (Book 5 – not a time travel story)
JL O'Grady and Kevin Allen's love story

THE THREE BROOCHES (Book 6)
A reunion with Kit and Cullen Montgomery

THE DIAMOND BROOCH (Book 7)
Jack Mallory and Amy Spalding's love story

Future Brooch Books

THE PEARL BROOCH
THE AMBER BROOCH

And More...

If you would like to receive notification of future releases
Sign up today at KatherineLowryLogan.com or
Send an email to KatherineLLogan@gmail.com and put "Sequel" in
the subject line

*   *   *

Thank you for reading THE DIAMOND BROOCH
I hope you enjoyed reading this story as much as I enjoyed writing it.
Reviews help other readers find books.
I appreciate all reviews, whether positive or negative.

AUTHOR NOTES

In October 2015 I was in New York City finishing *The Emerald Brooch* and preparing to run the New York City Marathon. Early one morning I was watching the wrap-up of the previous night's World Series game, and was curious about female sportscasters. This sparked a conversation with my son-in-law Chris and three of my grandchildren about female reporters and early baseball in New York City. One question led to another, and the idea for an early 1900s romance around baseball was conceived. Later that morning, Chris sent me a text: *Diamond Brooch = baseball diamond*. Bingo. I had a title and an idea for a plot.

The following spring I spent three hours with Tony Morante, Director of Stadium Tours for the New York Yankees. I went to the meeting intending to focus on the Yankees, but after talking with Tony, I decided to focus on the New York Giants, John McGraw, and Christy (Matty) Mathewson.

Matty would be a phenomenon today, another Aaron Judge. He was the first All-American boy and Christian athlete who refused to play on Sundays. He was so popular that a letter dropped in a mailbox in Omaha with no more address on the envelope than the numeral six was delivered to Matty at the Polo Grounds. Only one other American athlete exceeded Matty's popularity, and that was a horse—the great Dan Patch, an undefeated, record-breaking celebrity harness-racing horse (a major sport at the time).

Matty enlisted in the United States Army during World War I, although his wife Jane was strongly opposed. He served overseas in the newly formed Chemical Service, along with Ty Cobb, and was accidentally gassed during a chemical training exercise. He subsequently developed tuberculosis. Shortly before he died of the disease in 1925, at the age of 45, he told his wife, "Now Jane, I want you to go outside and have yourself a good cry. Don't make it a long one, this can't be helped."

Christy Mathewson and Ty Cobb were in the first class of inductees into the Baseball Hall of Fame, and John McGraw was in the second class. The McGraws and Mathewsons were great friends, and lived together for a time. They would have loved Amy.

The iconic photograph of Ty Cobb sliding into base while playing for the Detroit Tigers was taken either in 1909 or 1910. I found conflicting dates, which ultimately determined the year for this story. Cobb wore a chip on his shoulder the size of the Rock of Gibraltar, and it was said that he would climb a mountain to punch an echo. He and McGraw found each other despicable, but Matty may have been the only rival the misanthropic Cobb ever liked. Cobb and McGraw made up at Mathewson's deathbed.

The Provident Loan Society of New York was a pawn shop which had—and still has—a conscience. It was created during the financial panic of 1893, when J.P. Morgan, Cornelius Vanderbilt II, and others pooled their money to establish a not-for-profit organization to provide short-term loans at a lower rate than loan sharks. The business is still in operation and currently has five locations throughout New York City. Stephen Thomson is a fictional character who worked for the fictional Providence Loan Society, and what he did to the company's customers is fictitious.

The first issue of the *New York Herald* was published by William Gordon Bennett, Sr. on May 6, 1835. By 1845, it was the most popular and profitable daily newspaper in the United States. Later, the newspaper was managed by William Gordon Bennett, Jr., and at his death in 1924, the newspaper was acquired by the *New York Tribune*. When the newspaper's building on 6th Avenue was demolished in 1921, the clock was rescued and incorporated into the *New York Herald* monument located at Herald Square. The door to the clock tower has an owl motif, and Bennett was rumored to have been involved with the secret society, the Bohemian Club. He was flamboyant and known for erratic behavior.

Lillian Russell did sail on the *SS New York* in June of 1909.

However, I couldn't find enough information about that ship, so I used the Titanic's floor plans and many of its rooms for my fictional ship.

The T206 is perhaps the most studied and chronicled sports card set ever issued, and contains the most famous and expensive sports card ever issued, the T206 Honus Wagner. The cards were beautiful, extremely high quality, full-color lithographs. The artwork and color combinations on some of the cards are stunning. The standard measurements for this set are 1-7/16" x 2-5/8", although many issues vary in size. Several come shorter than 1-7/16" right to left, and longer than 2-5/8" top to bottom.

Amy's Riverside Drive mansion is based on the Schinasi Mansion, a twelve thousand-square-foot, thirty-five-room marble mansion located at 351 Riverside Drive, New York City. The mansion was featured in the USA Network Original Series *White Collar.*

The Polo Grounds stadium was demolished in 1964. The wrecking crew wore Giants jerseys and tipped their hard hats to the historic stadium as they began dismantling it. The site is now the home of the Polo Grounds Towers, a public housing project that opened in 1968. You can visit the site and see home plate.

This book could not have been written without the editing, research, and story development assistance of Faith Freewoman, Dr. Ken Muse, Lynn Wilson, and John O. Witt, LCDR-USNR (ret), and Dave Thome. Thank you so much!

I also want to thank my early readers: Keryn Aikman, Maria Diaz, Delphie Fielder Bland, Robin Epstein, Anne Marie Flynn, Annette Glahn, Cindy Gowans, Mary L. Johnston, Marjorie Lague, Stephanie Littlejohn, Holly J. McCann, Toni Mitchell, Jan Bowling Moutz, Rosanna Phelan, Rebecca Partington, Dawn Redmond, Paula Retelsdorf.

Printed in Great Britain
by Amazon